Sheila O'Flanagan is the author of ~~~~ ~~~~ ovels, including *If You Were Me, Things We* ~~~~ *Better Together, All For You, Stand By Me* and ~~ *Perfect Man*.

Sheila has always loved telling stories, and after working in banking and finance for a number of years, she decided it was time to fulfil a dream and give writing her own book a go. So she sat down, stuck 'Chapter One' at the top of a page, and got started. Sheila is now the author of more than nineteen bestselling titles. She lives in Dublin with her husband.

Sheila O'Flanagan. So much more than stories.

'Romantic and charming, this is a real must-read' *Closer*

'A big, touching book sure to delight O'Flanagan fans' *Daily Mail*

'A spectacular read' *Heat*

'Insightful, witty and full of fun . . . this is touching, tense and clever' *Irish Independent*

'A lovely book that will keep you guessing right up until the end' *Bella*

'Her lightness of touch and gentle characterisations have produced another fine read' *Sunday Express*

By Sheila O'Flanagan

Sheila O'Flanagan

Dreaming of a Stranger

headline
review

First published in 1997 by Poolbeg Press Ltd.

First published in Great Britain in 2003
by HEADLINE BOOK PUBLISHING

First published in paperback in Great Britain in 2004
by HEADLINE BOOK PUBLISHING

This edition published in 2015
by HEADLINE REVIEW
An imprint of HEADLINE PUBLISHING GROUP

1

Cataloguing in Publication Data is available from the British Library

ISBN 978 0 7553 3000 3

Typeset in Galliard by Palimpsest Book Production Limited,
Falkirk, Stirlingshire

Printed and bound in Great Britain by Clays Ltd, St Ives plc

Headline's policy is to use papers that are natural, renewable and recyclable products
and made from wood grown in well-managed forests and other controlled sources.
The logging and manufacturing processes are expected to conform to the
environmental regulations of the country of origin.

HEADLINE PUBLISHING GROUP
An Hachette UK Company
Carmelite House
50 Victoria Embankment
London EC4Y 0DZ

www.headline.co.uk
www.hachette.co.uk

I once read that a professional author is an amateur who wouldn't quit.

Thanks to everyone who believed in me and didn't let me quit.

Chapter 1

April 1981
(US No. 7 – *Woman* – John Lennon)

My lover and I sat side by side on the white Caribbean sand. The setting sun shattered into a thousand glittering diamonds as it hit the turquoise blue of the sea, and the only sound was the rhythmic thud of the waves as they broke upon the shore.

My lover and I sat in silence. There was no need for words between us. We were together in body and mind and it was perfection. The electricity between us charged the otherwise tranquil setting. But we would do nothing about that charge until the sun had finally slipped behind the gentle ridge of the island, its dying rays spilling blood into the sea. Then he would lean over to me and breathe quietly into my ear as he always did.

'Jane.' The words, coming from just behind me, broke into my dream and shattered it completely.

I looked up from the file that lay open on the desk in front of me. Jessica Fitzgerald laughed. 'If you didn't spend half your life in a daze you'd be a brilliant worker,' she said. She handed me a sheaf of papers. 'All these are fine. Can you get the confirmations out before lunchtime?'

I nodded at her. I was still halfway around the world, still in the arms of my secret lover on the white sands of the Caribbean. It was difficult to come back to the fifth floor of the bank's head office in Dublin, where the April rain drizzled miserably outside the opaque windows and there was no lover, secret or otherwise, in my life.

'Are you certain?' Jessica wasn't convinced, I could see it in her

1

eyes. I nodded once more, both to reassure her and to rid myself of the image of Sebastian lying bronzed and desirable on the beach beside me.

'I'll have them sent by twelve.' I glanced at my watch.

'Hope so,' said Jessica. 'And when you've done that I need you to do some photocopying for me.'

'Do you need that before lunch too?' I asked anxiously. 'Only I'm meeting Lucy at half twelve.'

'After lunch is fine,' said Jessica. 'Once you get those confirm-ations off.'

'Don't worry.' I watched while Jessica walked back down the long, open-plan area to her desk.

Jessica Fitzgerald was my boss. She was twenty-six years old, an assistant manager in the International Trade department of the bank where I worked and she was frighteningly efficient. But she was good to work for. She didn't make you feel stupid if you had to ask a question, she was always helpful and explained things thoroughly so that you were confident you knew what you were doing.

Some people said that Jessica was too helpful. That because she was so popular with her staff she had done herself no good in the further promotion stakes. The word in the bank was that you should always make sure that people knew less than you, that you kept an ace up your sleeve at all times, and that you were helpful, but not overly so. And that you exaggerated your own abilities as much as you possibly could.

At first I'd been scornful of people who said that, but in my two years in the bank I'd learned that they were probably right. I wanted to get promoted soon and I wanted Jessica to realise that I was promotion material.

I sat at my desk and tore along the perforated lines of the computer-generated confirmations. Although I'd told Jessica that I'd have them done by noon, it had been a busy day yesterday and there were hundreds of them. It meant working flat out to meet an almost impossible deadline.

They were gone by five past. I sighed with relief, stood up and stretched my arms over my head. I left the huge bundle of copies on Jessica's desk so that she could make a random check of some of them. Then I went to lunch.

The wind swirled around Baggot Street. It blew the rain directly into my face and whisked stray papers through the air. I pulled my grey, quilted raincoat around me and hurried down the street.

Lucy was already waiting for me outside Burgerland. She stood in the shelter of the building, calm and unruffled. Lucy would look calm and unruffled in a hurricane.

Lucy McAllister was my closest friend. We'd been friends since the day we met at St Attracta's Secondary School for Girls. I'd arrived at school the first morning feeling very alone. I hadn't gone to St Attracta's Primary School like most of the other girls, and I didn't recognise anyone in the crowd that swarmed around Class 1A. Everyone else seemed to know someone. A group of very pretty girls laughed in the corner together and glanced in my direction. I flushed with embarrassment, wondering if they were sneering at me for some reason. I looked around anxiously.

A small, fair girl sat at a desk near the back of the classroom and ignored everyone around her. She didn't look as though she was keeping a space beside her. She didn't really look at anyone very much. I took a deep breath.

'Are you keeping this space for anyone?' I asked. The fair-haired girl shook her head.

'D'you mind if I sit here then?'

'Feel free,' she said. 'Don't let me stop you.'

'I'm Jane O'Sullivan.'

'Lucy McAllister.' She looked around. 'Don't you know any of these people?'

'No,' I said.

'Me neither. It's weird not knowing anybody.'

I nodded. 'You didn't go to St Attracta's before?'

'The Holy Faith,' she told me. 'But St Attracta's is much more convenient for me, so my folks decided I should change. I didn't want to, really. I liked the Holy Faith.'

'I'm sure you'll make loads of friends,' I said.

She took a long look at the classroom full of girls and sighed. 'Maybe.'

After that, I couldn't think of anything else to say. I wanted to say something to show that I was bright and witty and that I was a good person to know. I pulled at a fingernail.

A tall, severe nun walked into the classroom, introduced herself

3

as Sr Elizabeth, the head, and began to talk to us about our responsibilities as adults.

Lucy yawned and Sr Elizabeth stared at her.

'In this school we expect our students to behave in a mannerly fashion,' said the nun. 'It is the height of bad manners to yawn when somebody is talking to you. You're Lucy McAllister, aren't you?'

Lucy nodded while thirty girls stared at her.

'Well, Lucy, it's nice to have you in St Attracta's,' said Sr Elizabeth. 'I hope you will spend your time here profitably and that you won't find it all *too* boring.'

Lucy flushed. 'Cow,' she muttered under her breath.

I gave her a sympathetic smile and she grinned at me.

It's funny how you sometimes click with another person. Lucy McAllister and I clicked. Despite the fact that we were completely unalike in looks – she was like a china doll with her fair hair, blue eyes and pale complexion and I was a sturdy, well-built redhead – we were the same sort of people.

We were both ordinary. Averagely clever, with average looks and an average background. We weren't as popular as the stunningly beautiful Stephanie McMenamin or her select group of friends, but neither were we avoided like some of the other girls. We never did so brilliantly in class that we were envied; but we were never sent to Sr Elizabeth's office with a note from the teacher to say that we were a complete waste of space. We were middle-of-the-road girls. We came from the same sort of families who lived the same sort of lives and we understood each other.

'What d'you want?' asked Lucy now as we stood in the queue for our burgers.

'Quarter-pounder, chips and Coke,' I said. 'No – wait – no chips. I'm trying to cut them out.'

Lucy laughed. Not a very caring laugh, I thought. 'Come on, Jane! You can never resist chips.'

'I'll have to,' I told her. 'I hardly fit into my jeans now and I can't afford another pair. I badly need to lose a few inches.'

'A small french fries will hardly make any difference,' said Lucy. 'There's nothing in it worth talking about anyway.'

'All the same,' I said as we inched forward. 'I'll just have the burger. It's all right for you – you never bloody well put on an ounce.'

4

Lucy grinned. 'Metabolism,' she said.

We brought our food to a white-topped table in the window. I shivered involuntarily as I watched the rain lash against it.

'So.' Lucy unwrapped her burger and daintily removed the dill pickle. 'Have you decided what you're going to do on Friday night?'

I made a face. 'Not really.'

'Oh Jane, for God's sake! It's your twenty-first birthday. You must have some ideas.'

I took Lucy's pickle and put it on my burger. 'No.'

'But you can't let your twenty-first go by as though it meant nothing.'

It was all right for Lucy. Her parents had thrown her a massive party. Although we were still close friends, her job at the temping agency meant that she met lots of different people. Easily enough to fill the room that Mrs McAllister had hired. And Michael, her older brother, had brought all his friends. I smiled at the memory. It had been a good night.

'It's my folks,' I told her. 'You know they've organised for us to go to the Walnut Rooms for dinner and a cabaret on Saturday night. They think it's very touching that my birthday and their anniversary should be on the same day.'

'I think it's bloody unfortunate,' said Lucy.

'Yes, well.' I robbed one of her chips. 'There's not a lot I can do about it. They've booked a table for twenty. Twenty! All of the aunts and uncles.' I took another chip. 'They think I'll like it.'

Lucy smothered a giggle. 'Sounds like a barrel of laughs.'

'Fuck off, McAllister,' I said.

She smiled at me and removed her chips from my reach. 'You're on a diet, remember?'

'I thought maybe we could just go out for a drink,' I said.

'Oh, Jane. We do that every week.' She crumpled her burger wrapping. 'Why don't we at least come into town and then maybe go to a nightclub or something afterwards? You, me and the twins.'

The twins, Brenda and Grace Quinlan, were our other old schoolfriends. They were like one person really, because they were almost identical and you rarely saw one without the other. But we got on well as a foursome and we'd stayed friends even when we'd finally shaken the dust of St Attracta's off our shoes.

5

'OK,' I said. 'Will you be talking to the twins or d'you want me to give them a call?'

'You'd better ring them,' said Lucy. 'I can hardly breathe in that office without them looking sideways at me. Thank God it's only for another couple of weeks.'

I didn't know how Lucy could stand going from office to office like she did. I liked knowing that I'd be meeting the same people every day and that I knew where everything was. Lucy was more adventurous than me.

'I'd better get back,' she said as she checked her watch. 'They give me such horrible looks if I'm late that I'm quite sure they're plotting something evil.'

I laughed at her. 'They're probably really nice people.'

'Huh,' said Lucy. 'They're solicitors. How can they be really nice people?'

I worked late that evening. International Trade was a busy department and there was always plenty of work to keep you past five o'clock if you wanted. I worked late whenever I could. I wanted the overtime and there wasn't anything else to drag me out of the office.

God, my life was dreary. Here I was, nearly twenty-one, and I hadn't achieved anything. I lived at home with my parents. I had a safe, but boring job in the bank. I didn't have any vices. I was still a virgin.

Lucy wasn't. Lucy had lost her virginity in France. When we left school she'd gone au-pairing for a year. Mam wouldn't let me go au-pairing although I desperately wanted to. We had a screaming match about it, but in the end I rang the bank and said that I'd be delighted to accept the position that they'd offered, and Lucy went to France on her own. It didn't bother her in the slightest. She wrote to me once a week to let me know how she was getting on, loving every minute of her time even if she thought that the two children she looked after were over-indulged little brats. Then, one day, a different letter came, falling over itself with underlined words and exclamation marks.

'*He was _tremendous_,*' she wrote. '*I knew that it probably didn't mean anything to him, because it's definitely _different_ with the French, but I just had to, Jane, I just had to. And he was so good-looking and so charming. He brought a bottle of wine and we went out into*

6

the country and we did it in the open air! I felt great about it. Mind you, I was terrified that Mme Lemartine would find out about it and send me home! I wasn't worried about getting pregnant, because I had sorted myself out about that the minute I met him! I just knew, you see! You just know, Jane, you'll understand yourself. Unless you and your latest have already done the deed! Write and tell me. In the meantime, I am having a great time with Étienne and I know that I'll be heartbroken when it's over.'

I crumpled up the paper. I was embarrassed that Lucy could write to me about it and envious that she had managed to lose her virginity in such a romantic way. And that she didn't seem to care that it was in a relationship that was purely for sex. Being in France had changed her outlook on life completely.

How many girls were virgins at twenty-one in this day and age? Hardly any, was my guess. I was one of them. Still. Despite my best efforts.

I snorted as I thought of my best efforts. In my entire life I'd had three boyfriends and none of them had been remotely close to dragging me to bed. Jesse, an American and my first love at seventeen (which shows that I was a late developer), lasted all of three weeks, the duration of his holiday in Ireland. Then came Frank. My relationship with Frank had been longer-lived but out of a Victorian novel. He was the sort of guy you'd never be afraid to bring home to your parents. He was too good to be true – scrubbed face, straw-coloured hair and a permanent expression of happiness. Frank couldn't cope with my moodier side and we split up after six months. Anyway, Frank wasn't The One, the man who would banish my imaginary lovers for ever. I hadn't met that man yet, although I yearned to find him. The one who would make me complete. The other half of myself. When I joined the bank, I almost fainted with the excitement of seeing so many men of my own age walking around the place. This was my opportunity, I thought. This time I would find the man of my dreams.

Actually, I found Dermot. It wasn't his fault that he couldn't live up to my imaginary lovers – to Sebastian or Nicholas or Rupert or Andreas. He did his best, but it wasn't enough. We split up after three months.

So here I was, without a man in my life for the last year. It was stupid to think that I needed a man to feel good. I told myself over and over again that I was happy just as I was, but I wanted someone. I needed someone to put his arms around me and to hold me and to make me feel loved. I ached with the need of finding him.

Mam and Dad were watching TV when I arrived home. I walked into the kitchen and draped my wet coat over the radiator. Pieces of the car that Dad was currently working on were laid out neatly on the kitchen table. Dad was the part-owner of a garage. I was probably the only girl I knew who could change an oil filter more quickly than she could shave her legs.

'You're very late,' said Mam. 'Your dinner will have dried out.'

'I didn't think you'd keep any for me,' I said. 'I told you I might be late when I left this morning.'

'I thought you'd ring and let me know.' She opened the oven door and took out the plate. 'You might want to make some gravy.'

The lamb chop was shrivelled and the potatoes dry. Mam was not a cook, she often said so, but she'd be hurt if I didn't eat it.

I brought my food into the living room with me and settled down in front of the TV. That way Mam wouldn't bother asking me about my day. She drove me nuts sometimes. She still treated me as though I was a child when I felt like an adult. Both my parents drove me nuts. They couldn't accept that I was a person in my own right now.

My birthday, for example. I probably wouldn't have had a big party anyway – I wasn't a party sort of person – but I certainly didn't want some family night out to mark my supposed coming of age. I'd been horrified when Mam told me of her plans but I hadn't the nerve, or maybe the heart, to say that I didn't want to be part of a joint birthday and anniversary celebration.

I sighed. I was very hard to please these days.

'Do you know who I saw in the shop today?' Mam worked part-time in the local supermarket.

I shook my head.

'That nice boy you used to know. Frank Delahunty.'

'Really?' I was indifferent.

'Yes. He didn't stop at my checkout but I recognised him straight away.' She looked pleased. 'Why don't you give him a ring?'

'Because I'm not interested in Frank Delahunty any more,' I

told her firmly. 'We split up. He went to London. He probably doesn't even remember me.'

'Of course he remembers you.' Mam looked affronted that anyone could forget her only daughter. 'He was very keen on you.'

'I suppose he was,' I said. 'But it wasn't to be.'

'Maybe now that you're older . . .' She sounded hopeful.

'No.'

'But—'

'No,' I said. Very decisively.

'Leave the girl alone, Maureen,' said Dad, coming to my rescue. 'If she isn't interested in the chap, she isn't interested.'

I must have been a terrible disappointment to my mother. She'd been beautiful when she was younger. Sometimes when she took out old photograph albums I'd stare at the snaps of her and wonder how on earth she'd produced a daughter like me. And, unlike me, she'd been popular with men. Not difficult, I suppose, when people said that you were a cracker. She was, too. Stunningly beautiful. Small and slender, with golden hair tumbling around her face. How could a woman like that look at her tall, well-built daughter and not wonder what on earth had happened? That was probably why she was always trying to find out about my boyfriends. She was afraid that nobody would ever find me attractive enough to marry, and she wanted me to get married.

I wanted to get married too, one day. But I wanted it to be to the right person, not someone Mam liked, the man who would love me through thick and thin. The man who would protect me.

I was an awful fool when I was twenty-one.

I met Lucy and the twins in O'Brien's on Friday night. Lucy and I arrived at the same time and went upstairs while we waited for the twins. They didn't get out of the department store where both of them worked until after six.

'What'll you have to drink?' I took my purse out of my bag.

'I'll get you one,' said Lucy. 'It's your birthday after all. And here . . .' She handed me a gaily wrapped package. 'Happy birthday.'

'Oh Lucy, thanks! Will I open it now?'

'Of course,' said Lucy. 'You're not thinking of sitting here all night without opening it, are you?'

9

I slid my finger under the Sellotape and unwrapped her present carefully.

'It's gorgeous,' I said as I held the delicate gold chain out in front of me. 'Really lovely.'

'Glad you like it,' said Lucy.

'Thanks, Lucy.' I kissed her lightly on the cheek and fastened the chain around my neck while she ordered the drinks.

'So how are your solicitors?' I asked as we settled into seats in the corner of the lounge.

'I'm sure there are loads of wonderful solicitors,' said Lucy, 'but I hate this job. Still, I was talking to Anna at the agency yesterday and she said that there were a couple of new jobs coming up soon. I told her I wanted something nice this time and she said she'd see what she could do.'

'Any preferences?'

'Human beings,' she said.

I laughed. 'They can't be that bad.'

'I don't want to talk about them,' she said. 'We're supposed to be having fun tonight.'

I drained my glass. 'My turn,' I said. 'Same again?'

The twins arrived as I came back from the bar with the glasses of beer. I got another couple for them and they handed over their present – a beautiful pale cream angora jumper and a multicoloured chiffon scarf.

'Happy birthday, Jane.' Brenda lifted her glass.

'Thanks.'

'So we've all finally made it to twenty-one,' grinned Lucy. 'We're all fully-fledged adults.'

'Tell that to my mother,' I groaned. 'She told me not to be home late tonight.'

The others laughed. Mam's concern for me was legendary. I suppose it was because I was an only child, but it was stifling all the same. Lucy's mother was far more relaxed than mine. Mrs McAllister never asked Lucy what time she'd be home. And the Quinlans' parents seemed to think that because the twins were together all the time it meant that they'd look after each other. I was the only one with parents who fussed.

'Brenda and I were thinking about getting a flat,' said Grace suddenly. 'What would you think of that?'

I stared at her. 'Would your parents mind?'

'I'm sure they'd prefer it if we stayed at home, but you can't live at home for ever. Besides, we want to live somewhere that's our own.'

'It's a great idea,' said Lucy. 'Maybe you and I should think of doing it, Jane.'

'We were kind of wondering if you would like to share with us,' said Grace. 'It'd be a lot cheaper.'

I looked at them in amazement. I'd never thought of leaving home before. Not to live in a flat, anyway. I assumed that I'd move out when I got married, but in 1981 Dublin girls didn't just up and leave and move into flats.

'What a brilliant idea,' breathed Lucy. 'It would be fantastic. I'd love to be out of our house. Michael's moved back home while he's saving up for the new bike and Joan and Emily are driving me crazy. My parents aren't too bad, I suppose, but the idea of living somewhere myself . . . what do you think, Jane?'

'I'd love it,' I said. 'Have you thought of anywhere?'

'Not yet,' said Grace, 'but we've been looking at the papers. If we get somewhere purpose-built, it would be best.'

'An apartment, you mean,' said Lucy. 'Not a flat.'

'Absolutely. We want to live somewhere nice. Not some crummy tenement in Rathmines.'

'Wouldn't that be terribly expensive?' I asked. I hadn't a clue about the cost of renting anywhere. It just seemed to me that a pretty, purpose-built apartment would cost a lot more than any of us could afford. It wasn't as though we were earning huge salaries.

'It would be OK if the four of us did it,' said Grace.

I shivered with anticipation. It would be fantastic to be four girls living together in an apartment. It would be freedom at last! We'd be able to do exactly what we wanted, whenever we wanted. I wouldn't have to account for every minute of my time. No more panicking on a Friday night because I'd had a couple of drinks and my clothes reeked of smoke from a pub. Mam went berserk whenever I came home smelling of drink or smoke. She immediately assumed that I'd been on a massive binge. It was terribly unfair of her. I'd only been utterly drunk once before, and that was such a disaster that I vowed never to get into that state again.

11

I shuddered as I remembered leaning over the toilet bowl while my parents stood outside the bathroom door ready to give me an earful when I could stand up again. God, that was awful. I hated being sick. I hated the loss of control. That was why I'd never drunk eight vodkas, two pints and a bottle of wine in a single night again.

'So what d'you think, Jane?' asked Lucy.

'I know my parents will go mad,' I said, 'but I'm all for it.'

'Great.' The twins looked pleased. 'Does anyone have a definite idea of where the apartment should be?'

'Not me,' said Lucy. 'Although something near town. I need to be near a bus stop so that I can get in early if I've got a job in some out-of-the-way place.'

'I don't mind at all,' I told them. 'Anywhere will do me.'

We spent until closing time talking about our flat. Our apartment. It was great. I finally felt grown up whenever I thought about living in an apartment. You couldn't really feel an adult when you lived at home. No matter what, you were always the child. I suppose it's difficult for a mother to think of a child as anything other than someone who needs their love and attention all the time, but I was ready to move on. I knew Mam wouldn't be happy about it. I knew there'd be a scene and I hated scenes, but it would have to be done.

When we were finally thrown out of the pub, Lucy insisted that we go to a nightclub.

'You can't possibly go home yet,' she told me. 'It's your twenty-first, Jane. It's appalling that you're not having a party.'

I sighed. 'I told you before – I'm not a party person.'

'I know, I know.' She looked at me in exasperation. 'But you've got to make the effort. Come on, let's go to Annabel's.'

The twins were all on for Annabel's and I gave in. I couldn't be a party-pooper all my life. We joined the queue outside. The doorman stared long and hard at me before he let me in. I looked too young, I knew. I was the youngest of the four by about three months but I looked at least a year younger than the others. The twins were both elegant girls. Tall and dark, they had a great sense of style. That was why they'd got jobs in the department store – they simply loved clothes. Lucy, who had looked young for her age in school, had found her look in France. Tiny and demure as a teenager, she'd blossomed in the last year. But I was still the same. I hadn't quite managed to tame my wild, curly hair or find a look that fitted me yet. I was growing up inside, but my appearance hadn't caught up with how I felt.

Annabel's was crowded. We pushed our way into the throng of people on the dance floor.

At least this was better than the cricket club dances of my teenage years. When we were at St Attracta's, everyone went to the cricket club disco on a Friday night and tried to meet the man of their dreams there. It never worked, of course. Blokes you'd never seen before would ask you to dance, hold you tightly in their arms and then leave you standing there like an idiot when the music speeded up again. I hated the cricket club but I always went. You knew that the night you didn't show up would be the night that *he* would be there.

We were so naive, I thought, as I danced around my handbag. What chance did anyone have of meeting the man in their life at a bloody disco?

'Would you like to dance?'

The lights had dimmed and the music was slow. He stood in front of me and smiled. The girls grinned at me and gave the thumbs up.

He put his arms around me and I leaned against his chest. He wore a denim shirt. I liked denim shirts. His aftershave was Brut.

But there had to be more important things in my life than love. I'd tried it, and I wasn't very good at it. Each time I'd gone out with someone, I'd truly believed that this was it. That it was for ever. Even with Jesse. I hadn't quite got the hang of simply going out and having a good time with someone. Was everyone as silly as me, I wondered, as I moved around the floor with him and tried to ignore the fact that the button on his shirt pocket was digging into the corner of my eye. Not Lucy – she'd had a few boyfriends since she'd come back from France, and none of them had lasted longer than a couple of months. Not the twins – they didn't seem to need men in their lives. They were different from other people. Not anyone else I knew. I was the sole idiot in town.

'Thanks,' he said as the music speeded up again. 'Would you like a drink?'

I shook my head. Suddenly I didn't want to be here any more. The girls were standing beside the bar.

'I've had enough,' I said. 'I think I'll go home.'

'Are you sure?' asked Lucy. 'It's only one o'clock.'

'I'm sure,' I said. 'Stay if you want to.'

'No,' she told me. 'I'm tired, too.'

We all left together and piled into a taxi outside.

'Riverview Estate,' said Lucy. 'Terenure.'

The driver nodded. I sat in the back with the twins while Lucy chatted away to him. I didn't listen to the conversation but leaned my head against the window.

Twenty-one. It had seemed very old when I was at school. Now I realised that it was nothing at all.

Chapter 2

April 1981
(UK No. 2 – *Making Your Mind Up* – Bucks Fizz)

I stood in front of the mirror in my bedroom and gazed in appalled fascination at my reflection. I looked like a Neapolitan ice cream.

Mam and Dad had bought me a watch for my birthday. It was a neat gold watch with a gold chain. They should have left it at the watch but Mam had also bought me the yellow dress. Some girls with flame-red hair could wear yellow dresses and not look ridiculous, but I wasn't one of them.

I couldn't understand my mother. She always looked so pretty herself, it was extraordinary that she didn't know what looked well on me. Whenever she bought something for me, I think that she saw herself in it. The yellow dress would have been perfect for her.

I thought about not wearing it, but that would have hurt her feelings. I sat at my dressing-table and wondered if there was anything I could do to salvage my appearance. What I really wanted to do was to wear a pair of jeans and a T-shirt, but that would have caused a riot.

My face stared back at me from the mirror. Grey-green eyes set wide apart, no cheekbones worth mentioning, generous mouth. At least I didn't have freckles. I hated freckles.

I rubbed foundation on to my cheeks and went heavy with the blusher. I didn't bother with make-up during the day but maybe I should have. It would make me better at using it at night. I brushed the silver eyeshadow on to my lids and loaded my lashes with mascara. Then I outlined my mouth with lip-pencil and filled in my lips with the red lip-gloss that had come free with *Woman's*

Own that week. I slid my cameo earrings on to my ears, hung Lucy's gold chain around my neck and put on my new watch.

I still looked like a Neapolitan ice cream.

Mam didn't say anything when I appeared downstairs. She must have thought I looked ridiculous. Compared to her, I was a complete mess. She wore a light green skirt with matching jacket and a white blouse. She looked great. Unlike any of the other mothers I knew, Mam was thin. Both Mrs McAllister and Mrs Quinlan were rounded sort of women. They looked like mothers. Mine still looked like a person. I wished she looked more like a mother. It would make it a lot easier for me.

We were late by the time we arrived at the Walnut Rooms and the rest of the family was already sitting at our table. We were escorted to it by a man wearing a dress suit and white gloves which I thought looked silly. I had never been to the Walnut Rooms before, since 'Patrons' were supposed to be over twenty-one. The rest of the family frequented it for birthdays or anniversaries or, in the case of Mam, a girls' night out with her sisters, Olivia, Judith and Joan, three times a year.

The 'Rooms' were really just one room, but it was huge. At one end was a stage and in front of that was a large dance floor, surrounded by tables. The backdrop to the stage consisted of hundreds of strips of foil paper in gold and silver, which fluttered in the draught of the room. Emblazoned across this in huge red lettering was 'Stevie Cleere and His Band' and the stage was ready for Stevie and company, silver coloured chairs awaiting their arrival.

Our table was near the stage. It was a big, round table, covered by two tablecloths, one pink and one mauve with a matching pink and mauve flower arrangement in the centre. It was all a little startling to the eye and clashed horribly with my yellow dress.

When we arrived all my relatives stood up and clapped which made me feel hugely embarrassed because people at the other tables turned around to look at us. I could feel my cheeks burn as I slipped into an empty seat. Aunt Olivia kissed me and congratulated the 'birthday girl', which again made me flush with embarrassment, and I squirmed uneasily. I looked around the table, trying to avoid the eyes of my relatives and smiling uneasily as I failed.

There were still two seats empty, which surprised me because, as far as I could see, everybody was there. Except Declan, I suddenly realised. Aunt Olivia was sitting beside me. 'Where's Declan?' I asked curiously.

'He'll be here later,' she said. 'He's picking up Ruth.'

Ruth? I didn't know any Ruth. She was not a McDermott, Mam's side of the family, or an O'Sullivan. I'd never heard of her before.

'Ruth who?' I asked.

'Good God, Jane, don't you ever listen to anyone? Ruth is Declan's girlfriend.' Aunt Olivia looked at me as though I were an imbecile.

'Nobody told me,' I said defensively. 'And I haven't seen Declan in ages.'

'Neither have I,' laughed my aunt. 'Since he met Ruth, I'm not sure he even knows we exist.'

They arrived five minutes later. I was sipping my Coke and listening to the conversation around me, when I saw Declan walk into the room, accompanied by a girl I presumed was Ruth.

An amazing girl. Declan was tall, just under six feet and Ruth almost matched him in height. Afterwards, I realised that it was probably because of her footwear, but the first impression was of a tall, thin, pale beanpole. Her hair was waist length and jet black, and fell in a straight sheet around her face. She wore a black T-shirt and long black skirt and a black shawl around her shoulders. She also wore spindly black shoes with an incredible heel which added inches to her natural height. The only colour she wore was provided by a huge silver cross hanging from her neck and her nails and lips, which were post-box red. She was incredible. I'd never seen anything like her before and felt even more foolish in my buttercup yellow dress.

'Hi everyone, this is Ruth.' Declan proudly introduced her as they sat down opposite me. He told her the names while she inclined her head graciously in the direction of each person, but didn't speak. 'And, of course, my Cousin Jane, the birthday girl,' he said cheerfully. I tried to smile. She looked at me as though I wasn't really there. 'Jane and I used to be great friends when we were children,' continued Declan blithely, 'but we don't see as much of each other now – do we, Jane?'

'No.'

Ruth opened her black handbag and took out a packet of cigarettes and a lighter. I watched her with interest. My parents hated smoking. She lit a cigarette, still without speaking, and took a long, deep drag. Then she exhaled the smoke very, very slowly. She turned and whispered in Declan's ear.

He smiled benevolently at her and kissed her on the forehead. I wondered if he'd noticed that she looked like Morticia in *The Addams Family*. Declan was such an ordinary-looking person, I couldn't believe that it hadn't struck him that his girlfriend was extremely odd.

'So what do you do, Ruth?' Mam smiled at her.

'I'm a hairdresser,' she replied. Her voice was husky and low.

'Really?' Mam made it sound as though she had always wanted to meet a hairdresser. 'Where do you work?'

'Peter Marks,' she replied. 'I'm a colouring specialist.'

I choked back a laugh. Colour specialist! Specialising in black, no doubt. All the same, I had to admit that she was attractive once you got used to the black. Her skin was flawless, her eyes (after you discounted the make-up) were sultry brown and her neck was long and graceful. Her hands, too, were long and narrow with perfectly shaped nails. As I looked at them, I curled my fingers into my palms to hide my own nails. I didn't bite them much these days but whenever I was nervous I picked at them and they were uneven in length.

The waiter came over and asked her if she wanted something to drink.

'A martini,' she said.

'And I'll have a pint,' said Declan.

Our family stopped looking at Ruth and began its own conversations. I decided to head for the Ladies.

I stood in front of the long mirror and felt more uncomfortable than ever. In comparison to Ruth, I looked childish. Even if she hadn't been there I would have felt silly but now my sense of discomfort was multiplied a thousand times. My face, which I had thought looked nice when I left the house, now seemed bland and uninspired. My thin-soled sandals were ludicrous. I felt a freak.

They were bringing around the starters when I arrived back at the table. My seat was between Aunt Olivia and Granny McDermott.

'You look very nice, lovey,' shouted Granny. She was a little deaf and shouted at everyone now.

'Thanks,' I said.

'I like the colour,' she said. 'Very bright.'

I wasn't sure whether this was really meant as a compliment or not. I gave her the benefit of the doubt.

'Thanks, Granny.'

'Reminds me of a dress I once had,' she continued. I sighed. Granny was a reminiscences person. Once she started, she just went on and on. I think that memories of things in the distant past were more clear to her than memories of things that had happened yesterday. She seemed to be able to conjure up people and places of her youth at will and retreat into their company. Or, as now, inflict their company on you. I listened with half an ear to the exploits of young Rosie McDermott and Ian and Glenda, without really hearing any of it.

Mam was talking to Joan about the supermarket. 'People continually try to just walk out,' she said. 'It's amazing. For the sake of a tin of beans or something. They need better security. And the kids try to rob the sweets all the time.'

Dad talked about cars. 'It was the carburettor,' he told Dick, Aunt Judith's husband. It was always the carburettor, I thought.

'Anyway,' said Uncle Kevin, 'I thought the best way to do it was to Rotavate the garden. Start from scratch. A big job. Worth it, though.'

'So I tried on the size fourteen,' said Dad's sister, Kathleen, 'and it wouldn't go near me! I was so embarrassed. Then she said, "Would madam like to try a larger size?" She said it loud enough for the whole damn shop to hear. So I told her no, that I didn't really think it would do for the larger lady.'

Judith nodded. 'Little upstarts,' she said. 'I won't go near any of those boutique places.'

'It looked lovely, though,' moaned Kathleen.

I applied myself to the egg mayonnaise. The conversation was inane. Who cared about dresses and carburettors and Rotavated gardens? I hoped I'd never become the sort of person who spent their time talking about their house. I wanted to be – different.

I watched Ruth, who pushed her food around her plate without eating it. I'd have loved to be able to ignore food like that, but once it was in front of me I had to eat it. That was probably why I wasn't a willowy beanpole.

'So how's the bank?' asked Declan suddenly, looking at me.

'Oh, OK, I suppose,' I said.

'Fed up already,' he teased. 'You're probably too intelligent for the bank.'

'Don't be stupid.'

'I'm not. You were always clever, Jane.'

'You're clever,' I said, blushing.

'Not like you.' There was real envy in his voice. 'I thought it was unfair the way you passed exams without studying for them.'

I laughed. 'Technique. At least we don't have to worry about them any more.'

'Thank God,' he said feelingly. 'I hated school.'

'I was glad to leave school,' said Ruth, suddenly joining in the conversation. 'It bored me rigid.'

'Where did you go?' I asked.

'Sisters of Mercy,' she said laconically. 'Bitches, all of them.' I looked around anxiously in case my mother had heard. She wouldn't approve of calling the nuns 'bitches'.

'Why?' I asked.

'Frustrated virgins,' said Ruth. 'It's not normal for women to lock themselves away like that.'

'But they're not exactly locked away, are they?' I asked reasonably. 'Not if they're teaching in the school.'

'Not all of them did,' she said. 'In fact, very few, I think. And they were probably considered racy.'

I laughed and she smiled. It changed her face completely. Quite suddenly, I liked her.

'So you work in a bank and you're bored. I work in a hairdresser's, but really I want to sing.' I looked at her in alarm, afraid that she might suddenly burst into song there and then.

'Professionally,' she added.

'Really?'

'Oh, yes.'

'Ruth is a brilliant singer,' said Declan. 'She's like a female Rod Stewart.'

I imagined he was right. That husky voice would sound great on a record.

They cleared away the plates and brought the soup. Aunt Olivia turned to me.

'How's the job?' she asked.

I wished people would stop asking me that. I answered non-committally. She extolled the virtues of hard work. I listened and said nothing.

The main course arrived but Ruth didn't eat her chicken. 'I'm a vegetarian,' she explained.

'That's silly,' said Donal O'Sullivan, who was on the other side of her. 'People need meat.'

'No, they don't,' Ruth said. 'You can get all the nutrients you need in vegetables.'

'Give me meat and potatoes any day,' said Kevin, to a rousing cheer from the assembled men. 'It might be all right for you lassies,' he added, 'but we men need our meat.'

Declan looked uncomfortable. I wondered if he was practising being a vegetarian because of Ruth. But he ate the chicken anyway.

The cabaret started. Stevie Cleere and his band played fifties music. Stevie was wearing a gold lamé coat and had his hair slicked back Teddy-boy style. My relatives loved him. I hated it. Declan and Ruth seemed oblivious. He watched her and she chain-smoked.

Then Stevie Cleere started playing requests. He called out a special one for 'The O'Sullivan family at table number three. A wedding anniversary and a twenty-first birthday! Best wishes from everyone!!' A spotlight spun in our direction and highlighted us. I was embarrassed but my parents were delighted. The band played a brief snatch of the *Anniversary Waltz*, then *Happy Birthday*, while the waiter brought a big cake over to the table.

Dad stood up and made a brief speech to the assembled O'Sullivans and McDermotts. He said that Mam had made him the happiest man in the world twenty-three years ago, and again twenty-one years ago, and that his family meant more to him than anything else. I cringed.

Once the cake had been handed around, various members of the family got up to dance. I stayed where I was with Granny O'Sullivan, Gramps McDermott, Declan and Ruth.

'Why don't you get up and dance?' demanded Granny, at the top of her voice. 'A young girl like you shouldn't be sitting down.'

'I hate dancing.' I had to remember not to shout back at her, but speak clearly. She hated being shouted at.

21

'No young one hates dancing. Your mother loved it. Always sneaking out to dances, she was.'

I looked at Granny in amazement.

'Wearing too much make-up and shiny skirts. I didn't like it, I can tell you, young Jane. I gave her a good talking-to.'

I loved the idea of somebody giving Mam a good talking-to.

'And what did she say?' I asked.

'You know the sort of thing. Girls have to enjoy themselves. I told her that doesn't mean staying out all night and kissing people on the street.'

'Who did she kiss on the street?' I asked.

'Martin Farmer,' she said. 'I never liked him. I was glad when she gave him up.'

I'd never heard of Martin Farmer.

'What else did she do, Gran?' This was a great opportunity to get information.

'All the things young girls do. Silly things.' Her voice trailed off. She had retreated into the past, her eyes were distant.

'You won't find out anything from Granny,' said Declan, suddenly turning around to me. 'She's too discreet.'

'Oh, I don't know,' I said. 'She's already told me about another of my mother's boyfriends – Martin Farmer. And I happen to know that she had someone called Fritz for a while. God knows how many else.'

'She still only married one person,' said Declan.

I made a face at him.

'Come on, Jane.' Dad came over to the table. 'Time for a dance with my daughter.'

'I'm useless at dancing,' I moaned but allowed him to take me on to the dance floor.

'You need lessons,' he said.

'Nobody dances like this any more,' I said. 'Lessons would be a waste of money.'

'No, they wouldn't. People will always like this sort of dancing. It might go in and out of fashion, but it will last longer than that shaking around you go on with.'

'I don't much like shaking around either,' I admitted.

'Your mam likes dancing,' he said. 'Always did.'

'She's good at it.'

'So would you be if you practised.'

'No, I wouldn't. I'm too – too lumpy.'

He held me away from him. 'Don't be silly,' he said. 'You're perfect.'

I suppose all fathers think their daughters are wonderful, but it was nice to hear my father say so. What's more, he almost believed it. I gave him a hug.

Stevie Cleere introduced 'Josefina – with a voice like spun gold.' She sounded like Edith Piaf. I hated Edith Piaf.

'You sing better than that,' Declan told Ruth, who looked pleased.

Around the table again people had switched places. Joan and Kathleen were beside each other and I eavesdropped on their conversation. Not deliberately, but my back was partially turned and I couldn't help hearing them.

'So if you like him, why didn't you bring him along?' Kathleen asked.

'Not to something like this,' said Joan. 'This is not my sort of thing, really.'

'Oh, I enjoy our get-togethers,' said Kathleen. 'We hardly get to see each other.'

'This family sees each other far too often,' observed Joan. 'The McDermotts know too much about each other. But if I said I didn't want to come, they'd go mad.'

'So what is he doing tonight?'

'I don't know. Sitting in front of the TV, I suppose. Missing me, I hope.'

They both laughed. I was in shock. It sounded like Joan had a boyfriend. The thought was horrifying. She was old. Joan, I thought, should either be married or single. People her age didn't have boyfriends. It was too ludicrous for words. She was nearly forty, for God's sake! She should have more sense.

I got up and went to the Ladies again. I sat in a cubicle, picking at my nails. What if I never found another boyfriend? What if I was still looking for someone when I was forty? It was a horrible idea. I should be out having fun tonight with people my own age. Not hanging around with desperate forty year olds.

I recognised Judith and Olivia's voices outside.

'He's besotted with her, of course,' said Olivia tensely. 'And she's just stringing him along.'

'But there's no harm in it,' said Judith.

'Of course not. Not yet, anyway. But I would so like him to go out with a normal girl.'

'She's probably very nice under all that black,' said Judith.

Olivia laughed. 'It's hard to tell, isn't it? It's simply that I imagined Declan would pick someone more – oh, I don't know.'

'More ordinary?'

'I suppose so.'

'He hasn't picked her yet,' said Judith comfortingly. 'It'll probably peter out. How old is he now?'

'Twenty-two,' said Olivia.

'He'll grow out of her. Or she'll change,' said Judith. 'How old is she?'

'I'm not sure. Something around the same, I suppose.'

'I'll bet you any money that by next year she'll have cut her hair and changed her colour scheme,' said Judith.

'Hopefully not to yellow,' said Olivia, and I could hear the laughter in her voice. 'Isn't poor Jane's outfit appalling?'

I froze.

'She's not a raving beauty, is she?' asked Judith.

'It's strange when you consider Maureen at that age,' said Olivia.

'Maureen was beautiful,' said Judith. 'I always envied her. She was so much prettier than the rest of us. Poor old Jane must feel like the proverbial ugly duckling whenever she sees her mother.'

'Oh, Jane will grow into herself,' said Aunt Olivia easily. 'Maureen never needed to. She just had an aura about her.'

'Do you remember Nick Maguire,' laughed Judith, 'and how he kept pushing poems to Maureen through the letterbox?'

'And she hated him.' Olivia laughed, too.

'Wonder what became of him?'

Olivia didn't answer, but I presume she shrugged, consigning Nick to the heap of Mam's spurned lovers.

'We'd better get a move on,' said Judith. They used the toilets, washed their hands and left. I waited for a few minutes before I moved. Then I wiped the tears from my cheeks.

I was outside my body for the rest of the night, an observer, not a participant. I could see myself sit around the table and laugh at people's jokes, dance with Dad and Noel, even once with Declan. But it was not me who was dancing with them, but somebody

24

being watched by me. I talked to Olivia and Judith and hated them while smiling at them. Hating their pity for me, knowing they were laughing at me all the time. I watched Ruth and filed away her poise and indifference to use myself at a later date. I watched them all as they mellowed through the evening until it was time for us to go home. I could see some of myself in some of them, in a movement or expression, but I didn't want to be like them, talking of their childhood and their houses and trivial things. I was beyond this and I now pitied them for the shallowness of their lives.

The drive home was quiet. We dropped Gramps back to his house where, contrary to his expectations throughout the evening, nobody had broken in and robbed him and where all was peaceful. Mam helped him get ready for bed while Dad and I sat in the tiny parlour. Dad nodded off while I read the paper, the silence of the room only broken by the solemn tick of the clock on the mantelpiece and an occasional snore from Dad.

He was cranky when Mam came downstairs to wake him up. She insisted on driving the rest of the way back home, which terrified me because she was an awful driver. It terrified Dad too, so he kept his eyes shut for the entire journey.

I climbed into bed and pulled the covers around me. It had been a dreadful night – no worse than I'd expected, but I knew now that I had to change my life. They were all sorry for me – I could see that. I needed to become someone else. Someone like Ruth. With panache. I couldn't play it safe any more. At the very least, I would go to Ruth's hairdresser's and get my hair cut.

It would be different when I moved out, of course. When I moved in with Lucy and the twins, I'd be able to spread my wings a bit more. I was going to take my life in my hands and do things. I was going to grow up at last.

Chapter 3

May 1981
(UK No. 12 – *Can You Feel It* – Jacksons)

I didn't get to see Lucy at all the following week. I was up to my neck in work and Jessica was a complete slave-driver. I checked letters of credit and sent off confirmations as though my life depended on it. On Friday night, the gang from work decided to go for a few drinks. Jessica said that she was buying – we deserved it. We arrived at the pub at half five and it was already crowded with bank employees. We found a table in the corner and nabbed a few seats. There were five people in our section – Jessica, Peter Mulhall, Lisa O'Toole, Alan Grant and myself. We got on well together although we were very different people. Jessica, Peter and I were the hardworking ones. Lisa really wanted to work in Personnel and Alan was lazy. But great fun.

'Did you hear about Ellen Henderson?' asked Jessica as she put her glass on the table. 'She resigned. She's going to work in RTÉ.'

'Doing what?' asked Lisa.

'Presenting a kids' programme,' Jessica told her.

We looked at her in amazement. 'Really?' I asked.

Jessica nodded.

'Fair play to her,' said Alan. 'I couldn't sit around making soppy jokes about kids.'

'You'd never last,' said Jessica tartly. 'TV works to a tight schedule. You're not exactly known for your timekeeping.'

We waited for Alan's reaction. 'I do my best.'

'Your best isn't exactly great,' said Jessica. 'What makes you late all the time?'

'Exhaustion,' said Alan. 'I live life to the limits.'

Jessica regarded him thoughtfully. 'If you live it to the limits like you've been doing lately, you'll be in trouble,' she warned him. 'I've got you off the hook twice already this month.'

Alan looked slightly abashed. 'I know. You're a pet, Jessica. I promise to be good in work if I can be bad outside it. Anyone for another drink?'

We nodded and Alan went off to order.

'He's mad,' said Lisa.

'Takes all sorts,' said Peter. 'And he's a bit of a laugh.'

I liked Alan. In my new, get-it-together life I half-wondered if he was the sort of guy I could go out with. I knew that he wasn't the sort of person I could spend the rest of my life with, but that was a separate issue. But there was no spark with Alan and you needed a spark.

He was frighteningly handsome. His hair was jet black and his eyes were navy blue. His body was tanned and muscular. I felt my heart race.

I didn't know him. I'd never met him before in my life. I met him in St Stephen's Green. I was feeding the ducks. He spoke to me and I knew then. The spark was there. I wanted him. No pretending.

'Are we going clubbing afterwards?' asked Alan as he returned with more drinks. 'There's a gang at the other end of the bar going out to Parks.'

'I don't mind,' I said. 'Whatever anyone wants to do.'

'I won't,' said Jessica, 'but don't mind me, I just don't like nightclubs.'

I was going to go to a nightclub. No more pretending that I wasn't interested. I was going to go and I was going to have a good time. I got up and went to the loo. Despite the fact that the pub itself had been done up last year, they hadn't bothered much with the toilets and the small area was crowded with girls trying to do running repairs on their make-up while others queued for the two cubicles.

'Fucking ridiculous,' said one girl. 'All these people and two fucking toilets. What do they think we are?'

I stood in the queue, grateful to be under the air-conditioner.

I always felt faint when pubs were crowded and when the air became thick with perfume, sweat and smoke.

I locked the cubicle door. Ever since the night in the Walnut Rooms, I expected to hear people talking about me in the Ladies. It was pathetic, really. I came out and redid my face. I pulled my brush through my hair and wondered how long it would take for it to grow again.

It had been a mistake to get it cut, I thought, as I looked at myself in the mirror. I'd got it done at lunch-time on Monday, but it hadn't been a good idea. My carrotty curls were gone and the hairdresser had created a much sleeker look which relied on masses of mousse and gel. It looked very stylish, but it wasn't me. I wasn't a short-haired person. I would be glad when it grew again.

I pushed my way back into the bar.

'Watch where you're going!' The voice was angry.

'Sorry,' I said.

'So you should be, you've nearly drowned me.' He looked at me, fury in his eyes.

'Oh, relax,' I told him. 'It's only a drink.'

'It was a drink that took nearly fifteen minutes to get,' he said.

I laughed. 'You mustn't come here very often,' I said. 'Look, if it makes you feel any better, I'll order you another one.'

'No, thanks,' he said. 'I couldn't allow that.'

'Why not?' I asked.

'Bit unfair,' he said. 'I only allow girls that I take out to buy me drink. I'm old-fashioned like that.'

'Well, you had your chance and you blew it,' I told him.

'Maybe you'll go out with me sometime and then I'll allow you to buy me as much drink as you like.'

'Maybe I will,' I said with a wink as I made my way back to our table.

'Is he from the bank?' I asked, indicating him as I sat down.

'That's Rory McLoughlin,' Jessica told me. 'He works in the dealing room.'

'The dealing room?' I said curiously. 'Where they quote us the exchange rates?'

'The very one,' said Jessica. 'Shower of assholes.'

Jessica so rarely criticised anyone that we looked at her in amazement.

'They are,' she said. 'Think they know everything. Paid too much money, and think they're worth it.'

'What exactly do they do?' asked Lisa.

'They buy and sell foreign currency,' said Jessica. 'You know how there can be a foreign currency amount on our letters of credit? Well, the dealers set the rate that we convert into pounds.'

'Oh.' Lisa nodded. 'Might be interesting.'

'It's very fast,' admitted Jessica. 'I was in the room a while ago. They spend the entire time shouting at each other.'

'Why?' asked Lisa.

'Because exchange rates change all the time,' Jessica told her. 'And if they don't buy or sell at exactly the right time they can lose money.'

'Sounds my kind of job,' said Alan. 'Especially if they pay better.'

'You have to be there all the time,' Jessica said. 'They start at eight in the morning.'

'Oh, my God!' Alan rolled his eyes in his head. 'The perfect job has just turned into a nightmare.'

We laughed. 'Actually, they can't do it for very long,' said Jessica. 'Because it's so high-powered and pressurised, they burn out.'

'I feel burnt out and I don't even do that work,' laughed Peter.

'You must have to be very good at maths,' I mused.

'Absolutely,' said Jessica.

'Rules me out, then,' I said. 'I only barely passed it in my Leaving.'

'How the hell did you get a job in a bank then?' asked Lisa.

'My incredible personality,' I told her. 'And they obviously thought that an A in history would be very useful!'

We ordered some more drinks. I was pleasantly mellow by now. I wondered if Lucy would drop in. She'd said that she might, but she was going to an interview at five o'clock and she might just go straight home afterwards. I looked at my watch. Almost eleven. The night had flown.

'Last orders!' shouted the barmen.

'One for the road?' I asked.

My colleagues nodded. I pushed my way towards the bar again.

'Stand clear, stand clear!' Rory looked at me in mock horror and moved away. 'It's the drink spiller,' he said.

'You spilled your own,' I told him. 'Don't blame me.'

I shouted my order across the bar. 'Are you sure I can't buy you one?' I asked.

He shook his head. 'Thanks, but no thanks.' He was drunk, but not very drunk. It took a moment for the blue eyes to focus on me again.

'What's your name?' he asked.

'Why?' I returned.

'I'd like to know.'

'Why?'

'I don't know. I'd just like to know.' He looked confused.

'Jane,' I told him.

'Jane.' He rolled the name around on his tongue. 'Jane.' He looked thoughtful for a moment. 'What rhymes with Jane?' he asked.

I shrugged. 'Plain springs to mind,' I said. It always did.

'That's too common, besides, it's not true,' he said. 'No – wait, I have it. Jane – hair aflame, shall we kiss, in a lane.'

'What!'

'It's a poem,' he said. 'I've entitled it "To Jane".'

'Thanks very much,' I said. 'You're very thoughtful.'

'Don't you like it?' he asked.

'It's the nicest poem anyone has ever composed for me,' I said as I paid the barman.

'Let me help you with the drinks,' said Rory.

'If you like.'

He came back to the table with me. The gang looked at him.

'I'm Rory,' he said. 'This is Jane.'

Peter grinned and winked at me. 'Peter,' he said. 'And Lisa and Alan. You know Jessica already.'

Rory furrowed his brow and looked at her. 'Of course I do,' he said gallantly, as he took her hand and kissed it. 'Jessica. I could never forget Jessica.'

'How nice,' she said.

He looked around at us. 'Do you all work for the bank?'

Alan nodded.

'And a great organisation it is, too,' said Rory. 'Don't go away. I'm getting my drink.'

He wandered off and I looked at the others helplessly. 'He just tagged on,' I said. 'Sorry.'

'Oh, he's all right,' said Jessica. 'He probably won't be back anyway. The dealers are a very cliquish crowd.'

But he did come back, carrying two pints of Guinness.

'We haven't seen you here before, Rory.' Jessica sipped her drink and looked questioningly at him.

'Oh, we usually drink in Larry's,' Rory told her. 'But this isn't a bad pub. Good company.'

Jessica dug me in the ribs and I tried to ignore her.

'So, where do all you guys work?' asked Rory.

'International,' said Peter. 'Not as exciting a job as yours.'

Rory looked pleased with himself. 'It's pretty intense,' he said, preening.

'D'you ever get to go abroad?' I asked.

'Sometimes,' said Rory. 'We go to London a bit. I was on a course there the week before last. And there's a forex conference every year. I haven't gone to that yet, but it's held in various countries. It's hard work.'

'Sounds it.' Peter couldn't keep the irony out of his voice.

Rory ignored it. He turned to me. 'How long have you been with the bank?' he asked.

Suddenly, I was interested in him. I don't know whether it was the blue of his eyes, or the lock of red-brown hair that fell into his right eye or even whether it was the scent of an unfamiliar aftershave which wafted from him, but the attraction was there. I felt myself straighten in the seat and look at him more closely.

'Couple of years,' I said, opening my eyes wide at him.

'I've never seen you before,' he said.

'Nor I you.'

We were silent for a moment. The others no longer existed as we looked at each other.

'Are you going anywhere later?' he asked.

'Perhaps.' I looked at the others. They looked back, unconcerned.

'Do you want to go for something to eat?'

I did, but I didn't want to abandon my friends. I looked at them quizzically.

'Not me,' said Jessica decisively. 'I have to get home. I'm getting up early tomorrow.'

'Nor me,' said Peter.

'I wouldn't mind a bite,' said Alan.

We stared at him, then he winced as Lisa pinched him.

'Come on then, Jane,' said Rory. 'There's a nice little restaurant around the corner.'

'D'you mind?' I asked the others.

'Absolutely not.' Jessica smiled. 'See you Monday.'

I followed Rory out of the pub. The air was cold, the warmth of the previous week gone. I shivered slightly and pulled my jacket around me.

'Cold?' asked Rory.

I shook my head. 'Not really.'

We didn't hold hands or anything as we walked side by side up the street, although we both stopped to look over Baggot Street Bridge. Rory rummaged in his pocket and took out a penny which he threw into the water. I watched him in amazement.

'I always do it,' he told me. 'Every time I cross the bridge. It's for luck.'

'What sort of luck?' I asked.

He smiled at me. 'Any sort, really,' he said. 'Luck in work, usually. But other things too.'

We stared at each other for a moment and I moved towards him, but he suddenly shuffled and thrust his hands into his trouser pockets.

'Come on,' he said. 'I'm starving.'

I walked along beside him, struggling to keep up with his long, ranging stride. He was an odd person, I thought, unlike anyone I had ever known before. Supremely self-confident, but strangely disconcerting.

'Slow down, can't you,' I pleaded breathlessly.

He stopped mid-stride. 'Sorry,' he said. 'I always walk quickly.'

The restaurant was Italian, small and dimly-lit. There were posters of Italian cities on the walls and lighted candles in Chianti bottles on the tables. It was pleasantly warm with an aroma of garlic and oregano. A waiter who wore a black suit with a deep red cummerbund and green bow tie approached us.

'Mr McLoughlin,' he said. 'So nice to see you.'

'Hi, Mario,' said Rory. 'Can we have a table for two?'

'For you, of course,' said the waiter. 'A nice, intimate table, perhaps?'

32

'That would be excellent,' said Rory.

We followed the waiter to a table at the back of the restaurant. He gave us a couple of menus. 'Would you like anything to drink?' he asked.

'A bottle of red,' said Rory. He looked at me. 'That OK?'

I nodded, still half reading the menu.

'Have you decided?' Rory asked me after a minute or two.

'The tortellini would be nice,' I said.

'And for you, as usual, the spaghetti?' Mario looked enquiringly at Rory.

'You know me too well,' said Rory. 'Perhaps I should have something different one day.'

'Perhaps this should be that day,' said Mario.

Rory looked at Mario and then at me. 'Perhaps.' He sounded doubtful. 'Oh, what the hell,' he said. 'Mario, I like the spaghetti. Give me the spaghetti.'

The waiter laughed. 'Whatever you want.'

I didn't know what to say to Rory. I looked at him carefully. He had a strong face, high cheekbones, high forehead, determined chin.

'So what do you do?' he asked me.

'Nothing as exciting as you,' I told him. 'International trade. I check letters of credit, that sort of thing.'

He nodded, but he wasn't listening to me. He closed his eyes.

He had incredibly long eyelashes, the sort any girl would die for. They looked unaccountably soft against cheeks with a five-o'clock shadow. He snored gently.

I looked around. Nobody was watching us. I kicked him softly under the table. He grunted, opened his eyes and looked around him.

'Wake up,' I said.

'What?' He looked startled. 'Oh shit, Jane – I'm sorry.'

'It's OK,' I said. 'You're tired.'

He pealed with laughter and this time people looked at us.

'I'm not tired,' he said. 'Well, a bit, I suppose. No, my lovely Jane, I've had about eight pints of Guinness tonight and if anything's wrong with me, it's that I've drunk far too much and I've been unbelievably unfair to you. I've dragged you to my favourite restaurant, I haven't been exactly wonderful company and I've had the absolutely disgraceful cheek to fall asleep. I'm very, very sorry.'

He looked down at his plate, but not before I saw a glint of amusement in his eyes.

'You're a terrible spoofer,' I said easily. 'You're not a bit sorry.'

He smiled and took my hand. His grasp was firm and confident, his palms dry.

'I am sorry I fell asleep,' he said. 'That was rude. But I'm not sorry I went to the pub – despite my best intentions – and I'm not sorry I stayed to drink more than I should have, because otherwise I wouldn't have met you and that would have made me even sorrier.'

He was amazing.

'I'm not sorry either,' I said, finally.

'Good.' He unfolded a napkin with a flourish. 'Now here comes Mario with our food – why don't we just eat up.'

The tortellini were wonderful, cooked in a gloriously light tomato sauce and bursting with flavour. I told Mario as much when he came to check on us.

'I'm so glad,' he said, beaming at me. 'I will tell the chef.'

'The chef is his brother,' Rory told me. 'They opened last year. It's incredibly good.'

'Do you eat here much?' I asked. 'He seems to know you very well.'

'It's the in-spot for dealers,' said Rory. 'We all eat here.'

'Are all dealers really clever?' I asked.

Rory grinned. 'I am,' he said, with that self-confident air that I was beginning to recognise, 'but not everyone is.'

'What do you do when you're not working?' I asked him. It was difficult to make him volunteer any information.

'I play golf,' he said.

I groaned. 'Not another one.'

'What do you mean?'

'Nearly everyone in the bank plays golf. It's so utterly boring.'

He shook his head. 'It's a brilliant game,' he told me. 'What else would have you out in the fresh air for four hours?'

'Almost anything,' I said.

'Ah, but so much business is done on the golf course,' said Rory. 'You play any other sport and you don't have time to talk. With golf, it's different.'

'Why would you want to do business when you're playing a game?' I asked.

He clucked at me. 'You've a lot to learn, young Jane,' he said. 'If you ever want to get on in business you've a lot to learn.'

I played around with my food. 'I don't know if I want to get on in business,' I said.

'Everyone does,' said Rory. 'Everyone wants to do well and make pots of money and if anyone says different, they're lying.' His tone was strong and sure.

'There are other things,' I told him. 'Like happiness.'

'Anyone who says money doesn't buy happiness is poor,' Rory commented. 'The only reason they say it is so you can feel good about not being able to afford three holidays a year and a house in Foxrock.'

'That's a terrible thing to say.'

'But true.' Rory sucked a strand of spaghetti from the fork and it sped into his mouth like an express train, scattering tomato sauce as it went.

We both laughed. He took my hand again.

'I like you, Jane,' he said.

'I like you too.' I looked at my plate.

Rory filled my glass with wine. It was smooth and slid down my throat with ease. The combination of wine and beer was making my head heavy. I'd have a hangover in the morning.

'Dessert, coffee?' asked Mario, clearing away our plates.

'Cappuccino,' said Rory. 'Do you want anything, Jane?'

'Coffee,' I said dreamily.

The walls of the restaurant were expanding and contracting. I blinked a few times to clear my head.

'It's very warm,' I said, closing my eyes.

'You going to fall asleep on me now?' asked Rory, who had suddenly come to life.

'No, no,' I said. 'Just resting.'

I don't remember drinking my coffee, but I remember Rory took me by the arm and steered me out of the restaurant. Mario bade us farewell and shook Rory by the hand.

'See you soon, signorina,' he called after me.

I ran my tongue around my lips. They were dry.

'Come on,' said Rory. 'I'll get you home. Where do you live?'

'I'm perfectly capable of getting myself home,' I told him, shaking my head in the cool night air. 'There's no need for you to put yourself to any trouble.'

I really wished I hadn't drunk so much. OK, some Fridays we did give it a bit of a lash, but it wasn't something I did regularly. Three drinks and a couple of Cokes was usually my limit. After all, I was a sensible person.

'I have absolutely no doubt that you'd be able to get home yourself,' Rory told me. 'But it's late and I don't think it would be a good idea to have you wandering around near the canal at this hour. So please let me see you home.'

'I'll get a taxi.' I clutched his arm and missed my step.

He caught me and drew me closer to him.

'We'll share a taxi,' he said, looking down at me.

He was not my usual sort of person. His face was too hard and he wasn't exactly good-looking. Interesting, maybe, but not handsome.

All the same, I looked into those compelling blue eyes. There was a magnetism there that I couldn't ignore.

He smiled at me and kissed me. In the middle of Baggot Street, with people around us, we clung together in our own world. His mouth pressed harder on mine and my body moulded into his. I might still be a virgin, I thought wildly, but I'm a good kisser.

He groaned slightly, and took his lips from mine. I looked at him thoughtfully. He tightened his hold.

'Now I'm definitely not letting you go home on your own,' he said. 'Where do you live?'

'Near Terenure,' I told him.

'That's OK,' he said. 'No problem.'

'Where do you live?' I asked.

'Blackrock,' he answered.

'But really, I live out of your way,' I protested. 'I can get a taxi myself.'

He let me go and held me at arm's-length. 'Is there some reason,' he asked in exasperation, 'that you don't want to share a taxi with me? Do I have B.O.? Am I so incredibly ugly that you don't want to be seen with me? Are you afraid that I'll lead you to a fate worse than death?'

I laughed at him. 'No.'

'Then for God's sake, woman, share a taxi with me.'

I bit my lip to stop laughing. He looked so funny in his mock anger.

'Of course I'll share a taxi with you,' I said. 'I'm just playing hard to get.'

'Oh, really,' he murmured, pulling me towards him again. 'How hard to get?'

'Not very,' I answered. 'Not very hard to get at all.'

Our progress along the canal was slow. Taxis passed us by, and we didn't care. I felt safe and secure in his arms, and I was happy to stop every few yards to kiss him. He tasted of wine and garlic and I supposed I did too. His aftershave was strong and masculine. His hold was possessive and fierce. But he never did more than kiss me, he didn't try to undo the buttons of my cotton blouse, he didn't even slide his hands under my jacket as I'd half expected. He kissed me with an intensity that was almost frightening, but which I returned.

The night air was cold, but I didn't feel it. I was tired, but I didn't notice. When we got to Portobello Bridge, Rory suddenly held me away from him.

'Better get you home,' he gasped, 'before I do something that I won't be responsible for.'

I raised an eyebrow.

'Witch,' he said and kissed me again. 'Witch.'

I held him closely.

He flagged down a taxi and we bundled into it.

I gave my address to the driver, while I burrowed into the crook of Rory's arm.

'I want to let you know that I'm not ready for a steady relationship,' he whispered into my ear.

I turned my head to look at him. 'Why not?'

'Because I'm a busy person. I work hard. I'm twenty-six years old. I'm not sure I'm ready to settle down.'

'Rory,' I hissed back. 'We've had a drink and something to eat. It's hardly a lifelong commitment.'

'So long as you understand,' he warned. 'I don't want you to get the wrong idea about me.'

'I like you,' I said. 'I won't get the wrong idea.'

But I more than liked him, I thought, as I finally slid between the sheets of my single bed that night. He interested me more than any other man I had ever met. There was an intensity about him, an energy that no one else I knew possessed. Whether he liked it or not, I was going to see more of Rory McLoughlin. I could feel it, and I knew that somehow our lives would slot together. Even if he wasn't ready for a steady relationship yet. Hell, *I* wasn't ready for a steady relationship. But I was ready for a bit of fun, and I was sure that Rory would be fun.

Chapter 4

May 1981
(UK No. 19 – *I Want To Be Free* – Toyah)

I didn't see Rory McLoughlin the following week. We were in a different wing of the building to the dealers and I'd never even been on the dealing-room floor. I'd seen pictures of it, of course: they always plastered them into the Annual Report, pictures of people holding two phones to their ears and trying to write at the same time. Progressive. Dynamic. Hard-working.

I was put out that he hadn't bothered to call, despite both our assurances to each other that we weren't looking for a long-term relationship. The least he could have done was phone me, I thought miserably. I tried to forget about him. I was still stuck in the groove of thinking that each man I met should be for ever. I did my best to shove him into the back of my mind and not to jump like a frightened gazelle every time the phone rang.

Jessica Fitzgerald teased me gently about him, although I swore to her that we had only gone for something to eat and that nothing had happened.

'Nothing?' she asked, her voice unbelieving.

'Not the sort of thing you're thinking about, anyway,' I returned. I took my pen and ran through a checklist of numbers.

'Stop pretending to work,' said Jessica. 'I can't believe you didn't get up to anything with Rory.'

'Why ever not?' I demanded. 'It's not as though he's really my type.'

'Because everyone wants to get off with one of the dealers,' she told me. 'They earn good money, they have a great life and most of them are good-looking.'

'Rory McLoughlin is not good-looking,' I informed her. 'Not

in my book, anyway. He's interesting, though.' I was pleased to be able to say all this without blushing.

'I'll be watching you,' she said, picking up a file from my desk. 'And if you spend your time taking personal phone calls, I'll know I'm right.'

I made a face at her retreating back. I was a bit disappointed that Rory hadn't called, although I didn't want to admit to it yet, not even to myself.

I bent over my letters of credit and read through the documents, turning over the sheets of paper with frantic speed.

Lucy's phone call distracted me.

'Busy?' she asked me, with the air of one who is not.

'Pretty much.' I glanced up to see if Jessica was watching me.

'Can you talk?'

'You talk, I'll listen.'

'Well, look, Jane, I think we should do the flat-hunting tonight and tomorrow. I can do it tonight, so can Brenda and Grace.'

'Do you have anywhere in mind?' I idly circled an error in the papers. Could nobody ever get things right? This would have to be done again.

'We've three,' said Lucy.

'Three!' I was surprised. I hadn't realised that the girls had gone so far without me.

'Yes. The ones I told you about off Waterloo Road. They look great, Jane. Real apartments. Then there's a flat in Donnybrook Village – that's the downstairs of a house – and there's a purpose-built flat over some shops on Morehampton Road. All very convenient for work, don't you think?'

'Convenient for me, certainly,' I said. 'But you're out in Tallaght.'

'Only until the end of next week,' Lucy said. 'Anyway, let's face it, Jane, I could be anywhere. So where I live doesn't really matter. Besides,' she coughed self-consciously, 'Dad is buying me a car.'

'A car!' I was overwhelmed with jealousy. 'A car!'

'Yes. It's my twenty-first present. He couldn't get it before now. It wasn't in.'

'Where's he getting it?'

Lucy was silent for a moment. 'Your dad's place,' she said.

I wished that my father, the garage owner, had bought me a car for my birthday. The watch Mam and Dad got me was lovely and I'd no reason to complain but a car would have been superb. Why, I wondered, couldn't my family have as much money as the McAllisters? My dad worked hard enough. It seemed terribly unjust.

'What sort of car?' I asked casually.

'Only a Mini,' said Lucy, but she could hardly keep the pride out of her voice.

'I'm delighted,' I said. 'That means we'll be able to drink and you can drive.'

'It means that I can live wherever we like,' Lucy reminded me. 'And I like the idea of Donnybrook. It's always seemed nice and classy.'

I laughed. Jessica glanced up at me and I immediately started checking papers again.

'Better than Rathmines, anyway,' Lucy said firmly. 'So can you meet us?'

'What time?'

'Sixish?'

'OK. Where?'

'Do you want to meet in the Burlington?' asked Lucy. 'We can look at the apartment there first and then walk up to Donnybrook.'

'No car yet?' I asked, disappointed.

'Not till tomorrow,' said Lucy. 'Your dad is giving it a service.'

'Good old Dad,' I said cheerfully. 'At least you'll be sure it'll go. Unless I find some important engine part lying on the table after tea. It has been known to happen.'

'Funny ha ha,' said Lucy. 'Look, I've got to go. I'll see you later, OK?'

'OK,' I said. 'Mind yourself.'

'*À bientôt*,' said Lucy.

I grimaced. Her habit of ending conversations in her newly-acquired fluent French always reminded me that she was the one who had spent the year away, not me. I wished, oh how I wished, that I'd made myself go. I hated the way she could chatter in French – not that there was anyone on the Riverbrook Estate who could chatter back, but it was amazing to listen to her all the same.

I looked at my watch. Four o'clock. I rubbed my eyes and sat back in my chair. Three flats to look at sounded great. I only hoped that I could persuade my parents that I wouldn't turn into some wild, permissive person as soon as I moved out.

41

I hadn't yet broached the subject of the flat with them. They couldn't actually do anything about it now, of course, I was old enough to make my own decisions, but I hated being at odds with Mam and Dad. This was still my greatest problem. That I hadn't been a rebellious teenager, that I hadn't really caused them endless nights of grief. I'd never dyed my hair, or worn outrageous clothes or safety pins through my nose. So when I told them that I wanted to do a perfectly simple thing like stay out overnight (as I had when Lucy had come home – we'd stayed at her brother Michael's place), or go away for a weekend, they always spent ages asking me to explain in minute detail where I was going and who I would be with. That's all very well when you're seventeen, but a bit much when you're twenty-one.

The only way Mam and Dad would ever see me as an adult was if I left home and lived my own life. It wasn't that I didn't care about them, didn't love them in my own way. It was simply that I couldn't possibly live with them any more.

I hated it when Mam complained about the state of my bedroom. It was my room, surely she shouldn't care if I left tights on the floor? I hated it when she criticised my hair. It was my hair, I could wear it however I liked. I hated it when she wanted to know where I was at every moment of the day. I wanted my freedom. The bliss of putting my key in the door whatever time of the day or night I liked and not hearing the whispered 'Is that you, Jane?' I couldn't wait to move into the flat.

The girls were already at the Burlington when I arrived. Brenda and Grace looked uncannily alike. They both wore their department-store skirts and blouses, blue skirts and blue and white striped blouses. I would bet anything that customers took a double take when they moved from Ladies' Separates (Brenda) to Evening Wear (Grace). They would wonder how on earth the salesgirl could move from one side of the floor to the other so quickly. Despite the fact that the girls usually wore their hair differently, they were identical tonight. I blinked at them. It took a moment to decide who was who.

'Hi, Jane,' smiled Brenda (the gold chain with the initial B the giveaway for those that needed it). 'Want a drink?'

Lucy looked anxiously at her watch. 'I said we'd be there by a quarter past six,' she said. 'It's nearly that now. Maybe we should just go?'

'I don't mind,' I said. I slipped my jacket back on. 'Let's head off.'

'The ideal thing about here,' said Lucy, as we reached Waterloo Mews, the apartment block off Waterloo Road, 'would be how near it is to everything. The hotel, the pubs, the shops—'

'And work,' I said. It would be ideal for me.

'What about the other flats?' asked Grace. 'Aren't we going to look at them?'

'Oh, sure,' said Lucy. 'But what do you think, girls? If this one is OK, will we just go for it?'

'If they'll let us,' said Brenda. 'I think this would be the best.'

'We haven't even seen it yet,' said Grace. 'Wait until we look first. It might be an awful tip.'

But the apartments were new, and still smelled of fresh paint and recently laid carpets. The block was five storeys high, in warm red brick with black wrought-iron balconies protruding from each apartment. The sun shone weakly, casting a watery glow across the face of the building.

I liked the look of the apartment block. It looked stylish and modern and I liked the idea of moving into a purpose-built block rather than taking over part of a house.

The letting agent was waiting for us in the lobby.

'There's a security camera.' He waved his hand in its general direction. 'Follow me, will you.'

We trooped after him.

'Third floor,' he said, 'it's quicker to take the stairs.'

The stairs were carpeted in pale green. I thought it might get dirty very quickly, and then I mentally slapped myself for such a domesticated, middle-aged thought.

'Number Thirty-Three,' intoned the agent. 'This way, ladies.'

We fell in love with the apartment instantly. It was impossible not to. The door opened into a small hallway, off which were four doors.

The agent flung one open. 'Living area,' he said. 'Very bright and spacious. Gets the evening sun.' The rays flickered over the floor.

'It's lovely,' I whispered to Brenda, who nodded. The room was decorated in pale blue and grey: china-blue wallpaper on which hung some pretty water-colour prints, smoke-grey carpet and natural pine furniture. The agent was right. It was a bright, airy room.

'Kitchen in here.'

The kitchen was a small room off the living room, a room to stand up in, not for sitting in. It was white and green, with white Formica cupboards with green handles, white ceramic tiles with a green leaf pattern.

'There's a waste disposal unit in the sink,' said the agent.

'Nice,' murmured Lucy.

He led the way back into the hallway. 'Bedrooms here.' He opened two of the doors. 'One slightly bigger than the other. Both with fitted wardrobes.'

We wandered around the bedrooms. Both were decorated identically, yellow and mauve. A bit bright for my taste, but pretty nevertheless.

'I like it,' said Brenda.

'And this is the bathroom.' He opened the last door. 'No window in here, but an extractor fan.' He switched it on as though it were an astounding feat of engineering.

'I love it,' said Grace.

'I'll leave you to look around for a few minutes,' he said.

We wandered through the apartment again, thrilled to bits with it. I'd no desire whatsoever to see any crummy half house in Donnybrook or a flat over shops. This was the one I wanted. I stepped out of the sliding doors on to the balcony. The evening sun was disappearing from it now, but later in the summer it would get the full benefit of its westerly aspect. Despite the fact that we were near Baggot Street and Leeson Street the sounds of the cars were muted and distant. Birds chirped at each other from the copse of trees in the grounds. It was perfection.

I turned back inside. The girls were still wandering around the apartment, exclaiming with delight over any little item that took their fancy.

'I bought it for you.' He looked at me.

'What on earth do you mean?'

'I want you to have somewhere of your own. A bolthole, if you like.'

'But Armand—'

'No, please, Jane. It is important. You are my life, you know that. But I am in France, you are here. It is necessary for you to have somewhere of your own, no?'

'Of course I want somewhere of my own. But I can't possibly—'

'No, please. A gift. From me. From the bottom of my heart.'

'Armand—'

'Jane, you cannot refuse this of me. Whether we stay together or not, this is still my gift to you. For all you have done. For the love you have given me.'

'It's too much.'

'Don't be silly. I already have two houses, a villa in St Tropez, an apartment in New York. Surely one little apartment here, in your town, is not too much? I want to give it to you. I love you.'

'I love you too.'

We melted into each other's arms. Time stood still. The evening sun slipped below the balcony as his lips found mine . . .

The twins returned to the living room, smiling. 'What do you think?' asked Brenda.

'I love it,' I said. 'I feel part of it already.'

'Me too,' said Grace. 'Isn't it cute?'

'And there's quite a lot of space,' said Lucy, who had come back into the room. 'It doesn't feel at all poky or anything, does it?'

'How much is it,' I asked, 'compared to the others?'

'Fifty pounds a month more than the house, thirty more than the flat over the shops.' Lucy checked her notebook.

'Can we afford it?' I asked. I knew, divided by four, that I could afford the rent. I was earning the most money and the rent on the apartment wasn't much more than I gave my parents, anyway. Of course, I'd have to pay for food and all the other expenses that I didn't have to worry about at home, but I knew I could manage. I'd got very good at managing finances.

'We can,' said the twins. 'Once we keep up our commission levels,' added Brenda. 'And we're good at selling. Did you know that the take in my department is up over ten per cent on this time last year?'

Brenda was extremely proud of her sales ability.

'And mine by twelve per cent,' said Grace. 'Although we have two new salesgirls as well as me.'

'And you, Lucy?' I asked.

'No probs,' said Lucy. 'I'm employed by an agency now, not the individual companies. I can manage.'

'So will we go ahead?' I asked.

Although Lucy had organised the viewing, everyone waited for me when it came to making the decision.

The girls nodded happily.

The agent was standing in the kitchen looking out of the window. I cleared my throat as I entered the room. He turned to me.

'Have you decided on anything, girls?' he asked.

'We'd like to take it.' I tried to keep my voice calm.

He smiled at me. 'Good,' he said. 'There are a few things we have to sort out.'

He listed all the things he needed. References, a bank statement, a deposit. I protested. He told me that they needed all these things to make sure that we didn't do a runner and leave the place in a mess.

'Once your references check out, then we'll be ready,' he told me. 'Then you can sign the lease and we're in business.'

'How long will all this take?' I asked.

'Only a week.' He smiled suddenly and looked altogether more human.

We had hoped that we'd have everything signed and sealed that evening, and it was a bit disappointing not to be given the keys there and then. But we resigned ourselves to it. Besides, I still had to break the news to my parents.

We had a celebratory drink in the Burlington. Lucy rang the other flat owners and told them that we wouldn't be out to look at their places, then we talked about housekeeping, division of labour and electricity bills.

Brenda and Grace said that they'd take the smaller bedroom, since they were used to sharing. Lucy and I were happy to take the other one, although the smaller bedroom actually had a bigger window, and I liked big windows.

I decided not to say anything to my parents until we heard back from the agent that everything was OK. We couldn't see what could go wrong, but I couldn't allow myself to believe that we'd actually got it until he rang.

I spent the next few days in a rash of feverish excitement, waiting for his call. Jessica put my edginess down to the fact that I hadn't heard from Rory, but for once in my life I wasn't pining for some man. The idea of the apartment was far more appealing than anything to do with Rory McLoughlin.

So when we bumped into each other in the staff canteen later that week I was offhand, and he looked surprised when I brushed by him without stopping to talk. From my vantage point at the table near the window I was able to observe him more or less unseen and I could tell that his eyes had followed me and that he was watching me.

Stuff him, I thought, as I speared a chip – why did they have to be so soggy, they drooped over the fork. If he's interested, he can do the running. If he isn't . . . well, if he isn't, there are plenty of people who are.

I didn't care that currently there weren't any interested men. Anyway, once we had our apartment I could see a vista of weekend parties and any number of men stretching out into my future.

Kevin Spencer, the letting agent, rang me the following Thursday to tell me that everything was in order and that I could sign the lease at lunch-time on Friday. I was the only one who could get the time to call into his office, and so I was the only one who was going to sign the lease. That meant that I would be the one responsible for it. The responsibility was awesome. This was the single most adult thing I'd ever done in my life.

So I called around, sat in the stylish office and waited for him to appear with his folder and his pens and I signed the lease on Apartment 33, Waterloo Mews, off Waterloo Road, Dublin 4.

I walked out with the keys, throwing them up and down in my hand, trying to look casual, until they slid out of my grasp and into the gutter. I scrabbled after them in a panic and pushed them safely into the side pocket of my handbag.

I phoned the girls, told them that I'd the keys, and asked them when they wanted to move in.

Lucy, Brenda and Grace all said that they could move in straight away. Brenda told me that her father had offered to move their things; Lucy had taken delivery of the car and said that she was already packed. I was the only one who hadn't even had the nerve yet to mention the subject at home.

Mam and Dad were already sitting at the dinner table when I arrived home. Mam took a plate of pasta out of the oven for me. I wished that she wouldn't bother making food for me. I was never sure what time I'd be home and it was ludicrous for her to cook meals that I might not eat. But she did, time and time again, despite my protestations. I eyed the congealed pasta in despair before realising that this was the last time. I could eat it with good grace because I wouldn't be coming home any more.

It was like plastic in my mouth, although I didn't know whether that was because it had dried out in the oven or because I was too nervous to eat.

I broached the subject when Mam poured out her second cup of tea.

'Lucy and I are thinking about moving into a flat.' I kept my voice ultra-casual.

'Don't be ridiculous,' said Mam. 'You don't need to move into a flat.'

'Why?'

'Because you've a perfectly good home here. There's no need for you to throw money down the drain renting a flat. Besides, they're all damp and horrible.'

'Not this one,' I said. I was still keeping my voice casual.

'You mean you've looked at one?' Mam was horrified. 'Without telling us first?'

'There wasn't any need to tell you anything,' I protested.

'Well, don't bother thinking about it any more,' said Dad. 'Your mam's right. It's an awful waste of money. Better stay here and save up for a house.'

They hadn't a clue.

'We're, um, actually thinking of moving in this weekend,' I mumbled.

'You're what?' Dad put his cup carefully into his saucer and regarded me thoughtfully. I hated it when he regarded me thoughtfully.

I cleared my throat. 'I'm moving into an apartment this weekend,' I told them. 'With Lucy and the Quinlan twins.'

'And you didn't think to discuss this with us?' Mam was angry.

'There was nothing to discuss, surely.' I tried to sound reasonable. 'I mean, I was going to move and so I went to look at the apartment and – well . . .' My voice petered out.

'It would have been nice to mention it at home before you did anything.' Dad folded his newspaper and put it on the table beside him. 'Why didn't you say anything until now?'

'No reason,' I said. 'We weren't sure we'd actually get this apartment or anything, so I didn't think there was any need to say it until—' I faltered. 'It didn't seem worth mentioning.'

'You're leaving home and you didn't think it worth mentioning,' said Mam. 'That's wonderful.'

I sighed deeply. I knew that the conversation would turn out like this. But this way, it was a *fait accompli*. There was nothing they could do. If I'd discussed it earlier, they would have found a thousand reasons why I should stay at home a bit longer. And I, feeling guilty, might have stayed.

'So where is this flat?' asked Dad.

'It's not a flat,' I said strenuously. 'It's a purpose-built apartment. It's lovely, Dad, really it is. It's off Waterloo Road.'

'Convenient for work,' he said. I shot him a grateful glance.

'You won't feel like you've even left work,' said Mam. She stood up and started to clear away the dirty dishes, crashing them into the sink. I bit my lip.

'When exactly do you intend to move in?' asked Dad.

'Over the weekend,' I said. 'Mr Quinlan said he'd move Brenda and Grace's things and Lucy can pile her stuff into the car.'

'Do you want a hand, then?' asked Dad. 'I suppose our car is big enough for almost everything.'

I smiled at him. 'Thanks,' I said.

'Is that all you have to say to her?' Mam abandoned her dishwashing and looked at Dad. 'That you'll help her move?'

'I don't see that we can exactly stop her, do you, Maureen?' he asked her. 'After all, she is twenty-one. She's an adult.'

Mam sat down. 'I know,' she said.

I didn't know what to say. Part of me understood how she felt but I had to live my own life. Dad could recognise that. Why couldn't she?

The atmosphere was a touch icy for the rest of the evening. Dad tried to keep it light, but Mam was fretful and annoyed. When I went to bed that night, I could hear the murmur of their voices through the wall. I supposed they were talking about me. I pulled my pillow over my head and tried to go to sleep.

When I came home from work the next day, I found most of my possessions neatly packed in brown cardboard boxes. I looked at Mam in surprise.

'I had nothing to do this afternoon,' she said lamely. 'I thought I'd help.'

I hugged her, and she buried her head in my shoulder. 'Be careful,' she said fiercely.

'Of course I'll be careful.' I looked at her in amazement. 'What do you take me for?'

She held me at arm's-length. 'It's not that I don't trust you,' she began.

'. . . but,' I added.

'But.' She smiled at me. 'OK, I trust you.'

'Thanks.' I kissed her on the cheek. 'Do you want to help me pack my clothes?'

Mam was a good packer. I don't know why, because it wasn't as if she ever went away anywhere. Maybe it was because she was naturally neat and tidy, but she folded my clothes far more professionally than I ever could myself. We took things out of my wardrobe and then she went into the spare room and called out to me that I had almost a hundred jumpers in there and how many of them did I want?

I followed her into the bedroom and looked at the mound of knitwear on the bed.

'Anything else in there?' I asked, peering into the wardrobe. I smiled suddenly, for there it was, where it had been for the past four years, my gossamer-light deb's dress. Still shimmering in the evening sunlight, still elegant.

'Don't suppose I'd fit into it now,' I said regretfully, looking down at my body.

'Oh, you probably would,' said Mam loyally.

'Don't think so,' I said. 'I've grown.'

We laughed, sharing the joke.

I selected some jumpers from the pile. 'I'll leave some of the others,' I told her. 'Anyhow, I might come back and stay the night from time to time. I might need some clothes here.'

She nodded, happy with my remark. I'd no real intention of returning home, but I owed her something.

The great move took place on Saturday morning. For the first time in about ten years, I was awake on Saturday before eleven o'clock. My eyes snapped open at about nine, and I was out of the bed and under the shower by half past. I stood under the

50

heavy flow of water, allowing it to course through my hair and trail down my body. I closed my eyes and dreamed of freedom.

We had already decided on the sequence of events. At the moment, I was the only one with a key. I would get three more cut on the way over to the apartment and be there by half past eleven. I told them that I would wait, that I wouldn't go into the apartment before they arrived, but the twins said not to be stupid, to go in and put on the kettle.

As it turned out, I was there by eleven o'clock. Mam and Dad both came with me – they wanted to see where I was living. I opened the door and showed them in, bursting with pride.

The sun hadn't yet come around to the living room and the balcony was still in shade. But the rooms were bright and new, and both my parents approved of the apartment. Mam particularly liked the intercom and video which meant that we could see someone at the door before we let them in. She thought it was superb security and I knew she felt better knowing that nobody could barge into our apartment unnoticed and unannounced. Dad liked the sink disposal unit. Both of them liked the balcony and promised some flowers in pots for it. Dad lugged my gear upstairs and I hauled the boxes into the bedroom that I was to share with Lucy.

Mam and Dad left before the others arrived and for that I was truly grateful. It meant that I had ten minutes in the apartment by myself, feeling proprietorial. I walked from room to room. It was perfectly silent in a way my home never had been. It seemed as though it was waiting for us to bring it to life.

I stood in front of the full-length mirror in the tiny hallway. Jane O'Sullivan, apartment dweller. Adult. It was great. I laughed aloud with the excitement of it all.

The shrill blast of the intercom sent me into orbit. When I stopped shaking I picked up the receiver. The video screen flickered into life. Brenda and Grace waved at me. I pressed the button and heard the buzzer of the main door as the twins disappeared from view. The intercom buzzed again and Mr Quinlan's face appeared. 'Let me in,' he said. 'I've got all their clothes!'

The Quinlans piled into the apartment, filling the hallway with luggage.

'What a lovely place,' said Mr Quinlan, giving it a cursory glance. 'Hope you'll be very happy here, girls.'

'Thanks, Dad,' said Brenda.

'I'll be off then,' he said. He didn't bother to stay and check out everything like my parents had. He seemed totally uninterested.

'See you, Dad,' said Grace. 'I'll phone you later.'

'Do you have a phone here?' he asked.

I shook my head. 'Not yet.'

'Oh well, the hotel is near enough if you need to call,' he said. 'See you, Jane.'

He picked his way through the hallway, climbing over the boxes.

'I'll pull them out of the way,' promised Grace. 'God, Jane, isn't this great!'

I hugged her. I couldn't help it.

'Where's Lucy?' asked Brenda.

I shrugged. 'No sign,' I said. 'Probably still in bed.' I walked over to the balcony and flung open the doors. 'Although how she could possibly sleep . . .' I stepped outside and leaned over the balcony rail. Behind me, I could hear the Quinlans pulling boxes around the apartment.

Outside, the sky was blue, the air warm. The traffic was a distant hum and there were no children's voices. We were in our sophisticated, adult world. 33 Waterloo Mews.

Lucy's green Mini hurtled up the road and screeched to a stop outside the block. She climbed out and looked up, pushing her blonde hair out of her eyes.

I waved frantically at her. 'I'll open the door for you.'

'Come down and give me a hand,' she yelled. 'I can't carry all this myself.'

More boxes were hauled into apartment 33, which was beginning to look like a construction site.

'Before we do anything,' Lucy reached into one of the boxes, 'let's celebrate!' She pulled out a bottle of Asti. 'Not exactly vintage champagne,' she said, 'but it fizzes and makes a popping noise.'

'Brilliant!' cried Brenda.

'I've got glasses,' I said. 'Dad gave me a collection. He gets loads of them from petrol companies.'

I rummaged around and found the box full of glasses. I tore off the cellophane and took them out.

'Better rinse them,' I said.

'Don't be daft,' said Lucy. 'It's alcohol. It'll kill any germs.'

She pulled the foil wrapper from around the cork. 'Ready?'

She eased the cork out of the bottle and it popped pleasingly. She filled the glasses. We stood in the middle of the living room and clinked the glasses together.

'To the apartment,' I said.

'The apartment,' the others echoed.

'To girls on tour!' cried Lucy.

'To us.'

We spent the day unpacking. It was very domesticated really and not at all exciting, but we had a great time. I hated hanging up clothes at home. By the afternoon, everything I possessed was neatly hanging on rails in the wardrobe.

We unpacked crockery and cutlery, our books and our clothes. Brenda played her cassette recorder at a level that probably would have had us instantly evicted, except that nobody had yet moved into the apartments beside us.

Ludicrously, for a Saturday night, we sat in. Lucy and I drove up to the Chinese takeaway and brought back curries and sweet and sour. We sat in front of the Quinlans' portable black and white, eating Chinese, drinking the wine we had bought and revelling in our freedom. Then we sat around in a circle, and talked until four in the morning before we fell, exhausted, into bed. I was happier than I'd been in ages.

Chapter 5

June 1981
(UK No. 13 – *Ain't No Stoppin'* – Enigma)

The rain fell unremittingly from the cloud-filled sky, splashed through the trees and cascaded across the pavements, forming wide oil-streaked puddles that filled the potholes in the roads. People scurried home, heads down, holding a sea of coloured umbrellas over them.

Raindrops plopped from the flat roof over the doorway of Waterloo Mews and joined the rivulet running frantically past the building; the torrent into which I stepped, soaking my feet completely.

I swore gently. It was not being wet that was the problem – I was wet through already – but it was the cumulative effect of being wet and cold in a month which was supposed to be summer that made me mad. I hated Irish summers. Each year, the promise of warm, sunny days. Each year, the reality of grey skies and stiff easterly winds.

I pushed open the entrance door and hurried up the stairs to our apartment, the plastic shopping bags bouncing off my legs.

The relief was immense when I finally got myself and my bags into the apartment. I shook my wet hair and slipped off my sodden coat and shoes. I opened the bathroom door. A forest of damp tights and drying knickers met me. I hung my coat on the back of the door, dumped my umbrella in the bath and carried my bags into the bedroom.

It had been a good day's shopping. I'd bought a new skirt and blouse in Pamela Scott's and a new pair of shoes in Fitzpatrick's. The skirt was lilac, calf-length but with a long slit up the side. It was both demure and seductive and, teamed with the crisp white blouse, it looked devastating. My shoes were lilac too, totally unwearable during the day but they would knock 'em dead at night. They were high-heeled, spiky and hard to wear, but I knew that they were fabulous. I didn't mind suffering for my appearance.

I made some coffee and drank it in the living room, as I looked out of the window at the dismal vista outside. The white plastic chair looked forlorn, a puddle of rain in its seat. The terracotta pots were miserable along the balcony, their purple and yellow pansies beaten into the clay by the sheer volume of rain. I leaned my forehead against the window and gazed into my coffee cup.

A month had passed since we'd moved in together and it was working well. A few minor quibbles about leaving half-opened bottles of milk on the table and not in the fridge; a bit of a barney over Lucy's habit of borrowing everybody else's make-up; occasional quarrels about whose turn it was to hoover the carpet, but overall we got on well together.

Sometimes days passed without us actually seeing each other. Brenda and Grace left first in the morning. They walked down to Grafton Street and always had a cup of coffee in Bewley's before they started work. So I sometimes missed them. I was the last to leave because my journey to work was the shortest. In fact, I probably spent the most time in the apartment. Lucy had a new (but not serious) boyfriend and she went out with him occasionally; the twins often went out at night together. I liked sitting in though, even when I was alone.

I was tired today. It was Saturday. The twins were at work and so was Lucy, currently temping in a travel agency. So I could afford to stretch out on the sofa and drape my legs over its padded arms. I had been out late the night before with the crowd from work. We'd done the pub and then Annabel's, which was now very convenient for me because I could stagger home. There was a reason for our revelry – Jessica had been promoted and was now manager of the entire department. One up for the working girls, I'd told her.

She'd grinned and said it was hard work. It was true, she told me, that you had to be twice as good for half the recognition. I was glad that Jessica's niceness hadn't got in the way of her promotion, it gave me some faith in the system.

Surprisingly, I was becoming more interested in work myself. Up until now, I had seen my job as simply a way to pay for my social life and I'd wanted promotion for the higher salary. But I was getting good at it, able to anticipate problems and stave them off and even to solve them when they did arise. I enjoyed the challenge now and I wanted to be busy. I liked having to call our correspondent banks in places like Caracas and Rio. It made me feel as though I really had a global job, instead of one situated in Dublin, Ireland. Jessica's promotion made me realise that I could get on too and believe in my work.

I lay down on the sofa and closed my eyes. It would be nice to be somewhere like Caracas or Rio now, I thought, listening to the incessant thud of the rain against the window. At least it would be warm.

The house was white, dazzling against the bright blue background of the sky. Its front was pillared and impressive; a flight of pink-tinged marble steps led up to a double doorway. Almond trees surrounded it, the nutty kernels wrapped in green fur. The scent of frangipani perfumed the air.

We sat around the pool, fanned by the breeze drifting up from the coast. The waiter brought long drinks in frosted glasses, decorated with an array of fruit.

My husband removed his sunglasses and took a drink.

'To you, my darling,' he said.

I raised my glass. 'Happy anniversary.'

We locked eyes. He stood up. His body was lean, sinewy, and sun-bronzed. He kissed me. It was deep and passionate. I groaned. We broke our embrace. He started to shake me by the shoulder. Why was he shaking me by the shoulder?

'Jane, wake up.' It was Lucy shaking me by the shoulder. I blinked at her, squinting.

'Wake up,' she repeated.

I sat up. It took a minute to orientate myself. I was angry at Lucy for dragging me out of my dream.

'What do you want?' I asked crossly. 'I was having a lovely dream.'

'Oh well,' she said, 'if you don't want to hear something miles better than the best dream you can imagine . . .'

I looked at her. I couldn't believe there was anything she could

56

tell me that was better than lying around the sun-kissed villa of Rio de Janeiro.

'When can you get your holidays?' she asked.

I shrugged. 'Not sure,' I said. 'I haven't actually put in for them yet although I'm supposed to. But everybody else had plans and I didn't so I didn't bother to fill in anything.'

'Can you get them next week?' asked Lucy.

'When next week?' I asked.

'Next Monday,' she said.

'Do you mean take Monday off?' I couldn't believe she was asking me to take Monday off.

She sighed deeply. 'Of course,' she said. 'God, you're thick.'

'If you told me what it was about,' I said tartly, 'I'd have a better idea of what I can and can't do. Anyway, I can't take Monday off because I haven't asked for it.'

Lucy looked at me as though I was mentally subnormal. 'If you want to go to Majorca you'll have to take it off,' she said.

I stared at her. 'Majorca?'

She bubbled with the excitement she had been suppressing. 'Yes. If you can get the holidays and if you have a hundred pounds to spare.'

'What do you mean?' I asked.

She smiled at me. 'There's a special offer in the travel agents,' she told me. 'A cancellation. We didn't get it until nearly closing time and by then it was too late to sell to anyone. For a hundred pounds a head, we can get an apartment in Palma Nova. Flight goes out tomorrow night.'

'Tomorrow night!' I felt like a parrot.

'Eleven o'clock.' Lucy flopped on to the floor and smiled at me.

We looked at each other like children who had broken into a sweet shop. I had two hundred pounds in my bank deposit account, even after today's shopping expedition. I could afford to go. I could go. If I could get the holidays. If I could get in touch with Jessica, perhaps. And if I could find my passport.

'Where's my passport?' I asked, in a panic. 'I need a passport, don't I?'

'Yes, you do,' said Lucy.

'But how will they get us the tickets?' I asked. 'If the flight's going tomorrow?'

'They'll leave them at the airport for us,' said Lucy. 'They do it all the time. I just go in and hand over the money and they give us the tickets and away we go.'

How could I get in touch with Jessica, I wondered frantically. I would have to let her know. If I went without telling anybody, they would probably fire me. But nobody else was on holidays next week, so it shouldn't be a problem. Unless they wanted to be pigheaded about it. Why should they be, though? After all, it wasn't as though there was any reason to stop me. Somebody else could do my work.

'I have to contact Jessica,' I said. 'I'll have to let them know.'

'Do you have a phone number?' asked Lucy.

'No. I don't think so. Maybe. I'm not sure.'

'Jane!' cried Lucy, in exasperation. 'Get your act together. Now can you go or not? Can you take the holidays, do you have the money, do you have a passport? Answer carefully, one at a time.'

I sat and gazed at the wall in front of me. 'I'm not sure, yes, yes but I don't know where it is.' I thought a bit more. 'I have no clothes,' I told her. 'Nothing summery, anyway. I bought stuff today but it's Irish weather stuff, not continental stuff.'

'It doesn't matter,' Lucy told me. 'You'll only be wearing a bikini and shorts.'

I shivered with excitement. 'I don't have a bikini,' I said blankly.

'Aaargh!' cried Lucy.

'OK, OK,' I said. 'I'm sorry. I'll get organised.'

I rummaged in my handbag. I knew that somewhere in there was Jessica's address. Maybe her phone number was there too.

'I'd better try and get Jessica first,' I said, emptying the contents of the bag on the floor. 'God, I hope I can go.'

Until now the furthest abroad I had been was a school trip to Brussels. It had been interesting, even fun at the time, but it was hardly in the same league. I couldn't imagine that tomorrow I might get on a plane, out of here and into the sun! It was almost too much to take in.

'Here it is,' I cried. 'Her address. And—' I paused triumphantly, 'her phone number!'

'Great,' said Lucy. 'Do you want to phone her now?'

'I'll go straight away,' I said. 'And I'll phone my folks as well. Oh, Lucy, this is brilliant!'

She smiled at me. 'I know,' she said. 'Will I look for your passport while you're phoning?'

'Yes.' I pulled on my wet coat. 'I think it's in the bottom of my bedroom locker somewhere.'

I raced out into the rain. I didn't mind that the back of my neck was cold and damp. We always used the phones in the Burlington whenever we wanted to make a phone call. The hall porter looked at me dubiously as I walked inside. I knew I looked a wreck but I didn't care.

Jessica was in, and was only too pleased to let me take two weeks' holiday starting Monday. 'Have a great time,' she told me. 'Send a postcard and don't overdo the duty-free.'

Mam was less enthusiastic. She wanted to know who the tour operator was, where exactly we were staying, why the other couple had cancelled, how we intended getting to the airport, what time the flight left and returned and how did Lucy know that there was a room in the hotel for us.

I tried to answer her questions, but obviously I couldn't tell her everything. I suggested that perhaps she and Dad might like to drive us to the airport and collect us when we got back. That way she'd be sure we left and sure we returned. Would that make her happy? I asked.

'Phone me tomorrow as soon as you have all the details,' Mam said. 'We'll see what we can do then.'

I hurried back to the apartment. Lucy was waving the green passport at me. 'Horrible photo,' she said.

'Get stuffed,' I told her. 'Jessica said yes! I can go!'

We hugged each other and danced around the living room. Suddenly the sound of the rain on the windows was welcome, a reminder of what we were leaving behind.

'How hot will it be?' I asked.

'I'm not sure,' Lucy told me. 'It was bloody hot in Paris last year, but I don't know what it will be like in the Med.'

The Med! It sounded fantastic.

'But it will be hot?' I asked anxiously. 'It's always hot in Spain, isn't it?'

'God, yes,' said Lucy. 'Like summer is meant to be.'

Brenda and Grace were green with envy when they came home to find us packing suitcases.

'You lucky cows,' said Brenda feelingly as she surveyed the piles of T-shirts and light summer skirts taking up the living-room floor. 'I'd love to be going on holiday.'

'Bitches,' said Grace. 'I hope it rains.'

She didn't mean it. The twins were two of the kindest people I knew. They offered us a selection of their own clothes. Decent of them, but Brenda and Grace were tall and willowy and, although I was tall, no stretch of the imagination would describe me as willowy. Lucy was smaller, and slight, but she borrowed a couple of long T-shirts which she said would look nice with a belt around the middle. 'Make a nice dress,' she said.

'Take lots of suntan lotion,' warned Grace. 'Everybody runs out of it.'

'It's cheaper over there,' said Lucy. 'So all the girls in the agency tell me, anyhow.'

'We can buy some in the duty-free,' I said.

Our cases were packed by nine o'clock. I laid out the clothes I wanted to wear tomorrow. I couldn't sleep that night. I tossed around in the bed and listened to the continuing rain. I couldn't wait for the following day.

Mam and Dad had agreed to drop us at the airport. They called around to the apartment at eight o'clock and Dad carried our bags down to the car. They hadn't been in the apartment since I moved in. Mam looked around with interest at the signs of our habitation – mounds of clothes waiting to be ironed, a scattering of books and magazines, Grace's clothes-design drawings. She examined the pots of plants on the kitchen window ledge and opened the cupboard door.

'You should have more vegetables,' she said.

'I'll eat them on holiday,' I promised.

The airport was crowded. Lucy found the holiday rep and asked about our tickets. My heart was pounding; I was terrified the girl wouldn't have a clue what we were talking about. After what seemed an age, Lucy returned, waving the tickets at me. So we were definitely going!

Long queues of people snaked around the check-in desks. We looked around for the one marked 'Palma'. It had the longest queue. I joined it immediately, terrified (stupidly) that somehow we might miss the flight if we didn't get in the queue straight

60

away. There were hordes of people in the airport and the noise and bustle was tremendous.

'You don't have to stay,' I told my parents.

Mam looked anxious. 'I should stay until you take off,' she said.

'That's not for nearly two hours,' I said. 'Don't waste your time. We'll be fine.'

'Come on, Maureen,' said Dad. 'Let's leave them to it.'

So they left. Mam hugged me and told me to have a great time. Anyone would think, I mused, that I was going away for good. It was only a holiday.

It took ages to check in, but finally we had our boarding passes and we went through to the duty-free.

'Don't buy booze here,' said Lucy. 'It's cheaper abroad. Everyone says so.'

'What should I buy?'

'We have to get sun protection, don't we,' said Lucy.

We stocked up with Ambre Solaire. I bought a bottle of *Charlie* and Lucy, who had a love affair with it since France, bought *Diorissimo*. I bought a huge bar of Cadbury's Fruit & Nut and Lucy bought an enormous Toblerone. Then we went to the bar and ordered Bacardi and Coke as a fitting holiday drink.

I felt a bit overdressed. I was wearing my olive-green jumpsuit which was very stylish, but not great in a crowded airport. Other people wore shorts and T-shirts. Lucy wore a light blouse and a pair of jeans, but she always looked comfortable and smart no matter what she wore.

As the hand of the clock pushed around towards eleven, I felt my stomach flutter with anticipation. We were still sitting in the terminal building at eleven-fifteen. People began to shift around in their seats, coughing, clearing their throats and looking at their watches.

Eventually the flight delay was announced. Our flight would leave at midnight. There were groans from the assembled throng, but Lucy and I didn't care. We ordered another couple of drinks.

'No point in worrying about it,' said Lucy. 'It happens all the time.'

I was glad that Lucy had the experience of her month at the travel agency behind her. She knew what was going on. Last week a couple had stormed into the agency, complaining that their hotel had been infested with cockroaches and that the food had been atrocious. Lucy confirmed that sometimes people ended up in awful accommodation, or the wrong apartment block or even, sometimes, the wrong resort.

'Still,' she said, 'unless you shell out a fortune for the holiday, why get into a frazzle about it?'

I knew that if my holiday had gone wrong I would get into a frazzle about it, but that was the difference between Lucy and me. She was always relaxed, no matter what happened. I let things get to me. Anything that went wrong, anything that didn't go according to plan, upset me. I was anxious now as I tapped my fingers on my thigh and looked out of the panoramic window at the huge aircraft coupled to the airbridge.

I presumed it was ours, but I wondered who on earth AirHols were. I had assumed that we would be travelling Aer Lingus. I had never encountered the charter flight market before.

'Want another?' asked Lucy, as she drained her plastic glass.

I shook my head. 'It'll send me asleep,' I said. 'Maybe later.'

Children were getting cranky. A baby cried, setting off another child. People looked around in irritation while parents anxiously tried to quieten their offspring.

We were delayed again. The people in the boarding area beside us filed on board the AirHols plane. I grimaced. That plane had been our plane. Hijacked, now, by the crowd at gate B26.

We watched it taxi slowly away from the building. We could see the movement of people behind the windows. It passed ponderously past our window and out of view. It was almost impossible to believe that this white painted bulk could ever get into the sky, let alone stay there.

Five minutes later it thundered along the runway and up into the night sky. Were we waiting for a plane to come in, wondered Lucy. If it hadn't arrived yet it would take at least half an hour, maybe even an hour, before we could board it.

'Let's have another drink,' I said.

While we sipped our drinks another plane, ChartAir, slid into the bay.

'Maybe this is it,' I suggested, half hopefully, half nervously. I was hopeful because I didn't want to sit in the airport for much longer, but nervous because ChartAir was painted bright pink and I had very little confidence in a pink aeroplane.

It was another half-hour before two air hostesses in pink uniforms and gold badges emblazoned ChartAir, called our flight.

There was a mass rush towards the gate as people struggled to get on to the plane first. Lucy told me to wait, that most people liked to rush but that there was no point. There were seats for us, she said, they were allocated, the flight wouldn't go without us. But I found it very difficult to sit calmly in my seat and watch people board the plane.

Eventually, the crowd thinned out and Lucy stood up. I jumped up beside her. We presented our boarding passes and walked down the airbridge to the plane.

Our seats were near the front. Bright orange upholstery clashed with pastel pink paintwork inside. I wasn't convinced about the safety of the aircraft. My only other flight had been Aer Lingus, with its pictures of shamrocks, harps and colleens on the inside of the plane and its Irish music piped through the cabin. ChartAir were playing Hits of the Sixties. It didn't seem quite in keeping with my idea of air travel.

They went through the same preflight routine, though, checked that we were belted in, banged the overhead lockers closed and pointed out the emergency exits – in the unlikely event that we would need to use them.

'Better be unlikely,' I muttered to Lucy as I read the safety leaflet. 'I'm too young to die.'

'Honestly, Jane,' Lucy was blasé about air travel, 'it's safer than travelling by car.'

'That's what everyone says,' I retorted. 'But at least the car is on the ground.'

'It's a pity it's dark,' mused Lucy. 'It's so much nicer when you can see what's happening.'

The plane rumbled along the runway. Images of crashes flashed through my head. I wished I hadn't read *Airport!* quite so recently.

'Do they use noise abatement procedures here?' I asked Lucy but she didn't bother to answer me.

The jet engines suddenly roared into life, their whine becoming more and more anguished. I could feel the plane wanting to move forward, gathering power. I gripped the seat. Then we were off and running, gathering speed with every second. It would be OK if we could travel like this and stay on the ground, I thought. I liked the speed, it was the height that bothered me.

Then we were in the air. The lights of the city formed a sparkling web of yellow and white far below us.

'Oh Lucy, it's gorgeous,' I breathed, then jumped with nerves as the undercarriage of the plane bumped into place. I clutched at her sleeve and she laughed at me.

'Relax,' she said. 'We're on holiday!'

I felt in the holiday mood now. The plane climbed higher into the blackness of the sky. Ethereal patches of grey cloud skimmed past the window. Already the land below was distant and invisible.

I settled back in my seat, feeling a little more relaxed and opened my magazine.

Lucy closed her eyes and let out a sigh.

Air hostesses rushed up and down the plane, offering drinks and more duty-free. Some people near the back started to sing and were asked to stop. I was enjoying myself immensely. They brought our meal around after about an hour and it was thoroughly disgusting. A limp lettuce leaf and some cottage cheese, followed by something that I couldn't identify but which might have been a sausage and then a pot of custard. I would have complained except for the fact that it wasn't really costing us anything.

'Airline food is always dreadful,' said Lucy knowingly. She hadn't eaten any of it. 'Especially charter flights.'

I dozed off after the meal, but it was hard to sleep with all the activity going on around me. The people in the seats behind us were a family and one of the children kept kicking the back of my seat. Every so often I turned around and eventually caught the culprit's eye. I looked stonily at him and he curled up, frightened.

Dawn was breaking as we touched down at Palma Airport. I nudged Lucy in the side and pointed at the sea. The Mediterranean. Even the name was full of glamour. The plane circled the airport. I could see the toy-sized cars and vans hurtling along the main road beneath us. I held my breath as we swooped down, watching everything magnify in size as we dropped from the sky. Then finally we landed, and I realised that the plane was still travelling very fast. The engines roared again and I held tight to the arm-rest. Quite suddenly the plane slowed down and taxied sedately to its resting-place.

It was ages before they let us off, but when they did the wall of warm air hit me like a physical blow.

'My God,' I said to Lucy who was just behind me. 'It's early morning and it's warm already.'

'Isn't it lovely?' She squeezed my arm. 'Don't you think it's fabulous?'

I revelled in the warmth. I couldn't believe that this was real, that Spanish people had this sort of heat in the air all the time.

'We've probably come at a warm time,' I said. 'It's not like this every day, I suppose.'

Mam had told me that the evenings would probably be cold. She'd insisted I pack an Aran jumper. If this warmth was anything to go by, the Aran jumper would be staying in the bottom of the case for the entire holiday. I hugged myself with delight.

We were here, in a foreign country, ready to have fun.

It wasn't exactly fun in the airport; it took nearly an hour before they piled us all into the huge blue and green coaches parked outside the building.

The tour rep clambered inside and fired off a volley of rapid Spanish to the driver who laughed sourly, then spat out of the door. The rep counted us a few times, then called out our names. It was like the school trip to Brussels all over again.

Eventually, though, we pulled away out of the airport and on to the main road.

I thought that Lucy was right and that we probably would be killed on the roads. The drivers drove with an abandoned enthusiasm that would have had them arrested at home. Nobody else seemed to notice except me. The tour rep was utterly unconcerned. She sat beside the driver and read through a ring folder, ignoring anything on the roads.

It was bright now. The landscape was rugged and dry. Tall, yellow apartments loomed from the centre of sandy fields. It was extraordinary.

Then, into sight, came the sea, sparkling as the early morning sun spilled on to it. Thousands of fragments of light breaking up as the swell of the water moved to and fro. I caught my breath at its beauty.

The light was so different, I thought. The air was clearer, without the grey that clung to Dublin. The houses were brilliantly white, with red and orange tiles and brightly coloured hibiscus in clay-filled gardens.

We passed an olive grove where a caricature of a Spanish peasant leant against a spindly tree. He wore faded denim dungarees and a torn straw hat, and he was drinking a bottle of water.

'This is fantastic,' I said. 'Absolutely fantastic.'

As we approached the resort, the tour rep began to tell us about the area. She warned us to keep topped up with sun protection cream and gave us other boring bits of information that were completely irrelevant.

Lucy and I were the last to get off the coach, the only two people staying in the Aparthotel Sol y Playa, a huge concrete building which stretched so high that it seemed to spear the blue sky above.

We lugged our cases into the foyer. The rep told us to come to her informal client get-together later that day and we ascended in a creaky lift to our room on the twelfth floor.

The view from our balcony was almost wonderful. Our vision of the sea was somewhat marred by the edifice of the Apartments Maria opposite, but we could still see a chink of the aquamarine water. Below us was the apartment's own square of blue, the pool, around which hundreds of sunbeds were arranged in a neat display.

I stood, barefoot, on the balcony and turned my face towards the sun. I felt like a flower beginning to unfurl.

Apartment 33 and the rain streaking down its windows was already a distant memory.

Our holiday had begun.

Chapter 6

July 1981
(UK No. 16 – *Piece of the Action* – Bucks Fizz)

I stood at the edge of the pool and curled my toes around the tiles. I bent my knees slightly and tried to ignore the searing heat of the sun on my burnt shoulders. Actually, they weren't so sore now although they had been agony a couple of days before.

We hadn't realised that the sun would be so strong. Tanya, the tour rep, had warned us at her client meeting about the sun and we took her advice to heart, at least as far as covering ourselves in suntan lotion was concerned. But we used oil, not cream, and it was like sitting in an oven carefully basted. We underestimated the burning power of the sun. We imagined it was the same as a very hot day at home, but after we got burnt we realised it was very, very different.

So two days into our holiday we had spent almost the entire day sitting inside the hotel bar, sipping drinks and looking at the sunbathers outside without being able to join them.

Since then we'd abandoned the oils, switched to creams and covered our shoulders and thighs. Now we had light tans, our skins were healing and we could spend time outdoors again.

I loved Spain. Palma Nova was a brash loud resort taken over by tourists in their twenties who just wanted to have a good time.

Lucy and I tried to visit places where Spanish people themselves might go, but there weren't too many of them. I'd assumed, part of my schoolgoing mentality, that if you visited a foreign country you should try and see some of it. But Palma Nova wasn't exactly a centre of culture. Still, once we accepted that we were only there for the suntans and nightlife, we had a ball.

We ate in the hotel each evening at seven o'clock, spending about an hour and a half over our meal. We always ordered wine because it was so cheap and because we felt incredibly sophisticated when the waiter topped up our glasses. Lucy tried to speak Spanish to him, and by now she had picked up a few words. He spoke French which was significantly better than his English so she managed to chatter to him in a mixture of both, much to his amusement.

His name was Salvadore and he was from Barcelona. He told us that we should visit his city which was 'muy, muy magnifico' and we assured him that we would. I meant it. I was sure that there were lovely places in Spain.

To satisfy my desire for exploration, we went on an excursion to the centre of the island, and to the capital of Palma where we visited the cathedral and the working port. Having done both of these things, Lucy declared herself finished with the cultural aspects of our visit and said that she was going to devote the rest of her time to sunbathing.

'And maybe I'll pick up one of these gorgeous men,' she said, as she rubbed after-sun into her reddened skin.

The men were a revelation. Some were skinny, weedy and unattractive, but there were a number of well-built, muscled bodies, tanned to a deep mahogany who paraded in front of us every day in the tiniest of swimming togs.

I leaned forward and dived into the pool. The water was shockingly cold after the heat of the afternoon. I stayed underwater, as close to the bottom as I could until I reached the other end of the pool where Lucy was dangling her legs. I pulled them gently, not enough to drag her into the pool which she would have hated, but enough to make her scream at me.

'Don't do it,' she yelled, 'or I'll kill you.'

'Pull her under,' called Jaime. 'She's too lazy.'

I waved at him and he wandered over to the pool.

'Come on in,' I said. 'It's lovely.'

'Yes, yes, I know,' he replied. 'Once you are in the water it is lovely. Only thinking about it is not so lovely.'

'A big strong man like you,' I joked. 'No problem.' I splashed a little water at him. 'Come on, Jaime.'

He thought for a moment, then belly-flopped into the water beside me, surfaced and put his arms around me.

I liked Jaime de Boer. We'd met him and his brother Wim earlier in the week. They had been drinking in the CocoLoco Tropical Bar when we walked in.

The CocoLoco was designed to look like a huge coconut. The tables were made of straw and the seats were shaped like halved coconuts. Palm trees grew inside the bar and brightly-coloured parrots and macaws squawked at the clients.

Lucy and I sat at the bar and ordered Tequila Sunrises. We were sipping the long drinks when the de Boer brothers started chatting us up. It was fun to let them – the brothers had superb manners.

They were both probably only after a bit of holiday fun but, Lucy told me, so were we. Not that much fun, I mouthed at her, but she just laughed.

So we talked to Wim and Jaime and went with them to the Razzmatazz Nite Club where we danced until three in the morning, when they took us back to the hotel, kissing us both in the foyer before they left.

We didn't see them the next day, but the day after that they turned up at the hotel pool and had turned up every day since. We had sunbathed together. It was much more exciting having Jaime rub sun cream into my back, instead of Lucy doing it. He would massage it gently into my shoulders and rub it carefully into the nape of my neck, before running his fingers slowly down my spine until I tingled with the pleasure of it.

Jaime pulled me under the water and wrapped his legs around my body. I pummelled him fiercely until he released me and I surfaced again, gasping for air.

'You didn't give me a chance,' I protested, but all he did was kiss me, slowly, on the lips.

I hauled myself out of the pool and sat beside Lucy, slicking my hair back from my forehead.

'Where are we going tonight?' I asked.

It was Friday. We were going home on Sunday and the brothers were going home later that night.

'CocoLoco,' said Wim who was busy plaiting Lucy's hair.

'We should go for a meal first,' said Jaime. 'It would be nice, don't you think?'

'Lovely,' I said. I was tired of the Aparthotel Sol y Playa's food but Lucy and I had eaten there every night because our food was paid for and we hadn't had time to save up for the holiday.

'Where will we go?' she asked.

'There's a nice restaurant near the beach,' suggested Jaime. 'It's called El Condor.'

'Is it English?' asked Lucy.

'Why do you want everything to be English?' asked Wim.

'I don't,' she protested. 'I simply wondered.'

'It's a mixture,' said Wim. 'We've eaten there a couple of times. There is a good variety of food.'

'Sounds OK to me.' I didn't mind where we ate.

'Good,' said Jaime. 'There is no point in going too early for eating. Maybe eight o'clock.'

'Eight?' said Lucy, aghast. Lucy loved food. Unfairly, she never put on an ounce of weight.

'It is more civilised,' said Wim. 'Eating early is silly. We will meet for a drink at seven and eat at eight.'

'That's fine,' I agreed.

'If we're eating later, then I'm going to have a snack now,' said Lucy firmly.

We laughed at her but she didn't care, so we followed her to the bar where she ordered an omelette. A *tortilla*, she said, pronouncing it torteeyah.

'I'll have a ham sandwich,' I said.

'*Un bocadillo con jamón*,' ordered Lucy.

I sighed. Lucy could be very irritating. All the waiters answered us in English.

When we'd finished, we sat by the pool again. I loved it by the pool. It was crowded and a bit noisy but I loved being warm and I loved swimming out of doors.

Every morning of our holiday I woke up expecting to find that grey clouds had rolled in over the sky and that the temperature had plummeted to the levels I was used to. But every morning I blinked in the brilliant sunshine and the temperature remained resolutely in the nineties.

Lucy and I would go down to the restaurant, usually too late for breakfast, but we'd order coffee and croissants which we took back up to our room and we'd breakfast sitting at our balcony table. It was blissful.

70

'Are you coming to the beach now?' Wim drained the beer which he had ordered.

Lucy and I exchanged glances. 'It's a bit late,' said Lucy. 'And we've got good spots at the pool. I'd prefer not to move.'

'Me either,' I said. 'But you go ahead if you want to.'

'I want to have a swim in the sea,' said Jaime. 'We'll see you later.'

'Fine,' said Lucy. 'Do you want a drink in the Coco before dinner?'

'That's an after-dinner place,' Wim objected. 'How about upstairs at the Eagle's Nest?'

We nodded. There was a lovely view from the upstairs of the pub.

'See you later, then.' I waved at them as they left.

Lucy and I sat in silence for a while. It was pleasantly peaceful sitting under the sunshade.

'Nice guys,' she said suddenly.

I nodded. I liked Jaime.

'Do you love him?' asked Lucy.

'What?' I was startled.

'Jaime – do you love him?'

'Do you love Wim?' I asked.

She shrugged.

'I don't love Jaime,' I told her. 'I like him. I like him a lot, but I don't love him.'

She sighed deeply. 'Thank goodness for that,' she said. 'I thought you'd fallen for him.'

'What d'you take me for?' I asked. 'We're on holidays. They're Dutch. What's the point in falling for him?'

'Well, you know you, Jane,' she said. 'You fall for everyone.'

I stared at her. 'Rubbish,' I said.

'It's not rubbish,' Lucy retorted. 'You're always falling for people.'

'No, I'm not.'

'Don't be silly.' Lucy traced her finger around her glass. 'You do.'

'Who?' I asked indignantly. 'Who, pray tell, have I recently fallen for?'

She had the grace to look slightly abashed. 'Not recently,' she said. 'But, Jane, you lose your heart too easily.'

She listed my boyfriends who seemed to me to be very few. Particularly since most of them had been so short-lived, I told her.

'But you were crazy about them at the time,' she pointed out. 'Each time you meet someone you think that this is it.'

I blushed. She was right. Every time I went out with someone, I would almost immediately visualise spending the rest of my life with him. I couldn't help it.

'What about you?' I asked. 'You were on and off again with Cian O'Connor for nearly two years.'

'But I never loved him,' said Lucy. 'I went out with him and sometimes I enjoyed it, but I never believed that this was my one true love or anything like that. You think that way all the time.'

'There's nothing wrong with thinking about it,' I said defensively.

'Of course not,' said Lucy. 'But you're only twenty-one, Jane. There's more to life than meeting a guy and getting married.'

'I know that,' I retorted.

'So you haven't decided that Jaime is the one for you and your life will be a wasteland if he leaves you.'

'I know that he is not the one for me and that he will be going back to Holland and I will never see him again.' I spoke the words clearly, enunciating each one distinctly so that Lucy would understand me. 'I am not stupid, Lucy.'

'OK,' she said. She looked worried. 'I'm concerned, that's all.'

I was touched by her concern but still irritated. Just because she had had a couple of no-strings-attached flings she felt that she could lecture me on men. *And* because she had lost her virginity to whoever he was in France, without losing her heart. I could do that too, I thought fiercely. Sex was a physical thing; it didn't have to mean a lifelong commitment.

'Don't get me wrong,' Lucy said. 'I don't mean to lecture you, Jane.'

'You're always lecturing me,' I said. 'But that doesn't mean that I'll listen to you.'

She grinned at me, and took me by the hand. I squeezed it. We understood each other.

'What are you going to wear tonight?' she asked, turning the conversation back to things that really mattered.

I wore a royal blue cotton dress which highlighted my tan and brought out the copper in my hair. I liked myself with the suntan, it made me look so much healthier and, I admitted to myself, prettier. I took the sun more easily than Lucy, although her dusting of honey was gorgeous and she looked almost Scandinavian with her long, blonde hair and golden skin. She wore an emerald green skirt and a deep pink shirt which would have looked awful at home but which was ideal on holiday.

I painted my lips scarlet and rubbed Vaseline over the lipstick to make them look wet and alluring. I hung my Majorcan pearl earrings from my ears and twirled in front of the mirror to admire myself.

'You're gorgeous,' said Lucy sarcastically. I stuck my tongue out at her.

'Let's go,' I said.

The Eagle's Nest was at the edge of the beach and a quieter pub than most of them because it didn't have a Happy Hour and it didn't sell cocktails.

Wim and Jaime were waiting for us. They looked superb in their faded jeans and white shirts, with their fair curly hair and bright blue eyes.

'Hello, ladies.' Jaime stood up and pulled two chairs out for us. 'What would you like to drink?'

We both had Bacardis while the brothers drank beer. We sat in silence, looking over the bay. It got dark quickly in Spain; the sea and sky were already black and the coloured lights of the town reflected off the water like glittering beads. The sea thudded gently against the beach beneath us with a rhythmic soothing sound which would soon be deafened by the music from the bars and the nightclubs. The breeze from the sea was warm and pleasant.

'Have you enjoyed your holiday?' asked Lucy, who could never stay quiet for very long.

'Oh, it was good,' Wim replied. 'Especially since we met you.' He leaned forward and kissed her on the cheek. Lucy offered him her lips and he kissed her again, while I squirmed in my seat.

'And you?' Jaime looked at me. 'Did you enjoy your holiday?'

'Oh, yes,' I replied, trying to ignore Lucy and Wim.

'Me too,' said Jaime. He leaned towards me but I picked up my glass and took a large gulp of Bacardi. So he didn't kiss me but he touched me gently on the back of the neck which almost sent me into orbit anyway.

I wondered whether Jaime expected to make love to me tonight. It was their last night. He hadn't suggested it before, even though I had met him alone for a drink once or twice while Lucy went off somewhere with Wim. But maybe he would feel that tonight would be the right time. He probably felt that he could get away with it more easily on his last night because he wouldn't have to face me the next day.

I took another sip of my drink. Did I want him to make love to me? It's hardly making love, I told myself sternly. It's just having sex. Would he want to have sex with me, then? And if he did, would I let him? The condoms which Lucy had handed me just before we left the apartment were in my bag. I had looked at her, horrified, as she had given them to me.

'Better safe than sorry,' she'd said, smiling.

I didn't know where she'd got them and I didn't ask. But she obviously intended going to bed with Wim. Where, I didn't know. I couldn't see us all going back to the Sol y Playa with Lucy and Wim in the bedroom while Jaime and I sat in the living room. I blushed as I thought about it.

Why was life so difficult, I wondered. Or was it me that made it difficult? It seemed straightforward enough for Lucy. See a man, go out with him, have a good time, say goodbye. Sex for me was all caught up with love and romance. I wondered if I was the last old-fashioned girl on the planet.

Of course, I didn't believe that you had to be a virgin when you got married. No, I thought you'd need to have a bit of experience, just so's you'd know what was what, but all these surveys that showed that girls had lots of partners before marriage scared me. How would I find loads of men to go to bed with? Anyhow, I couldn't let a man that I wasn't serious about see me naked. There were too many little podgy bits of flesh for that!

Lucy and Wim came up for air and smiled at us. My hands were shaking as I put my glass back on the table.

'Will we go and eat?' Jaime looked at me.

'I don't mind,' I said, and the others nodded.

We walked down the steps and on to the street. The pubs were all brightly lit now, drumming out music into the streets, flashing

74

neon lights to entice you inside. Shops were open, their merchandise spilling on to the pavement so that you couldn't help looking at it. Lucy and I had already bought sombreros, sunglasses, T-shirts emblazoned 'Majorca', flip-flops and huge donkeys to bring home to the twins.

The El Condor restaurant was at the end of the strip, tucked back a little from the street and with only a few tables outside.

'Out or in?' asked Jaime.

'Oh, outside,' I said.

I loved eating out of doors. It was great to eat with the warm evening air around you as you watched the nightlife.

We sat down at a table. The waiter came outside and handed us the menus.

The brothers knew what they wanted straight away. Jaime ordered a mixed salad followed by calamari. Lucy informed him that calamari was squid and he said that he knew that already but he liked it. She made an agonised face. Wim ordered soup and chicken. Lucy and I dithered over our choice until Wim demanded that we make a decision unless we wanted to starve. Eventually we decided to have salads for starters. Then we'd try the *paella*, because the food at the hotel had been very un-Spanish and we reckoned we should at least attempt a local dish. Jaime ordered two bottles of Rioja and some mineral water.

The waiter returned with our starters and I popped a piece of tomato into my mouth, wondering why they tasted so much better here. Mam would have been amazed by the amount of salads I was eating. I thought, although I wasn't sure, that my skin had improved because of it. I'd already resolved to change my eating habits when we went home.

The *paella* was nice too, although I didn't like seeing whole shellfish arranged around it. I could never eat anything that looked as though it might have once been alive. Lucy laughed at me as she expertly removed the meat and ate it.

We talked about home, about our jobs, about our families, about our countries. Jaime and Wim were very proud of The Netherlands and they had only good things to say about it.

'Amsterdam sounds lovely,' said Lucy, shovelling rice into her mouth. 'I'd love to go there some day.'

'But you must, of course,' said Wim.

She nodded and applied herself to her food again.

The wine was heavy and made me a little woozy. I drank some more mineral water. I wished that alcohol didn't make me so tired, it was very antisocial.

We finished our meal and called in at the CocoLoco for some cocktails. Then we played crazy golf on the little course beside it. Lucy was utterly useless at crazy golf but I was good at it and, despite the alcohol, won, much to everyone's surprise.

'Natural talent,' I said, with false modesty as I tapped the ball into the hole at the eighteenth.

'What do you want to do now?' Wim looked at Lucy and me.

'Whatever you like.' Lucy put her arms around him and pulled him close to her.

'Maybe we should split up for a while,' suggested Jaime. 'Jane and I will go for a walk and meet you back at the hotel later.'

'Fine by me,' said Lucy.

I bit the inside of my lip. Did Jaime have an ulterior motive, I wondered. Did he just want to get me on my own?

So what if he did, I told myself. Wouldn't I like to be on my own with him?

Jaime took me by the hand and led me away from the crazy golf.

'Where would you like to go?' he asked.

'I don't mind,' I said.

We walked towards the beach.

'It's not much of a beach,' said Jaime, as we stepped on to the sand. 'I think it's man-made.'

'Maybe.' I slipped out of my high-heeled sandals and walked barefoot on the sand.

'Give me those,' said Jaime, taking the sandals.

I walked to the water's edge and allowed it to lap gently over my toes.

'It's lovely and warm,' I said.

'I'm not going to paddle,' said Jaime. 'I will get my jeans wet and I have to wear them on the plane.'

'Are you sorry to be going home?' I asked.

He smiled. 'Yes,' he said simply.

We walked along the beach in silence. I enjoyed the feeling of the water on my feet. Earlier in the week the skin on my feet had peeled disgustingly, but now they were smooth and tanned. Healthy brown feet with smooth pink and white soles.

'Will you be sorry to go home?' asked Jaime.

I nodded. 'I like it here,' I said. 'I suppose I couldn't possibly live somewhere like this, but I love the weather.'

'It is a bit hot for me,' said Jaime. 'Every night it is so hot I cannot sleep.'

'I couldn't the first few days,' I admitted. 'But now I can. Anyway, we don't usually get to bed that early and you can sleep beside the pool.'

'Always the practical one,' Jaime said.

'I can't help it,' I protested.

'You should be not practical sometimes,' he told me.

'Impractical,' I corrected.

'Thank you,' he said.

We reached the crop of rocks that jutted out into the sea. It was dark here, and quiet, the sound of the town muted by the distance. I sat down on one of the rocks and examined my toes.

'What are you doing?' asked Jaime.

'Nothing.'

He sat beside me, and put his arms around me. Although I had been expecting it, I jumped.

'Jane,' he protested.

'Sorry,' I muttered. 'Didn't mean it.'

He caught me under the chin and turned my face to his. We gazed into each other's eyes. He was very attractive. I felt my heart begin to thump in my chest.

His lips came down on to mine, soft but demanding. I responded to him, wrapping my arms around his neck. He shifted position on the rock and pulled me towards him.

'Ouch,' I said as my sandals hit me on the back of the head.

'Sorry.' He fumbled around, trying to put them down somewhere.

'Give them to me.' I broke from his embrace and placed my sandals on a smooth-topped rock. I stood beside him and looked at him again.

He gripped me by the hair and I moved towards him. His body was warm and strong. I could feel myself tremble with desire for him. How much desire, I wondered, as his hands slid gently down my back. How much did I want him?

His hands moved downwards, to my buttocks, pulling me closer. I could feel him, hard, against me. Oh God, I thought.

He kissed me on the neck, on the shoulders, moved his head down to my breasts. I felt my nipples harden through the cotton of my dress as he brushed his lips over them. He clasped a breast in his hand.

'You're so lovely, Jane,' he said.

My dress was long, too long. He fumbled for the hem of it, trying to touch my thighs. I was shivering with lust, I wanted him more than I had ever wanted anyone in my life.

'Wait,' I said.

Deliberately, I pulled my dress over my head and stood in front of him in my snow-white bra and pants. He caught his breath as he looked at me. I felt in control now; this was my decision, my choice.

I undid the buckle of his belt and slid the zip of his jeans, pulling them down. He watched me in amazement.

'If we are doing this,' I said, keeping my voice steady and free of the embarrassment that I still felt, 'then you must wear something.'

The Dutch are very practical. He already had a condom in his jeans pocket and didn't need the one I'd carefully put in my bag.

Then we were moving together again, in a rhythm echoed by the waves on the sand. I felt myself open for him, accept him, feel him. It was an interesting experience, I thought. Pleasurable, yes, but not mind-blowing. Not what Lucy had written home about, but something that was worth doing. We were lying on the sand now, and he was on top of me, moving faster and faster until suddenly he cried out and was still. I quivered.

'You were fantastic,' he said. 'I have never known anything like it.'

'Really?' I said. All I had done was move with him. Was that all it took?

'Absolutely,' he said. 'It was the best thing ever for me.'

'I'm glad you liked it,' I said.

'Did you?' asked Jaime, who was now pulling his jeans on again.

I took my dress from its place on the rocks and pulled it over my head again.

'Yes,' I said. 'But I've got sand in my hair.'

'You look lovely with sand in your hair,' said Jaime. 'You are lovely.'

'I don't believe a word of it,' I said. 'You've probably got an even lovelier girlfriend at home.'

He smiled at me. 'No girlfriend,' he said. 'I promise.'

'Well,' I said, as I gathered my shoes, 'I don't mind if you have, Jaime. It was just a holiday thing between us, wasn't it?'

'But a good holiday thing,' he said anxiously. 'Don't you think?'

'A great holiday thing,' I told him, and kissed him on the nose. 'Now let's get back and find the others.'

Lucy and Wim were in the hotel bar. She had a self-satisfied smile on her face, and she looked questioningly at me as we sat down beside them.

'We went for a walk on the beach,' I said. 'What did you do?'

'Oh, stayed here,' said Wim casually. 'You were gone a long time.'

'Were we?' I asked. 'I didn't notice.'

'Too busy to notice,' said Jaime and I kicked him on the ankle.

Lucy giggled and I kicked her too.

We had a drink in the bar and then it was time for Jaime and Wim to go back to their apartment. We walked down with them, and sat on the steps, waiting.

Jaime kept his arm around me, while Wim held Lucy's hand.

Eventually, their bus arrived and they said goodbye. I was glad they were going tonight. Now that I had lost my virginity to Jaime, I was uncomfortable about meeting him again.

'Write to me,' said Lucy as Wim climbed on to the bus.

'Of course,' he said.

'Goodbye,' I said to Jaime, kissing him lightly on the lips.

'Goodbye,' he said. 'I'll always remember you.'

The bus drove away and Lucy and I stood side by side.

'Well?' she demanded, looking at me.

'Well, what?' I said nonchalantly.

'Well, did you?'

'Did I what?'

'Jane O'Sullivan, you look like the cat that got the cream. You must have!'

'Must have what?'

'You know perfectly well what.'

'Lucy,' I said. 'I took your advice. I didn't get too involved.'

She looked disappointed.

'All the same, he was a great lay!'

'Jane!'

'Well, let's face it, I'm not likely to see him again, am I? What else would you call it?'

'Did you enjoy it?'

'It was OK,' I said.

'Only OK?' Lucy looked disappointed for me. 'Wim was great!'

I thought about it afterwards. I had deliberately stayed uninvolved because Lucy was right, I lost my heart too easily and there was no future in losing my heart to Jaime de Boer. But I had freed myself from the shackles of my virginity and I was grateful to him for that. All the same, I still dreamed about the one true love, the man who would cherish me, and love me, and protect and care for me till the day I died. I wondered what he was doing now.

Chapter 7

August 1981
(UK No. 18 – *New Life* – Depeche Mode)

Two weeks after we came back from our holiday, Jessica called me into her office.

'I've some news for you, Jane,' she said as she sifted through a green-coloured folder. 'You're going to be transferred.'

'Transferred!' I looked at her in horror. I didn't want to be transferred. I liked my job in the International department and I was working really hard now. I knew that I was doing well, that my productivity (that awful word they kept throwing at us all the time) had soared, that I was getting more and more done in less and less time. I couldn't understand why they were transferring me. It was completely unfair.

'I don't really want to move,' I said, twisting the gold ring I'd bought in Majorca around my middle finger. 'I like it here, Jessica, all my friends are here.'

She smiled sympathetically. 'I realise that, Jane,' she said, 'and I know that nobody likes to move. But you have to take this as an opportunity. It's good for staff to be moved around. You know that I was in the Banking department before I moved here.'

'Is my work not good enough?' I asked nervously. Maybe it was only me who thought that my productivity had soared and I was making loads of mistakes. I didn't think so, but I couldn't think of any other reason to transfer me.

'It's nothing like that at all,' said Jessica. 'Absolutely not. I'm very pleased with your work, Jane, and I would prefer to keep you in the department if I could. But they need someone in Settlements and your name came up as a conscientious worker.'

I was glad my name was linked with conscientiousness, but that didn't make it any easier. And Settlements! Settlements sounded extremely boring.

'It won't be boring at all,' assured Jessica. 'And—' she paused, raising an eyebrow at me, 'you'll be next door to the dealing room.'

I made a face. For some reason, Jessica seemed to think that I fancied Rory McLoughlin. Ever since we'd headed off together from the pub she'd made barbed comments about him to me, despite everything I said to her. In spite of my own original premonition that we would have some sort of relationship.

'That was months ago,' I informed her. 'I haven't even seen him since.'

That wasn't strictly true because I'd seen him from time to time in the canteen, but I'd ignored him. If he was really interested in me he could come looking for me. The fact that he hadn't had convinced me that it had been a once-off thing and I didn't care. Besides, I was much more confident since my holidays. I really didn't mind too much about Rory McLoughlin.

'You and he made a great couple,' said Jessica wistfully. 'I thought it was the start of something when you went to eat with him.'

'You thought wrong, then,' I said coolly. I was pissed off with Jessica. She could have kept me in the department if she'd really wanted to. All this guff about Rory McLoughlin was just to salve her conscience. I didn't know why she wanted me out of the department, but she must have done. I wondered who my replacement would be.

I moaned to the girls when I went home that evening. It had been, for once, a glorious day and they were sitting on the balcony when I got home. Lucy was carefully trying to retain her tan, rubbing Johnson's Baby Oil into her legs, while the twins had smeared themselves with Hawaiian Tropic. The apartment stank of coconut.

I dragged a chair on to the balcony with them, enjoying the warmth of the sun.

'Almost like Spain,' said Lucy in satisfaction, as she stretched out her oiled and gleaming legs.

'Not nearly as hot.' I plopped down into the chair.

I poured out the story of my transfer and they were under-standing and sympathetic.

'Can't you say that you just don't want to go?' asked Grace, who was drawing on a large block of paper. I looked over her shoulder. It was a design for an evening dress and it looked stunning.

'That's lovely,' I told her. 'No, the bastards can transfer you wherever they like. If I complain, I could probably end up in a branch in Athy or something.'

'Better not complain, then.' Lucy closed her eyes.

'It's so unfair, though,' I moaned. 'I was getting on really well.'

'Maybe it'll be better in the new department,' said Brenda. 'Perhaps you'll like it even more.'

'I doubt it,' I said. 'And it means that I have to start making new friends again and everything.'

'I have to do that every time I start a job,' murmured Lucy. 'It's not so bad, really.'

She was now the secretary to the managing director of a distribution company. It was a three-month assignment while his own secretary was on maternity leave. Lucy enjoyed the job. The company had a beautiful suite of offices in a Georgian building around Fitzwilliam Square and they had a key to the park so that she could lie on the grass at lunch-time and bask in the sun. Because so much of the company's business was overseas, it was essential that Lucy could speak French and she was completely fluent by now.

'Maybe you should change jobs altogether,' suggested Brenda idly. She looked at Grace's drawing. 'If you make the collar a little higher here . . .' she suggested. Her twin nodded in agreement and her pencil flew over the paper, making the alteration.

'What could I do?' I asked. 'I'm not much good at anything.'

'I thought you were good at banking,' said Lucy.

'Oh, it doesn't mean much, really,' I said. I was depressed and nothing they could say would cheer me up.

'Rubbish,' said Grace, holding her drawing away from her. 'What do you think, girls?'

It was lovely. The evening dress was long and filmy, with a high collar at the back and a plunging neckline at the front. There was no doubt that the twins had real fashion sense.

'Can you make it up?' I asked. 'I bet you anything people would pay a lot of money for it.'

'It's only for fun,' said Grace.

Lucy opened her eyes, took her feet down from the balcony rail and looked at the drawing.

'Why don't you study design properly?' she asked. 'You'd do really well.'

Grace shrugged. 'I'd like to,' she said. 'But it would be too expensive. Maybe in a couple of years.'

'Frank went on to Milan to study,' I said, 'and I never heard from him again. I wonder how he's getting on.'

'Unless he's great, he probably won't make any money out of it,' said Brenda. 'Only one or two people break into the big time.'

'I'll tell you what,' I said as an idea came to me. 'Why don't you make up the dress and I'll wear it to our Christmas party, and when one of the top brass ask me where I got it I'll say that I have a friend who's in design. Maybe they'll give you a loan and set you up in business.'

Grace looked doubtful but Brenda thought that maybe it was a good idea.

'What we'd really like,' she confided, 'would be to have our own shop and sell clothes. Not all our own designs, of course, but expensive clothes.'

I could see how they would make it work. Both girls had developed a wonderful sense of style and looked superb no matter what they wore. Brenda and Grace could buy clothes from Dunnes Stores or Penney's and make them look as if they'd bought them from Pat Crowley or the designer rooms at Brown Thomas.

'Maybe I'll make it up anyway.' Grace, head to one side, looked critically at the drawing.

'If you make it, I'll pay for it,' I said.

'OK,' said Grace. 'You're on.'

We sat on the balcony until the sun slid down behind the tall houses opposite. Lucy went in to have a shower, she was meeting a few friends from the temping agency later. Brenda and Grace asked me if I'd like to go to the Burlington for a drink, but I decided to stay at home and read.

I was getting edgy again. I hadn't had a boyfriend in ages and it didn't look as if I'd find one soon. I was being transferred in work. Everyone else seemed to have an idea of what they wanted out of life but I didn't. The silence of the apartment when the girls had gone was oppressive. I pulled on a jumper and went outside for a walk.

I walked up Waterloo Road, then turned right on to Leeson Street and back along the canal. This was my regular evening walk. It usually took half an hour because I always sat on one of the seats and stared into the murky canal water, or watched the swans glide effortlessly along.

My stomach hurt and I knew that I was narky because I'd started my period. Its arrival usually made me feel depressed for a day or two, but I was quite relieved this time because I'd had the niggling worry that I might be pregnant. I'd kept the lid firmly on that idea as much as I could, but when I realised that I was nearly a week overdue I got into a terrible panic and prayed like a mad thing.

'Please, God, don't let me be pregnant, I'll never do anything like it again.' 'Please, Our Lady, I'm sure you don't want me to be pregnant, to bring an unwanted baby into the world, I swear I'll never do it again.' And finally, 'Please, St Jude, patron of hopeless causes, I promise, fervently, never to do it again.'

Once it had actually come, I realised that I'd been incredibly silly to have worried. We'd taken precautions, after all, and it was probably only my guilty conscience that had delayed it.

I was a mixture of relief and hormonal imbalance that evening and I went to bed early before the rest of them came home.

'It's a girl,' the nurse said, putting my child on my chest. 'Congratulations!'

My husband leaned towards me. 'You clever girl,' he said, kissing my sweat-soaked cheek. 'You have given us a daughter. This is the most wonderful day of our lives.'

My daughter was beautiful, with clear skin, deep blue eyes and a soft, downy covering of golden hair.

'We will call her Gloria,' said my husband. 'Because she is so glorious.'

'Don't be ridiculous,' I said. 'Her name is Samantha.'

'No, it should be Melissa.'

'Or Fiona.'

'Or Lucy.'

'Lucy is my friend. You can't call our baby by my friend's name.'

'Why not?' he asked, suddenly nasty. 'She's a wonderful girl and she's absolutely superb in bed.'

I snapped my eyes open, my heart thumping. Lucy was snoring gently in the bed opposite me. I was soaked in sweat because the room was sweltering. I crawled out of the bed and opened the window to let in a waft of warm night air.

I started work in the Settlements department the following Monday. I was very nervous as I took the lift up to the fifth floor and stepped out into my new department.

Rosaleen Corcoran, the twenty-nine-year-old Head of Settlements, came over to me as I stood uncertainly by the lift.

'Jane, isn't it,' she said brightly. 'Come on in. It's lovely to have you here. We're absolutely up to our necks, it's so busy.'

I looked around me. The Settlements area was large and everyone had a computer terminal on their desk. As yet we didn't have a computer in International Trade. There was a constant hum of noise and a clicking of keyboards as information was inputted into the system.

Rosaleen led me to a grey steel desk with its own terminal.

'This is your desk,' she said. 'What do you know about computers?'

I shook my head. 'Nothing, I'm afraid,' I said. I felt very stupid.

'Not to worry, we'll train you in. There are a number of different jobs you have to do and you'll be fully trained in everything. It's vitally important for you to be quick and accurate.'

She launched into a detailed account of my work and the work of everyone else in the department while I looked around me. My desk was in a good position, near the window so that I could look out over the city. The view was superb. I could see Dublin Bay in the distance beyond the jumble of houses, buildings and railway tracks. My old desk had been on the second floor of a different block and had simply overlooked other offices.

'We rotate people within the department,' said Rosaleen. 'It's for your own good and for security reasons as well. If we left people too long in one area, then they might become indispensable and we can't afford for that to happen.'

I nodded wisely.

'Now,' Rosaleen looked around her. 'Lorna Mulcahy will train you in, she's a good worker and a good trainer as well.' She called her over. Rosaleen told Lorna that I was to be trained on input and then left us.

Lorna was a tall girl, well-built, with heavy glasses and severely-cut hair. She didn't waste any time in small talk, but sat me down in front of the terminal and showed me the trading tickets and what to do with them.

It seemed simple enough to me, and I wondered why I'd been transferred to do such boring work.

Suddenly, Lorna let out a cry and waved a ticket at me.

'Asshole,' she said. 'Why do these guys insist on doing this!'

She showed me the ticket. The writing was illegible anyway, something I'd discovered already, but Lorna was adept at reading it. I didn't know what was wrong.

'He's put in a rubbish payment instruction,' she explained. 'This ticket shows somebody buying French francs and selling dollars. The instruction on the ticket is to pay the dollars to London and the francs to New York. Total rubbish. They have to pay the dollars to somewhere in New York and the francs to somewhere in Paris.' She held the ticket up to me. 'This is one of the commonest mistakes they make. They're so fucking careless.'

I was amazed at her. She was so annoyed about it all. It was just a mistake, I thought. Why make such a fuss about it?

Lorna pushed her seat away from the desk and strode towards the dealing room with me following in her wake.

I'd never been in the room before, and I looked in amazement at the activity. There were about fifty people in the room, sitting at long desks surrounded by flickering screens which were filled with a meaningless jumble of numbers. The noise was tremendous, the dealers shouted at each other and voices were coming from somewhere through loudspeakers. I hadn't a clue what was going on.

Lorna picked her way through the room and stood in front of one of the desks. Rory McLoughlin looked up at her, and at me.

'Well, hello, girls,' he said. He leaned back in his chair and hung his telephone over his shoulder. 'To what do I owe the pleasure?'

'This is Jane,' said Lorna, 'she's starting here today. And one of the things I am teaching her is not to accept this kind of fucking garbage from dealers.' She waved the ticket in front of him. 'What the fuck do you call this?'

I'd never heard so much swearing in one sentence before.

'Keep your knickers on.' Rory sat upright. 'What's wrong?'

'You're trying to pay fucking French francs to fucking New York,' said Lorna, 'and fucking dollars to London. Any chance you could give me an instruction that bears some fucking resemblance to the trade you've done?'

Rory laughed. 'I'm sorry, my sweet,' he said. 'I was thinking of something else. You know, it's fucking busy in here today, Lorna, and I'm writing fucking millions of tickets so if I get one wrong now and again, it's not a fucking crime. You don't have to come here and lose your head entirely, you know.'

'You're giving Jane a very bad example,' said Lorna. 'It's not our job to correct your mistakes.'

'But you do anyway, don't you?' Rory stood up and kissed Lorna on the head. 'I really am sorry.'

She was suddenly mollified and blushed. 'OK,' she said. 'Be careful next time.'

Rory looked at me. 'So you've joined us,' he said. 'Nice to see you.'

'You leave Jane alone.' Lorna punched him in the shoulder. 'She's a nice girl and she doesn't need any grief from you.'

'OK.' Rory winked at me. 'I'll see that I'm nice to her all the time.'

'He's OK, really,' said Lorna as we went back to our desks. 'In fact, he's one of the better ones. Most of them think writing the ticket is a waste of time. They're completely inaccurate and they don't give a damn. One day, all of this will be computerised anyway and they'll probably have to input the tickets themselves but, in the meantime, we do it.'

She sat down at the desk again.

'What would have happened if you didn't spot the mistake?' I asked curiously.

'The computer spits it out at you,' said Lorna. 'You can override it and tell it to accept the deal, but then someone else should spot it when the contract is printed. Rosaleen probably told you that we rotate around the department, so that one day you might be inputting and another checking contracts. Actually, I could have asked somebody else to take that ticket to Rory, but I reckoned you'd probably like to see the dealing room.'

'It's huge,' I said. 'And is it always so noisy?'

'Nearly always,' said Lorna. 'There's so much going on, you see.'

'And do people talk like that all the time?' I asked.

'Like what?' asked Lorna.

'You know,' I said. 'Swearing all the time.'

She looked at me in amazement. 'Does it bother you?'

'Not exactly,' I said carefully. 'We didn't have so much occasion for it in International Trade.'

Lorna laughed. 'You catch it from the dealers,' she said. 'They're really awful. And the only way to get their attention is to yell and shout and curse at them too. Otherwise, they'll leave you standing there and completely ignore you. You have to be tough to work here.'

We spent the rest of the morning inputting deals, then Lorna showed me around the rest of the department. She explained all the different jobs that I might have to do and introduced me to the different people. They seemed like a nice bunch, although I wished I was back in International Trade, doing what I was good at. It was terrible to be inexperienced again, not to know instinctively what was right and what was wrong in a given situation. I had to keep asking Lorna things and it made me feel very stupid.

I went to lunch with Lorna, a girl called Martina whose job I hadn't yet seen, and two other inputters, Clive and Seán.

Clive and Seán both wanted to be dealers. They said that there was nothing better than the buzz you got when you walked into the dealing room. And everybody knew that the dealers earned twice and three times as much as everyone else. Every time a vacancy arose, both Seán and Clive applied for it. They hadn't got it yet, but they were confident that one day they would.

'Do vacancies come up that often?' I unwrapped a rectangle of sugar and dropped it into my coffee.

'Fairly often,' said Seán. 'The dealers leave, you see. They get offered jobs in other banks for better money and they go. It's becoming a much more exciting job than it used to be.'

'Wasn't it always like this?' I asked.

Clive shook his head. 'Currencies used to have fixed levels against each other,' he said, 'but now they change all the time. The dealers have to buy and sell them and try to make money doing it. And it will get busier and busier. It's the job to be in.'

Not for me, I told the girls that evening. It was madness. I'd gone into the dealing room again that afternoon. It was obviously not as busy as it had been that morning because half a dozen of them were playing some sort of indoor cricket with a rolled-up newspaper and the side off a brown cardboard box.

'They're all completely nuts,' I said. 'Like children.'

Lucy was in good form because she was going to France with the MD for three days. They would stay at the Georges V hotel, which was the most exclusive in Paris, and everything would be paid for. We were all madly envious.

Grace was working on the evening dress. She'd bought a swathe of material in a magnificent jade green which she said would look fabulous with my eyes, and she pinned it on to a dressmaker's dummy which she'd also bought. The colour was fantastic and I couldn't wait to wear the dress. I'd given Grace the money for the material but she refused to take any payment for the dummy or for making up the dress. It would be a showcase of her work, she told me.

Brenda and Grace decided that they would open a shop together. Not immediately, they said, but some time within the next few years. They would work really hard and save as much money as they could.

'Maybe you should move back home,' said Lucy.

'Not yet,' replied Brenda. 'But if we buy the shop, then we might have to.'

'It doesn't cost us that much more to live here,' said Grace, 'but there'd be more space at home.'

It was true that the dressmaking was making serious inroads into the space in the apartment. The twins' bedroom was almost taken over by material, and we had to wear shoes indoors all the time in case we stepped on lost pins by mistake. But none of us wanted to give up the apartment. It was still the best thing we had ever done.

I was on one of my evening strolls when I bumped into Rory McLoughlin again. Somehow I'd expected that he'd make an opportunity to talk to me at work, but he never had. I felt a bit hurt when I thought about it, but I tried to dismiss him from my mind. All the same, I was thinking about him when I turned into Baggot Street to buy some milk and literally bumped into him.

'Hello there, Jane.' He caught me by the shoulders.

'Hi,' I said unenthusiastically. 'What are you doing around here?'

'We went for a pint in Searson's after work,' he said. 'I was going home. What are you doing?'

'Getting some milk,' I said.

'Bit of a trek in from Terenure,' said Rory.

I looked at him blankly.

'I'm sure there must be shops closer to you than here,' he added.

'Oh, I don't live in Terenure any more,' I said. 'I'm living in an apartment off Waterloo Road.'

'Really?' he asked. 'That's great.'

'Why?'

'You're very prickly, Jane,' he said. 'I think it's great when people move from home, that's all.'

'Have you?' I asked.

He looked abashed. 'Unfortunately not,' he said.

'I'd better get back,' I told him. He made me uncomfortable.

'Ah, don't go, Jane. Come and have a drink with me.'

'You've already had a drink,' I said.

'I've had two pints and a rock shandy,' said Rory. 'I can manage one more.'

'Look, I don't really see the point,' I said. 'It's not that I dislike you or anything, but—' I lifted my shoulders helplessly.

'Why does there have to be a point?' asked Rory. 'Come on, I'll tell you my life story if you tell me yours.'

Men were always asking me to tell them my life story, I thought. As if there was anything worth telling. I didn't know whether I wanted to go for a drink with Rory or not. I liked him, but I didn't want to be some sort of stopgap for him between real relationships. He obviously wasn't interested in me or he would have asked me out weeks ago. And, if the talk in Settlements was to be believed, he already had a girlfriend.

'Come on,' he said persuasively, 'one drink.'

I sighed. One drink wouldn't do any harm, I supposed, and I hadn't had a drink with a man since Jaime de Boer.

'Where do you want to go?' I asked.

'I'm easy,' he said. 'Anywhere you prefer?'

'The Burlington,' I said.

He made a face. 'That's not a real pub.'

'I know, but it's where I want to go. Take it or leave it.' I was being incredibly rude, I thought.

'I'd better take it, then,' said Rory as he linked me by the arm.

The hotel lounge was crowded and I sat down in a corner while Rory got the drinks.

'So, what do you think of Settlements?' He handed me a beer.

'It's OK,' I said, 'but I preferred it where I was before.'

'Change is good for you,' Rory told me, 'and any of the dealing areas are good fun.'

I didn't think deciphering a dealer's scrawl was particularly good fun and said so.

'We're all hopeless writers,' he said. 'But we make the money, so who cares?'

'Does anyone else in your family work in a bank?' I asked him.

'Don't be daft.' He took out a cigarette and lit it. 'Dad is an accountant. Mum is a housewife. Both my brothers work in offices but I don't exactly know what they do. I don't care, either. My sister is married.' He took a drag of his cigarette. 'No – I'm the one and only high-flyer in the family.'

'My dad owns a garage,' I said. 'Mam works in a shop.'

'My mother never worked.' He smiled lazily. 'Just as well, we'd never manage if she was out. Anyway, Dad had a heart attack last year so she's very concerned that he doesn't overdo things.'

I nodded and took another sip of beer.

I'd two glasses of beer while he had one pint and another rock shandy. He said that he tried not to drink too much on weekdays; it was only on Fridays that they went out and got mouldy drunk.

'I was pretty pissed when I took you to that Italian restaurant,' he said. 'I'm sorry about that, Jane, it wasn't very nice of me.'

'Oh, I enjoyed it,' I said offhandedly.

'It wasn't fair,' he said. 'I've been a bit embarrassed about it ever since. I didn't like to get in touch with you in case I'd done something really terrible.'

'You didn't do anything terrible,' I laughed.

'Sure?'

'Absolutely.'

'What did I do?' he asked.

I looked at him. 'Don't you remember?'

He studied the back of his hand. 'Not terribly well.'

'You kissed me,' I said.

'Really?'

I nodded.

'My breath must have been terrible,' he said. 'I'd drunk millions of pints and smoked hundreds of cigarettes. I'm sorry.'

'I'm not,' I said.

He smiled suddenly, and I liked him.

'So, what sort of kiss was it?' he asked.

'An ordinary sort of kiss,' I said.

'Like this?' He pecked me gently on the cheek.

'Not exactly.'

'Like this?' He kissed me lightly on the lips.

'Not really.'

He let out a deep sigh. 'I can't imagine what sort of kissing I was doing then,' he said.

'Like this,' I said, and kissed him.

'Jesus,' he said, breaking free. 'You'll get us barred.'

'You did ask,' I said.

'Maybe we should go outside and you could show me again,' said Rory.

We paid for the drink and walked out of the hotel. It had grown a little chilly since earlier, and I hugged my jumper to me. Rory put an arm tightly around me as we stepped out on to the street. We walked down towards the canal, and he led me to a tree on the canal bank.

'So,' he said, 'you were showing me something.'

I leaned up against the tree and kissed him again. Our lips parted and his tongue entered my mouth, exploring it, finding the gap between my teeth. I felt myself go dizzy with pleasure. He pressed closer to me and I held him tightly. He slid his hand under my jumper and touched my breasts lightly.

I could feel myself grow warm with wanting him. I squirmed with pleasure, pressing myself still closer.

'God, Jane,' he breathed into my ear. 'You're fantastic.'

'Thanks,' I gasped.

He moved away from me. 'I'd better stop,' he said. 'You drive me insane with desire.'

I giggled. 'Sounds good.'

'But not here and now,' he said.

'OK.' I tidied my jumper. I was shaking.

'You're some cool lady,' he said. 'Can I see you again?'

'You see me every day,' I said.

'No.' He stepped away from me. 'I didn't mean it like that, Jane. I mean, will you go out with me?'

'Of course I will,' I said.

He hugged me, fiercely. 'You're the most incredible person I've ever met,' he said. 'I want you all for myself.'

'I'm glad,' I said. 'Because I want you too.'

We looked at each other and he started to kiss me again. Even when I'd been with Jaime, I hadn't felt anything like this. If he'd asked me, I would have allowed Rory to make love to me on the spot, never mind where we were. If I wasn't in love with him, I most certainly wanted him.

'I'll walk you home,' he said. 'I won't be responsible for my actions if I don't.'

So we walked back to Waterloo Mews where he left me in the porch, depositing a very chaste kiss on my nose before he went. It was only when I went inside that I realised I'd forgotten the bloody milk.

Chapter 8

September 1981
(UK No. 1 – *Tainted Love* – Soft Cell)

I banged on the door of the bathroom and told Brenda to hurry up. The twins were going out with some of the girls from the department store where they worked and had hogged the bathroom since six o'clock. I was meeting Rory at eight and I wanted to wash my hair, have a shower and smother myself in perfumed body lotion. Lucy, unusually, had decided that she would stay in. Often, if I was going out with Rory, she would go out with the twins; once or twice she had come out with Rory and myself, but for some reason they didn't really get on and those nights were uncomfortable for all of us. Lucy seemed not to care that she wasn't going out with anyone. The job at the distribution company took up all her time; sometimes she even worked Saturdays. She hadn't been working this Saturday but she claimed that she was too tired to even consider going out.

Rory and I were meeting in Searson's and then going to his favourite Italian restaurant, La Bamba, where we had eaten that first night, for something to eat.

I looked at my watch. Nearly half past seven. I would be late. I banged on the door again.

'Keep your hair on.' Brenda emerged from the bathroom with a large pink bath towel wrapped around her. 'I'm finished.'

'About time,' I grumbled. 'You've probably used up all the hot water.'

It was a constant nightmare on Saturday nights. Last person into the shower usually ended up having a tepid flow at best. But since Lucy hadn't bothered tonight I was hopeful that there would be enough hot water left.

I stepped into the shower and the jet of water hit me. Warm, not scalding, but acceptable. I tipped a generous amount of shampoo into my hands and massaged it into my scalp. My hair was beginning to grow again, I noticed with pleasure. Although I'd enjoyed the experiment of having it short, I never really felt that it was quite me, and it was nice to be able to twist it into a little knot on the back of my head again. I smothered myself in Badedas gel, enjoying its herby smell. I stood under the flow of water and hopped around the shower trying to shave my legs. This was never very successful and I expected that one day I would fall, break a leg and drown under the water, but I did my best. I hoped that I hadn't left any tell-tale tufts at my ankles.

The water began to cool and I turned the taps off rapidly. I hated cold showers with a vengeance. I took my own towel from the back of the door and wrapped it around me.

'I have your hairdryer,' called Brenda from her bedroom. 'I'm nearly finished.'

I sat in front of the mirror in my bedroom and began to pluck stray hairs from my eyebrows.

'Here you are.' Brenda rushed into the bedroom. 'Sorry. Ours is broken.'

'I hope you have a wonderful time,' I said sourly.

'Get a grip,' said Brenda.

'Oh, sorry,' I said, truly contrite. 'I didn't mean to snap.'

Brenda smiled. She never took offence. 'No worries,' she said.

I dried my hair and applied my make-up. I'd learned a thing or two about make-up in the last few months and I could now apply it so that it looked very natural. I still tended to wear greys or browns on my eyes, but I didn't apply it as heavily and I could make my eyes look wider and brighter. When I was finished I was pleased with how I looked. I took my white blouse and lilac skirt from the wardrobe and put them on. Because we were only going as far as Searson's, I was able to wear the lilac shoes too.

I sprayed myself liberally with *Charlie*, behind my ears, on my throat, on my wrists, behind my knees and between my breasts.

Lucy was sprawled on the sofa in front of the TV when I walked back into the living room. She was wearing a pair of baggy jeans and a sweatshirt.

'You look great,' she told me.

'So do you,' I teased. 'Sure you don't want to come with Rory and me?' I didn't really want her to come but I had to make the offer.

'No thanks,' she said. 'I'm fine here.'

I felt bad leaving her sitting in on a Saturday night. After all, when we'd taken the apartment first we'd always gone out together. Now I was going out with Rory and the twins had something else to do, and I didn't think it was fair on Lucy.

'I honestly don't mind,' she said.

'But you're stuck here on your own,' I said.

'Jane – I don't mind,' said Lucy. 'Really. If I did, I'd say so.'

'I still think you should get a boyfriend,' I told her. 'It's not natural for you to be on your own.'

'I'm perfectly happy,' said my friend. 'Now will you go, you'll be late.'

I walked out into the late September air. The evenings were getting shorter and shorter now, the nights coming sooner and the air growing cooler. I hated the idea that we were moving towards winter. Once October came and the clocks went back, I always wanted to hibernate. It was so unnatural to get up in the dark and come home in the dark, and it made me ill-tempered.

But tonight was balmy. I'd flung a long white cardigan around my shoulders which was slightly at odds with my skirt's long slit. My shoes hurt, but they looked so good I pretended not to care. I was glad, though, when I reached Searson's, only five minutes late.

I hated being late. It wasn't part of my personality at all. If anything, I was the sort of person who would arrive early for dates and lurk in the toilets until the appointed hour.

I looked around for Rory but he hadn't arrived yet. Rory, unlike me, was rarely on time for anything. It drove me nuts.

My relationship with Rory was strange. It was very physical, although we hadn't gone to bed together. It was sparky. He was always testing me with weird questions or telling me dealing-room anecdotes. It was fun, because he knew how to enjoy himself and spent lots of money when we went out. But I wasn't comfortable with him yet and I didn't know how long we would last.

I sat down in a corner of the pub where I could watch the door and ordered a vodka and white wine.

I kept half an eye on the door and watched the other people in the pub. I always loved watching people in pubs, they never seemed to notice that they were being observed. I settled back in the red velvet seat and watched the couple opposite me. They were having a row. The girl kept her head down and stared at the table while he looked away from her, unconcerned. Every so often she took a tissue and wiped at her eyes. Poor thing, I thought. I wonder what he's done.

The doors swung open and I looked up expectantly, but there was no sign of Rory; the people coming in were a mixed gathering of men and women.

I glanced at my watch. A quarter past eight. Where the hell was he? He had, as far as I knew, intended to eat at half eight. Had he booked the table at La Bamba? I wasn't sure. It wasn't the sort of restaurant where you normally had to make a reservation.

He'd show up before half eight anyway, I thought. Rory liked his food. I would tell him that he was growing a paunch, and poke at it gently and he would grab me by the hands and tell me that it was more of him to love me.

But he still hadn't shown up by half past eight. I toyed with my drink, not wanting to order another until Rory arrived. Where on earth was he? It was unlike him to be quite this late.

I wondered if I should go down to the restaurant and see if he was there. Maybe I'd got it wrong. Maybe he'd said to me that he would meet me in the restaurant and that we'd go to Searson's afterwards. Suddenly, that seemed the most likely explanation. All the same, I thought I'd give him a couple more minutes. Just in case. Give him time to arrive at La Bamba, too.

So I waited until nearly twenty to nine before I got up. The barman looked at me sympathetically as though he thought I'd been stood up. I had been feeling a bit stood up earlier, but now I realised that I'd made a mistake I didn't feel too bad.

I walked down the street to the restaurant and pushed open the door. Mario greeted me effusively, as he always did.

'Signorina, most lovely to see you,' he said, clasping me by the hand. 'Where is Signor McLoughlin tonight?'

I felt the blood rush from my head. 'I – I'm not sure, Mario,'

I said. 'I was to meet him and I'm not sure where. But we were going to have something to eat here later, so I thought he might be here.'

'He has no reservation, signorina.' Mario looked concerned. 'And we are quite full tonight.'

'Would we need a reservation if we were to eat now?' I asked.

'I could make room for you, signorina,' said Mario.

'But I'm not sure of the time,' I said. 'I think I'd better leave it for now, Mario. I'll check out the pub for him.'

'OK,' said Mario. 'If he comes here, I will tell him.'

'Thanks,' I said and fled out of the restaurant.

I'd never been so embarrassed in my life. How dare he do this to me, I thought, holding my hands to my flaming cheeks. How dare he put me in this position. I stood on Baggot Street wondering what to do now. Should I go back to Searson's, where the barman would think I was mad? Should I wander around and hope to bump into Rory? I wasn't all that enthusiastic about wandering anywhere in these shoes. And where would I wander? Where could he be?

Perhaps, I thought, perhaps he'd had an accident. Maybe even now he was lying injured in the road. He must have had an accident, I thought. Otherwise he would be here. Or maybe he was sick. He'd had a bit of a cold yesterday, he'd been coughing down the phone lines which drove him mad. Maybe his cold was worse. We didn't have a phone so he couldn't contact me. Perhaps he was lying in bed now, fuming because he couldn't get in touch with me.

OK, I thought, that was the most likely thing. I'd walk to the Burlington, look up his phone number, and call his house. I didn't know his phone number by heart because I'd never had to call him at home. We arranged all our dates in the office. I knew his address though, so it would be easy to look up.

It took me ages to walk to the Burlington, because I now had a blister on my heel. This always happened with the lilac shoes, I thought viciously. I would have liked to take them off but I didn't think it would look good.

The Burlington was crowded. There was some sort of function going on and hordes of people swarmed around the foyer. The men were in tuxedos and the ladies wore brightly-coloured cocktail dresses and flitted around like butterflies.

I pushed through the crowd to the bank of telephone booths and picked up a phone book, easing my blistered foot out of my shoe as I did so.

The sheer number of McLoughlins made my heart sink. And, of course, although I knew Rory's address, I didn't know his father's name so I had to look through the entire list. Eventually I found it: Peter McLoughlin, the address and the phone number. I slid money into the phone and dialled.

The phone purred at the other end but nobody answered it. I stood there wondering whether anyone would answer, wondering whether Rory's parents were there, but there was nothing. Only the purring sound.

I replaced the receiver. Fuck you. I angrily brushed the hot tears from my eyes. Where are you?

I didn't know what to do. I went into the Ladies and sat in a cubicle. I tore off a strip of toilet paper and stuck it inside my shoe to protect my heel. Then I emerged and reapplied my lipstick. I would ring Searson's, I decided, in case he was there now. I looked at my watch. A quarter past nine. Maybe he'd said nine o'clock, not eight o'clock.

I phoned the pub and asked to speak to Rory McLoughlin. The barman called out his name. I could hear the hum of conversation in the pub, a sudden shrill laugh, then footsteps to the phone.

'He's not here,' said the barman.

'Oh,' I said. 'OK. Thank you.'

I replaced the receiver again. Obviously, wherever Rory was, it wasn't in Searson's or La Bamba. The only thing for me to do was to go back to the apartment. I'd get a Chinese takeaway and Lucy and I could sit together, eat and watch TV.

Pleased with my decision, furious with Rory and miserable that he hadn't shown up – for whatever reason – I called into the takeaway and ordered a chicken curry and a sweet and sour.

It was nearly ten o'clock by the time I got back to Waterloo Mews. I opened the apartment door carefully and walked into the living room. There was no sign of Lucy. Maybe she'd gone out. Maybe she'd decided to go into town and meet the twins after all. I went into the kitchen and put the food on the worktop.

A sound from the bedroom disturbed me. She'd gone to bed

already. Probably couldn't stand being at home alone. Poor Lucy. Sorry as I felt for myself, I felt sorrier for her.

I pushed open the bedroom door and stood, shocked. Lucy was in bed, all right, but she wasn't alone. I could see the outline of another person beside her, almost on top of her. I gasped audibly. As they realised that they were no longer alone, Lucy cried out in fright.

'It's only me,' I muttered, completely embarrassed. 'I didn't realise . . .' My voice trailed off.

I didn't recognise the man in bed with Lucy. He was older than her, a good deal older, in his thirties at least. He started to laugh.

'Shut up.' Lucy dug him in the ribs.

I stumbled back into the living room, tripped over my own feet and sprawled across the floor.

'Are you OK?' Lucy stood behind me, pulling her dressing-gown around her. I sat up and looked at her.

'I'm fine,' I said.

She gazed at me. 'I'm sorry,' she said. 'I wasn't expecting you home so soon.'

'Who is that?' I hissed. 'In the bedroom?'

She looked abashed. 'It's Nicholas,' she said.

'Nicholas?'

'Nicholas Clark. He's the MD of the company I'm working for at the moment.'

'Oh, my God.' I looked at her, aghast. 'Lucy, you told me he was married.'

'He is,' she said.

'Oh, Lucy!'

'Look, it's no big deal,' said Lucy. 'We're not madly in love or anything.'

'How could you?' I asked.

'How could she what?' Nicholas Clark walked into the room. He wore a black polo neck and tight-fitting jeans. Despite his greying hair, he was very attractive. I could see why Lucy had gone to bed with him.

'Nothing,' I muttered.

He put his arm around Lucy and kissed her lightly on the forehead.

'I'd better go,' he said. 'I'll see you Monday.'

'OK,' she said. 'Goodnight, Nick.'

'Goodnight.'

Nick took up a black leather jacket from the sofa and put it on. He waved at both of us as he went out the door.

I turned on Lucy and shouted at her. Had she no sense? What if she got pregnant? She was only going to get hurt, wasn't she? What about her future? What about Nick's wife? And family?

When I'd finished my diatribe I burst into tears.

Lucy looked at me calmly, went into the kitchen and filled the kettle. I stayed, sobbing, on the sofa. She returned five minutes later with cups of tea.

'It's not up to you to criticise me.' She handed me one of the steaming cups. 'It's my life, Jane.'

'But Lucy – you'll ruin it!' I cried. 'It makes no sense.'

We sat in silence for a moment.

'Do you love him?' I asked.

She sipped her tea and gazed into the cup. 'I don't know,' she said. 'I like him a lot, and I fancy him like mad, but I don't know whether I love him.'

'But he's married, Lucy!' I cried. 'How could you possibly even consider going out with a married man?'

'I didn't really mean to,' she answered. 'It just happened.'

'And was this the first time you—?'

She shook her head. 'No. We went to bed together last week. Remember when I was working late?'

'Where did you do it?' I asked.

'In his car.'

'Oh, Lucy.' I didn't know what to say.

She begged me not to give her grief. She told me that he was probably quite happily married. She didn't think that he would leave his wife and she didn't think she wanted him to. But there was something about him that attracted her and she couldn't get him out of her system.

'He's so sexy,' she said. 'Everything he does excites me.'

'But you should resist temptation,' I told her.

Lucy laughed. 'You sound like the nuns,' she said.

'They probably weren't entirely wrong,' I muttered.

'Look,' said Lucy, 'when he breaks my heart I'll come to you and say that you were right all along. But at the moment, we're together and that's that. I don't want to talk about it, Jane.'

'OK.' I was silent. I couldn't, absolutely couldn't, condone her behaviour. There was some girl out there, Nick's wife, who didn't know that her husband was sleeping with someone else. I couldn't take that. Nick would go home to her and kiss her and say that he'd been working late and she would never know that he'd been in Apartment 33, Waterloo Mews.

'She might not care.' Lucy interrupted my thoughts at exactly the right moment.

'Has he said that?' I asked.

She shrugged her shoulders. 'Only that they're going through a rough patch.'

'But Lucy, don't you think he's using you?'

'I don't know,' she said, making a face. 'I suppose we're using each other.'

I put my arm around her shoulder. She was my friend, my best friend and no matter what, I would stick by her. She took my hand and squeezed it. We sat together for a moment, then she looked at me and said suddenly, 'What the hell are you doing home now anyway? Did you and Rory have a row?'

The memory of my own evening, which had been completely blotted out by my discovery of Lucy and Nick, came flooding back. I bit my lip. I'd meant to say that we'd got our times mixed up and that I'd missed him, or something, but I blurted it out.

'He stood me up!' Then I burst into tears again.

Lucy put her arms around me and rocked me gently. She handed me a tissue while the tears flooded down my face. The shame and the humiliation of what Rory had done was almost too much for me to bear. I couldn't look at her.

'The bastard!' she said. 'I'll fucking kill him.'

Because she swore so seldom, it always sounded twice as bad coming from Lucy.

I sniffed, self-consciously. 'Maybe I made a mistake,' I said. 'Maybe I got the time wrong, or the place wrong.'

'If you'd done that, then surely he'd have come around here looking for you,' said Lucy. 'I'd have answered the door.'

'Maybe he did and you didn't notice.' I was suddenly hopeful.

'I don't honestly think so, Jane,' she said. 'If there was a chance

I'd say so, but Nick and I were in the living room until only a few minutes before you came in.'

'That was my only hope,' I said disconsolately. 'Unless he's been in an accident or something.'

'D'you think that's very likely?' asked Lucy. 'Was he driving?'

'No,' I said.

We sat in silence. The big clock on the bookshelf ticked loudly in the background. I sniffed.

'Was that Chinese I saw in the kitchen?' asked Lucy.

I nodded.

'What did you get?'

'Curry and sweet and sour.'

'Do you think it'll still be hot?'

'Enough, I suppose.'

'Come on, then,' said Lucy. 'I never knew a problem that wasn't solved by eating.'

So we ate the Chinese and opened a bottle of wine and sat in together, and I decided that best friends are absolutely essential to get you through life in one piece.

I didn't hear from Rory on Sunday, although I stayed around the apartment all day hoping that he might drop by. I couldn't believe that he wouldn't try to get in touch with me somehow and I still worried that something might have happened to him. I read through the Sunday newspapers carefully, looking particularly closely at the small stories in case there was one about a young man who had walked under a bus.

There was nothing in the newspapers and I had to assume that Rory was all right. I raged and wept all day Sunday, and the girls kept out of my way because I was in truly awful form. Lucy went home to her parents for the day and the twins went to a fashion show in the Mansion House, so I was alone with my thoughts. Horrible, vicious thoughts about what I would do to Rory McLoughlin when I met him.

I didn't sleep on Sunday night and I was out of bed early on Monday. I tried not to rush into work. The dealers were always at their desks by eight o'clock at the latest because the financial markets were already open on the continent and they had to be ready to trade, but none of the Settlements staff ever arrived before half past.

I usually strolled in about a quarter to nine, having allowed everyone else in the apartment to use the bathroom first. Today I could easily have been in by eight but I made myself sit down and have coffee even though I'd been first up.

I spent ages getting ready for work. I chose a calf-length black skirt with pencil-thin pleats and a figure-hugging cream top to wear over it. It was my most slimming outfit. The cut of the skirt hid my bulging stomach and its length hid my stocky legs. I dusted my face with translucent powder and blusher and applied a very light covering of eyeshadow. I didn't normally wear make-up to work and I didn't want to look as though I'd made a special effort, but I did want to look sexy and attractive so that Rory McLoughlin would know exactly who it was and what it was he had passed up.

I arrived at the fifth floor, walked over to my desk, switched on my computer terminal and pulled out my chair at the same time.

The rose was sitting at the edge of my desk in a small cut-glass vase. Propped against the vase was a gift card which simply said 'sorry'. It was signed Rory.

I felt the tears prick behind my eyes, and my bottom lip trembled. It was a lovely apology, but was it enough?

'Jane! What a lovely flower!' exclaimed Rosaleen as she walked past.

'Wish anyone I knew would send me roses,' said Lorna wistfully.

'It's only one rose,' I said. 'No need to get carried away.' But I lifted up the vase and sniffed at it appreciatively.

I sat at my desk and glanced through the paperwork without ever seeing what was written. Whatever it was that had prevented Rory from meeting me, he was upset about it. I wondered was he suffering pangs of guilt now, as he sat in front of his Reuters screen looking at the shifting numbers. Was he thinking about me, wondering whether I'd got the flower? Wondering whether I would forgive him.

It depended on why he had left me in the lurch, I decided. I touched the red petal. It was soft and delicate.

I waited almost half an hour before I picked up the phone.

'Dealers,' he said.

'Hi, dealers,' I responded.

'Jane.' He sounded worried.

'I got your flower.'

'Do you like it?'

'It's very pretty.'

Silence.

'I'm very sorry about Saturday night,' he said.

'So you fucking should be,' I told him angrily.

'Really, Jane, I am sorry.'

'Where were you?'

'My pal Jimmy rang to see if I would play football with him on Saturday afternoon,' said Rory. 'So I said I would. It was out in Greystones which was a bit of a pain, but it was a good game and we had a laugh. Then Jimmy went over on his ankle and we thought he might have broken it, so I had to bring him to Casualty and wait. You know yourself what Casualty is like. Hold on a minute, will you?'

The phone went silent and I could visualise him at the other end shouting an order to one of the brokers. It was almost impossible to have a conversation on the phone with Rory.

'Anyway,' he returned to the conversation a minute later as though nothing had happened, 'we were ages in Casualty and then I brought Jimmy home and we had a couple of drinks, and the next thing I knew it was nine o'clock. It was too late to meet you then, although I rang Searson's to see if you were there. Oh, fuck, Jane, I'll call you back in a minute.'

The phone went dead. I fumed at my desk for a few minutes, then started work. There was no point waiting for him to call me.

His touch on my shoulder made me leap like a gazelle.

'Hi, there,' he said. I swung around. He had never come out to me on the Settlements floor before.

'Hello.'

'I meant it when I said I was sorry,' said Rory. 'You mean too much to me to allow you to hate me.'

'I don't hate you,' I said. 'How could I hate you?'

'Easily,' said Rory.

'I never hate people,' I lied.

'Stand up,' he ordered.

'What do you mean "stand up"?' I asked.

'Exactly that.'

I sighed exaggeratedly, but carried out his request. I reached his shoulder. Rory was very tall. And strong. He played rugby and soccer, very unusually.

He put his arms around me. 'This is the bravest thing I've ever done,' he said, and kissed me in full view of everyone.

Chapter 9

October 1981
(UK No. 2 – *It's My Party* – Dave Stewart/Barbara Gaskin)

The Hallowe'en party was Grace's idea. She said it was atrociously bad form that four girls living together hadn't yet had a major party. Hallowe'en, she argued, was the perfect time and, what was more, we could make it fancy dress.

I wasn't keen on the idea of a fancy dress party. I always liked getting dressed up for parties, but not fancy dress. I could never think of anything to wear.

Brenda and Grace said that there were loads of things you could wear, and they were ready to make anything we wanted. Brenda decided to go as Robin Hood, Grace said that she would go as Maid Marian. I pointed out that we should all go as ghosts or vampires, but the girls refused anything sepulchral. Lucy got into the spirit of things and said that she would go as Mary Shelley.

I had no ideas whatsoever. The twins told me that I would have to think of something pretty damned quick if I wanted them to make me an outfit.

We sat in the apartment as the rain washed down the patio door. It had rained solidly all week and we were immune to the noise of the sluicing water. Lucy was compiling a list of invitees.

She had decided to ask about a dozen people from the distribution company. A few sales reps (mainly men), a couple of secretaries (girls) and a mixture of other people from the office, including Nicholas Clark.

'How about Mrs Clark?' I asked archly.

'Get stuffed, Jane,' said Lucy.

Most of the twins' invitees were female, because most of the staff in the department store were female. They'd asked about ten people and only two of them were men.

'It's up to you to redress the balance,' giggled Brenda. 'You can ask only men, Jane.'

'No problem,' I said confidently. 'Although I'll have to ask some of the girls as well.'

But I was lucky. There were a lot of men in Settlements, and I wanted to ask some of my International Trade friends too. By the time we had finished compiling the list, we had about forty names.

'Will they all fit in here?' I asked, looking around the apartment. 'There isn't a whole lot of room.'

'Better to have it too full,' said Lucy. 'Probably half the people won't arrive anyway.'

I was getting more enthusiastic about the idea. It would be a bit of fun.

Rory thought so too when I told him about it. 'I'll come as Antony,' he said, 'you can be Cleopatra.'

'Aren't people always going to fancy dress parties as Antony and Cleopatra?' I asked.

'I don't mind,' he said. 'Go as whatever you like.'

I wasn't sure whether he actually meant it or whether he was annoyed with me. The problem with Rory was that it was difficult to work out what he meant sometimes. He would get offended at something trivial, and ignore something which I thought a horrible insult. Our relationship was prickly, but fun. That was why I liked going out with him. He was unpredictable.

My parents liked him. The week after he had stood me up – an episode which had already become a standing joke – I suggested that we might drop in to see my parents on the way to the movies.

Mam was delighted to see me with a good-looking man like Rory and she was thrilled when I told her how well he was doing in the bank and what an important job he had. Dad liked him too, although he was less convinced about the job.

'Sounds mad to me,' he said, wiping his glasses, 'but times are changing, I suppose.'

I sighed deeply. My parents spent a lot of time talking about changing times.

'Do you want to see some photos of Jane when she was younger?' Mam beckoned Rory to sit down beside her.

'We haven't time, Mam,' I moaned. 'Really, we haven't.'

'Of course we have,' said Rory wickedly. 'I'd love to see photos of you, Jane. Before you got all old and wrinkly.'

I made a face at him as Mam went off to get the photo album.

'She was a lovely baby,' she said, as she opened the book.

'Oh, not baby photographs,' I complained. 'Really, Mam.'

But Rory exclaimed over them all. Pictures of me in my pram (I thought they'd have long been thrown away), my first day in school, my First Holy Communion (looking almost saintly, I thought), my Confirmation, holiday snaps, family snaps, and a photograph of me in my deb's dress, holding Michael McAllister's hand.

'Who's that?' asked Rory.

'Jealous?' I teased.

He squeezed me and leaned toward me. 'Of course.'

'It's Lucy's brother,' I told him. 'He's married now.'

Michael McAllister had married an absolutely stunning German girl called Ulrike whom he had met in London. Ulrike was the typical German, blonde hair, blue eyes and rosy cheeks. We pored over the photographs for a while. I was surprised to see how much I had changed over the last few years. I was still a well-built person, but I had lost a lot of the puppy fat I'd had earlier. My face was thinner too, and altogether more adult. Funny, when I was seventeen I thought I'd known so much. I'd been so sure of my opinions. Now I realised that I'd known nothing at all.

My parents insisted on telling Rory stories about me as a child. How I'd fallen from the garden shed into the rosebushes beneath, emerging with ripped skin and covered in blood so that Mam had almost fainted when she'd seen me; the night I had walked in my sleep and had tried to get out of the house and into the back garden because I thought that the flowers needed to be watered; the time when I had eaten four jam doughnuts at one go and had been sick all over the kitchen floor

'I wish you'd stop giving away all my secrets,' I said. 'Come on, Rory, we'll be late for the movie.'

'What are you going to see?' asked Mam.

'*The Empire Strikes Back*,' I said glumly. 'I'd rather go and see something a little less like a western.'

'It's a good movie,' said Rory unrepentantly. '*Star Wars* was good, Jane, you have to admit that.'

'I thought it was garbage,' I told him. 'But I'll sit through the sequel for you.'

'That's my girl,' he said.

We left my parents and drove into town. Rory had his father's car, a silver Golf. Next year he would be getting a company car.

The movie was OK, I thought, nothing special. Rory never tried to kiss me or hold me in the cinema, his attention was totally focused on the screen. Occasionally he would drape his arm across the back of the seat and twist my hair, but in an absent-minded sort of way. He bought loads of popcorn which he ate throughout the movie, offering it to me from time to time.

But he kissed me after he drove me home. He parked in the shadow of the huge beech tree which had given the apartment block its name, and reclined the driver's seat.

Rory was a superb kisser. He could drive me to a frenzy with the touch of his lips. His tongue nuzzled me as he breathed gently into my ear. I wondered sometimes where he had learned, because he could do things to me that no one else had ever done. When I was with him, close to him, I never wanted to leave him.

His hand travelled up my thigh, barely caressing me, sliding to the inside of my leg and higher. I caught my breath as he touched me and I felt myself quiver. I reached for him, under his shirt and ran my fingers through the matted hair of his chest. Our breathing was fast, impatient. I wanted to make love to him. I was glad that I had done it already, with Jaime, because now I knew what to expect.

'We'd better not,' I gasped, as he undid the buttons of my blouse and cupped my breasts in his hands. 'Not yet, Rory.'

'Why not?'

'Do you have anything?' I asked.

He was silent. 'No.' He broke away from me.

We looked at each other. He looked away first.

'I want to sleep with you, Jane,' he said. 'I love you.'

I had waited to hear him say the words. Sometimes I wondered if he ever would say them. He was so self-possessed, so independent, so interested in work and his friends and life in general. I was afraid that he wasn't really interested in me.

111

'Really?' I asked.

'Of course,' said Rory. 'Who wouldn't?'

I moved towards him again, and he buried his head in my breasts.

'I'll do something about it for the next time,' I said.

'Promise?' he asked.

'Yes.'

I did up my blouse, straightened my skirt and reclaimed my shoes from under the car seat.

'Do you want to come in for coffee?' I asked.

He declined. He'd better get home, he told me. His father went mad when he was out with the car.

I went to the family planning clinic after work the next day. They were very nice to me, very understanding and put me on the Pill. I walked out of their building feeling self-assured and in control.

When I got back to the apartment I saw Dad's car parked outside and my heart beat faster. My parents never called around to me. What on earth could be wrong?

Lucy and Dad were sitting at the table in the living room drinking tea. Dad stood up the minute I walked in and I felt that he could see straight through my bag to the packet of pills which were burning a hole in it.

'What's the matter, Dad?' I asked, seeing the immediate worry on his face.

'Your mam is in hospital,' he said. 'They're doing tests on her.'

I was white-faced. 'Why?' I asked.

'She had pains in her chest,' he told me, 'and the doctor decided that she had to stay in.'

'Oh, my God.' She had already died of a heart attack in my mind. I couldn't help imagining the worst. I swayed on my feet.

'She'll be fine,' said Dad. 'I came over to take you in to see her.'

I hated going to the hospital. Hospitals reeked of illness and death.

Mam didn't look too bad when I saw her. I tried not to look at the drip hanging from her arm and searched her face for any signs of tiredness instead. She said that she felt fine now and was embarrassed at being in bed. There was nothing wrong with her, she told us, she was probably just tired.

Rory was great that week. He came home to the apartment with me every day and waited with me until Dad called around to take me to the hospital. He didn't try and pressure me into going out anywhere. He could see how worried I was.

And I was worried. Shaking with fear, in fact. I had never, ever thought that either of my parents might become ill. Not at this stage in their lives when they were still quite young. I wanted Mam to be all right. I wanted them to find nothing wrong with her, though I was secretly convinced that it was hopeless.

As it turned out, I need not have worried. Our fears about heart attacks were entirely unjustified. Mam had torn a muscle in her chest. They kept her in to be certain, but everything was OK.

We had Sunday lunch together for the first time since I'd moved out. Dad drove us out to the Downshire House Hotel in Blessington. We'd often gone there when I was smaller and when we'd been for Sunday drives around the lakes.

We sat at a corner table in the dining room and waited for the menus.

'I'm glad you're OK,' I said, looking at Mam. 'I was really worried.'

She smiled at me. 'I knew there was nothing really wrong,' she said. 'I felt it. And, of course, I prayed to Our Lady.'

I tried to hide my impatience. Although I prayed in times of crisis myself, I didn't really believe in God any more. And I could never understand why Mam prayed to Our Lady and to the saints. Still, I'd done it myself when I thought I was pregnant so maybe it was just a case of covering all the bases. If you were going to pray at all, you should go directly to God.

'What are you having?' asked Dad, looking down the menu.

'The sole,' I said. 'And the *gratin* potatoes.'

'Are you sure you want fish?' asked Mam, who thought that fish was a penance food.

'I like sole,' I told her. 'We have it at work quite a bit.'

'I like your boyfriend,' said Dad casually. 'Have you known him long?'

'Since before I went on holiday,' I replied. 'But I only really started going out with him after we came back.'

'Just be careful.' Mam folded and unfolded her napkin.

'What on earth do you mean?' I asked.

'Exactly that. Don't let him do anything you don't want to.'

'Really, Mam!' I was annoyed with her.

'Well, it's important to keep yourself for the right man,' she said.

I blushed hotly.

'Maybe he is the right man,' I said.

'Maybe he is, but you'll have to be sure,' said Mam. 'You don't want him to take advantage of you.'

'He won't take advantage of me.' I looked down at the table. 'Nobody will.'

'Make sure of that,' said Dad firmly.

What would they say, I wondered, if they knew that their darling daughter had already been taken advantage of, as they put it? Willingly been taken advantage of in a completely reckless holiday romance. Poor Rory was bearing the brunt of their parental angst.

I played with my cutlery and tried not to get flustered, but I was glad when they started gossiping about the family. I didn't really listen, although I heard what they were saying. I was wondering whether Rory would become part of our family. Would he be included in the gossip this time next year?

I was sure now that Rory was the man for me. We had our differences. He was notoriously late for things; if he didn't enjoy something then he would walk out and leave. He didn't suffer fools gladly and he worked (in my view) far too hard, but he was definitely the one for me. We liked the same things – if not the same movies. We liked restaurants and pubs, we liked reading thrillers, we liked cars. We liked travel and we wanted to have lots of money. Since I'd worked in the bank, I'd realised how many people had money and had a better life because of it. And now I was used to money. Not having it myself, but seeing it every day in the numbers which came across my desk. Rory bought it and sold it and I transferred it around the world. It seemed to me that if I was rich, I would be happy.

I was happy now, though. Or I would be, I thought, if I had something to wear for our fancy dress party tonight. I sat on the edge of my bed and chewed the corner of my lip. I'd spent the week in and out of the hospital so I hadn't had time to think about the party. Brenda mentioned it occasionally to me but I'd been too distracted to worry about it. I'd told her that I'd think of something. But here I was, two hours to go and nothing to wear.

The apartment looked great. Brenda and Grace had bought witches, masks and cut out ghostly shapes from white paper and stuck them around the walls. Lucy had hollowed out pumpkins which she'd bought in Kilmartin's in Baggot Street and we had filled baskets with fruit and nuts. We were going to light candles instead of using the lights. It would look great, I thought. We'd bought gallons of Pedrotti and made fruit punch for the guests, who were expected to bring the rest of the drink themselves. We were half hopeful that they would actually arrive in time and not spend the entire night in the pub first. We'd suggested nine o'clock. Nine o'clock. It was seven and I still hadn't decided what to wear.

I'd thought that I would be able to dress up as a clown or something, but when I saw Brenda, Lucy and Grace's costumes I knew that my clown effort would look tacky and juvenile.

Grace was Maid Marian, in a long flowing dress and a blonde wig. Brenda dressed up as Robin Hood in a green pointed hat, green tunic, leggings and boots. They'd made the outfits themselves and they looked fantastic.

Lucy barged in wearing nothing but her bra and pants but she had her dress over her arm and her hair was a sheet of gold.

'Have you thought of anything yet?' she asked brightly.

I shook my head. 'Looks like I'll just be in jeans and a jumper,' I said.

'You can't do that!' Lucy was shocked. 'It's our party. You have to dress up.'

'But as what?' I asked. 'I can't think of anything.'

She rummaged through my wardrobe, pulling clothes off hangers.

'What about the green dress?' she asked. 'The one Grace did for your Christmas party?'

'I can't wear that yet,' I said. 'Don't be daft. Besides, there'll be people from the bank here. I can't wear it now and wear it again at Christmas.'

I pulled out the drawers and tipped the contents on to the bed.

'Why don't you wear your pyjamas?' asked Lucy. 'That'd be good. The men would like that. Wear as little as possible.'

'Rory would enjoy that,' I said.

'Here you are, Jane.' Brenda burst through the bedroom door carrying a swathe of silver chiffon. 'You can be a sort of ghost.'

I took the material from her.

'What is it?' I asked.

'We ran it up during the week,' she told me. 'You were so tied up because of your mam and everything. We didn't really know what to do, so this is just a ghostly outfit.'

'Oh, Brenda,' I said, touched that they had bothered. 'Thank you.'

She smiled. 'Don't mention it. I think it'll look lovely on you.'

I held it up against me. 'It's great. Thanks again.' I let out a sigh of relief. Luckily I had something.

I brushed my hair back from my head and secured it with a beaded comb. I did my sultry make-up look, silver eyeshadow and pillar-box red lips. I varnished my nails and wore my mauve shoes. I felt a bit underdressed in comparison with the others. Lucy looked fabulous as Mary Shelley, and the twins were brilliant. But I could hardly complain.

'You look fine,' said Grace.

'Rory won't be able to keep his hands off you,' promised Brenda. 'He'll think you're great.'

He did. He arrived before everyone else. I answered the door and he whistled appreciatively. He slid his arms around me. 'Good enough to eat.'

'Well, you needn't try eating her now,' said Lucy tartly. 'She's supposed to be keeping an eye on the sausages.'

We were cooking cocktail sausages for later. I gave a shriek and went to check them.

People arrived reasonably promptly and soon the apartment was thronged. It looked fantastic with the flickering candles and the eerie pumpkin faces.

Despite my best efforts, we had ended up with more women than men but that didn't seem to bother anybody. The music was loud but nobody complained. We'd invited the occupants of the apartments all around us. Everybody brought drink so that there were piles of bottles and cans in the kitchen.

Nick Clark arrived with a bottle of champagne which he popped and passed around between as many as he could. He looked extremely handsome and I could see why Lucy fancied him. He was older than anyone else there and he looked at us as if we were a bit crazy, but we were young and we were having fun.

Jessica, Peter, Damien and Alan had all come from International Trade. Rory invited all of the dealers along because I told him we wanted lots of men, so the room was full of them, still using all their jargon so that nobody had a clue what they were talking about.

Still, they were very bright and outgoing and kept the party fizzing along nicely. Shane Goodman, the corporate foreign exchange trader, was chatting away to Nick, telling him that he should be hedging his dollars forward. Nick nodded wisely, as though it meant something to him.

Brenda and Damien sat in a corner of the room, each with one half of the same apple in their mouth. Grace chatted happily to the guy who lived in the apartment upstairs. We had never even met him before; his name was Greg and his parents owned the apartment. He was doing engineering at college. I told Grace to hang on to him; it looked like he was loaded.

The sausages were very successful. When I brought them into the living room everybody fell on them. The buzz of the conversation grew louder, we kept the music fast and upbeat and we reckoned that the party was going well.

'I haven't spoken to you all evening.' Rory interrupted my conversation with Jessica and pulled me into his arms. 'Everyone is having a great time but I'm left talking to people I don't know.'

'You were nattering away with the other dealers,' I told him. 'I knew better than to interrupt you. All this garbage about cross rates and swissy prices and arbitrage and long bonds.'

He laughed at me. 'I'm sorry, what do you want me to talk about?'

'Oh, I don't know,' I said, putting my arms around his neck. 'My beautiful body, maybe?'

'I could talk about that all right.' He pulled me closer to him. 'But why talk about it? Why not do something about it?'

'Like what?' I whispered, nibbling at the end of his ear.

'You're driving me crazy,' he said, 'absolutely crazy.'

'Jane, what have you done with the bottle opener?' cried Grace. 'You had it last!'

Reluctantly, I slipped away from Rory and found the opener.

Lorna was looking through our selection of music. 'Anything slow?' she asked me. 'I want to dance with Martin.'

'Who's Martin?' I asked.

She nodded towards one of the reps Lucy had invited. I couldn't see why she wanted to dance with him, not my type at all, but I gave her a slow and smoochy tape which she slipped into the cassette recorder.

I allowed Rory to fold me into his arms. It was as though we were alone together. We clung together, barely moving. I rested my head on Rory's chest. He stroked my back. I was perfectly at peace.

'Having a good time?' I looked up at him again.

His dark blue eyes glittered in the candlelight. He leaned forward and kissed me.

I knew that I would make love to him that night. I was ready, he wanted to, we would have the opportunity. Well, maybe. If we could find a place in the apartment that wasn't already taken by somebody else.

I led him to our bedroom. It was empty, apart from the mound of coats on the beds. I locked the door behind me.

'Are you sure you're ready?' asked Rory.

'Of course,' I said.

I wondered if he thought that he was my first lover. As far as I was concerned, he was. Jaime wasn't a lover, he was my experience.

I lowered the straps of the slip over my shoulders.

'Take it off,' he commanded.

I let it fall to the floor, trying to keep my stomach sucked in as much as I could. I was happy that my body was in better shape than it had been a couple of years earlier, but my stomach was still a disaster area.

'Take them all off,' said Rory.

I wasn't embarrassed. I stood naked in front of him.

'God,' he said. He pulled off his own shirt and trousers. Somebody banged on the bedroom door.

'Go away,' I shouted.

I heaved all the coats on to Lucy's bed and we got into mine. We burrowed under the covers. Rory kissed every part of my body that he could reach. I reached out and grasped him.

118

'Be gentle with me,' he whispered, and I giggled. I was glad that he had made a joke, it made it easier.

Rory was more aggressive than Jaime, more dominant and quicker. But he held me tightly afterwards, stroking my hair, my back and my thighs. He told me that he loved me.

'But will you respect me in the morning?' I asked mischievously.

'I will still love you in the morning,' said Rory.

It was the most romantic thing anyone had ever said to me. If ever I had any doubts about Rory McLoughlin, they had been banished that night. He was the man for me. I wanted to marry him.

Chapter 10

November 1981
(UK No. 20 – *Why Do Fools Fall In Love?* – Diana Ross)

An icy wind whistled up Burlington Road, swirling dead leaves on the pavement, making my eyes water. I hugged my fleecy jacket around me and tried to insulate myself from the bitter cold. It was cold enough to snow, and they had forecast it last night, but this morning the sky was clear and blue. Frost glittered crisply on the pavements. It had stayed deceptively sunny all day; only when stepping outside did you feel the deadly bite of the Arctic wind.

I scurried across the road and let myself into the apartment, my freezing hands hardly able to hold the key. One day I would buy myself a new pair of gloves. I usually bought them around Christmas every year and lost them by January.

Greg from Apartment 43 ran down the stairs as I came in. He nodded at me, asked was it cold and, when I said yes, shivered in anticipation. I liked Greg. We had seen him a couple of times since the party. He'd called down to the apartment once or twice, simply to chat. He still seemed interested in Grace, although he had the same problem as all men did with the twins. It was impossible to know which one he was dating. The twins were beginning to take more of an interest in men, too. Until now, they had seemed to be totally happy with each other's company, very disconcerting unless you knew them. But Grace had been out on a couple of dates with Greg. Brenda went out very occasionally with one of the buyers in the department store.

Our lives were progressing very satisfactorily, I mused, as I skipped up the stairs to the apartment. Rory and I saw a lot of each other. I loved him more and more every day and I think he felt the same way. Sometimes I was plagued with doubts. He was such an active person, had so many different things to do. He didn't talk about us very much. Sometimes I panicked because he was never on time for anything and had to be reminded if we were going anywhere. But he said that he just had a short attention span; it was because of work, nothing to do with me.

We had been to my parents' house a couple of times. Rory was always extremely courteous to Mam, and to any of my relatives we happened to meet there. They all thought he was the nicest young man they had ever met.

The only person he didn't really get on with was Lucy. I thought that Lucy was plain jealous of the fact that I had a stable, loving relationship while she was still having an affair with Nick Clark. She never said anything to me, but I knew that she wanted Nick to leave his wife and move in with her. It worried me. I wanted Lucy to be happy. I was so happy myself, I couldn't bear to think of her being badly treated or miserable. Maybe it'll work out, I thought, as I opened the apartment door. Maybe by next year we'll all be in happy relationships. None as happy as mine, though.

The heating was on in the apartment which meant that someone was home already. I pushed open the living-room door and walked inside.

Lucy sat at the pine table, her head in her hands. I dropped my bag on the floor and rushed over to her.

'Lucy,' I said, 'are you all right?'

She shook her head, her blonde hair a curtain which hid her face.

'What's the matter?' I asked.

She sniffed loudly, and a tear dropped on to the table in front of us. I hadn't seen Lucy cry in years.

'Come on, Lucy, you can tell me. I'm your best friend.' I pulled up a chair and sat beside her. I took her wrists in my hands and tried to tug them away from her face.

She looked up and shook her hair back. Her eyes were red and her cheeks blotchy and swollen from her tears. She looked awful.

'Tell me,' I ordered.

'That bastard!' She sniffed again and a tear slid out of her eye and down her cheek. She scrubbed at her face with a crumpled tissue.

'Who?' I asked, already knowing the answer. 'Nick?'

'Of course, Nick,' she snapped. 'Who else?'

'What has he done?'

She buried her head in her hands again. I watched her anxiously.

'Lucy?' I said softly. 'What has he done?'

He's got her pregnant, I thought to myself. It was the one thing I feared for myself and the only thing I could imagine that would send Lucy into this despair. Bad enough for me, though I could always marry Rory. But what on earth would Lucy do?

'His wife is pregnant,' she cried suddenly. 'His fucking wife is pregnant.'

I looked at her and sighed deeply. Not as bad as if she were pregnant.

'How could he?' She looked up at me. 'How could he? He told me he wasn't sleeping with her any more.' She started to cry again, great gulping sobs. 'He said that they hadn't had sex in over a year. That's a joke. Her baby is due in April.'

'You couldn't expect him not to have sex with her,' I said, trying to be reasonable. 'They're living in the same house.'

'But he said that he didn't sleep with her,' sobbed Lucy. 'He swore he didn't sleep with her.'

I didn't know what to say. All along I had imagined that this was how the affair would end, but I couldn't say 'I told you so' to Lucy. I wanted to, but I couldn't say it. I kept quiet. I wished there was something I could do.

She hiccoughed, and wiped her eyes again.

'Would you like a drink?' I asked. 'Brandy, whiskey, vodka – tea, coffee?'

She shook her head. 'It's like when you're a kid,' she said, 'and you do something your mother doesn't approve of. And she says that it'll all end in tears. And it does, Jane, it fucking does.'

I wanted to cry, too. Lucy was my friend – I cared about her. I wanted to kill Nick Clark myself.

'He's not worth crying over,' I told her. I knew that the words were trite and stupid. 'You'll find someone else, Lucy.'

'I don't want someone else,' she sobbed. 'I want him, Jane. I love him.'

I put my arms around her and hugged her. I knew how she must feel. If Rory ever two-timed me, I would feel like this. But

I was lucky, because Rory loved me and you don't cheat on people you love. So Nick, the bastard, hadn't loved Lucy and hadn't loved his wife either.

'How did you find out?' I asked. 'About her being pregnant?'

She gulped. 'He told me,' she said. 'He said he couldn't see me on Thursday because he was going with her to a prenatal class.'

I wanted to choke him.

'Don't worry, Lucy,' I said helplessly.

'I'm not worried,' she said. She stood up and walked over to the window. 'I'm just so very fucking stupid.' She leaned her head on the glass. 'You warned me, Jane. You warned me against him and I didn't want to listen. But you were right.'

I shifted uncomfortably in my chair. Knowing I was right was one thing, being told it was different.

'I just didn't think it would work,' I said. 'I might have been wrong.'

She smiled at me, a watery smile. 'But you didn't lecture me and I'm very grateful. You were right and you said what you had to say and you left it at that, Jane. I really appreciate it.'

I was embarrassed. 'Come on, Lucy. You'd do the same for me.'

'I won't have to,' she said. 'You've got Rory. You're lucky.'

I didn't say anything. I was lucky and I knew it. Men like Rory didn't come around every day.

'Why don't we go out?' I suggested. 'Have a few drinks, get something to eat – just the two of us? We haven't done that in ages.'

She made a face. 'I don't really feel like going out,' she said. 'I've got a bit of a headache and I look awful.'

'So take some Panadol for your headache and wash your face,' I told her. 'Come on, Lucy. Let's do it.'

So we went to the Leeson Lounge and had a few vodkas, then wandered along to La Bamba for something to eat. Mario welcomed me as a favoured customer now, as I was, because I went there so often with Rory. It was funny but before I met him I had hardly ever gone to a restaurant for something to eat. Captain America's had been the limit of my sophistication. But I was growing used to walking in to La Bamba and having my coat taken and the menu put in front of me while Mario went off to get mineral water without being asked.

'It's my treat,' I told Lucy when I saw her look at the prices in the heavily-bound menu. 'Have whatever you like.'

We had ravioli and lasagne and tons of smelly garlic bread which cheered us up immensely. I was a little show-offish with Lucy. I asked Mario to recommend a decent wine, not plonk, to prove to her that I was now the sort of person who drank decent wine. I wanted to show her the kind of life I led with Rory. We had a good time. We called into Searson's for one on the way back to the apartment and were in giggling form by the time we got home.

Lucy was in a better mood the next morning. She decided to tell the agency that she wanted to switch jobs, that she couldn't work for Nick's company any more. She dropped me outside the bank before driving into town so that I was early and able to get a lot of work done before the deals of the day filtered through.

It was one of the hectic days. The dollar soared against the Deutschmark, interest rates were all over the place and the dealers shouted and screamed at each other, wrote illegible tickets and frantically tried to make money.

Rory and I had intended to go for a drink after work, but I knew that it was highly unlikely. On days like this, the dealers went off together to talk about their trades, and where they thought the markets were going, and how they had managed to turn a loss-making situation into a profit-making one.

Half of the talk was nonsense and I rarely joined Rory if he was going out with the lads. I got irritated listening to them. They thought they knew everything. I secretly felt that they knew nothing.

I hardly got to talk to Rory at all that day, just a brief hello when I went into the dealing room with a query on a ticket. So the next day I was delighted when he left a note on my desk which read '*Sorry, too busy to think, do you want to go to London for the w/e, love, Rory.*'

I rang his extension and said 'yes' and he told me that he had already organised the tickets. He'd arranged to meet some clients over there, he said. They were going to a football match on Saturday, but we would have Friday night together and most of Sunday.

I was a little put out at this. An evening and half of Sunday wasn't much, but at least he'd asked me, and he'd bought the tickets.

Mam phoned me at work that afternoon. I was busy and I didn't have much time to talk but I had to tell her.

'He's what?' she asked. I could hear amazement in her voice.

'He's bought tickets for us to go to London,' I told her, 'for the weekend.'

'This weekend?'

'Of course.' I altered a trade ticket. One of Rory's. He'd got the currencies mixed up.

'So I suppose you're going then?'

'Why not?' I asked.

'Where are you staying? With friends?'

'No,' I told her. 'The Inn on the Park. It's a very flashy hotel, Mam, and Rory's paying for that too.'

'That's very nice of him, I suppose.'

'Of course it is.' I cradled the phone on my shoulder as I inputted data. 'Rory's very good to me.'

'I know that,' said Mam. 'I like him. I'm just not sure that—'

'Mam!' I interrupted her. 'We'll be fine. I'll be fine. Don't worry.'

'It's not that I'm worried,' she said, 'but—'

'Listen to me.' I interrupted her again. 'We're going away for the weekend. Loads of couples do that. It's quite normal. Please don't spoil it for me.'

I could almost see her frown. I heard her sigh and I grinned to myself. She wanted to ask me about the sleeping arrangements, but she was silent and I wasn't going to volunteer anything. I was an adult. I could make my own plans. Besides which, I was taking my pill religiously every evening before I went to bed and I was confident that at least I wouldn't get pregnant.

Of course when Rory and I got married, then it would be different. I would wait for a year or so, there was no point in starting a family too soon, but I wanted to have children. I was an only child, so I wanted to have at least two, but I wasn't sure about it. I'd seen films of women in childbirth. It seemed awfully painful and I wasn't into pain.

We caught the six-fifteen to Heathrow. I hadn't been to London since I was a child, when Mam and Dad had taken me over for Easter. We'd gone on the ferry. We'd seen all the sights, done all the tourist things. I still remembered the hugeness of it all compared with Dublin.

I liked London. I liked the variety of the buildings, the incredible number of people, the bustling, hurrying nature of the city. We took a taxi to the hotel. Rory had been given some sterling by the bank for expenses, so it didn't cost us anything.

The hotel was fantastic. A liveried doorman stood outside the entrance and held the door open for us. A porter brought our bags up to the room. I bounced up and down on the double bed while Rory raided the little fridge and opened a snipe of champagne.

This would be the first time that we had spent the night together. We had, of course, made love again since the night of the Hallowe'en party, but only a couple of times, and there had never been the opportunity for us to spend an entire night together.

'What do you want to do?' I wriggled suggestively on the bed.

'What do you think?' Rory grabbed me.

After a very satisfactory interlude Rory suggested that we have a shower.

'Together?' I asked.

'Of course,' he said.

We stood under the jet of water together, revelling in the warmth. Rory tipped some shower gel into the palm of his hand and smoothed it all over me, starting at my shoulders and finishing at my ankles. It was exotic and sensuous. I did the same for him, working the soap into a white lather in the black hairs of his chest. We held each other closely, our bodies slipping against each other.

'I love you, Jane,' he said. 'I really love you.'

'I love you too,' I said.

We went to the hotel restaurant for dinner. It made La Bamba look cheap. The tables all had crisp white linen tablecloths. Waiters glided between them, carrying plates covered in silver domes. The menu was written on expensive parchment. I felt that we should be whispering, it was all so lavish.

We sat in a companionable silence observing our fellow diners. They were mostly businessmen in navy and grey suits, but at the table directly opposite us sat a middle-aged woman, beautifully dressed, impeccably made up and elegant. She added colour to the somewhat drab diners.

We went back to the room and sat on the bed watching TV. It was very loving and I felt as though we were married already. Mrs Rory McLoughlin. It had a good sound to it.

I'd expected that we would spend the whole night making love, but Rory fell asleep after the first time and snored gently beside me. I rolled him over on to his side, but he kept rolling back again. Eventually though, he turned towards me, put his arms around me and slotted beside me like a spoon as we both fell asleep.

He was to meet his London clients early the next morning. They were taking the Tube to Highbury to watch Arsenal play. I had absolutely no interest in football whatsoever. Dad had never followed a particular team so it never really entered into the equation at home. Any time he did watch football, it was in the pub. None of my boyfriends had any interest either, so terms like 'offside' meant nothing to me. Rory couldn't believe I knew so little. He knew the name of everyone on the current Arsenal team, Arsenal teams of the past, other clubs team members had played for and every manager the club had ever employed. I thought it was a load of rubbish and said so.

However, I left him happily wearing his Arsenal scarf on Saturday morning and went shopping. I walked down to Piccadilly Circus and then up Oxford Street, calling into every single shop on the way. I liked shopping in London, the sheer number and size of the shops was breathtaking. I spent all day in the shops. I was utterly exhausted by the time I made it back to the hotel, weighed down with plastic bags full of goodies. I wasn't sure what time Rory would be back. He'd said that he was going for a few pints after the match so I lay back on the bed and waited for him to return.

By seven o'clock, I was fed up and hungry. I knew that Rory lost his sense of time when he'd had a few drinks. But I thought it would be different when we were away together. I watched *Columbo* and ate the large Toblerone from the minibar.

By eight o'clock, I was really pissed off. What could they be doing? Surely he would remember that I was on my own and come back.

By nine, I had looked at the room service menu and ordered a burger and chips. Rory was paying for the room, he could pay for the food as well, I decided, as I speared a chip in anger.

By ten, I was worried about him. London wasn't like home, after all; anything could have happened to him. Perhaps he'd forgotten where he was staying,

He arrived back at around eleven, eyes red, cheeks flushed. He reeked of stale beer and cigarette smoke. His scarf was wrapped loosely around his neck and he staggered through the door. He smiled at me before he flopped down on the bed.

'Where on earth were you?' I asked.

He yawned widely and stared at me.

'Where were you?' I repeated.

'On the piss.' He grinned vacantly. 'Had a great time.'

'I'm very glad,' I said tartly. 'I thought you'd be back before now.'

He opened his eyes to look at me. 'Why?'

'I just did.'

'We were at a match,' he said, as though that explained everything. 'How could I be back before now?' He closed his eyes again.

'Have you had anything to eat?' I asked.

He snored gently in reply. I poked him in the back, but he simply rolled over and ignored me.

I watched him lying there, and felt angry and frustrated. What was the point of coming to London together if we were going to be apart all day – if he was going to sleep the minute we got together again? Did he not find me attractive? Was there something wrong with me? Obviously there must be, because otherwise he would have drunk two pints and come back to the hotel.

I climbed into bed beside him and lay there wide awake, a rigid mass of anger and confusion.

We had to check out by noon the next day, and our flight was at two-thirty. I woke him at eleven. He prised his eyes apart and looked at me blearily.

'Wha' time?' he asked.

'Time to get up,' I said shortly.

He reached out and pulled me to the bed. 'Come back in,' he said.

'No.'

He sat up. 'What's the matter?'

I was horrified to realise that I was on the brink of tears. I bit my lip and turned away from him.

'Jane?' He caught hold of my arm. 'What's wrong?'

'I thought you'd be back earlier last night,' I said, choking back a sob. 'I waited for you for ages.'

'But you knew I was at the match,' he said, his voice surprised. 'You knew I was with the lads. We went for an Indian afterwards.'

'How was I to know that?' I asked.

'You should have guessed.'

I suppose I should. Impossible for a gang of men to get together at a football match and not get pissed and go for something to eat.

'I didn't realise,' I said lamely.

'Silly girl,' said Rory. 'Come on, we've time.'

I fell towards him and climbed back into the bed. Our love-making was fast and frantic.

We barely had time to check out. I was embarrassed, certain that the receptionist knew that we had just made love. It was a rush to get to the airport. Our flight was on time. Rory was very considerate towards me, asked me if there was anything I needed, insisted that I sat beside the window, pandered to my every whim. When the air hostess asked if there was anything we wanted, he asked for Panadol.

When I was back in the apartment that evening I couldn't decide whether I'd enjoyed the weekend or not. I had certainly enjoyed the flights over and back. I loved aeroplanes, even though take-off scared me. I'd enjoyed our exquisite dinner on Friday night, but I still felt peeved that Rory had left me all day Saturday on my own, that he couldn't really understand why it had bothered me.

Still, it was part of getting to know each other. And it wasn't as though he was having fun all the time – he was with clients, after all. But if we did decide to get married, I hoped that he'd give up this desire for football and drink and realise that I was far more important to him than either.

Chapter 11

December 1981
(UK No. 10 – *Wedding Bells* **– Godley & Creme)**

We were all going home for Christmas Day. Given the chance, we would have stayed in the apartment and had Christmas dinner together, but we knew that our parents would go absolutely mad if we did.

We decorated the apartment, though. We pooled our money to buy a small tree which we stood in a wastepaper bin, propped up with books. It smelled gorgeous; the entire apartment was enveloped in the heady, outdoor smell of the fir tree. Brenda and Grace made wreaths of holly leaves and fir cones, and I bought a big inflatable Santa Claus which we blew up and stood in the corner of the room. The presents were placed in a pile under the tree.

It looked very festive and it would have been wonderful to spend Christmas Day there, but we decided that it wouldn't be worth the hassle to try and insist. Anyway, none of us would have been able to cook the dinner.

The week leading up to Christmas was hectic. The Settlements staff night out was on the Thursday. We got merry in Henry Grattan's, stuffed ourselves with food in a Chinese restaurant and finally fell down Leeson Street. It was a brilliant night. I got back to the apartment at about four o'clock.

Lucy woke me at half past eight, just as she was leaving. I hauled my eyes apart and looked at her through the gelled clump that was my hair.

'It can't be time to get up,' I moaned and she laughed unsympathetically.

'You woke me up when you got in,' she said heartlessly. 'I'm enjoying waking you up now.'

'Bitch!' I called after her retreating figure, throwing back the bedcovers and staggering into the bathroom.

Why on earth did we go out on a Thursday night, I wondered as I massaged shampoo vigorously into my hair and tried to stay standing under the spray of water. Whose idea was it?

Not only had we gone out on Thursday night, but tonight was the official bank party. This was for all staff; it was the one to which I would be wearing the dress that Grace had made, and it was held in the Shelbourne. I had been looking forward to it, but the way I felt now I wasn't quite so sure. I couldn't see how I could possibly stay awake long enough to go to another party.

I made hundreds of mistakes at work that day. For some reason, I was totally unable to remember the code for sterling and kept trying to input any sterling transactions as Irish pounds. The computer rejected them each time with a beep which was instantly recognisable. Rosaleen kept looking across at me. I know that she was counting the number of errors I made.

I wasn't the only one, of course. Settlements was full of white-faced people who could barely keep their eyes open. The dealers rang the phones simply to wake us up.

My phone rang. It was Rory. 'How are you today?'

I grunted at him.

'That bad?'

'I feel terrible,' I said. 'My eyes hurt, my head hurts and I can't input anything right. Rosaleen keeps looking at me and I'm sure she's going to write something awful on my appraisal.'

We had our annual staff appraisal every Christmas. Our annual bonuses were paid depending on how good the appraisals were. I'd hoped that mine would be good. I knew that I'd worked hard and that I was accurate and careful. All the same, I was afraid I could blow it all today.

Rosaleen had been at the party, but she'd drunk 7-Up in the pub and had gone home after the Chinese. Rosaleen didn't believe in having fun.

'Don't worry,' Rory told me. 'You'll be fine.'

I did feel better later on that evening and I had another shower before I got ready for the party.

Lucy did my hair for me. It was long enough to put into a neat French plait at the back of my head, which instantly made me look older and more sophisticated. I did my make-up carefully, applying just a touch of khaki eyeshadow to the corner of my eyes before filling the rest with my usual grey. Brenda had bought a lovely blusher a few days earlier which she said would look great on me, so I tried it out. It did look good. It made my cheekbones look higher and my face thinner.

Grace helped me into the green dress. She was very hopeful that somebody would like it and I was sure that they would. I just wasn't certain that, despite my assurances, I could get someone in the Lending department interested enough to consider advancing the twins money for dress design.

The high collar at the back suited me and my hairstyle. I wore earrings which Aunt Olivia had given me for my twenty-first, drop pearls in a silver setting. I put on the silver chain that Rory had bought me the week before – a pre-Christmas present, he'd called it, then smothered myself in Chanel's *Cristalle* which I had bought on the way to London. I borrowed Grace's silver gate bracelet because I didn't have any silver bracelet of my own and I wanted to keep my jewellery consistent.

'Let's look at you,' she said. I stood up and twirled around. The bodice of the dress was tight and the skirt full. It was a good party dress, I said, although I'd have to be careful not to eat too much, otherwise I might burst.

'Have you put on weight?' demanded Grace as she hauled at the zip.

I had to admit that I was a few pounds heavier. Going out with Rory meant eating and drinking more and I wasn't getting any exercise except sex. I was determined that I would diet after Christmas.

Rory called around for me in a taxi to bring me to the party. Although we thought we would be early, there were plenty of people already at the bar. We pushed our way through the crush to get a drink.

'Hair of the dog.' Rory handed me a Bacardi and Coke.

'I need the entire dog,' I muttered.

He went off to join the dealers while I stayed with my own crowd. Jessica came in, looking very pretty in a black cocktail dress, accompanied by Neil Dawson from the Baggot Street branch. Lorna had made a real effort and was wearing her hair differently, in a softer, much more feminine style. Michelle wore a long, slinky ballgown which made me feel that Grace's dress was too fussy. But everyone had admired it so far and, when I told them all that my flatmate had made it, they were really surprised.

I stayed chatting to Jessica while Neil wandered off.

'How are you getting on in Settlements?' she asked, sipping her drink.

'Not bad,' I told her. 'But I preferred International Trade.'

'Really?' she said. 'I thought you liked the people in Settlements better.'

'Not really,' I said. 'They're OK, but there's nobody like you, Jessica. Nobody who takes an interest.'

'I thought that one person was taking an interest.' She nodded over at Rory who was deep in conversation with Shane.

'Oh,' I said. 'I didn't think you meant Rory.'

'He's taking quite an interest though, isn't he?' she said wickedly. 'It's the talk of the bank.'

'Is it?' I was surprised. 'Loads of people in the bank are going out with each other.'

It was difficult for it not to happen. There were so many people of a similar age that inter-office affairs were going on all the time.

'But Rory is such a good catch,' said Jessica.

'You said that to me before,' I told her. 'Anyone would think you fancied him yourself.'

She blushed furiously and I looked at her in amazement. 'You *don't* fancy him yourself, do you?'

She shook her head vigorously. 'I'd better tell you,' she said. 'I went out with him once.'

I looked at her in shock. 'When?'

'When he first joined. It was ages ago, Jane, and we only went out twice. He was younger than me and it didn't work out. But I've stayed fond of him.'

'He never said anything,' I told her.

'He's probably forgotten,' said Jessica blandly.

I supposed it was reasonable to assume that Rory had gone out with other people in the bank, but I'd never asked him about it. I'd tried to talk to him once before about his previous relationships, but he was always dismissive about them, said they didn't matter. I hadn't realised that Jessica could be one of them.

'It really meant nothing,' she said again, uncomfortably. 'I shouldn't have mentioned it.'

'It's OK,' I said. 'Don't worry about it.' I wasn't worried. Jessica wasn't Rory's type.

The hotel staff came around at that point and tried to usher us in to the dining room. I moved with the throng. I sat at a table with the Settlements crowd and the dealers were at the other side of the room, but that didn't matter because I knew that Rory and I would get together later.

Helium-filled silver balloons were tied to the backs of the chairs. A huge Christmas tree, decked with shining balls and sparkling white lights, took up the corner of the room. We all crowded around the tables, exclaiming in delight.

'Love your dress, Jane,' said Martina. 'It's absolutely fantastic.'

'Sure is,' said Rita. 'Where did you buy it?'

'My flatmate made it for me,' I told her. 'She wants to be a dress designer.'

'I wish she'd design something for me,' said Martina. 'It's the nicest dress I've seen.'

I was pleased, both for me and for Grace. 'I'll tell her that,' I said. 'Thanks.'

After the meal we got up and danced. I stayed with my own crowd for an hour and then Rory came to claim me. We danced together, a public affirmation of our status as a couple.

It was the best Christmas party ever. In the raffle I won a £10 voucher for Brown Thomas, although I couldn't imagine what I could possibly buy there for a tenner, and Rory won a bottle of sherry, which he said that I could bring over to Mam and Dad for Christmas.

'My parents don't drink it,' he said. 'I know your mum likes sherry.'

'She'll be thrilled,' I told him. 'Thanks.'

I'd met Rory's parents a couple of weeks earlier. They seemed nice enough people, but his mother was more distant than mine and I couldn't help thinking that his father rather looked down on me. Rory had two brothers and a younger sister, although I hadn't met any of them yet. That was the one thing that bothered me about our relationship. If it was to be The One, if we were to get married, surely I should meet his family first. It wasn't as though they could stop us, of course. I simply felt that it would be the proper thing to do.

Rory's family wasn't as close as mine, though. Mam, Aunt Liz, Aunt Olivia and Aunt Joan met regularly. The various cousins knew each other very well. When we were smaller, we holidayed together a lot. The McLoughlins weren't like that at all. Rory had aunts and uncles, but he said he didn't see them much and he never thought about them. I couldn't imagine a family like that.

He held me close as we danced together. I could feel the warmth of his hand, smell the musky scent of his aftershave, sense his breathing with the rise and fall of his chest. I rested my head on his shirt and he held me still closer.

The church was crowded for Midnight Mass. Outside, frost glittered and sparkled on the black tarmac. Inside, fan heaters blasted warm air on to the congregation. A huge crib took up one side of the altar.

'*Adeste Fideles.*' The choir began the hymn, filling the church with rich sound. The priests marched in a procession around the church, carrying a doll to symbolise the Christ child. Father O'Herlihy, the parish priest, laid it in the manger.

It was a ritual that had been part of my life since I was nine years old and first deemed old enough to be allowed to go to Midnight Mass. I looked around me. I hadn't been to Mass since I left home. As I didn't believe in God and thought the ritual was very silly, there didn't seem to be any point, but there was something very comforting about Midnight Mass. I listened to the priest and felt guilty about my relationship with Rory. But we would be married one day, I thought. We love each other. It's right for us to sleep together. All the same, I felt terribly uncomfortable. Why did the Church have to make us feel like sinners all the time? Surely if there was a God He didn't want people to go around in a perpetual haze of guilt.

When we got home Dad made us Irish coffees and Mam heated up some mince pies. It was lovely. We wished each other a Happy Christmas and went to bed.

The smell of roasting turkey wafted up to my bedroom in the

morning. It was one of those aromas which brought me back to my childhood.

I was standing in the kitchen, watching Mam peel potatoes.

'Why do you take the skins off?' I asked.
  'Because you have to do that to roast them,' she told me.
  'Why are you scraping bits out?'
  'They are the eyes. You have to get rid of them.'
  'But they'll be blind!' I cried. 'They won't be able to see.'

I smiled at the memory as I walked into the kitchen again.

'Can I do anything to help?'

'Peel some potatoes,' said Mam, and didn't understand why I started to laugh.

I peeled potatoes, prepared the sprouts and scraped the cranberry sauce out of the jar and into a sauce boat.

'Are you going to wander around in your dressing-gown all day, or are you going to get dressed?' asked Mam.

'I'm going to get dressed, of course,' I said. 'But we have to give presents first. I always do that in my dressing-gown.'

She smiled at me. 'OK,' she said, wiping her hands on her apron. 'Let's see if your dad is ready.'

Dad was sitting in the living room watching *Miracle on 34th Street*.

'Do you want to do presents?' I asked.

He nodded, so we sat down in front of the tree and exchanged gifts. I watched my parents anxiously. I had spent a lot of time trying to get something they would like.

Dad was delighted with the stereo headphones I bought him. He liked to listen to music and watch TV at the same time, which drove Mam mad, so I had decided that this way he could do both. Mam was a bit put out to see that she only had a box of chocolates as her gift, until she opened the envelope inside the gift-wrap and saw a voucher for a full-day beauty treatment at one of the Grafton Street salons.

Her face lit up and she kissed me on the cheek. I knew she would like it; she always looked so well when she was made up and dressed up but she never spent time on herself these days.

Mam had bought me a lovely silver-blue jumper, decorated with

136

silver stars. Dad had bought me a book. I opened the present that Rory had given me the day before. I knew that it couldn't be anything like an engagement ring, because the box was too big, but secretly I hoped that it might be. It wasn't. It was a beautiful gold chain from which hung a wishbone.

'How pretty!' exclaimed Mam.

'That chap really likes you,' said Dad.

I slipped the chain around my neck and wished Rory was with me now. I felt a great ache of longing for him. I wondered if he had opened my present to him, a huge watch which told the time in almost every capital city in the world.

I went upstairs, had my shower and dressed in the new jumper and a black velvet skirt I'd bought especially for Christmas. I brushed my hair into a new style so that it fell over one eye. Looks cool, I thought.

When we sat down to dinner, Mam suggested that I pin it back out of my eyes.

'It's meant to be like that,' I said peevishly. I wasn't used to being criticised. In the apartment, we gave each other tips about how to look better, but we never told anyone to brush their hair out of their eyes.

In fact it was quite strange being home. My bedroom didn't seem like mine any more. I'd taken the pictures off the wall when I moved out. The wardrobe was empty except for the few bits and pieces I'd left behind and what I had brought with me for the three days I was staying at home. Mam and Dad had assumed I would stay with them until I went back to work, and I didn't have the heart to say that I wanted to go back to the apartment.

But after three days I was mad to go back. It was hard to be treated like a child when I was used to making my own decisions. I went down to Lucy's house on St Stephen's Night, just to get a break, and my parents wanted to know what time I'd be back. She said it was just as bad at her place, and the two of us wondered whether we could return to the apartment straight away. But we couldn't. It would have broken their hearts.

The day after St Stephen's Day, all the aunts and uncles came over for dinner. It was a traditional family get-together, held in a different house every year. I looked around at all of them and was a bit saddened that I didn't have any brothers and sisters. When

I got married, Christmas in my house wouldn't be the same huge social gathering. Sisters stay close, I thought, watching them. Brothers can sort of take it or leave it.

I looked at my watch and wondered whether Rory would call. He was in Scotland for Christmas. His family owned a house there and spent every Christmas 'holed up in the highlands', as he called it. There wasn't a phone in the house, so he couldn't call easily. The nearest phone was in the village, three miles away. He said he would try to phone, but that if it was raining he wouldn't bother. I told him that he'd better bother. I'd checked the weather forecast. It was pouring, apparently.

I sat and tried to join in the conversation but I was bored with it. I didn't care that Phoebe Sinclair's eldest daughter had got a first at university. I didn't even know who Phoebe was. It turned out she was an old school friend of Aunt Olivia.

'And Juliet O'Hara's girl has gone to live in the States,' said Aunt Liz. 'She married a doctor.'

'I never liked Juliet,' said Mam. 'She was a snob.'

'Only because her family were rolling in it,' reminded Aunt Liz. 'Do you remember, they had a girl who came in and cleaned for them every day?'

Mam nodded. 'They treated her like a slave,' she said. 'She was a lovely girl.'

'Do you remember Agnes Delaney?' asked Aunt Olivia suddenly. 'I saw her in town the other day. Pasted in make-up and trying to look half her age. Actually looked twice it.'

'Stop being bitchy,' I said. 'You're assassinating every character of your youth.'

Aunt Liz laughed at me. 'You'll enjoy doing that when you get older, young Jane,' she said. 'Bet you could say a few choice things about people you went to school with.'

I pursed my lips, then smiled. 'Stephanie McMenamin – tart,' I said brightly.

'Jane!' exclaimed Mam.

'Well, she was,' I said. 'I never liked her. Always showing off.'

'Didn't she get married?' asked Mam.

I nodded. 'She has a baby daughter and she's expecting her second,' I said.

'My God!' said Aunt Olivia. 'She's only your age.'

138

'Yes,' I replied. 'She got married the year we left school – to the same guy she was going out with since she was about fifteen. Kurt Kennedy. She lives on Riverview Estate.'

I had seen Stephanie a few times since we left school. At first I had been madly envious of her. A gang of us had gone to the church the day she married Kurt and had watched jealously as she had walked down the aisle looking radiant, her blonde hair swept up and her long veil trailing down her back. Kurt had looked debonair and handsome and I remember thinking that I could fancy him myself.

The last time I saw Stephanie she'd been pushing her daughter in a pram, hurrying for a bus. She hadn't looked half as glamorous then.

I knew about marriage. I knew it wouldn't always be perfect. That there would be days when I would probably regret it. Days when it would be a hassle. But I still wanted Rory to ask me.

'What about you?' asked Aunt Joan, breaking into my reverie. 'Are you thinking of getting married yet, Jane?'

I blushed. 'Not yet,' I said.

'Are you sure?' teased my aunt. 'You don't sound convinced.'

'Tell us about your boyfriend,' demanded Aunt Olivia. 'What's he like?'

'Really,' I protested, 'you sound as if you're vetting him or something.'

Mam laughed. 'They're just raging because you've a handsome young man dancing attendance on you,' she said. 'They think he sounds great.'

'Have you been telling them?' I asked.

'Just a bit,' she said. 'Well, you *are* my daughter.'

'His name is Rory,' I said. I didn't need much encouragement to talk about Rory. Saying his name conjured up his face. This was the longest I had gone without seeing him since we started going out together. I told them about him, how hard he worked, how generous he was, how good-looking he was.

'He sounds great,' said Aunt Liz warmly. 'But don't get married too young.'

'Who said anything about getting married?' I demanded. 'We've only been going out together.'

Aunt Liz shook her head knowingly.

'She's right,' said Mam suddenly. 'Don't rush into anything, Jane. Enjoy your life.'

'I *am* enjoying my life,' I said forcefully. 'I'm having a great time in the apartment with the girls. We go to work during the day and go out at night.'

'Every night?' Mam sounded concerned.

'Don't be daft,' I said. 'You know we don't. But we go out at the weekend, sometimes together, sometimes with boyfriends, and it's great.'

Aunt Olivia nodded. 'I would have loved to live in a flat on my own when I was younger,' she said wistfully. 'You're very lucky, Jane.'

'I think so, too,' I said, and got up to answer the phone which had begun to ring.

'I thought you'd never call,' I said to Rory. 'I've missed you.'

'Sorry,' he said. 'I couldn't really get away before now. What are you doing tonight?'

'I'm sitting in with my family. They're reminiscing about the old days and telling me to have fun while I'm young.'

'Sounds OK to me,' he said cheerfully.

'I told them I was having fun,' I said.

'I thought you were missing me,' he said. 'How can you be having fun?'

'Well, I usually have fun,' I amended. 'When will you be home, Rory?'

'I'll be back on New Year's Eve,' he said. 'Do you want to go out?'

'Of course I do,' I said. 'What did you have in mind?'

'Oh, anything once it's with you,' he said, making my heart somersault.

'You say the nicest things,' I told him.

'I know.'

We chatted for a while longer and then I went back into the living room.

'I know you want to have fun,' said Aunt Liz, looking at my happy face. 'But it seems to me that he has you in the palm of his hand. I take it that was your Rory.'

'That was my Rory.' I sat down and tucked my legs under me. 'He misses me.'

They laughed. 'Who misses whom?' asked Aunt Olivia but I ignored them.

On New Year's Eve, Greg from Apartment 43 invited us up to his place for a party. We accepted with alacrity, although I told Lucy that I'd be seeing Rory first.

'No problem,' she said. 'We're all going to the Burlington for a drink then straight up to Greg's place.'

'Straight up?' I asked.

'Straight up,' she answered. 'I promise we won't barge in on you.' She winked lasciviously and I made a face at her. But I was glad that Rory and I would have some time on our own in the apartment.

He called around at half past eight, looking incredibly desirable in his denim jeans, denim shirt and black leather jacket. I felt myself melt the moment he walked through the door.

The girls went off to the pub, telling us that they would see us later.

'Don't forget to come to the party,' reminded Lucy as they walked out of the door.

'We won't.' I closed the door behind them, delighted to be on my own with Rory at last.

We fell upon each other as though we had been apart for years. We laughed at ourselves and our desire. I opened a bottle of wine and put on some music and lay in his arms, happier than I had been in days.

It felt so perfect. So right. I closed my eyes and allowed him to stroke my cheek.

'I have a present for you,' he said suddenly.

I sat up. 'Another one?' I said. 'You're spoiling me.'

'I've nobody else to spoil,' he said. 'Besides, I like giving you presents. You're like a child when you get something.'

'You're the only one who gives me presents,' I said. 'And I do so love them.'

'Well, I was going to give you this one on Christmas Day,' he said, 'but then I couldn't give it to you and not be there.'

'Hand it over,' I commanded. 'Give me the goodies.'

He laughed and took the box out of his jacket pocket.

I knew at once that this was it. It had to be. I schooled myself not to be disappointed if it was another chain, or a bracelet or a pair of earrings. Rory might not be ready for marriage yet. He might think that we were too young. He might think that I would like a small gift of jewellery. Not a ring. He wouldn't know that I would be devastated.

I opened the box and looked inside. The ring nestled against the navy blue velvet, sparkling gently. The diamond was very beautiful. It was a solitaire in a raised setting and it glittered in the lamplight.

'Oh Rory,' I breathed. 'It's fabulous.'

He searched my face. 'Do you like it?'

'Oh, yes.'

'It's an engagement ring,' he said.

'I can see that,' I told him.

'I wanted you to be sure what it was.'

'I'm certain what it is,' I said.

'So?' asked Rory.

I took the ring out of the box and slipped it on to my engagement finger. I turned my hand from side to side so that shafts of light sparked out from the diamond.

There were tears in my eyes as I looked at Rory. 'I love you,' I said.

'But will you marry me?' he asked.

It was the question I had been waiting for since I was about thirteen, when I realised that girls got married. And Rory, my beloved Rory, had asked me. We hadn't casually chatted about it and decided to get married one day in a very sensible sort of way. He had bought a ring and given it to me and asked me.

'Of course I'll marry you,' I said, looking up at him again. 'I've always wanted to marry you.'

We went into the bedroom and made love. I wore nothing but my engagement ring in bed.

'I love you,' I said.

'I love you,' said Rory.

We were still there in each other's arms at midnight. We heard the sounds of people entering Greg's flat above, the steady hum of voices, the thud of music and the shrill laughter of a party. But we stayed where we were, content to be together. So when they stopped the music and started counting down to the new year, we were still together, holding each other tightly.

I was engaged to be married, I thought proudly. Engaged to Rory. My new life was about to begin.

Chapter 12

February 1986
(UK No. 1 – *When The Going Gets Tough* – Billy Ocean)

Jessica dumped a file on my desk and grinned sympathetically. 'Busy?' she asked.

I looked up from the documents I was checking to see if she was joking. I was very busy. 'What does it look like?' I demanded. 'I'm up to my neck. I'll never get this lot finished by five o'clock.'

'That can wait,' said Jessica. 'I need you to check these now.'

I glanced at my watch and then at the file. It was crammed with paper.

'Turnstone Industries,' I said. 'That's Jake's.' I looked over at the empty desk where Jake Loomis normally sat.

'But Jake is at the conference and I need someone to do this now,' said Jessica.

'I know Jake is at the conference,' I snapped, feeling rage well up inside me.

I'd wanted to go to the conference. It was called 'International Banking in the Eighties' and, even allowing for the hype of the brochure, it had looked very interesting. I meant to ask Jessica about it as soon as I saw the brochure but she was at a meeting so I left it on my desk for later. I couldn't find it the next day. I looked around for it for a while, then Rory rang me about something or other and I forgot all about it. Until Jake Loomis casually mentioned that he was going. He'd taken the brochure from my desk. 'I assumed you weren't interested,' he said blandly when I challenged him about it. I thought about making a fuss and demanding to go too, but it wasn't worth it. I was spitting mad all the same.

After I married Rory, the bank transferred me back to International Trade because they needed someone with experience in the department. Most of the people I'd originally worked with had either resigned or been promoted to other areas. Jake Loomis had come from Personnel and he was ambitious. I knew more about the work than he did, I was more conscientious than he was and I was more efficient than him – but he was the one at the conference and I wasn't.

'Jane?' Jessica was staring at me.

'I don't see why I should have to—'

'Jane, I'm not asking you, I'm telling you.'

I gritted my teeth. 'Fine.'

I pulled the file towards me and started work. None of the documents was properly checked and everything was out of sequence. That little shit, I thought bitterly.

I flew through the work. I had to. Rory and I were going out tonight and we were leaving on the dot of five. Rory would go crazy if I was late. Bill Hamilton, the most senior executive in the Corporate Treasury division, had invited a number of people to dinner in his house. We were included because Rory had been promoted at Christmas. So we couldn't be late.

I still had a couple more documents to check when Rory rang me at ten to five from reception.

'I'll be down in a minute,' I said. 'I'm almost finished.'

But it was nearly ten past by the time I hurtled down the stairs and into the marble foyer. Rory's face was black as thunder as we hurried down to the car park.

He was already sitting on the edge of the bed when I emerged from the shower. He looked great in a new charcoal grey Hugo Boss suit, pale cream shirt and Pierre Cardin tie. He tapped his watch and sighed.

'All right, all right,' I said. 'I'll be ready soon. Keep your shirt on.'

'I don't want to be late,' said Rory. 'This is a very important dinner, Jane.'

'I know it is.' I switched on the hairdryer. 'I won't be long.'

We had plenty of time. The invitation said half-seven for eight and it was only a quarter to seven now. He was driving me nuts. Rory, who had never been on time for anything in his life before, was now the one telling me to hurry up!

I did my face and took the purple satin dress from the wardrobe. It was last year's dress but it was one of my favourites. It made me feel very sexy and sophisticated and that was how I wanted to feel in front of Rory's colleagues.

'Do up my zip,' I asked Rory, who still sat on the bed.

'Breathe in,' he said, as he hauled at it.

'I am.'

'Breathe in a bit more.'

I sucked in my breath and he tugged the zip.

The fabric rucked unflatteringly around my stomach even though I tried to smooth it out, and it strained across my chest. I looked as though I'd explode through it any minute.

Rory looked at me critically. 'You're letting yourself go a bit.'

'Give me a break,' I said as I tugged at the dress again. 'I haven't worn this in ages. It's probably just a bit of weight since Christmas.'

'Christmas was eight weeks ago,' he informed me. 'You should have lost any pounds by now.'

'Well, I haven't,' I snapped, annoyed with myself for putting on weight and annoyed with him for being so direct about it. 'And I can't possibly wear this dress. I'll have to find something else.' I was close to tears. I had been so organised and now it was all a shambles. I was going to have to rethink my entire outfit – if I ever got out of this bloody dress. I was embarrassed about putting on weight although I usually added a few pounds in the winter. I lost them again in the summer but that wasn't much use now.

I was irritated at the way Rory was looking at me – as though I was some fat lump trying to squeeze into a dress five sizes too small. This dress was my size. Usually.

'I'd better wear the black,' I said, rummaging around in the wardrobe. 'It's stretchy.'

'I never thought I'd see the day when you would be going for comfort, not style,' said Rory.

'Fuck off, will you,' I said in temper. 'There's nothing wrong with the black dress.'

'It's a boring dress,' said Rory. 'Anyone can wear black.'

I couldn't stand Rory criticising how I looked. I never said anything derogatory to him about his appearance. I ignored him and pulled it off the hanger, smoothing it out on the bed.

146

'Well, I can't wear it,' I said. 'There's a stain on it.' I wanted to kick and scream in frustration.

By the time I'd found a suitable dress (navy blue, a couple of years old and normally slightly loose on me) Rory had decided that we were late. He hustled me into the car and ignored the fact that I'd stepped in a puddle, so my feet were wet. I didn't say anything but switched the heater on full blast to try and dry them.

He gunned the car along the dual carriageway. The driving rain smashed against the windscreen and the wipers raced across it frantically. I shivered. I wasn't looking forward to tonight any more.

The panic of having to race around and find something else to wear had given me a headache. I leaned back in the comfortable seat of the BMW and closed my eyes. I tried to relax my shoulder muscles and breathe slowly, but I was terribly tense and I couldn't seem to empty my mind like you are supposed to.

'Fuck!' exclaimed Rory and swerved suddenly.

I snapped my eyes open. 'What's wrong?'

'Fucking cyclists. No lights – in this weather. He deserves to be knocked down!'

I peered out of the back window but I couldn't see anyone. 'You didn't hit him, did you?'

'Don't be ridiculous. If I'd hit him, he'd know all about it.' Rory slammed the car into fifth.

I said nothing. It wasn't worth talking to him when he was in this sort of mood.

Bill and Karen Hamilton lived in a five-bedroomed, detached, redbrick house off the Stillorgan dual carriageway. It was an exclusive development of only twenty houses, all slightly different and designed to appeal to people with money. They had integrated garages, landscaped gardens and mock-Georgian porticoes over the front doors. The cobble-locked driveways were big enough for two cars and most of the people living in Huntswood Heights owned two cars. All of the houses had high hedges or trees enclosing their gardens, keeping them very private.

'Come on,' said Rory, as he switched off the engine. 'Let's hurry.'

We ran up the driveway together, holding our coats over our

heads. It was a horrible night. I pressed the doorbell and heard it chime at the back of the house.

Karen Hamilton opened the door. She was a stunning girl who looked considerably younger than thirty-three, which was how old Rory had told me she was. She was tall and thin with a long, graceful neck and a perfect oval face. Her hair was almost jet black and cascaded down her back in rippling glossy waves. She had dark brown eyes and black straight eyebrows. Her skin was flawless and glowed with a tan from a winter week in the Canaries. She wore a red wool dress which clung tightly to every curve of her body, its plunging neckline accentuating the deep V of her breasts. A ruby pendant rested in the hollow and drew your gaze inexorably towards them.

Rory's eyes almost popped out of his head when he saw her.

'Hello, Karen,' I said, when he failed to speak.

'Jane.' Karen's voice was low and throaty. 'It's wonderful to see you.'

A bit of an exaggeration. Karen Hamilton had only met me once before. The way she spoke it was as though her only joy in life was seeing me again. I smiled at her.

'Come in,' said Karen, 'before you get soaked.'

We stepped inside the house. The hallway was wide and the carpet deep and warm. The walls were papered in a creamy abstract design hung with prints from the New York Metropolitan gallery, lit by unobtrusive spotlights.

'We're in the lounge.' Karen sashayed down the hallway ahead of us.

The other couples were already there and I felt Rory's intake of breath as he realised that we were the last to arrive. Bill Hamilton stood in front of the gas effect fire, a glass of whiskey in his hand.

'Ah, Rory.' He put the glass down on the mantelpiece. 'You made it. And the lovely Jane.' He extended his hand and I took it. He shook hands with a firm, decisive grip.

'What can I get you?' he asked.

'Could I have a Bailey's with ice?'

'Certainly,' said Bill. 'And you, Rory?'

'Gin and tonic, please.'

I looked around the room while Bill busied himself with the drinks. It was huge, divided by double doors which led to the dining area. The understated décor could only have been achieved with a lot of money.

'Do you know everyone?' Bill asked me, as he handed me the drink.

'She knows me,' smiled Graham Kirwin, the Chief Dealer and Rory's boss. 'And she knows Suki.'

Suki was Graham's wife, a beautiful Eurasian girl he had met when he was working in Frankfurt. I had met her once or twice before, but I didn't know her very well.

'Hi.' She smiled.

The others introduced themselves. All of the men worked in the Treasury department. All of the wives were drop-dead lovely. I felt clumsy and unattractive in my navy-blue dress.

'Well, now that we're all here, I'd like to congratulate Rory McLoughlin on his recent promotion,' said Bill as he lifted his glass, 'and all of you for putting in such a good year for the bank.'

'Hear, hear,' said Bernard McAleer.

'And I'd like to thank the wives, especially,' said Bill. 'Sometimes wives have to put up with an awful lot. Late hours, hard work, et cetera. So I'd like to thank them too.'

'Absolutely,' said Lorraine, Bernard's wife.

What a load of crap, I thought. All the same I raised my glass and smiled at Bill. He was about forty, going grey, and with a paunch which was escaping over the top of his expensive trousers.

'Of course, Jane still works for us.' He smiled at me. 'And you're doing very well, I believe.'

'Thank you,' I said. He was patronising me. I hated being patronised. I wasn't doing that well. I'd been promoted last year but I reckoned it was well overdue. I was good at my job, but it was very hard to feel that it was important when Rory earned nearly three times as much as me – before bonuses. Bill made some more comments about the bank and its staff and how wonderful we all were. I supposed they taught them all that motivational stuff at their management meetings. I shifted uncomfortably from one foot to the other.

'So, tell me, Lorraine,' said Karen as she moved across the room and adeptly divided the men from the women, 'where did you get that fabulous outfit?'

149

'It's a Karl Lagerfeld,' she said. 'I bought it in London.'

'It looks superb on you,' said Karen.

'Yours is lovely too,' said Linda Sherry. Linda was the most ordinary-looking of the girls; the only one who didn't look as if she'd stepped off a catwalk.

'Thank you, my dear,' said Karen. 'I bought it in Terenure, would you believe.'

'Really!' Lorraine looked surprised. 'Very elegant.'

'Thanks. It's a nice shop, near the village. Called *Les Jumelles*.'

'Oh, I think I know it,' said Linda.

'I do,' I said. 'The girls who run it are friends of mine.'

I was delighted. The shop, which the twins had opened a couple of years ago, was obviously attracting the right sort of clientèle. These women could afford to spend money.

'Did you buy that dress there?' asked Lorraine, as she arched one of her fine eyebrows.

I blushed furiously. Lorraine was making some sort of dig at me and I didn't like it.

'No,' I said shortly.

There was a moment's silence, then Suki asked Karen about her recent holiday.

My attention wandered from the conversation and I looked around the room again. Everything in it was of the highest quality. The carefully polished fittings shone. The carpet, like the one in the hallway, was deep. I was conscious that my heels were making little marks in it.

The wives continued to chat about holidays. Karen had been to the Canaries. Lorraine and Bernard had been skiing in Kitzbühl.

'It was brilliant,' said Lorraine. 'The snow was fantastic and the nightlife was even better. Some of those ski instructors!' She laughed knowingly.

'I've never been skiing,' I said regretfully, deciding that I should make an effort to join the conversation, 'although Rory says we must go some time.'

'Go now while you don't have children,' said Lorraine. 'Once you start a family, you don't get a moment to yourself.'

'Don't talk to me!' said Linda cheerfully. 'Do you know what Charlie did the other day?'

She launched into a story about her son, a tin of paint and the cat next door. Linda was good at telling stories and she had us in fits of laughter.

'Another drink, girls?' asked Bill. We nodded.

'I meant to give up drink for January and February,' moaned Lorraine. 'I put on far too much weight over Christmas.'

'I think you look great,' said Fiona Roche. 'A bit of weight suits you.'

Actually, Lorraine looked like a stick insect to me. I couldn't imagine how she thought she was even slightly overweight. I could see her shoulder blades clearly through her dress. They started to talk about diets and I listened carefully. Tomorrow, I thought, I would start one of my own. No more crisps or sweets in front of the TV. What I needed was less food and more exercise.

When we'd first married, Rory and I joined a squash club. Neither of us was very good but we had fun bashing the ball around. But now Rory was far too busy to bother with squash and I'd stopped going to the club on my own. I'd start again, though. Maybe when Lucy came home she would join the club too. The last time I'd talked to her she hinted that she was thinking of returning to Ireland. She'd spent the last few years in Paris as a PA to the director of an Irish company there, but she was tired of France and she said she was looking for a job at home. She'd visited home quite a bit, and I'd been over to Paris a couple of times which was fun, but I missed our easy companionship at home. She'd gone to France shortly after I got engaged, to forget about her disastrous affair with Nick Clark. She'd stayed because she liked it so much. Then, being Lucy, she'd found a boyfriend and moved in with him. I got the impression, the last time we talked, that the relationship was floundering and I wondered if that was why she'd hinted at coming home.

I yawned, and quickly covered my mouth with my hand.

'Don't tell me you're tired!' exclaimed Karen. 'Or is our conversation boring you?'

'No, not at all,' I said hastily. 'I think it's the heat from the fire.'

'It was such a cold night I rather thought you'd like some warmth,' remarked Karen. She leaned down and lowered the setting on the gas fire. 'Is that better?'

'It's fine,' I replied in embarrassment. 'There was no need to lower it for me, honestly.'

'Oh, I like to give my guests whatever they want,' she said, making me feel as though I'd just put her to an immense amount of trouble. 'Do you want to go in and eat?'

I said that I would love to eat, although I wasn't very hungry. I still had a headache and my stomach was queasy, but the others said that they were starving. Karen smiled brilliantly at Bill and asked him if he was ready for food.

'I thought you'd never ask!' he cried.

'Excuse me a moment, then,' said Karen, and disappeared into the kitchen. I admired her ability to be a wonderful hostess and to cook a meal for us all while being so relaxed. If it was me, I knew that I would be in a complete tizzy, running in and out of the kitchen, with a red face glowing from the steam.

Karen sauntered back into the room a few minutes later, smiled radiantly at us and led us into the dining room.

'This looks great.' Linda sat down at the shining mahogany table.

'Appearances are everything,' laughed Karen.

I knew what Linda meant. The table was beautifully presented. The wood gleamed warmly, the cutlery shone and crystal wine glasses sparkled under the subdued lighting. A lovely floral centre-piece gave off the faint scent of orchids.

'What's for dinner, darling?' asked Bill, as he unrolled his napkin and shook it vigorously.

'Wait and see,' said Karen.

The door to the kitchen opened and a girl walked into the room, carrying two bottles of wine. I almost fainted when I saw her because I recognised her instantly. It was Louise Killane, one of the girls I had gone to school with. I squirmed in my chair. What on earth was she doing here?

'Louise is our chef this evening,' said Karen.

I looked up in surprise. I had assumed that Karen would be doing all the cooking herself. I didn't realise that people actually got somebody in to do the cooking for them. And Louise Killane! I hadn't seen Louise since we'd left school and I had no idea what she had planned to do. But obviously she'd studied cookery, even though as far as I remembered she hadn't done Domestic Science at school.

She took the wine to the sideboard, opened the bottles and poured a little into Bill's glass for him to taste.

'Perfect,' he said. 'Go ahead.'

She poured the wine delicately into the glasses. When she came to my place I saw the flicker of recognition in her eyes, but she said nothing, just filled my glass.

'She's a wonderful cook,' said Karen, when Louise had left the room. 'She does a lot of private functions and parties. I was at a charity dinner recently and Louise had done the cooking. Absolutely superb.'

I was interested to taste Louise's cooking, although I was still feeling dodgy and the drink hadn't settled my stomach. I despaired of my recent habit of getting headaches and feeling ill whenever I went out. I couldn't understand it.

Louise came back into the room carrying bowls of soup. The bowls were a delicate white porcelain, decorated with a simple gold band. My heart sank as I saw the soup.

'Leek and potato,' Louise murmured as she put the bowl in front of me. Green soup, I thought, as I looked at it. I hated green soup. The only soup I liked was vegetable or tomato. I had a big psychological problem with green-coloured soup, especially when a blob of white cream sprinkled with chives floated on the top of it.

I took my spoon and swirled the cream through the liquid. Now that food was in front of me I felt queasier than ever.

I took a piece of bread from the basket that Karen had passed around and buttered it. Perhaps if I had a bit of bread I'd feel better.

I ate the bread and toyed with the soup. Louise would feel hurt if I didn't drink it. That was the worst of soup. With a main course you could play with the food and hide the bits you didn't like under something else, but a full soup bowl was a dead give-away. All the same, I drank about half of it and hoped that it would be enough.

Louise didn't say anything when she came back to collect the bowls, but I heard the quiet intake of breath when she saw mine. I felt terrible about it.

'So, Jane,' said Graham. 'How are things in International Trade?'

I looked up from the table and smiled at him. 'Very well,' I said. 'We're very busy.'

'That's good news,' said Graham. 'And your team is getting the work done?'

'Absolutely,' I replied.

'I think you're great to keep working,' drawled Fiona. 'I couldn't.'

'I like working,' I said defensively, even if it was only half true.

'I do a lot of voluntary work,' said Lorraine, 'but I feel that I should leave paid work to people who really need it.'

I felt as though I had been slapped.

'But, of course, we all have children,' said Linda, smiling at me. 'When Jane has a family, she'll probably find it far too demanding to keep working.'

I looked gratefully at her. 'I expect you're right,' I said.

'How old is your eldest now, Bill?' Don stretched back in his chair.

'Would you believe Gary is nearly fourteen?' said Bill. 'I can hardly believe that myself.'

Karen certainly didn't look old enough to have a fourteen-year-old son. She looked in great condition. She must have worked out every day to keep a figure like hers. I resolved to join a gym myself as soon as possible.

The door opened again and Louise carried the dinner plates to the table. 'Poached salmon,' she said, placing the plate in front of me.

Oh Louise, I thought despairingly, why couldn't you have cooked something else?

Normally I liked salmon, although it wasn't my favourite fish. But it sat there in the middle of the plate covered in golden butter and the smell of it made me want to be sick.

Why did I feel so bloody awful? Please, God, I begged, please don't let me be sick tonight. Rory would never forgive me. Louise spooned some tiny buttered potatoes and some creamed carrots on to the side of my plate.

'Thanks,' I whispered. She smiled, very faintly, at me.

I couldn't keep my mind on the conversation. I listened to the words but I couldn't join in. I was concentrating on eating as little as possible but trying to arrange the food so that nobody would notice. I was hot, my head was pounding and I could feel my scalp sweating. I knew that my face was burning. I wiped my

154

damp palms on the side of my dress. The buzz of chatter around the table was loud and it seemed to echo around the room. I sipped the glass of mineral water beside me.

'Of course, Singapore is such a fabulous place,' Suki said, her voice coming from a great distance. 'Have you ever been to the Far East, Jane?'

I shook my head, unable to trust myself to speak without throwing up. I'd never lost the horror I had about being sick, the terror of feeling my stomach heave and being able to do absolutely nothing about it. I could see it now, being sick on top of that beautiful table. Spraying the flower arrangement with vomit. I closed my eyes.

'Excuse me a moment,' I said, and dashed upstairs to the bathroom.

I threw up into the toilet basin, gasping for breath as my undigested dinner came out the way it went in. I tried desperately to be sick as quietly as I could. My head felt as though it would explode, but I felt a bit better. I flushed the toilet and sat on the edge of the bath for a few minutes. After a while I stood up and splashed some cool water on my face. I squeezed some toothpaste from the tube on the bathroom shelf and rubbed it on to my teeth with my finger. Then, with a shaking hand, I redid my lipstick. I checked my dress to make sure that I hadn't spotted it but it was OK.

I went back downstairs again and rejoined the dinner table.

'Are you all right?' asked Linda as I took my seat beside her.

'Of course.' I kept my voice as firm as I could.

Rory looked at me quizzically: 'What were you doing up there?' he muttered. 'We were going to send up a search party.'

'Nothing.' I looked down at the plate in front of me.

Louise had replaced the salmon with dessert – a sumptuous, rich, chocolate gateau. My heart fell when I saw it. I'd been hoping that maybe Louise wouldn't have done a dessert, that she'd bring out a cheeseboard which I could have ignored.

Everyone else tucked in with gusto. I picked up my fork and cut a sliver. As a chocolate cake it was superb. As something to put into my sensitive stomach it was a disaster. I only ate half, and made a joking comment about having to diet.

'It's a bit late now,' guffawed Rory, 'since you can't fit into your clothes.'

I looked at him in horror. How could he say something like that in front of other people? How could he make fun of me in this way? He was telling them the story of the purple satin dress. The girls laughed. I tried to pretend that I didn't care. I'd kill him when I got him home.

'But the dress you're wearing is beautiful,' said Linda, when they had finished laughing.

'Rory is right, though.' I tried to sound unconcerned. 'I really must lose a few pounds.'

'I know a few good diets,' said Karen. 'I'll copy them for you, Jane, help you lose that surplus.'

'That's very decent of you, Karen,' said Rory as he smiled at her. 'I'm sure Jane would be delighted.'

When I killed him I'd do it slowly.

'Why do we worry about our weight so much?' asked Lorraine. 'Men don't care at all. Look at my husband.' She gazed fondly at Bernard, who was an advertisement for good eating. 'He's a bit on the plump side but it doesn't seem to worry him in the slightest.'

'Men look better with a bit of bulk,' said Don Roche.

'I agree.' Bill patted his ample stomach, the result of too much corporate entertainment and too little exercise.

I hoped that Rory would never end up like that. I felt sick again.

Louise came around with coffee and put a salver of mints on the table. She took away my half-eaten chocolate gateau without a word.

'Would anyone like a brandy or a port?' asked Bill.

I nodded. A brandy might settle my stomach.

'Are you sure?' asked Rory. 'You don't usually like brandy.'

'I thought I'd have one this evening,' I said shortly. 'You don't mind, do you?'

'Not at all.' He looked at me curiously.

The golden liquid seared its way down my throat. I sipped it carefully as I felt it warm me.

Karen led us back into the lounge, where we sat around the coffee table. I'd found it easier to sit up at the dining table. The sofa was very deep and soft and I felt uncomfortable.

They talked about the bank, gossiped about the staff, chatted about holidays, while I concentrated on not keeling over. I looked down at my engagement ring and watched the sparkling of the diamond come in and out of focus. I closed my eyes.

It happened quite suddenly and I couldn't prevent it. With an abrupt heave, I felt myself be sick again. I stood up, knocked Fiona's glass out of her hand and threw up all over the pale pink carpet. I stood there, like a character in a horror movie, spewing dinner in every direction.

The girls leaped out of the way, while the men looked on in shock.

'I hope it wasn't the salmon!' cried Karen.

I couldn't answer her, I was too busy being sick. I wanted to die with the shame of it.

Rory put his arms around my shoulder. 'Are you all right?' he asked, his voice tight.

I couldn't answer him. I heaved again, splattering the sofa.

'I'm sorry,' I gasped, as I finally stopped. 'I'm truly sorry.'

'Don't worry about it,' said Karen, her voice insincere. 'It'll be fine.'

I had disgraced myself and my husband. No matter what concern Rory was showing now, he would be absolutely furious with me later and I could understand that. Of course, it wasn't my fault but that was hardly the point.

'Do you want to go upstairs?' asked Bill.

'A bit late for that,' said Karen.

'Maybe we'd better just go.' Rory was dangerously calm. 'I'll take her home. I'm terribly sorry, Bill, Karen.'

'Not your fault,' said Bill. 'Can happen to the best of us.'

Karen went into the kitchen and returned with kitchen towel and a bucket of water. She started to try and clean her carpet.

'Let me do that,' said Rory.

'No – it's fine, I'll do it.' Karen looked as though the McLoughlin family had already done enough.

The other men tried to ignore it. The girls clustered around me sympathetically.

'You will be all right,' said Suki, in her lilting voice. 'Are you feeling better now?'

'Yes,' I said, although I still felt absolutely awful.

'Come on, then,' said Rory grimly. 'We'd better go.'

'I'll get your coats.' Bill left the room.

We were hustled out into the rain and I was grateful for the cold night air.

'Get in,' said Rory as he opened the car door.

'I'm sorry,' I said miserably.

'Why didn't you say you weren't feeling well before we went out?' he demanded. 'You could have stayed at home instead of embarrassing me like that.'

He switched on the ignition and the car sped down the road. I leaned my head against the cool window.

'I didn't do it deliberately,' I said. 'I felt OK earlier.'

'So why did you have to wait until we got to Bill and Karen's before making an exhibition of yourself?' he demanded. 'Really and truly, Jane, you've probably destroyed my career.'

'Don't be fucking stupid.' I lifted my head to look at him and felt dizzy again. 'It was an accident, that's all. Bill said it could happen to anyone.'

'Bill was trying to be diplomatic,' snapped Rory.

I wished it hadn't happened. I would never be able to meet those women again without dying of shame. I understood how Rory felt.

He went on and on at me in the car. He moaned at the show I'd made of myself and of him. 'And we were late getting there,' he said as he opened our front door. 'My God, Jane, if you wanted to ruin my life you went the right way about it.'

I stood in the hallway and looked at him. 'It wasn't my fault,' I said again. 'Can't you get that into your head? You're going on at me as though I deliberately decided to puke on somebody's carpet. Don't you realise that I am absolutely, completely and utterly mortified? You keep talking as though it's only you that's upset. Well, I'm fucking upset and I don't feel well. So piss off and leave me alone.'

I stormed upstairs to our bedroom and fell on to the bed in a paroxysm of weeping.

Rory didn't follow me. I could hear him stalk around downstairs, slam the fridge door shut, turn on the TV. I was really sorry about what had happened but I wasn't going to let him blame me. As though I could have done anything about it. He could have been more sympathetic, I thought miserably. He could have cared more about the fact that I was sick than the impression we were making.

Those bloody people were probably laughing at me. My back was coated in sweat again. I lay on the bed and wanted to die.

Eventually, I went downstairs again and took a couple of Hedex.

'They'll probably make you even more sick,' said Rory.

'Nothing left to be sick with,' I mumbled as I swallowed a capsule.

He put his arms around me. 'I'm sorry,' he said. 'I didn't mean to get at you. It wasn't your fault.'

I smiled lopsidedly at him. 'Thanks.'

He kissed me on the head, although it was a very half-hearted sort of kiss. 'Come on,' he said, 'I'll put you to bed. Let's hope you feel better in the morning.'

I slid beneath the duvet and allowed the coolness of the pillow to soothe my burning cheeks. I hoped I'd feel better in the morning, too. Right now, I was afraid I was going to die.

Chapter 13

March 1986
(UK No. 11 – *How Will I Know* – Whitney Houston)

I stood in front of the mirror in the bedroom and looked at my naked body. I could see the difference. At least, I thought I could see the difference. I hoped that the almost imperceptible swell from my breasts to the bottom of my stomach was because of my pregnancy and not because I was fat anyway.

It had taken three more days before the penny dropped. Even though Rory and I had talked about starting a family and I'd stopped taking the Pill about six months earlier, I simply hadn't realised that I was pregnant. Now that I finally was, I wondered whether it was such a good idea. I didn't know if I was ready. I was even less sure about Rory.

Rory was determined to make as much money as he could before he was thirty-five. He got into the dealing room by half past seven every day, checked the news reports and thought of clients to call and of new and more inventive deals he could show them. He was more wrapped up in work than in his home life but I couldn't blame him. Dealing was very intense. I'd no doubt that he loved me but I often wondered if it came to a choice between me and a foreign exchange deal which he would choose. I tried to participate in his work life as much as I could. I entertained clients with him whenever he asked, which was rare. I wanted to be a supportive wife.

Rory was thrilled when I told him I was pregnant. I was surprised at how happy the news made him. He wanted to go out for a meal to celebrate. I reminded him what had happened the last time we went out together and he laughed at me. In some ways I think he was pleased that he could go to Bill Hamilton and say, 'Bill, the reason my wife puked all over your beautiful home was because she's pregnant.' It was a lot better than thinking I might have done it because of the food.

Karen Hamilton rang me after Rory broke the news.

'I'm thrilled for you,' she said. 'Having a baby is a wonderful experience.'

If it was all that wonderful, I'd thought, feeling sick at the time, why hadn't she had a few more? Afraid that she wouldn't regain her superb figure, probably.

'And when your baby is born, I hope you'll join one or two of my committees, Jane. We do a lot of work – fund-raising, that sort of thing.'

I gave her a non-committal answer. It wasn't that I disliked Karen but I didn't feel comfortable with her, and I really didn't want to become part of her set. I hoped that she'd told Louise Killane why I'd been ill. I didn't want her to think it was because of her cooking.

I rummaged through my wardrobe. I could still fit into some of my clothes, but most of them were beginning to get a bit tight around my waist and I knew that sooner or later I was going to have to buy maternity clothes.

No clothes shopping today, though. I'd things to do. Exciting things like collecting trousers from the dry cleaners and getting my shoes heeled. Then I would come home and cook Rory's lunch. Rory would be back from golf by about two and he'd be ravenous.

I took down my tracksuit bottoms and a sweatshirt from the wardrobe and put them on. Rory was always starving when he came home from golf. I hadn't regained my appetite yet. I wasn't sick any more but food held absolutely no interest for me. It seemed to me, too, that Rory was eating more. He kept suggesting that we go out to eat, to save me cooking, but I'd no interest in going out.

I hoped that the lethargy would pass, but right now I was exhausted all the time. I think it was because we were so busy in work and I used up all my energy there. I wanted to get my revenge on Jake for going to the conference instead of me, although the opportunity hadn't presented itself yet. It was important for me, too, to stay efficient at work. I didn't want them saying that I was taking advantage of being pregnant. Actually, I was pretty useless at being pregnant. It wasn't much fun for Rory either, because he was such an outgoing person and he didn't like the fact that I wanted to be at home all the time, but he tried to be understanding. He succeeded mostly, but I stretched his patience sometimes.

I collected the laundry and my shoes and then made Rory's lunch. He wasn't home by two o'clock, which was irritating, because the spaghetti bolognese was nearly ready and I couldn't stand the smell of it. I sat curled up in the living room and read *You and Your Baby*. The photographs were very off-putting.

Where the hell was he? The clock on the mantelpiece ticked solemnly. Three o'clock. I turned off the ring under the sauce and threw the pasta into the bin. He'd probably stopped for a couple of pints. Maybe he'd decided to have something to eat as well. He could have bloody rung me to let me know.

The spring sunshine filtered through the curtains and across the polished pine floor, showing up a film of dust. My fault, of course.

I should do a bit of housework. Even if I was feeling a bit down, that was no reason to allow the house to go to rack and ruin.

Our house had been brand new when we'd bought it. It was about a mile outside Rathfarnham village in a small development around a tiny green. I'd enjoyed decorating it. I had great fun picking wallpapers and curtains, carpets and rugs. I felt very grown-up.

The phone rang and I jumped out of the chair. At last, I thought. He would be ringing to say he was on his way. I grabbed the receiver.

'Jane?' The voice was breathless and crackling.

'Lucy? Is that you?'

'Who do you think it could be?' she asked.

'You haven't called in ages,' I complained.

'I have been *très très* busy,' she said. 'Sorry, Jane.'

The last time Lucy had rung me was New Year's Day.

'What's new?' I asked, cheered at the sound of her voice.

'I'm coming home,' she told me.

'Really?'

'Really.'

'That's great news, Lucy.' I was really pleased. 'I can't wait to see you. Have you got a job here or anything yet?'

'Yes,' she replied happily. 'I sent off a few CVs back in January and, believe it or not, one of the companies has made me a brilliant offer. It's a great opportunity to come home.'

'What about Eric?' I asked.

162

Eric was Lucy's French boyfriend. She'd been living with him for the past two years.

'Eric and I have split up,' she said abruptly.

'Oh Lucy,' I said. 'I'm sorry.'

'It's not so bad,' she said. 'I knew that it wasn't going to work, Jane. That's why I didn't marry him.'

All the same, I could hear the disappointment in her voice.

'Any news yourself?' she asked.

I didn't think it was the time to tell her I was pregnant. 'Nothing that can't wait for a good old natter when you come home,' I said brightly. 'When are you coming?'

'Sunday week,' she told me.

'Do you want me to pick you up?' I asked. 'Or are your parents doing it?'

'Would you meet me?' She sounded pleased. 'That would be great. I'm coming in at a quarter past three.'

'I'd love to meet you,' I said. 'What's your flight number?'

She told me. 'It'll be fun being back home,' she said. 'It's funny, but I only started missing it in the last few weeks and now I can't wait to get back.'

'Where are you going to live?'

She groaned. 'I'll have to move in with my folks for a couple of weeks,' she said. 'I don't have anything else. But I want to buy an apartment somewhere. I've got used to apartment living over here.'

'It's not quite the same,' I laughed. Lucy lived in a beautiful apartment in a town outside Paris. The building was old, the rooms were huge and the apartments reached by a rickety old iron lift which creaked its way up each storey. I'd visited Lucy's apartment twice and had absolutely loved it. I could see why she was entranced by living in France. Saint Juste was exactly like a fairytale town, with narrow cobbled streets, tall cream-coloured buildings and little corner shops. Then, about a kilometre from Lucy's apartment, was a very modern train station with efficient trains which could hurtle you to the centre of Paris in about half an hour.

'I'll phone you again before I leave,' said Lucy. 'You can help me house-hunt when I come back.'

'Love to,' I said.

I replaced the receiver and hugged myself. I was delighted that Lucy was coming home. Since she'd gone, I didn't have a close girlfriend any more. I met the twins, of course, but it wasn't the same thing. Those girls were like one person. They didn't need a close friend. We had some laughs, but I never felt that I could confide in them the way I could in Lucy.

I heard a meow outside the kitchen. A chocolate-coloured tabby sat on the back step and pawed at the glass of the patio.

'What do you want?' I asked as I opened the door.

The tabby stalked into the house, wrapped himself around my legs and left half his coat on my tracksuit. I leaned down and stroked him on the head.

I didn't know where the cat had come from, but he had turned up about a year ago, soaking wet and mewing pitifully. I'd taken him in and fed him, much to Rory's disgust.

'You'll never get rid of it,' he told me sourly.

He was right. The cat adopted us. He turned up every day for a feed and spent hours lying on the windowsill outside the kitchen catching the rays of the sun.

I liked him, though. He was company. I liked the way he would roll around in the grass, the way he chased butterflies, the way he shinned up our side wall and looked, disdainfully, at the dog next door.

I'd christened him Junkie because he ate absolutely everything. Any food that we would have thrown out, Junkie eyed as a gourmet meal. Food that you'd never have considered giving to a cat – cheese, yoghurt, tomatoes and pasta – Junkie ate it all. None of this poached fish or chicken lark for him.

'Want some bolognese?' I spooned some of Rory's dinner into the cat dish.

Junkie purred appreciatively and set to work as he demolished the food and vibrated with happiness at the same time.

'Glad someone appreciates it.' I wandered back into the living room.

I lay down on the sofa and closed my eyes. A few minutes later, the purring furball that was the cat jumped on to the sofa beside me and settled down for a sleep too.

The lights flickered and gleamed over the still waters of the Caribbean. A warm south-westerly breeze fluttered through the palm trees. I sat on the pier and sipped my margarita.

He came up behind me and touched me on the shoulder. I jumped.

'Why are you alone?' he asked.

'I don't know.'

'The most beautiful girl in the world and you are sitting in the dark drinking alone. That cannot be right.'

'I'm not alone,' I told him. 'My husband is here.'

'Really? And where might he be?'

I gestured vaguely towards the bar. 'Getting a drink, probably.'

'I see.' His hands were gentle as they massaged my shoulders.

'Please don't do that,' I said.

'Somebody should,' he told me.

The sound of the car pulling into the driveway jerked me awake and I sat upright, causing the cat to leap from the sofa and meow with fury.

'Sorry, Junkie,' I gasped. I rubbed my arm which he'd caught with his claws and glanced at the clock. Gone six. I'd been asleep for ages and the light was fading. I heard the heavy thud of the car door closing and the sound of Rory's key in the front door.

I blinked a couple of times to clear the sleep from my eyes. I'd be casual when Rory came in, I thought, even though I was furious with him. What sort of time was this to come home, when he had departed for his round of golf at eight-thirty this morning? He had left me on my own all day which was completely unfair.

He poked his head around the living-room door. 'Hi,' he said.

I knew at once from the sound of his voice that he'd been drinking. This made me even more annoyed.

'Where have you been?' I asked him.

'Where do you think?' He came into the room. 'Playing golf.'

'Until now?' I asked. 'Bit of a long round.'

'Don't be silly,' he said. 'We played our round. We had to wait for half an hour for the tee, then we got going. Very slow, though. A lot of people on the course. Then we went for something to eat afterwards.'

'You might have told me you were going for something to eat,' I said. 'I made you spaghetti bolognese.'

'Oh.' He looked discomfited for a moment. 'Doesn't matter, I can eat it now. I'm starving again.' He sat on the edge of the sofa.

'I'd a great round,' he said. 'I played a brilliant lay-up shot to the third and then a super little pitch to within, oh I'd say three inches of the hole for a birdie. The lads were raging. Then, at the fifth—'

'I don't really care,' I interrupted him. 'I'm sure you had a wonderful time. Although it seems to me you spent more time on the nineteenth than on the course.'

'Oh, give it up, Jane,' he snapped. 'Of course we had a couple of pints afterwards. It's not a crime.'

'Well, you shouldn't have driven home,' I said. 'It's not right.'

'Christ Almighty, listen to her. You've become such a moan, it's not real. All you ever do is nag at me.'

'I don't.' I was hurt. 'I'm merely saying that you shouldn't drink and drive.'

'What you're saying is that you don't want me to drink at all,' said Rory. 'That's what you're saying.'

'No, it's not. Not at all. I don't mind you having a drink but there's a time and a place. And it's not fair, you going off on the piss on a Saturday leaving me completely on my own all day.'

'You probably slept through the whole day,' said Rory. 'That's all you ever do – sleep.'

Tears stung the back of my eyes. Of course I slept a lot. I was pregnant and I was tired. It was dreadfully unfair of Rory to claim that my tiredness was the reason he'd been out all day.

'You could have rung me,' I protested. 'You could have called and said that you wouldn't be back for lunch.'

'If I'd done that you would have moaned at me more,' said Rory. 'Nobody else's wife gets into the rage that you do.'

A tear slid down my cheek. 'I don't get into a rage,' I said forlornly.

'You never stop giving me grief,' said Rory. 'No matter what I do. You hate the fact that I'm in work so early, you hate the fact that I have to meet clients for lunch, you hate coming to dinner parties with me—'

'I don't hate dinner parties,' I protested.

'Tell that to Karen Hamilton,' said Rory.

There was an angry silence. 'You know perfectly bloody well that I puked at Karen's party because I am pregnant with your child,' I said. 'You're being horrible, Rory.'

This was always his ploy when he came home a bit pissed. Attack is the best form of defence, he'd told me once. Generate an argument about something else and you'll distract attention from whatever it is you're defensive about.

He stalked out of the room and I could hear him running the water for a shower. The state he was in he'd probably slip and drown, I thought bitterly, and I wouldn't care.

I sighed deeply. I knew that I was right. I went around the house closing the curtains and switching on the lights. Junkie curled up in front of the fire. I made myself some tea and toast.

I listened to the sound of the running water upstairs and fumed silently. His life would have to change with the arrival of the baby. It was all very well to be out and about whenever he felt like it, but he couldn't continue on like that when our child was born. There would have to be more give and take. The trouble was, that wasn't the way he'd been brought up. His mother had been the sort of woman whose life had revolved completely around her home and family. She was a brilliant cook, made all her own clothes and had the house sparkling clean all the time. Her two other sons, Jim and Paul, were well looked after. They didn't have to do anything around the house and neither did Rory's father. His contribution was the weekly pay cheque. It was all very different from my own upbringing. Rory and I used to have terrible arguments because I'd try to get him to do a bit of ironing or hoovering. As far as he was concerned, it was nothing to do with him. The most I managed to get him to do was the occasional bit of cooking and to put his dirty washing in the laundry basket instead of on the floor.

I pulled the sofa closer to the fire. I could understand why he would be fed up with my tiredness, I was fed up with it myself. Rory returned to the living room wearing his dressing-gown.

'Is there any food left?' he asked shortly.

'There's still some bolognese in the pot,' I said, 'but I'll have to make more pasta.'

'Don't bother,' he said. 'I know how to make pasta. You sit there with your feet up.'

I couldn't figure out whether he was being sarky or not. It was always hard to tell with Rory. I switched on the TV and watched Noel Edmonds.

Rory came in with a plate of spaghetti bolognese which he perched precariously on the arm of the sofa. 'Sure you don't want some?' He waved a forkful of pasta in front of me.

I shook my head.

We sat in tense silence. Rory took the remote control and flicked through the channels, never staying on one for more than a minute. I didn't say anything when a blob of bolognese slid off his fork and landed on our cream-coloured sofa.

It was a horrible evening. We couldn't be nice to each other. I was too annoyed and Rory kept falling asleep because of the drink. His eyes were bloodshot when he was awake.

I made more tea at half past nine, and shook him by the shoulder to see if he wanted any.

'Leave me alone,' he muttered.

I wanted to cry. Was this what it was all about? I asked. Was this it? Was this what I'd expected when the priest asked, 'Do you, Jane, take Rory?'

My wedding day had been perfect. It was the stuff that dreams are made of. I'd really believed that everything I wanted had come true.

We'd got married on the June Bank Holiday weekend. The sun blazed from a clear sky, not even a cotton puff of cloud marred its brilliant blue. I could feel the heat from the pavement through the thin-soled sandals I was wearing, and I was immensely glad that I'd decided against the huge taffeta ballgown that Mam had liked and had chosen the mid-length lace dress that Grace preferred.

She designed and made my dress, of course. Off-white, calf-length, lace over silk. A little sequinned bolero jacket over it, no veil but an arrangement of silk flowers in my hair.

I was ecstatic that day. Rory actually gasped when he saw me and I knew that, for once, I did look beautiful.

'The bride always looks beautiful,' Mam said, with tears in her eyes, 'but you are really lovely, Jane.'

We hugged and kissed and I felt closer to her than ever before.

The reception was in the Burlington. I'd spent so much time there when we lived in the apartment, it seemed the natural choice. We had a ball, the food was great, the band fantastic and nobody had made a fool of themselves which had to be a first for any wedding I'd ever been at.

Then we went on honeymoon – a two-week idyll on Lanzarote which suited us perfectly. Since then, Rory wanted his holidays to be less sun and more action, but our honeymoon had been perfection.

We stayed in a self-contained villa in a very upmarket complex near Playa del Carmen. We lay in the sun together, swam in the pool together, sat on the beach together, spent every moment together and not once had we been bored or tired or annoyed with each other.

So why was I so bloody miserable now, when it had been so wonderful in the past? Maybe we were just going through a phase. Perhaps my hormones were messed up because of the baby. Perhaps Rory was feeling the strain too. Maybe I was so caught up in myself that I was ignoring my husband. The books and magazines warned against that. Against allowing your husband to feel neglected and unwanted. Was that what I was doing to Rory?

Hard to ignore him now, though. He lay on the sofa, his head back, snoring loudly. I prodded him in the side.

'Why don't you go to bed?' I suggested.

'I don't want to go to bed,' he said, eyes wide open. 'I don't need to go to bed. I want to watch *Match of the Day*.'

I sighed. He was so dogmatic when he was drunk.

'Watch what you like, then,' I said. 'I'm going to bed.'

I climbed under the duvet and pulled the pillow around my head. From the room below I could hear Jimmy Hill's voice commentating on the match. I wondered whether Rory was awake or asleep down there.

I nodded off and awoke with a start at two in the morning. The bed beside me was still empty and I sat up in confusion. Then I remembered and wondered whether Rory could possibly be awake downstairs, or whether he had fallen asleep watching TV. Or whether he had gone out. He was quite capable of going out again if he got into a black enough mood.

I pushed the duvet away and padded downstairs.

Rory was stretched across the sofa, still asleep. I turned off the TV and looked at him critically. Did I want him to wake up and come to bed now? His snoring would keep me awake. Better to leave him there. He'd only get narky if I woke him, anyway.

So I went back to bed and, for the first time in my married life, slept alone.

Chapter 14

April 1986
(US No. 5 – *West End Girls* **– Pet Shop Boys)**

I stood in the Arrivals building at Dublin Airport and waited for flight EI 875 from Paris. I loved to stand in the terminal building and look at the destinations on the boards – Milan, Rome, New York, Boston, Madrid, Copenhagen – all seething with the excitement of a new place to go, new people to meet. When I drove into the car park and stepped out of the car, I was immediately infected with the desire to get up and go. Anywhere, just to leave my humdrum life behind and escape into the skies. Preferably to somewhere warm and sunny.

It was a miserable day today. The clouds were heavy and low, there was a persistent drizzle and a cool, easterly breeze.

I'd dressed up to go to the airport, much to Rory's amusement. But I didn't want to be put to shame by Lucy's French chic and I didn't want her to walk through the sliding doors and see a fat, frumpy matron waiting for her. I wasn't really fat or frumpy yet but I was very sensitive about my size. I'd begun to talk to my baby too, disconcerted when Rory caught me out, although he always laughed when he did.

Things had improved between us since the night when he'd slept on the sofa. I'd come down the next morning to find him making breakfast and looking sheepish. He'd apologised profusely, promised never to drink and drive again and looked so miserable that I kissed him and told him not to worry, that it was probably my fault as much as his.

Then we'd gone upstairs and made slow, languorous love. Since then, he had gone out of his way to be caring and understanding and I felt much, much better.

But I was still glad that Lucy was coming home because I'd missed her a lot.

The board flickered and 'Landed' appeared against her flight. I stood at the barrier and scanned the crowds for her.

She looked great and I felt a pang of envy as I saw her. She was wearing a tight pair of 501s which must have been ironed on to her and a very French navy and white striped T-shirt. Her hair, which she had always worn straight before, fell down her back in a mass of thick, golden curls.

I was very glad that I was wearing a pair of black trousers and a long emerald green jacket which hid my slight bump. I waved vigorously at her and she hurried towards me, almost killing someone with her trolley.

She kissed me, French fashion, on each cheek, then held me by the shoulders and looked at me.

'You look *fantastique*,' she cried. 'Absolutely great. You've got a glow about you.'

I laughed at her enthusiasm. 'You do too,' I said. 'And a lot more *fantastique* than me. I love your hair.'

'Mmm,' she said. 'I love it myself. I got it done in a salon in Paris. Girl called Genevieve. Brilliant hairstylist. Makes me look like a bit of a blonde bombshell, doesn't it?'

'And how.' I looked at her trolley. 'Is this all your luggage?'

She nodded. 'Not much, is it?' she said. 'For four years away.'

'Travelling light,' I smiled.

She made a face. 'I left stuff behind. I couldn't bring it with me.' Tears glistened in her eyes and I hugged her.

'Don't worry about me,' she said, sniffing. 'You know and I know that Eric was not the man for me. I, my dear, am a businesswoman. I don't have boyfriends. Just partners. And escorts.'

I smiled at her. 'Maybe you'll meet someone here,' I said.

'I truly don't care,' said Lucy as she pushed the trolley towards the exit. 'This new job will keep me very busy. You know, I'm not sure that I was cut out to be married.'

I put the money in the automatic parking machine and took our exit ticket.

'Which is strange,' continued Lucy, 'given that we spent so much time dreaming about it when we were younger.'

'Dreams are always a lot better than reality.' I helped her throw her cases into the boot of the car.

She looked at me curiously. 'You don't mean that, do you, Jane?' she asked. 'I thought you and Rory were very happy.'

I smiled brightly at her. 'Of course we are,' I said. 'I didn't mean for a minute that we weren't. I'm merely saying that you think and dream about something, and then it happens and it's not half as good as when you imagined it, that's all.'

I started the car and we drove out of the airport and on to the motorway. I liked driving fast and the motorway was the only opportunity I ever got to indulge. Rory had warned me about speeding. He said that there were Garda cars stationed along the road with speed guns to trap unwary motorists, but I didn't care.

'Horrible weather, isn't it?' Lucy peered out of the window.

'What was it like in Paris?' I braked sharply as we reached Whitehall in about three minutes.

'Dry,' she said. 'But not particularly nice. It will be in a couple of weeks, though.'

'Won't you miss it?' I asked.

'Probably,' she said. 'But you have to decide what you want to do. I didn't want to live in France for the rest of my life. I'm a Dub at heart.'

She leaned back in the passenger seat and yawned. 'Nice car.'

I nodded. 'Company car,' I told her. 'It's great. We don't have to worry about petrol or maintenance or insurance, the bank looks after it all.'

'Sounds wonderful,' said Lucy.

'It is,' I said.

'How's Rory's job going?'

'Very well,' I said. 'He's really busy. Remember I told you he got promoted before Christmas? It means he's out a lot, but he enjoys it.'

'And how about you, you're still working?'

I nodded and accelerated through the amber lights at Bolton Street.

'Yes, and I'm doing OK. I don't think I'll ever be as committed as Rory, though.' I shot her a sideways glance. 'And I'll be taking a bit of time off this year.'

'Time off!' she exclaimed. 'Why?'

'Don't be thick,' I said. 'Why do you think?'

She looked at me in amazement. 'Are you pregnant?' she demanded.

'I'm surprised you didn't notice straight away.' I laughed.

'Oh, Jane.' Lucy hugged me and I almost swerved into a cyclist. He shook his fist angrily at me and we giggled.

'Shit,' I said. 'I could have killed him.'

'No, you couldn't,' said Lucy confidently. 'Jane, I don't believe you're going to have a baby!'

'Why not?'

'It's such a grown-up thing to do.'

I laughed. 'I know. I can't believe it myself, really.'

'So tell me all about it. When is it due?'

'Around September,' I told her. 'They're not a hundred per cent sure, because my dates are a bit mixed up. But sometime around then.'

'Brilliant,' said Lucy. 'So how have you been? Are you sick or anything?'

I related the tale of the disastrous dinner party at the Hamiltons'. Lucy roared with laughter.

'If you ask me, they could do with someone puking on their carpet,' she said. 'She sounds like a right bitch.'

'Even so.' I gestured at an Alfa that had cut in front of me. 'I felt terrible about it.'

'And poor old Louise Killane serving the food,' said Lucy. 'Bet she thought she'd poisoned you.'

'I know,' I grinned at her. 'I was so embarrassed. But Karen let Louise know that it was because I was pregnant. Not something I'd want to happen again, though.'

'Never mind,' said Lucy. 'People understand.'

I drove on through the city. Lucy kept up a commentary on the changes since her last trip home. The traffic in Terenure was heavy, even though it was Sunday. 'Lots of new houses being built around here,' I told Lucy. I pointed out the twins' shop. The facade of *Les Jumelles* had recently been redecorated and it looked very exclusive. Lucy nodded approvingly at it.

We drove past St Attracta's school. A huge new extension had been built since we'd been there, taking over a chunk of what had once been the nuns' garden where they'd grown herbs and neat little rows of flowers. The field past the sports ground had been sold, and a development of red-brick townhouses now overlooked the school.

It had changed a lot since we were there, nearly ten years ago. Sometimes it seemed like a whole lifetime and other days I could close my eyes and remember it as though I'd only just left.

'Wonder who the head nun is now?' mused Lucy, as we turned past the school and drove on to the Riverview Estate.

'I don't know. Remember we said that we'd have a reunion five years after we left?' I said. 'And we never bothered.'

'I think there was a reunion last year,' said Lucy, 'not just our year, a school reunion. I'm sure Emily mentioned it.'

I shrugged. 'Going back isn't such a good idea,' I said. 'I don't really care what happened to most of them.'

'Jenny Gibson got married,' Lucy told me. 'She's living in London.'

'Is she?'

'Yes, in Greenwich. Somebody met her, can't remember who. Married an English guy.'

'What about the other one of that gang? Camilla McKenzie.' I pulled up outside Lucy's house.

'Don't know,' said Lucy. 'Haven't heard a thing about her. Funny, isn't it? Those girls were the absolute bane of our lives and now we don't know a thing about them.'

I hadn't seen Mrs McAllister in ages. Her hair was greyer, but she still looked the same as ever. I smiled at her and she waved at me. Then she ran down the garden path and hugged Lucy fiercely.

'Lovely to see you, Jane,' she said, over Lucy's shoulder. 'Do you want to come in for a drop of tea?'

I shook my head. I'd better get back home. Rory hated being in the house on his own. I waved goodbye to Lucy, arranged to meet her for lunch on Tuesday and drove back to Rathfarnham.

My husband sat in an armchair, legs over the sides, watching rugby. He had a bowl of crisps beside him and a can of beer in his hand. He was completely relaxed.

I planted a kiss on his head.

'So Lucy is home.' He offered me some crisps.

'I'm meeting her for lunch next week.' I took a crisp, sniffed it and decided against it. 'I'm glad she's back.'

I met her for lunch in FXB's the following Tuesday. She had two weeks to herself before starting her new job, and she wanted to go apartment-hunting. Living at home was already driving her demented. Mrs McAllister gave her a lot of stick over my marriage and pregnancy. She thought that Lucy was missing out. I told Lucy to stay free and single as long as she could and my friend grinned and told me she'd do her best.

'Where do you want to live?' I asked her, as we sipped our coffees after lunch.

'I'm half thinking of something the other side of town,' said Lucy. 'Maybe Clontarf or Howth.'

'Oh, don't do that,' I protested. 'That's miles away.'

'I'd like the coast,' Lucy mused, 'but this side of town is so expensive.'

'Why don't you want to be near Terenure?' I asked. 'Don't you like it?'

'It's not that,' Lucy confided, 'but if I was within easy distance of home, then Mam would always be asking me to drop by and I couldn't take it. Easier if I'm a bit further away.'

We decided to look at apartments the following Saturday. Lucy was armed with colour brochures and a vague idea of what she wanted.

'They're very small,' said Lucy doubtfully, as we wandered through the first block, a white painted scheme known as 'Bayview'. The apartments were a lot smaller than the one we had shared at Waterloo Mews. The one bedroom was barely big enough for a wardrobe, there was no chance of putting even a tiny table in the kitchen and the living room was completely dominated by a round table. There was no spare space whatsoever and Lucy shook her head. 'No way,' she said.

We drove up and down the coast looking at apartments. Ones that had a view of the sea, today an angry green topped by frothy white waves, were much more expensive than those that didn't. Every floor had a different price. Most of them had maintenance agreements which were expensive. We despaired of finding anything within Lucy's budget.

'It's not as though I'm being a cheapskate,' she complained, after yet another block failed to live up to the description in the brochure. 'I only want something with a bit of space.'

She had been spoiled by the Saint Juste apartment, with its high-ceilinged rooms, shuttered windows and polished wooden floors. The little boxes we were being shown didn't match up to what she had left behind.

'What about this one in Sandymount?' I suggested.

'That's second-hand,' said Lucy. 'We'll have to make an appointment with the auctioneer.'

'Maybe the owners would let us have a quick look around,' I said hopefully. 'We can always make an appointment for another viewing if you like it.'

So, more in hope than expectation we drove down the road, over the track at Merrion Gates and towards Sandymount. The apartment actually overlooked the sea, so we expected that it would be too expensive and we weren't very optimistic as we rang the bell.

The disembodied voice of a girl told us to come on up, it was the top floor. This amused us as the block was only two storeys high.

A pretty young girl carrying a baby on one hip and holding a toddler by the hand opened the door to the apartment.

'It's chaos at the moment,' she said. 'Sorry, you won't get a very good impression.'

Although the apartment was a mess and needed decoration, it was much bigger than the ones we had looked at and Lucy raised an eyebrow at me. The living area was a big square room, with a dining table in an alcove at the end. There was enough space for a small table in the kitchen, and there were two bedrooms, one double room and one with just enough space for a bed.

'We're moving back to Galway,' said the girl, whose name was Anita. 'We're both from there, we came here because my husband was working on a long-term contract and this was convenient. But I'm glad to be going back. This place is OK, but it's no place to bring up a couple of kids. The sooner we sell, the better.'

Lucy and I agreed with her. When Lucy talked about the price of the apartment, Anita said that she hadn't actually considered anything about it; the auctioneer was looking after everything.

We decided that Lucy would contact the auctioneer on Monday.

'What did you think?' she asked, as we got back into the car.

'I liked it,' I told her. 'It was a lot bigger than some of the ones we looked at. And she wants to be out soon.'

It sounded ideal and it wasn't really that far away. Lucy couldn't wait for Monday to contact the agent.

'Why don't we do a bit of shopping before you go home,' she suggested. 'Rory isn't expecting you too early, is he?'

I shook my head. 'When I told him I wanted the car to go house-hunting with you, he arranged for his pal Niall to pick him up. They've gone golfing out in Royal Dublin. He won't be back for ages.'

'Let's go back to Blackrock then, and have a mooch around,' said Lucy.

Lucy was a fantastic shopper. She breezed into shops, picked clothes off the racks and carried them all to the changing cubicles. Whenever a sales assistant told her that she could only bring two articles in with her, Lucy fixed her with a withering glare and said that she anticipated buying much more than that if the clothes were up to standard.

Amazingly, most of the assistants gave in. Lucy told me that everybody brought loads of clothes into the changing-rooms in Paris.

'We're far too humble,' she said. 'You don't buy a skirt or a blouse there, you buy a look. They let you try on everything. And they don't look at you and pretend something suits you if it doesn't. They're brutally frank.'

'If you want brutally frank, then you should call into Brenda and Grace,' I told her. 'Brenda once told me that I looked like a sack of potatoes in a dress I tried on.'

'Always known for her tact,' laughed Lucy. 'We might be a bit late for the twins, though, it's five o'clock.'

'They stay open until six,' I said. 'If you want to go there, we'll go.'

So we hurried back to the car. We'd bought nothing in Blackrock, much to the disgust of the sales assistant who was left to hang half a dozen skirts back on the rails. I drove to Terenure. There was a small car park behind the twins' shop – a luxury in the village. It wasn't a very big shop but the girls had made the most of the space. Clothes were arranged around the walls, hanging in what looked like tall, doorless wardrobes. It looked less like a shop and more like somebody's house.

'*Bonjour*,' said Lucy.

Grace looked up and shrieked in delight. She dropped a bright yellow dress on to the floor. 'Shit,' she said.

'Is that any way to treat a friend?' asked Lucy as she held out her arms.

Grace hugged her. 'I didn't know you were back,' she said.

Brenda abandoned her customer and came over to hug Lucy too. 'Visiting or home?' she asked.

'Home.' Lucy pecked her on each cheek.

I looked around the shop. All the subtle signs of a prospering business were there. The quality of the decor, the designer clothes, an ambience of understated money. Of course, if they were selling clothes to Karen Hamilton's friends, then they must be doing very well.

Lucy told them about the apartment. 'I hope I'll get it,' she said. 'It's me, somehow.'

'How's the baby coming along?' Brenda asked me.

'Cooking away.' I patted my bump.

'Isn't it amazing that you're the only one of the four of us to get married?' mused Grace. 'You'd imagine that we'd have a better hit rate than that.'

'I keep having disastrous affairs,' laughed Lucy. 'If I could find the right man, then maybe I'd be married too.'

'And you two are always far too busy,' I pointed out. 'Besides, how could one of you get married and the other one not?'

'That's one of the things about being a twin,' commented Brenda ruefully. 'We can't seem to let go of each other.'

'Thank God you managed it anyway, Jane.' Grace smiled. 'How's the high-flying husband?'

'High-flying on the golf course at the moment,' I said. 'But otherwise doing well.'

'Have you been to Jane's house yet?' Brenda asked Lucy. 'It's gorgeous.'

Lucy shook her head. 'Not yet.'

'You can come for tea during the week,' I told her.

'Admire what a hardworking husband can provide,' laughed Brenda.

'It's not just him,' I said, irritated suddenly. 'I work too, you know.'

There was a moment's uncomfortable silence.

Brenda chewed the bottom of her lip and Grace slotted a few hangers into spaces on the rails. I looked at them.

'I do work,' I said. 'I know that my job isn't as exciting as Rory's, or as having a shop, or doing whatever it is Lucy has been doing in France, but I do have a job which paid me a bonus of five hundred pounds last year, so please don't scoff at me.'

'We weren't scoffing,' said Grace. 'Honestly, Jane.'

I wiped my forehead, ashamed at my outburst. 'I know,' I said. 'I'm sorry.'

'Don't worry about it.' Grace patted me on the shoulder.

But I did worry about it, I couldn't help it. The twins were completely caught up in the shop, Lucy had a great job and had been offered an incredible salary in her new position and everyone seemed to think that Rory's job was so much more important than mine.

I lived in his shadow. He was a high-profile person and I was only his wife. It wasn't fair. I worked very hard.

When the baby was born they would look at me and say, 'There's Jane McLoughlin and her baby.' I would be linked with the child for ever. Nobody would see me as Jane, in my own right, ever again.

'You're very quiet,' said Lucy, as I drove her back to her house.

'I'm fine,' I said. 'It's been a hectic day and I'm feeling a bit tired.'

'I'm sorry.' Lucy was contrite. 'I didn't think. You're probably worn out, Jane. You should have said something.'

'I don't really get that worn out,' I said. 'It comes on me suddenly.'

Lucy sat silently beside me. What was she thinking, I wondered. That her friend was a misery and a bore? Mind you, she had always called me a bit of a bore. Yet there had been so many times when we were boring together. When we didn't get Valentine cards, when we panicked about the debs' ball, when we dreaded going to the disco. Those were the days, of course, when Lucy was a fragile china doll and looked shy and demure. Then we became more interesting, got boyfriends, rented our apartment. Lucy had her affair with a married man, then disappeared to France. She'd carried on doing interesting things while I had subsided into a sea of domesticity with my husband and my house.

I knew that I was probably over-reacting, I knew that I was being very stupid, but I honestly couldn't help it. It would be OK when the baby was born, I decided. Once I cradled my son or my daughter in my arms, everything else would fall into place. In the meantime, all I had to do was get through the next few months without cracking up.

Chapter 15

May 1986
(UK No. 15 – *A Kind Of Magic* **– Queen)**

I whistled under my breath as I waited in the reception area for Rory to descend from the lofty heights of the fifth floor. I'd finished work for the day but he was still trading. The dollar had gone nuts today so the dealers were very busy. I didn't mind sitting in peace, if not in comfort, down at reception. I wasn't comfortable because the leather seats were slung too low and, once I'd lowered myself into one, I found it almost impossible to get back out.

I leafed gently through the *Irish Times*, finished the Simplex and was having a go at the Crosaire when Rory finally emerged from the lift. I smiled at him. He looked distracted – his russet hair stood up in demented spikes on his head.

'Hi, sorry I'm late.' He peered over my shoulder at the crossword. 'Knave of Hearts,' he said. 'Nine down.'

'I would have worked it out.' I folded the paper. 'Lift me out of this goddamned chair.'

He grinned as he hauled me out of its green leather depths.

'Like taking a hippo out of a mudbath,' he commented cheerfully.

'Thanks.'

I felt fine these days and had a lot more energy but I wished that I would stop growing. I wasn't eating that much, but I still seemed to bloat a bit more every day. I was terrified that my baby would be so huge that I would never be able to deliver it.

I sat in the passenger seat and fiddled with my skirt. It had seemed comfortable that morning when I'd put it on, but now it was irritatingly tight and I couldn't seem to get it to sit properly.

'Stop fidgeting.' Rory pulled out of the car park and into the evening traffic.

He switched on Radio 4 to listen to the news. I would have preferred music. My attention span had shortened dramatically over the past few weeks and I found the news no longer interested me at all. I closed my eyes and ignored the flood of talk as I allowed myself to be lulled by the movement of the car.

Rory swung into the driveway. I jerked into wakefulness and Junkie leaped hysterically on to the wall.

'One day you'll kill him.' I got out and rubbed the cat's head. Junkie purred happily as his entire body vibrated with pleasure.

'Too right,' said Rory sourly. He always talked disparagingly about the cat, but I knew that deep down he liked him. Sometimes when I was upstairs, I could hear him talking to Junkie in the affectionate tone he usually only reserved for me.

'Sit down and relax,' he said, as we got inside. 'I'll make dinner tonight.'

This offer was so unexpected that I knew immediately something was wrong. Rory never cooked unless forced into it.

'What have you done?' I asked.

He looked hurt. 'Why should I have done anything?'

'Because you never cook otherwise.' I sat on the sofa and slid my skirt over my bump, sighing with relief.

'Sit there and I'll bring you a cup of tea,' said Rory.

There was definitely something up and I wanted to know what it was. I was useless at waiting for things, I needed to know straight away. But Rory busied himself in the kitchen, clattered cups and saucers and tripped up over the cat. I grinned to myself as I heard him swear. Junkie would have removed himself from Rory's range immediately. The cat always disappeared out of the target zone when Rory fell over him.

'So,' he said, as he settled on the sofa beside me and handed me a mug of tea. 'How was your day?'

'Fine.'

'Tiring?'

'They're all a bit tiring now.' I sipped my tea and waited for him to get to the point.

'You'd prefer to be on maternity leave already?' he asked.

'Not exactly.' I wriggled my toes. 'But a day off would be nice, I suppose.'

'How about a week off?'

I regarded him curiously. 'No point,' I said. 'I'd get bored sitting at home and Lucy can't take any time off work at the moment. She's up to her neck.'

'And you think I wouldn't take time?' asked Rory, sounding wounded.

'You're busy too,' I reminded him. 'That bloody dollar.'

He beamed at me.

'What?' I demanded. 'Stop doing your Cheshire cat impression and tell me what on earth you're going on about.'

'How would you like to go to Portugal for a week?'

I looked at him in stunned silence. 'Portugal?' I said finally.

He nodded.

'You and me?'

He nodded again. 'More or less.'

I looked at him intently. 'More – or less?' I asked.

'You and me, definitely,' he said. 'Think about it, whitewashed villa, your own pool, bougainvillaea falling over the walls, warm sun . . .'

'There is a catch to this, Rory McLoughlin,' I said. 'What is it?'

'My parents,' he said, making a face.

'Oh, Rory.' I knew I looked horrified. 'Not your parents.'

I'd never managed to get on with the McLoughlins, which was a pity. I didn't know why I wasn't the girl for their son, but for some reason I felt that they thought he could have done better. Peter McLoughlin was a decent enough man, but he always ignored me; Eleanor McLoughlin didn't really like me at all. I felt that she tolerated me but that she would have liked a more elegant daughter-in-law – and a more pliant one. I knew that she disapproved of the fact that we hadn't tried to have children before now and that she blamed me for that.

Still, if you weighed them up against the idea of a week in the sun, maybe it wasn't too bad a deal. The burgeoning spring had made me long for warmer weather. Portugal in May would be perfect.

Rory watched me anxiously. I knew that he was worried that I didn't get on with his parents. I could see that he was afraid that I wouldn't want to go on holiday with them.

'How come?' I asked finally.

'Week's golfing holiday,' Rory told me. 'Good deal for four. Dad found out about it and asked if we would like to go.'

'Us?' I asked in amazement. 'You and me?'

Rory had the grace to look abashed. 'He asked me originally,' he admitted. 'But the holiday was for four. Actually, he thought we could get another couple of men, but Mum wouldn't let him go without her. So he suggested you might like to come along.'

I'd known all along that Mr McLoughlin wouldn't have thought of me.

'Mum wanted you to come, though,' said Rory hastily.

I smiled. 'I'm sure she did.'

'Honestly, Jane. She said she didn't want to be stuck on some rotten golfing holiday and that you could probably do with a bit of time off.'

I was touched by his mother's concern. Maybe I'd misjudged her.

'So?' said Rory.

'Of course I want to go,' I said. 'Are you mad? Provided that there isn't a problem about me flying and provided I can get the time off. When would we go?'

'Saturday week,' he said.

I looked at him, my eyes full of excitement. 'Really?'

'Really.'

'Oh, Rory!' I hugged him. 'I love you.' I lifted my face so that he could kiss me.

I wasn't quite so keen on him when he woke me at six o'clock on the Saturday morning. I found it hard to sleep through the nights now and I'd fallen into a sound sleep at five. So it was hard to drag myself out of bed even with the promise of the holiday ahead of me.

It wasn't so bad once we were in the airport waiting for our flight to be called. Eleanor McLoughlin sat knitting, oblivious to the excitement around her. She was cool and aloof, completely self-contained.

I fell asleep on the flight, the first time I'd ever managed to sleep on a plane. I missed the breakfast. I half-opened one eye as they came around but couldn't wake up properly, so by the time we touched down at Faro I was refreshed and ready for action.

The sun was already high in the sky, washing the Mediterranean town with brilliant light. The heat was welcome and enticing.

We'd hired a car. A minibus brought us from the airport to the car-hire office a mile down the road. Mr McLoughlin grumbled that the car should be available at the airport and that we shouldn't have to travel anywhere. Rory told him not to be daft. Mrs McLoughlin ignored both of them and took out her knitting again. I couldn't believe that she would come to Portugal and knit. She told me that it was a christening robe for my baby and I felt a chill of horror. I knew that Mam expected that I'd use the family christening robe, the one in which all of the McDermotts had been christened. A row for the future, I thought glumly.

But I wasn't going to let any of this bother me while we were on holiday. I stood, quite happily, outside the car-hire office and waited for Rory to organise everything while I revelled in the warmth.

Rory emerged from the office with the keys to the Ford Escort, a selection of maps and the keys to the villa. He spread the map out over the bonnet of the car and sketched out the route to Albufeira.

'It's quite straightforward,' said Rory. 'Along here, then here. It's easy enough.'

'Wouldn't it be better to go this way?' suggested his father, pushing his horn-rimmed glasses up on his nose. A sheen of sweat had broken out on his forehead.

'No, look. This way, then this and this.'

'But if we turned here, then—'

'Dad! I'm driving.' Rory was irritated. 'I'll choose which way we go.' He refolded the map.

They loaded the golf clubs into the car, then couldn't fit in the cases and had to reload and start again. Mrs McLoughlin got into the car and sat there, like an empress.

'Don't forget to drive on the right side of the road,' said Mr McLoughlin. Rory didn't deign to reply.

Rory was a good driver. It didn't bother him that he was driving on the opposite side of the road. He put his foot down once we reached the main highway and we sped off into the sunshine.

The sunroof was open and a cool breeze fanned our faces. Rory's mother knitted, the needles clicking in continuous rhythm. Mr McLoughlin kept up a monologue about the last time he had come here golfing, and how well he had done and how good the courses were. He had an irritating voice. I tried to block it out.

I leaned back in the seat and ignored Rory's parents, gazing instead out of the window at the passing scenery. We could have been anywhere because main roads are pretty much the same everywhere, but suddenly we would see a sign saying 'Apartmentos' or 'Jardimeria' and I knew that we were abroad. Our villa was about three kilometres past the town of Albufeira, so we drove past the supermarkets and shopping centres, bypassed the town and continued along the coast road.

The sea glittered invitingly, showering us with sparkles of sun. The sand, when we could see it, was pale and soft. I felt a thrill of anticipation run through me.

We drove past the turn for the villa, ended up going another couple of miles too far and had to turn around again. Mr McLoughlin moaned that Rory hadn't read the map properly. Mrs McLoughlin's knitting needles stopped temporarily until the issue was resolved. We found the turn this time. Our villa was a few hundred metres up a steep hill.

'You won't be able to walk up this hill, Jane.' Rory's mother eyed me speculatively.

'Of course I will,' I said briskly, 'once it's not too hot.'

The villa was named 'Beach Villa', which had made me imagine some awful seaside resort holiday house. Nothing could have been further from the truth. It was a two-storeyed whitewashed building with a red roof and a profusion of brightly coloured flowers growing in the very green garden which surrounded it. A couple of almond trees shaded the entrance and Rory used the cover of the trees to protect the car.

We piled out on to the sandy driveway. I exclaimed in delight at the balmy temperature of the air and wandered away immediately to look for the pool.

It was on the other side of the villa, bathed in clear sunlight, blue and beguiling. I could hardly wait to get in. Reluctantly, I went back to the car to unpack.

Rory and I took a bedroom upstairs at the front of the house. His parents took one downstairs near the back. I opened the cases.

Rory had already retrieved his shorts and gone for a swim. When I heard him dive into the water, I decided to abandon the unpacking and go for a swim myself.

I felt self-conscious in my black maternity swimsuit, but neither of Rory's parents was there to see me and I slipped happily into the water.

'This is divine,' I gasped, bobbing around.

'Nice, huh?' Rory swam towards me and grabbed hold of me. 'Better than being at home?'

'Much.' I turned on to my back and allowed the water to support me. 'This is bliss.'

'We'll have to get a lounger to fit you,' he teased, as he poked me on my bump.

'Sod off,' I said lazily. 'Although I won't be able to tan my back because I can't lie on my stomach. I'll go home brown at the front and white behind.'

Rory chuckled. 'As long as you go home relaxed,' he said.

Overcome with love and affection, I kissed him fiercely on the lips. I broke away when I realised his parents were standing at the edge of the pool watching us.

The days passed in a tranquil routine. Every morning Rory and his father would get up at seven-thirty, have breakfast and disappear off to whatever golf course they were playing that day. His mother ('do call me Eleanor, dear') got up shortly after they left, had her own breakfast and went for a walk. I got up at about ten, brought my fruit and cake on to the verandah, put on the coffee machine and breakfasted overlooking the pool. That was my favourite part of the day, sitting in the warmth, shaded from the sun, totally at peace.

Wouldn't it be great, I thought, to live like this. To eat papaya and watermelon for breakfast, outdoors in the sun. To spend the day reading books, listening to tapes, occasionally exercising the mind with a crossword. I knew that I'd get bored eventually, but it was a very appealing idea.

The men usually arrived back by about two or three o'clock.

Rory would instantly belly-flop into the pool, showering me with icy water, and laugh at my shrieks of horror. Eleanor would get in for a dip too, swimming daintily across the pool in a stylised breaststroke. I preferred to be in the pool by myself although Rory begged me not to get in unless somebody was around – just in case.

'In case what?' I asked him, one day. 'If I get into difficulties, I can't see how your mother can help.' The idea of Eleanor diving in to save me was ludicrous. Eleanor never dived into the pool, but descended elegantly down the ladder at the side, splashing herself all over with water first. Then she would launch herself across the water, head dipping and rising with each stroke. She always looked uncomfortable, as though she was hating every moment. Once she got out she'd immediately change into a dry bathing costume, rinse the other one out and hang it over the line to dry.

'Wonderful drying here, isn't it, dear?' she said, on the third afternoon.

'Yes, it is.' I glanced up from my book.

'Of course, if we only got this weather at home, we wouldn't need to come abroad, would we?'

I squinted at her. 'No, I suppose not.'

'Ireland is such a beautiful country. So green. Such magnificent scenery. Such wonderful places to see. These foreign places are all very well but it's not the same, is it?'

I agreed that, no, it wasn't the same. I wanted to say that if we got this sort of weather at home then we wouldn't have countryside that was so green but I hadn't got the will to argue with her. Besides, she obviously wanted to talk. We hadn't had any conversations up until now. Despite my tentative overtures, she'd stuck her head in magazines and romantic novels or immersed herself in knitting.

'So, Jane.' She settled back into her sunlounger and placed a huge straw hat on her head. 'When will you resign from your job?'

I looked at her in amazement. 'Resign from the bank?' I asked. 'I don't plan to.'

'When you have the baby I presume you will resign,' she said. Her tone implied that I'd no choice in the matter.

I rubbed some factor six on to my arms. 'I don't think so,

188

Eleanor,' I said neutrally. 'I like working. Anyway, all women work these days.'

She laughed, a short barking laugh. 'Don't be silly, Jane, no woman likes working.'

I wanted to be fair to her. I'd thought about it quite a bit lately. I was going to take an extra month's unpaid leave after my baby was born, but I'd definitely decided to go back to work afterwards. I liked walking into the office in the mornings, knowing that there would be problems during the day that it was my responsibility to sort out, that there were schedules to be kept and deadlines to be met and that I could do all of this. I supposed that if we had more children I would feel differently about it, but at the moment Rory was so involved in work that I had to be as well, otherwise I would be crucifyingly lonely. All of my friends worked. I didn't want to be the odd one out. No one gave it up after just one child. Besides, it gave me financial independence. All my life I'd wanted to feel free; if I were to depend on Rory for every penny, I'd be trapped.

'I wouldn't mind giving it up, sometime,' I admitted finally. 'But I don't want to resign yet.'

'It's hardly fair on either your husband or your child,' said Eleanor, her eyes glinting.

'What's not fair?' I asked. It was none of Eleanor's business what we did.

'Rory has a very difficult job,' she said. 'He works hard, long hours. You don't seem to realise that. He needs comforting when he comes home, and you don't provide that, do you?'

I looked at her in amazement. 'I don't know what you're talking about,' I said. 'I provide him with love and companionship and I look after our home. What more do you expect?'

'Do you have the dinner ready for him when he comes in?' she demanded. 'I always have done for Peter.'

'Well, maybe your husband comes in at the same time every night,' I snapped. 'Unlike your son, who doesn't come in the same time any night.'

'Are you accusing him of something?' she asked, a red spot of anger on each cheek.

'Of course not.' I tried to keep my temper in check. 'I'm just saying that his job means he doesn't come home at the same time every evening, that's all. So there's no point in me preparing meals for him. Anyway, he either eats in the canteen or out with clients, so he's not hungry. If he's going out after work then it's up to him to get something to eat. If he's coming home with me, then I'll make something for him.'

'And how do you propose to manage when our grandchild is born?' Eleanor asked me. 'Farm him out to a baby-minder?'

She spat the word baby-minder as though it was a word of abuse.

I wiped traces of sweat from my brow. I wasn't sure whether it was the heat of the sun or the heat of my anger that had caused it.

'Our baby will be well looked after.' I kept my voice as calm as I could. 'I will look after him or her to the very best of my ability.'

She smiled at me in a sort of pitying way. 'It's your ability I worry about, dear,' she said.

I resisted the temptation to throw my book at her.

'Why are you concerned about my ability?' I asked.

'It's your attitude. I know you slept with Rory before you married him. I don't think that's the behaviour of a responsible woman.'

'What exactly do you mean by that?' I asked. I was shaking.

'I mean that a girl who sleeps around is not exactly ideally suited for motherhood.'

'I didn't sleep around,' I said furiously. 'I *did* sleep with Rory. He is your son. It was our choice.'

'I found some of those things in his pocket, you see,' she said. 'When I took his suit to the cleaners. Disgusting things.'

I wanted to laugh now. The look of horror on her face was hilarious.

'Eleanor,' I said gently, 'people do sleep with each other before getting married, now. You didn't like me doing it, but I did it with Rory. And I married him. We love each other.'

She still didn't look very happy. 'I expected it of him, somehow,' she said. 'But I don't think it's right for girls.'

'Even if you don't,' I tried to keep the exasperation out of my voice, 'it doesn't make me an unfit mother.'

'It's everything,' she said. 'The work thing. You know nothing about being a mother.'

'Neither did you!' I exclaimed. 'What experience does anyone have?'

'I had younger brothers and sisters,' said Eleanor. 'I knew how to care for children.'

I sighed deeply. 'So what?'

'You have no brothers and sisters,' she said. 'What do you know?'

'Don't be bloody silly,' I said. 'Not everyone has brothers and sisters – does that make them bad parents?'

'I'd be happy to give you my expertise,' she said, as though I hadn't spoken. 'I'll be able to stay with you if you like.'

I hoped that the shock wasn't too clearly written all over my face.

'I'll manage myself,' I said. 'Thank you.'

She sat back, looking self-satisfied. She had expected me to say this, I realised. She was a weird woman. She watched me, but I'd nothing more to say to her. I didn't want to talk to her. I wanted Rory to come home and rescue me.

Naturally they were late back. I spent the rest of the day feeling irritated both with her and with Rory. When he eventually did arrive back, I hustled him into the bedroom and started crying. I sobbed that his mother hated me, that she wanted (despite hating me) to live with us, that she thought I would be a hopeless mother, that I was a hopeless wife and that, probably, I was a tramp.

Rory comforted me, wiped away my tears and told me not to be silly. I sniffed and told him that his mother was a cow.

'She doesn't mean to be,' he said. 'She's anxious, that's all.'

'I'm anxious too,' I said. 'But I don't go around slagging other people off.'

'Come on, Jane.' He put his arm around me. 'Don't let her spoil our holiday.'

But she had put a damper on it, and I didn't enjoy sitting at the opposite side of the pool from her as she clicked away at her knitting or read her magazines.

She couldn't destroy the glorious weather, though, and the sense of wellbeing that lying in the sun gave. She had a point about not working, I thought ruefully. It would be easy to slip into an indolent lifestyle.

I walked down to the shop at the bottom of the hill one morning to buy some chocolate milk. I'd developed a craving for it, but we had run out and I couldn't wait until Peter and Rory returned to get it. So I slipped on a pair of espadrilles and took off.

It was very hot, and I half-regretted my impulse. But it was nice to walk along the narrow road, smelling the scent of the flowers and listening to the chirping of the cicadas. It was also nice to be free of the tyrant of the villa. The shop was cool and pleasant, a small corner shop, stocked with overpriced imported foods and very cheap fruit. I bought my chocolate milk, half a kilo of cherries and walked back to the villa.

Eleanor stood under the almond tree looking down the road.

'Where were you?' she demanded.

'I went for a walk.' I headed towards the pool.

'A walk.' She spat the words at me.

'Yes, you know, one foot in front of the other.'

'You went down to that shop, didn't you?'

'Sure I did.'

'Rory told you not to.'

'Rory told me nothing of the sort. You told me I wouldn't be able to walk up the hill, and you were wrong.'

'You're red in the face, you're breathless and it was far too hot to go anywhere,' said Eleanor.

She was right about being red in the face and breathless. The last few yards had seemed like a mile and I was tired. But I wasn't going to admit it to her.

'You see?' she said triumphantly. 'You can't deny it!'

'I don't deny being a bit out of breath,' I said. 'You'd be out of breath if you'd walked to the shop and back.'

'It was a stupid thing to do.'

'Oh, give me a break!' I cried. 'I stopped on the way down and on the way back. I took my time. I was fine. I'm pregnant, Eleanor, not a bloody invalid!'

'You could have killed my grandchild,' she said. 'It was a stupid, selfish thing to do.'

'Oh, fuck off,' I said, tired of listening to her.

Eleanor stared at me in horror. She opened and closed her mouth a couple of times, then turned around and stalked into the villa, slamming the door behind her.

192

I didn't care. I sat out in the sun and read my book. I drank the chocolate milk and ate a mountain of cherries. It was bliss.

When Rory came back I told him about the contretemps, hustling him over to the other side of the pool, out of earshot of the downstairs bedroom.

'She's only doing it because she's concerned,' he said placatingly.

'Concerned to stick her nose in,' I retorted. 'She's driving me around the bend.'

'She had a point,' said my husband.

'Oh, come on, Rory,' I said. 'You'd swear that I was suffering from some awful disease. Women in Portugal get pregnant too, you know. They have to walk around in this heat.'

'Well, yes, but they're used to it,' he said. 'You're not.'

'I was fine,' I said. 'But if you feel like that about it, I won't walk down there any more.'

'I would feel better about it,' admitted Rory. 'I'd hate anything to happen to our baby.'

Rory always called it 'our baby' now. I was amazed at how paternal he had become, reading the books, asking umpteen questions, wanting to find out about everything. I hadn't thought he would be so interested and said so.

'Why shouldn't I be interested?' he asked me.

'I don't see you as the paternal type,' I said.

'Jane!' He was shocked. 'Why not?'

'Your way of life,' I said, suddenly speaking about things that had bothered me for a long time. 'Early to work, often late home, golf, football, everything.' My voice quavered. I felt tears prickling at the back of my eyes.

'So, you think I'll be a rotten father, do you?' he asked. 'Just because I'm out and about a lot. You're as judgmental as my mother.'

'I don't mean to be.' I felt terrible. 'I'm just surprised you're taking such an interest in the finer details.'

'I am interested,' he said. 'This is my first baby.'

I turned to look at him. 'I should hope so,' I said.

He got up and dived into the pool. I sighed. I'd annoyed him and I hadn't meant to. I wasn't handling my husband very well these days.

The mood of the holiday changed. The sun still shone, the sea still sparkled but there was an undercurrent that hadn't been there before. I blamed Eleanor, of course. Stupid, meddling, interfering old bat. Each day I sat on the opposite side of the pool to her, engrossed in my book. Each day she sat in the shade of the verandah, eyeing me speculatively. She hated me. I knew she hated me.

Our final evening was a nightmare. Up until now, we had gone our separate ways at night. We drove to Albefueira together but ate in different restaurants. On the last night, Rory decided that we should all eat together. I could have killed him. Despite the arguments, he obviously didn't realise how deep the antipathy was between his mother and me.

So we went together to the Restaurant Stella Maris (chosen by Eleanor because she liked the name) and we talked uneasily about trivial things. I let the conversation bypass me as I picked at my chicken *piri piri* and gazed out over the sea. It was too dark to see anything other than the reflection of the town's lights, but I could hear the soothing rhythmical thud of the waves breaking on the shore and I allowed them to calm me.

'—when Jane gives up work.' His mother's words reached through to me.

'What?' I said, looking up.

'I was talking about how much easier it will be when you give up work.' Eleanor smiled at me. It wasn't a real smile, the corners of her lips barely lifted.

'We've talked about this before.' I put my knife and fork down carefully on my plate. 'I won't be giving up work. Not immediately.'

'Of course you'll have maternity leave,' said Rory.

'And then I'll be going back to my job,' I said. If they could only hear me at the bank, I thought in amusement. Nobody there saw me as a career woman.

The sea breeze wafted towards us and lifted the corner of the paper tablecloth. I fiddled with the piece of plastic that kept it on the table.

'I don't see any reason for you to keep on at that job,' said Peter. He took out a packet of cigarettes and lit one. I liked the smell of cigarette smoke in warm air, although I hated it at home. 'Our Rory makes enough money for you, doesn't he?'

'It's not a question of that, Peter,' I said calmly. 'It's a question of earning my own money.'

'Rubbish!' Eleanor was tight-lipped.

'It's not rubbish,' I said. 'I like to earn my own money.'

'It's all this wanting everything.' Peter inhaled deeply. 'Why should you want to work when you don't need to work?'

I found it difficult to believe we were having this argument.

I wished Rory would say something, but he sat there slicing his peppered steak into bite-sized morsels, head down, ignoring his parents.

'Because I spent five years of my life being educated to work,' I snapped. 'And I'm not going to sit around and vegetate all day.'

'It is not vegetating,' said Eleanor, her eyes flinty. 'I spend my time at home.'

'I rest my case,' I said, taking a sip of wine.

There was a brittle silence. I almost laughed from sheer terror. Peter and Eleanor looked furious.

'You're not going to sit by and listen to this, are you, Rory?' asked Eleanor. 'You're not going to let her insult me.'

My husband looked at me, his eyes pleading. 'I think you were a bit out of order there, Jane,' he said.

Great, I thought. He supports her, not me. I couldn't believe it.

'I think you're wrong, darling,' I said coolly. 'Your mother has spent the entire holiday insinuating that I'm not good enough for you, not good enough for our baby and not good enough for my job. I'm more than good enough for all three. I don't intend to give up work. Maybe I'll change my mind, but I don't want you to decide it for me now.'

'I don't think Mum meant to insult you,' said Rory.

'Don't you?' I asked.

I sipped at my mineral water. My throat was dry and I was close to tears but I was proud of the way that I didn't allow them to fall.

'I think I'll go back to the villa.' I pushed my chair back from the table. 'I've had enough of this shit.'

I stalked off into the dusk, hurrying through the throng of people crowding the narrow streets. The tears were falling now. They slid down my cheeks and dripped from my chin. I pushed past the brightly lit stalls selling handicrafts, roasted almonds and souvenirs.

'Jane! Wait!' Rory caught up with me and held me by the wrist. 'Where do you think you're going?'

'Back to the villa. I said so.'

'Oh Jane, this is silly.'

We stood face to face.

'Not to me, it isn't,' I said.

'Mum didn't mean it the way it sounded,' he said. 'And you've over-reacted.'

'Bullshit! She meant every word. And I haven't over-reacted. I've listened to her sniping at me at every available opportunity. Trying to tell me what to do. How to live my life. Do you know that she thinks I'm some sort of tramp for sleeping with you before we got married? She doesn't seem to think it's any problem for you, of course. She doesn't like me, she's never liked me and she's a stupid bitch.'

'Jane, I won't have you saying things like that about my mother.' Rory was angry.

'Why not?' I asked. 'She says things like that about me all the time.'

'She doesn't, Jane, she doesn't.'

'Huh.' I wasn't going to be placated. Rory usually did a good job of trying to placate me. I usually listened to him. But I'd had enough of his mother.

'I want to go back to the villa,' I said.

'I can't leave them in the restaurant,' said Rory. 'They're expecting us back there.'

'Well, you can go back if you like but I've no intention of sitting around with them.'

'I'll drive you back to the villa,' said Rory tiredly. 'Let me get the car keys. I left them on the table.'

I waited in the town square while he went back, no doubt to explain away my behaviour as hormonal. I sat on a warm stone seat and listened to the sounds around me. Various languages were being spoken, the different bars pumped out music, birds chirped in the trees, fooled by the brightness into thinking it was daytime.

Rory returned with the keys. 'Come on,' he said shortly.

I followed him to the car. We drove back to the villa in silence.

196

'I'm going back to town to bring my parents home,' he told me, when I'd opened the door. 'I'll see you later.'

'Fine,' I said.

I sat on the balcony of our bedroom overlooking the pool. It was almost silent, just night-time sounds. I didn't care about what I'd said to Eleanor. I was fed up with her. I was fed up with people telling me what to do. I was twenty-six years old, old enough to live my life without interference from anyone. I supposed that one day I might like to leave work, but that would be when I decided, not Eleanor McLoughlin. I leaned my head against the smooth, white wall. I wished Rory had been more supportive. It was frightening to think that he was, in some way, under his mother's influence. He should have told her to butt out.

I got up from my seat and went back into the bedroom. I sat in front of the dressing-table, scrupulously removed all my make-up and threw the cotton wool across the tiled floor in temper.

The bed wasn't very comfortable and I'd found it difficult to sleep in it. I couldn't sleep now. I lay there, staring at the ceiling.

It was at least an hour later before I heard the villa door open and the murmur of voices downstairs. The kettle was filled, I could hear Eleanor asking if anyone wanted tea. They must have both said yes because it was ages before Rory came to bed. He tiptoed around the room, swearing softly when he stubbed his toe on the wicker chair in the corner.

I waited for him to put his arm around me as he usually did, but he rolled on to his side immediately and pulled the sheets up around his shoulders.

Be like that, I thought furiously, anger coursing through me. Be like that.

I didn't sleep that night, I was too angry, too warm, too uncomfortable. As the early morning light filtered through the thin curtains I resolved never to set foot inside his parents' house again. And that my baby wouldn't be christened in Eleanor's christening robe.

Chapter 16

June 1986
(UK No. 2 – *Holding Back The Years* – Simply Red)

Lucy moved into her apartment in the first week of June. I wanted to help her, but I couldn't lift anything. I'd stopped growing and I was immensely grateful for that, but I still felt huge and I hated not being able to tie the laces on my trainers properly. She told me not to worry, that she had somebody to help her. I was glad. I'd felt that I was letting her down in some way.

'It's OK, Jane.' She'd rung me at work for a chat and I was glad of the break. 'David will help me.'

I scanned through my memory to recall someone called David but drew a blank.

'Who's David?' I asked.

There was silence for a moment and I wondered if I'd insulted Lucy by forgetting someone in her family.

'I met him while you were on holiday, Jane,' she said enthusiastically. 'He's really nice.'

'Oh, Lucy!' I started to laugh. 'I remember once you told me that I fell in love too easily. Do you remember? When we went to Majorca? And look what's happened since then – I've got married and you've fallen in love more times than I can count.'

'I said that because you are hopelessly romantic,' Lucy told me firmly. 'I don't always fall in love. I might fall in lust occasionally but that's entirely different. I've never met anyone that I thought was the one for ever.'

I felt a bit sorry for Lucy. She was doomed to search for perfection. But perfection never happened. I asked her to give me all the details about her new boyfriend, but she said that she'd tell me next week. Would I come over for dinner? She was asking the Quinlan twins as well.

'Do you want me on my own, or Rory and me?' I asked.

'It's a girls' night,' she said. 'Just the four of us. Like old times.'

I was looking forward to it. Sometimes I thought that the best days of my life had been living in the apartment with the girls, doing whatever we liked, having fun, occasionally behaving badly. Now my life was boringly suburban; my greatest social occasion this week had been a trip to the supermarket and then my pre-natal class. I hadn't even gone to Lisa O'Toole's departmental transfer booze-up on Friday, because by the end of the week I was shattered.

I was becoming more and more terrified about the baby. I was scared stiff about the birth, despite the kindness of the nurses at the hospital. I couldn't help remembering all those films of women screaming in agony, hair matted, wet from the sweat oozing from every pore. Even though the video they'd shown us portrayed the birth as a peaceful process, I knew that it would hurt. I was frightened of the pain.

Rory came to one of the classes with me, then said he'd seen all he wanted to see and refused to have anything more to do with it. I couldn't blame him. If it hadn't been for the fact that I had to go through it, I wouldn't have wanted to watch either.

Jessica told me not to worry, and to ask for the epidural; everything would be fine. I didn't believe her.

I didn't let anyone know how frightened I was. I told myself that women had done this for generations and that I could do it too, but I wondered whether I was really ready for it. I couldn't talk to Mam about it, I was too embarrassed. I wouldn't have dreamed of speaking to Eleanor McLoughlin. She'd already earmarked me as a failure, anyway.

I still hated Eleanor. Since we'd come back from our holiday I hadn't spoken to her, although Rory had been home to see them a couple of times. He'd come back with the christening robe and handed it to me.

'You see, Jane, I told you she cared.'

I took the fine knitted garment as though it was a time bomb. 'I have a christening robe,' I told him. 'It's a McDermott family tradition.'

199

I'd already made up my mind to use the McDermott robe. Mam would be very disappointed if I didn't. Eleanor had made me determined to use it anyway, and I didn't care if there was an almighty row. I was still annoyed at Rory for siding with his parents. I was sure I'd heard him murmuring phrases like 'highly-strung' and 'under pressure' to his mother on the plane as we flew home.

My relationship with Rory had altered subtly. I felt as though he had let me down. Sometimes, in the darkness of the night when his arm lay across me and his slow, steady breathing filled the air, I knew I was being stupid. When he rang my extension to say he'd be leaving late and would I be OK on the bus, I knew that I wasn't. I was a mess of turbulent emotions and I couldn't decide whether it was because of the pregnancy or because I was having a nervous breakdown.

It was a relief to go to Lucy's for dinner. The girls had known me all my life and I could let my hair down with them.

I arrived with a bottle of wine and – as a tribute to my domesticity – a cheesecake which I'd made. I also brought Lucy a house-warming gift, a watercolour of the Arc de Triomphe.

She hadn't done anything to the apartment yet, but it showed signs of her personality. The pine furniture was new – very like the stuff she'd had in Paris. I recognised some of the pictures on the walls.

'Come in,' she said, 'welcome to my new home.'

I sat on the edge of an armchair and looked around.

'I haven't got all my furniture yet,' said Lucy. 'I know it's still a bit of a mess, but I feel great about it.'

'It looks more you already.' I handed her the wine and the cheesecake.

She peered under the tinfoil at the cake.

'Oh, lovely,' she exclaimed. 'Food!'

'It's the only thing I can make,' I told her. 'I fake being brilliant at home by doing this.'

'Looks gorgeous.' She sniffed appreciatively at it.

I gave her the watercolour and she tore off the gift wrapping.

'Oh, great.' She smiled. 'I'll put it on the wall straight away.'

'You don't have to. Wait till you decide exactly where you want it.'

'I want it covering that ugly spot over there.' She nodded at the opposite wall. 'I'm not sure what happened, but it seems to me like there was a bit of a domestic crisis and she threw something at him and missed. There were a few patches like that – they're hidden behind the ones I've hung up already!'

Lucy rummaged in a cardboard box and produced a hammer and a nail. 'Watch how handy around the home I am.' She banged the nail into the wall with great enthusiasm.

The picture looked well and it hid the stain.

'So,' I said, settling back into the chair, 'tell me about your new lover.'

'He's not a lover yet,' said Lucy wickedly, 'but I want him to be. Actually, Jane, he's really nice.'

'Nice?' I said.

Lucy shrugged in her Gallic way. 'Nice,' she repeated. 'Comforting. Stable. Caring.'

'Sounds perfect,' I said wryly. 'Is there anything about him that isn't – nice?'

'Sod off, Jane,' said Lucy companionably. 'He's different to my usual man, that's all.'

The doorbell rang. The twins arrived, Lucy kissed them and they, too, proffered bottles of wine and a house-warming present. They had bought her a bagful of scatter cushions. I immediately claimed some to put behind my back.

'Is that chair uncomfortable for you?' asked Lucy anxiously.

'No, it's fine now,' I said. 'Honestly, Lucy. I'm OK.'

In fact, now that we were all together, I felt like the odd one out. Deep down I was envious of my friends. Lucy, as always, was like a sylph, in tight jeans, a peach-coloured silk blouse and hair cascading around her face. Brenda Quinlan wore a red linen dress which emphasised her hour-glass figure and Grace wore the same dress in jade. All three of my friends looked young, healthy and slim. I was wearing a light, elasticated skirt and a huge T-shirt. I felt like an elephant in a flower garden. At least I still had a dusting of my Algarve tan. It made me look less washed out and dowdy, but I was horribly aware that I hadn't managed to shave my legs in weeks and that little hairs were poking out of my support tights.

'So.' Brenda tossed her black hair out of her eyes. 'How do you like being back in Dublin, Lucy?'

'It's great,' she said. 'I'm glad I've got this place, the job's

201

going well – I'm paid far too much for what I have to do, but who's complaining? – and I like being home again.'

'It's nice to have you back,' said Grace. 'Isn't it strange for us to be together in an apartment again?'

It was. When the twins had come in and sat down it was, for a brief moment, as though we were back in Waterloo Mews.

'We've come a long way since then.' I glanced involuntarily at my bump.

'You certainly have,' giggled Brenda.

'You've done more than me,' I objected. 'With the shop and everything.'

'How is the shop?' asked Lucy. 'I meant to call in again, but I've been up to my neck moving.'

'Doing really well,' said Grace. 'We've been selling more and more of our own stuff, which is fantastic. We're wondering if, maybe, we should move into town.'

'It's more difficult in town,' I observed. 'The rents are so high.'

'That's the problem,' agreed Brenda. 'We haven't really decided yet.'

'Are those your own designs?' asked Lucy, waving at the girls' dresses.

Grace nodded. 'Thought we'd try them out today.'

'They're lovely,' I said warmly. 'I wish I could find something nice to wear.'

Grace looked sympathetically at me. 'There are places that do elegant maternity things,' she said and immediately made me feel that I was wearing the wrong sort of clothes.

'Have you ever done anything for a pregnant woman?' I asked her.

She shook her head but eyed me speculatively. 'Maybe I could try,' she said. 'What would you like?'

'Oh, just a nice sexy number,' I laughed. 'Something that would make me look like Jerry Hall.'

Hysterical laughter greeted this statement and I stuck my tongue out at them.

'I might be able to do something,' mused Grace. 'I'll have a try. Why don't you come down to the shop next Saturday?'

'OK,' I said.

Lucy went into the kitchen. I sat back and listened to the twins chatting about the shop and clothes and designs. They were smart and businesslike.

Lucy carried two huge bowls of salad into the room.

'I catered for summer,' she said as she plonked them down on the table. 'I forgot it was June in Ireland!'

The day wasn't very summery – not exactly cold, just overcast and dull.

Lucy opened the big windows overlooking the sea. Her one disappointment about the apartment was that it didn't have much of a balcony, just a strip of concrete surrounded by a wooden railing, barely enough room for a chair.

'D'you remember the time the nuns invited our year to tea in the convent?' asked Grace, as Lucy poured coffee.

'Could I ever forget!' Lucy laughed.

It had been an exercise in checking our vocations. We were served tea and sandwiches while Sr Elizabeth talked about the 'call from God'.

I giggled at the memory. 'I was terrified I'd actually got the call. For nights afterwards, I dreamed that God had called me and I'd have to go into the convent.'

Grace shuddered. 'Can you imagine? A little room and a huge crucifix hanging on the wall! That'd terrify anyone.'

'None of our year did get the call, did they?' asked Lucy.

We looked at each other blankly.

'Don't think so,' said Brenda. 'Got lots of other things maybe, but not the call.'

'I hated school.' Lucy leaned back in her chair and yawned. 'People bossing you around all the time and girls like Stephanie and Camilla to make you feel totally inadequate.'

'Will you ever forget those discos?' Brenda laughed. 'Weren't they absolutely awful? Standing around waiting to be asked to dance.' She shook her head at the memory.

'You two were always OK, though,' I said to the twins. 'You always had each other.'

'I'm not sure if that's good or bad,' said Brenda. 'We can never make up our minds about it, either. You know, I sometimes wonder if either of us will ever get married. We're so busy and we never get the time to go out.'

'What about you, Lucy?' asked Grace as she speared an ear of baby corn and dropped it into her mouth. 'Will you ever get married?'

I was surprised to see the faint stain of colour on Lucy's cheeks.

'I don't know,' she said uncomfortably. 'I keep thinking I might but I'm never convinced about it. Not like you, Jane.'

They all looked at me, the married woman. It was funny how people thought you changed when you got married. I still felt the same person as I'd been years ago, but the girls now seemed to think that I'd some special, secret knowledge about relationships that they lacked.

'Marriage isn't everything.' I blushed, realising that I sounded completely disillusioned. 'But it's OK.'

'Only OK?' Lucy looked disturbed. 'I thought you were very happy.'

'Oh, I am!' I nodded my head vigorously. 'I am happy. Don't get me wrong. It's just that you become part of a couple and people see you in that light. And there's a whole load of other shit like your in-laws and everything.'

I recounted the experience with Eleanor McLoughlin. I hadn't told anyone about it before and it was a relief to tell an audience which was basically on my side.

'The old bitch!' exclaimed Grace, with feeling. 'Who does she think she is?'

I shrugged. 'I always knew she didn't like me but I never realised that it ran so deep.'

'But that's terrible, Jane.' Lucy sounded horrified. 'Why didn't you get Rory to tell her to butt out?'

'He doesn't know how,' I said. 'I didn't think so at first but he seems to be a bit in awe of her.'

'I wouldn't have put up with it,' said Brenda. 'Cow.'

I smiled at them. They had already made me feel a million times better about it. It wasn't a crime to want to work for a bit longer, although Eleanor acted as though it was.

'But don't keep working if you're exhausted,' said Grace. 'Give yourself a break.'

'I'll work until I feel I should stop.' I grinned at her. 'After all my talk, I'll probably be knackered straight away!'

Brenda asked me what it was like to be pregnant. I refused to tell them on the grounds that we were about to have dinner and I didn't want to make them sick.

Lucy had prepared *coq au vin* as her tribute to France. She was a great cook.

'Why did you leave?' asked Brenda. 'I thought you loved France.'

'I did.' Lucy handed around some hot bread. 'It's a great place to live and my job was wonderful, but when I split up with Eric I couldn't stay there any more.'

'It seems a pity to have to change your life completely because of some man,' remarked Grace.

Lucy shrugged. 'I was probably ready to change, anyway. I know that Eric and I finally broke up because he was seeing someone else, but I'm not sure we had a long-term thing going anyway.'

'Why not?' asked Brenda.

'I don't know,' Lucy answered. 'I loved lots of things about Eric but I'm not sure I really loved him. Just as well, really. I was disappointed about leaving my job because the salary was great and I had a terrific amount of responsibility, but I was lonely. Anyhow, I wanted to come home.'

'I wonder do all relationships come to a natural end,' said Grace thoughtfully. 'You know, ten years and suddenly you've both changed too much. A different partner for different periods of your life.'

'Have you felt like that, Jane?' asked Lucy lightheartedly. 'Like you've had enough of Rory, that you've outgrown him?'

'Sometimes,' I said. 'But you get through that. Then sometimes I know that we'll be together for ever.'

'How lovely,' said Brenda, and she meant it. 'It must be great to be so confident.'

I felt lucky. Lucky that I'd a wonderful husband, a nice home, and would soon have a beautiful child. They might all be happy in their own way, but it wasn't the same. Lucy didn't have anyone to come home to, to share her hopes and her dreams. The twins had each other, but it could never be the same as having someone you could hold in the middle of the night, who you knew loved you.

'So,' said Lucy, clearing away the dinner things. 'Here we are, nine years since we left school and still friends.'

'A major achievement,' said Brenda. 'I haven't seen anyone else from school since we left.'

'Jane met Louise Killane a few months ago,' laughed Lucy.

'Did you?' asked Brenda. 'How was she?'

I giggled uncontrollably while the twins looked at me in amazement. 'Tell them,' I choked, looking at Lucy.

She recounted the horror story for them, and they shook with helpless laughter.

'Poor Louise,' I said, wiping the tears from my eyes. 'I bet Karen gave her hell.'

'Do you remember Anne Sutherland sending herself the Valentine card?' said Grace. 'She hadn't even disguised her writing.'

'I nearly did that once,' I admitted. 'I was so depressed when all the others had them.'

'I've only ever got one card in my whole life,' said Lucy. 'That was the year we left school. I never found out who sent it.'

'The first year we got married, Rory brought me to Paris for Valentine's Day,' I said. 'Remember, Lucy, we met you in Montparnasse.'

She nodded. 'He was incredibly romantic,' she said.

'Last year he gave me one of those jokey ones,' I said. 'You know, about loving me even though I was old and wrinkly. How romance lives on.'

'I suppose you can't keep being romantic all the time,' offered Grace.

'From Paris to a jokey card in four years,' I said. 'Not bad, huh.'

They didn't know whether I was serious or not. Neither did I really.

'Anyway, Lucy.' I got up and walked around to stretch my back. 'Tell us about your new love.'

The twins looked amazed. 'Already!' gasped Brenda.

Lucy made a contorted face at me.

'Very mature,' I said. 'Very *avant-garde* businesswoman with her own flat.'

'Come on, Lucy,' said Grace. 'Reveal all.'

'His name is David Norris,' said Lucy. 'He's an architect. I met him when I was wandering through one of those tile showrooms. I was looking for something for the bathroom. It needs to be completely redone. Anyhow, I bumped into him beside the discontinued lines.'

'Sounds very romantic,' observed Grace.

'Lucy McAllister, you are the only person I know who could pick up a man in a tile shop,' I said.

'I didn't pick him up,' she said primly. 'I actually dropped one of the tiles I was looking at and it shattered. Pieces of ceramic all over the place. Very embarrassing. A salesman came racing over and David said it was his fault.'

'Wow,' breathed Brenda. 'Chivalrous.'

'He's quite well-known in the shop because he recommends it, so it was no problem,' said Lucy. 'I asked him for a coffee.'

'How do you have the nerve to do things like that?' I asked.

'Easy,' she said. 'The worst that could have happened was that he would say "no". Anyway, we went for coffee and got talking. He asked me out. I said OK. That was all there was to it.'

'So where have you been?' I asked.

'The movies, once or twice,' she said. 'Dinner. Things like that.'

'How come you've turned into this *femme fatale* when you were such a drip at school?' I complained. 'We were hopeless at getting dates, then. How have you managed to change so much?'

Lucy considered the question. 'I think it's because I don't care as much,' she said seriously. 'When we were at school I was always afraid of what other people thought. Now I don't give a toss.'

'Fair enough,' said Brenda.

'So, is this a serious relationship?' asked Grace.

Lucy blushed. 'Maybe.'

'Lucy!' I looked at her in amazement. 'You're having a serious relationship with a nice man.'

'Nice?' asked Brenda.

'She called him nice when I arrived,' I said.

Lucy grinned. 'I know, I know. I've always had relationships with totally unsuitable men which ended up going down the toilet. Cian O'Connor – a disaster. On, off, on, off, hopeless. Nick Clark.' She flicked a look at me. 'Jane was right about Nick. Didn't care about me at all, just used me. Then Robert Maher. On the rebound, doomed to failure. Then Eric the frog.'

'Lucy!'

'Well, he was a toad,' she amended, amid laughter.

It was good to be with the girls again, I thought, listening to the conversation. This was the sort of thing I'd missed in the years of Lucy's absence.

'We should meet regularly,' I said suddenly. 'Once a month or something.'

Lucy nodded. 'It's a good idea.'

'Will you be able to get out when you've had the baby?' asked Grace.

'Of course,' I said. 'Rory will be a model father. He told me so.'

'Why don't we try and make a regular date?' said Lucy. 'Like the first Friday of the month.'

'That's your Catholic upbringing,' laughed Grace. 'First Friday, indeed.'

But we decided that it would be a good idea and made a date to meet again. In my house, this time, I suggested. After all, I would be like an even bigger elephant by then, and I mightn't even be able to drive.

I was more nervous behind the wheel these days. Rory had offered to drive me to Lucy's but I wanted to go myself. He was relieved when I returned home and I was touched by the concern in his face.

'You were longer than I thought,' he said, as I handed him the car keys.

'Girl talk,' I told him as I went upstairs to bed.

Chapter 17

July 1986
(UK No. 1 – *Papa Don't Preach* – Madonna)

'Have you thought about moving house, lately?' Rory looked up from the *Sunday Times* and pushed his Ray-Bans to the top of his head.

We were sitting in the back garden, soaking up a glorious Sunday afternoon in July. I'd woken up at six that morning to the sound of the birds shouting at each other from the branches and lumbered out of bed to look through the window. Already, the sun spilled over the rooftops opposite and slid across the garden. I stayed out of bed and had an early breakfast as I waited for the sun to come around the house and on to the back garden.

Junkie loved sunny weather. He stretched out in the grass, stomach facing skywards, sleeping peacefully. Occasionally the buzzing of a passing bee would wake him and he'd jump into life, stalk the bee in a frenzied bout of chase and stop around the garden before collapsing in an exhausted heap beneath the cherry blossom tree.

'Where do you want to move to?' I put the magazine supplement to one side.

'Somewhere bigger,' said Rory. 'In a better area.'

'What's wrong with this area?' I asked. 'It seems OK to me.'

'It's very young,' said Rory. 'I'd like to live somewhere older and more settled.'

'We're young,' I told him. 'And when this baby grows up he or she is going to want somewhere to play – with kids around the same age. This place is ideal.'

Rory sighed. 'I'm not suggesting we move into a geriatric ward. I'm merely saying a better area would be a good idea.'

I nudged Junkie with my toe. 'He won't like it.'

'Jane, you're talking about a cat,' said Rory. 'He'll go where the food is.'

Rory had a point. The way to Junkie's heart had always been through his stomach.

'Do you really want to move somewhere else?'

Rory leaned back in his chair. 'As senior forex manager, I think I should be living somewhere consistent with my status,' he said pompously.

I looked at him in surprise. 'Have you been promoted again?' I asked. 'Why didn't you tell me before now?'

'It's not official,' he admitted. 'Bill told me Friday. It has to be ratified.'

'Oh, Rory.' If I'd been able to leap from my chair I would have. 'That's brilliant news.'

'I thought you'd be pleased.'

'I'm pleased for you,' I told him. 'I'm thrilled for you.'

'Anyway, this means more money and I thought you might prefer to live in something better than a three-bed semi.'

Our three-bed semi was a very nice house and I'd felt comfortable there from the moment we moved in. But if there was a chance to move up, then I supposed we should take it.

'Where had you got in mind?' I asked.

'Don't care,' said Rory. 'Foxrock, maybe.'

I made a face. 'I don't know Foxrock at all. Couldn't we go somewhere I know?' I liked Rathfarnham. I liked the village and the countryside. It was close enough to my parents without being uncomfortably close.

'Where do you know?' asked Rory.

'Here.' I shrugged at him. 'Wherever.'

'I'd like to be nearer the coast again,' he said. 'I'm not mad on the mountains. How about Dun Laoghaire or Blackrock?'

'I really don't mind, Rory,' I said. 'But it depends on what sort of house you're thinking about. Anyway, we can't move until the baby is born.'

'I know that,' he said. 'Give me some credit.'

I went into the house, poured some more orange juice for myself and brought out a can of lager for Rory. I hadn't really thought about moving house before, although I'd muttered once

210

or twice that we wouldn't have half enough space when the baby was born.

That was the thing about Rory. I'd make a casual remark and then, one day, before I knew where I was, he'd acted on it. It would be great to have a bigger house, though where I'd find the time or the energy to clean it I couldn't imagine. My energy levels had fallen quite dramatically in the last week, coinciding with another leap forward in the size of my bump. My gynaecologist, Mr Murphy, said that I was cooking up a wonderful baby. I was happy that he was pleased with my progress, but I wished my wonderful baby wouldn't grow so much. Or that it was a bit less active. The baby had started kicking and moving so much now that I felt seasick. I couldn't wait to have my body back again. I was fed up sharing it.

'Rory thinks we should move house,' I told Mam the following weekend when I called around for a visit. I was feeling a bit guilty because I hadn't dropped around to her in ages, and the last two times she had called around to see me I'd been out.

'Not right now, surely?' she said as she filled the kettle. 'You need your rest, Jane. You look very washed-out.'

Why did my mother always have to make me feel under the weather? I was feeling OK. I didn't think I looked washed-out. In fact, I'd brushed Egyptian Wonder over my face simply so that she wouldn't be able to say that I looked washed-out or peaky.

'We weren't thinking of moving straight away,' I told her. 'But he's been promoted again and he thinks this would be a good time to move.'

'He works hard, doesn't he?' said Mam.

'He enjoys it,' I replied.

We went into the back garden with our tea. The weather had stayed warm, although not very sunny. The garden was beautiful. Mam and Dad had grown into gardening in the last few years. They lavished loads of care and attention on the flowers and shrubs that had once grown higgledy piggledy around it. Now the various colours complemented each other and the shrubs were neatly trimmed. I liked sitting there. Strange, I thought, I always did feel more relaxed at home now. When I came in the door, I reverted to being my mother's daughter instead of a woman in my own

211

right and, although this usually drove me crazy, I enjoyed it now. Besides, Mam always made me tea, gave me apple tart or fussed over me. If it had been a regular occurrence it would have been tedious, but at the moment it was brilliant.

'I was thinking of buying a car,' I said to Mam.

'Really?' She leaned towards me. 'What sort?'

'I don't know yet,' I said. 'I thought I'd ask Dad if they've anything in.'

The garage was doing well. Dad was working more, not less, now but they'd been able to hire additional staff and he and Mam had gone on holiday last year for the first time in ages.

'Something small,' I said. 'I don't need anything too flashy.'

I asked him when he arrived home and he scratched his head thoughtfully. There were a couple, he told me, Metros and Fiestas, if I was interested. Why didn't I drop down during the week?

I agreed. 'You can bring me home afterwards,' I told him.

The following Thursday, Rory left me at the garage. He was going on to Woodbrook for a game of golf with Bill Hamilton. 'Don't get anything silly,' he warned me.

'Like what?'

'Like Lucy McAllister.'

I laughed. Lucy had bought a little yellow MG which she drove around the city like a lunatic. I supposed the years in France had changed her method of driving. I'd always thought that I drove quickly, and I did, but I drove safely too. Lucy was an erratic driver. She stopped to do her make-up in traffic, ate croissants at the wheel and read the newspapers when in a jam. But she got away with it because other drivers appreciated a blonde in a sports car. They would have blasted me out of it with the horn.

I strolled into the garage, past reception and into the workshop. Dad was looking underneath the bonnet of a Corolla, shaking his head. That meant nothing, Dad shook his head no matter what was wrong with a car. It was something they obviously learned in mechanics' school.

'Terminal, is it?' I teased, kissing him.

'Nothing that I can't fix,' he said. 'Do you want to see some cars out the back? Be careful you don't trip over anything.'

I'd loved coming to the garage when I was small because it was

212

nearly impossible to walk through it without getting covered in oil and grease. Mam had never been able to say anything because, of course, Dad would come home covered in oil and grease too. It was the only time I ever had a legitimate excuse for getting filthy.

The garage was cleaner now and more carefully laid out. I was able to walk into the large yard at the back of the building without once tripping over a hubcap or brushing against an oil drum.

'There's a Micra over there, quite nice,' said Dad. 'Low mileage, lady owner. And we've two Fiestas. And a Metro.'

I looked at them all. Any one of them would have done, they were all ideal second-car material. It would have been nice to say that I wanted a Porsche or an Aston Martin or anything fast and steamy. It was terrible to think that I would have to be so sensible as to buy a neat little one-lady-owner car.

The road was long and dusty, the red sands sweeping across it. I shifted the car into fifth gear and kept the needle at eighty. It was vital that I made good time. They needed the material and they needed it now. It was no good to say that I'd been delayed. Excuses would not be tolerated. I glanced in the rear-view mirror. The Lotus was catching up, gaining on me. I stamped down firmly on the accelerator and was rewarded by a surge of power from the Mercedes. My car was bigger, more powerful. I could keep ahead of the Lotus. I sensed, rather than heard, the sound of the gunshot. I ducked involuntarily. They were getting closer. Whoever it was, he could drive. I tried to drive still faster, glancing down at the speedometer and watching the needle push further and further along the dial. The road curved suddenly and I hauled the wheel around with a screech of protesting tyres. The Lotus was still behind me. There were fifty miles to go. I would have to deal with the Lotus and deal with it now. I decelerated and allowed it to draw level. I could see him now, dark, sloe-eyed, determined chin. He looked across at me and I half smiled at him. Then I hauled at the steering wheel again and took him broadsides, sending the Lotus careering off the road and down the steep incline to the valley below. I was an excellent field operative. I always had been.

213

'So what do you think?' asked Dad.

I opened the door of a Fiesta. 'I like it,' I said. 'It looks like the sort of car I need. Not, maybe, the sort of car I'd like.'

He laughed in understanding. 'I know,' he said. 'But you've got to compromise.'

'Unfortunately.' I smiled at him. 'Do you want to discuss the sordid aspect of money?'

'You definitely want this one?'

I nodded.

'Sure?'

I nodded again.

'Then it's my present to you.'

I stared at him. 'I can't accept this,' I said. 'It's far too much.'

'I want to give it to you,' said Dad.

I remembered once being pissed off with him because Lucy's father had given her a car and he, the garage owner, hadn't given me one.

'I can afford to buy it, Dad,' I said.

'But I'd like to give it to you.' His face shone with pleasure. 'I know that when you were younger, we really didn't have the money to send you on all the trips you would have liked and we couldn't buy you all the things you wanted, but I can give you this car now. And I'd like to do it. Think of it as a present for the baby.'

'Oh, Dad.' I hugged him. 'Thank you.'

'It's my pleasure,' he told me. 'I love you, Janey. I want you to be happy.'

I released him. 'I am happy,' I said.

'Are you sure?'

'What on earth makes you ask that? Of course I'm happy. Why shouldn't I be? I have a great home, a great husband, I'll soon have a great baby and I now possess a great car. And, of course, I have wonderful parents. What more could a girl ask for?'

Dad puffed a bit. I was surprised at him. We rarely exchanged anything but trivialities, never any innermost feelings; certainly we never got emotional with each other.

'Your mam is a bit worried, that's all,' he said gruffly. 'We're concerned that you're running yourself around too much.'

'Mam is always concerned about me,' I told him. 'The last time

I was at the house she said I looked peaky. I couldn't possibly have looked peaky, I was wearing make-up.'

He laughed. 'It's just that Rory works so much and he always seems to be out,' he said.

I bristled, although I tried not to show it.

'It's because he works so hard that I can afford to buy the car, if I want to. And we can afford this baby and we can probably buy a new house as well,' I said. 'I can't begrudge him a couple of evenings out playing golf.'

'We were afraid you might be lonely.'

'Don't be silly, Dad.'

I kissed him on the cheek to show him that I hadn't taken offence, but I was shaking inside. Why did my parents think that my life with Rory wasn't as it should be? We'd had difficult times but, overall, it was going well. Why should they think otherwise? I'd never complained to them.

I collected the car at the weekend, drove it home and parked it with a flourish behind the BMW in the driveway. Rory came out to have a look at my acquisition. He peered under the bonnet as though he knew what he was looking for, revved the engine a couple of times and told me that it seemed to be OK. I pointed out to him that my dad did own a garage and that he should know a thing or two about cars. Rory nodded wisely and continued to look it over. I let him, it was easier than arguing with him.

Lucy and David called around at the weekend. I'd rung her earlier in the week to check if they were definitely coming and she'd said of course, they couldn't wait. And I couldn't wait to see the man whom she'd seen every day for the past six weeks. This was so totally unlike Lucy that I was intrigued.

'They're here,' called Rory, hearing the MG pull up.

I struggled into my baggy trousers and loose-fitting top and hurried downstairs to greet them.

David Norris was a short, slightly overweight man with fair curly hair and round glasses. I was surprised. Every other man Lucy had gone out with had been very handsome. He was wearing sand-coloured trousers and a slate-grey shirt. He looked very ordinary. I couldn't see what it was that had captivated Lucy.

She looked incredible tonight. Her hair was caught up in a

velvet bow and was gathered to one side of her head. She wore a pink and blue dress, short skirt, tight under her buttocks. Her eyes sparkled and her skin glowed. I had never seen her look like this before.

'Come in.' I kissed her on the cheek. 'Lovely to see you.'

'This is David.' She introduced him by dragging him by the hand and presenting him to me like a child showing off her best friend.

'Pleased to meet you.' I held out my hand. His grip was firm and decisive.

'Come through.' I led the way towards the back of the house. 'Do you want to sit in the garden for a while?'

We sat outside on the small patio behind the house. It got the best of the afternoon and evening sun and was warm and sheltered. David looked at it approvingly.

'I feel you're weighing up the house,' I laughed. 'Can I get you a drink or anything?'

'Beer, if you have it,' he said.

I brought out cans of beer. Rory and David started to talk about golf.

'You're making a big mistake, dating a golfer,' I teased Lucy. 'Have you noticed the way they spend hours talking about one single shot? How they drove off superbly, played a wonderful iron shot from the fairway, chipped neatly on to the green and sank a six-foot putt?'

'Jane! I didn't realise you were listening!' Rory grinned. 'Another drink, David?'

'I'll get them.' I got up and went back to the kitchen.

Lucy followed me. 'What d'you think?' she hissed when we were out of earshot.

'He's not like I expected,' I admitted.

'What did you expect?'

I wasn't sure what I had expected. Someone more suave, perhaps, more determined. David Norris seemed terribly laid-back. He listened to Rory, allowing him to expound his ideas on golf without ever interrupting him. He didn't impose himself on the company, rather became part of it. I liked him. Living with Rory was like living with a bomb about to go off. I was used to someone who was convinced he was always right, that his opinions were the only possible ones to hold, that life was for living to the utmost all the time. All dealers were like that. They had to be super-confident in their own abilities at work and it rubbed off at home too. It came as something of a shock to realise other men were more relaxed than Rory.

'He's very nice,' I told Lucy.

'He's not the best-looking man in the world,' she said, waiting for me to contradict her.

I was happy to. Not handsome, I told her, but attractive nonetheless.

'Come on, Jane, we're friends,' said Lucy. 'He's not good-looking at all. But he's such a decent person. I haven't known a decent bloke in ages.'

She sounded so distraught, I hugged her.

'I think he's lovely,' I told her. 'And he's awfully polite. He's sitting there listening to Rory going on and on and he hasn't clocked him one yet.'

'He's not into violence,' grinned Lucy. 'He's very peace-loving.'

'I hope he's not a vegetarian,' I told her. 'You'd never be able to live with him.'

She smiled at me. 'No, he's not,' she said. 'Although he's very concerned about the things that we eat. Not too much red meat, lots of vegetables, things like that.'

'How will you cope?' I asked playfully. 'Anyhow I'll get good marks, I'm doing Dover sole for dinner.'

'How are you eating, yourself?' asked Lucy.

'Fine.' I poured some milk into a glass. 'I can't eat a lot in one go because I get dreadful heartburn, but I'm not sick or anything. I suppose you can't really be too sick at this stage, you wouldn't be able to lean over the toilet.'

'Jane, you're disgusting,' said my friend. 'Give me some more beer and I'll bring it outside.'

We spent a very pleasant hour in the garden until dinner was ready and I told everyone to come back into the house. I'd set the table with care. I'd bought a floral centrepiece, remembering how pretty Karen Hamilton's had looked.

They complimented me and I flushed with pleasure. It was nice to be a foursome, I thought. I was glad that Lucy had found somebody that she cared about.

They were perfect for each other. They were on the same wavelength. They even finished each other's sentences. It was as though they had known each other for years.

'Where do you live, David?' I asked, during a lull in the conversation.

'I'm renting a place in Donnybrook at the moment,' he said. 'I bought a house there and I'm renovating it in my spare time. So I need to be somewhere nearby.'

'Do you actually do the work, then?' I asked, in surprise. 'I thought that architects only did the drawings.'

'Oh, I don't plaster or lay bricks or anything like that,' said David. 'But I can do a certain amount. I enjoy it.'

'What do you actually design?' asked Rory.

'I'm with a company that does corporate work,' David told us. 'Office blocks, that sort of thing.'

'Sounds really interesting,' I said. 'What are you working on now?'

'An office park development out in Sandyford. You should come and see it.'

We said that we would. I was interested in the idea of designing something and seeing it being built. It must, I thought, be very satisfying to see your drawing actually take shape on the ground. Much more satisfying than checking letters of credit, or worrying about the staff holiday rota.

The dinner was a success. Despite Rory's usual attempts to hog the conversation and David's natural reticence, there were no awkward silences or moments when I wondered why on earth I bothered. We played Trivial Pursuit afterwards. Rory and I narrowly beat David and Lucy.

They left about midnight. Lucy hugged me, told me to look after myself and then whispered again, 'Do you like him?' I gave her the thumbs-up as they got into her car and she roared away down the road.

I wished that Rory would look at me the way David looked at Lucy, although in my current condition it was asking a bit much. But he'd never looked at me like that, as though I was the only one in the world that mattered. He had a very pragmatic approach to life – see something, want something, get something. He regarded me as his partner and he did care about me, but he didn't show it and I wished he could.

I shook myself, trying to banish the thoughts. Was I envious of Lucy? It didn't make sense. She was in the first flush of another infatuation and I knew that the infatuation stage didn't last very long. I was the one to be envied, I told myself. I was the one who, one day soon, would have it all.

Chapter 18

I sat in front of my dressing-table mirror and outlined my lips with Rouge Absolut lip colour by drawing a neat line around the contours of my mouth. I blew myself a kiss, then filled in my lips with deep red gloss. I loved red lipstick, it was daring and looked well with my colouring. I leaned my head forward and shook my hair so that it fell in a cloud of copper around my face. Over the last few years the colour had lightened; it was more red-gold than pure carrot now and I liked it. For the first time in my life, my natural riot of curls was fashionable and I luxuriated in the feeling of not having to spend hours in a hair salon to make it look right.

I took the cream knitted suit out of the wardrobe. I'd spent a fortune on it, far more than I should have. It was, after all, a maternity dress. I felt good in it. Not (obviously) thin, but just a little bit sexy. It was so long since I'd felt desirable that it was worth paying the money for that feeling alone.

It was a pity that Rory couldn't be here to see me like this. He'd put up with me dossing around the house in tracksuits and sweatshirts for months. A pity he couldn't see me looking feminine and alluring now.

He'd gone to New York, a sudden crisis, nobody else could go. I had been incandescent with rage.

'Surely there must be somebody!' I yelled at him. 'You're not indispensable. What would they do if you dropped dead?'

'That's a completely different scenario, Jane, and you know it,' he snapped. 'I have to go. It's my job.'

I cried and sniffled until my face had gone blotchy and I'd given myself an attack of hiccoughs.

'Here.' Rory gave me a glass of water. 'Drink this.'

I drank the water and set the glass down on the coffee table.

'It's a terrible time for you to be away,' I said. 'The worst.'

'Jane, the baby isn't due until the end of September. You'll probably be late anyway and I'm only going to be away for four days – at the absolute most. If I could get out of it, I would, believe me, but I can't.'

'It's not the baby!' I retorted. 'You'll be in plenty of time for the baby. It's Lucy's wedding!'

Rory grimaced. 'I'm very sorry about Lucy's wedding,' he admitted. 'I truly would like to go, I know she's your best friend. But I can't, Jane. I just can't.'

I sat in the corner of the room and sulked for almost a day. How could Rory be away for Lucy's wedding? How could he leave me alone on such a day?

Lucy had rung me three weeks after our dinner date. 'Guess what?' she said.

'What?' I was fed up with Lucy because she hadn't phoned sooner.

'You'll never guess,' she said, a thrill of excitement in her voice.

'If I'll never guess, you'd better tell me.' I was annoyed at myself for sounding so ratty. I resolved never to get pregnant again. It didn't suit me at all. I was getting more and more cranky with every passing day.

'David and I are going to get married.'

'Lucy!' I dropped the potted plant I'd been holding. 'You're joking.'

'Why should I be joking?' she demanded.

There was no reason why she should be joking. I was simply stunned at the news. I couldn't believe that she was finally getting married. And to David. Whom she had known only for a few months!

'When?' I asked, wondering whether I would have regained my figure for the big day. Probably if I did all of those exercises, religiously, I could manage.

Lucy cleared her throat. 'The end of August,' she said. 'It was the soonest we could get.'

'Lucy!'

'What's the point in delaying it?' she demanded. 'We both know we're doing the right thing, we both want it, and there's no need for us to wait. Anyway, I don't want to wait. This is it, Jane! This is the one, I know it.'

'I'm delighted, Lucy.' I sounded half-hearted and I knew it. What was the matter with me? I should be delighted for my best friend. I should be pleased for her.

'You sound pissed off,' she complained. 'I thought you'd be pleased for me, Jane.'

'Lucy,' I said firmly, 'I am truly, completely, absolutely thrilled for you. You've just given me a shock and, in my condition, I have to be careful of shocks!' I laughed to prove I was joking.

'That's all right, then.' She sounded relieved. 'I thought you might give me grief. I've already had that from Mam.'

'Doesn't she approve?' I asked curiously. I would have thought that Mrs McAllister would be only too pleased to get Lucy finally married. She had moaned at her daughter about it often enough.

'It's not that she doesn't approve of the marriage, she doesn't approve of the speed,' explained Lucy.

'She'll get over it,' I said confidently. 'But didn't you have to give loads of notice to get married?'

'He asked me the first week we met,' she said. 'And I said yes and we went to the priest straight away.'

'Why didn't you tell me?' I asked.

'Because I was afraid that we were moving too quickly,' she answered. 'I didn't want to tell anyone until we were going out for more than seven days.'

A week! She had agreed to marry him after only a week. How could she have been sure? I hoped she wasn't making a terrible mistake but I kept my thoughts to myself.

'Joan and Emily will be my bridesmaids,' she said. 'I'd love to ask you, Jane, but they'd be disappointed if I didn't have them.'

I expected Lucy's sisters to be bridesmaids and I said so. Besides, I would have looked like a battleship staggering down the aisle behind her.

'Where are you going to get your dress?' I asked.

'I was hoping the twins might make it,' she said. 'I haven't asked them yet and I know it's not what they usually do, but maybe they wouldn't mind. I'm going to drop down to *Les Jumelles* today and check them out. I didn't want to go without telling you.'

'Thanks,' I said.

'Jane, isn't it wonderful to be completely in love?' Lucy was on a cloud of happiness. 'Isn't it the most perfect thing?'

I wondered if she thought it would be perfect when her husband expected her to clean the ring around the bath after he had used it. I chided myself for being so cynical. Honestly, I told myself crossly, you can't see the good side of anything.

I was miserable when Rory said he'd be away for the wedding. I drove him to the airport the night before but I didn't bother to go into the terminal building with him. It was totally unlike me. I knew that he was annoyed and I drove home feeling fragile and unsure of myself. I tried to convince myself that I was over-reacting and that everything would be all right when the baby was born.

But for some reason I sat in front of the TV that night and cried my eyes out, even though *Cheers* was hilarious.

I felt better the next morning. I'd had an amazingly good night's sleep, probably because I could roll all over the bed. I woke up feeling refreshed and looking forward to the wedding.

The twins were driving me to the church. I was ready by two, pleased with how I looked and glad that the day was almost warm, though hazy. I looked through photographs of my own wedding day while I waited for them to arrive. I'd changed a lot since then, I thought. I'd looked so young, so innocent.

Innocent my foot, I remembered. There I was in snowy virginal white and I had been having the most erotic sex with Rory. Maybe that was what was wrong with me now; our sex life had dwindled impossibly in the last three months. I'd lost interest in it, and I was terrified that Rory had lost interest in me, because he never pestered me about it.

Oh well, only a few weeks to go. Please God, I prayed, let me be on time. The idea of going a couple of weeks overdue was too awful to contemplate.

The Polo van emblazoned with *Les Jumelles* pulled up outside the house and the twins emerged wearing their latest outfits, the power shoulders, nipped waists and vibrant colours of Versace.

'We've only taken one or two of his lines,' explained Grace. 'But we thought these would be ideal.'

'You look great,' I told them. 'I thought you'd be wearing something of your own.'

'If we'd had time,' Grace said. 'But we didn't have anything spectacular lined up and Lucy wanted us to do the wedding dress and bridesmaids' dresses. She didn't give us an awful lot of notice, you know.'

I hadn't seen Lucy's dress yet. I hadn't wanted to see it in advance.

'I'll bet she looks lovely,' I said.

'Lucy is the one person I know that grew up to be more beautiful than she was at school,' commented Brenda. 'She was pretty then, but too cute. She always looked five years younger than she actually was. But now she's really lovely.'

I half-hoped she'd say something complimentary about me, but she didn't. Fortunately Grace told me that my dress looked great.

'Thanks,' I said. 'I got it in BTs. It cost a fortune.'

'Worth every penny,' said Grace. 'Clothes are so important.'

I knew exactly what she meant. The right clothes were like a key to unlock your inner self. Wearing the right thing made you feel confident, wearing the wrong outfit left you unsure. I was confident as we arrived at the church to wait for Lucy.

St David's Church was built on land that had once belonged to the religious Brothers who had built the boys' school. It was one of the early modern churches, erected a few years after Riverview Estate, to cater for the ever-increasing population. It was low and round, rather like a squat cake. I hadn't been in the church since the Christmas after my wedding. It was still the same. It smelt of beeswax and candles and the lingering traces of incense.

Lucy had arranged little floral bouquets at the end of every pew, peach and white posies of carnations. The altar was decked out in peach and white too – it was Lucy's favourite colour combination.

I remembered walking up this aisle myself. The trouble with weddings, any wedding, is that it reminds you of every other one you've ever been to and it reminds you of your own. I wished fiercely that Rory was with me now and that I could slip my hand into his while the two of us remembered, together.

The congregation murmured. The sun shone through the stained-glass windows, scattering coloured light over us. A purple shaft fell on the end of my dress, illuminating it. The organist played softly, background hymns, until suddenly there was a flurry at the back of the church and Lucy began her walk.

I turned to look at her as she approached. She held her father's arm, staring straight ahead, dignified and aloof. Her golden hair was twisted high on to her head, and fell in soft tendrils around her face, which was hidden by the short veil. A diamond band in her hair glittered with a thousand different colours. The dress that the twins had designed was raw silk, slightly off-white, tight at the bodice and flared into a tulip shape in the skirt. She was stunning. Tears of happiness for her welled up in my eyes. Why do I always cry at weddings? I asked myself, surreptitiously fumbling in my sleeve for a tissue. Grace handed me one as a tear rolled down her cheek too.

The wedding Mass started. Grace, Brenda and I were to say the Prayers of the Faithful. I hoped I could say my prayer without stumbling. I felt very diffident about being in the church since I didn't go to Mass any more. But I was happy to stand up and pray that Lucy and David would have a long and happy life together.

Lucy winked at me as I stepped down from the altar and I had to stifle a giggle. It was like being at school again, when the nuns sat in the congregation and watched us as we prayed. We'd pass the time by whispering jokes to each other. We tried to get somebody caught laughing by Sister Elizabeth, which meant a tongue-lashing in the head nun's office afterwards.

Mrs McAllister and Mrs Norris brought up the offertory gifts. I looked at David's mother with interest. A short, plump woman with a round face. David looked rather like her and I wondered if he would end up a fat little barrel of a man. Don't be horrible, I told myself. He looked great now – black tie suited him.

Then the ceremony was over. The organist swept into *The Wedding March* and Lucy and David strode down the aisle together, smiling broadly. I cried again, of course, but then nearly all of the women were sniffling. We couldn't help it, it was in our nature.

'We cry because we know what she'll have to put up with,' said Valerie, David's sister, who was married with three children. I liked Valerie, who was a cheerful no-nonsense sort of person.

'You're very cynical,' I told her, and she said rubbish, she was being practical.

'Doesn't Lucy look absolutely heavenly?' said Mam. 'I must go and talk to Mrs McAllister. I do like her hat.'

I thought it was terrible myself – a pink and white fondant creation – but parents have different views on appropriate wedding dress.

The reception was in a marquee in the Norris family home, which was in Stillorgan. The wedding was being held at such short notice that Lucy and David hadn't been able to book a hotel they liked. So Lucy had ordered me to ring Karen Hamilton and get Louise Killane's number. Lucy phoned her to see if she could organise the catering. Louise was delighted. Her company, 'Celebration Cuisine', specialised in weddings, she told Lucy. And she'd be delighted to offer a special discount to an old friend.

The photographer tried to organise us for a group photo. I seized the opportunity to talk to Lucy, went over to her and hugged her. 'You look fantastic.'

'Thanks, Jane. Isn't it great?' She beamed at me. She was having a wonderful time.

'I'll talk to you later,' I said and melted back into the crowd.

It took about half an hour before we left the church grounds. The priests of St David's never let confetti be used outside the church, so we'd brought rose petals and flung them over the happy couple. Stray petals lay on the tarmac, splashes of pink and yellow against severe black.

Although the Norris family home was relatively small, its corner site meant that the garden was about three times the size of its neighbours'. I'd wondered how a marquee could possibly fit into a suburban garden, but there was plenty of room. The red-and-white striped tent took up most of the lawn. A red-and-white striped canopy linked the tent to the house. The only big problem was the mad queue for the loo when we all arrived. Women clustered around the bathroom door in various degrees of need, but thankfully they let me go first.

Only thirty people had been invited for the meal, and they were close family and a very few friends. The twins and I were Lucy's only guests. David had invited a couple of fellow architects but that was all.

Two long trestle tables were set up for the guests, at right angles to the main table. Louise had done great work. The tablecloths were shining white, decorated with fresh flowers and thin swirls of silver and gold ribbon. The cake stood on the top table, not a traditional wedding cake, which Lucy didn't like, but a huge chocolate *Sachertorte* gleaming with rich chocolate icing.

Classical music wafted from the CD player discreetly positioned in the corner of the tent.

Louise had excelled herself with the food: little smoked salmon parcels to start with, arranged temptingly on a bed of iceberg lettuce and topped with a sprinkling of dill; carrot soup (thank God she'd given green soup a miss) served with the most delicious white crusty bread, still warm so that the butter melted into it; lemon chicken for the main course, delicately flavoured with a hint of tarragon, and finally, for dessert, a pyramid of profiteroles and cream.

It was the best wedding meal I'd ever tasted and the most food I'd eaten at one go in months. Thank God, I thought, that the knitted suit was a dress and jacket and that I didn't have to cope with the waistband of a skirt.

I watched Lucy during the meal. Her face shone with happiness and she looked completely at ease. I hoped that she would be very happy with David. He looked very content sitting beside her. He smiled and joked, but always turned back to her, checking on her, completely devoted to her. Did Rory ever look at me like that, I wondered. Somehow, I didn't think he ever had the time to look like that any more, eyes soft and caring. Rory was in too much of a hurry.

I asked him, sometimes, of course. 'Do you love me?' I'd say, gazing at him, and he would reply, with a hint of exasperation, 'Don't be stupid.'

Then I would ask again and he'd tell me that of course he loved me, and could we get back to watching TV or we'd miss the best part of the movie?

The passion would come back, I promised myself. After the baby.

'Finished?'

I looked up at Louise and nodded. She took the empty plate away from me.

'Wasn't that a fantastic feed?' said Grace. 'I didn't realise that Louise was so talented.'

'Neither did I. I didn't exactly do her food justice the last time I ate it,' I said. 'And to set up the company herself. I never thought she had it in her.'

'Goes to show,' laughed Grace. 'St Attracta's girls – lots of get up and go.'

Grace was right about St Attracta's girls. The twins were becoming more and more successful and Lucy had led a very varied working life. Her present job was earning her a staggering salary which shocked me when she told me. Louise's catering company was obviously thriving. And me – well, I had a good job too, I supposed, and a successful husband. But, as I looked at the others, I wished I'd done a bit more with my life. That I hadn't rushed into marrying Rory. Not because I didn't love him, but because being married to him was such hard work.

I got up from my seat and made my way to the bathroom. I locked myself inside and sat on the edge of the bath. I was worried about myself and the way I always seemed to criticise my own life. In my childhood, Mam would have slapped me across the back of the legs and told me to go out and play if I got into a mood like this. Mam didn't have time for introspection.

I redid my make-up and went back to the marquee. They had begun the speeches. Mr McAllister welcomed David into the family.

David's own speech was short and eloquent. He told us that he had known the very moment he had met Lucy, that very first second when she had, he said, thrown a ceramic tile at him, that they were meant to be together. She captivated him in that instant and he would remain captivated for the rest of his life.

Lucy blushed but we could see the pleasure in her face. Mrs McAllister beamed at her new son-in-law.

The speeches over, we went to the bar which had been set up in the conservatory at the side of the house. The evening was warmer than the day had been; the sun suddenly broke through the layer of cloud that had covered the sky earlier. People murmured in pleasure at the warmth of the conservatory and crushed together to get their drinks.

'Hello, Jane.' Michael McAllister bumped into me.

'Michael, how are you?'

He smiled. 'Great. And you? No need to ask, I suppose.'

I looked down at my stomach and made a face. 'Getting bigger every day.'

'When are you due?'

'Three and a half weeks,' I said, 'they think. I can't wait for this to end.'

He nodded. 'Ulrike was overdue with our first,' he told me. 'We thought young Karl would never make his appearance. But she was exactly on time with Helena.'

'I'd like to be early rather than late,' I commented. 'But every-body is different. Is this Karl?'

A small boy who looked irritated at being dressed in a pair of green velvet shorts and green velvet jacket tugged at Michael. He was an attractive child, fair, like both his parents, with Lucy's clear complexion.

'Dad, can I wear my jeans now?' he asked.

'No,' said Michael.

'Why?'

'Because I said so.'

Karl wandered off, scuffing his feet along the ground.

'You do your best,' sighed Michael. 'But they never appreciate it. I'd better find Ulrike, he's going to give her hell.'

She deserves it, I thought, dressing up the poor boy in a velvet suit. He probably felt a right idiot.

I met Louise and apologised to her in person for my awful behaviour at Karen's dinner party. Louise laughed it off, although she admitted that she had nearly thrown up herself when she realised that one of the guests had puked all over the living-room floor.

'Green soup,' I told her. 'Never serve green soup.'

She laughed with me and said that it was popular. 'But if I ever do any catering for you, I'll remember.'

Eventually I got talking to Lucy, who had been flitting around her guests like a butterfly.

'I hope you're really happy,' I said. 'You're having a great day, anyway.'

'Thanks, Jane. It's good fun, isn't it? I'm sorry Rory couldn't make it.'

'So am I,' I said dolefully. 'It's not quite the same being at a wedding on your own. He's sorry to miss it. He told me to give you a kiss for him, but I think I'll pass that message on to David.'

'Don't you think I'm incredibly lucky?' asked Lucy. 'I mean, isn't he perfect?'

I grinned at her. 'Perfect,' I said seriously.

'We'll stay close friends,' said Lucy. 'Both of us being married won't change that.'

'Of course it won't.' I was shocked at the thought.

'Good,' she said. 'Look, I'd better go and talk to Aunt Marjorie. She gets fidgety if she's left on her own.'

I glanced at my watch. Nearly seven. People would soon arrive for the evening entertainment. My parents, who hadn't come to the meal, would be along. A friend of David's was DJ for the night – Lucy promised that he was good. I wondered if Rory would be available if I rang the New York office. I desperately wanted to speak to him. I saw Mrs Norris, and asked her if I could make the call. I'd pay her, I assured her. David's mother told me I could call Australia, if I wanted. She was too happy to care. There was an extension in the bedroom, if I wanted some privacy.

I dialled the number of the bank.

'Dealers.' The voice sounded as though it could be in the next room.

'Could I speak to Rory McLoughlin?' I asked.

'Hold the line a moment.'

Thirty seconds ticked away before he came to the phone. I watched the second hand sweep across the face of the clock.

'McLoughlin.'

'Hi,' I said.

'Jane? Are you all right?' I was glad to hear the concern in his voice.

'Of course I'm all right,' I said. 'I simply thought I'd give you a call to say hello.'

'Jane, this is not a good time. I'm very busy.'

I bit my lip. 'I'm sorry,' I said. 'It's just that I miss you.'

I could hear the sigh coming across the Atlantic. 'And I you,' he said perfunctorily. 'But I'm up to my neck, Jane.'

'I won't delay you. I'll see you soon.'

'Jane – Jane, take care of yourself.'

'Yeah, sure.'

I replaced the receiver. In the middle of all the romance, Rory's distracted indifference was hard to take.

David's friend was a good DJ. He played a lot of old seventies numbers, especially for Lucy and David, he said. To recapture their youth. It was strange to think that some of the songs which were so fresh in my mind were now over ten years old. It didn't seem that long since we were dancing to them in the cricket club.

I wished he'd stop playing ballads. Something with a bit of go in it would be better. He'd depress us all if he stuck with the sad songs. They were just an excuse for David and Lucy to hold each other tightly in the middle of the dance floor.

My parents arrived and waved at me from the opposite side of the tent.

Emily McAllister, Lucy's twenty-three-year-old sister, looking almost as lovely as Lucy in her peaches-and-cream bridesmaid's dress, danced with David's brother, the best man. They gazed into each other's eyes. What were the odds, I wondered, on another sister marrying into the Norris family?

Mrs McAllister took off her hat and left it on a chair. I couldn't see it lasting the night.

Mr McAllister danced with his other daughter, Joan.

Michael and Ulrike danced with their children.

The DJ speeded up the music and the floor was crammed with people. I wished I could dance, but I didn't have the energy.

Lucy took off her veil. Her hair had begun to come down but she didn't care.

The tent was very warm and the air was stuffy. The smell of the canvas was very strong. I went outside and walked in the night air for a while, sipping my orange juice. After my baby was born, I was never going to drink orange juice again.

'What are you doing out here?' David Norris came around behind the marquee. I almost spilled my drink.

'Having a break,' I told him. 'It's so warm in there.'

'Lucy couldn't see you and she was worried that you mightn't be feeling well,' he explained.

'I'm fine,' I said. 'A little bit tired, that's all. It's been a super day.'

'Hasn't it?' He smiled at me. 'Thanks for your present, by the way.'

'It was nothing.' We'd bought them a video-player. Rory got it at a discount from one of his clients.

'Coming back inside?' asked David.

'In a few minutes,' I said. 'I'm fine, David, really.'

It was peaceful in the garden. When we moved house, I was going to tell Rory I wanted one with a huge garden like this. Without the marquee taking up so much space, it would have been fantastic. Probably need a lot of looking after, I supposed, but worth it in the end.

Jane O'Sullivan, I thought, how middle-aged. Thinking about gardens. You're only in your twenties. I still called myself by my maiden name when I talked to myself – it came more naturally.

I went back inside the tent. The atmosphere had hotted up, the dancing was more frantic and it was extremely warm. I took off the knitted jacket and sat down on one of the folding chairs.

The music was Glenn Miller and my parents were jiving. I shook my head at them in amusement. Mam had always been a great dancer.

David's brother was dancing with Joan. Brenda and Grace were talking about fabrics. Lucy was dancing with Mr Norris.

I wanted to dance myself. I would, for the last dance.

'Come on, Jane, a quick one for the girls!'

Lucy pulled us on to the dance floor, Brenda, Grace and myself. We stood together, like old times.

We sang together, holding hands high above the crowd. We hugged each other again.

'Got to go and change,' murmured Lucy.

They were going to Crete for their honeymoon, leaving in the morning. They'd refused to say where they were spending the night but we guessed they were going to the airport hotel. The flight was at eight in the morning and, as Lucy was not a morning person, she'd like to be as near as possible to the airport.

She returned wearing an ecru linen jacket over a pair of red culottes. She had taken down her hair and had tied it back into a ponytail. She looked about fifteen.

'So let's make a tunnel of love for the happy couple!' cried the DJ.

We formed an archway with our arms and Lucy and David ran under it while the DJ played *Congratulations!* over and over again. When they reached the end, Lucy turned and threw her bouquet into the crowd. If I hadn't jumped out of the way, I would have caught it. As it was, Emily pounced on it, squealing with pleasure.

Lucy and David disappeared. The marquee buzzed with animated conversation.

I was chatting to Brenda when a white-hot pain seared through me. She didn't notice anything, she was still laughing about some incident. I could feel the tent revolve around me and then the pain hit me again, as though someone was driving a skewer through me. I grabbed my stomach and gasped. In slow motion, I could see Brenda stare at me in horror. The pain ripped through me again and I think I screamed. I looked down and saw that my beautiful cream knitted dress was stained bright red with blood. I sank slowly, agonisingly, to the floor.

Chapter 19

September 1986
(US No. 4 – *Take My Breath Away* – Berlin)

I heard the siren of the ambulance as it raced up the road. The sound broke through the fog that surrounded my brain. Other guests at the wedding had gathered around me, then Mam rushed to me and I felt her cradling my head in her arms, murmuring words of comfort to me. The pain cleaved its way through me, hot and sharp.

I was afraid. Afraid for me and afraid for my baby. Strange how I'd regarded it as something of an encumbrance but now, when I knew that I might lose it, I felt closer to it than ever. I tried to communicate with the baby, to say that it would be all right, that I would stay alive, that we would both survive. But with every stab of pain I felt even more terrified.

The ambulance men got me on to a stretcher and into the vehicle more quickly than I would have believed possible. Mam climbed into the ambulance with them. I closed my eyes. My breath echoed around my head, rasping in my ears. I tried to regulate my heartbeat, to calm myself, to do my breathing exercises. I wondered whether those damned breathing exercises helped when you were losing your baby.

I didn't want to lose it. I didn't want to die.

They were ready for me at the hospital and rushed me through the corridors to the theatre, where Mr Murphy was waiting.

I opened my eyes to see him standing over me.

'Hello, Jane,' he said gently. 'Things not going exactly to plan, are they? But don't worry. You'll be fine.'

'My baby,' I croaked.

'Don't worry about your baby, Jane. We'll look after your baby.'

'I don't want to lose my baby,' I said as I tried to focus on him. 'Make my baby be OK.'

'We'll look after you,' he repeated as he moved away from me.

I stared upwards. The blinding white lights of the theatre made my eyes water.

'You'll just feel this for a moment.' The doctor injected me. My eyes blurred. I knew that he was there, I could sense him but I couldn't see him. I had to stay awake to protect my baby. It was important to stay awake.

'This is my daughter.'
  'What a beautiful girl.'
  'Yes, isn't she?'
  'So pretty.'
  'And talented. She's top of her class in school, you know.'
  'Really?'
  'Oh, yes. Very clever.'
  Then the teacher came over to us.
  'Get away from that child.'
  'But she's my daughter.'
  'She's not your daughter. She's Mrs Norris's daughter.'
  'Lucy's child. No. She's not Lucy's child.'
  'She's not your child.'
  'She is! She must be! She's my daughter.'
  I fought with them. I raised my hand as they tried to take her away from me and cried 'No!!'

My eyes snapped open. The wall in front of me was pastel pink. I thought I saw my mother's face leaning over me, but I wasn't certain. My eyes fluttered closed again.

Where was I? I couldn't remember exactly what had happened. The fragments were all over the place. Something had gone wrong but I couldn't remember . . . I opened my eyes again. I remembered, now.

'How are you, Jane?' Mam's face, clouded with anxiety, looked into mine again.

'I think I'm all right,' I said. Then, with trepidation, 'My baby.'

'She's fine.' Mam's eyes were full of tears. 'She's beautiful.'

'Where is she?'

'They have her in an incubator at the moment,' Mam said. 'But they don't think she'll be there for long. She's lovely.'

'What happened?' I looked at her in bewilderment. 'What went wrong?'

'Your placenta started to come away,' said Mam. 'There was no reason. It happens sometimes – one in a hundred and twenty births, Mr Murphy told me. You were lucky, we got you to the hospital really quickly.'

'Good,' I said, and fell asleep.

It was bright when I woke up again. Mam was dozing in the chair beside me. I moved my arm and the drip dragged. I lay still, trying to assess the damage to my body. My stomach ached. It was strange not to feel the baby inside. My baby was born, it was somewhere in the hospital. No, *she* was somewhere in the hospital. I remembered Mam saying that 'she' was all right.

I cleared my throat. Mam jerked into wakefulness. I smiled at her.

'How are you feeling now?' she asked.

'I'm OK,' I said, more strongly. 'I think I'm OK.'

She got up and kissed me. 'I'll get a nurse,' she said.

I didn't care about me. I only wanted to know about my baby.

'Your daughter is still in the incubator,' said Mr Murphy. 'But not for long. You'll be able to see her soon. You're doing well.'

'Has anybody called Rory?' I asked suddenly. 'Does he know?'

'We phoned him last night,' said Mam. 'He'll be here later.'

I wanted to see my husband and I wanted to see my baby. I didn't feel as though I'd had a baby. I wasn't sure she really existed.

They took me down to the IC unit after a while. I looked at her, in the Perspex container and I wanted to reach in and take her in my arms. She looked so tiny and so vulnerable, although actually she was pretty big for a premature baby. The nurses said it was just as well she'd come early. She would have been huge, otherwise.

Rory arrived that night, looking dishevelled and with stubble on his face. He burst into my room, startling me.

'Jane!' He put his arm around me. 'Jane, I'm so sorry I wasn't here. Are you OK?'

236

I nodded.

'What happened?' asked Rory.

'You don't want to know. Something to do with my placenta. It's too horrible to think about.'

'Were you doing anything to cause a problem?'

'Of course not.' I shook my head. 'One minute I was fine – dancing with the girls – the next—'

'Dancing! Jane, really!'

'I wasn't doing anything very energetic,' I protested. 'It couldn't have been the dancing.'

'I'm going to find a doctor and ask exactly what happened,' said Rory. 'They should have warned you.'

'It doesn't matter,' I said. 'Not now.'

'Of course it matters.' Rory walked around my bed. 'Look at you!'

'I'm OK now,' I said, trying to placate him. I was feeling tired. I was fed up having the drip attached to me, my arm was sore and so was my stomach. I was afraid to look at my stomach because apparently they staple you back together after a Caesarean and I wasn't sure I could cope with staples.

'Have you seen our baby yet?' I moved gingerly in the bed.

He shook his head. 'I came straight here.'

'Ask one of the nurses to take you to Intensive Care,' I told him. 'She's lovely, Rory.'

When he came back, he was beaming all over his face. 'She's gorgeous!' he exclaimed. 'A beautiful baby.' He put his arm around me. 'You're a clever girl.'

Clever wasn't exactly the word I would use. I'd nearly ruined Lucy's wedding. They had delayed their flight until the following day to be sure that I was all right. Lucy had phoned her mother the next morning and Mrs McAllister had told her about me. I was annoyed with Mrs McAllister, she should have let Lucy go on her honeymoon without fussing. The delay meant that they had to fly to London and then to Crete. They'd sent me a huge congratulations card from the airport.

Rory and I fell asleep together, he in the chair, holding my hand. I felt closer to him than I had for ages.

They brought my daughter to me the following day and I took her in my arms for the first time. She was so tiny, I thought, and so wonderful. I looked at her smooth, soft skin, her blue eyes and the covering of downy red-gold hair. I picked up her tiny hands, with their perfect fingers. It was hard to believe that I'd once been this small myself.

We hadn't decided on a name. We'd thrown a few around but hadn't yet found one that we both liked. Then, as I looked at her, one of them came back to me. Clodagh. My daughter Clodagh.

I told Rory when he came in later that day. He made a face at first but then walked around the room saying 'Clodagh McLoughlin' over and over until he proclaimed himself happy with it.

'How would you like Eleanor as a second name?' he asked.

'You must be joking,' I said.

Eleanor and Peter came in that evening to see me. I could tell that Eleanor thought I was totally inadequate. Her own daughter, Sandra, had produced three perfectly healthy children without any problems whatsoever. Three eight-pounders, all born after short labours.

Eleanor peeped into the crib beside me, and sniffed.

'She'll be a carrot-top like you,' she said.

'I know.' I wasn't going to let Eleanor upset me.

Peter pulled back the blanket a little. 'She's a dote,' he said, and I smiled at him.

They sat uncomfortably in the room, unable to think of anything to say but not willing to leave. I would have made conversation but I couldn't think of anything to say either.

'That the mother-in-law?' asked one of the nurses, after they left. I nodded. 'You can always tell the mothers-in-law,' she said as she took my temperature.

Rory looked uncomfortable when he came in the next day. He brought me a selection of magazines, the knitting I'd been attempting, and my Walkman.

'Hope that's enough to keep you occupied,' he said.

I was occupied enough, I told him. There were so many things I could do besides simply lie there. I had to learn how to bath my baby, how to change her, how to feed her. I hadn't got the hang of feeding her yet. Then there were 'parenting' classes. I would go to one tomorrow; right now I was still confined to bed.

'Wish I was in bed,' said Rory, robbing a grape from the bunch Eleanor had left me.

'How are you getting on at home?' I asked.

He shifted uneasily in the seat. 'Fine,' he said. His tone was unconvincing.

'What's the matter?' I asked. I knew that there was something wrong, something he didn't want to tell me.

'I've got to go back to the States,' he said. 'I'm sorry, Jane. I'll be home in a couple of days.'

I looked at him in horror. 'You can't do that!' I exclaimed. 'What about us?' Clodagh lay in her crib, totally unconcerned.

'I'll be back before you're out,' said Rory. 'It is, literally, a couple of days. The nurses said you'd be here until the weekend.'

I could feel myself want to cry. 'But, Rory,' I wailed. 'You'll be leaving us on our own.'

'Hardly on your own,' said my husband. 'Be reasonable, Jane. You're in a hospital with hundreds of other people. This is probably the best time for me to go to New York.'

He had a point but I didn't want to concede it.

'It's not fair,' I grumbled. 'Everyone else will have husbands visiting them every day and I'll be on my own.'

'Don't be silly,' he said. 'Your mother is in every day. Your aunts are in every day, I met Grace and Brenda Quinlan as I arrived. You're hardly on your own.'

'It's not the same,' I said mutinously.

We were silent. Clodagh sighed deeply and Rory went over to peer in at her. He stroked the side of her cheek. He loved the baby, I could see that. His eyes crinkled into tenderness whenever he looked at her. Suddenly I felt selfish and mean. It wasn't his fault he had to go to the States. Probably he would have preferred to be at home. I was only making things harder for him.

'I'm sorry,' I said. 'Of course you must go.'

He sat on the edge of the bed and kissed me on the forehead. 'I don't want to, Jane, you must understand that. I'd much prefer to be at home lounging in front of the TV.'

'I know,' I said, although Rory hardly ever lounged in front of the TV. 'When would you fly out?'

'Tonight,' he said. 'I'll be back by Friday, Jane. Honestly.'

He looked like a child, begging me.

'All right, all right,' I smiled. 'I believe you.'

'You're a wonderful wife,' he murmured. 'And I'm very proud of you.'

I was proud of myself. Not many women would be as understanding as me, I thought later as I flicked through *Cosmopolitan*. We had a truly adult marriage. I didn't need Rory beside me every moment of the day to know that he loved me.

All the same, Mam and Dad were horrified that he had to go away. Mam thought it was dreadful and that he should have told the bank that he couldn't go. I made the point that it was as well he went now, that at least I was in hospital being looked after. Better now, in fact, than next week when I was at home. Besides, he was going to get time off next week.

Dad didn't say anything, but he looked worried all the same. I wished that people would stop looking at me as though I was some piece of china that would break. I was fine now, the doctors all said so.

But I was miserable the next day. It was very lonely knowing that Rory was in the States, that no one would be coming in to see me until later, and that my stomach felt as though it had been trampled on by a herd of wild buffalo.

I lay back on my pillows and tried to read my magazine, but I was tired, and sore and fed up. I couldn't even pick up my baby because I still couldn't move properly and I didn't have the strength to take her out of her crib. I felt absolutely hopeless. I closed my eyes and a tear trickled down my cheek.

'How is my most favourite girl in the whole world?' The door to my room burst open and I opened my eyes in surprise, scuffling underneath my pillows for a tissue to dry them.

All I could see was a huge flower arrangement hiding the man who carried it.

'Sorry I couldn't get in earlier, but I only got back to Dublin today. How are you feeling?'

The flower arrangement moved towards the shelf and I watched it with interest. He put the bouquet down and looked at me.

'Oh, my God!' he said. 'I'm terribly sorry. I've got the wrong person.'

He was tall and thin. He looked underfed. His soft brown hair was unfashionably long, tousled and unkempt. His eyes were brown too, huge in his lean face. He wore faded denim jeans and a lumberjack shirt. He looked shocked.

'Who were you looking for?' I asked, horribly aware that my cheeks were streaked with tears. Maybe he wouldn't notice, I thought; probably women who had just given birth cried all the time anyway. He'd think, hopefully, that they were tears of joy.

'My sister,' he said falteringly. 'I thought she was in here.' He broke off to look at me intently. 'Have you been crying?' he asked. 'Have I butted in at an awful time?'

I shook my head. 'No, no, I'm fine,' I said, wiping under my eyes. 'Absolutely fine. No problems at all. Everything's fine.'

'That's good,' he said uneasily. 'I thought maybe you weren't fine. It happens, doesn't it? Sometimes you think it's going to be the best experience of your life, and of course it's not!'

'It *was* the best experience of my life,' I said firmly.

'Really?' he asked. 'I always thought it was very painful.'

I smiled faintly. 'I don't know, exactly. They knocked me out.'

'The best way,' he told me. 'Great idea.'

'Not in tune with modern thought,' I said. 'Not in tune with the birth experience.'

He laughed. He had a rich, resonant laugh which seemed to come from deep within him.

Clodagh started to whimper.

'Oh Lord,' he said contritely. 'I've woken your baby. I'm terribly sorry.'

'Do you think you could hand her over to me?' I asked. 'It's just that I can't actually get out of bed yet.'

'Of course,' he said. 'Don't worry.'

As he walked to the crib, I was filled with a sudden sense of foreboding. What if he was one of those people who try to kidnap babies? If he took my baby and ran out of the room, would anyone be able to stop him? Would anyone notice? My heart raced fearfully as he bent to pick up Clodagh.

'What a gorgeous baby,' he breathed as he lifted her carefully in his arms. 'Isn't she wonderful?'

'I think so,' I said. 'Can you give her to me, please?'

He handed my baby to me, nestling her carefully into my arms.

Clodagh pursed her lips and opened her clear, blue eyes, looking straight into mine.

'Hello,' I said. 'Howyah doing?'

She blinked at me and yawned.

'I'd better be going,' the man said. 'I'll leave you to it, shall I?'

I smiled at him. 'Thanks,' I told him. 'Don't forget your flowers.'

'Gosh, yes,' he said. 'There'd be war if I forgot the flowers.' He picked up the bouquet and took out a yellow rose.

'Here,' he said, proffering it to me. 'For you.'

I raised my eyebrows at him. 'For me?'

'Of course,' he said. 'For my intrusion. I'm sorry again.'

'No problem,' I said as I watched him walk out of the room. 'No problem at all.'

I got out of bed the next day and had a bath. The water seeped its way into every pore of my body, cleansing me. I felt a million times better after it. Mam had been to the house and had brought me more nighties and some make-up. I told her that I hardly intended getting made up in hospital, but she said it was for the day I left so that I'd look nice in the photographs.

I half expected Peter and Eleanor to show up together, but they didn't. Jessica called in though, her face clouded with concern. She cooed over baby Clodagh and asked probing questions about my health, which I dismissed. She told me to take every second of maternity leave that I could, and to take the month's unpaid leave I was entitled to as well.

Much to my surprise, Karen Hamilton also dropped in, looking radiantly beautiful in her lime-coloured Escada jacket over a Lagerfeld skirt. Rory would be pleased when I told him she'd called. He liked the idea of being good friends with the boss's wife. Karen told me to join a gym once I got out of hospital to get my figure back in shape. I didn't like to say that it had never actually been in shape in the first place.

'It's the only way,' she said as she flicked back her mane of black hair. 'Otherwise, you'll simply let yourself go. Those little wads of flesh won't disappear of their own accord. You have to work at it.'

I told her I would think about it and promptly forgot about her.

I was tired by the evening. Mam and Dad called in but I wasn't in the mood for casual conversation and they left after a short while. I could hear them talking to each other in low voices outside the room. I'm sure Mam was worried about me.

I wished so much that Rory was with me. It had seemed such an easy thing to say that it was all right if he went away, but I missed him hugely. This was a point in our lives when he should have been there. It wasn't fair. I hated his job.

There was a tap at the door, and a head poked around it. I looked up. It was the man from yesterday.

'Hi,' he said. 'Mind if I come in?'

'Not at all.' I was curious. What did he want?

'I thought I got you at a bad time yesterday and I wanted to see how you were today,' he said. 'Are you OK?'

'Why does everyone seem to think there's something wrong with me?' I exploded. 'I've had a baby! Millions of women have babies! Why should there be anything wrong?'

He shrugged, his brown eyes direct. 'No reason,' he said equably. 'I thought you were upset yesterday, that's all. And I wondered if there was anything I could do to help?'

'I really don't see that it's any of your business,' I said icily. 'If I want to burst into paroxysms of tears, then surely that is my prerogative.'

'Absolutely,' he said. 'Without a doubt. I'm terribly sorry – I seem to have made things worse. Janet says I do it all the time.'

'Janet?'

'My sister. The girl next door. She's always complaining that I keep putting my foot in it. I can't help it, it's my nature.'

He looked so hangdog and contrite that I couldn't help laughing.

'You didn't put your foot in it,' I said. 'You just got the wrong end of the stick.'

'Good.' He sat on the edge of the bed. 'How's the baby?'

'She's great,' I said enthusiastically. 'Feeding like a horse.'

'That's good.' He peeped in at her. 'Aren't they superb like that?' he asked. 'So tiny and dependent?' His voice softened. 'So much promise. They could grow up to be anything they choose.

'So.' He sat back on the bed again. 'Where's her dad?'

'That's a very impertinent question,' I said as I leaned back against my pillows. 'What business is it of yours?'

'None whatsoever,' he admitted cheerfully. 'I just wondered what Dad looked like.'

'Do you think I'm an unmarried mother or something?' I asked. My wedding and engagement rings were in the ashtray on the bedside locker.

'Not at all!' He looked surprised. 'I wouldn't have imagined you to be unmarried at all. Not that there's anything wrong with it if you are,' he added hastily.

'Her father is in New York,' I told him. 'He'll be back the day after tomorrow.'

'Good,' he said. 'Because I'm sure you wish he was here.'

'Of course I do,' I said. 'But he's very busy at work just now and he's taking next week off to look after us, so I can't exactly begrudge him two days away now.'

'I suppose not,' said the man, 'but I bet he hates to be away from you right now.'

'I know he does.' I looked him straight in the eye. He met my glare without flinching.

'Have you decided on a name for your baby yet?' he asked.

'Clodagh,' I said, and wondered as I did so why I was even bothering to talk to him.

'Lovely name,' he said. He glanced at his watch and exclaimed in horror. 'Look, I'd better be going. Got to see the sister. Take care of yourself.'

He disappeared as quickly as he had come and I shook my head. Maybe tomorrow I would knock on the door of the next room and see his sister, Janet. I wondered what his own name was, surprised we hadn't got around to such pleasantries yet. We seemed to have got around to so much else! Actually, although I pretended to be annoyed with him for dropping in, I was quite pleased to see him. It was great to talk to somebody different for a change and it was nice to have such an attractive man visit me. And he *was* attractive. In other circumstances, like if I wasn't married and hadn't just had a baby, I would have found him extremely attractive. I shook my head as I thought about him. I was losing my marbles.

When I peeped around the door of the next-door room the following day, his sister had already left. Gone home, the nurse told me – lovely girl, beautiful baby, easy delivery.

Easy delivery! While mine had been a disaster. I still couldn't rid myself of my feelings of inadequacy about Clodagh's birth.

Probably if it had all gone wrong at home, privately, I wouldn't have minded so much. But it had been so spectacular. I grew hot with embarrassment as I remembered keeling over at the wedding. All those people watching me. It was horrible.

He popped his head around the door again later that day.

'Your sister has gone home.' I looked up from my magazine.

'I know,' he told me, 'but I was driving by and I thought I'd see how you were.'

'There's nothing wrong with me,' I said impatiently. 'And I don't see why you have to keep calling in here. I don't even know who you are!'

'Oh!' He looked surprised. 'My name is Hugh McLean,' he said, as though that explained everything.

'Should it ring a bell?' I asked. 'Are you famous?'

'No.'

'Are you a doctor?' I suddenly realised that this could account for his turning up again at the hospital.

'No.'

'So why are you here?'

'I don't know.' He walked into the room. 'I know it's awfully cheeky of me but I'm interested in you.'

'How dare you!' I was really angry.

He flushed, the colour staining his lightly tanned cheeks. 'Not that sort of interested,' he said. 'Interested that you were OK. That's all.'

I looked at him carefully. 'It's a bit strange,' I said, 'don't you think? You wander in here by mistake and I can't get rid of you and now you tell me it's because you're interested in me. I find that terribly offensive.'

He didn't seem to be the sort of person to take offence. 'It sounds awful, doesn't it,' he agreed. 'But I was concerned.'

'Why?' I couldn't understand him.

'Because you were bawling your eyes out when I came in and I thought you might do something terrible.'

I put my head to one side. 'You mean – like I might top myself or something?'

He looked embarrassed. 'Something like that.'

I laughed, suddenly, the first real laugh in months. 'I'm not that sort of person.'

'That's a relief.' He did look relieved. As though he'd actually believed it.

'So you don't have to worry.'

'Good,' he said simply. 'Because I was worried.' He scratched his chin thoughtfully. 'Do you mind telling me why you were crying?'

His cheek was incredible.

'Of course I do,' I said. 'It was a private moment.'

'A sad private moment?'

'Look!' I exclaimed. 'Are you some kind of psychiatrist or something? Has somebody sent you in here to make a not-so-subtle appraisal of me? Does my family think I'm off my rocker?'

He bit his upper lip to stop smiling. 'No.'

'Well, do you mind telling me what bloody concern it is of yours whether I weep into a bucket, kill myself, or not?'

'I don't know,' he said.

I sighed. 'You're very kind,' I said. 'At least, I think you probably are. But really, none of this is any of your business. I was unhappy. And it was because my husband had to go away. That's all. But I'm going home on Friday, he'll be back to collect me and everything is going to be fine. So it's really decent of you to care but there's no need.'

He walked around the bed and looked out of the window at the jigsaw of rooftops and chimneys. He thrust his hands into the pockets of his jeans and turned to look at me.

'I don't know what came over me,' he said. 'I really don't. I've been dreadfully intrusive and I know, don't tell me, that you're probably very vulnerable right now.'

'I'm not a bit vulnerable,' I interrupted him.

'Oh.'

I grinned. 'Actually you have cheered me up immensely,' I said. 'So you can believe that you've done some good. Are you a trainee Samaritan or something?'

'No,' he said. 'Just an idiot.'

'Well, Idiot,' I said, 'thanks for looking out for me, but there really was no need. I'm miles better now.'

He exhaled deeply. 'Good.'

'So please don't feel the need to call in again. It's not a great idea. If you bump into any of my family they'll think I'm having an affair.'

He shook his head. 'I don't think so,' he said.

I laughed. 'Maybe not. Anyway, please don't call in again. I'm not at my best entertaining men when I've just given birth.'

'Nice seeing you, though,' he said, walking towards the door.

'And you,' I told him.

I thought about him after he had left. Such a strange person. Interesting, though. Why had he continued to call in and see me? Did he really think I might do something dreadful? I smiled inwardly at the thought. How could I even consider anything like that with the most beautiful baby in the world sleeping right beside me?

It was great having my own baby. A part of me, I could see that she was a part of me. I loved the way her eyes squeezed closed in sleep and the way she clenched her tiny fists. I loved the touch of her peachy soft skin and the silky feeling of her hair. I loved it when she nestled close to me. I loved her, completely and entirely.

Rory arrived home on Friday morning and came straight to the hospital from the airport. The week had been a bit chaotic. We hadn't expected Clodagh's arrival to be quite so sudden so we hadn't bought the cot and the pram and the car seat and the changing mat and all the other paraphernalia that babies need. Mam and Dad had done the running around, buying whatever we thought of.

I was ready now, though. I'd showered and washed my hair and had dressed in my favourite maternity trousers which didn't look too bad at all with a new white blouse worn over them. The blissful part was that they were now too big for me. There was buckets of room in them. Hah! I thought. Jane regains control of her body at last!

I used the make-up that Mam had brought in, carefully applied the foundation, the eyeshadow, the blusher and the lipstick. I clipped on my huge gold earrings and my bracelets, and I pulled my hair back from my head with a velvet ribbon. I was delighted at how I looked.

So was Rory. He'd been so used to my indifference about my appearance over the past few months that I must have seemed like a butterfly emerging from a chrysalis to him. He kissed me deeply on the lips, told me that he loved me and gave me a bottle of Dior's *Poison*.

I bundled blankets around our daughter, who looked like a doll in her pink sleeping-suit, and picked her up confidently. Already I'd grown used to her. I couldn't imagine what life would be like without her. In the last week, she had become much more a part of my life than she ever had when she was inside me.

She snuggled down into the blankets and closed her eyes tightly. She was so lovely, I almost cried again. But I'd made a resolution not to cry any more. It could be misconstrued.

One of the nurses took a photograph of us before we left. She told Rory that he had a wonderful wife and a beautiful daughter and Rory agreed with her as he put his arm around me.

I was glad to get home again. The house was my cradle, my comfort. I was happy to see my own bed, to have my own things around me again. I settled Clodagh into her Moses basket and made sure that she was well wrapped up. Then I went upstairs and threw all my washing into the laundry basket. Rory's suitcase was on the bed, but I hadn't the energy to unpack for him too. Anyway, I was absolutely dying for a cup of tea.

So I threw my own case into the back of the spare cupboard and closed the door on it. I'd already forgotten about the shrivelled yellow rose which still lay inside.

Chapter 20

April 1990
(UK No. 1 – *Vogue* – Madonna)

The shrill ring of the telephone woke me. I rolled over in the bed and reached out for the receiver as I blinked in the watery morning sunlight.

'Hello.' My voice was still heavy with sleep.

'Good morning,' said Rory. 'Happy birthday.'

I blinked again and looked at the clock. Seven o'clock. 'Good morning,' I said. 'How are you? How are things in Frankfurt?'

'Busy.'

'Too busy?' I pulled myself up in the bed, waking up properly.

'Not too busy,' he said. 'I'll be home in time, I told you that.'

'That'll be a first.' I tried to sound as though I was joking.

'I wouldn't miss your party,' he said. 'I organised it, didn't I?'

'Of course you did,' I said. 'I'm looking forward to it.'

'I'll see you later then,' said Rory. 'Enjoy your day.'

'Thanks.' But he'd already replaced the receiver.

I stretched in the double bed. The door opened and my daughter walked in.

Clodagh was wearing her Care Bear pyjamas and carrying her blue teddy.

'Can I get in?' she asked.

I held out my arms and she ran at the bed, jumped on to it and burrowed under the duvet.

'I'll go to sleep,' she said as she squeezed her eyes closed and stuck her thumb into her mouth. Clodagh was a chip off the old block when it came to bed. She enjoyed her sleep. Other mothers

I knew were exasperated by the fact that their children woke up at the crack of dawn every morning. Usually I had to wake Clodagh, even at weekends.

She curled into the crook of my body and slept. Her long eyelashes fluttered over her creamy skin and her strawberry-blonde hair curled around her face.

People said that she looked like me, but I couldn't see it. I thought that she was the image of Rory. She had the same determined features, even in sleep, the same high forehead and the same bright blue eyes. She had my colouring, but even then she would be lucky enough never to be called 'carrots' at school, her hair was too fair for that. She was not exactly a pretty child but she was striking and, naturally, I thought she was very intelligent. She had Rory's quick brain. She was good at numbers, she asked sensible questions and she was incredibly self-possessed. But I liked her best like this, curled up against me, needing me. She was like a little angel.

'Get a grip,' I muttered to myself as I slid carefully out of the bed so as not to disturb her.

I sat in front of my dressing-table and looked at myself in the mirror. I was thirty years old. How had that happened? I couldn't believe I was thirty! When, during the previous week, I sat back and thought about my impending birthday, I wondered where on earth my twenties had disappeared to. I could still clearly remember leaving school, that part of my life hadn't dissolved into the mists of time as I thought it would. I could visualise the teachers, the students, Sr Elizabeth, all as precisely as the day I left. If somebody had insisted that I write down a list of all the girls in my class, I was sure I could have done it. And yet here I was, thirty years old. Thirteen years since I left school. Married for eight years. A mother of a three-and-a-half-year-old girl. It seemed utterly impossible.

I peered into the mirror to check my hair. At Christmas, I'd noticed that the occasional grey hairs were becoming more noticeable and now they seemed to be increasing geometrically, every day another couple, to annoy me. It seemed ludicrous to have grey hairs on my head when I felt so young. At seventeen, thirty had seemed an absolute lifetime away. Now that I'd reached it, I knew that it was nothing.

All the same, my birthday present to myself was a morning at the hairdresser's, getting a decent colour to hide the unwanted grey streaks.

I stood up and looked at myself full length. I was in better shape now than I'd ever been, my work-outs at the gym had seen to that. The bulge of my stomach had flattened and I had a waist again. I wasn't perfect, of course, but leaner and fitter. Strange that, as I got older, I should acquire the shape I'd wanted when I was a teenager. I went to the gym three times a week now, and it made a huge difference. I'd decided against Karen Hamilton's gym though, because I really didn't want to see her every day. She kept asking me to go to lunches with her, or help to organise charity functions. It wasn't that I didn't care about the charities, but Karen was so overwhelming that I could only take her in small doses. I was in her good books at the moment because I'd helped her organise a dinner last week which had raised twice as much as she'd originally hoped. The down side of that success was, I knew, the chance that she'd try and get me to help with the next event too. Karen was not the sort of person to take no for an answer easily, and of course Rory always tried to get me to do whatever Karen wanted. If it kept her happy, it kept Bill happy, he said. And Bill was still the Group Treasurer.

Triona Bannister arrived at eight o'clock. She was Clodagh's nanny, although perhaps 'nanny' was exaggerating slightly. She came every second week to look after Clodagh. The arrangement suited us perfectly because Triona had another part-time job and I wasn't out and about enough to need someone to look after my daughter all the time. Triona lived about a mile away. I'd met her in the library when she was looking at the 'Wanted' notices. She had four younger brothers and sisters, she'd baby-sat as a teenager and she was looking to continue baby-sitting as much as possible. That way, she said, she could study, work and earn money at the same time. In addition to her part-time jobs she was going to college at night. I didn't know where she got the energy. She had lots of references, including one from one of my neighbours, and so I'd given her a trial. Clodagh loved her. Unfortunately, Triona was going to the States to work from June to September. I'd be sorry when she left us, especially as I was thinking of going back to work full-time myself. I was fed up with doing bits and pieces with Karen Hamilton. Last month, I'd told Rory that I was going to get a job. 'Outside the home,' I put it.

'You're what!' he exclaimed, looking at me as though I was subnormal.

'I want to work again, Rory,' I said. 'I need to have something to do.'

'But Clodagh will be going to school next year,' he said. 'Surely you can wait until then.'

At first that was what I'd thought myself. After all the tantrums I'd thrown when I was pregnant about not giving up work, I'd been forced to stop after Clodagh was born because I'd managed to end up in hospital again two months after her birth, this time with appendicitis. When I got out of hospital I resigned from the bank. I couldn't cope with both work and Clodagh, I just couldn't.

I didn't mind looking after Clodagh at first. She was a very alert baby, always looking for someone to play with her. I enjoyed taking her for walks, to the mother-and-baby swim, playing silly games with her, acting idiotically. It was fun.

Then the lunches with Karen were organised, I joined the gym and took up art classes. So I needed someone to look after Clodagh, at least some of the time. Triona was the answer to a prayer and I was able to fit in the things I wanted to do while she minded Clodagh.

The only problem was that I was bored. I didn't want to work with Karen Hamilton. I wanted to earn my own money again. I enjoyed being with Clodagh, but I couldn't be with her every minute of the day. I was starting to go mad. The afternoon that I found myself standing in the supermarket in front of the vegetable display with no real idea of why I'd gone there in the first place, I knew that I had to get back to work.

Rory didn't agree with me. I didn't know why he was so set against it although his mother might have had something to do with it. He insisted that there was no need for me to work and that I should be at home with Clodagh.

'None of the other girls work,' he said. 'Why should you?'

'Because I'll go barmy if I don't,' I told him.

'That's ridiculous,' said Rory. 'Karen Hamilton isn't barmy.'

'If that's what you believe,' I said bitterly. She'd driven me nuts that day. She'd got into a flap about whether the tablecloths for a lunch should be pink or green. I couldn't see that it mattered either way and said so. She'd told me that I just didn't understand.

Eventually, after heated discussion, Rory and I decided that I would get a job once we'd arranged something suitable for Clodagh.

I wanted her to go to a kindergarten of some sort. I'd been to a kindergarten myself when I was a kid and I thought it would be better for her than being on her own. Rory was sure that she would be better off at home and that we should get someone in to mind her. I said that I would check things out and let him know but I didn't want her to be on her own in the house with someone. I was determined that it would be a crèche or a kindergarten.

When I started to look for a job, I didn't realise how difficult it would be. I supposed I'd been lucky when I was younger – I'd waltzed into the bank with no real effort. But there were lots of people looking these days. I wanted to take any job, just to get out and start working again, but Rory told me that I should wait for a suitable job. His idea of a suitable job was one where I'd have plenty of time to be at home whenever he wanted. We argued about it, but he won. He told me that the bank would be looking for temporary workers later in the summer and if I could hold out until then, he knew that they'd offer me something.

It wasn't exactly what I'd imagined, but it was better than nothing and, deep down, I was glad that I would be working at something that was even a little bit familiar. After nearly four years out of the business world, my confidence was a little shaky.

'I'm going to get my hair done this morning,' I told Triona, as she hung her coat in the cloakroom. 'I'll be back by lunch-time.'

'OK, Jane,' she said. 'Is Clodagh awake yet?'

'What do you think?' I called as I put on the kettle. 'It's about time you got the little madam up.'

I waited until Clodagh had run downstairs in her bare feet to kiss me before I left the house. The traffic into town was busy. I parked my Honda Civic in the Setanta Centre and walked across to the Royal Hibernian Way where my current hairdresser worked. Practised, I supposed, was a better way of putting it. ZhaZha's

253

Hair Sculpture was more like an operating room than a hairdressing salon. It was hi-tec all the way, everything in grey and chrome and no chintzy bits to make the austere atmosphere more homely. But I rather liked it that way. I hated salons where the junior who washed my hair made inane conversation about my probable holidays or the state of the weather. In ZhaZha's they didn't speak unless they were spoken to. It made everything much more peaceful.

But today I would have liked something a bit friendlier. I pointed out the grey hairs to Sabrina who peered through the rest of my hair disdainfully, pulled up lengths of it and looked disappointed. She was thinking 'another old bat' and wondering how to tell me that they really only wanted young, trendy people in her salon. I felt out of place in the grey and chrome, suddenly too old for it.

Was this how it was going to be from now on, I wondered, frantically. Always feeling too old? Soon I would be as bad as my parents, hankering after the good old days.

God, I was like that already. As I sat in front of the mirror and watched Sabrina snipping away at my locks, I realised that I didn't recognise any of the songs that were being played in the background. I was an old fogey. I shuddered at the thought.

Sabrina used an all-over colour on my hair. 'They're not too obvious, anyway,' she said patronisingly. 'You're lucky you're not very dark.'

I paid by credit card and left. Why should I feel bad about it? Karen Hamilton had her hair done here, so did Lorraine. They were both dark – and no way could it be natural. So snotty Sabrina must have her quota of greying women. I couldn't be the only one. But I knew that I'd never go back to ZhaZha's again.

I drove back to our house in Dun Laoghaire. From now on I would get my hair done here, I decided. Somewhere cosy in the town centre would be a damn sight more convenient anyway.

Our house was one of five, built half a mile outside the town. It was new when we bought it, a couple of months after I had my appendix out. It still looked new, although the saplings that I'd planted in the front garden had begun to grow and were now covered in spring-green leaves. Each house was slightly different although all were red-brick and all had a built-in garage. They weren't anything spectacular from the front, but they were big houses with plenty of room and a reasonably-sized south-facing garden with a conservatory.

It was the conservatory that had persuaded me, even though I'd no interest at all in moving house at the time. But the sun shone warmly through the glass, and I could see myself sitting in a room which was as much part of the garden as the house, and I agreed.

Rory employed a gardener to landscape the back garden, which was a good idea because I would never have made it so pretty. It had colour all year round, although summer was my favourite time when the Californian lilac and the fuchsia and the roses were all in bloom.

I liked my house, but I'd preferred our home in Rathfarnham.

Triona and Clodagh were in the garden when I got in.

'Oh Jane, I do like your hair!' cried Triona.

'Really?' I was pleased that she'd noticed.

'It's lovely. The colour really suits you.'

'Is it that different? I want it to look natural,' I said.

'It does,' said Triona, 'but the colour hides those few grey hairs.'

Ouch, I thought. I hadn't realised that Triona had noticed the grey. I'd fondly believed that only I'd seen them.

'You haven't forgotten about tonight?' I asked her.

'Oh no, of course not,' she smiled. 'I left my overnight bag upstairs.'

Rory had organised a big birthday dinner for me in The Copper Beech restaurant. He'd invited twenty guests. I was really looking forward to it. I was forever going to dinner parties with him, but I'd never been to one which was for me. Most of our dinner parties were work. Tonight would be for fun.

Well, almost for fun. I had put my foot down when I realised that half of the guests were to be either Rory's bosses or his clients. 'I can put it on expenses that way,' he told me. 'Bill thinks it's a great idea.'

I threw a fit. My birthday was not some marketing exercise, it was my birthday. If he only wanted to bring people that he worked with, then he could cancel it. I wasn't interested. He sighed, exaggeratedly, and told me that he had also invited Lucy and David Norris, Brenda and Grace Quinlan, and Jessica and Neil Dawson. I was afraid that Lucy, Brenda and Grace would feel intimidated by the number of bank people present, but there wasn't much I could do about it.

Lucy was delighted anyway. 'I hardly ever get out,' she said. 'I'm looking forward to it.'

David Norris had set up his own company two years earlier and Lucy was working for him. They were, she said, only now starting to make money and it was a great treat to know that they could go and feed their faces at someone else's expense.

Brenda and Grace, whose boutique was now absolutely booming, were also delighted to be invited out. 'We never have time, usually,' said Brenda. 'And anything we ever go to is tiny little hors d'oeuvres carried away before you eat them. It's because of the models, of course: you can't tempt them with real food.'

I was looking forward to a bit of time with the girls. We hadn't got together since Christmas.

I was in great form that evening when I put on my black trousers and body and my multicoloured Frank Usher sequinned jacket. I left my hair loose in a cloud of copper unsullied by any grey.

'You look fantastic,' Triona told me as I came downstairs.

'Lift me, lift me,' cried Clodagh, so I did, hoping that she wouldn't try and pick all the sequins off the jacket.

It was half past seven. The restaurant was booked for eight. Rory's plane had been due in at six-thirty, but I'd phoned the airport and it had been delayed. It had landed at seven, they told me cheerfully.

I wasn't sure whether or not I should go to The Copper Beech and be there in case the guests arrived on time. I was pretty sure none of them would, they were notoriously late for everything, but it would be awful for someone to show and for neither Rory nor myself to be there. And by the time he got back, had a shower and changed, it would be half eight at least.

If only he didn't always put me in these situations. Nothing with Rory was ever cut and dried. There was always some moment of high drama to mess things up. But if I went to the restaurant now, before Rory, he'd probably get on his high horse and ask me why I hadn't waited.

I made my decision. I'd go.

It was just as well I did. Lucy and David were arriving as my taxi pulled in front of the mews building. I called to them as I handed over my fare.

'Jane!' cried Lucy. 'It's great to see you. Happy birthday!' She threw her arms around me. 'Now you know what it's like,' she said. I'd sent Lucy a card for her thirtieth birthday and enclosed tickets for the theatre. She'd phoned me one day when I was out and left a message on the answering machine to say that she would speak to me when she had got over the trauma of her new age.

'Hello, Jane.' David kissed me on the cheek. 'Where's Rory?'

'On his way,' I said hopefully. 'He was in Frankfurt all week, only got back this evening. I decided I'd better come on ahead.'

I led the way inside. They had reserved the upstairs dining area for us, the tables arranged side by side.

The Copper Beech was the in-restaurant of the moment and it was patronised by what Lucy called the 'glitterati'. It wasn't a very big restaurant but it was tastefully decorated, with bare walls covered in murals, natural wood tables and an uneven stone floor.

'I've never been here before,' said Lucy. 'Nice, isn't it?'

I nodded. 'Rory does buckets of entertaining here,' I told her. 'It's like the staff canteen to him.'

'Nice canteen your husband has,' said David. 'We must set up something like this at home, Lucy.'

'Our canteen is the kitchen,' she said. 'Beans on toast my speciality.'

'How's business?' I asked.

'Pretty good,' said David. 'Busy, thank God.'

'How do you like working for him?' I asked Lucy.

She squeezed me by the elbow. 'He's the best boss I ever had an affair with,' she whispered.

We sat down at the tables and the waiter brought us drinks. I hoped that Rory wouldn't be too late, it would be so embarrassing if people I barely knew arrived. I'd met all of the clients he had invited before, but I still felt that he had a bit of a nerve turning my birthday into a works outing. I turned around when I heard footsteps on the iron stairway, hoping it would be him.

Bill and Karen walked in. I was surprised to see that they were on time. Karen looked simply stunning, as always. She wore a tight lycra dress and a long red jacket. Her black hair had been cut into a shorter, softer style.

'Happy birthday,' she cooed, kissing me on the cheek. 'Welcome to the thirties club.'

'Thanks.' I accepted the perfectly-wrapped present she handed me. 'I'm so glad you could come.'

'Where's the husband?' asked Bill. 'Hiding somewhere?'

'He'll be along shortly,' I told them. 'He only got back from Frankfurt tonight.'

Bill nodded and lit a cigar.

More people arrived, bank people I knew. They were served with drinks while I fluttered around greeting them, wondering where the hell Rory was. I was tense and, so far, not having a good time.

Then he swept into the room, looking handsome and relaxed, and managing to embrace everyone in his welcome. He shook hands with the husbands and kissed the wives and eventually made his way over to me.

'Sorry I'm late,' he whispered. 'The bloody traffic was terrible.'

Now that he was here I was able to relax, and I stopped feeling as though I had to look after Bill or Karen or Graham or Suki. I joined Lucy and David who were sitting in the corner.

'I would have preferred a little party of my own.' I waved apologetically at the gathering in front of us. 'But Rory was organising something for the bank anyway, and he felt that this was as good an occasion as any.'

'You must do it for me, darling,' Lucy said to David. 'A big meal and line up all your builders.'

We laughed.

'I love your hair,' said Lucy. 'You've coloured it, haven't you?'

I told her about the grey and she nodded in understanding. 'Happens to us all.' She ran her fingers through her own hair.

'At least you can't see yours,' I told her.

'Nothing like a good colour.' She winked.

Then the Quinlans arrived, followed by Jessica and Neil. The conversations buzzed around the room as people grouped themselves in little bunches.

Finally the waiter appeared, sat us down and handed us the little menus that said 'Happy Birthday, Jane' on the front.

I felt very important. It was good to be the guest of honour for a change. I looked around at everyone. Although I still classed

Lucy and the twins as my closest friends, I kept in touch with Jessica and I did see a lot of the other wives. Some of them used the same gym as me and, of course, I often met them at Karen's charity lunches or at one of the bank's corporate hospitality functions.

They were not the sort of people I could get very close to. I wanted to fit in with them, but for some reason I never felt on the same wavelength. I didn't understand why, unless it was that I was never convinced that I, Jane, was the sort of person who could spend a fortune on a dress or a pair of shoes and still have enough money for a facial or a hairdo afterwards. The O'Sullivan household had been frugal. Money was never wasted. Although I'd always thought I would enjoy spending it, I felt guilty every single time I did. Especially because I still considered it to be Rory's money. Maybe I wouldn't feel so bad when I was earning myself.

'So where are you going on your summer holidays this year?' asked Grace, leaning across the table. The twins were dressed in their own creations tonight and they looked great.

'I don't know.' I shrugged. 'It depends on my husband.'

Rory turned towards me. 'What depends on me?' he asked.

'Our holidays,' I told him. Last year we'd gone to the South of France and stayed in a *gîte* a couple of miles from the coast. We'd talked about the States this year. Rory wanted to bring Clodagh to Orlando.

'The way work is going, we'll be lucky to get away at all,' said Rory. 'Isn't that right, Graham?'

Graham nodded and said that Rory was the hardest-working individual on the team.

'By the way,' he asked my husband, 'did you clear the outing with Jane?'

'What outing?' I asked.

Rory looked daggers at Graham. Whatever the outing, he didn't want to ask me about it now.

'Trip to Edinburgh the week after next,' said Graham. 'Golfing. Just the lads. A bit of a laugh.'

'He didn't mention it,' I said cheerfully, 'but I never stop him going anywhere.'

Beside me, Rory breathed a sigh of relief. He didn't know that

I would kill him when I got him home. We'd planned to go for a few days down the country ourselves the week after next. I was looking forward to it. Not just the break, but the opportunity to spend some time alone with Rory. We hadn't spent time alone in so long, I sometimes felt that we were two separate people who shared the same house. When we talked, we never seemed to talk about our hopes and our dreams but about the plumbing or the car or Clodagh. I knew that I couldn't expect romance all the time, but a little bit would have been nice. When he'd told me about the birthday dinner, I thought that was very romantic until I realised that half the bank would be there. Now it was no different to the millions of other functions we attended, except for the fact that everyone had been forced to buy me a present, which was very embarrassing.

'You and Rory must come to dinner with us soon,' said Lucy. 'We haven't been out together in ages.'

'You and I must go out to dinner together ourselves,' I told her. 'I haven't had a decent girls' night out in I don't know when.'

'Great idea,' said Brenda, who had overheard. 'How long is it since the four of us went out?'

I shook my head. 'Months.'

'Exactly,' said Brenda. 'Months. And we're supposed to be friends.'

'We did well for a while but we've let it slip lately,' agreed Lucy. 'I keep meaning to ring people, but I don't.'

'Me too,' I said. 'I'm always afraid you'll be too busy.'

'I'd never be too busy to go out with the girls,' retorted Lucy.

The food in The Copper Beech was delicious. I felt absolutely stuffed by the time dessert was finished, a lovely strawberry and cream pie. Then the waiters returned with bottles of champagne and Rory stood up and proposed a toast to me.

My cheeks flushed with embarrassment as he called me his 'beloved wife' but I was glad he used the words and glad that he felt he could say them in front of other people.

'To Jane!' he said, raising his glass.

We drank champagne and liqueurs and people swapped seats and talked to each other. It turned into a very pleasant party. Jessica came and chatted to me about children; she was now pregnant with her third. She wanted to know when I'd have another one. I grinned and said never. I presumed that this was because of the trauma of Clodagh's birth, but I felt terribly guilty about it because I remembered how much I'd longed for a brother or sister when I'd been young. But the thought of being pregnant again, sick and fat, which was exactly how I'd felt for the entire time, was too horrible to contemplate. Linda Sherry joined us and I allowed Jessica to talk baby talk with her while I kept half an ear on their conversation and watched the other people at the party.

Everyone seemed to be having a good time. People sat around in relaxed groups and chatted to each other, while the waiters whizzed around making sure that everyone had enough to drink. I looked around for Rory. He was talking to a girl who had been introduced to me as Amanda Ferry, the new Corporate Treasury dealer. I wondered over and over how the women put up with the chauvinistic ethos that dominated most dealing rooms. It was still a male preserve, all about money and power and egos. I imagined there'd been a few sharp intakes of breath when Amanda had joined the dealing room. She was tall and very striking, with auburn hair, almond-shaped grey eyes and olive skin. She had a fantastic bust. I wondered who would be the first to take her out. They'd probably put bets on it among themselves. She'd sat between Graham Kirwin and Bernard McAleer during the meal and they'd vied for her attention. I'd noticed her talking to Leo and then Bill and then one or two other men whom I didn't know very well, and now she was talking to Rory. She laughed suddenly and leaned towards him. Rory smiled at her and squeezed her arm. He caught me looking at him and jumped back like a child caught with his hand in a sweet jar.

I waved at him and he came over to me. 'Enjoying yourself?' I asked.

He nodded. 'It's going well, don't you think?'

It was going well. People were having a good time.

'Have you met Amanda?' He gestured towards her. She'd turned away from us and was talking to David Norris.

'You introduced us earlier,' I said. 'Nice girl.'

'Very bright,' said Rory. 'Sharp.'

'Good,' I said.

We looked at each other for a moment.

'Do you want another drink?' he asked.

'Any more champagne?'

He smiled at me. 'Sure.' He kissed me fleetingly on the lips and disappeared to get more champagne. I grinned to myself.

Lucy came over and kicked off her high-heeled shoes.

'God, I can never wear these,' she sighed. 'And I do so like to look tall.'

'Nice shoes,' I said.

'Ancient,' Lucy told me. 'About five years old. I can't afford anything new at the moment.'

I stared at her. 'Money problems?'

She shook her head. 'Not really, Jane. It's simply getting the business going. It's taking all our spare cash. It'll all work out in the end, I'm sure of that, but we're a bit strapped at the moment. And there's our own house, of course. Every additional spare bit of cash goes on that.'

They'd bought a lovely old house in Howth, but it needed a lot of repair work to make it habitable.

'How is the work going?' I asked.

'Slowly,' groaned Lucy. 'I'd love to be able to walk into the kitchen and not have a piece of the ceiling fall in on top of me.'

'It'll be worth it in the end,' I said. 'Your house will be much nicer than mine when you've finished.'

'Oh Jane, your house is lovely,' protested Lucy.

'But it's new and doesn't have much character,' I said. 'It's a good family house, but not a beautiful one.'

'Character is all very well but I'd adore an en suite bathroom,' laughed my friend. 'You really will have to come out and see me, Jane. Not you and Rory, just you.'

I looked at her suspiciously. 'Why not Rory?'

'You said earlier we girls didn't get together enough any more. Well, you and I are even greater friends than we were with the twins. We need to keep in touch.'

'I know,' I said. 'To be honest, I suppose I've felt that maybe you'd be bored with my company now, Lucy. After all, I'm not doing anything much and all I'd do is natter on about Clodagh and the cat.'

'I like hearing about my goddaughter,' said Lucy. 'She's a lovely baby.'

'Not a baby now,' I said. 'An *enfant terrible*.'

'Bring her with you,' said Lucy.

'Don't you want to have a baby of your own?' I asked curiously.

'Not yet,' she laughed. 'Not after your experiences.'

'You get over it,' I said. 'Almost.'

Rory and David came over with glasses of champagne for us. Rory told stories about his flight back from Frankfurt, David told tales of architects' nightmares and then Grace and Brenda came and talked about horrible customers.

'Huge, fat, blobby women trying to get into our size twelves,' giggled Grace. We all laughed. I was merry with drink. It was ages since I'd drunk more than a glass of wine; tonight I'd had at least three, and champagne as well. I was light-headed and everything seemed fantastically funny. I staggered over to talk to Karen for a while, then back to Lucy, then more people joined us; David had disappeared, Grace and Brenda looked a bit drunk and we started swapping old school stories. It was a long while since I'd had such a good time.

It was past midnight before people started to disperse. I slipped downstairs to the Ladies to repair the ravages of the night. I didn't look thirty, I decided as I squinted at myself in the mirror. I still looked young.

'Well, I don't think they can possibly be happy.' David's voice carried into the Ladies, and I stopped, my lipstick halfway to my mouth.

'Of course they are.' Lucy sounded abrupt. 'You just don't like Rory, do you?'

'No, I don't. He's pompous and self-centred. I would never organise a birthday party for you and then invite all my clients.'

'Maybe you would,' said Lucy and pushed open the door. She looked surprised to see me, and a little worried.

'Hi,' she said. 'I didn't know you were here.'

'Running repairs,' I said lightly. She disappeared into a cubicle and I hurried upstairs again.

'There you are!' Rory put his arm around me. 'We're going down Leeson Street.'

'Who's we?'

'The gang. Bill and the lads, their wives, Amanda.'

I looked around for the twins. 'Are you coming?' I asked.

Brenda shook her head. 'I'd love to,' she said, 'but we've a busy day tomorrow and I can't go to the shop feeling like death. We'd better give it a miss.'

'You two used to be great clubbers,' I protested.

Brenda laughed. 'Before we got sense.' She gathered up her bag. 'We'd better go, Jane. Give us a call. Happy birthday.'

I gave her and Grace a hug and then Lucy appeared at the top of the stairs.

'Going clubbing?' I asked. She looked over at David, who had preceded her. He shook his head almost imperceptibly.

'Guess not,' said Lucy. 'Busy day tomorrow.'

Why did they all think they had such busy days? Tomorrow was Friday. The dealers would all be at their desks at eight, however late they stayed out tonight. I was disappointed in my friends. Jessica had left earlier, unable to stay awake because of her pregnancy.

So I said goodbye to the twins and Lucy and David and went to Buck Whaley's with a dozen of the guests, where I drank myself silly and passed out in the corner. I only vaguely remembered Rory carrying me upstairs to bed at half past three in the morning.

Chapter 21

May 1990
(UK No. 17 – *I Still Haven't Found What I'm Looking For*
– Chimes)

I sat in the conservatory, legs tucked underneath me, Junkie curled up at my feet and my book open on my lap. The scent of lemon thyme floated in the air and a gentle breeze from the open skylight stirred the fronds of the potted ferns. There weren't many flowers in the conservatory. I preferred it as a place to sit in the sun than as somewhere to grow plants. It was sunny outside but the wind was from the north-east and cool, so the conservatory was the nicest place to be that afternoon. I loved being there, curled up in the wicker chair, on my own.

Soon, Triona would be back with Clodagh. My daughter would run into the room and throw herself at me and the fragile quiet of the day would be shattered. Of course I'd be glad to see her, I missed her when she was away. But in the meantime, the silence of the conservatory was very peaceful.

I stared out at the garden and watched the wrens hop across the lawn. The birds fed nervously in our garden, aware that it was cat territory and always keeping an eye out for Junkie.

His tail switched lazily as it hung down from the chair, and his nose twitched. I wondered what he was dreaming about. I glanced at my watch, my birthday present from Rory. Time seemed to be passing so slowly today. Surely I should be up and doing something? I wondered what time Rory would be home this evening.

Last night there'd been a terrible row. He was late home, not drunk, just late, and I screamed that I was fed up with him treating our home like a hotel and me like an unpaid servant. He roared back at me, listing all the things he'd ever done for me, as he dragged me around the house and showed me what a beautiful home he'd provided. Then Clodagh woke up and started crying which upset me and upset Rory.

But we didn't make up and slept back to back, rigid in the bed. I didn't fall asleep for ages. I lay there, tears dripping on to the pillow, as I wondered why we couldn't appreciate each other any more.

Of course, David Norris was to blame. His careless words to Lucy were still clearly etched in my mind. David thought my husband was self-centred and pompous. And sometimes I did, too. I kept asking myself over and over 'does it matter?' So what if he was those things, if he was also a good and loving husband and father? The trouble was that I couldn't decide whether he was a good and loving husband and father any more. He was good to us. He adored Clodagh. He loved me. There was just something not quite right and I was frightened.

Tears welled up in my eyes again but I wouldn't let them fall. I was a stupid, selfish woman. I lived in some damned dream world that wanted everything to be like a fairytale. Life wasn't like that. It was hard. And a lot harder for most people than it was for me.

When Triona and Clodagh returned I was scratching Junkie under the chin. Clodagh showed me the stones she'd gathered on the beach and Triona offered to make coffee. We sat around the island worktop in the kitchen while they told me about their day and I listened to Clodagh's happy chatter. She pushed her hair out of her eyes as she displayed her stones, laying them out carefully in neat rows in front of me.

'She's very bright,' Triona told me. 'She talks a lot and she talks a lot of sense.'

I hoped that she hadn't talked to Triona about last night's row. She'd clung to my leg, her eyes wide and terrified as I'd hissed malevolent words at Rory and she'd cried when he stormed into the bedroom and slammed the door behind him.

For her sake we couldn't have any more rows like that.

He arrived home early and walked straight upstairs. Clodagh and I were sitting together in the living room playing *SuperMario*. I listened to his footsteps overhead as he walked across the bedroom. I tried to guess his mood from his tread, but it was impossible.

When he came downstairs he was wearing his tracksuit. He flopped down on to the sofa and allowed Clodagh to jump on to him, tickling her until she squealed for mercy.

'I left something on the table for you,' he told me shortly.

My heart was thumping as I went into the kitchen. I didn't know what he might have left me. It was an envelope containing reservations for a weekend in the Park Hotel in Kenmare for two people. Our weekend away, delayed because of his golfing trip to Edinburgh. I hadn't said a thing to him about it, even when he'd packed a bag on the Thursday evening and told me he'd be back by Sunday. I walked back into the living room.

'Is this for me and you?' I asked.

'Naturally,' he said. 'I said we'd go away, and we're going.'

I looked deep into his eyes. 'Thank you,' I said as I sat down beside him. He hugged me briefly and turned on the TV.

We went the following weekend, leaving Clodagh with Rory's parents. I hated leaving her with Peter and Eleanor. I still didn't get on with them very well, and I didn't like the way they tried to influence Clodagh. But they'd offered to take her and I couldn't very well turn them down.

Clodagh didn't mind because Eleanor and Peter's house was full of toys that they kept for all their grandchildren. 'We'll be back on Sunday night,' promised Rory as he kissed her goodbye.

I settled into the leather seats of the Mercedes and slid a CD into the deck.

Dire Straits filled the air and I closed my eyes. Rory was a good, dependable driver and I trusted him completely. The Mercedes was a great car to snooze in.

We drove as far as Matt the Thresher's almost without speaking, but it was a relaxed silence without the tensions of recent weeks.

We had French onion soup and crusty rolls in Matt's, followed by a coffee for me and a pint for Rory. 'I'm only having one pint, so don't get your knickers in a twist,' he told me as he ordered it.

'I wasn't going to.' I sipped my coffee.

The drive from Limerick to Kenmare was tortuous. Lots of

traffic and, once we had reached Killarney, long and twisting roads through the mountains.

Eventually we reached Kenmare, strung out at the beginning of the peninsula. Rory drove through the main street, swearing softly at the parked cars in the middle of the road. Finally he swung in through the gates of the hotel and pulled up outside the door.

A porter helped us with our cases. The room was beautiful, L-shaped with a small sofa, table and TV in one part and two beds side by side in the other. I flopped down on the sofa and yawned widely.

'What do you want to do tonight?' asked Rory as he sat on the edge of the bed and slid off his shoes.

I put my arms behind my head. 'I don't mind. Eat, drink and be merry?'

'Do you want to have a shower before we go down to dinner?' he asked.

I nodded, and sat upright. 'Oh, yes. I'm sticky from the drive down.'

The water in the shower was hot and powerful. I massaged shower gel into my body and turned around under the spray. The bathroom door opened and Rory appeared. 'Mind if I join you?'

I shook my head and he got into the shower. Rory's body had changed over the last few years. Business lunches, dinners, entertainment had all added a few pounds around his waist. I poked his more rounded belly with my finger. He caught my hand and pulled me towards him.

It was a long time since we'd showered together. When we were married first, we shared the shower every weekend. I liked it – the warmth, the closeness, the water cascading over us. Sometimes we'd make love, sometimes not, but it was always a supremely sensuous experience. Now Rory massaged shower gel over me, his hands gliding expertly around my body. I quivered with pleasure and kissed him on the chest.

We made love in the shower and then again on the bed. Rory was strong and passionate. I loved the passion, but it was the togetherness that made me happiest, the knowledge that he wanted me.

He held me tightly to him afterwards, cradling me in his arms as he rocked gently back and forwards. We dozed together, at peace. I woke with a start about twenty minutes later and wriggled out of Rory's arms to dry my hair. The hum of the dryer woke him, and he dressed while I wrestled with my hairstyle.

He wore casual trousers and a cotton shirt. I put on a light pair of blue trousers and white blouse and draped myself with jewellery. We looked good together as we walked into the dining room.

'Do you still want to go back to work?' Rory asked, as he sipped his glass of Pinot Noir.

I nodded. 'Funny, I wasn't that keen on it when I started and then I got interested. When I left, I missed it like mad. I still miss it.'

'I can't understand you,' said Rory. 'I'd have thought that most girls would love to be able to swan around and do what they liked.'

'You'd think that until it happens to you,' I told him. 'But I need to feel that I'm doing something.'

'Having a good time is doing something,' he objected.

'Not worthwhile, though.' I poured myself some more wine. 'Even though it might be boring work, it'll still be something I'm doing for myself.'

'Don't you think that rearing Clodagh should be enough?'

'You sound like your mother.' I laughed. 'I love her – but all day, Rory? Can you imagine what it would be like to talk to a three-year-old all day?'

He laughed, too. 'I suppose so. Here, fill your glass.'

We lingered over the food and talked to each other for what seemed like the first time in months. Then we went to the lounge and sank into the low armchairs, drinks in our hands.

There were a fair number of people sitting in the lounge already, in couples and in groups. Rory knew one of the couples, Kieran and Antonia Woods. Kieran was the treasurer of a company which dealt with the bank. I sighed deeply as my husband went over to talk to him. Abandoned again.

My gaze roamed around the room and out into the hallway where more people were arriving. I swirled my Bailey's, watching the liquid adhere to the side of the glass, allowing the ice cubes to clink against each other.

When I looked up again, I was surprised to find the man standing at the bar looked vaguely familiar. He was tall, rangy and his business suit looked as though he had put it on by mistake. He wore tortoiseshell glasses perched on the edge of his nose, and carried a jacket and very battered briefcase. He was out of place in the refined elegance of the Park Hotel and yet very attractive in a dishevelled sort of way. He moved out of my line of vision and I frowned. I knew that I knew him, but I couldn't remember where I'd seen him before.

Rory returned, Kieran and Antonia in tow. 'Kieran was wondering if I'd like to go golfing with him tomorrow,' he said, as they sat down beside me. 'But I told him you wouldn't let me bring my gear.'

'I'm sorry, Kieran,' I said, 'but it's a get-away-from-it-all weekend. We couldn't do that if he brought it all with him.'

'You should take up golf yourself,' said Kieran. 'I'd say you've got a lovely little swing.'

'The last time I came home late, she had a great little swing,' joked Rory. 'She got me on the edge of the head.'

They all laughed. 'You must teach me that move,' said Antonia. 'I could do with it myself.'

We spent the evening with them. At first, I was aggrieved that Rory had brought someone over to join us but Kieran and Antonia were entertaining company, and I didn't feel as if talking to them was hard work.

Antonia had a son around the same age as Clodagh so we chattered about our children, sharing gossip and tips. Antonia was a beautician who ran a salon from her house in Rathgar.

'I must call in to you sometime,' I said.

'Any time.' She smiled. 'You have great bone structure.'

'Thanks,' I said, even though I knew that she was just being kind.

We stayed in the bar until nearly midnight. My eyes were closing as we walked up the stairs to our room.

We pushed the beds together to make an enormous and comfortable double bed. We fell in beside each other, kissed perfunctorily and then both fell instantly asleep.

The following day was glorious. The sun blazed out of the blue sky, dotted with fluffy white clouds. The air was warm and balmy and the countryside green. We went for a walk through the town and across the bridge, stopping to watch the river speeding its way to the sea.

'Isn't it beautiful?' asked Rory. I nodded in agreement. I could see why people lived in the country. The pace of life seemed to have slowed already, local people nodded in greeting to us as though we were known to them, and the air was clear and sweet.

I was starving by lunch-time so we went into a pub and ordered soup and sandwiches. Then we went back for the car and drove through the winding countryside to Sneem. I bought a toy woollen lamb for Clodagh, an Aran jumper for Mam and a blackthorn walking-stick for Dad. Rory laughed at me for buying presents to take back to Dublin.

We didn't eat in the hotel that evening, but in a local restaurant where the food was plentiful and full of flavour and where nothing was too much trouble for the owners.

'Don't you feel that you could live like this all the time?' said Rory, as we strolled arm-in-arm back to the hotel.

'You're joking!' I glanced at him and saw that he was smiling. 'You'd never be able to live somewhere like this,' I told him. 'It's far too tranquil for you.'

'I suppose you're right,' he said. 'But I wonder. Maybe in a few years, when I earn enough money, we could retire.'

'You'll never retire,' I said positively. 'No matter how much money you earn. You like it too much.'

'I don't know,' he said, as we turned up the gravel driveway. 'We burn out, you know.'

'Oh, yeah! And if you burn out from foreign exchange trading, you'll still probably want to do something like it.'

'You hate my job, don't you?' said Rory.

'Not hate it,' I told him. 'I resent it.'

'Why?' he asked. 'It pays the bills, it gives us a good life and – at the moment, anyway – I enjoy it.'

'I know you enjoy it,' I said. 'You enjoy it too much, I think. You'd prefer to be at your desk than at home.'

He made a face. 'Not really. But when I'm dealing, it's the most important thing in the world. I can't think of anything else. All the same, have you noticed me giving a damn about exchange rates this weekend?'

'Since they can't move at weekends, it's hardly relevant,' I retorted.

'I didn't look at today's papers for yesterday's closing prices,' he protested and I leaned my head against his shoulder and told him that he was a wonderful person.

We sat in the lounge again and sipped our drinks. I felt perfectly in tune with Rory as we sat there. When he went to the Gents, I got up and went over to the bar to order again.

'A pint of Heineken and a Bailey's,' I said as I leaned against the bar counter.

'Hello again.'

I turned around, recognising his voice. Of course, I thought, looking at him. He was wearing jeans and a denim shirt tonight and that made him easier to identify, even though the haircut was so much tidier and the glasses changed the shape of his face.

'What are you doing here?' I asked abruptly.

'That's a wonderful greeting.' He smiled and pushed the glasses up on his nose.

'I'm sorry.' Why was I rude to him? 'I'm simply surprised to see you.'

'I'm surprised to see you,' said Hugh McLean. 'How's your daughter?'

My tone softened. 'Clodagh is lovely,' I told him. 'A beautiful child.'

'She was a lovely baby,' he said. 'Really lovely.'

I smiled. 'All babies are lovely,' I said. 'How is your – niece, nephew?'

'Niece,' he said. 'Cliona.'

'Do you see her often?' I asked, making conversation.

'Quite a bit,' said Hugh. 'I'm her godfather.'

'Do you have any children of your own?'

He threw back his head and laughed. 'Not that I know of,' he said, wiping his eyes. 'I certainly hope not.'

I looked embarrassed. 'You married?'

'Not.' He looked incredibly cheerful. 'No one will have me.'

'Why?' I asked. 'You talk too much?'

'Not at all.' He sounded wounded. 'You know I hardly ever open my mouth.'

I grinned at him. 'You never shut up every day I saw you.'

272

'But I cheered you up,' he told me. 'Come on, I did cheer you up.'

We looked at each other for a moment. His eyes were soft. I turned away and picked up the drinks. 'It was nice seeing you again,' I said. 'I'd better get back with these.'

I felt his eyes follow me across the room. I wondered why on earth he disturbed me so much. Why he seemed to be able to see right through me, to my soul.

You're being fanciful, I told myself, taking a gulp out of the Bailey's.

Rory returned and sat beside me.

'I was thinking of converting the garage,' he said.

'What?' My mind was on other things.

'The garage. I thought we could convert it.'

I stared at him. 'Into what?'

'Another room, Jane. What did you think?'

'Don't be daft, Rory. We've four bedrooms, a living room, a dining room, a kitchen and your study. We've also got a utility room and a conservatory. What on earth do you want more rooms for?'

'When the family grows a bit.' He winked at me.

I made a face at him. 'I'm going back to work, darling. The family can wait a little longer.'

'Don't you think it would be nice to have another room downstairs?'

I shrugged. Rory loved talking about changing the house. It was part of his nature to want to change things all the time. He was never content to leave them as they were.

He continued to talk about the extension and I half-listened to him as I tried not to look in Hugh McLean's direction.

A girl came into the bar, looked around and joined him. I observed them from beneath my eyelashes.

She was average height, quite attractive in an understated sort of way, in a charcoal-grey suit and smart red shoes. She carried a folder which she opened out and gave to Hugh. They looked through it, pointing out items of interest to each other. Hugh nodded from time to time.

So, a business acquaintance and not a girlfriend, I decided. Although he might be attracted to her. When he wasn't reading through the folder he was watching her. Maybe they were down on business but he was hoping to get her into bed, I thought. Maybe he was already dreaming of the moment when they would slide into those very comfortable beds together and he would put his arms around her.

Jane! I was horrified at myself. What on earth was I doing, thinking about the man like this? I hardly knew him. I didn't have any right to make up his life for him. Besides, she might be happily married and completely uninterested in him.

He looked up then. I wasn't quick enough to drag my eyes away so I pretended that I wasn't looking at him, but past him. I yawned exaggeratedly. The faintest trace of a smile hovered around his lips and he bent his head to the folder again. I felt my face redden with embarrassment.

'Do you know them?' asked Rory suddenly.

'Sorry?'

'Those people over there – do you know them?'

'Why?'

'Because you're staring at them, Jane.'

I turned around in the sofa until I was practically facing Rory. 'No, I don't know them,' I said, keeping my voice level. 'But he looks vaguely familiar to me. I thought he might have been some-body from the bank.'

I was a good liar. I could keep my voice neutral and unexcited.

'He was staring at you, too,' said Rory.

I shrugged. 'Probably because he noticed me looking at him. Anyway, they're definitely not from the bank. You'd recognise them, wouldn't you?'

He nodded. 'No, I don't know them. Oh, who cares! Do you want to go to bed?'

I nodded. 'Isn't it amazing how sleepy you get in the country?' I said.

'God knows why, we haven't done anything all day,' said Rory.

'Good for you.' I grinned and followed him out of the bar. I didn't look back at Hugh although I was sure that he was watching me.

We made love that night again, doing immense good to our averages, which had slipped alarmingly of late. It was great to be desired and wanted by Rory. I loved holding him, being held by him, being close to him.

I stood by the window, looking out on to the bay. He came up behind me, softly, so that I jumped at the touch of his hands on my shoulders.

'You look lovely,' he whispered, kissing me on the cheek.

'For you,' I breathed. 'It's easy to be lovely for you.'

'I want you so much,' he said.

'I want you too.'

He began to slide the clothes from my body. My linen jacket, my silk blouse, my cotton skirt, until I was naked before him. I hadn't turned around while he did this, enjoying the anonymity of it. I could feel his skin close to mine, the warmth of his body.

'Oh Rory,' I whispered, turning finally to face him.

The face was not Rory's but Hugh's, smiling down at me in silent mockery. I screamed, but no sound came from my throat. I put my hands up to protect myself, but he caught them and then forced his face down on mine to kiss me.

I struggled against him and shouted, 'No!'

'Jane! Jane! Wake up!' Rory was shaking me. The sheets were wrapped around me and I couldn't free myself.

'You're OK! Don't worry!'

I looked at him and remembered who I was and where I was.

'Sorry,' I mumbled. 'Nightmare.'

'Eating too much rich food,' he snorted. 'Are you OK?'

I nodded.

He yawned. 'It's only half three,' he said. 'Let's get a bit more sleep.'

I rolled over in the bed, shaking. The dream had been very vivid. I didn't know why it had come to me like that, but it seemed so real that it frightened me. So unfair on Hugh McLean too, I thought, as I pulled the sheets around me again. He wasn't the type to force himself on anyone.

My sleep was dreamless and sound after that. I woke up when I felt Rory slip out of the bed to have his shower. I lay there, cocooned in its warmth. It was great to know that I could lie there and that Clodagh wouldn't come running in at any moment.

I lay there half awake, half asleep, revelling in my laziness until Rory switched on the hairdryer and startled me into full wakefulness.

We planned to leave after breakfast so that we wouldn't be too late arriving at his parents' house to collect Clodagh.

I strolled into the dining room while Rory brought the morning papers from reception. I chose a seat near the window at the opposite side of the room from Hugh McLean, who was reading a book at a table on his own.

He looked up as I walked by and nodded to me as I sat down. I smiled very briefly at him, the memory of my previous night's dream very clear in my mind. I couldn't understand why he had invaded my dreams like that. He was very attractive but not really my type. That scruffy, academic look was not for me. But his face was arresting. You couldn't help being drawn to him.

I ignored him and then Rory entered the room and sat down in front of me, blocking my view of Hugh. I was relieved. We ate our breakfast, chatted and went up to our room to collect our bags.

Hugh and his girlfriend walked past as we settled our bill.

'Nice to see you again.' He waved at me.

I opened and closed my mouth, unsure what to say.

'Meet you in another few years, perhaps,' he said as he opened the door.

Rory didn't hear the exchange. He was signing the credit card voucher.

It was six o'clock when we finally arrived back at the McLoughlin family home.

Clodagh squealed with excitement when we walked in and ran the length of the hall to me. I picked her up and swung her in the air.

'Be careful with the child, she's only just finished her tea.' Eleanor came into the hallway, her lips pursed.

'Did you have a nice tea?' I asked Clodagh, who immediately made a face and said no.

Eleanor looked annoyed and I stifled a giggle. 'Good girl, Clodagh,' I muttered under my breath.

We stayed for almost an hour. Peter wanted to show Rory their new alarm system and security lighting. Peter was paranoid about being burgled and the house was protected like a fortress. I often wondered how they would ever get *out* in an emergency.

I always enjoyed coming home, even if I'd only been away for a couple of days. Clodagh ran upstairs to check on her toys and I unpacked our bags.

It had been a lovely weekend, I mused, as I unfolded our clothes. If only we could have more of them, maybe we could be closer to each other. The romance of our relationship had long since disappeared under the day-to-day living of our lives and sometimes it seemed as if we were just two people sharing the same house. But we had been lovers at the weekend, doing simple things for each other, finding pleasure in each other's pleasure. I loved Rory. I was going to make more time for us. It was up to me to make sure that we were as happy as we deserved to be.

I went to bed that night on a cloud of happiness and dreamed of my husband and my child.

Chapter 22

June 1990
(UK No. 14 – *Nessun Dorma* – Luciano Pavarotti)

The country had gone World Cup crazy and so had everyone in the bank. They'd organised various different trips to see Ireland playing in Italy and Rory had gone on almost every one. It wasn't something I felt I could complain about. Everyone I knew wanted to go to the matches. All the same I was sick to the back teeth of football and, even though I wanted Ireland to win as much as anyone else, I was relieved when we were finally beaten and our lives got back to normal.

I sat in the living room on the last Friday in June and spread out our holiday snaps in front of me. Our holiday plans had been entirely disrupted by the World Cup. I'd suggested to Rory that maybe I could go with him to a match and stay on in Italy. He'd looked so horrified that I hadn't pressed matters, but I still wanted a holiday. I'd enjoyed the weekend away with Rory so much that I thought two weeks with him and Clodagh would be magic.

I still hadn't started working yet although I'd gone for an interview with the bank and they'd assured me that they would get back to me soon. That was nearly three weeks before and I presumed that the World Cup had disrupted the recruitment programme as it had disrupted everything else. When Rory was home we had some fierce battles. I wanted to watch Wimbledon and he wanted to watch soccer. Our second TV, in the bedroom, was black and white and neither of us wanted to give way and be the one to retire upstairs. Rory pointed out that it was easier to tell which tennis player was which because they were on different sides of the net; soccer players, he said, were all over the pitch; it was much harder to follow the game in black and white.

This was true, and so I was the one who usually ended up in the bedroom. He'd bring in a gang of his mates and they would sit in front of the TV, drinking cans of beer and eating microwave popcorn as they screamed abuse at the players.

Clodagh loved watching the football and would scream at the TV as much as Rory, to his great amusement.

'She's a great little girl,' he said to me one night as we curled up in bed. 'Maybe it's time for her to have a brother or sister.'

His words chilled me to the core.

'Not yet.' I ran my fingers up his chest. 'But one day.'

'You should have another baby soon,' he said. 'Clodagh will be at school before it's born and you don't want too much of an age gap. It wouldn't be fair on either of them.'

'I'm not ready,' I said.

'Oh, come on,' said Rory. 'You were fine the last time. A little hiccough at the end but you came out of it OK, didn't you?'

'I nearly died,' I told him.

'Don't exaggerate.'

'You weren't there.' I rolled over so that my back was to him. 'It wasn't my finest hour.'

'But you can't put it off for ever,' he objected. 'And we agreed that we should have a couple of kids.'

'I know, I know,' I said. 'And we will. Just not yet.'

He sighed and laid on his back. I pulled the pillow around my face. I wasn't ready to be responsible for another person yet. It would stop me from going back to work too. I knew Rory didn't want me to go back but I had to do something. Mam had always worked and I was used to the idea. It hadn't done me any harm, after all.

So I wasn't going to have a baby yet, whatever Rory said. Maybe in another couple of years.

I woke up the next morning with a runny nose and scratchy throat and wondered why I always managed to get colds in the summer. I spent the day being irritable at Clodagh and then guilty at my irritation. Her eyes filled with tears as I told her that no, she couldn't have another bar of chocolate. I shouldn't have given her one in the first place. I was trying to be the sort of mother whose children preferred fruit as a treat, not sweets.

In the end I did something which was probably even worse and brought her to McDonald's where she had a great time eating burgers and chips and almost exploded trying to suck up her strawberry triple thick milk shake.

I called in to the chemist on the way home and bought some lozenges for my throat and Night Nurse for my cold.

I met my next-door neighbour as I arrived home. Claire Haughton worked in a stockbroking company and I rarely saw her, but today her black Mazda MX3 was parked in the driveway and she was eyeing her garden with some concern.

'Hello.' I nodded at her.

'Hi,' she said.

Claire and her husband Martin had lived next door for a year and a half but we had very little contact with them. The last time I'd spoken to Claire was in the pub at Christmas when we'd bumped into them, all four of us a little the worse for drink.

'Nice day.' I fumbled in my bag for the house keys.

'Huh.' She put her head on one side. 'Do you know much about gardening, Jane?'

'Not a lot.' I grinned at her. 'When we moved in, Rory got a friend of a friend to do our garden. All I'm supposed to do is take up the daffodils in the summer and plant them again later in the year. I usually forget. But I did manage to get a nice display of pansies in a few pots on the patio.'

'I took the day off because I thought I might do something with this.' She indicated her garden with a broad sweep of the hand. 'But I don't know what to do, really.'

'Why don't you get someone to do it for you,' I suggested. 'Then all you have to do is pay the bills.'

'It seems a bit of a cheat,' said Claire. 'I know that it's a good idea but my parents have a lovely garden and they do it all themselves. I really would feel so ashamed to say that I couldn't.'

She looked so distraught that I laughed at her.

'Why don't you come in for a coffee and you can look at mine and see if it gives you any ideas?' I offered.

She smiled at me. 'Love to.'

We took our coffee into the conservatory while Clodagh ran out into the garden and started kicking a football around the lawn.

'We needed grass for her to play on,' I said. 'Given the choice, I might have paved it all over but a bit of green is nice.'

'I'd no interest at all until recently,' said Claire, 'then I went home and my folks' place looked so lovely that I realised that I'd neglected mine shamefully.'

'You don't have time to do it, though, do you?' I asked. 'You leave early in the morning and it's usually late when you get back.'

Claire sighed. 'I know. I'd love to have a job where I didn't have to get in to the office until ten o'clock and I could leave at four. When I was at school they used to tell us that computers would make our lives easier and we'd all have much more leisure time. All computers have done is connect everybody in the world so that if someone in the States is awake, I have to be awake too! Madness! Sometimes I wonder if we've made any progress at all.'

'But you must like it surely?' I asked her. 'Otherwise why would you do it?'

'I do like it.' Her face lit up. 'Only it doesn't exactly leave you with time to do things like the garden. I'm always entertaining clients or going to company presentations and things like that.'

'You sound like Rory,' I said unsympathetically. 'He's always complaining that he has to spend hours in the office, but he loves it really.'

'He works in foreign exchange, doesn't he?' asked Claire.

I nodded.

'Those guys are lunatics,' said Claire. 'I don't know how they do it.'

'Neither do I,' I told her. 'And I don't know how I put up with it either.'

She laughed at me. 'What did you do before you had your baby?' she asked. 'I'm sorry, but I've forgotten her name.'

'Clodagh,' I supplied. 'Oh, I worked in the same bank as Rory.'

'An inter-office romance.' Claire chuckled. 'How lovely.'

'What about you?' I asked. 'How did you meet Martin?'

'He works in one of the companies I research,' she told me. 'I met him at a presentation.'

'So,' I said, 'they're worth going to after all.'

'Sometimes.' Claire drained her cup and stood up. 'Can I go outside?' she asked.

'Of course.'

We wandered around the garden. I told her the names of some of the shrubs and the flowers. It *did* look very appealing, especially compared to Claire's which was just a square of lawn dotted with weeds. Junkie eyed us with interest from his perch on top of the garden shed.

Claire kept up a stream of idle conversation. It was nice to talk to someone new, I was sorry that I hadn't ever talked to her before. You could hardly count Christmas; people never talked at Christmas, just came out with a stream of seasonal clichés.

'Come to the garden centre with me,' she suggested. 'You can help me pick out a few plants.'

'You should have the garden ready for them,' I told her. 'Have your sites prepared.'

'All I want to do is to chuck down a few colourful flowers,' she said. 'I'll leave the long-term stuff until I've done a bit of work. But a few bright things would be nice, liven up the front and back a bit.'

'OK.' I was pleased that she'd asked me.

'I'll go and get my bag,' said Claire. 'Will we go in my car?'

'I have to bring Clodagh,' I reminded her. 'So it'll have to be mine, is that all right?'

'Sure.'

I swept *Mr Men* books and fluffy toys out of Claire's way as she got into the car. 'It's a run-around,' I explained apologetically. 'Not really a car for adults.'

'It's fine,' she said. 'It'll get us there.'

She wasn't used to a car that carried children. I could see her looking at the boxes of tissues, the moist wipes and all the various bits and pieces that I needed if I brought Clodagh anywhere.

'It must be a bit of a job for you,' she remarked as I unbuckled my daughter from the child-seat.

'What?' I asked.

'Bringing her places.'

'It's not so bad now.' I lifted Clodagh out and set her down on the gravel outside the garden centre. 'When she was a baby it was an absolute nightmare. Everywhere we went we had to bring stuff to feed her and change her and keep her warm. It used to take hours to get her organised. Now I can simply strap her in. Mind you,' I added as I grabbed a hold of her and removed the gravel from her hand, 'she's at an awful age now. She wants to be in absolutely everything. You know, they say you need eyes in the back of your head – well, you need eyes all around your head with her.'

Claire laughed. 'She's lovely.'

We spent a very pleasant half-hour as we strolled around the centre and picked out some plants for Claire's garden. I enjoyed myself immensely. I was surprised at how much I knew about gardening after all. I managed to steer her away from high main-tenance plants and get her to buy stuff that didn't need much looking after.

Eventually she made her purchases and we loaded up the car with a selection of bedding plants and a few shrubs.

'It must be wonderful having time to do this,' said Claire, as we unloaded her purchases and carried them through to her back garden.

'It's OK,' I said. 'But you get bored after a while.'

'Are you bored?' she asked as she placed the little pots in a row across her patio.

'I want to go back to work,' I told her. 'I was never particularly fond of it, but I do enjoy meeting people and it's very difficult being at home all the time.'

She nodded. 'I can imagine.'

'Working life isn't designed around women with children,' I said. 'Despite the fact that hordes of married women work.'

'Companies are making the effort,' said Claire.

'Some are.' I picked a few leaves off the privet hedge. 'But you're really a second-class citizen if you're a working mother. You know the way a company expects you to give your time whenever it wants. It's so difficult if you've got a kid. They get sick at the most inconvenient times, and you have to put them first. If you try and do that at work there's always going to be a conflict.'

'I suppose so,' said Claire. 'Sometimes I think I'd like a kid myself but every time I do I get into a panic.' She smiled. 'We've been married three years so I feel as if I should. I don't think I'm ready yet, though. But my biological clock is ringing alarm bells all over the place.'

'How old are you?' I asked.

'Thirty-three,' she said.

I was surprised. I'd assumed that she was younger than me. She certainly looked it.

'It's great having a child,' I told her. 'But it does change your life completely. Anyway, you've loads of time.' I glanced down at my watch. 'I'd better go back home,' I said. 'I promised Rory I'd make him a meal this evening and I'll have to get started.'

'Of course,' she said. 'I'll get on with this. Maybe we could have a chat again some time.'

'Love to,' I told her. 'Come on, Clodagh.' I dragged my daughter away from the flowerbeds. She'd managed to get clay all over her.

'See you again,' said Claire.

I washed Clodagh's face and hands and changed her into a pair of cotton jeans. She looked positively angelic with her hair caught back in a tiny ponytail and her face scrubbed clean and glowing. She sat in a corner of the kitchen and teased Junkie. The cat put up with an incredible amount from Clodagh without ever scratching her. When he had had enough, he simply got up, stalked upstairs, hid under one of the beds and went to sleep.

I was roasting a chicken for Rory's dinner. He'd complained when he rang earlier that he hadn't been out to lunch once this week and that I hadn't made him anything to eat in the evening either. He was wasting away. I told him that it would be good for him to lose a pound or two, but he said that he was perfectly proportioned.

Over the last year or two I'd improved my cooking skills and now I quite enjoyed chopping and slicing in the kitchen. I was going to rub the chicken with garlic and do a lemon sauce to go with it. Rory liked roast chicken.

The aroma of cooking filled the house. I loved the smell of roasting from the oven especially when it was liberally laced with garlic. I took my book into the conservatory and read it while the dinner cooked.

Rory said that he'd be home by six, but I knew that he'd almost certainly be late. He rarely got home before half-past, so I'd timed dinner for about a quarter to seven. When he hadn't arrived home by seven I was annoyed.

I didn't get *madly* annoyed until eight o'clock. I hadn't realised that it was so late because the evening was bright and sunny and

I'd been so absorbed in my book that I hadn't noticed the time going by.

'Where are you?' I looked at the phone. 'Why haven't you called?'

That was his other bad habit. If he knew he was going to be late, he didn't ring until the very last minute.

The chicken smelled gorgeous and I was starving. Clodagh had fallen asleep on the sofa, her thumb stuffed into her mouth. I carried her up to bed and undressed her without waking her.

There was no point in getting into a rage with Rory. I went back downstairs, carved myself a couple of slices of chicken, took a couple of roast potatoes and sat down in front of the TV.

It stayed bright until past ten o'clock. I varnished my nails, pillar box red, and sat with my hands outstretched in front of me as I waited for them to dry.

What pub had he gone to, I wondered. Larry Murphy's? Searson's? Where was his latest haunt? I hadn't a clue. I thought about ringing one of the pubs to find out if he was there. I actually took out the phone book and looked up the numbers but I didn't have the nerve to phone. I'd always despised women who rang their husbands or their boyfriends in pubs. Especially as the men concerned would so often shake their heads at the barman and refuse to take the call. No, I would wait for Rory to come home in his own good time.

He hadn't returned by midnight but I wasn't worried because closing time was half past eleven and he wouldn't leave the pub until twelve. I tried to recall his exact words that morning. 'Home by six,' he'd said. 'Nothing planned. Do something nice for tea, there's a love, I'm dying for a bit of good grub.'

So I'd done something nice for him to eat but he had failed to make an appearance. Typical, I thought, as I went upstairs to bed.

My mother had never slept when I was out late at night and I found it hard to sleep when Rory was. Even when I knew that he was out on business, I could never fully relax and fall into a deep sleep. Usually I dozed, waking at every noise, expecting him to come in at any moment.

I dozed on and off until two o'clock in the morning. By then I was worried. What if he'd had an accident? The last time I'd worried like this was before we'd married and he hadn't shown up for a date at all. But that was different. Now he was my husband.

I rolled over in the bed. What if he'd had a crash? I could see him lolling in the driver's seat of a car which had careered into a lamppost. If he'd gone to a club, surely he would have called. I whimpered with worry and with rage.

Dawn was breaking when I heard the sound of his key in the door. He stumbled on the stairs and I heard him swearing softly. He pushed open the bedroom door.

I pretended to be asleep. I heard him undress, his shoes fall to the floor with a thud. I could sense that he had simply stepped out of his clothes and left them lying on the floor.

He smelled of stale cigarette smoke and alcohol. I couldn't stay quiet any longer. I turned towards him.

'Where the hell were you?' I asked.

'Out,' he said.

'Out where?'

'Met some people.' He closed his eyes.

'Rory!' I shook him, but to no avail. He snored gently.

He got up for work at seven o'clock as usual. I'd fallen asleep at six, listening to the dawn chorus and the hum of the milk-float as it had driven down the road. I heard him shuffle into the en suite, banging the door.

I was sitting up in bed when he emerged, rubbing his hair with a towel.

'What happened to you last night?' I demanded.

He looked at me, still unable to focus his eyes properly. He yawned.

'Nothing.'

'Something must have happened,' I told him. 'You were meant to be home at six.'

'I was,' he smirked. 'I didn't say six p.m.'

The smile annoyed me even more. 'Rory, where the hell were you? You didn't call, you didn't tell me you'd be late. What happened?'

'Nothing,' he said again. 'We had to go out with some clients. They came to a meeting at four and we went for a drink with them. Then Andrew suggested we had a bite to eat. We couldn't refuse them, so we went for a Chinese. Everybody was in good form so we went to a club afterwards.'

'For God's sake!' I exploded. 'You went to a nightclub?'

'Why not?' asked Rory. 'We were having a good time.'

'You're pathetic,' I snapped. 'Nightclubs. You're a married man, Rory McLoughlin, you shouldn't be spending your time in nightclubs.'

'Why not?' he asked. 'At least they're a bit of fun.'

'Sugar daddies go to nightclubs,' I said.

He laughed at me. 'What would you know about them? You won't ever go.'

'I went to Buck Whaley's for my birthday,' I protested.

He picked up his suit from the floor and hung it up. 'Once or twice a year you might go into a club,' he said. 'It just so happens that I have to go as part of my job. There's nothing I can do about it. It doesn't make me a sugar daddy.'

'Well, what do you call a bunch of men who stand around in a nightclub?' I demanded. 'Eyeing up the women?'

'There were some lovely girls there all right.' He took a clean shirt out of the chest of drawers. 'Some really lovely girls.'

I knew he was trying to annoy me and he was succeeding.

'So you had a good time then?' I asked. 'Your boys' night out?'

'It wasn't just boys,' he said. 'Two of their girls came along and so did Amanda.'

'Well, I hope they had a good time too.' I felt a total frump at the thought of my husband in a nightclub with three women and an indeterminate number of men.

'It wasn't anything,' he said. 'Only fun.'

'So you had fun while I sat in with your daughter,' I said bitterly.

'What would you have done if I'd come home?' asked Rory. 'Sat in with me.'

He was right but I couldn't see what difference that made.

'I'm late.' He straightened his tie. 'And I'll have to get the Dart into work.'

'Do you want a lift to the station?'

'No,' he said. 'I need the walk.'

He left the house, slamming the front door behind him.

The bedroom door opened and Clodagh slid into the room.

'Where's Daddy?' she asked, her eyes big and wide.

'Gone to work,' I said.

'He didn't come in and kiss me.' Her bottom lip trembled.

Rory always kissed her goodbye. That was her signal to come into the bedroom for her morning cuddle.

'He was late,' I said. 'Come on in.'

She wriggled into the bed beside me. 'I don't like it when he doesn't come in and kiss me,' she said.

'Neither do I,' I told her, cuddling her close.

We lay together in the bed, our eyes closed. I hoped that Rory had an absolutely massive hangover. I hoped that his head was pounding and that he would have a very busy day and that he would lose money. He hated losing money.

Clodagh and I slept for nearly two hours. We spent the day cleaning the house and then I let her play computer games for as long as she liked. This was a real treat for her, as usually she was restricted to half an hour. But I didn't have the energy or the inclination to tell her to stop.

I removed my nail varnish and fed half of the chicken to Junkie who loved the garlic and mewed for more.

Rory arrived home at half past five. I heard the roar of the car in the driveway and stood, motionless, at the sink where I'd been filling the kettle.

He came into the house and went upstairs immediately. When he walked into the kitchen he'd changed into a pair of jeans.

'Home early,' I said.

'Couldn't stay the pace,' said Rory. 'Any food left?'

I turned to look at him.

'You mean yesterday's dinner?' I asked.

He sighed. 'Yes, yesterday's dinner,' he said.

'There's some.'

'Look,' he said, 'I really want to go to bed and get some sleep but I decided that I'd better come in here and face the music first. So will you just get on with it and chew me out and then I can go to bed.'

'What do you want me to say?' I asked.

'The usual stuff,' he said. 'About how hurt you are that I didn't call, how foolish I am to go on the piss, how inconsiderate I am to come home drunk.'

'It hardly seems worth the effort now, does it?' I asked.

'No, but you might as well say it because it'll make you feel better.'

'What would make me feel better,' I tried to keep my voice steady, 'would be if you behaved like any normal husband and came home after work.'

'I did come home after work,' he said triumphantly. 'Unfortunately my work meant having to stay out late.'

'Overtime?' I murmured.

'Exactly,' he said. 'I'm sorry I was late. Now is that OK?'

'Not really,' I told him. 'Why didn't you phone?'

'I knew you'd ask that,' he said. 'I didn't phone because no one else was phoning. I didn't see the point. I knew you'd guess what had happened and you did guess, didn't you?'

'Of course I guessed.' I walked into the living room. 'But I'd prefer to be told by you.'

I waited for him to follow me, but he didn't. I heard him filling a glass with water.

Was I being unreasonable, I wondered. Did Martin, next door, arrive home in the middle of the night and expect Claire to guess where he had been? Maybe it was Claire who arrived home in the middle of the night in that relationship, though. Did Lucy's husband do it? I doubted that very much. I didn't think that David Norris was the type to go to a nightclub at all. How did Karen or Linda or Lorraine or Fiona react when their husbands rolled in as the birds were beginning to sing in the trees? Did they simply say, 'Had a nice time, darling?' and go back asleep, or were there rows in their households too? Was I the only one who objected?

I went back into the kitchen. Rory was staring out of the window into the back garden watching Junkie roll in the grass.

'It doesn't matter.' I put my arms around him.

'That's my girl.' He smiled and kissed me on the forehead. 'I am sorry, you know.'

'Sure.' I leaned my head against him.

We stayed like that for a moment, then he held me away from him. 'I'm going to bed if that's all right with you,' he said. 'I didn't get much sleep last night.'

'I guess not.'

'So – goodnight.'

'You'd better say goodnight to Clodagh,' I said.

He went in and kissed her too, then went up to bed. I could hear the sounds of his snores drifting down the stairs so I closed the bedroom door and sat down in the living room with Clodagh.

'Is Daddy sick?' she asked, her voice full of concern.

'A little under the weather,' I said.

'What does under the weather mean?' she asked.

'He's sick,' I said.

'Read me a story,' said Clodagh, dismissing Rory and his possible illness.

So I sat and read *Cinderella* and wondered whether or not the Prince had ever gone on the lash after their marriage and what Cinderella would have done in the circumstances.

Chapter 23

July 1990
(US No. 18 – *You Can't Deny It* – Lisa Stansfield)

St Stephen's Green was crowded. Hordes of people sat on the grass in a multicoloured display of bright summer clothes against the manicured green lawns. The fountains played in the summer sun and the sparkling drops turned into miniature rainbows. Children leaned into the water and floated plastic boats across the fountains. Ducks quacked furiously on the ponds as they fought for the crusts of bread that were thrown to them. The music from the lunch-time band recital floated across the park, cheerful and spirited.

I walked through the Green. I loved it when it was crowded like this. Once lunch-time had ended, it would be quiet. The men and the boys would put shirts on to backs which had been exposed to the sun and girls would pull their skirts down from the hitched-up position on their thighs.

I was meeting Lucy for lunch in Captain America's. It was ages since either of us had been there. Because of the sun and the clear blue sky, I wore a T-shirt and a short skirt and revelled in feeling good.

Lucy waited for me in Grafton Street, sunglasses pushed into her hair. I felt sorry for her; she was wearing a smart business suit and blouse, which looked very stylish but was not necessarily the most comfortable dress for the scorchingly hot day.

'Hello there,' I said.

'Hi, Jane. Gosh, you look cool.' She looked wistfully at my T-shirt and skirt.

It was hot inside Captain America's too.

'Any chance of a window seat?' asked Lucy hopefully.

'You're lucky,' the waitress told her. 'Someone's just leaving.'

We were shown to a table near the open window where we could look out on to the bustling street below. A juggler stood on the pavement surrounded by a knot of people as he threw silver clubs into the air. The waitress left us with the huge laminated menus and disappeared.

'What are you having?' I asked Lucy.

'Plain burger and chips,' she said. 'I feel that in this weather I should be having a salad, but I'm absolutely starving.'

'Two plain burgers, two chips,' I ordered when the waitress returned. 'And could I have a glass of milk, please?'

'Coke for me.' Lucy handed over her menu and leaned back in her chair.

'How was your meeting?' I asked.

She'd been meeting the bank manager to discuss the affairs of David's company.

'Not bad,' she said. 'We've renegotiated our loans at a better rate and that'll help the cash flow.'

'How's the business going?'

'Quite well,' she said. 'It's still a bit knife-edge and I'm worried that it won't work out, but I think it will. David has a lot of contracts and he's very good.'

'I'm glad,' I said. 'How do you like working with him?'

Her eyes lit up. I'd never in my life seen anyone as much in love as Lucy Norris. Her marriage hadn't lost the sparkle that had been there at the start. It was strange, I thought, that a girl like Lucy, who could have had any man she wanted, had chosen the very plain David to be her husband. And that they were so mad about each other.

'He's great to work with,' she said. 'We don't live in each other's pockets. I do all the administration and he does everything else. He sits in his office, I answer the phones so I don't see him all the time, but it's great. People say that husbands and wives find it difficult to work together, but it's perfect for us.'

'That's wonderful,' I said.

'We just seem to match so well,' she said. 'He complements me and I complement him.'

'Lucky you.'

'He never loses his temper, he's always appreciative of whatever I do.'

'What a paragon,' I murmured.

'Jane!' She looked at me quizzically. 'Are you being a touch sarcastic?'

I blushed. 'I suppose so,' I said. 'Sorry.'

The waitress returned with our drinks, which saved me from having to explain myself to Lucy straight away. When the girl had left, Lucy looked at me, hurt in her eyes.

'So why be nasty?' she asked.

I didn't meet her gaze. I looked out the window at the juggler who was now throwing flaming torches. I was fighting with myself, not knowing exactly what I wanted to say to my friend.

'Jane?'

I looked across at her and picked at my nails, a habit I'd never managed to break.

'I think Rory and I are going through a bit of a difficult patch,' I said finally. It was the first time I'd admitted this, even to myself. I was horrified to find that my voice was shaking.

Lucy didn't say anything to me. She took a sip of her Coke and regarded me thoughtfully. I pulled the petals off the carnation in the little vase on the table.

'How difficult?' she asked finally.

I twirled a lock of hair around my fingers. I was afraid to speak in case I would cry.

Our burgers arrived. I loaded some mayonnaise on to the side of my plate and shook salt and vinegar liberally onto my chips.

Lucy was silent, waiting for me to speak. I coughed a couple of times.

'Not too difficult,' I said eventually. 'But it's getting to me a bit.'

Lucy popped a chip into her mouth. 'It's hot,' she gasped, her eyes watering. 'What exactly is the problem?'

'He's out a lot,' I said. Then it all came flooding out. He enjoyed being at work more than being at home, he loved going for a pint with the lads, he spent nearly every Saturday playing golf, he'd spent half the summer in Italy watching football. I was a drudge, a bore, a dullard. We'd spent a great weekend away in Kenmare a couple of months ago, but it had been downhill all the way from then.

'Why do you think this has happened?' asked Lucy.

I wiped the tear from my eye. 'I don't know.'

'Maybe it's a temporary thing,' said Lucy. 'You know, like the seven-year itch.'

'We've been married for eight years,' I said bitterly. 'Oh Lucy, I don't know what's wrong, exactly.'

'Has everything always been OK until now?' she asked.

I chewed the inside of my lip. 'Sort of.'

'What d'you mean, "sort of"?'

'We had a bit of a dodgy run when I was pregnant,' I told her. 'But once Clodagh was born, everything seemed to get back to normal again. I don't think it's deliberate, Lucy; I think he just feels that once he brings home the money, then that's enough.'

'It's not enough,' said Lucy.

'You've never liked him, have you?' I asked.

There was an uncomfortable silence while Lucy debated what she should say to me. She had never criticised him in front of me before, but I knew that David and she must have talked about him. I could still hear David's comments on the night of my birthday.

'I think he's very self-centred,' said Lucy. 'Maybe not intentionally, but self-centred all the same.'

I didn't like to hear this from her. I wanted her to say that her marriage was the same as mine and that there was nothing even slightly strange about Rory's behaviour. That all men were self-centred. But she didn't. She just looked uneasy.

'I'm probably a bad person to ask,' she said. 'I'm so bloody happy with David that it colours my judgement.'

'What about Eric?' I asked. 'How did you feel when it started to go wrong with him?'

'Eric was different,' Lucy told me. 'I never really loved Eric.'

She'd lived with him for over two years. She must have loved him.

'Come on, Lucy,' I said.

'Seriously,' she said. 'I didn't love him. I fancied him like crazy; you know I always have had a thing about French men since Étienne, and I was certainly besotted by Eric, but I don't think I ever loved him. Not in the way I love David.'

I sighed. 'So, what made you decide to split up with Eric?'

'Well, because of Chantalle,' Lucy reminded me. 'He was two-timing me.'

I wondered if it could be possible that Rory was two-timing me. I didn't think so, he wouldn't have the time. I was pretty sure that he told me the truth about where he was most of the time, and I never got the impression that there was another woman. He was far too interested in bloke-ish things. No, whatever else Rory was doing, he wasn't having an affair with someone.

'What about going back to work?' asked Lucy. 'You've been thinking about that for a while. Have you got any further with it?'

I told her about the interview with the bank. I'd expected to hear back from them before now and their silence was ominous. I supposed that I was out of date for working with a bank now; things had changed dramatically over the last few years and maybe it would take too long to retrain me.

'Besides,' I continued to Lucy, 'Rory keeps harping on about another baby.'

'Jesus, Jane,' said Lucy, 'what do you think about that?'

'You know how I feel,' I said. 'I don't want one yet. I know that women are meant to get over the pain instantly, but I can't get over the terror I felt and I'm not ready. Some day, I hope. Really, I do – I'd like Clodagh to have a brother or sister, but not yet.'

'Have you talked to Rory about it?'

'I don't talk to Rory about anything,' I said abruptly. 'We talk about things but neither of us is listening to the other one.' I sighed deeply. 'I suppose I'm as much to blame, Lucy. I don't try to understand him.'

Lucy looked doubtful. 'Maybe he's not the understandable type,' she said.

I dipped a chip into some mayonnaise and ate it slowly. 'Why doesn't it work out like you expect?' I asked. 'All I ever really wanted was to be married and have a family and live happily ever after. Nothing more than that. I expected to have a job, because we always had jobs in our family. I expected that my job wouldn't be as exciting as my husband's but that I'd enjoy it, anyway. I thought I'd have a couple of children and that childbirth would be simple. I thought I'd lead a normal life, Lucy.'

'You probably are leading a normal life,' said Lucy. 'How many women are truly happy?'

'You're truly happy.' I made it sound like an accusation.

She looked abashed. 'I know,' she said. 'And I'm really lucky. But then I was happy when I didn't have boyfriends either, Jane. I enjoyed myself a lot as a single person. Actually, the only times I was truly unhappy was when Nick told me his wife was pregnant and when I caught Eric cooing to Chantalle on the phone.'

I laughed. Lucy smiled at me. 'I'm glad to see you laugh, anyway.'

'You've cheered me up,' I said. 'I guess I'm going through a phase. Not exactly happy with everything, but a damn sight luckier than most.'

'It's funny, isn't it,' said Lucy, 'how women only gauge their happiness by how well their relationship is going. Men can be happy no matter what, but with most women it's different.'

'Except for you,' I pointed out.

'I'm a lot happier now than I was before I met David,' said Lucy. 'It's a whole different plane of happiness.'

'You're a happy sort of person,' I said. 'You were always the optimistic one. I'm the sort of person who thinks the glass is half empty, not half full.'

'You need to get out and have a good time,' Lucy told me. 'And I know what we should do.'

'What?' I asked.

'We'll go to a fortune-teller,' said Lucy. 'Then you'll be able to see the light at the end of the tunnel.'

I'd never been to a fortune-teller before, and I didn't think it was a very good idea. What if she told me something absolutely dreadful?

'It's a bit of fun,' said Lucy. 'We used to do it all the time in France. There was this girl, Simone, she was brilliant. It was on her advice I took the job back in Dublin.'

I couldn't believe that Lucy would do anything as important as changing jobs simply on the say-so of a fortune-teller. I looked at her in blank amazement.

'I didn't think you believed in that sort of rubbish,' I said sternly.

'I don't.' Lucy spooned more mayonnaise on to her plate. 'Well, not exactly. Sometimes they tell you useful things but mostly it's for a laugh.'

'And do you know one here?'

She nodded. 'I've gone to her. I went before my wedding. She's a Belgian woman who lives in Sutton. She's very good.'

'Oh, Lucy!'

'Seriously, Jane. She told me that I'd have a long and happy marriage with the man of my dreams.'

'Oh, for goodness sake!'

'I've been married for nearly four years and it is happy,' said Lucy. 'So she was right.'

'Did she also tell you that the man of your dreams would be tall, dark and handsome?' I teased.

Lucy grinned. 'No, but she said that he would build me my home.'

Lucy and David's house in Howth was still under construction.

'How long was this supposed to last?' I asked.

'Unfortunately she didn't give a deadline,' sighed Lucy, 'but she was right.'

I was still doubtful about going to a fortune-teller. I was afraid that my future would hold something terrible and I felt that I could cope with it better if I didn't know about it. I could see Lucy's charlatan making up some horrible story that would actually come true. How could anyone who had been educated by the nuns believe in fortune-telling? Anyway, the Belgians were hardly the sort of people who were fortune-tellers, I thought. If Lucy had said that this woman was Romanian or Hungarian I might have had more faith in the enterprise.

All the same, I agreed to go and see her. Lucy arranged appointments for us the following week and I told Rory that he'd have to be home early, because I was going out with Lucy and somebody had to mind Clodagh.

'You're always going out with that bloody woman,' said Rory. I could hear the buzz of the dealing room behind him; someone was shouting, 'At thirty, at thirty,' at the top of his voice. 'Hold on,' Rory said. I heard him shout, 'Ten done,' and then he was back to me. 'I'm very busy,' he told me. 'I'm not sure what time I can make it.'

'I'm meeting Lucy at seven o'clock,' I told him firmly. 'You'll have to be home by half past six. Surely you're not so indispensable that you can't make it home early one day out of five?'

He gave in, with ill-grace, but gave in all the same. I was in a frenzy, worrying whether or not he would really make it home on time because I didn't trust him not to decide to go for a pint anyway. When I heard the car pull into the driveway at twenty-five to seven, I breathed a sigh of relief.

Clodagh was already bathed and in her pyjamas. She looked good as gold with her hair and skin gleaming and clutching her Enid Blyton book for Rory to read to her.

He swung her into the air and told her that she was wonderful, then asked me what I'd made for dinner.

I hadn't done anything, I told him, but there were plenty of microwave meals in the freezer and all he had to do was heat one up. He looked at me as though I'd lost my head, but just told me to have a good time and not be too late home. His comments reminded me of my mother. I told him I'd be a good girl and then kissed him on the head. His hairline was receding, I noticed. A few years ago, that kiss would have been planted in his hair; now his forehead was much higher. I'd only noticed tonight how much his hair was thinning.

Lucy's house was just before Howth, overlooking the sea. The entire place had fallen into total disrepair before the Norrises had bought it, and it was currently held together by scaffolding and plastic sheeting. I parked carefully in the driveway, out of range of falling masonry, and tooted the horn. Lucy came to the doorway.

'Come on in,' she called, 'it's perfectly safe.'

I didn't like to disagree and picked my way carefully across the garden.

'It's perfectly safe,' repeated Lucy. 'We wouldn't be living in it if it wasn't.'

The only habitable rooms were the kitchen, David's office and the bedroom. I looked around at the half-built walls and didn't envy them.

David was sitting at the kitchen table, architect's drawings open in front of him.

'Hi, Jane,' he said absentmindedly.

'Hello, David.' This man disapproved of my husband. I liked him very much but it was hard for me to be civil to him.

'Have a good time,' said David, as he looked up at Lucy.

'Thanks, darling.' She gave him a kiss on the lips and he responded to her. I turned away and gazed out at the garden.

Lucy and David had a much longer garden than Rory and me. The lawn stretched back towards the sea and was bathed in evening sunlight. It would look lovely when the house was completely renovated and the garden cultivated.

'The garden is the last on my list,' said Lucy when I told her this. 'What I want is to be able to go from room to room without finding bits of plaster in my hair.'

I drove to Mrs Vermuelen's house, directed by Lucy. I still had no faith in the ability of a Belgian woman to divine my future.

'She's very strict about her clientele,' Lucy told me. 'She sees people only by appointment and only through personal referrals.'

'Who referred you?' I asked.

'The personnel manager in my last company,' said Lucy.

It seemed extraordinary to me that such a range of people went to fortune-tellers.

'What does she do?' I enquired. 'Palms, tea-leaves, cards?'

'Tarot cards,' said Lucy.

'I don't see how cards can tell you anything,' I said. 'It's pure chance which card turns up.'

'Exactly,' said Lucy. 'Chance and fate.'

We rang the doorbell. I was surprised to feel my heart thumping in my chest. Would this woman have anything worthwhile to tell me? She'd probably get it all wrong, anyway. I'd taken off my wedding and engagement rings and left them at home. I wasn't going to give her any clues.

A girl aged about seventeen opened the door.

'Have you come for fortunes?' she asked in a bored voice.

Lucy nodded and the girl showed us into a waiting-room. 'She's the daughter,' Lucy explained. I grunted. The daughter obviously thought we were idiots.

There was another woman sitting in the waiting-room, reading a magazine, for all the world as though she was sitting in a dentist's surgery.

I picked up a copy of *Hello!* and skimmed through the pages, examining pictures of Princess Diana looking absolutely miserable, Jane Seymour showing off her home and the latest Valentino fashions.

Lucy went in first. I continued to read the magazines and wondered what on earth Mrs Vermuelen could have to tell me. It'll all be mindless mumbo-jumbo, I thought. I should have stayed at home and saved my money.

Finally Lucy emerged, smiling, and told me to go ahead in. I shook my head in disbelief at myself and walked through the doorway.

I'd expected that the room would be dark and that there would be astrological pictures all over the place. But, in fact, it was a very ordinary room with a pale blue carpet, cream walls and blue curtains. The only concession to the paranormal was a beautiful chart of the Zodiac which hung on one of the walls.

'Hello,' said Mrs Vermuelen as she looked searchingly at me.

She was about fifty, a dumpy, matronly woman with salt-and-pepper hair and bright green eyes. She didn't look in the slightest bit like a psychic. I smiled at her. Even if she was going to take my money under false pretences, it was difficult not to warm to her.

She stared at me in silence for a while, keeping her hands on her cards. Then she smiled.

'What is your name?' she asked.

'I thought you were working that out,' I said facetiously.

'No,' she said.

'It's Jane,' I told her. I wasn't impressed. I didn't think she'd need to know my name.

'OK, then, Jane,' she said. 'I will do a reading for you. I want you to shuffle the cards.'

I stifled the urge to giggle. It was all so silly. I shuffled the cards and handed them back to the fortune-teller. I couldn't believe I was doing this.

She began turning them over, talking to me in a matter-of-fact voice.

'You are an only child,' she said. I looked at her in surprise. 'You come from a happy home.' Well, yes, I suppose I did. 'You are married.' So far it was probably all good guesswork, although I wondered how she knew I had no brothers or sisters.

She touched another card. 'Your husband is a professional man. He works hard.' She looked at me intently. 'He neglects you.' I shifted uncomfortably in my seat. 'You are concerned mostly with your home and your husband,' she said. 'And with money. You are well-off.' Oh, come on, I thought, this is ridiculous. She's telling me stuff that applies to practically anyone. Lucy and I had already decided that women were concerned mostly with their relationships, and she could tell I was well-off by the fact that I was wearing a rather nice Mondi suit. I should have worn tatty old jeans.

She went on: 'You are at a crossroads in your life.' I looked down at the cards in front of her. They were very pretty, with pictures of events on them. I tried to see the one she was looking at now. It said 'The Fool'. I nodded my head. That's exactly what I was, I thought.

'You will soon embark on a new chapter of your life,' she said. 'A totally new situation for you.' She touched another card. It showed a tower being struck by lightning. 'There will be sudden changes.' She looked up at me. 'Not necessarily ones you will like. A complete alteration in your life.'

Perhaps she meant I would get a job and go back to work. That would be a complete alteration in my life.

She went on: 'There are a lot of people in your life,' she said. 'Mostly helpful to you. But I would advise you to look out for a dark woman. A professional woman. She means you no harm, but she may disrupt your life.'

I thought about it. I didn't know any dark, professional women. I knew dark, unprofessional women like Karen and Lorraine, but I didn't think that these were the sort of people Mrs Vermuelen was advising me against.

'A man will feature in your life,' she said. 'Important. Not your husband.'

I shot her a glance. 'What way will he feature?' I asked. 'Romantically?' These fortune-tellers always expected you to want to know about romance. I bet they thought that once they mentioned a mysterious dark stranger, everyone believed them.

She shook her head. 'I do not think so. Not in this reading. But he is there and he is important. Maybe you can encourage him to be romantically involved.'

I blushed. 'I don't think so,' I said. 'What sort of man is he?'

She pointed at a card, the King of Cups. 'He is warm-hearted, friendly. A cheerful man,' she said. 'Pleasant. Not interested in money. Loving.'

301

Definitely not Rory, I thought. I welcomed the idea that there was a romantic warm man in my future. Maybe I would have an affair myself. I clamped down on the thought. I was being silly. That was the problem with having a fortune told. You went and looked for things to make it come true. Imagine if I tried to get off with some casual male acquaintance, just because this woman had said a man would be important in my life!

'You will have decisions to make,' said Mrs Vermuelen. 'You will doubt your ability to make the correct one, but you will. This will change your life and its direction. Things will not continue as they are. There will be some unpleasantness.'

'None of this is very encouraging,' I said gloomily.

'You will find happiness,' she told me resolutely. 'You will be pleased with the choices you have made and they will be the right ones. You must not let yourself be swayed by monetary matters.'

Easy for her to say, I thought. God knows how much she's raking in every day.

'So I'm not going to win the lottery!'

'There is no great money in your cards,' said Mrs Vermuelen. 'Although you will not want for anything. There is a time of reflection, of contemplation. You must re-evaluate things.'

I was doing that already, I thought. She was saying all the things I often said to myself.

'There will be a short holiday,' she told me. 'And a visit to a hospital, but nothing serious.'

I wondered did they always tell you about holidays and illness. This was a dreadful waste of money.

'You need to reach into your heart, Jane,' she said intently. 'You must decide what it is that you want from life. You cannot afford to settle for second-best.'

I smiled at her. 'I don't.'

'You must find your own happiness,' she told me. 'There is nothing wrong with wanting to be happy.'

For no reason, I felt the sting of tears in my eyes and I swallowed deeply. 'And will I be happy?'

'You can be,' she said. 'The ingredients are there. You must make the correct choices. Not, perhaps, the ones you think you should make.'

She told me more, but I forgot it almost as soon as she said it.

I was thinking of her words. *There's nothing wrong with wanting to be happy.* It sounded like something a psychiatrist would say.

Lucy was waiting for me when I came out.

'Well?' she asked.

'I am allowed to be happy,' I told her. 'I have to beware of a dark woman. I'm going on a short holiday. I've to watch out for a visit to hospital that won't be serious, and there's a warm and romantic man in my life. Oh, and there are going to be dramatic changes which will all work out for the best.'

'Wow!' said Lucy. 'Sounds OK.'

'Do you think so?' I asked. 'I'll tell you how I see it. Some dark woman barges into me on the street, knocks me in front of a car. I spend a couple of days in hospital, but return feeling OK. The dramatic change is that I go back to work and my warm-hearted boss gives me the sack.'

'Unbeliever,' said Lucy. 'I, my dear, am a cool-headed business woman who will reach the dizzy heights of success aided by my loving partner. I too will be going on a short holiday, from which I will return refreshed and with new ideas which will earn me a lot of money.'

'My fortune showed money to be conspicuously absent,' I told her.

'Probably because you're well-off already,' said Jane. 'Come on, do you want to pop into the Marine for a drink?'

We drove to the Marine Hotel and took our drinks out on to the back lawn which stretched down to the sea. There was a wedding reception and a bridal couple stood in the middle of the lawn holding hands while friends took photographs of them. They looked radiantly happy. Her dress was traditional, long and pure white, and she wore an equally traditional long white veil. He was in a morning suit. They gazed into each other's eyes.

Rory and I had looked into each other's eyes like that on our wedding day. I hadn't been able to keep my eyes off him and he hadn't been able to keep his hands off me.

We stayed until the sun had slipped down behind the water and then I drove Lucy home.

'Off you go and earn lots of money with your dazzlingly brilliant husband.' I smiled at her.

'Off you go and pursue happiness.' She smiled back.

'Meet you for lunch again in a couple of weeks?' I asked.

She nodded. 'Give me a call. We'll see how Mrs Vermuelen's predictions have worked out.'

She got out of the car and let herself into the house. I drove back to Dun Laoghaire, across the tollbridge and along the coast. I thought about my fortune and laughed nervously to myself because, even though I didn't believe it, I was worried about the sudden changes that Mrs Vermuelen predicted. Changes I might not like? I thought of all the changes I might not like but couldn't think of anything awful. And this dark, professional woman. Was that Claire Haughton, I wondered, and, if so, why would she harm me? And what about a holiday? Maybe Rory would bring me for a surprise weekend away. Paris, perhaps, or Rome. He'd done that a couple of times when we were first married. The hospital bit was worrying. I was a bit of a hypochondriac, although living with Rory had half-cured me. I realised that men never got colds, they got flu, and they never got indigestion, they had heart attacks. Listening to him complain had made me realise that occasional twinges meant nothing. All the same, I didn't like the idea of having to visit a hospital. I hated hospitals. But she said it wouldn't be serious. I shook my head. It was all gibberish! A loving stranger would be nice, all the same, I thought wistfully, as I turned into the driveway. But I didn't need a loving stranger, I had a husband. And I was going to make sure he knew I loved him tonight. I shook back my hair, straightened my shoulders and went inside the house. Rory had fallen asleep on the sofa, a tin of beer on the floor beside him and the newspaper on his head.

I sighed deeply. Romance doesn't last for ever, I told myself as I tidied up around him. And he'd probably had a hard day.

Chapter 24

August 1990
(US No. 2 – *If Wishes Came True* – Sweet Sensation)

I was spraying the roses in the back garden when Claire Haughton peered over the top of the dividing wall. I jumped back in shock. I was wearing my Walkman and singing along to *Queen's Greatest Hits* so I didn't notice her until I casually looked up. I switched off the tape and slipped the earphones from my ears.

'You scared the life out of me,' I said.

'Sorry about that,' said Claire. 'Are you busy, or can I pop in for a second?'

'Of course.' I expected her to come around to the front door. Instead, there was a scrabbling sound and Claire swung her leg on to the wall. She pulled herself into a sitting position on top of it and then dropped lightly into my garden.

'Good God,' I said, 'that was very athletic.'

'I work out in the gym,' said Claire. 'It's the least I can do.'

'I work out, too,' I told her, 'but I haven't put it to such practical use.' I put down my bottle of rose spray. 'What can I do for you?'

Claire tossed her hair out of her eyes. 'I'm hoping it's more what I can do for you,' she said. 'Once you don't think I'm imposing.'

'Not at all.' I was curious to hear what she wanted.

'The last time I was talking to you, you said that you were interested in getting back to work,' said Claire. 'I was wondering if you'd got a job yet?'

I shook my head. 'The bank I went to phoned me up and offered me two weeks' contract work which might or might not have been renewed,' I said. 'Two weeks is no good to me. I'd have to make alternative arrangements for Clodagh, and it would

305

cost me as much as I'd earn. It's not worth my while. I need something longer-term.'

'What exactly is your experience?' asked Claire.

I gave her a résumé of my career. It didn't sound much, condensed for someone's benefit, and I supposed that it wasn't much really, but I tried to make it sound more interesting. After all, I'd spent a lot of time on the phone to banks all around the world – surely I could make that sound important when I told people about it.

'So you had a reasonable amount of responsibility,' said Claire.

'I suppose so,' I said.

'But you can't type or anything, can you?' she asked.

I laughed a little. 'Actually, I can. But the thing in the bank – at least when I was there – was to deny that you could, because then you were sent off to the more mundane jobs. Nowadays I suppose it's OK, because computers are so much a part of everything and people need to be able to use them, but when I started, if you said you could type you were thrown into a typing pool and it was bloody difficult to ever get out.'

'So you can use a keyboard.'

'I'd be a bit rusty but I suppose it wouldn't take long to get up to speed,' I said. I looked at her curiously. 'Is there a point to all this, Claire?'

'Of course,' she said. She rubbed her nose as though undecided about what she should say.

'Look,' I said, 'if you know of a job, please tell me about it. I won't say that it's anything to do with you, and if I don't get it there won't be any hard feelings.'

She smiled at me. 'It's not like that at all.' She made her decision. 'A few of us are leaving the company where I work to set up on our own. We'll be providing private and corporate financial services. We need an office manager, someone who can organise us, organise the office, do the paperwork, that sort of thing. If you have computer experience, that would be great.'

I looked at her on a rising tide of excitement. This would be ideal. I couldn't think of anything I'd rather do more. But I hadn't any computer experience, not the sort Claire meant, anyway. I was good at computer games but it wasn't exactly the same thing.

'I'd be very, very interested,' I told her, trying to sound enthusiastic without sounding desperate. 'It would be perfect for me. If I had a full-time job, I would organise something for Clodagh and I'd be able to give my time to the job.' I decided that I'd have to come clean about the computer skills. 'But I've never used a personal computer,' I told her. 'I'd need to learn.'

She made a face. 'It's a drawback, Jane.'

'I learn very quickly.'

'It wouldn't be a great salary.'

'I don't care.'

'Never say you don't care, Jane,' she told me. 'Say that it should be commensurate with experience.' She rubbed her nose again. 'How about I have a chat with the others and see what they say? I can't guarantee anything, honestly I can't, but I'll certainly get back to you by next week.'

'Claire, that would be brilliant,' I said. 'I appreciate you thinking about me.'

'Oh, we need someone who won't cost the earth,' said Claire bluntly. 'We can't afford to pay anything great, yet.' She glanced at her watch. 'I'd better go. I've got a few calls to make.' She grasped the top of the wall again and hauled herself upwards. 'I'll be in touch,' she said and swung back to the other side.

I kept our conversation to myself. I didn't want to tell Rory, in case nothing came of it and he laughed at me for getting my hopes up. I'd asked him to check with the bank again and see if anything was likely to come up, but he'd said that there was nothing yet. It didn't bother me quite as much in the summer, because it was great to be able to be outdoors whenever the weather was fine, but I wanted to have something definite before the end of the year. It seemed to me that time was simply racing by and I hadn't managed to achieve anything yet.

I spent the week in a state of suppressed excitement, which was something I hadn't experienced in years. Every time the phone rang, I hoped it was Claire to tell me that they wanted me to work for them. It was only when I was waiting for a call that I realised how often it did ring. Usually Rory would answer it, because it was normally for him. Now we were practically tripping over each other to pick it up. He looked at me very strangely as I tried to grab the receiver one evening.

'Are you expecting someone to call?' he asked. 'You've made a dive for the phone each time it's rung tonight.'

'No,' I replied nonchalantly. 'It does ring a lot though, doesn't it?'

'People are always looking for me,' he said. 'The currency markets don't stop moving, you know.'

I yawned. I was fed up with the currency markets. I half listened to his conversation as I watched the news.

'No – no – I can't. Well, of course, I'd – yes – yes – you know I do. No – no – absolutely not. Naturally. Yes – yes – yes. Don't be silly. Yes.' A laugh. 'Yes – no – yes – maybe.'

'Funny conversation to be having about the dollar,' I said idly when he had replaced the receiver. He looked at me angrily. 'Are you eavesdropping on my phone conversations?' he asked.

'No, I'm not,' I retorted. 'I couldn't help hearing you. All I said was it was a funny conversation to be having about the dollar. God, you're sensitive.'

I flounced out of the room and ran upstairs to check on Clodagh. She was lying in bed, her red-gold hair fanned out on the pillow, her face completely composed, an arm flung out over the bedclothes. I retrieved her blue teddy bear which had fallen out of the bed and tucked it in beside her. She stirred and sighed softly.

Rory was behind me. He put his hands on my shoulders and led me out of the room and into the bedroom. He kissed me, fiercely, on the lips. I was surprised at his passion and excited by it. He slowly undid the buttons on my cotton shirt and eased it from my shoulders. I stood in front of him, glad that I was wearing one of my snow-white bras and not one of the bunch that had gone a murky blue since I'd washed them with a couple of pairs of Rory's navy socks by mistake.

He undid the bra and removed it. I watched him intently. There was a desire in his eyes that I hadn't seen in months. I opened his shirt and ran my fingers through the hair on his chest. He groaned softly and pushed me on to the bed.

Our lovemaking was urgent and demanding. Because we had left our bedroom door and the door to Clodagh's room both open, I'd a feeling of illicit excitement about it and I had to restrain myself from crying out when most I wanted to. We lay there together for a moment, then he kissed me tenderly on the throat.

'You're a wonderful wife.'

'I love you,' I said.

He closed his eyes and lay across me. He was a bit heavy, but I wasn't complaining.

Claire phoned at lunch-time the next day. I hurried in from the garden when I heard the shrill ring echoing from the house.

'Can you come to an interview?' asked Claire.

'When?' I asked.

'This evening, if possible.'

'What time?'

'Five – six?'

I thought about it for a moment. If Rory could be home in time, then I could make six o'clock.

'Where do you want me?'

'Our office is in Merrion Square,' she told me. 'Could you make it there?'

'By six o'clock,' I said. 'Sure.'

She gave me directions. I would be meeting one of the other partners, a man called Stephen Reynolds. Claire told me that he was very demanding but very fair. She told me not to try and mislead him in any way. She'd given him details of my career, but could I bring a CV along with me?

I was dismayed by that because I didn't have one. I didn't tell her that, of course, but I spent half the afternoon meticulously typing a CV, trying to keep it honest while emphasising all the good things about my career.

I rang Rory and asked him to be home early. He told me that it wasn't possible, that he was supposed to be meeting clients after work. I explained about the interview but he was unsympathetic.

'I'm not trying to belittle you in any way,' he said, 'but the fact is that I'm earning the money here and you're only doing it for fun. I have to meet the clients, I can't put it off.'

'But Rory, this is important to me.'

'You'll have to come up with something else,' he said. 'I can't get home before eight o'clock.'

I was furious with him. He was always meeting clients. I couldn't see any reason why he wouldn't defer one meeting once. Or why he couldn't send somebody else. In the early years of our marriage,

309

he told me that he had to go to all the meetings because Graham or Bill couldn't go, and he wanted to do anything they wanted so that he would be noticed and get promotion. Now he was a senior member of the dealing-room staff, but he was still the one who met the clients.

I didn't know what to do about Clodagh. It wouldn't do to turn up at an important interview with my daughter. I rang home, but Mam was obviously at work and the number rang and rang without anyone answering. I thought about Lucy but I couldn't ask her to look after Clodagh; she was working herself even if she was at home.

Finally I rang Triona's house. I remembered that she had a younger sister and, even though it was a complete off-chance, thought she might be able to help. Triona was so good and so competent, I thought that any sister of hers would be good enough for me. Her mother answered the phone and said that Pat would be home in half an hour and she'd get her to give me a ring. It would have to do, I thought. If the worst came to the worst I would turn up with Clodagh, although I couldn't see that it would help my chances of getting the job.

When the phone rang at half past four I raced to answer it.

'This is Pat,' said Triona's sister. 'I believe you're looking for a baby-sitter.'

I told her the situation, that I would need her for a couple of hours. I'd pay her the flat rate, I said; all she had to do was keep an eye on Clodagh. She said it was no problem, she'd be here by five. I thanked her profusely, delighted that I was out of a mess.

The next half-hour passed in a frenzy of anticipation. I badly wanted to get the job. I stood in front of the wardrobe, surveyed my clothes and tried to pick something suitable for an interview. Something that made me look confident and reliable. I wasn't sure about a lot of my clothes. They were very expensive, but they were either casual or very formal. I didn't have much in the way of business suits and I felt that wearing a suit would be the best way of looking quietly competent. In the end I decided to mix and match, wearing a navy jacket and beige skirt. I kept my jewellery to a minimum, a simple gold chain, tiny earrings and my wedding ring. Looking at myself in the mirror I decided that I looked the part of an office manager. Not too flashy, not too frumpy. My hands were sweating by the time the doorbell rang and Pat arrived.

My first instinct was to tell Pat that the interview had been cancelled. She didn't look to me the type that could look after herself, let alone my precious daughter. In fact, she reminded me a little of my Cousin Declan's one-time girlfriend Ruth. Pat was dressed all in black as Ruth used to, although Pat emphasised the darkness of her clothes by wearing very pale make-up and blood-red lipstick. Her skirt was long, almost sweeping the ground, and she wore black lace-up boots. Worst of all, as far as I was concerned, were the four earrings she wore in each ear and the diamond earring on the side of her nose.

'Hi,' she said. 'I'm Pat Bannister.'

I looked at her without speaking. If I told her to go away, I would be reinforcing my prejudice. She could be a perfectly nice girl. She probably was a perfectly nice girl. But could she be trusted to look after Clodagh?

At that moment Clodagh herself ran into the hallway. She stood beside me for a moment, looked at Pat and said, 'Why has that girl got a ring in her nose?' loudly and distinctly.

I couldn't help laughing and Pat joined in.

'Why have you got a ring in your nose?' I asked, as she stepped into the hallway.

'I like it,' she said. 'It gives me character.'

Not the sort of character I was used to, but she was a nice girl. Why did she have to ruin her appearance like that? I kicked myself for becoming so middle-aged so quickly.

'Have you baby-sat before?' I asked.

'Lots of times,' said Pat confidently. 'Don't worry, Mrs McLoughlin, I'll take good care of her. Won't I?' She looked at Clodagh, who was staring at her with undisguised interest.

'I should be home by seven,' I told her. 'My husband isn't expected back until eight but don't be surprised if he does show up. I've left some food in the fridge for Clodagh. If you want anything yourself, feel free. There's some ham there if you want to make a sandwich.'

'Thanks,' said Pat, 'but I've already eaten. I'm a vegetarian, anyway.'

Probably accounts for the waif-like looks, I thought, although the pale face was definitely more made-up than natural. Oh God, I thought, please let this girl know what she's doing. I didn't want to leave my daughter in the hands of some loony teenager. But despite the make-up, Pat Bannister's voice was confident and assured, and I felt that she had common sense and judgement. At least, I hoped she had.

'Do you know how to use the video?' I asked. 'She's got loads of tapes and things if you want to keep her amused.'

'We'll be fine, Mrs McLoughlin,' said Pat. 'It's only for a couple of hours. I can cope. Please don't worry.'

'How old are you?' I asked.

'Fifteen,' said Pat. 'But I'm a very mature fifteen.'

I smiled. I remembered being fifteen, too. God, I thought, I'm twice as old as this girl. She probably sees me in the same light as her own mother. I shivered at the thought.

I got into the Civic and backed carefully out of the driveway. I had the address and phone number of Claire's offices in my bag. I hoped that I would be on time.

I was almost twenty-five minutes early. I wondered should I go into the office straight away, but dismissed the idea. It would look too keen, I thought. So I sat in the car until five to six, listening to 98 FM and practising being interviewed.

The offices were in the basement of a Georgian building. There was no name-plate or distinguishing feature outside and I hoped that I'd got the right place. I was very tense. I took a deep breath and rubbed the palms of my hands against my skirt. I rang the bell.

Claire herself opened the door. I was glad to see a familiar face. She showed me to a small office off the hallway and told me to wait. Stephen would be in to see me in a couple of minutes, she said. I sat in the office, gazing around me, nervously clearing my throat from time to time. It was very quiet. I could hear the occasional murmur of voices and, once, the shrill of the telephone but otherwise it was silent. I coughed and the noise seemed to echo around the room, bouncing off the walls back to me. Why am I doing this, I wondered. I didn't need this job. I didn't need to put myself through this. I desperately wanted them to like me, to think me good enough, but it wouldn't be the end of the world if they didn't. Would it?

The door opened and Stephen Reynolds walked in. He was a huge man – tall, broad-shouldered and heavy. His face was slightly pudgy, with a double chin. But his eyes were clear and direct and looked straight at me.

'Mrs McLoughlin,' he said. 'Pleased to meet you.'

I took his proffered hand nervously, afraid that my clammy handshake would put him off. But he didn't seem to notice. His grip was firm and determined.

'Come into my office,' he said and I followed him meekly along the hallway, up some stairs and into another room. Stephen's office was at ground level. It was a small, utilitarian room. The walls were beige, without any pictures or charts and the only furniture was a pine desk, a swivel chair and a couple of computer monitors. He looked around, then went outside and brought back a chair for me.

'Sorry,' he said, 'we're not up to strength on the equipment yet.'

I smiled tentatively.

'Did you bring a CV?' he asked.

I handed it to him. He read through it carefully, taking his time, looking up at me occasionally.

'So you left work after the birth of your child,' he said. I thought that there was accusation in his tone.

'I was very sick,' I said. 'My baby was born early.'

For a moment he looked sympathetic. 'But you're ready to get back into the workforce again, Claire tells me.'

I nodded enthusiastically. 'Absolutely. I've enjoyed being at home, but I'm ready to work again.'

I was sure he wanted to ask me whether I was going to get pregnant again but I'd read somewhere that it was discriminatory to ask women that. He didn't risk it.

'You don't have PC experience,' he said.

'No. But I'm ready to learn,' I told him.

He leaned back in his chair and looked at me. 'I'm sure you are, Mrs McLoughlin. But I can get plenty of school-leavers who are already computer literate.'

I took a deep breath. 'I'm sure you can, Mr Reynolds,' I said. 'And I know that there are hundreds of people looking for a job. But I'm ready to work hard to help this company do well. I'm experienced at dealing with people, and I have got mainframe computer experience, so I'm not entirely computer illiterate. I think I could be an asset to you, if you'll give me the chance.'

I was proud of the way I managed to say all this without letting my voice quiver with the timidity I felt.

'That's very ambitious of you,' he said.

'I'm not ambitious in the sense that I want someone else's job,' I said. 'But I'm a quick learner and I know I can do this. I'm prepared to go on a computer course to learn enough to be able to cope. I'm prepared to do that in my own time.'

'At your own expense?' He lifted an eyebrow.

I thought about it for a moment. 'I'll pay for the course if you reimburse me after six months' work,' I said. 'If I haven't worked it out by then, well, I'll never work it out. If I have, then it would be only fair to pay for the course.'

He laughed then. 'You seem shrewd enough, anyway. If we offer you a job, when can you start?'

'I have to organise something for my child,' I said. 'I haven't done that yet, but I suppose it would only take a couple of weeks. Anyway, if you want me to do anything in the evenings I'd be happy to take work home until I can start here.'

'What do you think is a fair wage?' he asked.

I didn't know what to say to that. I mentioned my last salary at the bank, wondering whether that was incredibly high or incredibly low. It was higher than they were prepared to offer me, but not much. When I thought about it a bit more, I realised that my salary was exactly one fifth of what Rory had earned last year. Not including his bonus.

Stephen Reynolds stood up. 'I'll send you a letter confirming what we've said,' he told me. 'I'd like you to start the first week of September. That should give you enough time to organise yourself. If there's anything I need you to do in the meantime, I'll give you a call. If you can organise yourself to attend a computer course, then do it. I don't think it need take you that long. One or two days usually does it.' He extended his hand again. 'Welcome to Renham Financial.'

'Thank you,' I said. I was dizzy with the speed of it all. When I'd gone for an interview with the bank for my first job it had been weeks before I'd heard back from them, and that was to tell me that I was on a panel from which vacancies would be filled.

This man had just offered me a job on the strength of my cobbled-together CV and a fifteen-minute interview.

I walked on air to the door. I didn't see Claire Haughton but I wanted to hug her. What a wonderful person, I thought, floating back to the car. Imagine, one little conversation with her had changed my whole life.

Suddenly the fortune-teller's words came back to me. That there would be changes in my life, not necessarily pleasant, but necessary. The interview hadn't been particularly pleasant but it had been necessary. And I'd done well at it. I was so pleased with myself. All this time, I'd been scared of trying to get a job again because I knew that things had changed and I was afraid that my qualifications were out of date. But they weren't. And once I'd done a computer course, I'd be back on top in no time.

I didn't even care that the traffic around Merrion Square was so awful that it took me nearly forty minutes to get home.

Pat and Clodagh were playing in the garden when I let myself in. There was no sign of Rory yet but it was only seven o'clock. I walked out to join the girls.

'Guess what,' said Clodagh. 'We're playing princesses.'

'Are you?' I waved at the hair-band made of tinfoil in her hair. 'Is this your crown?'

'No,' she said derisively. 'It's my tiara.'

I stifled a giggle and turned to Pat. 'I hope she behaved herself.'

'Oh, she was an angel,' said Pat, who was flushed under her white make-up. 'She did exactly what she was told all the time, didn't you, my little princess!'

'Of course. Because I'm good,' stated Clodagh.

'You're very good,' I said. 'But now it's time for you to have your bath and go to bed.'

'I don't want a bath. I want to play with Pat.'

'Pat has to go home now,' I told her. 'You have to have your bath.'

She looked mutinous but gave in. I paid Pat and thanked her for coming at such short notice.

'No problem,' she said. 'Any time. She's a great kid.'

Rory's Mercedes turned into the driveway as Pat walked down it. He got out of the car, briefcase in his hand and looked at her in amazement. She smiled at him, waved at me and walked down the road.

'Who on earth was that?' he asked, as he stepped into the hallway.

'Pat Bannister,' I told him. 'Triona's younger sister. She was baby-sitting.'

'Baby-sitting?' he queried. 'Why should she be baby-sitting? How come you let a girl like that look after Clodagh?'

I looked at him in exasperation. Surely he could remember that I'd been to an interview. I'd assumed that he was home a bit early because he was interested. Obviously, I was wrong.

'She minded Clodagh while I went to my interview. And she's not "a girl like that"! She seems to be a very nice, capable young lady,' I said.

'Looked like a total spacer to me,' he said. 'Is she on drugs or anything, do you think?'

I held my temper. 'Don't be stupid,' I said. 'Why are you home already? You're early.'

'Clients didn't turn up.' He sat down on the sofa and turned to the TV page in the newspaper. I nearly screamed with annoyance.

'So you could have been home at five, after all?'

'I didn't know they hadn't turned up until a few minutes ago,' he said. 'I wouldn't have been able to leave earlier. What's for dinner?'

I stared at him in disbelief. 'I haven't had time to do anything yet,' I said. 'I didn't know if you'd want dinner or not. You could have been eating with your bloody clients. And how could I make dinner when I was out getting a job?'

He stopped looking at the paper and looked up at me instead.

'You got a job?' he asked, amazement in his voice.

'Don't sound so surprised,' I said. 'Why shouldn't I have got a job?'

He didn't answer that part. 'So what about Clodagh?' he asked.

'Maybe you'll have to give up your job to mind her,' I retorted.

He laughed. 'Why, what are they paying you?'

I told him and he laughed again. 'You won't have enough to cover her child-care expenses.'

'She's going to school next year,' I said. 'That's not the point.'

'You'll still have to get someone to look after her in the meantime. And school will finish much earlier than you, I suppose. I think you're being very silly, Jane.'

'I'm not being silly,' I said. 'I'm doing something I've wanted to do ever since I left work.'

'I just don't understand you,' Rory sighed. 'You never particularly liked the bank when you were there, but as soon as you gave it up you'd swear that it was the most important thing in your life. Well, I have to remind you that your child is the most important thing in your life, and you should be a bit more responsive to her needs.'

I looked at him wordlessly. I couldn't think of anything to say.

'It's not as though you need the money,' he continued. 'You have everything you could possibly want. I never scrimp or tell you that there isn't enough. So I can't see why you can't be like Karen or Lorraine and be content with what you have.'

'Because I wasn't brought up like that,' I said, perilously close to tears. 'Because I want to earn my own way, like my own friends.'

'Like Lucy and those dyke twins,' said Rory.

'Brenda and Grace are not dykes,' I snapped.

'Bit odd, don't you think?' said Rory. 'Both of them over thirty and unmarried. From what you say, hardly ever a boyfriend.'

'They've had boyfriends,' I said. 'But they're twins. And even if they were dykes,' I added, 'that's no reason to be snotty about them. Karen and Lorraine buy things in their shop.'

'Karen and Lorraine are lovely girls,' said Rory. 'But sometimes they take friendship a bit far.'

'They don't shop in *Les Jumelles* because of me,' I shouted. 'They shopped there before they knew us. So it's nothing to do with you or me.'

I flounced out of the living room, slamming the door behind me. There was a crash and a tinkle as a pane of glass fell out of the frame.

'Oh, fuck!' I cried.

Rory opened the door and put his head around it. 'Temper, temper,' he said. 'D'you need help to clear it up?'

'No,' I snapped as I picked up the pieces of glass. I wanted Rory to understand, but he wouldn't. I wanted time to be me again and not just his wife or Clodagh's mother. I wanted to be able to say

317

that I was going out for a drink with people from work, even if I never actually went. Surely he could understand that.

'Tell me about your job,' he said, in bed that night. So I told him about the interview, about Stephen and Claire and about having to do a computer course.

'And you said you'd pay for it?' he asked incredulously.

'They'll reimburse me,' I said. 'Once I'm in the job a while.'

He sighed into the darkness. 'You're awfully naive,' he said. 'They'll use you until they can stand on their feet and then they'll get someone else.'

I couldn't see the point in them doing that and said so. But Rory only sighed again and rolled over in the bed. I lay beside his sleeping body, unable to sleep myself. They weren't going to use me, I wouldn't let them. Besides, I would be good at this job and I would make myself indispensable. Working at home all day made you good at prioritising things and it made you organised. I would be the very best office manager they could have, and in six months, not only would they pay for my computer course, they would offer me a raise.

I smiled to myself. Maybe I wasn't such a pessimist, after all. And maybe I was ambitious, too. Already I could see myself as some sort of director. I snuggled down beside Rory and tried to sleep, but my dreams were of huge computers, blank screens and the awful feeling that I hadn't a clue what I was doing.

Chapter 25

September 1990
(UK No. 16 – *Listen To Your Heart* – Roxette)

It took me only a week to settle into my new routine. I enrolled Clodagh in a playschool which she absolutely loved. I was very relieved that she liked it, because the first day I left her I was so utterly racked with doubts that I almost rang Renham Financial and told them that it was all off, that I couldn't possibly leave my child. But she walked into the bright, sunny room and stood there, mesmerised by the coloured drawings and the child-sized tables and chairs, and she was instantly ready to join in. In fact, I was slightly put out at how quickly she adapted. I'd steeled myself for some tears and a wobbling chin. But it was me who felt bereft leaving her, not the other way around.

I felt bad about Triona Bannister, because I would have to find somebody to look after Clodagh each weekday after school and Triona couldn't do that. But she said not to worry, that she could do her other job full-time now if she wanted and that she knew somebody ideal. Audrey Bannister, Pat and Triona's mother, was the new childminder, and she collected Clodagh after school and brought her back to the Bannister house. There were another three Bannister children: Toby, Caroline and Donie, aged ten, eight and five respectively. Audrey adored children, she told me, and was only sorry that she hadn't been lucky enough to have a few more. But (and she whispered confidentially to me) her body had decided that Donie would be the last. She chatted to me non-stop when I was there and I liked her a lot. I was perfectly happy for Clodagh to be looked after by her, especially as she was used to Triona and Pat already. Clodagh loved the Bannisters' home as much as she loved the playschool. She liked having other children around her and she was adored by Caroline, who followed her round the house like a mother hen.

'Caroline has Ninja Turtles,' Clodagh informed me, one evening. 'And she doesn't have to put her crayons in a box.'

I was relieved that Clodagh was happy. It helped to ease my guilt.

I told myself that the new arrangement was better for both Clodagh and me. And in a lot of ways it was, because when I was with her I enjoyed her company so much more. Because I wasn't playing with her all day, I was much more prepared to play when I came home at night, even though I was often tired.

The tiredness came from the fact that everything was so new. I'd done a two-day intensive computer course, learned how to use the new products and was pretty pleased at how quickly I picked things up. But it was very different going into the office and looking at a heap of files and hoping that I'd managed to input them correctly into the computer. I didn't have too many disasters, although one day Stephen came in and spilled something on the keyboard which jammed it and I couldn't save any of the work I'd done that afternoon. He didn't want me to leave the machine switched on in case someone came in and accessed the files, so he insisted in switching it off there and then. I felt sure that there must have been a better way, but I didn't know one at the time and so the following day, when the keyboard had cleared itself, I had to do the work all over again.

Claire was wonderful to work for. She treated me with courtesy and understanding and never made me feel that I owed her anything for finding me a job. She was incredibly efficient and superb with clients. I was awed when I listened to her on the phone. One day, I promised myself, I would be that confident.

My work was mostly administrative, keeping files up to date, making appointments, phoning suppliers, that sort of thing. I didn't have to give any information over the phone although, as I listened to the others, I began to pick up bits and pieces which I stored away in my mind for future reference.

Rory was amused by my work, but grateful for it too. Because I wasn't at home all day, more or less waiting for him to come home, I didn't snap at him or hound him and so I suddenly found that we were having fewer arguments over what time he came home at and where he had been. He was right about one thing though – by the time I'd paid for Clodagh's school and Audrey Bannister, I hardly had any money left for myself. But at least it was my money, earned by my own efforts, and I was proud of that.

We were sitting watching TV one night – Clodagh had been put to bed – when Rory announced that he was going to the States the following week.

'What for?' I asked.

'Golfing,' he said, looking sideways at me to see how I would take this news.

I wasn't sure how to react. I hated it when Rory went golfing. It was a great holiday for him, but I was left behind to run the house while he had fun.

'Who are you going with?' I asked.

'Usual gang,' said Rory. 'The lads.'

I picked at my nail varnish and managed to peel off an entire strip of red colouring. I sucked my finger and went to get some nail varnish remover.

'When are you going?'

'Sunday.'

'I'm surprised the bank can do without you.'

Rory leaned over and put his arm around me. 'Come on, Janey,' he said persuasively. 'You don't mind, do you?'

I wriggled out of his armlock and stood up. 'What about our holiday this year?'

'We can't go anywhere at short notice while you're working,' he pointed out. 'I did say this before, you know.'

I made a face. 'I know.'

'So you don't mind, do you?'

'I mind,' I said. 'But I won't try and stop you, if that's what you mean. Nothing I could say would stop you anyway, would it?'

'If you threw enough of a tantrum,' said Rory. 'Then you might stop me.'

'Really?'

He looked worried.

'Don't look like that,' I said. 'I won't throw enough of a tantrum. Go ahead, I don't mind.'

I didn't mind as much as I thought I would. A week with Rory away would give me time to relax in the evenings without feeling that I had to cook for him or do things for him. When he was there, I always felt I should be providing something for him, but I never quite knew what. It would be nice to do my own thing for a week.

So Clodagh and I dropped him out to the airport on Sunday morning and even carried his clubs into the terminal building. I didn't see any of the others, but Rory said that they'd probably checked in already and were undoubtedly propping up the bar.

'Do you want to have a drink before you go through?' I asked, holding Clodagh tightly by the hand to stop her running off into the throng of people.

'If you like,' said Rory indifferently.

I scrunched up my nose. 'Probably not,' I decided. 'She's dying to run around the place and we'd never get to sit down in peace.'

'All right, then.' Rory nodded. 'I'll go along through to Departures.'

'Come on, Clodagh,' I said. 'Let's see Daddy going to the plane.'

We walked with him as far as we could and then he kissed me lightly on the cheek. 'I'll be back in a week,' he said. 'You have the name of the hotel, in case you need me.' He swung Clodagh into the air and she squealed with pleasure. 'Be a good girl,' he said. 'You never know what Daddy might bring home if you're a good girl.'

'A present?' she asked, eyes shining.

'Only if Mummy tells me you've been good. I won't bring anything back to people who aren't good.'

'I'm very good,' said Clodagh very definitely.

We laughed and Rory walked down to the departure gates while Clodagh and I stood at the huge windows and looked out at the aeroplanes. I still loved airports and I loved looking at the planes.

I stepped down from the aircraft. The heat wrapped itself around me as I stood on the tarmac. The silver-grey Rolls Royce slid across the ground towards me. A chauffeur got out of the car and opened the rear door. The man who emerged from the car was tall and dark although there was a sprinkling of grey in his hair, but it was distinguished and not ageing. He was immaculately dressed, an Armani suit and tie, Gucci shoes, Ralph Lauren sunglasses. We stood motionless for a moment and then he ran towards me, abandoning formality as he clasped me in his arms and hugged me.

'I've missed you, Jane,' he said.

'And I you.'

'How could you stay away so long?' he asked.

'I didn't want to.'

I was protected in the circle of his arms. He led me to the car and we sat inside, cocooned from the outside world by the opaque windows. The car sped through the highways, through the streets, to the house.

Whitewashed – they were always whitewashed in this corner of the world. Welcoming, because it was not a mansion, only a small house.

The chauffeur left us and we sat together on the terrace, over-looking the pool.

'Don't ever leave me again,' he said, taking off the Armani jacket.

'Never,' I whispered as I unbuttoned his shirt.

'Mummy, I want to go to the toilet,' wailed Clodagh as she tugged at my skirt.

I shook my head and the dream dissolved. What was I at, I wondered in disgust, dreaming ridiculous dreams at my age. Who was this strange man in the Armani suit? At least my taste was changing. When I was younger, my dream men were fishermen's sons. Now they were business tycoons.

This is reality, I thought, unbuttoning Clodagh's jump suit. More useful than unbuttoning imaginary men's shirts.

We visited Mam and Dad on the way back from the airport. Mam was forever complaining that she didn't see enough of us and so she was delighted when we arrived on the doorstep, Clodagh holding a bunch of flowers for her.

Dad was sitting in front of the TV watching *Star Trek*. Mam and Dad had bought a video at Christmas, and Dad was actually very good at using it. Unlike me. I normally managed to record speedway racing when I meant to video a romantic movie. Dad had an impressive library of films he had recorded perfectly. But he'd bought the *Star Trek* video. Being a Trekkie was his secret vice, something that he had never admitted to before. Now he'd come clean and had bought every video of every episode, and drove poor Mam around the bend because he watched them whenever he could.

I curled up on the sofa beside him while Mam and Clodagh went into the kitchen to arrange the flowers.

My parents were a happy couple. Their marriage had grown stronger over the years, they were in tune with each other. They must have had their share of rows, although I didn't remember them.

They didn't seem to need other people, they were perfectly happy in each other's company. Dad still went to the pub on Saturdays to watch football; Mam was content to work in the supermarket, although she said that she would be retiring soon. She wanted to spend more time in the garden.

I enjoyed being at home with them. Clodagh went for a walk with Mam while I watched *Star Trek* with Dad. I'd loved watching it with him when I was small. I'd wanted to do my hair like one of the girls – in an intricate weave on the top of my head. I'd cried when Mam told me she couldn't do it.

Captain Kirk saved the planet and I made a cup of tea. There were milk chocolate mallows in the biscuit barrel and I took one, eating all the chocolate first, then the mallow then the biscuit as I'd always done.

'That's a perfectly disgusting way of eating a biscuit,' observed Dad, who bit his straight through.

'Nonsense,' I said happily.

'So tell me, where is Rory playing golf?' Dad wanted to know.

'Florida,' I said. 'Lucky sod.'

'Why didn't you go, too?' he asked.

'Because it's a men-only trip,' I said. 'And besides, I'm at work now.'

He looked at me curiously. 'Why did you want to go back to work?' he asked. 'I thought you were happy.'

'Not you, too.' I sighed. 'Why does everyone think there's something wrong with me because I want to do something for myself? I couldn't stay at home all the time, that's all. I know I should have baked cakes and done domestic things, but I was never much good at it. I missed work when I left.'

'Your mam was the same,' said Dad. 'Always out working. But there was a difference. We needed the money.'

I nodded. 'I know it's not like we need the money. But that's not the point. I wanted to earn some of my own, anyway. It's probably very silly.'

'You're putting yourself under a lot of pressure,' he said. 'Having to get up and get Clodagh out and then race home to collect her again.'

'She'll be going to primary school next year and I'll have to run around then, anyway,' I told him. 'Besides, I'm very organised about it.'

'Organised about what?' Mam pushed open the door. Clodagh bounded in, her hands full of stones.

'Look what I collected,' she said proudly. 'Stones.'

'Well done.' I took one from her.

'Organised about what?' asked Mam again.

'Getting Clodagh out to playschool,' I said. 'Clodagh, put the stones down on the fireplace before you drop them.'

'You don't need to work,' said Mam.

'You sound like Rory,' I said dryly.

There was an awkward silence, the sort when everybody is afraid to speak for fear of saying the wrong thing. Mam patted her hair and fiddled with her necklace while Dad rewound the tape on the video machine. Clodagh dropped the stones on to the fireplace and they clattered against the marble.

'Be careful,' I said sharply. 'You'll break something.' She recoiled at the tone of my voice.

'I'm going to work because I need to do something for myself,' I said. 'Not really because we need the money. Rory understands.'

My parents said nothing. Clodagh and I left soon afterwards and, although I kissed Mam and Dad goodbye as usual, I was annoyed with them.

We were very busy in the office the following week. Claire had secured a couple of new clients, Stephen was at meetings all week and I spent nearly all my time answering the phone and producing statements. Although there were lots of set-up costs that still had to be taken into account, it looked as if the company had made a profit for the month, which pleased everybody enormously. We were in high spirits, joking about being rich, when the phone rang on Thursday afternoon.

'Renham Financial,' I said in my best telephone manner.

'Is that you, Jane?' The voice was distorted and faint, the line crackled.

'Yes, Jane speaking,' I said. 'Who's that?'

'Jane, it's Audrey Bannister.'

Audrey! I felt my heart pound. If Audrey was ringing, then there must be something wrong. What could have happened?

'What's the matter?' I asked jerkily.

'Don't panic, Jane,' she said. 'Everything will be all right. Clodagh had a bit of an accident, that's all. I'm ringing from the hospital.'

Hospital. I moistened my lips and felt sick. 'What happened?'

'She was playing in the garden and she slipped and banged her head. She's OK, Jane, but she was a bit dazed and she cut herself on the edge of the paving slabs.'

'Oh, my God,' I said. 'Is she conscious?'

'Of course she is,' said Audrey. 'Honestly, she's fine. But she wants you and I said I'd call.'

'I'll be there as soon as I can,' I promised. 'Tell her I'm on my way.'

My hands were shaking as I replaced the receiver. This was my worst nightmare. The others looked at me in concern.

'Is everything all right?' asked Claire.

I looked at the mounds of paper on my desk waiting to be processed and filed. Rory had told me that this would happen one day, that I would have to leave the office because of my responsibilities, and he was right.

'Clodagh has cut her head and she's been taken to hospital,' I said shakily. 'I have to be with her, Claire.'

'Of course you do.' She looked at me sympathetically. 'Don't worry, we'll tidy up for you.'

'I'm terribly sorry,' I said. 'I know it doesn't look good to rush out like this but—'

'Will you stop worrying and go,' ordered Stephen. 'There's nothing here that can't wait for a day. Go on, Jane.'

I looked at them gratefully and gathered up my bits and pieces. It was a blustery day and my hair whipped around my face as I hurried across the square to my car. Please let her be OK, I begged, turning the key in the lock. Please let her not be frightened. The car misfired and cut out. I tried to calm myself and started it again.

I bobbed and weaved in and out of the traffic, and caused one irate motorist to bang the horn and gesticulate rudely at me as I cut in front of him. I didn't care. It only took fifteen minutes to get to the hospital.

Clodagh had already been stitched when I arrived, and she was sitting on a trolley holding a teddy bear in her hand. When I saw her I wanted to cry, she looked so small and vulnerable. There was a huge bump on her head and the skin was angry and sore. They had shaved a section of her hair so that she looked like a surprised scarecrow.

I ran to her and hugged her. She whimpered a little and a tear slid down her cheek.

'She'll be fine, Mrs McLoughlin,' said the nurse. 'She was very brave.'

'Were you?' I was almost in tears myself.

'Of course she was,' said Audrey, who was standing beside the nurse.

'Can she come home now?' I asked.

The nurse said yes, they had checked her X-ray and she was fine. She rubbed Clodagh on the back and told her again how brave she was.

'I'm terribly sorry,' said Audrey, as we walked back to the cars. I carried Clodagh who was quietly sucking her thumb. 'They were playing chasing and one thing led to another. Before I knew what had happened, she had gone over with a thump. I brought her to the hospital straight away.'

'It wasn't your fault,' I hastened to reassure her. 'It could as easily have happened at home.'

'I feel responsible,' said Audrey. 'She was in my care.'

'Don't be daft.' Audrey looked so worried that I felt sorry for her. 'It was one of those things. She'll be proud of the scars.'

'They said that you won't notice it too much once her hair grows back,' Audrey told me. 'I'm sure they're right. It wasn't such a big cut, just deep.'

'Please don't blame yourself,' I said. 'What did you do with your own children?' I looked around as though they should be in the hospital grounds somewhere.

'Left them next door with Nancy,' sighed Audrey, 'with strict instructions to sit still and do absolutely nothing.'

I laughed. Audrey's children were not the sort to sit still for very long. 'You'd better retrieve them,' I said. 'I'll bring Clodagh home and we can sit down and watch TV together. Can't we, Clodagh?'

She nodded, still sucking her thumb.

'Phone me later and let me know how she is,' said Audrey.

Clodagh and I sat together on the sofa watching *The Den*. She still looked very pale. I was worried sick about her. Everyone knew that hospitals were madly understaffed these days. What if she was really concussed or something? I resolved to watch her like a hawk.

Of course, the nagging voice inside my head told me, this would never have happened if you hadn't insisted on going back to work. Clodagh was in the Bannisters' instead of at home that afternoon because of my job. Otherwise, she would have been playing safely in her own back garden. I leaned back on the sofa, arms around Clodagh, and closed my eyes. What was the best thing to do now? Should I give up work because it was unfair on Clodagh? Should I pretend that I wasn't overcome with guilt?

The doorbell rang at nine o'clock. Claire stood there, a box of Jelly Tots in her hands.

'I brought these for the invalid,' she said as she stepped inside. 'How is she?'

Clodagh was still sitting on the sofa but she looked a lot brighter. She perked up immensely when Claire gave her the Jelly Tots.

'My goodness!' exclaimed Claire. 'You do look as though you've been in the wars.'

'They had to cut off my hair,' said Clodagh proudly 'And I've stitches.'

'Really?' marvelled Claire.

'And everyone says I'm brave.'

'You certainly are,' said Claire. She turned to me. 'You'd better take tomorrow off, I suppose,' she said. 'We can manage for one day.'

I looked at her gratefully. 'Thanks,' I said. 'Would you like a cup of tea or anything?'

She nodded and I went into the kitchen to put the kettle on. How would I tell her that I'd probably have to give up work? I couldn't do it straight away, of course, I would have to give them time to find someone else. I felt terrible.

'Do you feel that this is all your fault?' asked Claire as I handed her the cup.

'Sort of,' I said.

'It's not,' Claire told me. 'She would have been playing, no matter what.'

'I know,' I said. 'But Claire, I should have been there for her. If it had happened at home, then *I* would have brought her to hospital and none of it would have been so terrible for her.'

'She seems to have got over it quickly enough,' remarked Claire.

'I know,' I said again. 'But I still feel that it's my fault.'

'I hope it doesn't affect how you feel about working for us.' Claire put her cup gently on to the saucer. 'We like you, Jane. Stephen thinks you're extremely good. We wouldn't like to lose you.'

I flushed at the compliment. 'Thanks.'

'I'd better be going,' said Claire. 'I'll see you in the office on Monday.'

'OK.' I walked to the door with her.

By Sunday, when Rory was due home, the bump on Clodagh's head had subsided. She still had a peculiar lopsided look because of her hair and the plaster, but she had recovered from her experience and she was proud of her injuries. She insisted on going to the Bannisters on Saturday afternoon to show them her wounds, much to my relief and amusement. I'd been afraid that she wouldn't step inside their house again, but she proudly brought me to the spot where she had fallen, looking for bloodstains, and finding them on the paving-stones.

The Bannister children were awed by her plaster and her hairdo. Caroline promised to mind her when she next came over. Toby insisted on showing her his appendix scar, and Donie told her that he'd once nearly had stitches but didn't. He'd love stitches, he said enviously.

'Will you be leaving her again on Monday?' asked Audrey anxiously.

I nodded. 'I'm not sure about going on working,' I confided, 'but certainly for another couple of weeks.'

'I'll be delighted to have her,' Audrey assured me.

I dressed Clodagh in her favourite jeans and sweatshirt on Sunday to go and meet Rory. I brushed her hair until it shone and tied it back with a velvet ribbon. She preened in front of the mirror, still proud of her scars.

'Come on, Madam,' I said. 'We'll be late.'

I drove Rory's car to the airport because he hated travelling in the Civic. I think he felt that a car littered with childish debris was beneath him.

The arrivals hall was crowded with people but I saw Rory instantly, standing at a meeting point as he waited for me. Clodagh ran to him immediately and he picked her up and held her high in the air.

'What in God's name happened?' he asked, as he looked in shock at her head.

I explained and he was furious.

'What was that woman doing, letting them play somewhere dangerous?' he demanded. 'Clodagh could have been seriously hurt.'

'It was an accident,' I said, able to be calm myself now. 'They were horseplaying, Rory, you know how kids are.'

'I know how other kids are,' he said. 'Rough.'

'Don't be silly.' I didn't want him to argue about it in front of Clodagh. 'Come on, let's go home, we can talk about it then.'

I slid a tape into the deck and listened to Clannad. The haunting music soothed me.

I drove steadily. Rory wasn't a good passenger, and he'd draw sharp breaths if I overtook other cars or cut in front of someone. I knew that he was a better driver than I was, so I never tried to compete.

There was a sailing ship on the river near the tollbridge, its white sails neatly furled around the masts, proud and majestic on the water. It was lovely to see, a pleasant change from the usual grey or white painted boats.

I pointed it out to Clodagh who looked at it in awe. 'It's a pirate ship,' she said, her eyes wide. 'Prob'ly pirates on it.'

I loved the drive once we reached the coast. I loved to watch the sun on the water and the curve of the bay stretching out into the distance.

When we got home, Rory left his case on the bed while he went for a shower. He said he was exhausted and jet-lagged and that the shower might wake him up. I unpacked his bag while he showered, and wondered why on earth he couldn't learn to fold shirts properly.

Then I went downstairs and made some tea, while Clodagh hopped from foot to foot and asked about her presents.

'You'll have to wait until Daddy comes downstairs again,' I said. 'I don't know what he's brought us.'

He'd brought a baseball shirt and cap for her and she was entranced by them. Predictably, he had bought me a bottle of perfume, *Paloma Picasso*, in its distinctive round bottle.

'Thanks, darling,' I said, kissing him.

'No problem,' he said.

He asked Clodagh about her accident, but she was getting bored with it by now and her answers were perfunctory. He waited until she had gone to bed later that evening, before quizzing me further about it. There was nothing more to tell, I said to him. She was playing, she fell, she cut her head. There was nothing Audrey could have done to stop it happening, it was one of those things.

He didn't look convinced. 'And what about Friday?' he asked. 'Did you go to work?'

'Of course not,' I said. 'Claire said it would be OK to take the day off. Anyway, Clodagh's fine now.'

'It wouldn't have happened if you'd been here,' said Rory obstinately. 'I still think you should have been.'

'Rory McLoughlin, I cannot understand you!' I cried. 'What is so wonderful about having me stuck at home? Besides, Clodagh loves the playschool and she loves Audrey's children and it has to be miles better for her than being stuck here with me. So don't give me that sort of crap.'

I could see he wasn't happy but he said nothing. He was besotted with Clodagh, of course. She was the most important thing in his life, and the idea of her being hurt in any way was almost too much for him to bear. But he would have to get used to it; she wouldn't go through life without being hurt. Physically or emotionally. Women are, I thought, as we got ready for bed. For some reason, we always manage to be hurt in some way or another. And being female meant physical pain. I knew, I'd had dreadful stomach cramps all day.

So I was glad that Rory didn't want to make love that night but simply pulled the duvet around him and burrowed under it. The jet-lag had definitely caught up with him. He was snoring before his head even touched the pillow.

I lay on my side of the bed and closed my eyes. Suddenly, I remembered that Mrs Vermuelen had predicted a short hospital visit. Was this it, I wondered, my eyes snapping open in amazement. Had she been right after all? I shivered with fear. If she was right about this, then what else could she have been right about? She'd predicted changes in my life and I'd got a job. She'd predicted a hospital visit, and I'd had one. I pulled the duvet around me. I was scared and I didn't know why.

Chapter 26

October 1990
(UK No. 19 – *From A Distance* – Cliff Richard)

The weather had taken a turn for the worse. A screeching wind howled around the office, forced its way through the gaps beneath the doors and wound its way around my legs. We didn't have any central heating in our part of the Georgian building – one of the reasons why the rent was reasonable. Stephen had bought an electric heater but, although it warmed the air, it was no protection against the icy blasts of wind. I shivered as I sat at my desk. My feet were cold, the tips of my fingers were cold and my nose was freezing. I'd forgotten, until I went into the office that day, what a cold person I actually was.

I blew on my hands to warm them and my fingers flew over the keyboard as quickly as accuracy would permit. I would allow myself a cup of coffee, my third of the morning, when I finished this report for Claire. I was drinking far too much coffee, but it helped to keep me warm.

The phone rang, startling me. It had been a quiet morning so far and its strident tone shattered the peace.

'Renham Financial,' I said.

'Hi, it's me.'

It was a couple of weeks since I'd heard from Lucy, and I should have called her before now. But I'd been so busy that, every evening after I made dinner, I simply flopped in front of the TV, unable to move. Rory had nicknamed me Couch, as in couch potato, but I didn't care. He wasn't much better, I told him, as he channel-hopped with the remote control.

'How are you, Lucy?' I held the phone between my ear and my shoulder and tapped away at the keys. I was adept at this by now.

'Great,' she said. 'There's a hole in the kitchen wall, the wind is howling around the house and the plumber has left us with no heating. Otherwise, it's wonderful.'

I laughed. 'I'm freezing, too,' I said. 'Our heaters are not exactly the furnaces of hell.'

'How would you like to get away from it all this weekend?'

A lovely thought, since it was Monday. 'Where to?'

'Barcelona,' she said smugly.

'Lucy! Are you going there?' I asked. 'You lucky devil!'

'We can both go if you like,' she said. 'It's only for two days. David is doing a presentation next week for a building he's hoping to design. He wants some samples of a particular ceramic tile and it's manufactured in a factory near Barcelona. It would be possible to get them sent over, but David is terrified they won't arrive in time and he'd like someone to meet the manufacturers, anyway. He can't go because he's meeting people on Friday night and he can't get out of it. So he asked me, and the airline is doing a two-for-the-price-of-one fare over, so I thought maybe you'd like to come.'

'Oh Lucy, how utterly fantastic,' I said. 'I love the way you ask me to go away on unexpected holidays with you.'

'This is not a holiday,' she said sternly. 'This is a business trip. I am an important business woman and I expect you to treat me like one. Besides,' she added, 'my fortune said that I'd be going on a brief holiday – and so did yours. I just thought I'd help it come true for you.'

Those damned fortunes! I thought angrily. I'd almost forgotten about them again, now Lucy was reminding me. All the same, it was a great opportunity. Anything to get out of the icebox that was Dublin.

The office seemed to warm up instantly. We chatted for a while longer and then I hung up. I didn't like to spend too long on the phone, and I hated it if Claire or Stephen walked in when I was on a personal call.

They were very relaxed about calls. Claire had casually told me that there was no problem about making them, but that she assumed I wouldn't abuse the privilege. I hated the thought of her even suspecting that I might abuse anything to do with Renham, and I made as few calls as I could. And I didn't like taking too many incoming calls, either.

I didn't get that many. It wasn't like when I first worked in the bank. Then friends from other departments, or Lucy or the twins, rang nearly every day.

I hadn't seen the twins in ages. I was getting very remiss about my friends, I thought. I would make a trip to *Les Jumelles* next week. I could probably do with getting a couple of new outfits for Christmas.

Christmas. I sighed. Once you were halfway through October, you couldn't help thinking of the festive season ahead. Rory had already given me a couple of dates for my diary. The bank always had a variety of functions at Christmas, and wives were expected at some of them.

'I don't suppose you'll be doing that much entertaining in your office,' he teased, as I wrote the dates in my diary.

Nobody had said anything about it yet but I didn't suppose we would. Our clients were mainly private individuals although we did have a few companies. I guessed that we would probably send a few bottles of wine or brandy to our best customers. The office party would be a riot, I mused. Claire, Stephen and me. A far cry from the hundreds that made up the bank's office party. Of course, there had been a whole range of events then – the official party, the department party, the section party, the occasional boozy lunch. I sighed for my lost sense of irresponsibility.

Still, a weekend in Barcelona sounded romantically irresponsible. I hoped that Rory wouldn't get too uptight about it. He hated me going away anywhere without him. It didn't happen very often, certainly not as often as he disappeared on golfing or business trips, but when I'd spent a weekend in London with Mam the previous year he'd been completely lost on his own. He'd been so unsure of how to cope with Clodagh that he'd spent the weekend at his parents' house.

I managed to get home reasonably early and cooked a chicken stir-fry which I knew he liked, so that he would be in a properly receptive mood when I told him. He tucked into his food happily and then stretched out on the sofa. Once he was perfectly relaxed, I casually mentioned that Lucy had asked me to go to Barcelona with her for the weekend.

He sat bolt upright and stared at me. 'Barcelona!' he said. 'What the hell do you want to go there for?'

'Because it's a foreign city.' I beamed at him. 'Because Lucy asked me and because I don't even have to pay for the air fare.'

'When would you go?'

'We can get a flight out on Friday evening through London,' I told him. 'I'll go straight from work. The return flight is Sunday afternoon.'

'It hardly seems worth the effort,' he said.

I explained about the ceramic tiles and he nodded. 'I suppose it's a nice opportunity. Even if you will be rushing around like a mad thing.'

'It'll be a break,' I said. 'I haven't been away at all this year.'

'Whose fault is that?' asked Rory, but at least he had the grace to flush slightly. I didn't even need to mention the World Cup, it went without saying.

Clodagh was wide-eyed when I said that Daddy would be collecting her from Audrey's on Friday, because I would be away until Sunday. She nodded wisely but I don't think that she actually understood. But I wasn't worried about her, because she was so adaptable. It wouldn't bother her in the slightest if I went missing for a couple of days.

Friday was cold but bright. The sky was a watery blue and the wind was still icy. According to the weather forecast, the weather in Barcelona wasn't hugely better. I packed a couple of heavy jumpers in my small case and, full of hope, a couple of long-sleeved T-shirts. I'd arranged to meet Lucy at the airport and leave my car in the long-term car park.

She was waiting for me as I hurried into the building. I was wearing a pair of black velvet leggings, a creamy-white jumper, black ankle boots and a black leather jacket. Lucy wore jeans, desert boots, a chunky angora jumper and a russet-coloured suede jacket. We both looked as if we were in our twenties. Well, Lucy certainly did and I hoped that I did too.

I wasn't scared of take-off any more, although I always tensed when the plane started its race along the runway and held my breath for those few moments when it seemed that it would never quite make it off the ground. I leaned my head against the window and watched the lights of the city fall away beneath us before settling back in my seat.

Lucy took out a map of the city. 'This is where we're staying,' she said, circling an area of the map. 'We'll have to get a taxi out to the factory; it's a few kilometres outside the city. Our appointment with Señor Casals is at ten o'clock tomorrow.'

'Is the factory open on Saturday?' I asked in surprise.

'Not to manufacture,' Lucy told me, 'but he'll be there to show me the tiles. And he'll have our samples ready, I hope.'

'Sounds OK,' I said. 'It'll be something different at any rate.'

'You sound as though you long for something different,' remarked Lucy.

I shrugged. 'You know how it is. Everyday living is so boring, especially in the winter. Up in the dark, home in the dark, can't get outside.'

'You wanted to go to work,' Lucy reminded me.

'I know,' I said. 'And I'm very glad I did. But I'd love something exciting to happen to me, for once. I lead a very predictable life.'

'You know the old saying,' said Lucy. '"Be careful of what you wish for, you might get it".'

I laughed. 'All I want is a tiny little bit of excitement,' I said. 'And I'm getting it right now, by going on this trip.'

We sat back in our seats, drank our coffee and read through our magazines. The flight to Heathrow was exactly on time, and so was our flight to Barcelona. We'd checked our luggage straight through, so we didn't have to hang around waiting for it in London.

'What's the betting it ends up in Madrid?' asked Lucy as we fastened our seat belts on the Iberia flight.

I already felt as though I was in a foreign country. The air hostesses offered us Spanish newspapers, and there was a different atmosphere in the plane, a slice of Spain sitting on the tarmac.

We flew uneventfully through the blackness of the evening. When we felt the plane begin to descend, I looked out of the window and saw the pattern of the city below us. We flew in over the buildings and then out over the inky sea to make our final approach.

Barcelona Airport was much prettier than Heathrow. It was light and airy with polished marble tiles and a sophisticated decor. As usual, our cases were the last to appear. I'd already begun to panic, assuming that they had, at the very least, been left behind in Dublin.

'Here we are,' said Lucy, as her case bounced out, closely followed by mine. 'Let's go.'

It was surprisingly warm outside. Not the intense humidity of summer, but a balmy evening breeze fluttered through the air. It was definitely a million times warmer than the temperature we'd left behind. We got a taxi outside the airport. If it hadn't been getting late, Lucy would have insisted on the bus or the metro – she didn't believe in getting taxis if public transport would do – but we were both tired and the taxi was a welcome luxury.

'Hotel Galina,' Lucy instructed him. '*Avenguida del Paral-lel.*'

She couldn't speak much Spanish but she could get by. My own command of the language went as far as '*Dos San Miguel*' (essential for any holiday) and '*Gracias*'. I really should learn to speak foreign languages, I thought, but I didn't have the ear for them that Lucy had.

The *Avenguida del Paral-lel* was one of the long streets that dissected Barcelona. It stretched from the beautiful *Plaza d'España* at one end down to the port and the *Paseo de Colon* at the other. It was not one of Barcelona's expensive streets but, according to Lucy who was reading her guidebook, it was a night-time street with clubs and shows.

'I don't especially want to go to a club or show,' I said.

'Don't be boring, Jane,' said Lucy. 'You'll go to whatever we can!'

The Hotel Galina was near the end of the street, a few minutes' walk from the port. It was a small hotel, aimed at the business traveller who didn't want to spend too much money. The concierge handed us the key to our room and waved us in the general direction of the lift.

Our room was very ordinary, a couple of single beds, TV, minibar and a small bathroom. The decor was cream and brown and not exactly inspiring, but it was immaculately clean and bigger than we'd expected.

I opened the curtains and looked out of the window. There was a small balcony outside, so I pushed open the patio door and walked out. It was still pleasantly warm. I sighed with pleasure as I felt the heat. There was no view from the balcony as we backed on to a jumble of apartments, and all I could see were shuttered windows and oblongs of light. The sounds of TVs and the occasional roar of a motor-bike broke the stillness of the night.

When we'd unpacked, we went downstairs to the tiny bar in the hotel. There was no one else sitting there, but we ordered a couple of drinks and sat chatting inconsequentially to each other. It was great to be away with Lucy again. At midnight we went to bed, much to the relief of the barman who was probably afraid that he would be left with two drunk women on his hands.

Lucy had set the alarm for eight o'clock the following morning and I groaned as it buzzed me into wakefulness. Lucy groaned too; neither of us were morning people. I stepped out on to the balcony while Lucy had a shower. It was still quite warm, although the sky was overcast. It would probably rain, I thought glumly. I hadn't brought an umbrella.

But by the time we had both showered and had a breakfast of croissants and coffee, the clouds had disappeared and the sky was a radiant blue. We stood on the pavement outside the hotel and gasped with pleasure at the real heat in the sun.

'My goodness,' I said, 'I thought it would only be mildly warm. This is positively hot.' I slipped my jacket from my shoulders. 'I'll be too warm if I wear this.'

But we carried our jackets anyway, unable to believe that it would stay so pleasant.

The factory was, as Lucy said, outside the city. We had to take a taxi. It would have looked very odd to arrive on a bus.

Señor Casals was waiting for us. I'd imagined a much older man, I hissed to Lucy, as he left his office for a moment to get coffee. He was young, in his early thirties, I guessed, and very, very good-looking. He wasn't tall, but he had smooth, tanned skin and thick black hair with only the faintest sprinkling of grey at the temples. He had brown eyes which turned even darker when he talked. I knew that I was looking at him like a teenager at a pop star, but I couldn't help it. He was the most attractive man I'd ever set eyes on. His voice was deep and fluid, his foreign pronunciation of English words adding to its charm.

He showed us around the factory, pointed out the various processes of making the tiles and said that he hoped his designs would be the ones that David Norris chose. Lucy talked about prices and consignments and deliveries to him, and I admired her business acumen. I would have given him the contract simply to see him again.

Really, Jane, I told myself as I watched him, you are behaving like a schoolgirl. But I couldn't help it; there was a magnetism about him which made me want to forget that I was a married woman with a four-year-old daughter.

'This is your first visit to Barcelona?' he asked Lucy, as she finished the meeting with him and took the heavy box of tiles from his desk.

'Yes,' she said. 'It seems a lovely city.'

'Oh, but it is,' he said. 'We think, the most beautiful city in Catalonia. And in all of Spain, of course.'

I knew, vaguely, that the Catalans considered themselves to be completely different from other Spaniards. They spoke a different type of Spanish and there had been trouble when they tried to establish themselves as a separate entity from Spain.

'That will not happen,' said Señor Casals when I mentioned it. 'But it is important for us to be different. Our people are different, our culture is different, our language is different.' He smiled. 'You must allow me to take you to dinner tonight,' he said to us. 'It would be a very great honour.'

Lucy and I exchanged glances. 'That would be lovely,' said Lucy, a shade too quickly. I wondered if she found him as desirable as I did.

'I will meet you at your hotel,' he said. 'I will book a restaurant for us. For nine o'clock.'

Lucy's face fell and I grinned. She was still fond of her food – nine o'clock was far too late for her.

'We eat late in Barcelona,' he told her, reading her face correctly. 'But perhaps you would prefer earlier? Eight o'clock, maybe?'

'That would be fine,' said Lucy. 'We look forward to seeing you.' She dazzled him with a smile. 'May we telephone for a taxi from here?'

'Oh, please do not trouble yourselves with a taxi,' he said, consternation in his voice. 'I will drive you myself.'

'There is no need for that, Señor,' said Lucy. 'We will be happy to get a taxi.'

But he would have none of it, and of course we were delighted to be driven back to the hotel by him. We relaxed in the soft leather seats of his car and listened while he pointed out sights of the city to us.

'You will go sightseeing?' he asked.

'Yes,' I said, although I knew that Lucy wanted to go shopping.

'You must see the *Sagrada Familia*,' he told us. 'One day, perhaps, it will be finished, but it is strange to see a cathedral which is so beautiful and so old. And look at our buildings, they are very fine.'

He pulled up outside the Hotel Galina. 'I will be here for you at seven-thirty,' he said. 'We can go for an *aperitif* before dinner.'

'Wonderful,' said Lucy as we scrambled out of the car.

She said nothing until we got back to the room and she put the box of tiles safely at the bottom of the wardrobe.

'Isn't he absolutely gorgeous,' she said dreamily. 'Wouldn't you run off with him?'

I nodded. 'And his voice.' I sighed. 'Pure poetry.'

We sat and drooled for a while and then I told her that we should do some sightseeing, so we changed into our jeans and I pulled on a long-sleeved T-shirt and tied a sweatshirt around my waist. It was actually hot outside now. The sun washed down on to the streets, reflected off the buildings and brightened the pavements. Lucy took out her guidebook and we worked out our route to the *Sagrada Familia* Cathedral.

It was an incredible building, like a sandcastle that was being washed away by the tide. Designed by Gaudi, the four turrets built in his time reached for the sky, topped by their coloured gilt crosses. The other side of the cathedral, where work still continued, mirrored those turrets but in a more modern style. The effect was startling.

Then Lucy wanted to go shopping and so we took the metro back to the shops. She bought some shoes in delicate soft leather which, I informed her, would be totally impractical at home; and a long linen skirt which emphasised her tiny waist. She bought a book on Spanish architecture for David. Fortunately it was English, but she didn't check that until she had already paid for it. 'It wouldn't have mattered,' she said. 'The pictures are enough.'

I bought myself another leather jacket, this time in a pale silver grey, and a Barcelona FC football shirt for Rory. I bought a doll and a pretty yellow dress for Clodagh and a box of rich chocolates for my parents.

We strolled along another of the long, wide streets, so that Lucy could take photographs of the incredible wavy buildings that were so much a feature of the city.

'They must have all been on drugs when they were designing them,' I said, looking up at a particularly crazy one.

'Probably,' agreed Lucy, 'but aren't they brilliant?'

There were other sights I wanted to see, but Lucy started to moan that she had a blister on her foot and so we caught a metro back to the *Paral-lel* and the Hotel Galina.

We had coffee at another pavement bar there, like children unable to give up a special treat.

'Isn't it wonderful?' sighed Lucy. 'Can you imagine sitting out in the middle of O'Connell Street trying to drink a cup of coffee now?'

'Not any time,' I said. 'You'd be killed by the fumes before you froze to death.'

Both of us took an age to get ready for dinner. Lucy washed her hair again and gelled it, so that she could plait it into a neat braid which fell to her shoulders. She was a mixture of innocence and sophistication. Her eyes gleamed softly out of her perfectly complexioned face. She wore a black Quinlan Lycra dress which hugged her figure like clingfilm and made me madly envious of a body which had not been subjected to the rigours of pregnancy.

I wore a pale green skirt and matching shirt. It was a pretty outfit, but not as alluring as Lucy's. I brushed my hair into a loose cloud of curls and went a bit heavy on the lip gloss.

We are both being very silly, I thought as I blew kisses to myself in the mirror.

I looked down at my hands. The diamond of my engagement ring sparkled in the light and the gold of my wedding band glowed warmly. I hadn't thought about Rory all day.

Ferdinand Casals called for us at exactly seven-thirty. A chauffeur was driving him, and Lucy and I exchanged surprised glances as the car pulled up outside the hotel. Obviously the tile business was doing well, Lucy murmured.

'Did you come to this part of the city earlier?' he asked, when the driver stopped in the old quarter.

Lucy nodded. 'We looked around. It's very – ancient.'

He laughed. 'It is the oldest *barrio* of the city,' he said. 'There is a restaurant here which I think you will like. But first we will have our *aperitif*.'

He led us to a small bar in a sidestreet. It had marble-topped tables with wrought-iron legs.

'What can I get you to drink?' he asked.

We both ordered gin and tonics and he went up to the bar to

get them. We looked at him as he stood there in his charcoal suit, impeccably dressed.

'I wish David could look like that,' sighed Lucy. 'But every time he wears a suit, he looks like he found it at the bottom of the wardrobe.'

'Rory has some very expensive suits,' I mused, 'but they don't sit on him like they do on this man. God, he's attractive.'

We giggled again.

He came back with the drinks and talked about Barcelona and the tile business and his family. He talked in a completely uninhibited way, telling us that he was divorced which was a shame on him and his family. He did look unhappy about it and I felt I should ask him more.

'We were married very young,' he said. 'I was twenty-one and she was twenty. We changed too much.'

'Do you have any children?' asked Lucy.

His eyes lit up. 'A son,' he said. 'Andreas. A fine boy.'

'I have a daughter,' I told him. 'She is four years old.'

'You look far too young to have a daughter.' He lied beautifully. 'You look hardly old enough to be unchaperoned.'

Lucy and I broke into a fit of giggles which I thought was terribly childish of us, but we couldn't help it.

'It is true,' he protested. 'You are two lovely ladies.'

'Thanks,' said Lucy, wiping her eyes. 'And you are a charmer.'

'Sorry?'

'You try to charm us like birds off trees,' she smiled. 'And you are succeeding very well.'

'I'm glad,' he laughed. 'I'm having a good time. It's not often I go to dinner with two ladies who are not from my family.'

'I'd say you go to dinner a lot with single ladies,' I told him. 'A man like you must have many girlfriends.'

He shook his head. 'I have no time,' he said. 'My business takes so much of it. I wonder which is right, to spend time working or to spend time in leisure? What do you think?'

'If you have money, then you don't have to worry about working,' said Lucy, 'and it can be leisure.'

'But it's nice to do something with your time,' I said. 'You can't sit around doing nothing.'

He nodded vigorously. 'And I like to be busy,' he said. 'It is

343

probably what destroyed my marriage. However,' he put his glass on the table, 'let us not worry about these things now, but go and have a wonderful meal in La Cocina.'

We followed him out of the restaurant and back into the streets, Lucy on one side of him, me on the other. We linked arms with him and I shivered at the warmth of his body close to mine. I didn't recognise the scent of his aftershave. You are an awful idiot, I told myself, as I hurried to keep in step with him.

The restaurant was tucked away behind the Town Hall, in an old stone building. The proprietor greeted Señor Casals like an old friend, which he was. He used this restaurant a lot, he told us – the cooking was superb.

I don't remember much about the meal. Ferdinand – we were on first-name terms by now – ordered for us, traditional cooking which was heavy and full of flavour. He chose Spanish Rioja to accompany the food and it was rich and warming. He told us about the city and the people, how they always asked if you were a Catalan and not a Spaniard. His voice was hypnotic and the words spilled comfortably between us.

I wanted to go to bed with him. I'd never felt that about anyone since I'd met Rory. The attraction I felt now for Ferdinand was exactly the same as I'd felt for Rory when I'd first known him. I was ashamed of feeling like this, but I couldn't help it. Lucy was attracted to him too, I could see it in her eyes. Every so often we would glance at each other and a look of complete understanding would pass between us. Inside me, feelings that had lain dormant for years stirred uncomfortably.

I shivered. What had I come to that I was having thoughts like this about a man I'd only just met? Who was nothing to do with me and who I would never meet again? I shouldn't feel like this, I told myself, I should be moved by his attractiveness but I shouldn't feel this slow, burning longing to throw myself at him. And it wasn't love, of course, it was simply physical desire. I understood, briefly, how men could be tempted when they were away on business. I wondered, not for the first time but with a lot more concern, whether Rory had ever felt like this when he was away.

I was sorry I thought of Rory. That made me think of Clodagh, too. Both of them would be sitting in front of the TV. Rory – if he thought of me at all – secure in the knowledge that I would come home from this break having enjoyed myself with my girlfriend of nearly seventeen years. He certainly wouldn't imagine that I was having erotic fantasies about Ferdinand Casals who was, I realised, flirting outrageously with us.

It was great to feel desirable again, though, and that was why I encouraged him. I didn't feel desirable with Rory any more. It wasn't his fault, of course. Time had muted the mad passion but I was amazed that I could still feel the way I did. It was a heady experience.

He brought us back to the hotel and kissed us both on the cheeks. I felt his lips burn against me as though he were branding me. It was hard to break away from him. I wanted to hold him and be held by him.

'I think he fancied you,' said Lucy as we undressed for bed that night.

I sat in front of the mirror and removed my make-up carefully.

'Don't be daft,' I said. 'He flirted with both of us.'

'But it was you he concentrated on,' she said. 'I could tell, Jane. There was a rapport between you.'

'There was nothing between us,' I said as I relived his final, casual kiss. I touched my cheek as I spoke, still sensing him. 'But he was some operator.'

'He was devastatingly attractive.' She slipped out of her dress and folded it neatly before putting it into her case. 'Men like that aren't safe to be let out alone.'

'He didn't try anything, though.' I brushed my hair.

'No,' said Lucy. 'Just as well.'

'Do you think David will like the tiles?' I asked.

'The what?'

'The tiles. The reason we came here.'

'I'd forgotten about the tiles,' admitted Lucy. 'My mind is still full of Ferdinand.' She shook her head. 'Yes, I think the tiles are fine. But I'd better get David to come over the next time. I wouldn't be responsible for my actions with a man like that if I was on my own. I mean, I'm mad about David but Ferdinand has such a physical presence . . .'

'Just as well I came, then,' I said virtuously. 'I was able to protect you.'

She eyed me dubiously. 'Oh yes?' she said. 'And who will protect the protector?'

I dreamed of Ferdinand that night, a hotchpotch of a dream that included all the men I'd ever known, even Jesse, my first boyfriend. Jesse stood in front of me telling me that I was a wanton woman and that he was going to divorce me, while Rory was the solicitor I engaged to look after my interests. I was disturbed by the dream; it preyed on my mind even the next day as we boarded our flight and left Barcelona behind us.

I was glad to get home to a takeaway pizza which Rory had ordered and to sit beside him on the sofa eating it and watching Inspector Morse on TV.

'Did you have a good time?' he asked, as I cut myself a triangle of pizza.

'Fine.'

'Did Lucy get her tiles?'

I nodded, my mouth full. 'What did you do?' I asked, when I'd swallowed the food.

'Nothing much. I was out last night, I left Clodagh with my mum. She enjoyed it.'

'Where did you go?'

'Nowhere special. Few drinks, that sort of thing.'

It must have been nice for him to go out and know he didn't have to face my wrath if he came home pissed.

'Did you miss me?' I snuggled up to him.

'Of course,' he said. 'Jane! I can't eat pizza with your head in the way.'

I sat up again. He was right, of course.

Chapter 27

November/December 1990
(UK No. 6 – *We Want The Same Thing* – Belinda Carlisle)

November was the month I hated most. Dark, dreary, cold and usually grey, it settled on me like a cloud. The days were still getting shorter, the weather bleaker. I never had any energy in November, everything was a chore. I often wondered what it was like in Barcelona in November, whether the air was still vaguely warm and whether the sun still shone on the crazy buildings. I thought about Barcelona a lot, not about Ferdinand Casals who had been relegated to the back of my mind along with my other schoolgirl crushes, like Bryan Ferry and Eric Clapton, but about the light of the sun, the gaiety of the people, the buzz of the city. It contrasted all too starkly with the driving rain and the huddled bodies of Dublin.

Rory gave up drink in November. Not on a permanent basis, merely to give his body a rest before the ravages of December. The dealers spent December in a virtual haze of alcohol, with business lunches almost every day and business dinners or drinks almost every night. Usually that meant I saw more of him in November, but this year was particularly busy and he never seemed to make it home before eight in the evening. Then he'd throw himself down on the sofa and close his eyes.

I thought that maybe he was becoming burnt out. They said it happened to dealers. Living on the edge all the time suddenly became too much to handle, and they couldn't keep going. Rory had been living on the edge now for ten years and I felt that it was too long. Even though he'd been promoted, he still traded. Often, when people were promoted they became backroom people, or administrators, but Rory didn't want that. I wondered now if he wouldn't prefer it to constantly trying to outguess what was going to happen in the increasingly volatile currency markets.

I wanted to talk to him about it, but I couldn't. There was something off-key about Rory in November. He came home, sat down, watched TV or fell asleep. He played with Clodagh and he talked to me, but as though he were really somewhere else. I felt our relationship slipping through my fingers, like water from a cupped hand, but I didn't know what to do about it. We were two people living in the same house, each with a private agenda that the other knew nothing about.

We'd have to confront it, I knew, but not now. Not until after Christmas and the New Year. So I struggled through the dank and dreary days of November in a half-world of happiness and misery that I couldn't do anything about.

The bank's annual Christmas party was the first Friday of December. This was not the staff party, but a dinner for the bank's clients which the more senior staff and wives attended. I usually enjoyed it. It was the one bank function that was fun and Rory was always in good form. This year it was in the Berkeley Court and so, the Saturday beforehand, I drove across to *Les Jumelles* to see if the twins had anything in stock that would turn me into a sex siren for the night.

I brought Clodagh because Rory was playing squash with Bill Hamilton. I remarked sourly that Bill would probably have a heart attack on the squash court – he was just the right age for it and getting heavier all the time. Rory laughed and said that if Bill did keel over he, Rory, was next in line for the job, so maybe it would be killing two birds with one stone. I liked it when Rory joked with me, it was rare these days. So I didn't mind when he drove off laden down with his kit-bag to beat Bill.

Clodagh was in a dreadful mood, wriggly and contrary. She didn't want to get into her car seat and cried that she wanted to go with Daddy. Her current personality was obstinate. No matter what we wanted her to do, she wanted to do the opposite. She wasn't happy about anything. Her favourite word was 'No'. I hoped that she wouldn't try to pull Brenda or Grace's beautiful clothes off the hangers or throw a screaming fit in the middle of the shop.

Les Jumelles wasn't the sort of shop where women brought four year olds. It was an exclusive shop, with breathtaking prices which most women seemed quite prepared to pay.

I turned into the car park of the shop and switched off the engine. Clodagh refused to get out of her car seat.

'Come on,' I said impatiently. 'I'll bring you to McDonald's on the way home if you're good now.'

The books didn't agree with bribery, but it was my only weapon. Clodagh got out of the car.

The shop was full. Well-dressed women clustered around the rails of silks and satins, swooped on the best designs and carried them off to the changing rooms.

'Hi, Jane!' Brenda pushed her hair out of her eyes. 'It's a bit manic in here today. The party season, you know.' She dropped to her knees and smiled at Clodagh. 'How's my favourite little girl?'

Her favourite little girl clung to my leg and buried her face in my skirt. I shook my head at Brenda. 'She's not in a good mood today. Temper tantrums. Little devil.'

Brenda laughed at me. 'She's lovely,' she said. 'Why don't I bring her into the office and she can play with some of the materials? Would you like that, Clodagh?'

My daughter nodded, trotted off with Brenda and left me to rummage through the rails in search of the perfect dress.

'You should have rung and said you were coming.' Grace appeared by my side. 'I would have put some things aside for you.'

'I wasn't going to come today,' I said. 'I thought I'd another week before the bank do, but I realised this morning that it was next Friday. Anyway, I like milling around like this, it whips up the buying frenzy.'

'Anything in particular you'd like?' asked Grace. 'Do you have anything in mind?'

I shook my head. 'Once I look thin and gorgeous, that's all that matters.'

'No problem,' grinned Grace. 'Let's have a look at the thin and gorgeous rail.'

She selected a few different dresses for me, all beautiful and all horrifically expensive. She chose my favourite colours, purple, green and royal blue. But she also included a gold lamé dress with a matching jacket that was different to anything I normally wore. I fingered the material and held it against me.

'I'm not sure it'll go with my hair,' I said as I carried it into a changing room.

'Trust me,' said Grace.

The dress fitted perfectly and it looked great with my hair. I preened in front of the mirror as I turned around to check how I looked from every angle.

'It's lovely.' Brenda peeked in at me.

'I know,' I said. 'It's so completely different from what I usually wear that I feel odd.'

'Buy it,' she said.

'Is that your expert boutique manager advice?'

'Absolutely.'

I bought the jacket and dress and stood at the desk while Brenda wrapped it in tissue paper and slid it into the exclusive dark green *Les Jumelles* carrier bag.

'You'll look fantastic at the party,' she promised me.

'Thanks.' I signed the credit card slip. 'We must get together some time soon, we haven't been out in an age.'

'After Christmas,' said Brenda. 'We're up to our necks now. Open on Sundays from next week.'

They worked hard for their money, I thought, as I collected Clodagh from their office.

'I'll give you a buzz after Christmas,' I told them. Brenda nodded. She was already attending to another customer. Grace called a 'goodbye' after me as I led Clodagh out of the shop.

'McDonald's,' said my daughter immediately.

I sighed. 'Soon,' I promised. 'I'm going to buy some shoes first.'

Clodagh started to cry. 'McDonald's,' she sniffled. 'You said.'

So I drove back to Dún Laoghaire, joined the throng of people queuing at the counter and bought her a burger and chips. She ate like a horse when she wanted to, but every day her tastes changed and so food that was perfectly acceptable on Monday was hated on Friday. McDonald's was a constant, though. I was starving myself so we both tucked in to Big Macs and chips.

When we'd finished, I dragged her across to the shopping centre where I managed to buy a pair of shoes and a bag. I was sure that I would look good on Friday. Last year, Karen Hamilton had worn a long multicoloured dress with a deep slit down the cleavage and a deeper slit up the side. All of the men, both from the bank and their clients, had spent the night looking at her. Whenever she took to the dance floor or walked up to the bar, their gaze followed her. Rory had tried to pretend that he didn't even notice her, but I saw his eyes almost pop out of his head when she brushed past him at one point.

My dress would not have that effect, but it was pretty and it suited me. I'd look like a corporate wife.

Pat Bannister baby-sat for us on party night. She arrived at seven, as I was putting the finishing touches to my make-up and Rory was pacing around the bedroom begging me to hurry up. He was meant to be there early because he had to greet his clients. I ignored him and continued to outline my lips with lip pencil before colouring them in with lipstick.

'Why don't you just slap it on?' he demanded, as I blotted it on a tissue.

'Because it lasts longer this way,' I told him, filling in the colour again. He sighed in an exaggerated fashion and looked pointedly at his watch.

'All right, all right,' I grumbled. I sprayed myself liberally with *Dune*. 'I'll be ready in a minute.'

I looked into Clodagh's room. She was already asleep, tired by her day out, her eyes squeezed shut and her teddy bear grasped in her hand. She was such an angel when she was asleep, I thought, a lump in my throat as I looked at her. I kissed her on the forehead and she sighed gently. I pulled her quilt over her and tiptoed out of the room.

Pat was sitting in front of the TV reading *Hard Times*.

'Still forcing you to read that dreadful book?' I remembered how much I'd hated it at school myself.

'I quite like Dickens,' said Pat, 'although I'm not mad about this one, myself. I loved *Great Expectations* though.'

'Enjoy it, then,' I said. 'I preferred Arthur Hailey, myself. You know where we are if you need us. There's plenty of food in the fridge if you get hungry. We'll be back about two.'

'That's fine.' Pat looked up from the book again. 'I'll probably go to bed around midnight.'

'OK, then,' I said. 'Goodnight.'

I hurried out into the driveway where Rory was already impatiently revving the engine of the car.

'We're late,' he said sourly.

'They won't even notice,' I said.

The Berkeley Court was crowded with people. Most of them were in dress suits and were with the bank; the bar was packed, and people thronged around the foyer too. The women were like tropical birds strutting around the hotel in their party clothes. Brightly-coloured dresses stood out among the tuxedos and the black cocktail numbers. I felt gaudy but striking in the gold lamé. I'd been to the hairdresser's that day and had my hair pulled into an impressive chignon on the back of my head, secured by a diamanté clip in the side. My height was always an advantage at dressy occasions. I could carry the extravagant outfits well.

'Jane, how wonderful to see you.' Bill grasped me by the hand. 'We thought you'd never get here.'

'Sorry,' I said, 'my fault. Gilding the lily.'

'You look super,' he said. 'What can I get you?'

'I think Rory has gone to get me a drink,' I said. 'Perhaps later, Bill.'

Not that it mattered. The entire night was paid for by the bank, which meant a free bar for the evening. I was driving home, of course. Rory would drink tonight but I wouldn't. I'd allow myself a gin and tonic before the meal and a glass of wine with it and then I'd switch to Ballygowan. It would have been nice to get blazingly drunk at one of Rory's parties, but I knew that I never would.

'Hi, Jane.' Karen Hamilton, looking fabulous in cerise velvet, wandered over and took Bill's arm. 'I rather think there's a man over there you want to talk to,' she murmured to him and he left us alone. 'How's Clodagh?'

'She's fine,' I said. 'And Gary?'

'He started college this year. Amazing how time flies.'

'Isn't it?' I said.

'Clodagh must be starting school soon,' said Karen idly.

'Next year,' I said. 'She's going to playschool at the moment.'

'Bill tells me you're working again.'

'A financial company,' I said. 'Small. Nothing special.'

'Rather you than me,' said Karen.

'I enjoy it.'

We made desultory conversation for a little longer, then we were joined by Bill again and a couple of the bank's clients. I looked around for Rory who was chatting to a rounded, bald man who looked as if he might explode out of his tux at any minute. This was the part of the night that I disliked. Rory always abandoned me to talk to someone else and, although I understood his motives, I hated being left with people I didn't particularly like.

Luckily, we moved fairly quickly into the banqueting room. It was wonderfully decorated in silver and gold. A huge Christmas tree sparkled with thousands of fairy lights at the top of the room. Rory steered me towards our table. I sat down at my place and looked at the name beside me. I opened my eyes wide in surprise and checked it again. There was no sign of any of our guests yet, so I asked Rory if they were all particular clients of his.

'We share them around,' he told me. 'Conor Donnelly will be at my table, he's one of my better clients. I've got Richard Dennison as well, that should keep you happy. And Kieran Woods and Antonia.'

I nodded. 'And this one?'

'Some credit client. I'm not sure who. He accepted at the last minute and they put him at my table.'

At that point Richard Dennison and his wife, Susan, arrived and we shook hands with them. I knew them quite well by now; we had gone to dinner with them a number of times. I liked Susan. She was in her mid-twenties and taught French. Richard was fifteen years older than her, and absolutely besotted by her. They had a daughter a couple of months younger than Clodagh.

We kissed, continental fashion, on each cheek. But with Susan it was a genuine greeting.

'You look great,' she said, sitting down. 'Love the dress. Where did you get it?'

Les Jumelles.

'That's where I picked this up,' said Susan. 'But – I'll let you into a secret here – last January, in their sale. They always have a fantastic sale.'

'I know,' I said. 'I bought some stuff last January myself. But I wasn't smart enough to buy a cocktail dress.'

'That's really pretty.' Susan looked admiringly at my dress. 'Distinctive.'

'I'm never sure that's a good idea,' I said. 'Distinctive sounds like it should be nice but it's a major disaster.'

'No, it's nice,' said Susan. 'Are we terribly early or is there a reason that there's nobody else at this table?'

'I don't know.' I fiddled with the cutlery. 'I hope they sit down soon. I'm starving.'

A crush of people walked into the room, checking the table plan at the doorway and making their way to the tables. Conor Donnelly and his wife, Lisa, joined us, followed by a man introduced to us as Fergal Slattery and his wife, whose name I didn't catch. The final guests arrived a few moments later.

'I'm terribly sorry,' said Hugh McLean. 'Were you waiting for us?'

'Not at all.' Rory stood up and extended his hand. 'Rory McLoughlin. I'm with the Treasury team.'

'Hugh McLean,' he said, shaking hands. 'And this is Denise.'

Denise was a pretty girl who couldn't have been more than twenty. She had soft brown hair, brown eyes and a flawless complexion.

'My wife, Jane,' said Rory.

I held my breath as he took my hand. 'Delighted to meet you,' he said. He smiled, a tiny smile that only barely turned up the corners of his lips.

We sat down and the Managing Director of the bank made a brief speech of welcome. Then the food was served.

No matter how wonderful, the food at a Christmas party is always predictable. The first parties you attend are always such novelties that you don't mind turkey and ham, followed by pudding. After a few years of the same food every year, I'd grown blasé about it. But I was hungry and I tucked into the pâté with enthusiasm.

Susan Dennison chatted away to me, talking about her daughter and asking me questions about discipline which, given Clodagh's current form, I felt ill-equipped to answer. I replied to her but with only half a mind on the conversation. I was too much aware of Hugh McLean sitting in the seat beside me.

How on earth had he managed to get here? Rory had never

mentioned him as a client of the bank and obviously didn't know him anyway. Why did this man keep turning up? He had a power to disturb me for reasons I didn't understand.

He was attractive, but I'd grown out of his sort of attraction. He seemed interesting, but not especially to me. He was kind. I suppose he'd been kind to me. I shook my head, recalling those few days after Clodagh's birth, when Hugh had breezed into my room every day. A most peculiar man, I'd thought then.

I shot surreptitious glances at him as I ate, careful to look at him only when his attention was directed at his companion. I wondered whether she was his wife or his girlfriend. I thought they were talking rather too much for her to be his wife. She wasn't the same girl I'd seen him with at the Park. He hadn't been married, then. No one would have him, he'd said. He looked quite different tonight. He'd abandoned the run-down look for a far more groomed appearance. His shirt was crispy white with a winged collar over a thin black bow tie. His dress suit was brand new, with impeccable creases. The tortoiseshell glasses gave him a slightly distracted look, just enough to stop him looking completely in control.

He caught my eye as the waiters cleared away the soup bowls. I flushed slightly and tried to glance away, but it was too late. He cleared his throat and spoke to me.

'How is your daughter?' he asked.

'You're always asking about my daughter.' I folded and refolded my napkin. 'She's fine.'

'Then how are you?' he asked.

'Fine.'

'And your husband is fine too, I suppose?' he said.

'Of course.'

'Did you enjoy your stay at the Park?' he asked.

'It was—'

'Fine?' he supplied.

'Very enjoyable,' I said. 'A lovely hotel.'

I picked at a fingernail and looked at the table. I really didn't know what to say to him. It was like meeting someone with whom you'd had an affair. Or so I imagined. But I hadn't had an affair with Hugh, I'd hardly even spoken to him. Why did I immediately feel guilty when I saw him?

The girl, Denise, tapped him on the arm. He turned away from me and talked to her, leaving me sitting staring into space. Susan talked to Rory. I watched the waiters bustling around the room, choreographed by the head waiter. It must be difficult to cater for a huge party like this, I thought, as I played with my name card. There were about two hundred people here tonight.

'Penny for them,' said Hugh.

I turned to look at him. 'I was thinking that there's a lot of hard work involved in catering,' I said.

'I'm sure there is.'

I was convinced that he was laughing at me. I didn't know why.

'How is it that you were invited tonight?' I asked bluntly. I supposed I should have been more polite to someone who was obviously a good client of the bank, since only good clients were invited to the party, but I didn't see him like that.

'We're clients,' said Hugh simply.

'I guessed that,' I said. 'I wondered in what capacity.'

'In the borrowing capacity.'

I nodded. 'Rory said you were a client of the Credit department,' I said. 'What do you do?'

He relented. 'I own a bookshop. Well, a few bookshops. I've amalgamated them into a chain. You may have noticed. CityBooks.'

'Oh yes.' I'd seen one of the shops in Dún Laoghaire. It looked very inviting, with a period façade and a huge display of books attractively placed in the window.

'We've three shops now,' said Hugh. 'Dun Laoghaire, Sutton and Rathmines. We're hoping to open more at some point. The bank has lent us the money to do the refits and make sure that the design is the same in them all. Give them the corporate look.'

'I've seen the one in Dún Laoghaire, although I haven't been in it,' I said. 'It looks very attractive.'

'Obviously not attractive enough if you haven't bought anything yet,' he said.

'I buy magazines more than books.' I told him. I felt a complete philistine.

Just then, Denise attracted his attention again. I wished that dinner was over and that the dancing would start. It was very difficult to be trapped beside someone like this. Susan spoke to me and I turned to her gratefully, keeping the conversation going with her throughout the main course and right through the dessert as well. It was easy enough to do, because Susan could talk for ages about the students she taught or about her daughter. All I had to do was to ask the right question and she would be off and running, leaving me to nod and agree with her whenever necessary.

Rory didn't talk to me at all during the meal, but I didn't expect him to. He was working, after all. He swapped golfing stories with Conor, Kieran and Richard which kept them all amused. Sometimes they made a fourball together, so they were close as friends as well as clients.

It seemed forever before the tables were cleared and the band got up to play. They started with some sixties music which had a lot of people up and dancing straight away. Rory looked at me and raised an eyebrow in silent query and I got up and started dancing with him.

'Who's the guy beside you?' he asked me as we twisted on the dance floor.

'His name's McLean,' I said breathlessly. 'He owns some book-shops. He's apparently just got a loan from the bank for refurbishment.'

Rory nodded. 'I can place him now. Did we meet him before? He looks familiar.'

'He was at the Park last Easter when we went down,' I said. 'You accused me of knowing him.'

Remembrance dawned in Rory's eyes. 'And did you?' he asked.

'Don't be silly.' I spun around him in a flurry of gold.

We sat down after a few minutes and Rory asked Antonia to dance. Hugh danced with Denise, and they laughed happily together.

The band was good. Most people got up and danced. Rory got up with another client's wife. I tapped my foot under the table, even though I was sitting down. Then Richard asked me to dance, then Conor, then finally I sat down again and drank some Ballygowan.

I smothered a yawn guiltily with the back of my hand, then glanced at my watch. Midnight already.

They played some slow music. Rory and his pals were propping up the bar as they smoked cigars and drank brandy. He looked over at me and I smiled at him.

'Would you like to dance with me?' Hugh stood beside me.

'I don't think so,' I said.

'Why ever not?'

'I'm tired.'

'Why do I get the feeling you don't like me?' he asked.

I looked up at him. 'I don't know,' I said honestly. 'I don't dislike you. You make me uncomfortable.'

'Why?'

I looked down at my lap. 'I'm not sure.'

'Come and dance with me and we can talk about it,' he suggested. 'I don't like to think that I'm making someone uncomfortable.'

'What about your girlfriend?' I asked.

'Denise is my sister,' said Hugh. 'She's my partner in the bookshops.'

I felt silly. He was a client, after all. I stood up.

'I love your dress,' he said.

'Thank you.'

His hand was on the base of my spine, hot through the thin fabric. Only hot in my mind, because his other hand, in mine for the waltz, was cool and dry. He was a good dancer. I moved with him around the floor.

'So why do I make you uncomfortable?' he asked again.

'Because you met me when I was feeling down,' I told him. 'And seeing you reminds me of that time. It embarrasses me.'

'I'm truly sorry,' said Hugh sincerely. 'I didn't mean to upset you then. It seemed like a good idea at the time.'

'Oh, I was upset anyway,' I said. 'And you did cheer me up. But I suppose people don't like being reminded of difficult times.'

He spun me around. 'Why was it difficult?'

'You know why. I told you then. Rory was away, I'd had a difficult birth, I felt – lonely.'

'You looked it,' he said. 'That's why I kept coming in.'

'I know. And thank you.'

'It was nothing. Denise always says that I like interfering in other people's lives. Sorry if I interfered in yours.'

'You didn't,' I said. 'You were very kind.'

He made a face. 'I don't want to be known as kind,' he said. 'I want to be known as a daredevil, risk-taker.'

'That's my husband,' I told him gently.

'Ah.' He looked searchingly into my eyes. 'And how is the husband?'

'You asked me that already,' I said. 'And I answered you. He's fine.'

'So tell me about your daughter, then,' he said. 'Since everything is OK in the husband department.'

So I told him about Clodagh and chatted about my life and he was very easy to talk to. He didn't judge but simply listened. I found myself telling him stupid things, about how I felt going back to work, about my envy of Lucy and the Quinlans, but he didn't tell me that I was foolish or selfish, he merely held me as we danced and nodded encouragingly from time to time.

When the band changed the tempo of the music, I thanked him and went to refresh my make-up. Lisa was in the Ladies and asked me about Hugh.

'A credit customer,' I told her. 'Nice guy.'

'Very attractive,' she said, 'in a laid-back sort of way.'

'He owns a few bookshops,' I said. 'I don't think he's very, well, businessman type.'

'You get tired of the suits after a while,' she said. 'I long to meet someone who isn't turned on by a balance sheet.'

I laughed at this but knew what she meant. I told her about Ferdinand Casals. 'There's a man you would have liked,' I said. 'Businessman with a difference.'

'Not really,' she told me. 'They're all the same underneath. It's a power thing.'

I supposed she was right, which was disappointing. Would Ferdinand have been half as attractive to me if he was a farmer in an olive grove? Probably not.

Rory was dancing with Amanda Ferry from the dealing room when I got back. They were doing some very vigorous jumping about. I'd have to warn him about the danger of having a heart attack. He was the right age.

The music seemed very loud. I wondered would anyone notice if I sloped off to the foyer for a while. There was nobody at our table anyway, they were all dancing.

I went outside and sat in one of the deep sofas. It was blissfully quiet.

He sat down beside me five minutes later. 'Are you all right?' he asked, concern in his voice.

'Are you following me?' I opened my eyes.

'Of course not,' said Hugh. 'I went to the Gents. Saw you sitting here. Thought you might be feeling unwell.'

I sighed. 'You're always thinking I'm unwell.'

'Sorry,' he said.

'And you're always apologising.'

'Always is a little strong,' he said. 'We don't meet that often.'

'I know.' I hung my head. 'Forget it.'

'Forget what?'

I shrugged. 'I don't know. You're very difficult.' My voice rose. 'You're different to other men I've known.'

'I'm so glad,' he murmured.

I looked at him. 'Why?'

'You know lots of people that I don't particularly like,' he said. 'I'm glad I'm different.'

'There's nothing wrong with commerce,' I said sharply. 'You mightn't like the bankers or the accountants or the solicitors but they're the people who make life tick. No doubt you think it's immoral to earn money.'

'Not at all,' said Hugh. 'I don't run my shops for charity.'

I was deflated. 'I suppose not. You get me at dodgy moments in my life. I'm the one who should apologise to you.'

'Don't worry,' he said. 'It's water off a duck's back to me. I don't get involved. I interfere but it's harmless, really.'

I gazed at him. 'Why do you interfere with me?'

'I don't know,' he said. 'I can't help it.'

'Why?'

'You always look as though something dreadful is about to happen,' he said. 'As though some awful event is waiting to destroy you. You have this hunted look about you.'

I was shocked. 'I do not.'

'You do,' he said. 'And that's interesting.'

'Well, you're not very good at expressions.' I stood up. 'Rory is probably hunting for me as we speak. I'd better get back inside.'

'Sure,' he said. 'It's a good party.'

In fact, Rory was dancing with Amanda again. They'd been joined by a gang of the dealers and their girlfriends. I joined in, kicking up my heels and shaking my head until the clip in my hair flew off and nearly took Rory's eye out.

'Good party,' he said that night when we were in bed.

'Very good.' I pulled the duvet around me.

'I'm sorry I didn't get much opportunity to dance with you,' he said. 'You were brilliant at the end there.'

'I'm always brilliant,' I said tiredly, as I closed my eyes.

He pulled me towards him in the bed, rubbed his hand on my stomach and allowed it to slip into the warmth between my legs.

'Too tired,' I mumbled.

'Oh, come on, Jane.'

'Really, Rory. I'm exhausted.'

'It's not too much to ask, is it?'

'In the morning.'

'Great,' said my husband and rolled over. He was snoring within thirty seconds.

Chapter 28

January 1991
(**UK No. 10** – *You've Lost That Lovin' Feeling* – **Righteous Brothers**)

It was a busy week. The Civic packed up on Monday, and Dad couldn't send anyone around to pick it up until Tuesday. He told me that there was something wrong with the clutch and that he wouldn't have whatever the part was until the end of the week. I was in a perpetual rush then, getting Clodagh off to playschool, getting into work and then hurrying out on the dot of five to pick her up again. I was sort of pleased when Rory announced that he'd got to go to London on Thursday, because it meant that I'd have the Mercedes. He was getting the early morning flight, so I told him I'd drop him at the airport, bring Clodagh to school and go into work myself afterwards. Rory was unusually pissed off about going to London. He said he was far too busy in work to be losing a day wandering around the City. He'd be back some time on Friday; he'd give me a call.

Thursday was hectic. It was pouring with rain at six in the morning, Clodagh didn't want to get out of bed and Rory was grumpy. He'd been late home the previous night, but he hadn't been in a pub – there were no stale smells of tobacco and alcohol clinging to his suit, but his eyes were red from staring at the Reuters screens so late.

We didn't talk on the way to the airport. Rory drove because he reckoned we'd get there faster that way, Clodagh fell asleep again and I wondered whether I'd ever get the nerve to talk to Rory about the state of our marriage.

We had to talk, no question. I just wasn't sure what to say.

That I knew something must be wrong? That I knew that Rory was fed up with me? That I still loved him but that I couldn't go on like this? That he would have to choose between his career and me? I didn't want to ask the last question. I was afraid he'd choose his career.

I left him at the set-down point. He kissed me perfunctorily on the cheek, said he'd ring and then disappeared along with all of the other men in business suits. I slid into the driver's seat and headed back across town.

The rain sloshed against the windscreen of the car, and I needed the wipers on at full speed to cope with the torrent of water. I hurried Clodagh into school, holding my coat over her and cursing the weather. I was still wet by the time I got into work. Fortunately, the mad scramble ended in the office and, amazingly, it was quiet that day. I'd managed to get up to date on all of the day-to-day stuff, Claire was in meetings most of the day and Stephen was in the States. Claire popped her head around her office door at about four o'clock and told me to go home if I wasn't busy. 'No need to hang around,' she said. 'I'll be here for a while and I'll answer the phones, if you like.'

'Great.' I tidied my desk. It was nice to get off early for once. I ran across the street to the car. It was still pouring with rain.

I cursed when I realised that I'd got a ticket, but then remembered that it was Rory's car and that he could probably get the bank to pay for it. I crumpled the pink and white paper and put it into the glove compartment. Rory was madly untidy. The compartment was a jumble of tapes and CDs, half-opened packets of mints and miniature bottles of aftershave. There were a couple of other parking tickets in there, too. With a bit of luck he wouldn't notice this one. I pushed it in towards the back and felt the soft, yielding material. More rubbish, I thought, as I pulled it out. It was a stocking. A black silk stocking.

I was sick on to the passenger seat. I couldn't help it. A sudden heave over which I had no control brought my food racing back up my throat, burning it. I couldn't do anything to stop myself and the foetid pool landed on the empty leather seat beside me. After it happened, I didn't know what to do. I sat in the driver's seat, shivering with the cold and the shock. My face was wet but I didn't know whether it was with sweat from being sick or with tears. And the smell clung to me. I didn't know what to do about the vomit. There wasn't anything to clean it with. My car always had plenty of tissues for emergencies, but Rory's hadn't. I looked around in confusion. The smell was so awful that I knew I would have to do something. If I stayed in the car, with that, I would be sick again.

So, in the end, I used the evidence to clean up. I stretched the sheer black stocking between my hands and used it to scrape the mess out of the car. I didn't know what to do with the stocking afterwards. Part of me wanted to keep it, to confront Rory with it, maybe even to throttle him with it. But I couldn't keep it, and eventually I dumped it out of the window.

I don't remember the drive home. I remember that, at some point, the rain eased off but I left the wipers racing across the windscreen in a frenzy. I remember that, as I waited for the railway gates to lift at Merrion, *Unchained Melody* played on the car radio. I also remember that, despite the temperature outside, I was very hot, that a rivulet of sweat ran from my temple to my chin and that my hands were clammy on the steering wheel. But I don't really remember the details of my drive. One minute I was in Merrion Square then, suddenly, I was at home, fumbling for my house keys.

I sat in the kitchen and cried. I cried until my eyes were so sore that I couldn't stand the salt tears, until my cheeks were swollen and until I felt positively sick again. I leaned forward in the chair and rocked with my grief, with the shock of Rory's betrayal and with the knowledge that I was a fool. I buried my head in my arms and sobbed like a child.

I cried because I knew that Rory was having an affair, and that the affair was the only thing that could explain all the late nights, and the whispered phone conversations, and the fact that he didn't seem to care that we hadn't made love since before Christmas. I didn't know whether to hate him or to hate me for driving him to it. I was a useless wife, a hopeless mother. I wasn't there for him when he needed me.

How long had it been going on? I wiped the tears from my eyes and went into his den to search for more evidence. At the back of my mind lingered the very faint hope that there could be a rational excuse for Rory having a sheer black stocking in the glove compartment of his car. I vaguely remembered Dad once saying that stockings had been used as emergency fan belts on cars. I couldn't imagine that a slinky 7-denier would be much good as a fan belt and I wasn't sure that the Mercedes even *had* a fan belt, but it was the only hope I had.

Rory's den was as messy as the car. It wasn't really an office, more a place where he kept all his bits and pieces. His golf clubs were propped up in the corner, against the small filing cabinet. There was nothing in the filing cabinet, just American Express dockets and old copies of the *Financial Times*. There was a desk in the office, too. The top drawer of the desk was locked and I pushed and pulled at it frantically. I was convinced that there was evidence in the desk. I searched the den for the keys as tears fell down my cheeks. The keys of the desk were in the filing cabinet. My hands shook as I opened the drawer. It was empty, except for an electric razor. I scrabbled around in the drawer. It didn't make sense to lock it if there was nothing in it, but I couldn't find anything. I pressed against the side of it, looking for secret panels. Suddenly I realised that I was making a complete idiot of myself. This was an ordinary desk, there couldn't be any secret panels in it.

I sat down in the swivel chair and closed my eyes. Maybe I was wrong after all. Maybe there was a perfectly rational explanation for the stocking.

The phone rang and I jumped in fright.

'Jane, are you coming to collect Clodagh?' It was Audrey Bannister. I looked at my watch. Half past six. I'd been in a daze, hadn't realised it was so late. I told her I'd be round straight away.

'Are you all right?' she asked, as she opened the door. I'd splashed cold water on my face and run a brush through my hair, but I knew that my eyes were still red and that my cheeks were blotchy.

'Upset stomach,' I said.

'You poor thing.' She looked anxiously at me. 'Will you be OK? You look wretched.'

'I'll be fine,' I said. 'I just need to lie down for a while. I think I ate something dodgy at lunch-time.'

'Rory can keep an eye on Clodagh,' said Audrey. 'You should go to bed.'

I nodded tiredly. Clodagh knew that something was wrong. She sniffed the air in the car. 'It smells of sick,' she said. I'd have to do something about it. I couldn't let Rory know I'd thrown up in his precious Mercedes.

'Don't be silly,' I said.

'Well, it does.' Clodagh was adamant. 'Sick, sick, sick.'

'Be quiet,' I said, but I could hear her muttering under her breath, 'Sick, sick, sick'.

I made her something to eat and then parked her in front of the TV without even checking to see what was on. I went back into Rory's den and opened the filing cabinet again.

The American Express dockets were jumbled together in a red folder. His business card was Amex, so there was every reason for him to have lots of receipts. There were loads of them. For Dobbin's and Gilbaud's and The Copper Beech. For petrol. For flights to London and Frankfurt. For the theatre. For the flower shop. I looked at the flower shop ones more closely. Flowers? To whom? Why? I was beginning to shake again. Was this it? Was this the evidence?

I looked at the dates on the restaurant receipts, but they didn't mean an awful lot. He could have been on business, it could have been anything else. Same with any of the others. How could I tell?

There was nothing else in the den. I don't know what sort of evidence I'd expected. Had I thought that, just by looking, I could have identified the receipts documenting his infidelity? It wasn't as easy as that. But the flowers – the flowers still bothered me. Every Friday since October. That was an awful lot of flowers.

I put Clodagh to bed and the phone rang again.

'Hi, Jane,' said Lucy. 'How are things?'

I really didn't want to talk to Lucy then. She'd guess there was something wrong.

'Fine.' I spoke carefully.

'I know it's a bit late but d'you want to go to the cinema tonight?' she asked. 'David and I were going and I've booked the tickets on my credit card, but now he can't. So I'm looking for another victim.'

'Sorry, Lucy,' I said. 'Rory's in London and I can't get anyone to mind Clodagh at this hour.'

'That's a pity. Oh well, never mind. Another time, maybe.'

'Sure.'

'Are you all right?' she asked. 'You sound a bit funny.'

'Headache,' I muttered. 'All day.'

'You poor thing.' Lucy was sympathetic. 'And here's me asking you to go to the movies. Probably the last thing you want to do.'

'I'll be fine,' I said. 'I'll take a few Hedex or something.'

'Well, look after yourself.'

'I will, Lucy. I'll give you a call. Maybe we can go to the cinema next week?'

'That'd be great. See you, Jane.'

'See you.' I replaced the receiver. I felt sick again.

I didn't sleep that night. I turned over and over again in the big five-foot bed and wondered what I should do. How could I confront Rory? What should I say to him? I was useless at arguing with him. He always managed to make me end up apologising to him. But this was his fault. His. I wished that I'd kept the stocking. He could hardly bluff his way out of that.

I wondered about the owner. What was she like? Where had he met her? How long had he known her? Who the hell was she? Was she a client, perhaps? Or somebody from the bank? Did everyone except me know about it? Was it true that the wife was always the last to know?

The worst question, the absolutely earth-shattering question, was – what had they been doing in the car and why was her stocking in the glove compartment?

Pictures of the unknown woman swam into my mind. Tall, blonde, willowy. Eminently sexual. A thin woman. Without a stomach. Or maybe Rory would go for someone dark. He liked dark women. Not fat, though. Not with hips or anything. Was it because of Clodagh, I wondered. Was it because my body was different? God, it couldn't be that, my original shape wasn't as good as my body now. I still went to the gym once, sometimes twice, a week. I thought I was in good shape. Relatively speaking. But I hadn't thought I was unattractive. Obviously I was wrong.

It was hard to get through the next day, but somehow I managed to get myself under control. I worked like a demon in the office, chivvying Claire and Stephen to make appointments, phone clients, do things they'd put off doing. I even tidied up Stephen's office which usually resembled a battle zone. When Rory called, unexpectedly, I was surprised at how calm I suddenly was.

'I'll be home tomorrow,' he told me. 'Sorry, Jane, I thought I might get back tonight but it'll have to be tomorrow.'

'No problem,' I said. 'Easier to pick you up tomorrow.' I wondered if his mistress was with him now, if it was all an excuse and they were lying together on some hotel bed, revelling in each other. Was she tracing her finger along his chest as I usually did? Was she kissing him behind the ear, which he absolutely loved? Was she – I couldn't bear to think of what else they might be doing. I felt my stomach churn, but I hadn't eaten since yesterday so I knew that I couldn't be sick again.

'See you tomorrow, then,' he said.

'Sure.' The tears were welling up again.

The question of how to confront him remained. Maybe I *had* made a terrible mistake. Maybe there was a perfectly rational explanation for the stocking. I sat on the sofa with my legs curled beneath me, rocking gently back and forward, and tried to think of a perfectly rational explanation. I couldn't.

Lucy called again that evening. 'How's the headache?' she asked. 'You sounded terrible last night so I thought I'd ring and check.'

'Better.' I looked at my still-puffy eyes in the mirror. 'I think it was a bug of some sort.'

'Why?'

'Because I still feel a bit shaky. I was sick last night,' I said.

'Is it something you ate?'

'I'm not sure, Lucy. Might be a touch of flu. I think I've a bit of a temperature, snuffly nose, sore throat, that sort of thing.'

'When is Rory back?' she asked.

'Tomorrow, sometime.'

'OK, then. Take care of yourself, Jane, you still sound rotten. Talk to you next week.'

I couldn't talk to Lucy about it yet. When I knew for sure, then I would talk to her, but not now. I couldn't share this pain with anyone, I held it close to me. I got through the evening somehow, but every so often, my thoughts and my grief fizzed together in my head so that tears suddenly welled up again and I'd scrub frantically at my eyes.

I practised meeting Rory. 'Hi, darling, how are you? You bastard!'

'Rory! Your girlfriend called. Can she see you in the car later?'

I'd spent ages getting the passenger seat clean. It smelled of disinfectant now. 'Rory, my love, I've missed you. By the way, did your girlfriend lose her stocking in your car? You bastard!'

Being angry helped, it meant I could block out some of the pain. But how would I feel when I met Rory face to face? The thought made my head swim. I didn't know how I would cope. Should I try and get more information first? Be absolutely, one hundred per cent certain?

I was baking a cake when he phoned on Saturday morning. I don't know why on earth I was baking, it was something I did so rarely that Clodagh watched me with great interest. I gave her some pastry to play with and she was rolling it into a long, doughy snake when the phone rang.

'I'll be in at two,' said Rory. 'Will you be there to pick me up?'

'Sure.'

'Everything OK?'

'Yes.'

'Clodagh OK?'

'Of course.'

'Do you want anything in the duty-free?'

'No.'

'See you at two.'

'We'll be there.'

I was trembling as I replaced the receiver. I put the cake in the oven, set the timer and told Clodagh that we had to go and pick up Daddy.

We stood in the arrivals area and waited for him. Clodagh jumped up and down to see him. My mouth was dry. He came into the arrivals hall, looking tired, and my heart leaped at the sight of him. Why? It made no sense. This morning I'd hated him, and now I'd give anything to make everything all right between us. He pecked me on the cheek and I wanted to recoil from him but he was my husband, I couldn't. At that moment, I wanted to bury my head in his shoulder and tell him that I loved him and that it was probably all my fault, and that it didn't matter what he had done, but now would he leave whoever she was alone and come back to Clodagh and me, be my husband again. I could make it all right – I knew I could.

We walked out to the car park together. He talked about the London trip. It must have been business, he couldn't have made up all of the stories.

'Accident?' he asked, sniffing the disinfectant as he got into the car.

'The usual.' I maligned Clodagh, who occasionally had bladder problems.

'Maybe we should take her to a doctor.'

'She'll be OK,' I said as I pulled out of the parking bay.

I didn't confront him. Not that evening, nor even the next day. I couldn't bring myself to do it. I still didn't know what to say, but I was alert now for clues and I found them. Not tangible clues, but his behaviour gave him away. So did the faint, lingering traces of *Samsara* which clung to him some nights when he had been working late.

I said nothing. I had to wait until I was ready. It helped that we didn't talk to each other very much any more. He didn't have to lie to me very often. Every night, as we lay together side by side, the tears would slide down my cheeks and saturate my pillow so that I would have to turn it over. But he never heard me cry and he never knew that I knew.

On Friday, two weeks later, he told me that he was going out to dinner. Meeting clients. The Copper Beech, he said. He wouldn't be too late. Would I come into town with him and take the car so that he could get a taxi home? No sense in risking being done for drink-driving. He'd become very serious about drink-driving since one of the dealers had been breathalysed on Baggot Street after a long lunch and had been prosecuted. I told him that it was no problem, I'd be happy to drive him into town. It was a lot safer than risking his licence, I agreed. He came home and showered and changed. He looked good in his Hugo Boss suit, even though his slight paunch had got a little bigger since Christmas.

'Who are the clients?' I asked, as we pulled out of the driveway. I sniffed the air. The faint aroma of disinfectant still lingered.

'The usual,' said Rory. 'Couple of guys from Hamburg. Boring, really.'

If it were true, then it could be boring. But I didn't know now whether he ever ate with clients or whether it was always with his . . . his what? Mistress. The word made me retch.

'Poor darling,' I said unfeelingly. 'What time will you be home?'

'We're having a drink beforehand, dinner at eight. Maybe a drink afterwards. Back by midnight, I suppose.'

'That's fine,' I said. 'I might go over to Lucy. She wanted to go to the cinema last week but I couldn't. Pat can stay on and baby-sit.'

'Good idea,' he said. 'Tell her I was asking for her.'

I knew then that he must be meeting his mistress. He never thought it was a good idea for me to see Lucy. He still didn't like her.

He got out at Searson's and I thought of all the times we'd met there ourselves in the past, as I watched him walk inside. I wondered whether she was already there. Perhaps she was sitting back in one of the seats, long legs crossed, elegantly waiting for him. She'd look at the door each time it opened, expecting to see him come in. Did she worry that I would ever find out? Did she care that maybe, some day, I would know about them and create a scene? I laughed to myself. I never created scenes, I wasn't the type.

Once, in school, our geography teacher, Miss Hennessy, had accused me of copying my homework. I told her I hadn't but she didn't believe me and she ranted and raved at me for ages, telling me that it was useless to copy other people's work and that I would never amount to much if I didn't put the effort in myself. And I let her shout at me because I couldn't think of anything to say to defend myself and it was easier to take the blame rather than to try and argue my corner. I didn't like causing trouble then and I didn't like causing trouble now. I didn't like people looking at me and whispering about me. The thought that people like Karen and Lorraine might know about Rory's girlfriend made me shiver.

I was shaking again. I spent a lot of time shaking. I wished he hadn't taken her to The Copper Beech. That was where he had taken me for my birthday. How could he do this to me? I drove home feeling utterly exhausted.

Pat was sitting on the sofa watching a video, Clodagh on her lap.

'I've got to go out again, Pat,' I told her. 'Can you stay until a bit later?'

'No problem,' she said. 'I'll just phone my mother.'

I left her to phone while I went upstairs and had a shower. I turned the heat up as high as I could and let the steaming hot water scald its way through my hair and to my scalp. I massaged shampoo into my hair until it foamed and lathered so much that the soapsuds ran into my eyes and stung them. I scrubbed myself with a loofah until my skin was raw and sore. I let the needles of water hit me on the chest, leaving red weals on my breast, and then I wrapped myself in a huge bath-towel and padded into the bedroom.

'Where are you going, Mum?' asked Clodagh, who had followed me upstairs.

'Out,' I told her.

'Out where?'

'Just out.'

'I want to go too.'

'Don't be silly. Here.' I handed her an old lipstick. 'You can get made up with me, if you want.'

We sat in front of the dressing-table and turned ourselves into creatures of the night.

Clodagh was beautiful. Glossy red-gold hair, big blue eyes, clear, bright skin. I loved her fiercely. I hugged her suddenly, strongly, and she wriggled away from me.

'You'll mess me up,' she complained.

I finished my preparations and went downstairs again. Pat was sitting in the living room in front of the roaring gas fire, her homework spread around her.

'You look stunning, Mrs Mac,' she said, looking up and eyeing me appreciatively.

'Thanks,' I said. 'One has to make the effort from time to time.'

'Where are you going?'

'Just out for a drink,' I said. 'I won't be that long, Pat.'

'A boyfriend,' she giggled. 'You wouldn't bother looking like that for Mr Mac.'

I gave her a withering glance and she dug me in the ribs. 'Only joking!' But I knew that she was wondering, her eyes gave her away.

'Mr McLoughlin is in The Copper Beech,' I told her. 'The number is on the notice-board. I'm not sure where I'll be, so if you need anything, ring him.'

I knew she wouldn't. Pat was the most capable person I had ever met. She'd changed her look since the first time she had come to the house. Now her hair had reverted to its natural nut-brown, and she didn't wear the pale make-up any more but brushed her cheeks with Body Shop beads.

I slipped into the car and drove back into town. It was cold now, the air temperature was way down and the stars glittered grimly in the black velvet sky.

I hadn't been to The Copper Beech since my birthday. Cars were lined up outside; obviously it was still doing well and still pulling in the business trade. Rory liked it because they knew him, deferred to him and called him by his name. Since the party, they'd been especially nice to him. They kept a good wine cellar, he'd say sometimes, sounding particularly pompous. Once, when he'd said something like that, I'd have hit him and we'd both laugh. 'But they do,' he'd say, defensively.

The doorman stood outside the rough stoned building. He smiled at me as I crunched along the gravel courtyard and clicked up the granite steps. I was another woman meeting her date.

The foyer of The Copper Beech was separated from the main restaurant by folding screens. A woman sat behind a high old lectern, a book of reservations in front of her. A pot of ink and a quill pen stood on top of the desk. A pair of half-glasses hung on a chain around her neck. She hadn't been there the night of my birthday party. I would have remembered her.

'Hi,' I smiled. 'Is Mr McLoughlin here yet?'

She looked at me in surprise and glanced down at her book. 'Mr McLoughlin?'

'Rory McLoughlin. I think the reservation was for eight o'clock.'

She was definitely put out by my question. I looked at her carefully.

'He may have only made the reservation for two,' I said casually.

She smiled in partial relief. 'Well, yes,' she said. 'His companion is with him.'

With those words my world disintegrated. I'd kept a faint hope that I was wrong, deep inside me. I'd hoped that maybe I'd arrive here, and Rory would be with clients from Hamburg, and I would have made a huge mistake. In my heart, I'd known that I was wrong but I couldn't help hoping. For a split second, I thought I was going to faint, then I became aware of the receptionist watching me. She looked worried. I wondered if they were used to confrontations in this restaurant. I wasn't going to confront Rory, she needn't have worried. I was going to walk up to him and say hello and walk away again. That way, he would know that I knew and he'd have to talk to me about it.

'I'm just here to give him something,' I said. 'Don't worry. He's expecting me.'

'He's at table five,' she told me. 'Behind the yucca plant.'

I looked around the screen.

My husband and his mistress were sitting opposite each other. He had his back to me so I couldn't see his expression, but she watched him, her eyes soft. I knew those emotions, I had looked at him like that once. As I stood there, she reached out and touched his hand.

Rage, hot and furious, coursed through me. Until that moment I'd still half-hoped that I was making a terrible mistake. That maybe there was an explanation and I just hadn't managed to find it. That Rory could not have been unfaithful to me. Maybe he brought girls out, but on a purely platonic basis. Maybe it *was* business. Maybe the stocking – well, I couldn't come up with a reason for the stocking, but it was always possible that there was something I hadn't thought of. But Amanda Ferry was looking into his eyes and there wasn't an innocent reason why she should look at him like this. The bile rose in my throat as I observed them.

Neither of them had seen me yet, I was still screened by the yucca plant. I breathed carefully, trying to stay calm.

Time was suspended as I walked across the granite floor towards them. It was as though I was walking through a tunnel. I couldn't see to the right or to the left of me. I was oblivious to the other diners, I couldn't hear the hum of their conversation. I stood beside them.

Amanda looked up and an expression of sheer horror crossed her face. Rory's own mouth had dropped open. He stared at me, dressed in my expensive purple velvet dress, my choker of pearls, my drop earrings and my hair, scooped into a plait at the back of my head and secured by a matching velvet ribbon.

We looked at each other in silence. I wondered, fleetingly, whether anyone in the restaurant was watching us. But they wouldn't know that there was anything wrong. To them, it might be a perfectly normal scene.

'Do close your mouth, Rory,' I said calmly. 'You'll be left like that.' I remembered hearing that line delivered in a movie years ago. I had thought it very effective then and it made me feel good to use it now. I was still shaking inside, but my hands were still and my voice was steady.

'Mushroom soup?' I inclined my head towards the bowl on the table.

He nodded, speechlessly.

'I hope you enjoy it,' I said. I picked up the bowl and emptied its contents over his head. 'You fucking bastard!'

I watched the contents of the bowl adhere to his hair and drip solemnly down his face. He cried out in shock. Amanda gasped in horror. I looked at her coldly. 'Bitch,' I said, although I almost felt sorry for her.

The restaurant was silent. It was the first time in my life that I'd ever created a scene, but I'd created one now.

A waiter hurried over and grabbed me by the arm.

'I'll have to ask you to leave,' he said.

I started to laugh; maybe there was a touch of hysteria in it.

'Of course I'll leave,' I said. 'There's no reason for me to stay here.'

We walked side by side through the hushed restaurant. My high heels clattered on the stone floor. I sensed rather than saw the eyes of the other diners follow me. From the flurrying behind me, I knew that another waiter had brought a towel over to Rory.

I pulled my coat closer to me as I walked back to the car. The waiter and the doorman both watched me as I left.

The car was cold and I was shaking as I sat in the driver's seat. I thought that I might be sick again but I managed to take deep breaths and stay calm. I closed my eyes and visualised them again. I'd thought over and over about the sort of girls that Rory might choose to have an affair with, but I wasn't sure exactly what sort of person his choice would be. Given his feelings about me working, I wouldn't have imagined a committed career woman, but that was what Amanda was. He'd talked about her at home from time to time, in a casual way. She was good, he'd said. Strong. She didn't take any shit from anyone. She got on well with the clients. I'd thought that Amanda sounded a decent sort of person.

I started up the engine and drove home. I parked a few streets away from the house and sat in silence.

If I'd wanted to destroy my marriage, I'd probably done it now, all right. What were the chances of Rory ever forgiving me for making such a fool of him? And in a restaurant where he was well-known! The folly of my action was coming home to me and I felt that I had made a terrible mistake. But I couldn't help it. When I saw them there, I wanted to do something to hurt him. To humiliate him the way he'd humiliated me. And it had been wonderful at the time. I'd had a sense of power and excitement and rage as I dumped the soup over him. It had been a fantastic moment. But the wrong thing to do. The thing to do, surely, was to have sat down and talked to him and been rational about it. We could have worked something out. It wasn't entirely his fault. Bitter tears rolled down my cheeks as I leaned my head against the steering wheel.

I cried for a while and then dried my tears. I would go home now, at any rate. I was freezing in the car.

'Did you have a nice evening?' asked Pat, as I walked into the living room. She looked at me curiously. 'Are you OK, Mrs McLoughlin?'

'Of course I am.' I rummaged in my bag for her money and handed it to her. 'Will you be all right getting home on your own?' I asked.

'Sure I will.' She pocketed the notes but still looked at me strangely. 'See you again, then.'

'I'll give you a call,' I said.

When she'd gone, I went upstairs and sat in front of the mirror. I knew now why Pat had asked me if I was all right: my mascara had streaked across my face and I looked as though someone had given me a black eye.

I smeared cleansing cream over my face and then removed it

gently with cotton wool. I looked awful. I slipped out of my clothes and into my dressing-gown, then went downstairs and took a couple of Hedex. My head was pounding now. I wondered should I have a drink as well. Maybe a few drinks. Maybe I should take all the tablets and a bottle of whiskey. That would give Rory a shock.

In the end, I made myself a cup of tea and brought it up to bed. At eleven o'clock, I turned out the light. I wondered when – if – Rory would come home.

I slept fitfully, dozing and then suddenly waking up with a startled jump. I waited for the sound of a taxi to pull up outside the house or the sound of Rory's key in the front door. Each time there was an unexpected noise, I was wide awake again.

The hum of the electric milk float woke me at seven o'clock. I blinked a couple of times as I looked at the gentle green glow of the alarm clock. The bed beside me was still empty. Rory had not come home. I suppose, deep down, I hadn't expected him to. I sat up in the bed, knowing that I wouldn't go back to sleep, knowing that I had irrevocably changed everything.

I hugged my knees to my chest. Oh God, I thought, through another flood of tears, what have I done?

Chapter 29

January 1994
(UK No. 7 – *The Perfect Year* – Dina Carroll)

'Happy New Year!' Lucy turned to me and flung her arms around me as the chimes of her carriage clock finished ringing in 1994. I hugged her, and then everybody at Lucy and David's New Year's Eve party hugged each other.

It was a great evening. We arrived about nine and Lucy handed around bowls of steaming hot chilli and crusty garlic bread. David played his *Hits of the Seventies* CD, and followed it up with Queen, Status Quo and (for the girls, he said) Abba. It was great fun. Lucy cracked open the bottles of champagne to toast the new year, and I sipped mine as I leaned my head against the French windows and gazed out into the darkness of Lucy's garden.

January was always difficult for me. It wasn't that I still felt anguished, although I didn't think the hurt would ever completely disappear, but it was hard not to think back and wonder how things might have been.

The scene was clear and vivid. I could recall every moment as though it were on videotape, running it in slow motion through my head.

Rory had arrived home at five o'clock on the day after I'd dumped the soup on his head at The Copper Beech. I'd sat around the house all day, afraid to move in case the phone would ring, not knowing where to ring myself or even who to ring, and wondered where on earth Rory had got to. I supposed that he was with Amanda and the thought chilled me. Was she comforting him about the fact that he had a deranged wife, or did either of them care? Was he revelling in my lunacy in having made a show of him, or was he humiliated beyond belief? Would he ever come home again, or had I driven him away for ever?

Every so often I'd go upstairs and check to see if all his clothes were still there. There was no reason why they shouldn't be, but I needed to check all the same. The Hugo Boss and Armani suits nestled in the wardrobe and his shoes gleamed on the shoe-rack at the bottom. I fingered the fabric of his suits, held his ties to my face and shook with nerves.

I was sitting on our bed when I heard the sound of his key turning in the lock. I moistened my lips and tried to steady the thump of my heart as it hammered against my chest.

I heard Clodagh run from the living room into the hall, and Rory pick her up and talk to her. Then the measured tread of his footsteps up the stairs and into the bedroom.

He was wearing the trousers from his suit and a woollen jumper which I didn't recognise. He didn't speak as he walked over to the wardrobe and looked inside. Then he took a suitcase from the top shelf and opened it on the bed.

'What are you doing?' I asked nervously.

He didn't answer. He took trousers from hangers and laid them neatly into the suitcase.

'Where are you going?'

He continued to fold his clothes.

'How long will you be away?'

He ignored me completely.

This had always been his way when we had a row. Freeze me out. I had to make him talk. I didn't want our marriage to end. I didn't want him to walk out on me. I could and I would forgive him for Amanda Ferry.

'Rory, can't we work something out?' I pleaded.

He looked at me as though I was an insect. 'I hardly think we have anything left to say to each other.'

'Of course we have,' I said. 'We have to talk about this.'

'You think there's anything to talk about?' he hissed at me. 'You humiliated me in a place where I have a reputation to maintain. I do a lot of corporate entertaining in that restaurant. You humiliated me in front of a fellow colleague. You made a spectacle of me and of yourself, and you think that there's something left for us to talk about. Don't make me laugh, Jane.'

'And what about you?' I asked him. 'What about you and Amanda Ferry? Don't you think we have something to talk about there?'

He gazed at me. 'Not really.'

Suddenly I was shaking again. 'Why "not really"?' I asked. 'What were you doing with her?'

'Having dinner,' he said.

'Oh yeah?'

It was like talking to a brick wall. He didn't want to discuss it, he wouldn't discuss it. He went on packing.

'Where are you going?' I asked.

'I haven't decided yet,' he said. 'But anywhere is better than here.'

'Why?' I asked. 'Why, Rory?'

'Why not?'

'Didn't we have a good marriage?' I said, even though I'd wondered about that so often myself. 'Did you hate it? Do you hate it?'

'We're different,' he said, as though that explained everything. 'We want different things, Jane.'

'But I thought we wanted the same sort of things,' I said helplessly. 'I thought we wanted a good life and to be together.'

'Being together isn't enough,' said Rory. 'You have to work to make life together a good thing.'

'But I did!' I cried. 'I tried. I thought you were happy, Rory. I never stopped you from playing golf or going for drinks or doing any of the things you wanted to do. What more could you ask from me?'

'You always looked down on me,' he said. 'From your lofty idealistic heights. You wanted to be well-off, but you never tried to get on with Bill or Karen or Graham or Suki. You never tried to be friendly to the girls, invite them over for lunch or anything like that. You went to the functions, but you never really wanted to go.'

'So you have an affair with someone in your office because I wouldn't ask Karen Hamilton over for lunch and because I thought all those things she dragged me to were crashingly boring. Makes sense, Rory.'

'Who says I was having an affair?' he demanded. 'Where did you get that information?'

'I didn't need to get that information anywhere,' I said. 'It was patently obvious to me when I saw you. Anyway, I found her stocking in the car.'

'Her stocking.' He looked guilty.

'Yes.' All the spirit suddenly evaporated from me. 'Yes, Rory, you left it in the fucking glove compartment.'

We looked at each other silently. For a moment, I thought our marriage would be OK. Rory would hold me and I would forgive him, he'd understand how I felt and then everything would be all right again.

It seemed a bit daft to want our marriage to be saved. After all, he'd been having an affair. He'd consistently, persistently deceived me. He had come home to me having spent an evening with her, and he had lied over and over again. And yet, right then, if he had said that he was sorry and that it had been a mistake, I would have believed him and I would have tried again. I'd have been different too. I'd have given up work if that made any difference, because my marriage was more important than anything else. I'd have tried really hard to be a good wife to him and to ensure that there would be no reason for him to have an affair. Because there must have been a reason, and I must have been part of it.

'I'm going to live with Amanda,' he said.

I looked at him, aghast. 'You can't.'

'I can,' said Rory. 'And that's what I'm going to do.'

'Do you love her?' I demanded. 'Do you?'

He shrugged lightly. 'Maybe.'

'You fucking bastard!' I cried. 'You don't give a toss for me or for Clodagh. What about her? You're just going to leave us, are you?'

'Jane, you made a show of me. Now, I admit that I should have told you about Amanda before now, and I know that it must have been a shock to you, but these things happen. There was no need for you to behave the way you did. We can't put it back together, Jane, and I don't want to. It never really worked, did it?'

We'd been married for ten years and he'd decided that it had never really worked. I couldn't believe it. I knew that there had been times when I was miserable in our marriage, when I wondered whether I'd done the right thing. But I knew that I loved Rory and that, even if everything wasn't exactly perfect, it was probably as good as it was going to get. I didn't believe in fairytales, after all.

I watched him pack and then sat in the bedroom while he drove away, and I couldn't believe that it had actually happened.

* * *

'Are you all right, Jane?' Lucy stood beside me, a glass of Ballygowan in her hand. Lucy was expecting her first baby in March. Once again she was on a cloud of happiness. She looked great, too. No morning sickness, heartburn or constant backache for Lucy. She continued on as though there was nothing different about her. Even her bump was a neat, round thing which she carried well.

I turned around to her. 'I'm fine,' I said. 'Just thinking.'

'Don't think,' said Lucy. 'Just have a good time.'

'I am having a good time,' I told her. 'Honestly, Lucy. This is a great party.'

'I hate it when I see you looking melancholy.' She squeezed my arm.

'Don't be silly,' I said. 'I'm reminiscing, I suppose, but I'm not melancholy.'

And I wasn't. Not any more. For six months after Rory left, I barely functioned. I kept expecting him to come back. I couldn't believe that I wouldn't hear the car pull into the driveway, and that he wouldn't come in, no matter how late. I hated sleeping in the big bed on my own; when I stretched into the empty space where Rory should have been, I would gasp with the pain of losing him.

Clodagh couldn't understand it. Every day she asked where Rory was. I told her that he'd had to go away to work and she accepted that for a while, but I knew I'd have to tell her the truth.

'Daddy's living somewhere else at the moment,' I said eventually.

She looked solemnly at me and pulled at her ponytail.

'Why?'

'Because he needs to live away from us.'

'Why?'

'Daddy and me—' This was awful. What the hell do you say? 'Daddy and I are not getting on together just now. You know, we're not friends at the moment.'

'You're not meant to be friends,' she said scornfully. 'You're Mammy and Daddy.'

She sat in a corner and drew pictures of him which she stuck on her bedroom wall.

I hated telling people about it. I didn't want them to know. I didn't cry when I told Audrey and Claire, but I broke down completely when I met Lucy.

'Oh Jane,' she said, and put her arms around me. 'The bastard.'

I told her the entire story. I couldn't bring myself to tell anyone else.

'I'd have throttled him with the fucking stocking,' she said. 'He never deserved you, Jane, never!'

The twins *looked* shocked, but I didn't think they really *were* shocked. They called him a bastard, too.

But the real trauma was telling my parents. Mam didn't believe it.

'Can't you patch things up?' she asked, over and over again. 'For the sake of Clodagh, at least?'

I hadn't told her about the stocking. I couldn't.

'There's nothing to patch up,' I said.

'But surely—'

'No. He's seeing someone else.'

She stared at me. This was something that happened to other people, not us.

'Who?'

I shrugged. 'A girl from the office.'

Dad wanted to kill him. 'Nobody treats my daughter like that,' he muttered. 'Nobody.'

I felt as though I was a permanent topic of conversation with everyone I knew, as though they were pointing me out and saying, 'Look, there's Jane McLoughlin, her husband left her.' I would have liked to have said that I threw him out, but he hadn't even allowed me to do that. I resented that. I should have been the one to tell him to leave, not the one who wanted him to stay. I despised myself.

'Come over and join the rest of us,' said Lucy. 'Don't stay here on your own.'

I smiled at her. 'I'm fine on my own, Lucy, I like it.'

That was true. I was used to being on my own now and I could cope with it. I didn't need anyone any more. Clodagh and I were a good partnership together, we understood each other.

When he first left, we found it difficult. I was in shock. I got up every day, went to work, came home, argued with Clodagh and went to bed. She kept asking for Rory, I kept saying that he was at work. Rory and I didn't speak for a month, and then he rang me and said that we had to talk.

He told me that he wanted to sell the house, that he'd give me

383

half of the sale price. He'd continue paying maintenance for Clodagh. He was efficient and cool and seemed to have totally forgotten that we had shared a house and a life for ten years. Claire Haughton told me to get a good solicitor and squeeze the bastard for every penny but I couldn't do that. I still felt that somehow it was all my fault.

Every night I cried myself to sleep. Every night I wrapped my hurt and my pain to me. Every night I asked myself why this had happened to me. All I'd ever wanted was to get married and to live happily ever after. It wasn't too much to ask, was it?

The pain and the hurt were always there, in the background, no matter what I was doing. I would be standing in line at the supermarket checkout and suddenly a longing for my husband and my marriage would well up inside me and I would almost cry out in my unhappiness.

Then, one day, it didn't hurt so much any more. Clodagh and I were in St Stephen's Green and she was throwing bread to the ducks, squealing with laughter and enjoyment every time one of them pecked at the bread. A warm breeze carried the scent of newly-mown grass and the sun was warm on our backs. Quite suddenly, it was good to be alive. I picked up my daughter and swung her around and she wrapped her arms around my neck and told me she loved me.

I explored my feelings from time to time. Like a person who's had a tooth out, I poked around at the gap in my life, always expecting it to hurt and being surprised when it didn't. Every so often, I would conjure up a picture of Rory and Amanda and it didn't send the dagger through my heart that it had done a few months earlier. It was more a dull ache, and I could cope with a dull ache.

We sold the house. It wasn't as much of a wrench as it might have been, because I'd never felt as happy in the Dún Laoghaire house as I'd done in the Rathfarnham one. With my half of the money, plus a mortgage which I took out, I bought a small townhouse nearer my parents. The house was nothing special – two bedrooms, a small living room and a kitchen/dining-room. It was about half the size of our previous house, but it was mine and I was happy. Rory and I divided the furniture between us. It was a horrible time, doling out chairs and sofas, lamps and pictures. Some of the pieces that I wanted looked awful in the new house so I stored them in the attic out of sight. I told him he could have the bed but he said that Amanda already had one and I bit my lip but bought a new one for myself. Now the house had a feminine personality. There were no golf clubs in the hallway, or grubby football jerseys in the laundry basket, or Kung Fu videos lying around the TV. It was weird at first, but we got used to it.

Clodagh wanted to know if Rory was dead. She'd heard about death at playschool. I told her that he was busy but that he was still alive and still loved her. It was hard not to rubbish him in front of her, to tell her that he was an unfaithful bastard and that he couldn't possibly love her, otherwise he'd never have left us. I wanted so much to say it, but I didn't. Then, when we had managed to be civilised to each other, he came and visited Clodagh and took her to McDonald's.

'Why can't you stay?' she cried, as he put his jacket on to leave the house again. 'I don't want you to go, Daddy!' She sat on the bottom stair and howled. I was crying too and Rory looked anguished.

'Why don't you stay?' I asked, as I swallowed the lump in my throat. 'We need you.'

'It wouldn't work, Jane,' he said. 'It couldn't work. I'm sorry.'

So I was left with a screaming child who wouldn't be placated and cried over and over again for her Daddy, until I felt like bringing her to Amanda's flat and dumping her on the doorstep.

That was my low point. If Clodagh didn't love me, didn't want me, then who could? I poured myself a brandy, then another and another and got pissed out of my brains curled up on the sofa. I passed out, Clodagh on my knee, and woke up at three o'clock in the morning freezing cold and with a stiff neck. I carried Clodagh to bed and crawled in beneath the duvet, both of us still dressed. It was a nightmare.

The next morning I woke up to hailstones drumming against the bedroom window and a hangover drumming against the back of my eye. I had to call in sick to the office. There was no way I could have made it through the day.

'I think I've got the flu,' I told Claire, not caring that I was lying to her.

'We need you back by next Monday,' she said firmly. 'I must have somebody I can depend on, Jane.' The warning in her voice was very clear.

I flushed with embarrassment. 'I'll be there,' I said. 'Tomorrow, if I can.'

But I took the next day off too and used the rest of the weekend to pull myself together. He's not worth going to pieces over, I told myself repeatedly. And Clodagh depends on you. She does need you.

'We're going to play charades.' Lucy broke into my thoughts again. 'Come on, Jane, you can be on my team.'

I was good at charades, I could think laterally. Lucy was hopeless. The Quinlans were brilliant, and we had to split them into different teams because Brenda could guess Grace's mimes instantly.

We fell around the room laughing and got drunk. After the charades, Lucy made coffee and most of the guests left. The twins and I were staying overnight, because we'd have had to drive across town and we were way over the limit.

'I'm going to bed,' said David, at about 4 a.m. 'If you girls want to sit up and gossip please feel free, but I can't keep my eyes open.'

'You must be exhausted, Lucy,' I said. 'You've organised all this, and you've been awake all night. Surely you want to go to sleep?'

She shook her head. 'I was asleep from three o'clock this afternoon until eight. I'm grand now. Not a bother. Anyway, I like staying up until I'm so tired I just pass out on the pillow. Otherwise it's so bloody uncomfortable I can't stand it.'

I nodded. 'When you can't lie on your side properly, it's awful.'

'I sleep on my stomach, usually,' said Lucy. 'I'm destroyed.'

We laughed at the picture of Lucy lying on her stomach now.

'You look great,' said Brenda. 'You hardly look pregnant at all.'

'Bitch,' I said. 'I looked like an elephant after seven months.'

'And you only managed eight months,' said Grace.

I shivered at the memory. 'Never again.'

'Really?' asked Lucy. 'Or are you just saying that?'

'Well, it would be a bit difficult for me to have another child in my current celibate lifestyle,' I said, 'and I can't see that changing in the near future. So it looks highly unlikely, but it doesn't bother me that much. I feel sorry for Clodagh though; she'd love a brother or sister.'

'Maybe you will find someone,' said Grace. 'You're only thirty-three, Jane.'

I looked at her, disbelief in my eyes. 'Yeah,' I said. 'And Prince

Charming will come along and sweep me off my feet. Me and my seven-year-old daughter. I can just see it, can't you?'

'Why not?' argued Brenda. 'You're still an attractive girl, Jane.'

I laughed. 'Thank you,' I said. 'But I'm a woman, not a girl now, and nobody wants a woman and a child. Besides,' I added truthfully, 'I'm perfectly happy as I am. I don't want anybody else.'

The three of them looked at me, not sure whether to believe me or not.

'Truly,' I said. 'I know I nearly cracked up when Rory left me . . .'

'The fucking bastard,' they said in unison. It was a standing joke with us that, whenever I mentioned his name, they added the next statement.

'. . . But I can cope now. I can more than cope.' I took a sip from my glass of wine. 'I know it sounds corny, but I'm happier now than I ever was before. I've got a lovely daughter – who is hopefully sleeping peacefully in her grandparents' house tonight – parents who are very supportive, a good job, and . . .' I looked around me, 'brilliant friends. So I don't actually need someone to come in and reorganise my life and try to mess things up for me.'

'But don't you miss having someone?' asked Brenda.

'Why?' I asked. 'Do you?'

The twins were still single.

'It's not the same,' said Grace. 'I know people think we're weird, but neither of us has ever met someone special. We have separate friends and occasional boyfriends, but we haven't been lucky – or unlucky – enough to meet someone to marry. But if you've been married, I can't help feeling that you'd always want someone.'

'Rubbish,' I said spiritedly. 'Rory McLoughlin sapped me of all of my confidence. His horrible parents hated me. He spent all his time working, in the pub, on the golf course or bonking his fucking girlfriend. I never knew where I stood with him. I was always rearranging my schedule to fit in with his. Now I only have to worry about Clodagh, and I don't actually have to worry about her. She's great. We plan things, we do them, we have fun. Nobody messes around with us. I don't need someone and I don't want someone.'

The amazing thing was that what I'd said was almost completely true. All my life, I'd believed that I needed a boyfriend or a lover or a husband to make me a complete person, to give me a sense of

387

worth. Now I knew that I could stand on my own two feet and that I didn't need anyone else. It was an exhilarating feeling. I tried not to let the thought (occasionally, at the back of my mind) that Rory was still my husband, and that he was still part of my life, ever bother me.

'I understand how you feel,' said Lucy quietly, 'but I'd be miserable without David.'

'You have a marriage made in heaven,' I told her sincerely. 'And if I'd been lucky enough to marry someone like David, I'd be miserable without him too.'

And that was the truth. David Norris was almost too good to be true. He was the New Man personified.

'Wait until the baby is born,' said Lucy darkly, when I said this. 'New Man, I don't think! If there's one thing about David, it's that he loves his sleep. I can't see him getting up in the middle of the night to see how Junior is getting on. Chances are, he won't wake up at all!'

'Clodagh was a demon,' I said, remembering. 'She howled for the first three months. I thought I'd never get to sleep again. And then, of course, I was sick.'

'Poor thing.' Brenda stretched out her long legs. 'When we went to visit you in hospital after your appendix operation, you looked so miserable.'

'I was,' I said feelingly. 'It's funny how quickly you recover from things, although I felt absolutely exhausted for ages.'

'I feel perfectly fine and then suddenly I want to collapse,' Lucy sighed. 'It's like all my energy disappears at once.'

'Mine is disappearing now,' yawned Grace. 'Thank God we're not opening the shop tomorrow. This idea of opening all the hours God sends is dreadful.'

'When does your sale start?' asked Lucy. 'I might go in and buy a few things. For life after the bump.'

'That's a terrible way to refer to your child,' grinned Brenda. 'We don't start our sale until the fourth.'

'I'll call in myself,' I told them. 'I need some new blouses for work.'

'Do you know who was in the other day?' asked Brenda, looking at me. 'Karen Hamilton. She hadn't been in for ages.'

'I haven't seen her in years,' I said. 'How does she look?'

'Wonderful,' said Grace glumly. 'She seems to get younger all the time.'

'Surgery,' I said confidently. 'Nobody could look as good as her naturally. Her son must be – gosh, he must be twenty-one or twenty-two, by now!' I looked around at them, horrified. 'Imagine knowing people with adult children! It's creepy.'

We laughed, but it was. I couldn't believe that I was thirty-three. It had been bad enough to be thirty! And still, inside, I felt about seventeen. I hadn't changed all that much.

'This will crack you up,' said Brenda, as she curled her legs under her knees and looked for all the world like a schoolgirl herself. 'Stephanie McMenamin's kid is in secondary school.'

We shivered with horror. To me, Stephanie – the most beautiful girl in our class at school – was frozen in time as a teenager.

'We're like a crowd of senile old women gibbering away,' said Grace, 'as though we were ancient old crones. We're only thirty-something, after all!'

'Would you do anything different?' I asked Lucy. 'If you were only a teenager again?'

She wrinkled her brow. 'It's hard to know,' she said. 'I wouldn't have worried so much about bloody exams, for a start.'

'You'd probably have to worry twice as much now,' I said.

'But so much worrying,' she said. 'And it didn't make a blind bit of difference to me, in the end. There are so many more important things.'

'What about you?' I asked Grace.

'Nothing,' she said simply. 'I'm happy.'

'Me too,' said Brenda. 'I suppose there's loads of things that you might do differently but I think my life has worked out pretty well. And you, Jane? What would you have done?'

I sighed. 'I suppose I wouldn't have married Rory, but that's hindsight,' I said. 'And if I didn't marry Rory then I wouldn't have Clodagh, so that's all wrong. I don't know, really.'

'So what's your New Year's resolution?' asked Lucy, standing up and rubbing her spine.

'To diet,' said Grace and Brenda simultaneously.

'To grow my nails,' I said, stretching out my hands in front of me. I didn't bite them any more, but I would have loved long nails.

'Why don't you just get them stuck on?' said Lucy. 'There are loads of places for that.'

'I did, once,' I said. 'Sculptured nails. Then I wanted to take them off and I had to buy a bottle of acetone to soak them in. While I was doing that, the doorbell rang and I jumped up and knocked over the little bowl it was in. The stuff spilled all over the table and over Rory's scientific, extremely expensive programmable calculator. It melted all the keys and they stuck together so that he couldn't use it any more. He went absolutely berserk!'

The girls laughed. 'You may laugh now,' I said, giggling myself, 'but he was absolutely furious with me. And, of course, I laughed when it happened, which made it worse. So it'll be long nails, naturally grown, for me. Also, I'm going to make a definite effort to improve my painting.'

I'd taken up art classes again the previous September in the local vocational school. I was quite good at it now, and was sneakingly proud of some of my watercolours. I harboured a very private dream that one day I would actually sell one, although I couldn't quite see anyone being daft enough to spend money on one. Still, it was a lovely thought.

'Girls, I'm going to bed,' yawned Lucy. 'It's been a great evening but my eyes are closing and I'll fall asleep here if I don't go upstairs.'

We all got up.

'Happy New Year,' I said again as I drained my glass.

'Happy New Year,' they echoed. We hugged each other before going upstairs to bed.

Chapter 30

February 1994
(UK No. 1 – *Without You* – Mariah Carey)

I met Rory for lunch in the National Gallery. I didn't want to meet him but he said that he needed to talk to me and he sounded so urgent that I agreed. I didn't like meeting him in public places. I always felt that people looking at us would know that we were a separated couple (although I knew that I was being ridiculous) and that they would be watching us curiously, wondering why we were together. I preferred meeting Rory in my house, when he came to pick up Clodagh. I was always in control in my house.

I liked the National Gallery. Quite often I would walk down Merrion Square and go in there at lunch-time, not to eat in the restaurant but to gaze at the paintings. I loved the portraits, people's expressions captured on the canvas since the eighteenth century. Had they ever dreamed that their pictures would end up in a public gallery rather than in the grand houses where they once lived?

My favourite was a painting of a nun. Among the dark oils of the gallery this was a bright painting, full of light and colour. The nun stood in a flower garden, her white veil perched on her head in a complicated continental arrangement that looked rather like a kite. I thought she might be a postulant because she was dressed completely in white whereas the nuns in the background were in white and black. She held a prayerbook and was gazing towards something outside the frame. She looked so peaceful that she made me feel peaceful too. I often wondered whether she was a real nun, or whether the painter – William Leech – had conjured her up from his imagination. The painting was called *A Convent*

Garden, Brittany. I had a copy of it at home in the kitchen but it wasn't the same as the real thing.

Rory was already at the gallery when I arrived. He was standing in the foyer, stamping his feet to warm them. It was freezing outside, bright and sunny but with a biting northerly wind. I handed in my coat and pulled my woollen hat from my head.

'I like your hair,' said Rory.

'Thank you.' We were always polite to each other.

'It suits you like that.' This was going beyond the call of duty, I thought, although I was pleased that he had noticed. My hair was shorter now, just above my shoulders instead of rampaging down my back, and it was cut in a neat bob. The curls had relaxed a bit over the last couple of years and I could wear it shorter without feeling silly.

'Do you want to go and eat?' he asked.

'It's why we're here,' I said calmly.

He didn't have the power to upset me any more. I didn't need to try and score points off him, which I'd done when we first split up and which I was never any good at anyway.

The restaurant was already full of people. We took our trays and joined the end of the queue. I was starving.

I had chicken and a salad while Rory chose beef casserole. He picked up a couple of individual-sized bottles of wine and put one on my tray.

'I don't want any wine, thanks,' I said as I replaced the bottle. 'I'm busy this afternoon and wine at lunch-time makes me sleepy.'

'It's only a small bottle, for God's sake!' he said. 'It won't kill you.'

'I didn't say it would,' I told him. 'I just don't want any. A glass of water is fine.'

He sighed exaggeratedly. 'Whatever you like.'

We took our food to a table and sat down. He had bags under his eyes, I noticed, and he looked tired. His hair was streaked with grey and it was thinning out even more on top.

'So, what do you want?' I jabbed a cherry tomato with my fork and squirted juice in his direction. It missed him by a whisker.

'Be careful,' he said sharply. 'You nearly got me that time.'

'Sorry,' I grinned. 'Accident.'

'Huh.'

I took a sip of water.

'Amanda and I are going on holiday this year,' said Rory. 'We're going to Florida and then to the Bahamas. We want to take Clodagh with us.'

I put down my knife and fork and looked at him. My heart pounded. One of the rules was that Clodagh didn't actually ever stay with Amanda and Rory. It was probably very stupid of me, but I couldn't stand the idea of my daughter sleeping under the same roof as the girl who had robbed me of my husband. Robbed? Another stupid statement. I knew she had done nothing of the sort. Rory had allowed her to steal him, an entirely different thing. But I still didn't want her as a surrogate mother to my child.

'You know our arrangement,' I said.

'Of course I know our arrangement,' said Rory impatiently. 'That's why I'm meeting you today. I want to change it.'

'No,' I said.

'Great,' said Rory. 'I'm offering our daughter the opportunity of a lifetime and you don't even give her a chance. You just say no. How do you think she'll feel when she hears she had the chance to go to Disneyworld and you didn't let her?'

'Thank you,' I said. 'I'm so glad to be cast in the role of wicked mother.'

'Oh, come on, Jane,' he said. 'I want to take her. I haven't had her for even a weekend since we broke up.'

'Since you left,' I reminded him tartly. I didn't want to behave like this but I couldn't help myself.

'I knew you'd be like this,' said Rory. 'You don't want me to have access to her at all.'

'That's not true,' I replied half-heartedly. 'I don't mind in the least you seeing her. I just don't want her to stay with you. Not when Amanda is there.'

'There's nothing wrong with Amanda,' said Rory. 'You'd swear that she was some evil monster, the way you carry on.'

I shrugged. 'Sorry,' I said. 'I can't help it.'

We ate in silence for a while. I thought about Rory's request. I should really let her go. Rory was right. But for her to be with them – as though they were a family unit. The thought made me tremble. People would think that Amanda was her mother! It was too much to take. I couldn't let her go, I just couldn't.

'You always were a selfish bitch.' Rory drained his glass of wine.

'Oh, come on, Rory,' I said impatiently. 'I'm not being selfish.'

'Yes, you are,' he said. 'You don't want her to go, so you say no. You don't care about what Clodagh wants.'

'Of course she'll want to go,' I said. 'I'm not stupid.'

'Then think about it,' he pleaded. 'It's only for two weeks.'

Two weeks without her. I'd never been parted from her for that long, before. But Rory looked so unhappy. He did love Clodagh, I knew that. He had always been mad about her. I sighed and bent over my food to hide the tears in my eyes.

'I'll think about it,' I said finally. 'When do you want to go?'

'Easter,' Rory told me. 'But she needs a passport and a visa.'

I nodded. 'She'll need it quickly, then,' I said.

'Thanks,' he said.

'I only said I'll think about it,' I reminded him. 'I'm not promising anything.'

'Thanks for thinking about it, at least,' he said. He took my hand and squeezed it. I jumped at the touch.

'Do you hate me that much?' he asked.

'No,' I said. 'I don't hate you at all any more.'

He smiled wryly. 'I'm glad.'

I removed my hand from his and looked at my watch.

'Better be getting back soon,' I said.

He nodded. 'Sure.'

We walked slowly through the gallery together.

'I'm just going to the Ladies,' I said. 'I'll talk to you soon, Rory.'

'OK,' he said. 'Thanks.'

I watched him leave the building, pull his wool coat around him and stride purposefully out on to the street. I didn't go to the Ladies but walked back into the gallery.

What should I do? I stared blankly at the canvases around me. What was the best, the fairest thing to do? To let her go, I supposed, but it was hard to make that decision. I didn't want to let her go.

I stood in front of the painting of the nun again. What would you recommend? I asked her silently. You should know, you're a nun. Should I let my daughter stay with my husband and his mistress?

It was unfair to call her his mistress. They'd been together for three years.

'I thought it was you.' I recognised his voice instantly and turned around. Strangely, I wasn't surprised to see him. He hadn't changed at all. A few extra lines on his face, maybe, but still the same glasses, the same tousled look, the same boyish grin.

'Hello,' I said. 'Where did you spring from?'

'I come here for lunch quite a bit. And you?'

'So do I.'

He looked around. 'Have you eaten yet,' he asked, 'or are you waiting for someone?'

'I've eaten,' I told him.

'Pity,' said Hugh.

'Why?'

'I'd have treated you, of course.'

'Aren't you meeting anyone yourself?'

He shook his head. 'Not today.'

'So you come here on your own?'

'Nice place to be,' he said. He looked at the picture. 'It's one of my favourites.'

'Mine too.' I smiled at him. 'I often wonder what she was like.'

'The nun?'

I nodded.

'She was a princess,' he said. 'A beautiful princess, obviously, since all the best princesses were beautiful. She was engaged to be married to a prince. And he wasn't exactly her choice. She was in love with somebody else. But she was promised to him and so she met him because she always did what she was told. She told her lover that she could never see him again because she was engaged to be married to the prince. Then she realised that she couldn't go through with it. But her lover had already killed himself because she had rejected him. So she joined the convent.'

'You made that up,' I said accusingly.

'Perfectly true,' he told me.

'I don't believe a word of it,' I said. 'She looks far too serene to be the sort of girl who has locked herself in a convent because she didn't want to get married. A girl who did that would look more – bottled up.'

'Actually, she's the painter's wife,' said Hugh.

'Really?'

He nodded.

'Not a nun then.' I smiled slightly.

'No.' He turned to me. 'They split up eventually.'

I turned away from the picture and began to walk back to the entrance.

'Oh, look, sorry.' He walked after me. 'Jane, I'm sorry if I spoiled it for you. I didn't mean it.'

I turned back to him. 'You didn't spoil it,' I said. 'I have my own thoughts about her anyway.'

'What are they?'

'Secret,' I said.

We stood beside each other. 'Where are you going?' he asked.

'Back to work.'

'Where?'

'Merrion Square. Five minutes away.'

'I'm going to Baggot Street,' he said. 'I'll walk with you.'

'If you like.' I collected my coat and hat, pulled the collar high around my neck and the hat low over my head.

'You look like a pixie,' he said.

'You're a nutter,' I told him.

The wind was icy and whirled down the street, catching dust and litter as it went. I shivered.

'How is your little girl?' asked Hugh.

'Getting bigger,' I said.

'She must be at school by now,' Hugh mused.

'For the past few years. She's seven.'

'My God,' he said. 'I wouldn't have believed it.'

'Same age as your niece,' I told him.

'I can't believe she's seven either,' he said despairingly. 'It only seems like last year she was born.'

I nodded. 'I know.'

'And your husband?' he asked.

My teeth chattered with the cold. 'What about him?'

'How is he?'

I shrugged and said nothing. Neither did Hugh. We walked in silence as far as Renham Financial.

'This is where I work,' I said. 'Nice seeing you again.'

'And you,' said Hugh.

'Maybe in another few years,' I said lightly.

'That's my line,' he said. 'See you, Jane.' He turned and was gone. I hurried down the steps to the office, feeling strangely alone. I tried to forget that Hugh McLean always turned up when I least expected him to. Well, of course, I never expected him to turn up. He wasn't part of my life, how could he be?

And yet – seven years. I'd known him that long. I remembered him as he barged into the room in the maternity hospital, carrying the bunch of flowers for his sister and going red to the roots with embarrassment when he saw me crying in bed. I smiled at the memory.

Some people just bobbed in and out of your life. Hugh certainly seemed to bob in and out of mine.

I thought about Rory's request for nearly a week. Eventually I decided to ask Mam what she thought, although that was a mistake. I called into the house to pick up Clodagh, who was now attending St Attracta's primary school. I'd never gone to the primary school, it hadn't been built until I was ten and Mam hadn't wanted to move me then. It gave me the shivers when I thought that my child would one day attend my old school, sit in a classroom where perhaps I'd once sat myself. I wondered whether or not the same desks were there, and if she'd ever sit at the one that said *Jane O'Sullivan was bored here 1975*. She'd look out of the classroom windows, but instead of seeing the rolling fields that had surrounded the school when I was there, she'd see rows of houses which had been built on the surrounding land, crawling halfway up the mountains in an ever-advancing army.

Our routine was simple. In the mornings I'd drop Clodagh at my parents' house, where she'd have tea and toast before walking to school. Then I'd pick her up on my way home in the evenings. Usually she'd be looking out of the window waiting for me so that I didn't have to go into the house every day. She'd run out, banging the front door behind her and streak down the front path, a leggy, coltish thing, long hair flying behind her, her bag bumping against her legs.

Clodagh hated it when I came into the house, because it always took me at least half an hour to leave. Mam would ask me how I was, tell me that I was working too hard and suggest that I buy a tonic. 'You're looking peaky,' was still her favourite expression.

I helped Mam dry some dishes while Clodagh watched *Blockbusters* and told her about Rory's request.

'And I hope you said no,' she said firmly.

I made a face.

'Oh Jane, you must have refused.'

I sighed. 'I wanted to, of course,' I told her. 'But it was very difficult to dismiss it outright. I'm sure Clodagh would love to go.'

'That's hardly the point, is it?' asked Mam. 'You can't possibly let her go.'

'That's how I feel,' I admitted, 'but I'm not sure it's the right way to feel.'

'He's asking you to let a seven-year-old girl go on holidays with him and his – his – fancy piece.'

I smothered a smile. In Mam's eyes, Amanda Ferry was a trollop.

'I know,' I said. 'But he's very good to Clodagh, and I'm sure that he'd give her a wonderful holiday.'

'My foot,' snapped Mam. 'I don't think you should expose her to that sort of thing.'

'It's hardly any sort of thing.'

'I don't think that girl should be in contact with your daughter,' said Mam. 'And that's that!'

'It's not fair to call her "that girl",' I protested mildly. 'She's probably a very nice person.'

'Oh, really,' said Mam. 'Then why did she steal your husband?'

'She didn't steal him.' I wondered myself why on earth I was defending Amanda when I absolutely detested her. 'Rory let her steal him, which is a very different thing.'

'If that girl hadn't got her talons into him, then he'd never have left you,' said Mam.

I shrugged. 'Maybe not. So maybe she did me a favour.'

'Jane!' Mam was shocked.

'Well, maybe she did. He was driving me round the bend before he left. Maybe it's just as well.'

Mam flapped the tea towel in the air. Her face was red with effort. I stacked the dishes neatly in the cupboard. They were new cupboards. Mam and Dad had bought a complete new kitchen a year ago and Mam loved her new pine and glass fitted look.

'I still think it's a bad thing for Clodagh to see the sort of goings-on that would happen on holiday with that pair,' she said.

'I don't think she'll see any goings-on, as you put it,' I said. 'They've been living together for three years. I'm sure they'll be able to restrain themselves in front of the child.'

Mam blushed; she hated referring, even obliquely, to sex. The idea that Rory and Amanda might be sleeping together was absolutely abhorrent to her.

'Well, you know my views,' said Mam. 'I'll let you make up your own mind, I won't interfere.'

I hugged her. Since Clodagh was born I felt much closer to her, I thought that I understood her better. I certainly understood how much she'd had to put up with when I was a child.

'Come on, Clodagh,' I called. 'Put your coat on, it's time to go home.'

In bed that night I made my decision. I would let her go. I didn't want to, but I couldn't always do exactly what I wanted. And I knew that Rory would look after her. He adored her.

He was thrilled when I phoned and told him, promised that he'd take very good care of her and that he wouldn't allow her to do things that I didn't let her do and that he'd make her eat all her greens. I told him that I never made her eat all her greens but he was welcome to try.

I told Clodagh the next day because we had to go and get her photograph taken and fill out her passport and visa applications. Her face lit up and I felt a heel for even thinking of not letting her go.

'Where will we be staying?' she demanded.

'I don't know,' I said. 'Daddy will tell you.'

At first, she thought that I was coming too and, when she realised that I wasn't, she said she didn't want to go. Secretly that pleased me, but I told her not to be silly, that she'd have a great time and that she wouldn't miss me one little bit. So she went around in a frenzy of excitement and couldn't wait until her Easter holidays. She marked off every day with a big red crayon, standing on the three-legged stool to reach the calendar and sticking her tongue out of the corner of her mouth as she ticked off the days.

In the meantime, the office was very busy. Claire was giving a presentation to a group of investors in a week's time and I had to prepare the documents, make slides and charts and organise the venue. So I was absolutely up to my neck. It was strange but, whenever the office was busy, it was manically busy and the phones never stopped ringing. We'd bought a new desktop publishing package, too, and I hadn't quite got the hang of it yet so that I kept having to look in the manual to see if I was doing things properly, which made it all twice as complicated as it should have been. Each time I had the document nearly right, the phone would buzz and I'd forget what I was doing and have to start all over again. Claire and Stephen loved it when the phones were hopping like this, because it meant lots of business. But today, particularly, it was driving me round the bend.

'Renham Financial,' I said as I cradled the earpiece between my ear and my shoulder and tried to point the computer mouse at the right icon on the screen in front of me.

'Could I speak to Jane, please?' asked the disembodied voice.

'Speaking.' I used my pleasant telephone voice.

'Hi, Jane, it's Hugh.'

I almost dropped the phone and I double-clicked the mouse on the wrong icon.

'Hugh!' I cleared my throat. 'How can I help you?'

'How can you help me?' He laughed, that rich deep laugh. 'You can help me by coming to lunch with me today.'

I stared at the phone as though I could actually see Hugh McLean's face on it. 'Lunch?' I asked.

'Yes,' he said. 'I'm going to the National Gallery for lunch and I thought you might like to join me.'

'That's very nice of you,' I said, in confusion. 'But I can't do that.'

'Why not?' he asked.

'Well, because – I just can't.'

There was silence at the other end of the phone. I could hear the crackle of static on the line.

'I'm sorry,' I said. 'I'll have to go. I'm very busy.' I hung up, my heart thumping.

Had Hugh asked me for a date? Hardly. Lunch wasn't exactly a date. And he knew that I was married, for goodness sake. He'd hardly be likely to ask me for a date if he thought that Rory and I were still living together. I glanced down at my hand. I didn't wear my wedding ring any more. When I'd taken it off first, there

400

was a faint pale line around my finger and I'd felt naked without it. But I couldn't still wear it when it didn't mean anything. Hugh wouldn't know that. So why did he want to meet me for lunch? Anyway, if he had wanted to ask me out (ask me out, what a juvenile expression!), he could have done so any time over the past seven years.

Come on, Jane, I said to myself. Get a grip. But all through the afternoon, as I wrestled with Claire's presentation document, his face swam before me, ruffling me, unsettling me.

I worked until seven o'clock. I phoned Mam to say I'd be late and Clodagh answered the phone. She told me that she was the best in her class at spelling and proceeded to go through her list of words beginning with W.

'You're very clever,' I told her proudly.

We bought takeaway pizza on the way home, hot and dripping with melted mozzarella cheese. Clodagh adored pizza although Mam always gave out to me when I bought it. She didn't believe that anything other than chops and vegetables was the right food for a growing girl. I reminded her frequently of the experiments she had done on me, bringing home trial runs of some very dubious fast food from the supermarket when she'd worked there. She dismissed this as irrelevant and reminded me that there was always meat in whatever she had brought home. I remembered some of the stuff that I'd eaten and doubted very much if the meat it claimed to contain had ever actually been part of a living animal, but it was no use, Mam was adamant. She'd always fed me properly. She'd never have made it as a vegetarian.

Clodagh, on the other hand, loved vegetables. Not green ones, but mushrooms and tomatoes and peppers and sweetcorn – all of which were on the giant-sized pizza we took home.

We ate it in front of the fire watching TV, getting topping all over our fingers and our faces and we giggled as we fought over the last piece. Like two children.

I checked her homework for her while she played *Sensible Soccer* on her Nintendo. She still loved soccer and watched it avidly on TV. I thought it might be a link with Rory that she wanted to keep. She supported Liverpool, although, she told me, she fancied Ryan Giggs.

She never played with dolls. She liked toy cars, football and computer games. She loved dressing up, but preferred wearing jeans and trainers. She played quite happily with both the boys and the girls on the road and was much more self-confident than I'd been as a child. She didn't let anyone mess her around. But when she went to bed, it was with her blue teddy bear tucked into the quilt beside her.

I hoped that I'd made the right decision about the holiday. I knew that I'd never forgive myself if she found out that she'd had the opportunity to go and I hadn't let her. But I was terrified that she'd prefer Rory and Amanda's company to my own, and that when she came back she'd ask me if she could stay with them more and more and then one day would move in with them altogether.

It was an unlikely scenario, I knew that. All the same, Amanda and Rory earned more than £100,000 a year between them, lived in a beautiful duplex apartment near Blackrock and would be able to give Clodagh everything she needed without even thinking about it. That's what scared me. If Rory ever decided that he wanted to have custody of Clodagh, I wondered whether any judge would really think me a more suitable parent. Sometimes I'd worry about it as I lay in bed at night, listening to the sounds of the house settling, creaking floorboards and strange gurgles from the cistern. It was never so bad in the daytime, when Clodagh and I were a kind of partnership, but I hated the nights. I'd always been a bit afraid of the dark and all my worst imaginings came to me then. I never dreamed good things at night any more.

Chapter 31

March 1994
(UK No. 2 – *The Sign* – Ace of Base)

I met him in the National Gallery again, by accident not design. It was one of those typically March days, one minute a blue sky and blazing sunshine and the next grey clouds and hailstones. I was walking back to work, past the gallery when the hailstorm began. I hurried inside to shelter. Lots of other people had the same idea and the rooms were full of those who probably wouldn't be there otherwise, so that there were groups in front of the paintings. I went to mine.

The nun was still there, still looking serenely out from her field of flowers. I thought of Leech painting his wife as a nun and wondered why their marriage had broken up. I sat on one of the seats and looked around me, still shivering a little from the sudden blast of cold. Then he walked past me, from the restaurant towards the door.

I thought he hadn't seen me at first because he strode by, hands deep in his pockets, staring at the floor. He stopped suddenly, spun around on his heels and looked back towards me.

His eyes lit up in recognition and he walked back to me, smiling. 'Hello again,' he said as he squashed himself between me and an elderly gentleman in a waxed coat. 'How are you?'

'I'm OK,' I said. 'And you?'

'Great.' He smiled.

We looked at each other for a while. I felt that I should say something to him but I didn't know what. He just looked at me.

We both started to speak at the same time and broke off.

'You first,' he said. I shook my head. 'No, you.'

'I was going to ask you if you'd like to lunch with me sometime,' he said. 'Since you gave me the bum's rush the last time.'

'I was surprised you phoned,' I said. 'That you even knew where to phone.'

He looked surprised himself. 'That was easy,' he said. 'The name-plate was on the railings.'

'Oh, I see.' I couldn't believe he'd noticed the nameplate, or remembered it.

'So?'

'Why did you ask me?' I turned to him. 'Why do you want to lunch with me at all?'

'I like you,' he said simply. 'I always have.'

'But I'm married,' I told him. 'You know that.' I didn't want to tell him about Rory and me. I wasn't able to. I was afraid that he'd think that I was looking for someone if I told him about Rory. I didn't want him to think that. I wasn't looking for someone. Not like that.

He looked resigned. 'I know you're married, Jane, that's not the issue. I'm not trying to have an affair with you or anything. For God's sake, I saw you in bed and didn't try to have an affair with you.'

I laughed. 'I don't think anybody could have, just then.' I looked at him seriously. 'But there's no point in us having lunch, Hugh.' It was the first time I'd ever said his name to his face. It felt strange. 'What good would having lunch with me do?'

'I'd enjoy it,' he said. 'You make me smile.'

I looked at him in astonishment. 'Me? Don't be daft.'

I didn't think I made him smile. Any time I ever met him, I seemed to be in floods of tears. Around us, people walked up and down the gallery's polished floor. They sat down or got up from the seat beside us and yet they only registered in the outer reaches of my mind. I liked Hugh. But what was the point in getting to know him? And if, by the remotest chance we started to have a relationship (I hated that word), where could it possibly go? I had a seven-year-old child; I had to be realistic about things.

'Why are you so afraid of a simple lunch?' asked Hugh.

I stared at my shoes. There was a ladder beginning in my tights. I twisted that leg behind my other leg to hide it.

'I don't think it would be a good idea.' I stood up. 'I'm sorry.'

He stood up too and walked towards the door with me. We walked side by side out of the gallery and on to the street.

'Are you happy?' he asked suddenly.

I was horrified to find tears in my eyes. 'Of course I'm happy,' I said, as a huge tear slid down my cheek. I turned away from him to hide it and hurried up the street. I felt him standing there, watching me. Please don't follow me, I prayed. Please don't.

For once, my prayers were answered. He allowed me to walk away from him without doing anything about it. Part of me wondered whether he would ring again, to apologise perhaps, or even to ask to see me. But he didn't. I didn't hear from him at all, and I told myself that it was just as well.

Clodagh and I went to the supermarket to get her photograph taken for her passport. She twirled around on the seat with excitement and stuck her tongue out in the last photo.

'What's this meant to be?' I asked in mock severity.

'A present for you,' she told me.

'Some present,' I said.

She still crossed off every day on the calendar. She smiled in satisfaction and said, 'Only ten more days, only nine more days,' while I tried not to let her see that it bothered me.

David Norris rang towards the end of the month to tell me that Lucy had given birth to a baby boy. Mother and child doing well, he told me.

She was in Holles Street, so I walked down the next day to see her. She sat propped up in the bed, reading *Hello!* magazine and looking fantastic. I hugged her and peeped into the little crib where the baby lay sleeping.

He was lovely, still wrinkled, not yet grown into his skin. He opened his eyes as I looked down at him, navy blue staring up at me. I touched his cheek. The skin was soft as a peach, the sort of skin I'd die for now.

'He's gorgeous,' I whispered to her. 'And you, you bitch, you look brilliant.'

'I'm actually knackered,' said Lucy. 'I've muscles where I never knew muscles existed before. I feel like every organ in my body has been taken out and put back in the wrong place.'

I laughed at her.

'It's no laughing matter,' she said. 'I'll never be able to walk properly again. And,' she hissed, 'I've got stitches.'

I shuddered. 'I don't want to know, Lucy,' I said. 'I've been through this already.'

'Yes, but you at least did it in style,' objected Lucy. 'You were carted away in an ambulance and knocked out for the entire episode. None of this pushing and shoving business for you.'

I grinned at her. 'Was it absolutely awful?'

'They say you forget,' she told me darkly. 'But I'll never forget.'

'Never mind,' I said consolingly. 'Have you thought of a name for him yet?'

'We keep tossing names around,' said Lucy, 'but we can't agree on one yet. The poor child will be known as X for the rest of his life, as far as I can see.'

'Loads of names will go with Norris,' I told her as I sat on the edge of her bed and idly flicked through her magazine. 'God, doesn't Cindy Crawford look fantastic?'

'Jane, please don't show me pictures of supermodels,' complained Lucy. 'I know I never looked like them but now I know I never will. It's a very depressing thought.'

'Sorry.' I put the magazine on a shelf. 'So what names have you come up with?'

She sighed. 'David wanted to call him Nicholas!'

Lucy's married ex-lover. I laughed. 'So what did you say?'

'I told him that he could call him after the bloke who first groped me in the back seat of a car if he wanted to, but that it wasn't my favourite name.'

'So what others?' I prompted.

'I'm not sure yet; we're going to make up our minds soon, though. We'll have to.'

I stood up. 'Whatever you call him, he's a darling,' I said as I peeked in at him again. 'And he doesn't look a bit like either of you.'

'I know,' she said, 'although I tell David that he looks like him after a few pints.'

'I'd better get back to work,' I said regretfully. 'But I'll call in and see you again.'

I hurried back up the square to the office, thinking about Lucy and David and how happy they were, truly delighted that she had such a lovely baby. It made me think of Clodagh, and how she'd been as a tiny scrap. And of Hugh McLean, who had visited us. I couldn't get Hugh McLean out of my head, although I tried to blank out thoughts of him every time they appeared. But I'd be in the middle of typing something, or answering the phone, and then suddenly I'd hear his voice in my head, or see his face in front of me as clearly as if he were really there. And I'd stumble over whatever I was doing and make a mess of it.

It was like being a teenager again, although if I were a teenager I could at least say that I had a crush on him or something. But I was too old for crushes! Too mature to act like a schoolgirl! Anyway, I didn't fancy him and I wasn't attracted to him. Not in that sort of way. I told myself this over and over again. There was no room in my life for men any more. They brought nothing but grief.

I thought about them all. Every man I'd ever known had made me cry. Jesse, Dermot, Richard – even Frank, Mr Nice Guy and the first man who had really mattered to me, had left me to pursue his career. And Rory had never stopped making me cry. Even now, when I didn't love him any more, a film or a song might remind me of a time when we *did* love each other, when everything was all right. I'd suddenly ache for something that I knew now I could never have.

They went on holiday the Thursday before Easter. The flight was in the morning so I took time off work and drove Clodagh to the airport to meet Rory and Amanda there. I could have driven her to their apartment the night before, but I didn't want to do that. I was shaking as I put her case into the boot of the car. She looked confident and self-assured as she clambered into the back seat, neatly dressed in her best jeans, jumper and jacket and wearing her Nike trainers. She had her own bag with her spending money in it and her passport.

It took no time to reach the airport. I parked in the short-term car park and walked with her to the departures area. She held my hand and I was comforted by the warmth of it in mine.

'I'll bring you back a present,' she promised as we walked through the sliding doors. 'I'll get you something really nice.'

'Thank you.' I scanned the crowds for Rory.

He was near the escalators and he was on his own. For a brief moment I thought that maybe Amanda had decided not to go, but that was ridiculous.

'Hello, there,' he called and Clodagh waved at him. I looked around for Amanda.

'She's in the café upstairs,' said Rory. 'She thought you'd prefer it if she was upstairs.'

'I don't mind,' I said nonchalantly, although my heart thumped and I was still shaking. I looked at Clodagh. 'You be a good girl,' I told her.

'I will.' She stared at me solemnly.

'And do whatever Daddy tells you.'

'I will.'

'And don't be any trouble.'

'I won't.'

'And have a good time.'

She beamed. 'Of course I'll have a good time.'

'OK, then.' I dropped down to her level. 'Give me a kiss.'

She flung her arms around me and kissed me, wetly, on the cheek. 'Why don't you come too?' she whispered. 'They'd let you come.'

'I'd love to,' I said, 'but I have to go to work.'

'Please come.'

'I can't. You won't miss me, Clodagh, you'll be too busy having fun.'

'I s'pose so,' she said, as she unwrapped her arms from around my neck. 'But I'll remember you all the time.'

'Good.' I planted a kiss on top of her head. 'So I'll leave you with Daddy.' I stood up. 'Look after her,' I said to Rory.

'Of course I will,' he said. 'She's my own daughter. I'm not going to let anything happen to her.'

I knew that he meant it and I knew that he would take care of her. But it was still hard to turn away from them and walk out of the building back to the car. I kept wanting to run back, especially to see Amanda. I didn't want her to touch Clodagh but I knew that I was being silly. I was proud of the fact that I'd let Clodagh go with them. But I still felt sick inside.

I dropped around to Lucy that evening, unwilling to sit at home on my own yet. She was feeding baby Andrew, patiently holding him against her, watching him carefully.

She smiled as I came into the room. 'I'm not very good at this yet,' she said, 'but I'm going to persevere for a while.'

'How are you feeling?' I asked as I sank into the armchair opposite her.

'Great,' she said, and she did look wonderful. Her golden hair shone in the warm light of the lamp beside her, and her skin was clear and flawless. She looked about twenty.

'You look fantastic,' I said enviously. 'How do you do it?'

'Make-up,' she laughed. She looked at me intently. 'How did it go this morning?' She knew how I felt about it, she'd been very sympathetic but had agreed with my decision to let Clodagh go.

'I was sick leaving her at the airport,' I said. 'I wanted to stop her and say I'd changed my mind, but I couldn't do that. She was looking forward to it so much. And Rory will be good to her.'

'But the idea of another woman with your child . . .' Lucy lifted Andrew gently on to her shoulder and rubbed his back.

'I know.' I bit my lip. 'But she's seven years old, Lucy, and she's a person herself. I can't try to stop her from seeing Amanda. If we lived in England, Rory and I would probably be divorced by now and he'd have married Amanda, and there'd be nothing I could do about it.'

'Will he stay with her, d'you think?' asked Lucy.

'I don't know.' I stood up and paced across the room. 'I think he loves her but who knows, really. I thought he loved me.'

We were silent for a moment. The clock on the mantelpiece ticked rhythmically. I pulled at my fingernails.

'Why do you think he got off with her in the first place?' asked Lucy.

'Why did Rory ever do anything?' I asked. 'He loves new things all the time, Lucy. That's why I can't be sure whether or not he'll even stick with Amanda. He used to change the car nearly every year. He was the one who wanted to move house. He was always looking for new things to buy. He changed his friends a lot. Except for the management at the bank, he went through phases of blokes being his best mate. He's not a very constant sort of person.'

'But you are,' said Lucy. 'So you'd think it'd work out, really.'

409

'You are the most constant thing in my life.' I sat down again. 'You're the only person I know that I still feel comfortable with. You never criticise or accuse me or try to change me.'

She laughed. 'That's because I know you. Anyway, you don't do any of those things to me either. That's why we're friends, stupid.'

I smiled. 'Suppose so.'

She handed the baby to me while she went upstairs. I cradled him in the crook of my arm. He was lovely, so small and so innocent. It was such a shame that he had to grow up, I thought. Into a person. Being a boy, he'd probably break some poor girl's heart. Why couldn't life be easier?

'You look very natural,' said Lucy as she came back into the room, a book in her hand. 'Sure you wouldn't like another one?'

I shook my head. 'Out of the question,' I said.

'But if it wasn't out of the question?'

'It is,' I told her. 'There's no point in thinking about it.'

She handed me the book. It was a photograph album.

'Our Debs' Ball,' she said, 'and our first holiday together. Remember?'

I looked at the pictures of us all. Lucy, the Quinlans, Stephanie McMenamin, Jenny Gibson, Louise Killane, Anne Sutherland, Camilla McKenzie, Martha Sheridan. We were all smiling, delighted with ourselves. And the holiday snaps. Lucy and Wim, Jaime and me. I closed my eyes as I remembered losing my virginity to Jaime.

'Great holiday,' I said, reliving the moment.

'Jane O'Sullivan, you're practically there again!' Lucy prodded me in the ribs.

'I remember it all so clearly,' I said. 'We were on the beach. I got sand in my hair.'

'And you came back with a smile like a Cheshire cat,' she told me. 'I knew that you'd done it.'

'Lucy!'

'Well, you had the glow,' she said.

I leafed through the photograph album, smiling at its memories.

'Don't you miss the sex?' asked Lucy suddenly.

I blushed furiously. 'What a question,' I mumbled.

'Well, don't you?'

Lucy had always loved it. More than me, I thought.

I made a face at her. 'Sometimes.'

'Have you gone out with anyone in the last four years?' she demanded.

'Don't be ridiculous,' I said. 'How could I?'

'Easily,' she told me.

'Lucy, you'll find out for yourself when Andrew is a bit older. You don't have a life of your own when you've got a kid. And I'm all that Clodagh has. I don't have time to go around meeting men.'

'You should make time,' said Lucy. 'It's not good to be alone.'

'That's rubbish,' I said. 'There's nothing wrong with being alone. I'm quite happy.'

'You think you are,' she said, 'but you're only coping, Jane. There's a difference.'

'Lucy, I'm perfectly happy. I enjoy my work, I get on well with my colleagues, I have a good relationship with my daughter. I have a nice house, a car that goes and a cat that curls up on my lap at night. What more could a girl ask for?'

She was silent for a moment. I'd stumped her now, I thought. Because if you were happy, then there wasn't any more that you needed. And I was happy.

'When we were younger, you always wanted boyfriends,' she said.

'That was different,' I objected. 'That was to prove something.'

'But don't you miss the companionship?'

I leaned back in the chair. 'That is where your entire argument falls down,' I told her. 'Rory gave me bugger-all companionship in the last couple of years of our marriage. Obviously because he was giving it all to Amanda Ferry. Golf trips that were supposed to be with the lads – he was taking her away. And I never even guessed, Lucy. Not once. Christ, I was stupid.' I shook my head at my own naiveté. 'And when he wasn't with her, he was with people from the bank. So when he came home, all he did was flop down on the sofa and fall asleep. Call that companionship! Mostly he just got in the way.'

'So why didn't you get out sooner?'

'Because I thought marriage was like that,' I said. 'Anyway, who cares now? I don't.'

She gazed at me sympathetically but I was immune to her sympathy. I was perfectly happy as I was, and I wasn't going to let her make me feel in some way inadequate because there wasn't a man in my life.

'We should go to the fortune-teller again,' she said suddenly.

'Oh, come on, Lucy!' I cried. 'That's a load of crap and you know it.'

'She told me about Andrew,' said Lucy obstinately. 'She's been right about everything.'

I'd never been back to Mrs Vermuelen after my first visit, I was too scared. She'd been right about some things and I didn't want to know about my future from her. Anyway, I still didn't believe in fortune-tellers. But Lucy went regularly and said that the woman was always right.

'Maybe,' I said finally. Lucy's silences were more persuasive than her words.

David came back just as I was leaving. He kissed Lucy, picked up his son and held him close. David was still one of life's sensitive souls. I envied Lucy, but there weren't many Davids around.

It was raining as I drove home. The windscreen wipers scraped back and forwards, pushing the water away. I hated this sort of weather and I detested driving in it. Car headlights dazzled me as I drove along the coast back towards the tollbridge. I could feel the wind whipping down the river as I drove across the bridge and a blast of icy air hit me as I rolled down the window to toss the change into the basket.

The house was cold and dark. It felt completely different without Clodagh, as though a whole chunk of it was missing. I wondered if my mother had felt like that when I left home. I pressed the button and the central heating sprang into life. The water whooshed through the pipes and immediately made me feel less alone.

Junkie was sheltering under the windowsill. I opened the kitchen door and he shot into the kitchen, an angry ball of wet fur. He slid across the tiled floor and crashed into his food bowl. He sat down and licked his fur, trying to rearrange it. I put some more food into the bowl and he fell on it ravenously.

I made myself a cup of coffee and brought it into the living room. I switched on TV and gazed unseeingly at the screen. Junkie followed me in and climbed on to my lap. I sat there like

412

a grandmother, sipping coffee and rubbing the cat's fur. It was soporific.

Did I need a man in my life? Was there room for one? Was there a part of me that needed one? What were they worth after all? None of them had ever done me any good.

I thought of Hugh McLean again, as I knew I would. He wanted to know me, but why? It was stupid of him to say that it was because I made him smile or because I interested him. Men didn't want to meet women for lunch because they interested them. They only wanted to meet women because they fancied them. Because they wanted to go to bed with them.

The idea that Hugh might want to go to bed with me gave me a sudden glow. Had I been missing out for the last few years? No, I decided suddenly. I hadn't. It would be all moonshine for a while and then suddenly it would all go horribly wrong, and I just wasn't going to let that happen to me again. It didn't matter who it was. Whether they seemed nice or not. Men hurt you, that was all they knew what to do. They wined you, dined you, took you to bed and left you. And it would never be any different.

The sun slanted through the chink in the bedroom curtains. I could see the fragments of dust float in the air. I yawned suddenly and stretched out in the bed. The stretch went from my finger-tips to my toes.

The bedroom door opened and he stood naked before me. Each muscle on his body was clearly defined. I gazed at him, enjoyed looking at him.

'Do I meet with your approval?' he asked.

He opened the curtains. The Mediterranean sun spilled into the room. I blinked at its brightness. He opened the windows and the scent of bougainvillaea filled the air.

He sat on the bed beside me. He touched my forehead and traced a line slowly down my face, my neck, between my breasts where he paused for a moment, looking at me. Then his finger moved lower, slower. I flinched involuntarily as it reached the base of my stomach. He smiled.

I reached for him and pulled him closer to me. He smelled of shower gel and Paco Rabanne. His face was smooth, clean-shaven. I touched his arms, the muscles were strong and hard.

413

He made love to me and I cried out with the joy of it and the passion. We lay together when it was over and he lit a continental cigarette. The smoke spiralled above me, blue and pungent.

'I have to go,' he said, and I nodded. I didn't know who he was. I'd never seen him before. I didn't want to see him again.

When I woke the next morning the rain was still beating on the window, drumming heavily against the glass. Junkie was curled into a little ball at my feet, purring with pleasure. I blushed as I remembered the dream. I'd blame Lucy for it, I thought, for reminding me of desires that I didn't need to have any more. I pulled the duvet around me and stayed in bed until the afternoon.

Chapter 32

April 1994
(UK No. 1 – *The Real Thing* – Tony Di Bart)

I wanted to collect Clodagh from the airport, but Rory said that he'd drop her back at the house. He'd take Amanda home first, he told me, and then call in with Clodagh. I spent all day waiting for her return. The flight was delayed by almost two hours – I rang the airport a few times to check on its progress.

I made shepherd's pie for her dinner because it was her favourite meal. I kept reminding myself that she would probably be tired and cranky and would want to go to bed straight away.

They arrived home about nine o'clock. I had had the central heating on all day so that the house would be warm enough for her. Rory held her in his arms. For a horrible moment I thought that something was wrong, but I could see that she was only sleeping.

'She's exhausted,' he told me. 'She didn't sleep on the plane, she insisted on watching the movies, but with the delays and everything she hasn't slept since yesterday. She fell asleep in the car.'

He carried her upstairs. I eased her out of her clothes. She didn't wake up, even when I slipped her pyjamas on to her.

'Did she have a good time?' I asked.

Rory nodded. 'A ball,' he told me. 'She enjoyed everything. Went on as much as she possibly could in Disneyworld. Wanted to go jet-skiing in the Bahamas – we didn't let her, of course, although she had great fun on the banana boat.'

'Banana boat?' I asked.

'Oh, a floating thing shaped like a banana,' he explained. 'You sit on it and it's pulled along by another boat. Goes quite fast. She had a great time on that. Met a few American kids on the beach, so she can speak a bit of Spanish now!'

'Did you enjoy it yourself?'

We were like strangers, really. Such courtesy, I thought. Never there when we lived together.

'I'm knackered,' he admitted. 'Looking after her is a full-time job.'

'I'm glad you think so,' I said. 'And how is Amanda?'

'Fine,' said Rory. 'She had a good time. She was very kind to Clodagh.'

I looked around uncomfortably. 'Good.'

'They got on very well.'

'You and Amanda can have one of your own,' I said tartly.

'We might,' said Rory. 'Clodagh has made us think that we might.'

His words made me feel sick. I could cope with the idea of them living together, but the thought of them being a family was completely different. Then Clodagh would have a half-brother or sister. I supposed they'd want me to let her stay over, then. Well, I wouldn't. She was mine.

'Amanda'll be wondering where you are,' I said. 'And you're probably tired yourself. Maybe you'd better be going.'

He did look tired. He stood up. 'Thanks for being so good about it all,' he said suddenly.

I stood up, too. 'It's OK.'

We were face to face. His eyes were still the same colour blue, still attracted me. Don't, I whispered to myself, fighting the urge to touch him. You don't love him any more.

He leaned towards me and kissed me on the mouth. I was shocked that he would think the same as me. I returned his kiss, remembering the familiarity of him, the taste of him. It would be easy, I thought wildly, to get him back. I could make love to him now, and then he would come back to me and it could be as it was before.

He held me closer to him and I could feel myself hungry with desire. We could be together again. I would forget everything that had happened. We were husband and wife still. He could move in tomorrow, and it wouldn't matter because we were still

416

Rory and Jane McLoughlin. We'd a perfect right to be together. Clodagh could have her parents back, her family back. She would love that.

He began to unbutton my blouse. His hand slipped beneath the cotton of my bra, touching my breast. I trembled. He groaned softly. I pressed against him and he slid the blouse from my shoulders.

'Oh Jane,' he said.

If he hadn't spoken maybe it all would have been different. If he'd said nothing, perhaps we would have made love there and then on the rug of the living-room floor, naked in front of the flickering gas fire. And then my life would have fitted back into the groove from which it had been so unfairly shaken. I could have become Jane McLoughlin again.

But he said, 'Oh Jane' and his words pierced through my desire and into the part of my brain that was practical and intelligent. I pulled away from him and started to rebutton my blouse.

'What's the matter?' he asked.

I stared at him. 'What's the matter!'

'You wanted to, I wanted to. Where's the harm?'

I stepped back away from him, folding my arms in front of me.

'You left me for another woman,' I said. 'You changed everything.'

'You're still my wife,' he said.

'Don't be stupid,' I said.

'You still want me.'

I clenched my fists until my nails dug into my palms. 'No.'

'Oh, come on, Jane. You were shaking with want for me.'

I was shaking still. 'No,' I repeated.

He stepped towards me. 'Why not?'

'Because you're living with Amanda,' I said. 'You know that. You've been living with her for years. You've just been on holiday with her. You can't surely expect me to—' I broke off. 'Don't you love Amanda any more?' I asked.

He shrugged. 'Oh, I love her,' he said offhandedly.

'Then why?'

'Because I still love you too, Jane.'

'Don't be ridiculous.'

'You're so desirable,' he said. 'You were always so desirable.

417

From the first moment I saw you, I wanted you. That first night I wanted to fuck your brains out.'

'Rory!'

'Sorry,' he said. 'But it's true. You had a great body and you used it, Janey. Then you went all uninterested.'

'I was uninterested because you were,' I said. 'You were never around. How could I stay interested in someone who was never there?'

'I'm sorry about that,' he said. 'I was wrong.'

'And you're wrong now,' I said. 'It's over between us, Rory.'

'Is there someone else now?' he asked.

'No,' I said.

'Stands to reason,' said Rory.

'Why?'

'You practically fell on me,' he said. 'You wouldn't have done that if you were getting it regularly.'

'I think you'd better go.' I thought I was going to faint.

'You think you're in the movies,' he said. 'People don't go just because you ask them to.'

I swallowed. 'Do you want to stay?'

'I want to make love to you,' he said. 'You want to make love to me.'

'No, Rory, I don't.'

He looked at me quizzically. 'You'll turn into a dried-up old maid,' he said, 'and nobody'll want you.'

'Rory, will you please leave.'

'Poor old Jane, they'll say. Frigid.'

'I'm not frigid,' I said.

'Not yet. You're still hot stuff now, Jane. But give it another few years. Then you'll be forty and you'll have no chance.'

'Why do you bring everything down to your level?' I asked. 'I think you should go, Rory. I'm sure Amanda is anxiously waiting for you.'

He laughed suddenly. 'It was a good try though, wasn't it?'

'Brilliant,' I said, trying to keep my voice under control. 'Thanks for giving Clodagh a great holiday. Now will you go?'

'Suit yourself.' He tucked his shirt back inside his jeans. 'See you, Jane.'

I stayed where I was. I heard the front door close and his car

418

roar down the road. Then I poured myself a brandy and port and knocked it back in one go. My legs buckled beneath me and I collapsed on to the sofa.

Clodagh woke up at midday on Sunday. She insisted on wearing her American leggings and her Miami Dolphins sweatshirt and put her baseball cap on her head backwards. She told me her stories about the States, about the fun she'd had and the places she'd seen. But most especially about Disneyworld, and the great time she'd had there. Rory and Amanda had indulged her completely. They'd gone to Paradise Island in the Bahamas where she'd spent every day on the beach. She looked tanned and healthy and she hadn't burned. Amanda had made her wear suntan cream, she told me. And a hat. She was a real nag. I laughed at that, although with some reservations, because it seemed to me that Amanda really had taken good care of her and I suppose that I'd half hoped that Amanda wouldn't have given a curse what Clodagh did.

'Did you like her?' I asked curiously.

'She was OK,' said Clodagh laconically. 'She played loads of games with me and she let me buy loads of clothes. But it wasn't the same as being with you,' she added.

'I'm glad to hear it,' I said. 'Now come on, we're going over to Granny's for our lunch.'

Clodagh complained about the cold although the weather was improving and the evenings were getting brighter. The cherry blossom tree in the front garden was laden with pink flowers which spilled down on to the grass and swirled on the driveway whenever the breeze picked up. I liked the way the evenings were getting longer, it made me feel as if I was emerging from a long tunnel. I always felt like this when winter finally began to give way to spring and the leaves reappeared on the trees. I loved waking up to a sunlit bedroom instead of the inky blackness of a December morning. I'd more energy in the springtime too; I became more optimistic.

I tried to forget about Rory's advances. It wasn't something I wanted to think about, or talk about, even with Lucy. I'd been afraid that I might give in to him, and that would have been a terrible mistake. But he'd said things that could be true and they niggled at me.

Was I becoming a dry old maid? Surely that was an outdated idea? I had a full and active life and I didn't need Rory to lecture me about it. Of course I didn't get out much after work, and maybe that was a problem. When I thought about it, I realised that it was ages since I'd been to the pub (except for a sandwich at lunch-time), or to the cinema or to a play. Maybe it was time to get out and about a bit more. But I couldn't abandon Clodagh, that wouldn't be fair.

I looked at the calendar. Lucy, myself and the twins hadn't got together since New Year. I'd been in *Les Jumelles* a couple of times since then, but the shop had been incredibly busy and the twins hadn't any time for idle gossip. The thing to do was to get them over to the house for a dinner party. Or better still, go out to dinner some evening. That was my problem; all my entertaining, such as it was, was conducted from home. I needed to be outside these four walls. I rang Lucy and asked her what she thought.

'Great idea,' she said. 'Leave it until the end of the month, because Andrew will be on bottles by then and I'll be able to dump him on David for the night.'

'Lucy, you don't dump your child,' I told her. 'I'm sure that's not a politically correct way of putting it.'

'I shall leave my husband to do his share of the joint parenting of our child,' she amended.

I rang Brenda at home. 'Love to,' she said.

We arranged the party for a Saturday night so that the twins could come and sleep late on Sunday. I was surprised at how much I was looking forward to it.

'Pick somewhere around the canal,' said Lucy. 'Then I can come across the tollbridge and we won't have to struggle with parking in town.'

'We should have it in Temple Bar,' I said. 'That's the in place to be.'

'Yeah, and they'll ask us for our bus passes or something,' said Lucy.

So we met in Searson's, which we'd done so often before. It seemed like a different pub altogether.

'Isn't this like old times?' grinned Brenda, as she came back to the table carrying glasses and mixers. 'How's the baby, Lucy?'

'He's great,' she said proudly. 'Although I don't know where the phrase "sleeping like a baby" comes from. My baby doesn't sleep.'

We laughed. It was good to be together again.

The pub filled up fairly quickly and a blue smoke haze drifted through the lounge. We'd booked a table in the Malaysian restaurant next door for nine o'clock.

'Time to get a few drinkies in first,' Grace said. 'A very important element of a girls' night out.'

'Does anyone have any news?' I tipped my Coke into the glass of Bacardi in front of me.

'Don't look at me,' said Lucy. 'I've done my bit. It's time for the twins to do something – like open a chain of shops, maybe. Buy out Brown Thomas, for instance.'

Grace Quinlan blushed furiously and Brenda looked down into her glass of vodka. Both girls looked so embarrassed and guilty that we knew there was something they had to tell us.

'What?' asked Lucy, staring at them. 'You've done something, haven't you?'

They looked at each other and giggled. When they did that it was hard to imagine that they ran a very successful shop and made expensive clothes to order for influential people. They looked exactly as they'd done the day they got into trouble at school for pretending to be the opposite twin. It caused great consternation at the time, because the one difference between them was that Grace could sing while Brenda could not. We'd had a practice for the school musical that day, some operetta which I couldn't remember now, but Grace had to sing a solo and when Brenda stood out front and belted out the number in one note, the music teacher had thrown a fit.

'So?' I asked, looking at them. 'What have you done now?'

'We're getting married,' said Grace, and burst into a fit of giggles again.

Lucy and I exchanged looks. It was hard to take them seriously.

'To whom?' I asked. 'Each other?'

Brenda looked at me. 'Don't be stupid,' she said.

'Well, Brenda, I just find it hard to believe,' I said. 'I didn't know you were going out with anyone. So are both of you getting married? Or just one of you?'

Lucy stared at them with her mouth open.

Brenda looked offended. 'If we'd realised that you'd be so surprised . . .' she said.

'Not surprised, shocked,' I amended. 'Come on, tell all.'

It was almost too good to be true. They'd gone to an Irish fashion presentation in London earlier in the year. There'd been a reception afterwards, lots of Irish people milling around. Brenda had met a man from the promotions board. Nice guy, she said, his name was Robert Driscoll. He said he'd look her up when he was back in Dublin. He was back two weeks later, his younger brother in tow because he knew Brenda had a twin sister and he thought that a double date might be better fun. Grace and Damien got on like a house on fire.

'Love at first sight,' said Brenda.

'Are you sure?' I asked, in disbelief.

'Why shouldn't I be?' she said.

Lucy and I were flabbergasted. All their lives, the twins had been a unit on their own. Now, finally, they were getting married. It was almost impossible to believe.

'Are you sure one isn't doing it because the other is?' asked Lucy.

Brenda smiled. 'Absolutely not,' she said. 'Really, Lucy, it's true.'

'Where are your engagement rings?' asked Lucy. Like doubting Thomas, she wanted proof.

The twins opened their bags and took out jewellery boxes. Inside were identical solitaire diamonds, glittering in the light, nestled in red velour.

'Why aren't you wearing them?' I asked.

The twins slipped them on. 'We wanted to tell you before you saw them,' said Grace. 'We couldn't just walk in and flash them at you!'

'It's fantastic news,' I said. 'I'm thrilled for you both.'

'Thanks, Jane,' said Brenda. 'And believe me, we're both madly in love.'

They looked it. There was a sparkle about them that made them radiate happiness. I'd seen the sparkle earlier but I'd thought, enviously, that it was because they were busy at work and having a good time being free and single.

'I'm stunned!' I said. 'So tell us all about your fiancés.'

Robert, the older brother, was a promoter of Irish goods abroad. They'd heard of him before, but never met him. Damien, the younger by two years, was a photographer. They'd seen his credits on pictures. So, Grace said, they weren't completely unknown to them. The twins spoke with all the excitement of first love. They fell over themselves to tell us about them.

'So are you going to have a double wedding?' I asked.

'Absolutely,' said Brenda. 'At the end of the summer. We haven't set an exact date yet. We haven't decided what sort of do we'll have.'

'I can't believe it,' I said. 'It's incredible.'

'I wish you'd stop saying that you can't believe it.' Grace looked amused. 'Why shouldn't two men find us completely and utterly desirable?'

'No reason at all,' said Lucy. 'What astounds us is that you found two eligible men out there. You know how it is when you hit thirty. They're all either married or gay.'

We ordered another round of drinks and then went into the restaurant for our food. There was no other topic of conversation besides the twins' news. Lucy and I tried on their engagement rings. I liked the look of the diamond on my engagement finger again.

The waiter brought us menus. We'd chosen Malaysian because none of us had ever eaten Malaysian food before. We hadn't a clue what anything was so we told the waiter to bring a bit of everything, as long as it wasn't too hot.

'And a bottle of Chablis,' I added. I still ordered it automatically. It had been Rory's favourite wine and I'd grown to like it.

'Where are you going on your honeymoons?' I asked, as we sat back in our seats.

'I'm not sure,' said Grace.

'Are you going to different places?' Lucy asked.

'We haven't really thought about it properly yet,' said Brenda.

'And have you bought different houses?' I asked.

'Give us a break!' laughed Grace. 'We will, but not yet!'

'My God,' said Lucy. 'That'll be the first time ever.'

'Will you be able to cope apart?' asked Lucy.

'Definitely,' they replied in unison.

The meal was great. Satay chicken on wooden skewers and neat little spring rolls with an individual bowl of sweet and sour sauce for starters; then beef in a coconut sauce which sounded awful but tasted gorgeous, and prawns and chicken. We asked for bowls and chopsticks for the authentic look.

'Means I'll hardly get any food,' complained Lucy, who wasn't great on coordination.

The restaurant was busy. There was a steady hum of conversation and the waiters and waitresses scurried around serving customers. I'd driven past The Copper Beech on the way to meet the girls, detoured especially to briefly stop in front of it. It was unchanged, the iron sign still swung over the door. I'd grown hot with remembered rage as I paused before driving on.

I wondered if they'd remember me if I went in – if the woman at the desk was still the same, and whether she'd shudder at the sight of me. I'd never found out what had happened afterwards. Rory would never speak about it and I couldn't blame him.

When Rory and Amanda moved in together, Amanda changed jobs. She went to work for another, smaller bank. Still as a dealer, still earning good money. Was she really thinking about having a baby with Rory? The thought made me go hot and cold.

'Wake up, Jane,' said Grace. 'We're talking to you.'

'Still dreamy old Jane,' laughed Lucy. 'What were you thinking about?'

'Oh, nothing,' I said lamely. 'What are you talking about?'

'You see?' said Lucy. 'You go off into a little world of your own. We're discussing whether or not to go to a nightclub.'

'A nightclub!' I looked at them in horror. 'You must be joking!'

'There speaks the sensible one,' laughed Brenda. 'The mother of the seven year old.'

'Do you want to go to one?' I asked Lucy. 'I haven't a clue where we should go.'

'It was a joke, Jane.' Lucy grinned. 'You really are hopeless.'

But they were laughing with me, not at me, and I didn't mind.

It was past one when I got home. Clodagh was spending the night at my parents' house, which was what she always did on the rare occasions I was out late. The last time had been New Year's Eve.

Although the house was empty now, the feeling was different from when Clodagh had been on holiday with Rory and Amanda.

I knew where she was now, that she would be asleep. While she'd been away, I lay in my bed and kept working out what time it was in the States so that I could imagine what she might be doing.

Junkie sidled up to me and rubbed against my legs. I bent down and scratched him under the chin and he stretched his neck, purring with pleasure. He sat down in front of his food bowl and looked expectantly at me.

'You can't possibly want food,' I said. 'I fed you before I went out.' But I put some food into the bowl and he ate it, gulping it down as though I might take it away at any moment.

I leaned against the worktop and waited for him to finish. He would go out for the night soon; he'd been in all evening, sleeping as he usually did, curled up in the turn of the stairs.

I was still amazed by the twins' news. I couldn't believe that they'd actually got themselves engaged. It was incredible. I'd always believed them to be completely uninterested in men. The occasional date for one or the other, sure, but never anything more serious than that. Sometimes Lucy and I had discussed what it would be like for one twin if the other married. She would be bereft, I said, dysfunctional. They would have to marry other twins, we'd decided, and it was hard enough to find one eligible man.

But they'd managed it. It just went to show that if you waited long enough the right man – or men – would come along.

And what sort of man are you waiting for? I asked myself, as I sat in front of the mirror wiping away my make-up. What sort of man could fit into my carefully constructed new life?

Nobody. I didn't care what the others were going to do. I didn't care how many daydreams or even ordinary dreams I had about men. I didn't care if Rory called me a dried-up prune. I didn't care that sometimes I sat at home and felt my aloneness cling to me. I didn't care that I was a single parent. I didn't care about any of that.

It would be so nice, though, to have someone in the bed beside me. That was the time I felt it. When I lay in the double bed, using only a sliver of its actual size. I didn't curl up. I slept in a straight line either on my stomach or on my side. It would be wonderful to have somebody to hold me then, and to protect me from the things that kept me awake.

I kept on having the dream again. Of the man I didn't know,

making love to me. It frightened me that I didn't know who he was. That I enjoyed the lovemaking so much. That I needed to dream the dream in the first place.

I don't want to need someone, I said to myself, holding on to the corner of the pillow as I'd done when I was very small. I can do it all by myself. Other people only let you down. I can depend on me, only on me. And Clodagh depends on me too. I don't have time for weakness or for wanting things I can't have.

Stop dreaming, Jane, I told myself firmly. Dreams don't come true.

Chapter 33

May 1994
(UK No. 15 – *Inside* – Stiltskin)

It was my favourite month. The air was warm again, the trees were dressed in shining green leaves and the flowers had come into bloom in the garden. My Californian lilac bush, something I'd grown in every place I lived, was covered in bright blue flowers with little yellow pinpricks of pollen. Junkie lay in its shade and ignored the occasional early bee which hovered in front of it, his head casually across his front paws.

The sun streamed through the bedroom window, making it easier to get up. Clodagh talked about school holidays and I wondered where I should bring her this summer. I wanted to take her somewhere myself. I wasn't trying to compete with Rory and Amanda, I said to my reflection in the bathroom mirror, I was doing my own thing as a mother.

I always got up earlier in the summer and I made an extra bit of effort to look good. God only knew why, there wasn't anybody in the office to look good for. But I liked looking well for me. I wore brighter clothes and coloured shoes. My winter wardrobe was greys and black. My summer wardrobe was a rainbow of colours, and I didn't care if they clashed with my hair. Today I wore a red and cream check suit and a cream hair-band in my hair to keep it out of my eyes, to let the sun get at my wintry pale forehead.

'You look pretty.' Clodagh came into the bedroom. Sometimes I could see myself in her now, especially when she was dressed in the St Attracta's uniform.

'Pull your socks up,' I said. 'Don't leave them hanging around your ankles like that.'

427

She sighed deeply and pulled up the socks. I stifled a grin. I was sure that I was echoing my own mother. I'd caught myself doing it so many times that it was scary.

'Come on,' I said, 'let's go.'

I dropped her at school and drove on to the office, playing my kd lang tape at full volume. I didn't expect to be busy today and I planned to go down town at lunch-time and do a bit of shopping. I hadn't been in town in ages because the weather hadn't been good enough, but I was looking forward to a stroll down Grafton Street and some window-shopping. I never came into town on Saturdays any more, it was too crowded and Clodagh hated it. Even though she liked clothes, she wasn't like some other children I knew who positively enjoyed trying things on. Whenever we went to town, she dragged out of my arm and wanted to go into Virgin Megastore or HMV to look at the computer games. When it came to clothes she usually came home and told me what she wanted and I tried, when possible, to get it for her.

But today would be shopping for me and for me only. I needed some new blouses, a lightweight skirt and maybe a jacket. Nothing designer, just something practical and smart for work.

I left the office at half twelve and strolled to the Stephen's Green Centre.

It was bright and crowded. Although I didn't like huge crowds, I enjoyed the bustling of the centre, of people in a good mood with things to do and places to go. I wandered through the shops humming to the music. Funny how they were always playing seventies hits these days; it was amusing to know all the words from the first time around.

I took the escalator to the first floor and leaned over the railings to look at the crowds below. I loved doing that, watching people when they didn't know that you could see them. Often you saw somebody you knew, like the dark-haired girl sitting at a coffee shop who used to work in the bank. I couldn't remember her name but she'd been in the Settlements department when I was there. She'd joined when I was on maternity leave.

Then I saw Hugh McLean. He was leaning against a shop window reading the *Irish Times*. I recognised him straight away, although he looked unusually smart. He was wearing a suit and tie. It was a good suit, the jacket was a neat fit and the trousers had a knife-edge crease down the middle. His tie was a splash of colour. As I watched him, he folded the newspaper and glanced at his watch.

It was one-fifteen. I left the balcony and walked down the stairs. If he was still there when I got to the bottom, I'd talk to him. That was the sort of mood I was in. The stairs were crowded with people, all of whom seemed to be going in the opposite direction to me.

He was still there. I thought about walking by, but that would be silly. I knew this man and I could say hello to him, there was nothing strange in that. I'd been stupid up until now. There was nothing wrong with knowing men, and he had said that men and women could be friends without it meaning anything. So I'd say hello to him, and we would chat casually and that would be that.

'Hi,' I said. My voice broke as I spoke and I cleared my throat and started again. 'Hi.'

He looked up, surprised. 'Jane. How are you?'

'I'm fine,' I said. 'And you?'

'I'm equally fine. What are you doing here?'

'Shopping,' I said. 'Browsing, really. And you?'

'Nothing much,' he replied.

We stood there awkwardly, neither of us sure what we were going to say next. The last time I'd seen him, I'd been crying. He was used to seeing me crying, not like this, not cheerful and relaxed. I realised that he had never seen me cheerful and relaxed before.

I smiled at him. 'Nice seeing you. I'd better get on and do my shopping.'

I turned away from him as the girl approached. She was drop-dead beautiful. Her hair flowed around her shoulders in a riot of chestnut curls and she wore an elegant terracotta-coloured suit. She was taller than me, even in her flat Italian shoes.

You cannot possibly be jealous, I told myself, as she kissed him full on the lips.

'Jane!'

I turned back to him. The girl was holding his arm. 'I'll see you again, Jane,' he said.

I nodded but I didn't think so. Not with that girl on his arm.

I spent more than I meant to. I bought a suit, like the one Hugh's girlfriend was wearing and a pair of jeans that hugged tight, but not too tight. I was probably being a bit optimistic about the jeans, but what the hell. At the last minute, I saw a floral body in Knickerbox which I thought would look great with the jeans and I bought it. I walked back up to Merrion Square, swinging the plastic bags as I went.

So he had a girlfriend now, I thought. He'd probably had a girlfriend for ages. Maybe even when I'd last met him. So if he had a girlfriend, and if she was as beautiful as the girl in the shopping centre, then there was no real reason for him to ask me out. Not for the sort of reasons I'd imagined. He really did only want to get to know me because – why? My mind, perhaps. Seeing the girl had helped me put everything in perspective. Up until now, I'd been looking at things purely from my own point of view. Strangely, today I could see things clearly for the first time in ages. It was as though a cloud had lifted from me.

I half thought he might phone that afternoon, although there was no reason why he should. All the same, I kept anticipating the ring of the switchboard and I answered every call with such efficiency that the light had hardly flashed before I was talking. But he didn't call and it didn't matter.

There was an exhibition of our art class's paintings that evening in the community hall. I told Brenda and Grace that they would have to show up to give a bit of moral support and pretend at least to want to buy one of mine. I'd three in the exhibition. They were all of Junkie. One of him stretched on the windowsill in the evening sun, eyes tightly closed. One of him curled up under the cherry blossom tree, paws covering his head. And one of him on his hind legs as he tried, unsuccessfully, to catch a butterfly. They were watercolours, nothing special, but pretty. I'd never bought a painting myself but I hoped against hope that someone would buy mine.

The twins showed up around eight. They were meeting the Driscoll brothers a little later. They hung around my paintings impressively until an elderly lady who had been dithering beside the one of Junkie on the windowsill finally took it up and bought it.

In the end I sold them all, which was thrilling. Clodagh and I went for a pizza on the strength of my earnings.

'Are you famous?' she asked, as mozzarella dripped down her chin.

'Practically.' I grinned. 'You can call me Picasso from now on.'

'Who's Picasso?' she asked.

I told her.

'Did he paint cats?'

'Possibly,' I said. 'Although you mightn't recognise them.'

He phoned the following week. I was busy at the time, but not so busy that I couldn't talk to him.

'Want to meet for lunch?' he asked.

'OK,' I said.

'Today?'

'I can't today,' I told him. 'But tomorrow, maybe?'

'OK,' said Hugh. 'The gallery?'

'What time?'

'Better be there early if we want a table. Half twelve?'

'Sounds great. I'll see you there.'

'OK.'

I exhaled slowly. I still wasn't sure what I was doing or why. Maybe it was the twins. Maybe hearing about their engagements had made me feel that I should try again. But try what, exactly? And what did he want me to try? Oh Jane, I told myself, you're an awful idiot.

I spent ages trying to decide what to wear. First I put on my new suit but decided that it looked far too new and too much as if I was making an effort for him. Besides, it was the same make as his girlfriend's. This was a friendly lunch. Nothing else. I wore my safe, green linen suit and a plain cream blouse. But I was nearly late for work because I spent so much time styling my hair, and I wore my favourite drop pearl earrings, the ones Rory had given me for our fifth wedding anniversary. I didn't wear my rings.

It was colder today, a sudden return to wintry weather. I wore my leather jacket over my suit and pulled it around me as I hurried down the street to the gallery. I looked around for Hugh but I didn't see him at first. I walked through the rooms.

He was standing in front of the convent garden painting. He was smiling as he looked at it.

'Hello, Hugh,' I said. The second time I'd used his name.

'Hello, Jane.' He smiled at me.

I liked his face. It was a better face now that it was older, it

431

suited him more. It was long, and still lean, lightly tanned. His eyes were brown pools, set deep. He wasn't wearing glasses today.

'Let's go, shall we?'

We walked in silence to the restaurant. We were early and it was still quiet.

'What would you like?'

'Lasagne and salad,' I said.

'Same for me,' ordered Hugh. We pushed our trays along the chrome counter.

'Would you like some wine?' he asked.

'Are you having some?'

'Yes,' he said.

I took a small bottle of Chianti.

Hugh paid for lunch. I wanted to split the bill.

'No,' he said. 'I've asked you loads of times. It has to be my treat.'

'I'd prefer if we split it,' I said. 'Really, Hugh.' The third time. It was getting easier to say his name.

'Really, Jane,' he said. 'It's not as though I'm exactly pushing the boat out here.'

I looked doubtfully at him. 'But I'd feel better about it.'

'Why?'

'I don't know, I just would.'

He carried his tray to a table and sat down. I followed him, clutching my money in my hand.

'Put it away, Jane,' he said. 'It's my treat.'

I sighed. 'OK.'

Now that we were face to face, I couldn't think of anything to say. It was exactly as it had been when I was younger, I was completely tongue-tied. How crazy, I thought. I'm a mature adult. He's a mature adult. There must be something we can talk about. I busied myself with my food, although I kept looking at him furtively. He was relaxed as he cut his lasagne with a fork, oblivious to me.

The restaurant was already filling up. The hum of conversation was getting louder all the time. If it got too busy, they would put other people at our table. We wouldn't have a chance to talk but it didn't seem to bother him.

'How are the bookshops?' I asked, after what seemed like an age of silence.

He looked up at me. 'Great,' he replied enthusiastically. 'We're half thinking of opening one in the city centre, but rents are astronomical and I'm not sure about the demand. It's cut-throat in town at the moment.'

'Does your sister still work with you?'

'Denise?' he asked. 'Yes, she manages the Sutton shop. Janet does the Dun Laoghaire one and I do the one in Rathmines.'

'Janet is the sister with the baby, isn't she?'

He grinned. 'She's had another one since you were in hospital,' he said casually, 'a boy. They named him after me, which I think is incredibly silly. I don't believe in calling children after anyone else. He's four.'

'I don't have any other children,' I said as I took a mouthful of wine.

It was months since I'd had wine at lunch-time. It was going straight to my head; I was seeing things at a distance, hearing things through cotton wool.

'Is Denise married?' My voice seemed to belong to somebody else.

'Oh yes,' said Hugh. 'She was married a couple of years ago. No children yet, although she probably will have them one day.'

'Is there anyone else in your family?'

He smiled at me. 'No.'

'You're not married, then?'

'No.'

'Not engaged?'

'No.'

'Going out with someone?' I could see her clearly, the chestnut hair, the perfect body, holding his arm in a possessive grip.

'On and off.'

'On or off at the moment?'

'Midway,' he said. His eyes crinkled with amusement . . . I felt like a child caught with a hand in a jar of sweets.

'The food is nice here, isn't it?' I said.

'Yes.' He still sounded amused.

I took a slug of wine and almost drained the glass.

'Do you mind if I sit here?' The elderly man had already placed his tray on the table beside us. Hugh looked up at him. 'Not at all,' he said.

'I don't want to interrupt,' said the man.

'It's no problem,' I said hastily.

He took his plate of fish and potatoes and put it carefully on the table. He sliced the potatoes into even pieces and popped a piece into his mouth, chewing carefully. I couldn't help watching him and I knew that Hugh was watching me. I smothered the desire to laugh.

'Are you finished?' asked Hugh, seeing that I'd put down my knife and fork.

I nodded.

'So am I.' He pushed back his chair.

'Oh, please don't leave because of me.' The elderly man looked perturbed.

'Not at all,' said Hugh. 'We were leaving anyway. We're quite finished.'

We went back into the gallery and strolled towards the exit, saying nothing. I stopped in front of another painting I liked.

'*The Ladies Catherine and Charlotte Talbot*,' read Hugh. 'Why do you like it?'

'Because they're only children,' I said. 'Can you imagine what it was like to be a child back in 1700, dressed up like that?'

They wore miniature adult dresses. The older child's dress was a blue and gold outer skirt over pink and gold beneath. A gold-coloured shoe peeped from under the dress, a gold buckle and a red heel. The younger girl's dress was a lighter material in green and cream. She had flowers in the apron of the dress and her sister was taking one. I could just see Clodagh in those circumstances – wearing jeans, T-shirt and trainers. She wouldn't have bothered gathering flowers, either.

I looked at my watch. 'I'd better get back,' I said.

'Sure,' said Hugh.

We walked in silence back to the office. The lunch hadn't gone as I'd expected. I thought he'd try and get me to go to bed with him. I was so stupid, I told myself as he said goodbye. Really bloody stupid.

I messed up my work that afternoon because of the wine. It made me incredibly sleepy. I couldn't believe that a glass and a bit could do so much damage. I drank loads of water from the dispenser and made myself half a dozen cups of coffee.

'Who was the guy I saw you with coming back from lunch?' asked Claire. She sat on the corner of my desk with a red file in her hand, swinging one of her shapely legs backwards and forwards.

'Nobody in particular,' I muttered as I slapped away at the keyboard.

'Very good-looking, from what I saw of him,' said Claire. 'Is he married?'

'Why on earth do you want to know that?' I asked, startled into looking up at her.

'Just wondered,' she said. 'All the good-looking ones usually are.'

'And so are you,' I said. 'And me.'

She stared at me. 'You don't seriously consider yourself still married to that bastard, do you?' she asked.

'You mean Rory?'

'Of course I mean Rory!' She actually looked quite angry.

'I am married to him,' I said. 'I might not want to be and he might not want to be either, but we are.'

'You're quite mad,' said Claire.

I tapped furiously at the keys on my keyboard.

'He tried to make love to me again,' I said quietly. She stopped swinging her leg and looked at me.

'Rory did?'

I nodded.

'And what did you say?'

'No.'

She breathed a sigh of relief. 'Thank God for that.'

'Maybe I should have let him.'

'Jane, are you in your right mind? He left you with a four-year-old kid, for God's sake! He's been living with some other woman for the past four years. Why would you want him back?'

'I don't know,' I said. 'I don't know.'

'Take a week off,' she advised. 'And see a shrink.'

She walked back to her office and slammed the door shut behind her. She had always cared about me. She had been very good to me. I leaned my head against the computer screen. I should never have gone to lunch with Hugh McLean.

Clodagh and I went to a christening on Sunday. It was my Cousin Laura's child, her third. Laura was the only girl in the family who'd had her first baby before she'd married. She'd only been twenty at the time. She didn't marry the father of baby Ben, but another guy, Sean Riordan, someone she'd only known for a couple of months. They seemed happy and this was their second child together. The first had been a boy, now aged three, whose name was Joe. This christening was for their daughter, Alexandra.

Declan and his wife, Anna, were the godparents. He hadn't married his crazy girlfriend, Ruth, but had chosen instead the sensible, pragmatic Anna. I hadn't seen them in ages. The last time I'd seen her Anna had looked middle-aged, but today she looked great. She'd coloured her hair, was wearing a fabulous new suit and had lost weight. Declan was extremely attractive with his silver-grey hair and light grey suit. They sat either side of Laura and Sean and smiled down at baby Alexandra.

There were four other babies being christened that day. I listened to the drone of the priest as the sun shone through the stained-glass windows and fell in dappled drops on to the altar. Alexandra roared as the water was poured over her.

Ben shuffled in his seat. He was very uncomfortable in his suit and tie and he pulled at the tie every so often. Each time he did this his grandmother, Aunt Kathleen, shoved him in the back. Joe played with a Transformer toy. Declan and Anna's two children sat in solemn silence as they watched the ceremony. Richard was ten years old, a tall gangly child, usually awkward and ill at ease. Rebecca was a pretty little thing, a year older than Clodagh, with the McDermott gold hair and tumbling curls. Clodagh sat beside me, yawning.

'Is it over yet?' she asked, as Alexandra's yells tore through the church.

'Soon,' I whispered.

'Did I cry?'

I looked down at her. 'No,' I said.

She'd been the best behaved baby at her christening. When the water hit her head, she'd opened her eyes in shock and her face had puckered up into a parody of a cry, but she'd been quiet.

'That's my girl,' Rory had murmured proudly.

We went back to Laura and Sean's house. It was on the Riverview Estate, a few doors down from the house that Stephanie McMenamin had bought when she married Kurt Kennedy, straight after school.

The younger members of the family, freed from the need to be quiet, raced into the garden and started chasing each other around the lawn.

The aunts sat together, chattering away and, as always, argued about some event in their past.

'You're wrong, you know, Liz, it was after John's wedding.'

'No, absolutely not, it was before. Because they went to Blackpool for their honeymoon.'

'I like your dress, Jane,' said Laura as she sat down beside me. 'It's really pretty.'

'I got it in town last month,' I said. It was taupe linen, buttoned up the front and reached almost to my ankles.

'It makes you look incredibly thin.' Laura stubbed her cigarette in the ashtray beside her.

'I'm not thin,' I said. 'I wish I was.'

'You look fabulous,' said Laura.

'You're not bad yourself,' I told her, although I was sort of lying because Laura looked washed-out. Her hair had lost some of its shine and her skin was dull.

'I'm so tired,' she said. 'For some reason, the baby keeps waking up at three in the morning and won't go back to sleep.'

I nodded sympathetically.

'It's funny, isn't it,' mused Laura. 'After all the things we said we'd do as kids, we've ended up like our parents.'

I looked at her.

'Me, for instance,' she said. 'Three kids, just like my own mother. And you, like yours, with one.'

I laughed. 'Never thought about that,' I said. 'But the difference with me is that I don't have a bloody husband any more.'

'And the difference with me is that my oldest kid has a different father.'

Aunt Elizabeth came over to us, camera in hand. 'I want to get a photo of my favourite nieces,' she said.

'I'm not your favourite niece,' I objected.

'All my nieces are,' she said.

I sighed but moved closer to Laura. The flash lit up the room. Alexandra wailed for a moment but then stopped. The sounds of the children playing wafted through the open window.

'Get away from my swing!'

'No!'

'Give me that ball!'

'It's mine!'

'Mine!'

'It's not yours, go away, I'm telling my mam.'

Laura walked over to the window.

'Keep it down out there,' she called. 'Ben, let Joe have the ball.'

'It's my ball,' objected Ben.

Joe started to cry.

'He's a cry-baby,' said Rebecca calmly. 'He's always crying.'

While they were arguing, Clodagh took the ball and ran to the end of the garden. 'It's mine now,' she said.

'Clodagh,' I called warningly.

'Anybody want some tea?' Mam came into the room carrying a tray laden with cups and saucers and a huge teapot. The women fell on it gratefully, the men ignored it.

I sipped a glass of wine. I was trying to get back on to wine. I'd had a revolting headache after my lunch with Hugh and I knew that it was because of the Chianti. I'd once drunk bottles of the stuff, with no ill-effects whatsoever. I was losing my touch with drink. And if, on the remotest off-chance, I went out to lunch with Hugh again, I didn't want to be made emotional and soppy by a single glass of wine. I wanted to have my wits about me. If I had any left.

Chapter 34

June 1994
(UK No. 15 – *Love Is All Around* – Wet Wet Wet)

I flicked through the travel brochure and looked at the pictures of apartments in the sun. Impossibly blue skies were mirrored in impossibly blue pools while scantily-clad people sunbathed. I was trying to find a picture of the San Carlos apartments in Cala d'Or, Majorca. I hoped they actually existed. I was a bit worried that they didn't appear in any of the brochures I'd picked up at the travel agent's. The San Carlos apartments were where Clodagh, Mam and I were going for a two-week holiday, and they weren't in the regular brochure because the tour operator had only recently obtained a number of them. It was a spur-of-the-moment holiday, at Mam's suggestion. Dad, Mr McAllister and a couple more of their friends were going to the States for the World Cup, and Mam felt that she should have a holiday too. So she asked me what I thought. I was more than happy to go on holiday and started to scout around for something. I'd seen the ad on the back of the *Irish Times* the previous week – a special offer – and I'd decided to go for it. What a turn-up, I'd thought, as I booked the tickets. Going on a sun holiday with my mother!

Claire walked into the office and I hastily thrust the brochure into my desk drawer. She'd been in a foul humour all week with an abscess on her gum which wasn't getting any better. She'd already been to the dentist during the morning and now she looked pale and ill.

'How are you feeling?' I asked solicitously.

She grunted. 'Not great. Don't ask me what he did to it.'

She took her diary from her office and brought it out to me. 'Can you cancel the rest of my appointments, Jane? Or try to, anyhow?'

I took the diary. 'I'll do my best.' Claire's schedule was always full. She was the hardest-working person I'd ever met.

'Claire?' I called to her. 'Is this for real?' I pointed to Hugh McLean's name, an appointment for four o'clock.

She looked puzzled. 'Of course it is,' she said. 'He's a new client.'

'When did he phone you?'

'Early last week,' she said. 'Actually, he called quite early in the morning. Before you were in. Why?'

'No reason,' I said. 'I know him, that's all.'

'Do you?' Claire's face lit up. 'Well, if you know him, Jane, maybe you can meet him.'

'What!'

'I don't see why not,' she said. 'He only wants to talk about some of his personal investments. He's looking for a valuation on some shares and a comparison of some products. You can find out exactly what his portfolio is and I'll do the work. I'd prefer not to cancel a new client.'

I looked uncomfortably at her. 'I'm not sure he'll want to talk about his personal finances to me,' I told her. 'I don't know him that well.'

'See how you get on.' She massaged the side of her cheek. She hadn't read any of the signs, totally unlike her.

I rang the list of clients and rescheduled her appointments. I didn't know what to do about Hugh. He hadn't called me since our lunch. I'd been mistaken about him, he obviously wasn't interested in me. Like all men, I thought bitterly, meet you and discard you. I knew I was being irrational about him, but I couldn't help it. Perhaps it would be easier to ring him and put him off. He wouldn't want to talk to the office manager about anything as important as his shares, anyway.

I phoned the number in Claire's diary.

'CityBooks.' The girl's voice at the other end was bright and cheerful. 'How can I help you?'

'I'd like to speak to Mr McLean,' I said. 'I'm calling from Renham Financial.'

'I'm sorry, but Mr McLean isn't in the store today,' she told me. 'If you'd like to leave a name and number, I can get him to call you on his return.'

'Is he due back today?' I asked.

'I'm afraid not,' she said. 'He's at meetings all day.'

'No problem,' I said. 'I can get him again.' I replaced the receiver and rubbed my nose. Well, he'd have to meet me and talk about the sordid details of his financial life. Tough.

At three o'clock, I went into our small bathroom and did my face. Liquid powder make-up, hazel eyeshadow, scarlet lipstick. And lash-lengthening mascara. I wasn't going to let him see me looking anything other than my best.

Claire had gone home at lunch-time but I bumped into Stephen as I came back into the main office. He stared at me. 'What have you done to your face?' he asked.

'I'm meeting one of Claire's clients,' I told him. 'I thought I'd better put on a bit of make-up.'

'Very nice,' he said vaguely. 'You look different.'

'Thanks.' I decided to take it as a compliment.

'I'm leaving the office now,' said Stephen. 'I've got a meeting at the Westbury in fifteen minutes and I don't think I'll be back here this evening. So I'll leave you to lock up if that's OK, Jane.'

'Sure,' I said. 'Have a good weekend.'

'You too.' Stephen hurried out of the building.

Hugh McLean arrived on the dot of four. I buzzed the intercom to let him into the building. He was carrying a bunch of flowers. 'For you.' He handed them to me.

'What for?'

'Does there have to be a reason?'

I buried my head in the bouquet. The scent was wonderful.

'I was trying to contact you earlier,' I said in my best office manner. 'Claire has gone home sick. Toothache. She can't meet you and I was going to cancel. She suggested that I talk to you instead, but obviously that's ridiculous.'

'Why?'

'Because I'm not an expert on financial matters,' I said. 'I can't tell you what you should buy and sell. I can tell you the value of what you currently own, but that's not necessarily a great deal of use to you.'

'That's partly what I need to know,' said Hugh. 'Why don't you do that, anyway?'

I got up from the desk and switched the telephone to Claire's office. Her room was small but neatly decorated in pale blue and cream. Her desk was white ash, empty of paper because she was so tidy. I switched on her computer terminal.

'Do you want to tell me what you have?' I asked.

He handed over a sheet of paper. I looked through his investments and then up at him again. His holdings were much greater than I'd imagined. If he wasn't exactly rich, he was very well-off.

'Some of them were left to me,' he said, seeing my expression.

I nodded wordlessly. When I'd finished his valuation, I pressed 'print' and handed him the results. He smiled when he saw them.

'Good,' he said. He sat back in the chair and looked around the room.

'How long have you worked here?' he asked.

'Four years,' I replied.

'Like it?'

I nodded. 'It's a good company and they're good employers. I've got a decent job here, and I'm a share-holder now.'

'Never think of changing?' asked Hugh.

I shook my head. 'I'm good at this,' I said. 'Most of the time.'

Hugh glanced at his watch. 'What will you be doing for the rest of the afternoon?' he asked.

'Nothing much,' I said and pressed a few keys on the computer simply for something to do.

'Would you like to come for a drink with me?' asked Hugh.

'I can't, I'm afraid,' I said, keeping my voice business-like. 'I have to pick up my daughter from my mother's house after work. They're expecting me by five-thirty.'

'It's only four-thirty now,' he said. 'A quick drink and you can still be on time.'

'I have to lock up the office at five,' I told him. 'Everybody else has gone for the weekend.'

'So we're alone together?' he said.

I stared at him. 'In this office, yes,' I said.

He grinned at me. 'What fun.'

'I don't see anything funny in it,' I said nervously. 'What did you have in mind for fun?'

'You, me, a little hanky-panky on the boardroom table?'

'Really,' I said. 'I think—'

'Jane, Jane!' He held up his hand. 'I'm only joking.'

His eyes were twinkling but I was annoyed with him.

'Well, it's not something to joke about,' I said coolly. 'You really shouldn't make those sort of jokes.'

'Then you really shouldn't wear those sort of clothes,' said Hugh.

I smoothed down my light woollen skirt with my hands. It was short but not too short. It fitted me perfectly, though, and I knew that it looked good on me. I wore it with a short-sleeved angora jumper in pale lilac which plunged rather more than I liked at the neckline but which had never given rise to any comment in the office before.

'Those sort of remarks aren't very businesslike.' I tried to keep my voice steady.

'Who cares?' asked Hugh.

I wondered whether he had been drinking. There was a devil-may-care attitude about him that I'd never seen before. 'I do,' I said. 'I'm a married woman, you know.'

Hugh came and sat on the edge of the desk, closer to me. I pushed Claire's swivel chair back from it and away from him.

'I find your marital state very interesting,' said Hugh lazily. 'It doesn't stop you from lunching with me, from flirting with me, but you use it like a shield against me.'

'I've never flirted with you,' I said, as I got up from the chair and walked across the room. 'And you were the one who asked me to lunch, even though you knew I was married. So don't give me that crap. You're the one who keeps coming on to me.'

'Do I?' he asked. 'I thought I was being nice to you.'

'You're all the same,' I cried. 'Bastards, all of you!'

He looked at me, astonishment in his eyes, as I ran out of the office and down the corridor to the bathroom, slammed the door behind me and pulled the lock firmly across. I'd never meant to flirt with him. I'd thought he'd fancied me and that had given me a bit of a boost, but I didn't want him to think that I wanted anything more. I was hopelessly confused about what I did want. Tears of embarrassment coursed down my face, leaving black track marks of mascara on my cheeks.

'Jane!' He knocked on the bathroom door. 'Are you in there, Jane?'

'Go away,' I said. 'You can leave the office, just close the door behind you.'

'Jane, don't be silly. Come on out.'

'No,' I said.

'Jane, this is ridiculous.'

'I know,' I said. 'You've made it ridiculous.'

'I'm sorry if I teased you. I didn't mean to, you know.'

'Oh really?'

'Really. Jane – come out.'

But I wasn't going to come out. Even if I wanted to, I was too self-conscious. And my face was a blotchy mess. God, I thought, you'd think by now I'd be able to function as a human being. Would I ever grow up? My ex-boyfriend Frank had done this to me once when we'd had a row. I'd locked myself into the kitchen at home then, as far as I could remember. The whole situation was farcical and I began to giggle helplessly. So much for my sophisticated office manager function!

It was quiet outside. I hadn't heard the office door close but I presumed he must have gone. I looked at my watch. I'd give him another five minutes and then I'd have to leave anyway. I splashed some water on to my face and scrubbed away the mascara with toilet roll. I still looked as though someone had given me a couple of black eyes.

I slid back the bolt on the door and walked outside, feeling like someone in a spy movie. He was sitting at my desk.

'Hi,' he said.

I bit my lip. I'd rubbed off the lipstick.

'I thought you'd be gone.'

'I couldn't go, not after making you cry yet again!'

I rubbed the side of my face. 'I'm sorry about that,' I said. 'I've been really stupid.'

'I suppose I should be apologising – yet again!' He smiled at me and his brown eyes glinted. 'I really don't mean to upset you, Jane and I was only joking. But it was in bad taste and that's what I'm sorry about.'

My heart was doing somersaults. This is crazy, I thought. He thinks I'm trying to have some sort of affair with him and he's trying to let me down nicely. And I think that he's trying to have some sort of affair with me. But I don't want to know someone who'd try and have an affair with a married woman. And I'm probably all wrong about him, anyway. I was always useless with men, absolutely hopeless. 'It's OK,' I said. 'Really.'

'Well, look,' said Hugh. 'I'll leave you alone and never bother you again if you'll just do one thing for me.' He stood up. 'Only one thing.'

'Sure,' I said, and smiled at him. 'I'll be pleased to.'

His kiss took me by surprise. His head bent towards me and suddenly his lips were on mine, soft and gentle, exploring my mouth. I gasped as his arm encircled my waist, drawing me closer to him. I breathed his aroma, tasted him, wanted him.

He held me even more tightly and I held him too. It was so long, so bloody long since I'd held anyone like this, been held like this. But he broke away from me first, still holding me, as he looked down at me breathlessly. He let me go so abruptly that I almost fell.

'I just wanted to see what it would be like,' he said.

I steadied myself by clutching at my desk. His eyes were almost black now and the hint of amusement was gone. I couldn't speak. I opened and closed my mouth but no words came out.

'But I shouldn't have done it.' He turned on his heel and walked out of the office.

The flight to Palma was delayed. We'd been sitting at Gate B27 for the past half-hour, and now it looked like we'd be there for at least another hour. People grumbled, muttered under their breaths and talked about the small print in the insurance policy.

'Hopefully we will be boarding the flight in about an hour,' said the slightly distracted air employee.

'Why aren't we going?' asked Clodagh. 'I want to go now.'

'Because the plane isn't here yet,' I said. 'You can't go until the plane arrives.'

Mam had never been on a sun holiday before. She hadn't been out of the country in over five years and her last flight had only been as far as Manchester. She fussed around with her bags and took out her magazine. 'This was for the plane,' she said. 'I'll have nothing to read on the journey.'

'It's not a very long flight.' I slipped my Walkman earpieces from my ears. 'They'll be interrupting you, serving you drinks and duty-free and food.'

'And the movies.' Clodagh looked up from her Gameboy for a second.

'There won't be any movies on this plane,' I told her.

'There was with Daddy,' she said petulantly. 'I'm not going if there isn't a movie.'

'Then you can just stay here,' I said, my patience close to snapping. 'In the airport, for two weeks.'

Her lower lip trembled and she looked to Mam for support. 'You'd better be good.' Mam used her peacemaking voice.

I put the headphones back on again. I was trying to learn some Spanish.

'*Dónde está la Oficina de Turismo, por favor,*' I repeated to the tape. '*Dónde están los servicios?*'

'You've asked where the toilets are.' Clodagh pulled me by the sleeve. '*Los servicios* are the toilets.'

I sighed and switched off the tape.

The plane arrived eventually and we filed on. Unfortunately, I didn't qualify for preferential treatment under the 'women and young children' rule any more, but Clodagh hopped around begging me to get up from my seat and join the queue.

'We have to wait until it's our seat number,' I explained, giving her a boarding pass. 'When they call these numbers, then we can board.'

Finally we were on the plane, seat belts fastened and ready to go. Clodagh peered out of the window. She wasn't impressed by the 737, she wanted a Jumbo. They'd flown to Florida in a Jumbo. But she liked the roar of the engines and the thunder of speed as we accelerated down the runway and cleaved our way through the clouds and up to the blue sky above.

'Of course, I've done all this before,' she said as she undid her tray and pulled it down from the seat in front.

'I'm sure you have, lovey.' Mam was indulgent.

I didn't enjoy the flight. There were too many children, all over-excited, all trying to run up and down the aircraft. I wouldn't let Clodagh out of her seat and she cried with frustration. We spent the entire journey quarrelling and when we finally landed in Palma Airport she refused to get out of the seat.

'Stay here then,' I said, as I lifted our hand luggage out of the compartment. 'I don't care.'

'Oh Jane, you're not being very nice to her,' said Mam. 'Come on, Clodagh, you don't want to miss the beach, do you?'

My daughter obeyed my mother and got out of the seat.

'Have a nice holiday,' smiled the hostess as we stepped out of the plane.

A blanket of heat engulfed us. I felt beads of sweat beginning to prickle the top of my forehead and I inhaled warm air and jet fumes.

'It's hot,' said Clodagh in surprise.

'Of course it's hot,' I said in delight. 'You're in the sun.'

'It's very humid.' Mam looked around and fanned herself with her magazine.

There was a baggage handlers' strike at the airport, and the arrivals hall was chaotic with people and luggage all over the place. I held on grimly to Clodagh. If she disappeared into the maelstrom, I would never find her.

The dispute was resolved while we waited but it was still an hour before our luggage appeared. We struggled outside to where the coach was waiting. The tour rep looked harassed.

The coach started up and chugged out on to the motorway. The rep blew into the mike a couple of times and then welcomed us to Majorca.

'I'm sorry about the hassle at the airport,' she said. 'There wasn't anything we could do about it. I hope it won't spoil your holiday.'

'What's left of it,' muttered a man behind me. 'We're already over three hours late.'

A muted rumble of agreement came from the back of the coach. People talked about suing the company and the airline and just about everyone. I leaned my head against the coach window and gazed outside as we sped along the motorway.

We were the second stop, which was a great relief because Clodagh wanted to go to the loo. It was a lovely block of apartments, only three storeys high, purple and pink flowers tumbling over the balconies.

Mam was exhausted and flopped on to the bed. Clodagh, after her emergency trip to the bathroom, rushed out on to the balcony. We overlooked the pool and she squealed in delight when she saw it. It was kidney-shaped, with a small wooden bridge across the narrowest point and a tiny bar nearby.

'Look!' she cried. 'Can I go swimming?'

'I have to find your things first,' I said.

'Oh, please now. Please.'

I grinned at her. 'All right.' I slapped some sun cream on her before she ran out. 'Be careful.'

She gave my words the weight they deserved. Clodagh was a superb swimmer, much better than I'd been at her age. As I looked out of the window, she ran to the pool and dived in, in one smooth movement. I sighed with relief. She was happy, anyway.

'Are you OK?' I asked Mam, who lay on the bed, eyes closed.

'Just hot,' she said.

'Well, change into something lighter,' I told her. Mam had insisted on wearing Irish clothes, although I'd told her she'd melt in Majorca. 'Why don't you have a shower?' I suggested. 'That'll cool you down.'

She went into the shower while I unpacked the cases and put away the clothes. So organised, I smiled to myself. When I'd gone on holidays first, I'd always lived out of the case. Now everything was neatly hanging in its place. I left out a light blouse and skirt for Mam and changed into shorts and a T-shirt. I looked out of the window again. Clodagh was deep in discussion with a couple of children, so I didn't have to worry about her.

'I think I'll go downstairs for a while,' I called in to the bathroom.

'Don't forget to put on some sun protection,' shouted Mam over the hiss of the shower.

What did she think I was? I'd been to the sun so many times

448

and she'd never been at all, yet she was the one telling me what to do. I shook my head.

There were some sun loungers in the shade and I sat down, allowing the heat to warm me through to my bones. It was blissful. I smoothed Protection 8 on to my face, arms and legs and stretched out on the lounger.

'Jane.'

I looked up, my sunbathing disturbed. Hugh was standing over me, casting a shadow across my body.

'Hello,' I said, not at all surprised that he was there. I'd always expected him to be there. He sat down on the edge of the lounger and ran his finger gently across my forehead.

'Hot?' he asked.

I nodded, lazily.

'Want to get into the pool?'

'Maybe.'

'I want you in the pool, Jane. And out here on the grass. And upstairs in the apartment. Everywhere.'

He bent towards me, his mouth met mine again and I recognised the familiarity of his lips.

I woke with a start, flustered by the intensity of the dream. The sun had dipped behind the apartment building and caused a shadow to fall over the lounger. It wasn't any colder, just shady, but I pulled myself upright and looked around me.

'Hello,' said Clodagh, seeing me move and running towards me. 'I thought you were going to stay asleep for ever. Like the sleeping princess.'

'I thought I was, too,' I said. 'Are you having a good time?'

She nodded vigorously. 'They're my friends over there,' she said. 'Natasha and Sonia and Martin. They're from Croydon. That's in England.'

'Good,' I said. 'Do you need any more sun cream?'

'On my nose.' She rubbed some on. 'They can't swim as good as me.'

'You're the best.' I kissed her and hugged her wet body against me. She squirmed away from me and ran, yelling, to the pool again.

449

Mam joined me from her seat under a nearby palm tree.

'Have you got used to the heat yet?' I asked.

'No,' she said, 'but I'm working on it.'

The San Carlos complex was fantastic. The three apartment buildings formed a circle around the pool and garden area. There were two restaurants in the complex itself and a small supermarket. Games were organised for the children, so I hardly saw Clodagh during the day and she was enjoying herself far too much to want to hang around me. Mam went to afternoon dances in the ballroom of the San Carlos Hotel next door. Every day the sun blazed down on top of us, and every day we went a little browner. Mam was worried about tanning. It wasn't safe, she warned, we were doing irreparable damage to our skin. But she still sat in the evening sun because there was nothing more soothing or relaxing than the warmth of its rays caressing your shoulders as you sipped a cooling drink.

Some days we went to the beach. Cala d'Or was a series of little coves, with sand running back deeply from the sea. We went to them all, Serena, Esmeralda, Es Forti and Cala d'Or itself.

The Spaniards themselves holidayed in Cala d'Or, the rep told us, and I believed it because there were far more Spanish people there than at any of the other resorts I'd ever gone to. They ran around the beaches chattering to each other, the words unintelligible. I was still trying to learn Spanish but, every time I switched on the tapes, I would be lulled to sleep by the voices repeating the phrases. I still hadn't got much further than asking where the toilets were.

Each night we ate in a different restaurant. Clodagh loved eating in restaurants, she enjoyed sitting on the terrace with a menu in her hand, having the power to decide exactly what she wanted to eat. Mam kept wanting to eat paella, which I didn't like but which they'd only do for two people. 'You have to, Jane,' she said, 'it's what the people themselves eat.'

She'd become immersed in Spanish culture and robbed my Spanish tapes whenever I wasn't using them. She did all the ordering of the meals, assisted by Clodagh. The waiters humoured them and I shook my head and stared into the distance when I ended up with squid instead of pork chops and octopus instead of chicken.

'It's all part of the experience,' said Mam, as she broke a prawn in half.

We stopped at the bar beside the crazy golf every evening so that Clodagh could play while we chatted. The barman got to know us and had our drinks sent over to us straight away. Bacardi for me, Tia Maria for Mam and Fanta lemon for Clodagh. I liked talking to Mam in the evenings, although I hated it when she talked about Rory.

'He ruined your life,' she said, after too many Tia Marias one night.

'No, he didn't.'

'Of course he did,' she told me. 'If it wasn't for him, you'd be happily married now.'

'How do you know?' I asked. 'I could have married somebody much worse and been even more miserable.'

'Do you mean you're miserable now?'

'Don't be silly,' I told her. 'Of course I'm not miserable. I was more miserable when I was married to Rory, only I didn't realise it at the time. But now, I'm happy. I've got a wonderful daughter.' I looked across at Clodagh who had nearly brained a German girl with her golf club.

'But he abandoned you,' said Mam. 'That was a terrible thing to do.'

'Mam,' I said, 'our marriage was falling apart long before Amanda Ferry.'

'You could have saved it,' she said, 'if it wasn't for her.'

'Maybe. Maybe not. How does anyone know?'

'I don't like to see you on your own, Jane. It's not right.'

'And why not?'

'Because every woman needs a man.'

'Oh, spare me that rubbish!' I exclaimed. 'It was that sort of thinking that made me marry Rory in the first place. Surely you don't believe that? Not in this day and age.'

'You'd be happier with a husband,' she said decisively.

'I wouldn't. Anyway, I can't marry again.'

'You could always live with someone.'

'Maureen O'Sullivan!' I cried. 'You can't possibly mean that. I thought you'd die rather than see me shacked up with someone.'

'I didn't mean it like that,' she objected. 'You know what I mean. In a proper relationship.'

'You sound like Oprah Winfrey,' I teased.

'I only want what's best for you, Jane,' she said. 'I've always only wanted that.'

'I know,' I said and squeezed her arm.

The barman came and sat down with us. It was a smallish bar, never very crowded. He preferred it that way, he told us in excellent English. He didn't want to be overrun with tourists.

'Are you from Cala d'Or?' I asked.

He laughed. 'No, from the mainland. Barcelona.'

'Really?' I asked. 'I've been to Barcelona.'

So we exchanged conversation about the sights of Barcelona and the people and the buildings, and we had a thoroughly enjoyable time while my mother went behind the bar and served the tourists.

He asked me to dinner a few nights before we went home. I told him that I couldn't possibly, but Mam pushed me into saying yes. 'You've only got one life,' she said. 'Have a bit of fun.'

I couldn't believe my mother. She'd never talked to me about having fun before. Her life had always seemed to be about responsibilities, this was a completely new side to her. So Mam and Clodagh went into the town to eat while Javier brought me in his Renault Clio into the mountains and to a Spanish restaurant where there were no tourists.

It was a small restaurant with ceramic tiled walls and quarry-tiled floor. The meat was on display in a refrigerated unit and you walked up to pick the piece you wanted. Then the chef took it away and cooked it. I had steak, very unSpanish, but so beautifully cooked that it fell apart when I cut it.

'So why are you here alone?' asked Javier.

I sipped the Viña Sol. 'Hardly alone,' I smiled. 'Three generations of women in my family together.'

'But you have no husband?'

'We don't live together any more.'

'I am sorry to hear that,' he said. 'It is a sad thing.'

It was wonderful to have dinner with a man again. The independent woman idea was great but I enjoyed being part of a couple. Javier was completely charming and utterly disarming. He complimented me on my dress, my hair, my suntan. He agreed with me on music and on films. He made me feel like the most important person in the world. And the best part was that I knew that I would never see him again, that this was one night that I could have all to myself.

We sat on the verandah outside the restaurant.

'Where do you live?' I asked idly, looking down at the white lights of the resort below us while the cicadas chirped in the background.

'An apartment,' he said. 'It's not a very nice apartment, but it is functional.'

He draped his arm over the back of my chair. I'd expected it and so I didn't react. Then he leaned towards me and kissed me on the cheek.

The cards were on the table, I thought. It was my decision and mine alone. I could go to bed with him. Dangerous, perhaps. No contraception, what about AIDS? I could thank him for a nice evening and go home. I didn't know what I wanted to do.

'I would not want to take you to my apartment,' he said, as we got into the car. 'It is too small. Not right for you.'

'Where do you want to take me?' I asked.

'To my boat,' he said.

'Your what?'

'My boat, it is tied up at the Marina.'

We drove to the Marina and to his boat. It was a small speed-boat, black and sleek. I raised an eyebrow at it.

'Expensive?' I asked.

'My hobby,' he answered.

I stepped into the boat, shaky from its movement and from the Viña Sol. Was I a total slut, I wondered. Would I burn in hell for ever?

He was a considerate lover. He brought me places I hadn't been in years, filling a need that had been dormant within me. We moved in rhythm with each other and in rhythm with the rocking of the boat on the water. When I cried out, my cries were echoed by the seagulls overhead.

It was dawn by the time I crept back into the apartment. I closed the door quietly behind me, wincing as it clicked. I tiptoed to the balcony and gazed out at the lightening sky tinged with orange. The waves broke gently against the sand in the distance. I smiled with pleasure.

'Did you have a good time?' I jumped guiltily as Mam's voice reached me. I peered back into the apartment. She was standing in the living room, looking out at me.

'Yes,' I said, conscious of my rumpled dress and tangled hair.

'Good,' said my mother calmly, and went back to bed.

Chapter 35

July/August 1994
(UK No. 3 – *Love Ain't Here Anymore* – Take That)

I returned home from my holiday tanned, happy and full of energy. I busied myself around the office driving Claire and Stephen nuts with my enthusiasm. Files that hadn't been checked in an age suddenly received my full attention, I made back-ups of the hard disk in the computer and I updated everyone's diaries so that no important meetings could be overlooked.

Every day that the weather was fine, I ate my lunch in the park in Merrion Square. I sat under a tree with my sandwiches and tin of Coke, read *Cosmopolitan* and *Marie Claire* and stretched my dusty brown legs to the faint Irish sun.

I hadn't felt so good in ages. I couldn't believe it was because of three nights of passion with Javier, but that had to have had some effect. I suppose it was the excitement of finding myself desirable in a purely physical way that I'd enjoyed so much. Nor did I care that, on the two occasions I'd gone to the sun without a husband, I'd had a holiday romance. Lifelong commitment was all very well, but a brief flirtation with passion was fun. It was great to have fun again.

Even Clodagh noticed the difference in me. She told me that I looked more sparkly and that I was laughing more. Mam hadn't said a word to me. The second night I'd met Javier – not until eleven o'clock – she'd told me simply to be careful and have a good time. She was a revelation to me. Instead of acting as my mother, she was my accomplice. I'd thought that she would lecture me, tell me that I was (at the very least) committing some sort of sin, that I could end up in all sorts of trouble, but she didn't. I was grateful to her, and for the first time in my life I appreciated her.

So when I got the phone call from Amanda Ferry one afternoon two weeks after our return, I didn't start shaking and quaking as I think I would have done earlier, but was able to talk to her in quite a sensible way. She was the one who sounded nervous, unsure of her ground.

'I wondered if we could meet for a chat,' she said. 'It's nothing exactly important, Jane, but I'd appreciate it very much.'

A year ago – six months ago – I would have dropped the phone and fled sobbing to the toilet. Now I listened to her calmly and said 'Sure, where and when?'

She didn't want to meet in town, she said. Or in Blackrock or Dún Laoghaire. Perhaps somewhere closer to me? Somewhere we could have a private conversation? I was intrigued. I wondered if she wanted to tell me that she was pregnant, carrying Rory's child. I didn't know how I'd feel if that were the case.

We decided on Johnny Fox's because the evening was bright and clear even if the air was cool. I drove up the mountains and parked opposite the pub. There was a wooden table outside and I sat there and waited for my husband's lover.

She was ten minutes late. Her bright red Alfa hurtled into the car park, sending up chips of gravel and sliding to a halt near the wall.

She was still very attractive, I thought enviously. Her dark curtain of hair was natural, no need to hide any grey there, and she wore a pair of pink cotton leggings and a long, white baggy jumper which emphasised the trimness of her figure.

Bitch, I thought, sipping my Budweiser.

'Hello, Jane,' she said as she sat down beside me. 'I'm sorry I'm late, I took the wrong turning.'

'No problem,' I said. 'Would you like a drink?'

'I'll get you one. What'll you have?'

'I'm OK for the moment.' I indicated my glass. 'But let me buy you one.'

She shrugged slightly, said she'd have a vodka and white, and I went into the bar to get the drink. When I came back, she was gazing out over the city while she puffed at a cigarette with short, jerky breaths.

Closer to, she was still attractive, but her face owed as much to art as to nature. The smooth skin was helped by her make-up, the colour of her eyes accentuated by kohl. She pushed her hair behind her ears in a jangling of silver bracelets and earrings and took a deep drag of the cigarette.

'Thanks,' she said, as I put the drink down in front of her.

We sat looking at the view together. I wasn't going to make whatever it was easier for her, although I was consumed with curiosity. I didn't think she could possibly be pregnant. For one thing she was far too thin, and nowadays it was practically a crime to be pregnant and either drink or smoke, let alone do both.

'I suppose you're wondering why I wanted to see you.' She sipped the vodka, leaving the mark from her glossy lips on the edge of the glass.

'I am interested,' I admitted.

'It's not awfully easy for me to talk about,' she said. She tapped ash into the ashtray and looked around us as though checking that we were alone.

'Why don't you just spit it out?' I suggested. 'It's easiest that way.'

So she told me, amid much puffing of her cigarette and drinking of her vodka and shredding of the beer mat in front of us, that she thought Rory was having an affair.

'He's never in.' Her voice quavered. 'And he's spent half the summer in the States at that fucking World Cup.'

I hid a grin. It didn't seem that long since I'd complained about the very same thing. God, I was glad that I wasn't living with Rory any more. I wished that I could divorce him, not to get married again, but to know that he was finally, irrevocably, out of my life.

'Has he been making any surreptitious phone calls?' I asked. 'You know the sort, where he puts the phone down as you walk into the room?'

She shook her head. 'Not that I know of. Oh Jane, I'm sorry to have dragged you up here to talk about this, but you've always been so good about it and I really don't have anyone else I could possibly turn to.' A tear slid down her face, along her chin and plopped into her empty vodka glass.

I found it hard to believe that I was sitting here listening to the woman who had stolen my husband crying because he might be having an affair with somebody else. It had the hallmarks of a comedy, but there was nothing comical about the way Amanda sobbed quietly beside me.

'Even if he is having an affair, there's nothing much I can do about it,' I said. 'If I wanted to.'

She looked at me, her eyes red. 'I thought he might be having it with you,' she said starkly.

'With me?' I looked at her in amazement. 'Amanda, the bastard left me!'

'But he talks about you,' said Amanda bitterly, 'all the fucking time. Jane this and Jane that, and Clodagh this and Clodagh that, until I want to throw something at him.'

'Rory does?'

'All the time,' she said again. 'So I thought maybe he wanted to get back with you and maybe you were encouraging him. I had to find out, Jane, to see where I stood.'

I shredded a beer mat myself. The scene in my living room, when he'd tried to make love to me the night they'd come home from the States, was clear and fresh in my mind. I could see him now as he stood in front of me, mocking me.

'I'm not having an affair with him,' I said. 'If you can have an affair with your own husband. Maybe I would have tried to get him back once, but not now. I don't love him any more.'

And this time, maybe for the very first time, my words were true. Other times, I'd told myself I didn't love him. Other times I'd been afraid that I might still love him. Still more times, I'd ached with a need for him that might have been love. But today I knew that I didn't love him any more, would never love him again. Even if he knocked on my front door tonight, carrying flowers and chocolates and airline tickets to somewhere wonderful, I would simply be bored by him. I'd moved on from Rory and I felt that a weight had been lifted from my heart.

The smoke from Amanda's cigarette spiralled in front of me. Poor Amanda, I thought.

'Surely you're out and about a lot,' I said brightly. 'Maybe it's just that your lives aren't coinciding very much at the moment. And I bet half your dealing room has gone to the World Cup.'

Nearly all of Dublin's financial powerhouses had been practically closed during the Italian adventure, and I expected that it was the same this time around.

'Oh yes,' she said. 'The lads are jetting back and forward like nobody's business. But Rory has stayed over there. He's been there for almost a month! He says he's meeting clients and I suppose he is, but it's not fair.' She looked guilty for a moment. 'I rang your office earlier and they said you'd been on holiday. So I thought that maybe you'd gone to the States with him.'

'Good God,' I said in amazement. 'I was in Majorca with my mother and my daughter.'

She started to giggle suddenly, slightly hysterically, and I laughed too.

'I really don't think he's having an affair, Amanda,' I said, hoping to God I was right. 'The last time I talked to him, he said that you and he were thinking of having a baby.'

She lit another cigarette from the butt of the first. 'Really?'

'He said that you'd thought about it when you brought Clodagh on holiday.'

'I do want a child,' she admitted. 'But he won't talk about it to me. When I mentioned it to him, he said that he already had a perfect child and he didn't need another one.'

I was furious at Rory's cruelty. I signalled a barman to get us another drink.

'How badly do you want a baby?' I asked. 'I always thought you dealers wouldn't have time for all that.'

'Oh, I wouldn't go on dealing if I had a baby!' Amanda looked shocked. 'I couldn't, I'd be too tired. God, it's tiring enough half the time. I'm twenty-nine, Jane, and I want to have one now.'

'And give up work?' I said.

'For a while.'

'I can't believe that Rory isn't interested,' I said. 'I'd a massive row with him because I wanted to go back to work after Clodagh. The only reason I didn't was because I went back into hospital to have my appendix out and I was too knackered to go back. Then, when I did eventually decide to return, he was dead set against it. I'd have thought he'd be thrilled to have you at home with your baby.'

'Apparently not,' she said.

'What about his mother?' I asked. 'The wonderful Eleanor?' She made a face. 'Eleanor doesn't like me very much.'

'Good,' I said. 'The old cow never liked me very much either.'

We had another drink as dusk fell and the lights of the city came on below us. There was no real comfort I could offer Amanda, because I didn't honestly know whether Rory was seeing someone else or not. I was a bit surprised, because in one of our bitter recriminatory conversations he'd told me that Amanda was everything he had always wanted in a woman. I couldn't believe that it had all changed for them so soon.

I waited until she had driven away before I started my own car, afraid that maybe she was so upset that she would stay and drink some more and have an accident on her way home. I laughed at myself for my concern. But I was concerned about her. Regretfully, I rather liked her.

Lucy was stunned when I phoned her the following evening.

'Didn't you want to scratch her eyes out?' she asked.

'Not really,' I said. 'To be honest, I felt sorry for her.'

'Jesus, Jane,' said Lucy. 'That's above and beyond the call of duty.'

'Well, I did,' I told her. 'The poor girl is going through exactly what I went through, and even if she was once my worst enemy, I wouldn't wish it on her now. Rory can be such a bastard when he wants to be.'

'So you don't care that she wants to have a kid?'

'No,' I said. 'She can have a dozen of them and I still wouldn't care.'

'Jane,' said Lucy. 'I think you're over him.'

'Lucy,' I said. 'I know I am.'

So there I was, thirty-four, and out of love with my husband at last. I could even play the songs that we had danced to without wanting to cry, to hold my head in my hands and wonder what had all gone wrong and why.

I sold another painting. I'd been commissioned to do it by

a woman who'd seen one of the ones I'd done of Junkie and wanted me to do one of her own cat. So I did and she paid me for it, and I went to *Les Jumelles* to spend the proceeds on an outfit for Brenda and Grace's weddings.

The shop was crowded when I called in on Saturday afternoon with Clodagh, who wanted to be somewhere else.

I looked through the racks of clothes for something simple but elegant. I still found it hard to believe that the twins were actually getting married.

I found the outfit I wanted, a floaty chiffon dress with faint cream and pink flowers and a pale green jacket to go over it. It conjured up pictures of English country lawns and afternoon tea and it made me look serene. It took more than my pay cheque for the painting to pay for it, but it was worth it. I bought a hat too, a kind of cloche in the same green as the jacket, and I thought that it finished my outfit perfectly.

'You look like Mia Farrow in *The Great Gatsby*,' said Brenda. 'It suits you.'

'I hope I'm a bit more robust than Mia Farrow,' I said. 'And I always thought Daisy was a dopey character.'

'Jane, girls who are dressed like nineteen-twenties rich young ladies don't go around using words like dopey,' complained Brenda. 'You don't live the part.'

'It doesn't matter about me, once you do,' I returned. 'How are the preparations going?'

Brenda groaned. 'Next month,' she said, 'and we're up to our eyes. I don't know how we'll get through it at all.'

'What about your own dresses?'

'Oh, we've got them,' she said. 'We didn't even attempt to make them. Wedding dresses are so much fuss and I know it's silly, but we don't want the bother. Besides which –' she broke off.

'What?' I asked.

'Nothing,' she said. I looked at her. The twins were up to something, I knew it by the expression on her face, but she suddenly distracted me.

'Guess who was in here the other day?' she said. 'Stephanie McMenamin. Stephanie Kennedy, I mean. She's improved again; she looked absolutely wretched for a while, but she'd had her

461

hair done and she'd dumped her kids with someone, so she had a bit more of a spring in her step.'

'Good,' I said.

'You look great too,' observed Brenda. 'There's colour in your cheeks and a bit of a spring in your step, too. Have you been getting up to anything?'

I blushed wildly and looked at her in confusion. She stared at me with delight. 'You *have* been getting up to something!'

'Not at all,' I said, composing myself. 'It's just the tan from my holiday.'

But Brenda continued to grin as she wrapped my jacket and dress in soft white tissue paper and slid it carefully into the bag.

I felt as though I was tying up all the pieces of my life. As though, quite suddenly, they were all falling into place and all finally making sense. Good things had happened to me and horrible things had happened and – not that I believed in a great plan or anything, any more – they were all part of what made me be the person I was. And I was an OK person. Not the loveliest in the world, or the most intelligent, or the luckiest or the most miserable. Still pretty average, really, but content with that.

The only part of my life that I hadn't tidied up was the part of it where Hugh McLean lurked. I didn't know what to do about him. I'd misread his signals time and time again. I still didn't know exactly what he'd wanted from me – a quick fling seemed the most likely thing, and yet he wasn't the type of person who'd want a quick fling. And he wasn't the kind of person who would deliberately try to break up someone's marriage. I wished I could figure him out and then forget him, but I couldn't quite do that. I hadn't dreamed about him for quite a while, though, which was a relief.

I'd put him to the back of my mind when Claire came out of her office, holding his file.

'Did you send off the analysis of this client's portfolio I did for him?' she asked me.

My heart missed a beat when I saw his name. 'Of course,' I said. 'I sent it the following Monday.'

'I think I should give him a call,' she said. 'I forgot about

462

him a bit, the file had somehow gone to the bottom of my pile. Can you get him for me, Jane?'

'Wouldn't you like to call him yourself?' I asked.

'But you spoke to him for me, didn't you?' said Claire. 'So you should call him and then put him through to me. OK?'

'OK,' I said, with leaden heart.

I didn't want to do this. I didn't want to ring his number and ask for him. I hoped against hope that he would be out of the shop and that the girl would take a message because then I could leave the number of Claire's direct line with him to phone. An absolutely taboo thing to do, to give either Claire or Stephen's direct line to anybody, but I'd do it and hang the consequences.

I punched the numbers on the phone and listened to the dialling tone.

'CityBooks.'

Shit, I thought as I heard his voice.

'Is that Hugh McLean?' I asked. What a way to talk to someone who has kissed you the way Hugh had kissed me.

'Yes,' he said. 'What do you want, Jane?' His voice was cool, impersonal.

'I've a call for you from Claire Haughton, one of our partners,' I said. 'You were due to meet Mrs Haughton the day you called into our office. She asked me to get you on the line.'

'Does Mrs Haughton know about us?' he asked calmly.

'Us?' I squeaked.

'You know, about me chasing you around the office and you locking yourself in the Ladies. That little incident,' he said.

'No. Absolutely not. Nothing,' I assured him.

'Can you ask Mrs Haughton to call me back tomorrow?' asked Hugh politely. 'I'm quite busy right now and I don't really have the time to talk to her.'

'Certainly,' I said. 'Is any particular time convenient?'

He considered for a moment.

'Perhaps it would be better if you arranged an appointment for me with her,' he said. 'I'd prefer to meet her face to face, especially as there are a couple of things I need to chat to her about. Tomorrow afternoon would suit if she has a free moment. Otherwise Friday?'

I called up Claire's appointments on the computer screen. Her diary was full for the next day, but she could see him directly after lunch on Friday.

'Sounds fine,' he said. 'Thank you for calling, Mrs McLoughlin.'

It sounded strange being called Mrs McLoughlin. Most people who knew me called me Jane. When I left a name with anyone any more, I reverted to Jane O'Sullivan.

I told Claire that Hugh McLean had made an appointment to see her and she was delighted.

'Means we've probably nailed him as a client,' she said. 'Well done, Jane.'

I wasn't sure she'd say well done if she knew exactly how Hugh and I had parted. It was not what she'd call professional. And Claire was very professional.

I was in a complete flap all day Friday. My new, composed self had disappeared under the stress of knowing that Hugh would be in the office. It wasn't, of course, that there was anything between Hugh and me; it was embarrassment at meeting him again, at having to be polite to him. I dressed down deliberately. I wore an old, very plain white blouse and an ankle-length pleated skirt. I didn't wear any make-up and only a little *L'Air du Temps* behind my ears. I looked demure.

I walked around the square at lunch-time, although the sky was grey and my light cashmere cardigan wasn't really warm enough in the easterly breeze. I rehearsed how I would greet him, how I would keep my composure, how I would be totally unfazed by him. It was an embarrassing situation, I told myself, but I could handle it with dignity and with self-respect. I would be totally in command.

It was exactly a quarter to two when I arrived back at the office. Hugh was due at two. Claire was already in her office making notes. I typed up some reports for Stephen, keeping one eye on the clock, and the other on the door. Stephen's writing was big and florid and much easier to decipher than Claire's, which was small and neat.

I was under the desk retrieving a page which had floated to the floor when Hugh came into the office. I heard the door open and I straightened up and whacked my head off the corner of the desk. For a moment I knew what they meant by seeing stars. The room spun around and my eyes filled with tears of pain.

'Are you all right?' he asked, concern in his voice.

'Yes,' I gasped. 'Just got a shock, that's all.' I took out a tissue and wiped my eyes. Brainy idea not wearing make-up, I thought. If I had done so, I'd have had mascara running down my face again!

'I've an appointment to see Claire Haughton,' said Hugh.

'I know you have,' I said. 'I made it.'

His mouth twitched. I couldn't believe that he was laughing at me. I buzzed the intercom and told Claire that Hugh McLean was here to see her. 'Send him in,' crackled her voice.

'Do you want to go in?' I asked. 'The second door—'

'I know which office,' he said. 'Thank you.'

I was furious with him and with me. Why had he chosen that moment to come into the office? Why was it that whenever I planned anything, tried to have everything just so, it never worked out like I'd expected. I sat in front of my screen, bleary-eyed from the knock on the head. I rubbed it gently; there was a bump at the back like a golf-ball. I'm probably concussed, I thought gloomily.

'Jane, can you bring in some coffee?' said Claire's voice over the intercom. I made a face but brought in coffee and biscuits. Hugh was sitting opposite her, looking relaxed. He was wearing the same suit as he'd done the last time, I noticed. Probably his only suit. It was the one I'd seen him wear in the Stephen's Green Centre, too. I felt better when I noticed that. He wasn't one of the sharp businessmen who wandered around the bank, the kind Rory associated with. Usually Hugh looked unkempt and uninterested in suits. He was a jeans and sweatshirt sort of person. I wasn't going to let him intimidate me.

I put the tray with the coffee and the cups and the Afternoon Tea biscuits on Claire's desk. Hugh was wearing his tortoiseshell glasses today. There was a fingerprint in the middle of one of the lenses.

He was with Claire for about half an hour. I sat at my desk and did my work but with only half my brain on it. I could hear the gentle hum of conversation coming from Claire's office, and the occasional laugh.

She escorted him to the outer office and shook his hand. 'I'm pleased to have met you,' she said. 'I look forward to doing business with you.'

'Thanks,' he said. He looked at me for a moment. 'Do you mind if I make a call?'

'You can use my office if you want some privacy,' said Claire, waving at her open door.

'Not at all,' said Hugh. 'I simply want to call my office. This phone will do fine.'

Claire smiled at him, a wide beaming smile that I'd never seen before. I wondered if he had that effect on everybody, made them all feel good. Hold on a minute, I told myself, he doesn't make you feel good, does he?

He phoned the bookshop and spoke to somebody there. I didn't listen to the conversation. I kept my head buried in a file, reading it carefully, totting up columns of figures.

I heard him replace the receiver. 'Thank you, Mrs McLoughlin,' he said.

I looked up at him, green eyes meeting brown. 'O'Sullivan,' I told him. 'My name is Jane O'Sullivan.'

The switchboard blinked at me and I answered it. I could see him still standing in front of my desk. I put the call through to Claire.

'Why have you changed your name?' he asked.

'Oh, I've just reverted to what it was before,' I said casually. 'That's all.'

'Why?'

'You remind me of my daughter,' I said. 'Always asking questions.'

'I think we should talk,' said Hugh.

I was sort of in control. Not completely, because my hands were shaking just a little and I could feel the beat of my heart, but he wouldn't have seen any of this.

'Talk about what?' I asked.

'Us,' said Hugh.

I stared at him. 'There is no us,' I said, as I hit the wrong key on the keyboard and obliterated half my work.

'Why not?' asked Hugh.

I shrugged.

'Meet me.' He looked carefully at me.

466

'Is there any point?'

'Meet me.'

'When?'

'Tonight.'

'You seem to think that I can take off whenever I like,' I said. 'I'm taking my daughter to her ballet class tonight.'

'While she's at ballet. You could meet me then. I do want to talk to you, Jane.'

'All right.' I was still in control. 'If you like. I'll meet you in the Rathfarnham Orchard at seven. Sharp.'

'OK,' said Hugh. 'See you then.'

He left the office and I released the breath that I seemed to have been holding ever since he had first entered. What had I done? I asked myself. And more to the point – why had I done it? It wasn't as though I was in Spain any more. I couldn't blame the sun or the sangria for being silly. But I wanted to go out with him. To see what it would be like. To get him out of my system. I couldn't count the lunch at the National Gallery, that was completely different.

It was a rush to get home, get Clodagh's things together and get out again that evening. She lost her shoes and her leotard and her bag. I ran around looking for them while trying to smudge a bit of lipstick on my lips and rummage for my thin gold chain and tiny pinhead stud earrings. I was still going for the demure look. I kept the skirt long – my ecru linen, and the top chaste – an oatmeal knit. I thought I looked particularly sensible in that outfit. I chivvied Clodagh until she yelled at me and finally bundled her into the car and drove down the road to her ballet class. I wouldn't have very much time with Hugh McLean. Her class was over at eight.

The sun shone on the white walls of the pub. I should have said that I'd meet him outside. It seemed a pity to go in out of the light. But it was still cool and I probably would have shivered my way through our conversation.

I pushed open the doors and peered into the interior of the lounge. He was sitting on a stool at the bar and I caught my breath. I'd tried to pretend that he wasn't that attractive, but he was. I wished that he didn't look so desirable, my knees had turned to jelly.

I walked over to him and sat on the bar stool beside him.

'Glass of Bud,' I said to the barman. Hugh closed his book and looked at me. He was reading *War and Peace*.

'Hello, Jane O'Sullivan,' he said. 'Glad you could make it.'

'I can't make it for long,' I said. 'I've to pick up Clodagh at eight.'

He glanced at his watch. 'So what are you doing – giving me an hour to make my pitch?'

I shook my head. 'I don't know what you mean,' I said. 'I don't really know why I'm here at all.'

He ran his finger around the rim of his beer glass. 'I have to confess I'm not too sure about it myself,' he said.

'You asked to meet,' I told him. 'What do you want?' I knew that I was being very rude but I couldn't help myself. I thought that if I was rude, then he wouldn't realise how nervous I was.

'The last time I saw you, you were Jane McLoughlin,' he said. 'Now you're Jane O'Sullivan. O'Sullivan is your maiden name, I suppose?'

'Maiden name,' I echoed. 'Sounds sort of spinsterish, doesn't it. My friends are always telling me that I'll end up a dry old spinster.'

'Why should you do that?' he asked.

'Because . . .' I sighed deeply. I wanted to tell him and I didn't want to tell him. I was afraid of breaking the shell I had built around myself. But Javier had already cracked the shell. I pulled at a fingernail.

'Don't.' He caught my hand in his. 'You'll be sorry afterwards. I always am.'

His hand was warm and dry. I resisted the urge to pick it up and kiss it.

'I left my husband,' I said, and then corrected myself. 'No. My husband left me. Another woman.' I thought about Amanda and smiled to myself. Not a victorious smile, just a knowing smile.

'Quite some time ago,' said Hugh.

I flashed him a glance. 'How would you know how long ago?' I asked.

'I heard,' he said.

I took my hand from his. 'How did you hear?'

468

'Dublin is a small city,' he said.

'But not that small,' I replied. 'So how?'

'My company is a client of your – ex-husband's bank. I discovered it in discussions with somebody there. Purely by chance, Jane.'

I was furious. How dared people talk about me! 'How by chance?'

'It was my fault,' he admitted. 'I said I'd met you at the Christmas party. The person concerned said it was your last, that you and Rory had split up.'

'I see. And did they tell you why?'

He shook his head. 'I didn't ask. I don't care why.'

'So you knew, when you met me, when you phoned me?'

'What do you take me for, Jane? Do you really think I'd try and pinch another man's wife?'

I didn't know quite what I felt. Relief, perhaps, because that was the one thing that had truly bothered me about Hugh. He knew that I was married but he'd still kind of chased me. And I wasn't happy about him being that sort of person. But he hadn't chased me as a married woman, he'd known that I wasn't living with Rory any more.

He was watching me carefully.

'But why do you want to—' I broke off, unsure.

'See you?' he supplied.

I shrugged. 'Whatever.'

'Jane, I told you before. I like you. I liked you when I thought you were married, but I like you better now you're not. I kissed you once because I wanted to, but it was the wrong time and the wrong place. I know that I keep making you cry – for which I'm eternally sorry – but I promise that I won't always make you cry. And I like the way you fight me all the time.'

I laughed. 'You'd get bored with that soon enough.'

'I only want to get to know you better,' he said. 'Nothing more.'

'Nothing?' I said.

'Not yet, anyway,' said Hugh.

'So what are you suggesting?' I asked.

'A couple of dates,' said Hugh. 'You know what dates are? Dinner, theatre, movie, drink – that sort of thing.'

'And nothing else?'

'Not unless you want to, of course.'

I might want to, I reflected, but that wasn't the point. Hugh was a nice man but did I want somebody in my life? It wasn't like Javier, I couldn't just dump him after a few days. And I was trying so hard, so very hard to get it all together all by myself. I could hear them say: 'Don't end up a dry old maid, Jane,' but I still wasn't sure. I couldn't be convinced. I didn't want this possibility, this dream to be as uncertain as all the rest.

'A date, then,' I said cautiously. 'Nothing extravagant.'

'Nothing extravagant.' He drained his glass. 'I'll phone you, shall I?'

I'd thought he would fix up something there and then. I was a bit surprised. 'OK,' I said.

'Fine.' Hugh got down from the bar stool. 'Well, I'll leave you in peace and I'll be in touch.' He glanced at his watch. 'You've plenty of time to pick up Clodagh.' He smiled at me and walked out of the pub.

Chapter 36

September 1994
(UK No. 2 – *Always* – Bon Jovi)

The blue and white KLM DC-11 banked slowly, tilting so that we could see the silvery sheen of the water beneath us and the tiny sail of a boat below. Our side of the plane was in shadow while the evening sun poured through the opposite side in great golden shafts. We were suspended for a moment between the sea and the sky and then the aircraft steadied itself, straightened up and began to drop slowly and gracefully towards the island.

We seemed to skim over the water only a few feet below us. I wondered, briefly and agonisingly, if the pilot had made a mistake but then quite suddenly the runway was beneath us and the plane bumped on to the tarmac, screaming as reverse thrust was applied to the engines and the aircraft jolted down to a slow roll.

The terminal building of Flamingo Airport was to our left, a bright pink building which was no bigger than a supermarket. Palm trees waved gently in the sea breeze and already I could sense that the air outside was warm.

The flight attendants opened the doors and the passengers scrambled to take down their luggage from the bins above. I stood up and stretched. Although this was by far the biggest plane I'd ever flown on, it was nearly twelve hours since we'd left Schipol Airport in Amsterdam. The delay in Caracas had been the worst. We wandered around the Venezuelan airport for almost an hour, looking at touristy dolls and T-shirts without wanting to buy anything. All the same, I could say I'd been to Venezuela now, and nobody need ever know that I hadn't been outside the rather grim terminal building.

But we were here, in Bonaire, the tiny Dutch Antilles island where Brenda and Grace were going to marry Robert and Damien and where Lucy and I were to be their witnesses.

We'd been shocked when the twins told us of their plans, although we understood why they wanted a Caribbean wedding. They didn't want hordes of relatives and they didn't feel that it was appropriate to have a wedding at home without inviting them. So they'd thought of the Caribbean idea – a holiday and a wedding all in one, as Brenda had put it.

None of us had heard of Bonaire before but Robert and Damien, both keen scuba divers, decided that this was the island for them. It was a scuba diver's paradise, with thousands of exotic fish and coral formations that could only be matched by the Great Barrier Reef. The twins agreed; they didn't much care where they went as long as the sun shone and the wedding was legal.

Then they'd sprung their bombshell. They wanted some friends to join them. They didn't want to get married completely on their own and they thought that Lucy and I would like the holiday.

'We can't come on your honeymoon!' Lucy objected, even as I watched her mentally calculate the cost of a transatlantic flight.

'We're not asking you to come on our honeymoon,' said Grace. 'We'll be spending a few days on Bonaire – to fulfil the residency requirements, and so that the lads can dive, but then we're going on to Aruba and Curacao. We'll be in the Dutch Antilles for two weeks. We're suggesting that you spend a week in Bonaire. At a different hotel.'

'A week!' I did some mental calculations myself. 'I can't really—'

'Our treat,' explained Brenda.

We stared at her speechlessly. Lucy was the first to find her voice. 'You mean – you want to pay?'

'We're getting a good deal,' grinned Grace. 'Damien is going to take hundreds of photographs, and one of the hotels has offered us very inexpensive accommodation, by way of encouraging him to do a bit of Bonaire promotion. We've got another good deal on flights, so don't think that it's costing us the earth. Besides,' she put her arms around our shoulders, 'we want you to be there. You've always been our friends, through everything. We were at both your weddings, we want you to be at ours.'

I felt tears of affection prick the back of my eyes. 'I don't know what to say.' I was absolutely stunned.

'Say you'll come,' said Brenda.

'There's one other thing,' added Grace. 'We don't expect you to come on your own, Lucy; after all, David would probably love the holiday too. So he's included in the package.' She looked at me and her eyes twinkled. 'As is anyone you might want to bring, Jane.'

I blushed to the roots of my hair and the others giggled. I'd told them about Hugh. My friend. Who was a man. Just a friend, though.

I still wasn't sure about Hugh and me. I didn't know whether we had a relationship or, if we had, where it might lead. I'd been out with him three times. To the cinema once, to see *Sleepless in Seattle*, at which I sniffed covertly – Hugh proffered a slightly crumpled tissue beneath the cover of the giant-sized popcorn; to a classical recital which was moving (but not, thank goodness, tear-jerking) and to dinner in Dobbin's, which was the nearest we'd got to a romantic evening. And in those three nights, he'd never once tried to do anything more than kiss me lightly on the cheek when I got out of his car. He always refused the offer of a cup of coffee, or a nightcap, and he left me wondering. I couldn't believe that he'd once kissed me, passionately, on the lips. I could only assume that he had done it for a reason of his own which I couldn't yet fathom. If he'd wanted me physically then, it didn't seem as though he wanted me physically now.

Yet it was good to go out with him. Javier had reminded me of how much I enjoyed turning up at a restaurant on the arm of a man, even one who had a paperback in his suit pocket, pulling the jacket out of shape. It was nice to be part of a couple.

He met Clodagh the night we went to the recital. I felt strange about him coming to our house, but he said that he'd collect me and I thought that Clodagh should meet him. Just in case.

She gazed at him with undisguised interest and he told her that he was pleased to meet her. She asked him questions, silly inconsequential questions, but he answered them seriously, making no concession to her age.

'Where are you going?' she asked us.

'To a concert,' I said as I slipped my jacket around my shoulders. 'You're to be good while we're out, no giving any trouble.

Do what Anne tells you.' Anne was her current baby-sitter, the girl next door.

Clodagh yawned, bored with my orders. 'I always do what I'm told,' she said.

When we returned, at midnight, she was awake. I peeped around her bedroom door as I always did and she stirred slightly in the bed. I walked over to look at her. Her eyes were open, focused.

'Is he your boyfriend?' she asked.

'I don't know,' I answered.

'Amanda is Daddy's girlfriend,' she told me. 'So I suppose you should have a boyfriend.'

'Do you like Amanda?' I asked.

'You're always asking me that.' Clodagh snuggled down under the covers. 'She's OK. I like your boyfriend.'

'Do you?'

'He's nice,' she said, as she closed her eyes. 'Not as nice as Daddy,' she added, opening them again. 'But he'll do.'

Despite Clodagh's approval, I didn't feel as though I could ask Hugh to come to Bonaire with me. Brenda and Grace urged me to do it. I knew that they thought it would be the ultimate in romance if I went to a wedding with Hugh McLean. Especially a wedding in such wonderful surroundings.

So I mentioned it to him, very casually, over the phone one evening.

'They suggested what!!' he exclaimed.

I repeated it for him. 'Of course you probably wouldn't be able to go anyway,' I added. 'Even if you did want to.'

'Do you want me to?' he asked. 'Would you like me to be there?'

I'd thought all afternoon about it, picturing myself on the Caribbean island with him and without him, watching the girls get married with him and without him, sitting in a restaurant sipping Piña Coladas with him and without him. If I wanted him to come, I wanted it to be for the right reason. Because I wanted *him*, Hugh – not just anyone. Although I couldn't trust myself to think it through properly, I wanted him to be with me. I didn't want to allow myself to think that I might be falling for him, because that would be crazy. I would be falling into the same old trap again, trying to live a dream that couldn't possibly come true. It was different for other people. Lucy was lucky. Maybe Brenda and Grace would be lucky. But my men had always been disastrous. Maybe that was my fault, but I wouldn't let myself be hurt again. That was why I was happy with Hugh, because he didn't try anything.

'I'd like you to come,' I said hesitantly. 'But, you know, as my friend.' I put a wealth of meaning in the word 'friend'.

'I see,' said Hugh. 'I'm not sure if I can make it, Jane.'

'Please,' I said, surprised at how much I actually did want him to come. 'I'd like it if you did, Hugh.'

He thought for a moment. 'OK,' he said. 'But I'm paying my own fare.'

Brenda was delighted he was coming and told me that they wanted to pay for him – they were paying for David; they had the money, for God's sake. But Hugh was adamant; he would pay for himself and the twins had to allow him.

He stood beside me on the tarmac as we looked up at the huge plane that had carried us halfway around the world. The warm air touched my neck and I shivered with the pleasure of it.

Brenda and Grace had arranged to meet us and bring us to our hotel. 'You lot are in The Golden Necklace,' she told us. 'We're in the one a little further away.'

'I don't care if we're on a shack on the beach,' declared Lucy, as she hugged me with excitement. 'This is absolutely fantastic. Aren't the girls the best in the world!'

It took a while to get through immigration. Lucy had lost the form they had given her to fill in on the plane. She finally found it, stuck in her wallet with the pictures of Andrew, and she pulled it out, scattering photographs over the immigration desk. The comfortable lady behind the desk picked up the photos and smiled.

'Your baby?' she asked.

Lucy nodded.

'Lovely, lovely,' she said as she stamped the form and waved us through.

We collected our luggage and walked outside. The twins and the Driscolls were waiting for us. Robert Driscoll allocated the taxis, and we were driven to the hotels; Lucy, David, Hugh and I to The Golden Necklace, which was only a few minutes' drive from the airport, and the twins and their fiancés to the larger, more modern Turtle Bay, a little further along the coast. The island was only twenty-seven miles long and, we discovered, almost a third of that was given over to a nature reserve.

Bonaire was a Dutch Antilles island. Apartments and houses built in the tall and narrow Dutch style jostled against the low, whitewashed, more usual Caribbean houses. The signs were a mixture of Dutch and the local dialect, Papiamento. It gave me the strangest feeling to find continental Europe in the middle of the soft, blue sea.

We checked in to the hotel, already warm, definitely tired but happy to have arrived. Lucy wanted to phone home to check on Andrew. Her only worry about the holiday was leaving Andrew with her mother. There were half a dozen phones at reception. I'd phone Clodagh in the morning, I said, before the wedding, when I knew that she would be in. Hopefully, she would be in bed by now.

The bellboy, tall and gangly and wearing the hotel uniform of brightly coloured floral shorts and shirt, showed us to our rooms. They were simply furnished, with tiled floors and stone walls, but when I opened the balcony and stepped outside, I caught my breath at the beauty in front of me.

A coconut tree swayed outside the window, the nuts clustered in the heart of the tree almost close enough to touch. Through the waving fronds, I could see the expanse of pure white sand which led into the azure blue sea. It was unspoiled and exquisite. It made the brochures look tacky.

Hugh stepped on to the balcony behind me and rested his hands on my shoulders. 'Perfect, isn't it?' he whispered in my ear. I nodded, watching as a heron suddenly swooped from the sky and, pulling its body into a long white spear, entered the water, then emerged with a fish between its beak.

'Did you see that!' I exclaimed. 'Did you?'

'Yes,' he said. 'Fantastic.' He let go of my shoulders and leaned over the edge of the balcony. 'There's a swimming pool over there.' He waved to the left. 'If you want to go swimming.'

'In a pool?' I said scornfully. 'When that sea is there? You must be joking.'

'Do you want to go for a swim?' he asked.

'Absolutely.'

'Come on, then.'

'Before unpacking?' I asked doubtfully.

'The cases will still be here when we get back,' he laughed. 'Come on, Jane.'

I opened my case and found my swimsuit. I held it in my hands, undecided. I was undecided about a few things, now that we were actually here.

The room had two huge double beds. I didn't know what sleeping arrangements Hugh intended. If he behaved the way he usually did, it would be separate beds and a goodnight peck on the top of my head, but I couldn't be certain about that. And I wasn't sure about changing into my swimsuit in front of him either. He'd see my scars, for one thing and my flabby stomach, which all the work in the gym couldn't get rid of, for another.

Hugh disappeared into the bathroom and emerged wearing a pair of fluorescent pink shorts and a lime green T-shirt. 'What do you think?' he asked. 'Suitable attire?'

'Brilliant.' I dived into the bathroom myself. My swimsuit was black with tiny white dots. It hid a multitude of sins, although it did plunge daringly between my breasts. I pulled a multicoloured sarong over it and slid my feet into a pair of sandals.

'Nice,' said Hugh appreciatively, as I pushed open the bathroom door.

We walked through the hotel and out to the beach, which was hotel property. There were a few deserted sun-loungers and half a dozen people sat in the now-fading sun at the end of the pier.

'Do you think it'll be warm enough?' I asked as I looked longingly at the silky blue water.

'Don't be ridiculous,' said Hugh and strode in. He dipped down beneath the surface and bobbed up again. 'It's wonderful!'

I undid my sarong and draped it on one of the sun-loungers. Then I ran into the water, sending up a shower of silver spray. I dived beneath it myself and struck out strongly. It was beautiful, warm and enticing.

Hugh swam out to me and I turned as he caught up with me. 'You're a good swimmer,' he said, in surprise, treading water.

'I love swimming,' I told him. 'I used to do a lot of it when I was younger, then I got out of practice. But Clodagh and I go every Saturday now. It's not the same though, is it, swimming in a pool full of chlorine as swimming in the Caribbean sea?'

I loved saying Caribbean. It sounded so exotic, so romantic. Even more romantic than The Med, I thought deliriously.

'I'll race you to that buoy over there,' said Hugh, and I nodded.

He was a strong swimmer too, but he only beat me by the length of his body. I caught up with him and grinned. 'By the end of the week, I'll be beating you.'

'Want to bet?' he asked as he made for the shore.

He floated lazily and I swam over to him.

'Enjoying yourself?' I asked.

'Wonderful,' said Hugh. 'Thanks for asking me to come.'

'Thanks for coming,' I said.

I kissed him. I couldn't help it. He righted himself in the water and looked at me, his eyes dark, unfathomable. Then he smiled suddenly and they were lighter, carefree.

'Come on,' he said, 'we'd better go back.'

I followed him out of the water and we sat for a while on the sand as the sun sank below the horizon in a flaming ball of orange and red, which spilled across the sea in an ever-increasing pool of colour. When it disappeared, quite fast because the sun sets quickly in the Caribbean, we went back to the room and we showered and changed ready to go downstairs.

We were to meet Lucy and David for dinner. It would be the first time that we'd got together properly as couples, although Hugh and David had engaged in long and deep conversations at the airport and during the flight while Lucy and I watched the movie. I'd wondered, uneasily, what they were talking about.

The hotel restaurant was built jutting out over the sea. The water lapped beneath us and boiled with the fighting of the fish for the scraps that the diners threw from their tables. Lucy aimed a bread roll into the water and watched as a cauldron of fish demolished it.

'Unreal,' she said in wonderment.

We had the obligatory conch chowder for starters, although I wasn't sure that either Hugh or I should have it – its aphrodisiacal properties were probably wasted on us. Then we had a local chicken dish, washed down with Californian Chardonnay, followed by some fresh fruit.

'Superb,' said David as he spooned the last piece of mango from the plate.

'Magnificent.' Lucy dabbed her lips with her linen napkin. 'I could grow to like this.'

'Me too,' I said as I yawned widely and covered my mouth in dismay. 'Sorry.' I looked around at them. 'I suddenly feel exhausted.'

David looked at his watch. 'Not surprising,' he said. 'It's three in the morning at home.'

'Is it really?' asked Lucy. 'No wonder I feel tired! I know I slept on the plane and so I thought I should be OK, but I'm terribly sleepy.'

My yawn had set up a chain reaction.

'Stop it,' ordered Hugh. 'I'm having a wonderful time and I don't want to go to bed yet.'

'Could be more wonderful there,' muttered Lucy and I kicked her, hard, under the table. Her muffled 'ouch' didn't go unnoticed but Hugh pretended to ignore it and took a cigar from his shirt pocket. He offered one to David and they both lit up and smoked while Lucy and I gazed into the sea and looked at the fish.

'Will we have a nightcap and then go to bed?' she asked eventually.

We got up from the table and walked down to the bar, which was practically on the beach. The barman was making cocktails, like Tom Cruise in the movie, shaking and jiving to the music from his ghetto blaster. The music wasn't terribly loud. I guessed the residents wouldn't want their peaceful idyll shattered by Salt-n-Pepa.

The men talked together while Lucy and I took our drinks down to the beach.

'Aren't the twins just great?' Lucy sipped her margarita. 'Who else would have arranged something like this?'

I shook my head. 'I'm so happy for them. They're such wonderful girls and I never, ever would have believed that they'd get married.'

'Just goes to prove,' said Lucy, 'there's somebody out there for everyone.'

I stirred my Long Island Iced Tea with a straw. 'Maybe.'

'Oh Jane.' Lucy kicked off her shoes and buried her feet in the sand. 'You know I'm right. What about you and Hugh?'

'What about us?'

'Isn't he right for you?' she asked. 'He's come on this holiday – you asked him to come. Surely that means—'

'I don't know,' I interrupted her. 'I don't know, Lucy.'

'But Jane—'

'It's not that sort of relationship,' I said.

'What!'

'We're friends, that's all.'

'Don't give me that, Jane. How could you be "friends" with someone who looks like that? Besides, he's a nice bloke. He's kind and considerate and he treats you well.'

'You found out all that on the flight over?' I asked, amused.

'I can see it, Jane,' she said. 'Same as I could see that Rory McLoughlin was a shit and always would be. But Hugh is different. Believe me.'

'Why didn't you ever like Rory?' I popped a maraschino cherry into my mouth.

'Because he stood you up,' she said. 'Remember the night you were meant to meet him in Searson's? And you came home and found me in bed with Nick?'

I shuddered at the memory.

'That bastard could have contacted you somehow,' she told me. 'But he didn't. He knew you'd be in Searson's waiting for him, but he didn't even bother to call. I know it all sort of went out of your head because of me, but I never forgot. And even though I couldn't say anything then, it bothered me. If he could stand you up when you were still mad about each other, what could he do later? That was the way I saw it.'

'I see,' I said.

'And he was such a pompous prick,' she said, using language that I rarely heard her use. 'Every time we met, he was always trying to prove that he was more intelligent, richer, knew more than anyone else in the company. And whenever you'd say anything, he'd sort of put you down.'

The tirade stopped. I looked at her thoughtfully. 'Did you always think that?' I asked.

She nodded.

'And you never said anything?'

'He was your husband, Jane.'

'Oh Lucy,' I said, and put my arm around her. 'I'm glad I know you.'

'Don't get soppy,' she said. 'Look, do you want another drink?'

I surveyed my glass. 'I'd better not,' I said. 'I'm falling asleep as it is.'

'Don't fall asleep before you have brilliant sex with Hugh,' she told me. 'It'd be such a waste.'

Just then, David and Hugh arrived down on the beach with another drink. I groaned but drank it anyway. I felt my eyes close and I leaned against Hugh for support.

'Jane, what have you done with my shirts?'

'Ironed them, of course.'

'My white ones?'

'Yes.'

'Where's my green one?'

'The one you put in the basket on Monday?'

'I only have one green shirt.'

'It's not washed yet.'

'For Chrissake, Jane, it's not as if I ask that much of you. A meal on the table in the evening and a clean shirt every morning. My God, what else are you doing all day?'

'It's only Wednesday. Why would I have washed your Monday shirt already?'

'Because that's what you should be doing. Look, I'll be late home this evening, I'm meeting a client.'

And Rory slammed the front door, the car door and gunned down the road.

I felt myself being lifted from the sand and carried to the hotel room. I knew that somebody, no – I knew it was Hugh – had placed me gently on the bed. I opened my eyes and saw him there, looking at me. I reached up and tried to touch his face but I couldn't quite reach and I couldn't speak either.

He slid my cotton blouse over my head and eased my skirt down my legs. So, I thought, he'll take advantage of me in my exhausted state. He pulled the sheet from the bed and rolled me underneath.

'Sleep well,' he said, and kissed me on the forehead.

Shit, I thought, before drifting into deep, dreamless sleep.

Brenda and Grace married Robert and Damien at four o'clock the following afternoon. We arrived at The Turtle Bay at half past three to find them sitting at the beach bar sipping long, interesting-looking cocktails.

'It's for the pre-wedding nerves,' Damien explained, his boyish grin wide and cheerful.

'Come on,' said Robert, 'have one.'

So we sat down and drank a cocktail each until it was time for the wedding.

The ceremony was conducted in the gardens of the hotel, a lush oasis of verdant lawns and tropical flowers. The officiating magistrate was a local woman, about fifty, her frizzy hair like a grey Brillo pad on top of her dark skin. She smiled broadly at us as she stood beneath the bower of pink, purple and yellow flowers. Behind her, a tiny fountain sent jets of sparkling water shooting to the sky so that they fell back to earth in diamond droplets, catching the sun and exploding into a rainbow of colours.

The twins were beautiful. Dressed exactly alike in white linen, with tiny red rosebuds twisted into their hair, they looked cool and virginal. The Driscoll brothers wore white suits, with black bow ties, which reminded me a little of characters in a James Bond film I'd once seen. Birdsong echoed around the garden, the ghetto blaster was quietly playing *The Four Seasons.*

When the magistrate asked, 'Do you, Brenda, take Robert?' and she replied, 'I do,' I felt my eyes water and a tear slid gently down my cheek.

'Goose,' murmured Hugh and slipped me another crumpled tissue. I sniffed and wiped my eyes, then cried again when Grace and Damien were pronounced husband and wife.

'You may kiss the brides!' The magistrate beamed at them and the Driscolls caught the twins and kissed them long and hard, to applause from the four of us and the small crowd which had gathered to watch the ceremony.

We signed the register, Lucy and I, and hugged the twins and their husbands. It was one of the most joyous occasions of my life.

We went for a celebratory drink in The Turtle Bay's terraced restaurant. A table was set out for us, decked in a bright pink tablecloth and laden with an arrangement of tropical fruit in a huge ice bowl which glistened wetly in the afternoon sun.

We didn't think we were very hungry, but we fell on the seafood starters and the tropical kebabs as though we hadn't eaten in days.

Robert opened bottles of champagne and we toasted each other in a silly, happy banquet that lasted until dusk fell around us and the sun slid again into the sea.

Later we went down to the beach again, carrying bottles of champagne and ice buckets, and sat at the edge of the water, letting it run between our toes and wash over our feet.

'This has been a marvellous day.' Grace lay back and got sand all over her beautiful dress.

'It's definitely the way to get married,' agreed Lucy. She turned to David. 'If I ever divorce you, you'll find me here marrying one of the divers.'

We laughed. We'd seen lots of divers today, strong and muscular men carrying full aqualung equipment as though it weighed nothing.

'It would have been the thing to do, ourselves,' commented David.

'Your wedding was good fun, though,' said Grace.

'Sure it was.' I nodded in agreement.

'God, Jane,' said Lucy, 'I bet you can never think of my wedding with anything other than horror!'

'Why?' asked Hugh. He'd been quiet all day, keeping just a little bit distant from the revelry, and I jumped now as he spoke.

'Because Jane practically had her baby at my wedding,' said Lucy.

'Did you?' Hugh looked at me.

I nodded. 'I almost gave birth to Clodagh in a marquee in Stillorgan,' I told him. 'It was not the best experience of my life.'

'You didn't look too bad on it,' he said.

There was silence in the group as the twins and Lucy looked at me in astonishment.

'How d'you know what Jane looked like?' asked Lucy. 'You wouldn't have known her then.'

Hugh and I exchanged glances and I answered. 'Hugh actually called into my room in the hospital by mistake,' I said. 'He was visiting his sister, who'd had a baby too. That's when I first met him.'

'Eight years ago?' said Grace.

Hugh cleared his throat. 'We didn't exactly know each other,' he said. 'It wasn't as though we were friends then, or anything.'

'All the same, isn't it a small world.' Brenda looked at me

trangely. 'That eight years on you're sitting here beside Jane, at our wedding.'

'Isn't it?' said Hugh equably.

'Anybody want a top up?' Damien brandished the bottle of champagne.

We held out our glasses to him, although I didn't really think that I could drink another drop.

'What are your plans for tomorrow?' Lucy asked Brenda.

'Nothing,' she said. 'We're going to lie here and bask in the sun, then we go to Aruba the day after.'

'David and I have joined up for a diving class,' said Lucy. 'I'm terrified, but it sounds like such fun, and they were showing a video of the marine life in that diving shop we were in this morning. I have to have a go. Are you going to give it a try, Jane?'

'Probably,' I answered, 'but I didn't put my name down yet.' I looked at Hugh. 'Do you want to try?'

'Sure,' he said. 'We'll sign up for tomorrow afternoon.'

The moon appeared on the horizon and cast its white light on to the water in front of us.

'Don't want to be party-poopers or anything,' said Lucy, 'but David and I are going back to our hotel. Maybe have a drink there, have an early night.'

Guffaws greeted this statement and Lucy blushed furiously. David grinned at her. 'It's all this romance,' she said. 'It's getting to me.'

'OK, then,' said Brenda, 'we'd better throw our bouquets.'

'Don't be daft,' I said. 'There's only Lucy and me here.'

'Come back up to the bar,' said Grace. 'We can do it properly there.'

We stood up and brushed the fine, white sand from our clothes. A great cheer greeted the twins as they walked into the bar. Brenda spoke to the barman and he shouted out to the crowd that the brides were going to throw their bouquets and all the ladies should gather around.

'You too,' hissed Lucy as she pulled me into the group.

'There's no point in me being here,' I objected. 'It's not relevant to me.'

But I stood beside her as Brenda and Grace climbed up on the narrow bar, balancing carefully in their high-heeled shoes, and casually threw their bouquets into the crowd.

It was inevitable, I suppose, that I'd catch Brenda's because she had thrown it directly at me. I grinned at her and waved.

'Free drink for the lucky ladies,' ordered the barman and presented me and the girl who had caught Grace's flowers with Piña Coladas.

Lucy and David disappeared.

'Come on,' whispered Hugh, 'we should go, too.'

We hugged the twins, told them to have a great time in Aruba and promised to meet them at the airport when they got home.

'We're delighted you came,' said Brenda, 'and it was lovely to meet you, Hugh.'

'Thanks for asking me.' He kissed the twins on their cheeks and shook hands with the Driscoll brothers.

Hugh and I walked in silence along the beach towards The Golden Necklace. I was light-headed from the sun and the champagne and still tired from the flight the day before. It had been a wonderful day.

I stumbled in the soft sand and Hugh caught me by the arm to steady me.

'You OK?' he asked, and I nodded but I held on to his arm, enjoying the warmth.

A diving jetty separated our hotel from The Turtle Bay. Coloured lights along the jetty danced in the night-time breeze. The diving boats bobbed in the water, waiting for the morning. Suddenly, I didn't want to go back to the hotel yet.

'Can we sit on the edge of the jetty for a while?' I asked.

'Sure,' said Hugh.

We strolled along the wooden planks to the end of the jetty and sat there with our legs dangling over the water. In the distance I could see a fluorescent purple light under the sea. 'It's a night diver,' explained Hugh. 'Some types of fish only come out at night.'

'I'd be scared to dive in the dark.' I shivered at the thought.

'Cold?' asked Hugh and put his arm around me.

I sat, immobile, in the circle of his arm. I could feel the rise and fall of his body beside me. Thousands of sensations surged through me. I moved towards him, very slightly, unsure of myself and of him.

'Cold?' he asked again. I looked up at him, into his brown eyes, half hidden by the shadows of the night.

'A bit.'

He held me tighter. 'Still?'

'A bit,' I said again.

His face was close to mine and I could hear his breathing now and smell his aftershave. I leaned my head towards him and I saw a flicker in his eyes before we kissed.

I'd been kissed more passionately before, more intensely before but never more urgently. Never with more unspoken promise, unspoken desire. And as we kissed, the ice that I'd tried to keep around me since Rory suddenly melted and coursed through me in a torrent of hunger and longing.

'My God,' said Hugh, as we parted. He held my shoulders, looking at me fiercely. 'Do you kiss like that all the time?'

'No,' I said. 'Only when I want to.' And I kissed him again.

'I love you,' he said, when we parted again.

I disentangled myself from his embrace and stood up. Hugh stood beside me. I gazed into the darkness of the sea and watched the reflection of the jetty's lights on the water. Hugh was close to me, but not touching me.

'Did you mean that?' I whispered, afraid of his answer.

He stood behind me, and wrapped his arms around me. 'I never say anything I don't mean.'

'But love?' I murmured.

'I loved you from the first moment I set eyes on you,' said Hugh. 'Crazy though that may seem to you, Jane. With your eyes all red and puffy in your hospital bed. You'd just had another man's baby and I wanted to kill him for leaving you on your own.'

'Don't be daft.'

'And I loved you when I saw you at the Park Hotel, and again at your Christmas party, and I've wanted you every day in between.'

I turned, still held by him. 'But you can't have loved me.'

'I loved you,' he said. 'Don't ask me why, Jane, because I don't know. What makes people fall for each other? When I talked to you, I knew. And I couldn't do a damn thing about it.'

'Really?'

'Really, Jane. And it's not just because you interest me or intrigue me or anything, it's just that I think we fit together. I know that might not sound the most romantic thing in the world, but it's true. And maybe you're still not ready to love someone.' He held me closer. 'I'll wait.'

But he didn't need to wait, because I knew that I loved him too. He was the right person for me. It was as though I'd found another part of me.

'I love you,' I said. The words sounded strange but right.

The mauve light of the night diver moved further out beneath the waves. The reflection of the jetty's lights rippled on the surface of the water. The air was still.

Then Hugh led me away from the pier, out of the night and into his life.

My lover and I sat side by side on the white Caribbean sand. The setting sun shattered into a thousand glittering diamonds as it hit the turquoise blue of the sea, and the only sound was the rhythmic thud of the waves as they broke upon the shore.

My lover and I sat in silence. There was no need for words between us. The only ones that mattered had already been said.

An unmissable read from **Sheila O'Flanagan**

When Steffie helps her two siblings organise a surprise wedding anniversary party for their parents her only worry is whether they'll be pleased. What she doesn't know is this is the day that her whole world will be turned upside down.

Jenny wants to be able to celebrate her ruby anniversary with the man she loves, but for forty years she has kept a secret. A secret that she can't bear to hide any longer. But is it ever the right time to hurt the people closest to you?

As the entire family gather to toast the happy couple, they're expecting a day to remember. The trouble is, it's not going to be for the reasons they imagined . . .

For more information visit www.headline.co.uk
or www.sheilaoflanagan.com

Have you read all of Sheila's irresistible novels?

If You Were Me

You're engaged to a great man. You're on a countdown to your wedding day. You stopped thinking about your first love a long time ago.

But what if one unexpected, forbidden kiss were to throw your life upside down?

Carlotta O'Keefe suddenly finds herself wondering if the girl she was would recognise the woman she has become.

She thought she was living a charmed life. But what if she's got it all wrong?

What if her past is meant to be her future?

Things We Never Say

A husband is afraid to say that selling the house his wife loves is the only option. . .

A son can't say how useful his ageing father's fortune will be when he's gone. . .

A woman hasn't said that even though they live thousands of miles apart, this man is always on her mind. . .

But if those things were said, the results might be surprising. As Abbey – and a whole family she knew nothing of – are about to find out in Sheila O'Flanagan's warm-hearted, thought-provoking and touching novel.

BETTER TOGETHER

Sheridan Gray has discovered a secret. . .

When journalist Sheridan loses her dream job, she's distraught. She's forced to relocate to the countryside. Her career is over. . . until she discovers that her landlady holds the key to a big story.

But the longer Sheridan stays in Nina's home, and the closer she gets to a certain handsome man in the town, the tougher it is to expose their secrets. When it comes to love or success, will Sheridan go with her heart or her head?

STAND BY ME

Dominique Brady's life changed the day she met Brendan Delahaye.

He was a man with big dreams and she was the girl he wanted to take with him. Madly in love, they married, Brendan's business hit the big time and they became the most powerful couple in Ireland.

Then one day Brendan disappears without a trace and Dominique's world is shattered. Will Brendan ever return? And if he does, will Dominique stand by her man?

**Wolf turns and jerks his head toward
the woman. "Dolly, you'll sleep
with the jeep."**

"We ain't thieves," the man says.

"'Course not," Wolf agrees enthusiastically, but shoots Dolly a meaningful look. "Anyway, we should at least get our goods out of the sun." The townie nods, saying nothing, and Wolf turns to me. "How 'bout helping us with these bags again?"

Something tells me I should leave right now and pretend I never had anything to do with a strange couple of travelers called Wolf and Dolly. Something tells me a man with a smile like his can only bring trouble. Maybe that something is what normal people call common sense.

But Papa always said I don't have a whole lot of that.

"Sure," I say. "Why not?"

Praise for
K. S. Merbeth and the Wastelanders

BITE

"A full-throttle, sand-in-your-eyes, no-holds-barred ride through a *Mad Max*–style wasteland where the bad guys become family. Finally, an underdog with teeth!" —Delilah S. Dawson

"Merbeth has created her own universe filled with destruction and not a small amount of grim, acerbic wit. Fans of Mira Grant's 'Newsflesh' series will be pleased by the smart writing."
—*Library Journal*

"Filled with dark humor, wit, and a realistic dystopian setting, *Bite* plays with the idea of who the good guys are in such a harsh world." —*Booklist*

"Merbeth's debut novel puts a unique spin on post-apocalyptic horror.... *Bite* flips the script."
—*B&N Sci-Fi & Fantasy Blog*

"Pure undiluted high-octane anarchy.... If you enjoy movies like ... *Mad Max: Fury Road*, or games like *Fallout 4* and *Borderlands*, then *Bite* is the book for you. Gleefully unrestrained and unrelenting, strap yourself in and enjoy the ride. *Bite* is here, let the mayhem commence!" —*The Eloquent Page*

RAID

"Merbeth returns to drag readers off of their couches and into the explosive, feverish Wastelands.... [An] edge-of-your-seat rush."
— *RT Book Reviews*

"Merbeth's fast-paced *Mad Max*–style adventure, set in a post apocalyptic desert, is difficult to put down."
—*Library Journal*

By K. S. Merbeth

Bite
Raid

The Wastelanders (omnibus edition)

THE
WASTELANDERS

K. S. MERBETH

This omnibus edition contains

Bite

Raid

www.orbitbooks.net

Onmibus copyright © 2018 by Kristyn Merbeth
Bite copyright © 2016 by Kristyn Merbeth
Raid copyright © 2017 by Kristyn Merbeth
Excerpt from *Afterwar* copyright © 2018 by Lilith Saintcrow
Excerpt from *Extinction Horizon* copyright © 2014 by Nicholas Sansbury Smith

Author photograph by Mauri Mobray
Cover design by Lisa Marie Pompilio
Cover copyright © 2018 by Hachette Book Group, Inc.

Orbit
Hachette Book Group
1290 Avenue of the Americas
New York, NY 10104
orbitbooks.net

First Omnibus Edition: October 2018

Orbit is an imprint of Hachette Book Group.
The Orbit name and logo are trademarks of Little, Brown Book Group Limited.

The publisher is not responsible for websites (or their content) that are not owned by the publisher.

The Hachette Speakers Bureau provides a wide range of authors for speaking events. To find out more, go to www.hachettespeakersbureau.com or call (866) 376-6591.

Library of Congress Control Number: 2018946390

ISBNs: 978-0-316-52707-1 (trade paperback), 978-0-316-52703-3 (ebook)

Printed in the United States of America

LSC-C

10 9 8 7 6 5 4 3 2 1

THE
WASTELANDERS

Contents

BITE

*For everyone who gave me shit about being
an English major* :P

I
Show Your Teeth

"Need a ride?"

His grin looks more like an animal baring its teeth. His teeth are yellowed and chipped, with gaps between showing where others have been knocked out. There's something starkly predatory about him, which is the first reason I shouldn't say yes.

The second is I'm small, alone, and unarmed. Any of those could be a death sentence in a place like this.

And there we have the third reason: By "a place like this," I mean a torn-up, full-of-potholes road running through the middle of nowhere. It's the only thing marking the landscape for miles. There's nothing but empty desert and the ruins of old cities in every direction. Nuclear war can do that to a place, I guess. But the point is, there's no one around to hear if I scream. Plus, even if someone did hear, chances are they wouldn't give a shit.

The fourth reason is the creepy lady in the passenger seat, who has blue hair and an assault rifle in her lap.

The fifth reason is the red-stained sacks of something-or-other sitting in the backseat.

The sixth reason is . . . ah, hell. Need I go on?

I scratch my nose, sniff, and spit. The rumble of the jeep is the only sound in the stagnant air.

It's obvious that getting in this jeep is a terrible idea. A sixteen-year-old girl like me could provide a hell of a lot of entertainment for someone with a sick enough mind. I must look like easy prey, with my ragged clothes and skinny body.

So naturally, my answer is—

"Sure, why not?"

When it comes down to it, I've been walking for days. The soles of my boots are collecting holes. The sand burns my feet during the day, and the world is dark and frightening at night. The sun has left my skin raw and peeling, and when it sets it sucks all the warmth away. I'm down to one can of food and less than two days' worth of water—not enough to make it back to town even if I wanted to go. Lord knows how far I'd have to travel to find more.

This jeep and its driver are smelly, creepy, and very possibly dangerous, but they're my only ticket out of here.

The stranger shows his teeth again. His eyes are hidden behind a pair of goggles too big for his face.

"Hop in then, kid."

I clamber into the backseat next to the reeking mystery bags, nearly tumbling onto them before I manage to squeeze myself into the tight space between the bags and the door. I place my backpack on my lap, my arms curling around it protectively. It doesn't hold much, just my canteen, one can of food, and a blanket my papa gave me, but it's all I have. I lean back with a sigh as the jeep starts moving. Sayonara, middle of nowhere! I might end up dead and dismembered in a ditch, but it'd be better than wandering aimlessly through this hellhole of a desert.

We pick up speed quickly, and I have to pull down on my beanie to stop it from flying off my head. A few strands of mousy hair poke out from underneath it, and I try to push them under again, but it's no use. I settle for holding the beanie with one hand and resting the other on the side of the jeep. The rank smell of the bags is getting stronger and stronger, making my eyes water. I blink it away and try to ignore it.

My attention shifts to the lady in the front seat, who still strikes me as pretty creepy. She was still and silent the whole time they waited for my answer, but now she turns around. It's impossible not to stare at her hair. It's very long, nearly waist-length, and oddly straight and sleek. I really don't understand how someone could have hair so perfect looking, or how and *why* her hair is colored electric blue. The color is incredibly vivid in the dust-colored world around us.

She has dark eyes that reveal an Asian heritage, and small lips painted a vibrant red. She's pretty, with a noticeably lady-like figure despite the wasteland garb covering her quite modestly. Her red lips are mouthing something, but I can't make out any words with the wind whipping around me.

I squint my eyes, tilt my head to the side, and give her a vacant stare. She stares back at me for a moment before turning around.

She doesn't try to talk to me again, and neither does the feral man. Apparently they don't care enough to ask where I intend to go. I'm just along for the ride, and that's fine by me. Wherever I'm going has to be better than where I've been.

If I had any common sense at all I'd probably want to stay on edge. But, at this point, I'm already in the jeep. Either they want to kill me or they don't, and I won't get much of a choice in it either way. So I decide to nap. What can I say? It's been a long couple of days.

I wake up with my face pressed against the lumpy garbage bags, and *wow* do they smell. The scent is invading my nostrils, pillaging my throat, and violating my poor brain. I gag and recoil, pressing against the side of the car and frantically wiping my face with a hand that is probably even dirtier. I don't know what the hell is in there, but I don't want it on or near my face.

Once I determine I'm safe from any obscene-smelling sub-stances, I realize the jeep is no longer moving, and my back-pack is no longer on my lap. The man and young woman are standing a few yards away from the still vehicle, having a quiet conversation. Neither of them is paying attention to me.

I adjust my beanie and climb out of the car, stretching out my bony limbs one at a time. My back cracks and both of the strangers' heads jerk toward me.

"Err," I say. The woman still has her assault rifle, and it's now pointed in my direction. I raise my hands and smile ner-vously. "My bad."

She relaxes when she sees it's just me, and the man displays that grin of his again. I notice my backpack in the dirt at his feet. In his hand is what I assume to be my last can of food. Unsurprisingly, it's beans. Despite how sick I am of goddamn beans, my stomach rumbles. But his other hand holds a really big knife that he must have used to pry the can open, so I decide not to comment.

"So you're awake," the man says through a mouthful of food. He swallows, sighs with unabashed satisfaction, and continues. "We were about to wake you up, but you looked pretty happy in there. You were drooling a little on the goods."

I wipe my mouth and feel my cheeks grow hot. He laughs, a hearty and surprisingly genuine sound. He bends down to grab my backpack off the ground and tosses it over to me. I can't resist the urge to take a peek inside, just to make sure nothing else is missing. Once I'm certain that my canteen and my papa's blanket are still inside, I sling the bag over one shoulder and smile at him.

"We found a little town," he says, jerking his thumb behind him. "Decided it was as good a place as any to stop."

"Oh, yeah, great," I say sincerely. "That works just fine. Thanks for the ride, mister."

He laughs again, this time for no good reason I can decipher.

"Right, kid," he says. "Mind helping us carry this?"

I glance at the gross bags in the back of the jeep. The thought of lugging them around is far from pleasant. I don't know what's in them, and honestly I don't want to know. But he *did* give me a ride, so...

"Sure."

"Good!" He grins again. "Don't drop 'em or anything, we're selling this shit."

I nod and wipe my sweaty palms on my jeans. Right, I can handle that. Probably.

The blue-haired Asian lady has been looking at me intently this whole time, and it's starting to make me uncomfortable. She has a weird blankness about her. Not a hint of emotion ever crosses her face, and she has an incredibly unnerving stare. It's like looking into the eyes of a corpse. I try to ignore her, but looking at the guy with the savage grin isn't much better. At least the woman combs her hair. The man's is in long brown dreadlocks, and obviously hasn't been groomed in an awfully long time.

The two of them move over to the jeep and start unloading. They pack my arms full first, and I scrunch my nose and try not to inhale too deeply. Once we all have as much as we can carry, we head toward the town.

Or, rather, toward the pathetic collection of shambling buildings we call towns around here. Like most, it's built over the ruins of an old city, and made mostly of crumbling walls and scrap metal. People have patched up half-destroyed shells of rooms with blankets and plywood and whatever else they can find. From the looks of it, no more than a couple dozen townies live here. They peek out of doorways and windows as we pass through the outer limits of town. I see mostly men, a handful of women, and not a single child, which is not surprising. The end of the world didn't exactly encourage people to go making babies left and right, and half of the ones that do get born won't make it past their first year.

I've only ever seen pictures of the great old cities, but it's enough to make me appreciate the sadness of what they've become. I thought the town I left was small and run-down, but now I know the people back there had it pretty good. These people are dirty, thin, wrapped in rags.

Hollow eyes in hungry faces turn to watch us, but they don't seem overly alarmed. Apparently this place is used to strangers, which is a bit odd. Most of these little towns can go months without seeing a new face. Three strangers arriving would've been a big old affair where I came from, and not a friendly one at that.

We walk for a few minutes, moving into what seems to be the heart of the town, an open space between some of the more well-kept buildings. The man dumps the bags he's carrying on the ground, and the woman and I follow suit. They produce wet thumps and small clouds of dust as they hit. I gratefully suck in fresh air while the other two survey the area. I'm not really sure what my plan is at this point, but these two seem to have some kind of goal, so I figure it can't hurt to stick with them for now.

"Where are they?" the woman asks. Her voice is nearly a whisper, and as flat and emotionless as her face.

"Not here," the man says, "which can't mean anything good."

I eye them, but bite back my question as a townie approaches. He's a tall, wiry, dark-skinned man with a commanding presence and suspicious eyes. He folds his arms over his chest and spits a gob of yellowish saliva that narrowly misses my boot.

The dreadlocked man beside me shoves his hands into the pockets of his ratty jeans, assumes a relaxed posture, and grins.

"Name's Wolf," he says. "We've got some goods here. You have anything worth trading for? Gasoline, maybe?"

The townie says nothing. He looks at us, scrutinizes the bags, and looks at us again.

"Might," he says finally. "What've you got?" He nudges a bag with one shoe.

Again comes that cruel display of teeth.

"Meat," Wolf says, overemphasizing the word.

The other man's eyebrows rise.

"Ain't seen that in a while," he says. "What's it from?"

"Couple o' wild hogs."

"Hogs," the townie repeats. He stares at the bags, his jaw working as if he's chewing on the information. "Lot of meat for a couple hogs."

"Fat ones," Wolf says dryly. "Look, you gonna trade or not?"

The man pauses.

"Let me think," he says. He seems to be carefully weighing each word. "I'll have to look at our stocks. Why don't you lot stay overnight? We'll talk in the mornin'."

"Meat won't stay good forever," Wolf says. It's hard to read his expression behind the goggles.

"Meat probably ain't good now," the townie says, spitting again. I have to hop to the side to avoid this one. "One more night won't hurt."

"Fine," Wolf says. He turns and jerks his head toward the woman. "Dolly, you'll sleep with the jeep."

"We ain't thieves," the man says.

"'Course not," Wolf agrees enthusiastically, but shoots Dolly a meaningful look. "Anyway, we should at least get our goods out of the sun." The townie nods, saying nothing, and Wolf turns to me. "How 'bout helping us with these bags again?"

Something tells me I should leave right now and pretend I never had anything to do with a strange couple of travelers called Wolf and Dolly. Something tells me a man with a smile like his can only bring trouble. Maybe that something is what normal people call common sense.

But Papa always said I don't have a whole lot of that.

"Sure," I say. "Why not?"

II
The Strangers

Carrying the cargo is sweaty work, and by our second trip into town I think I'm starting to smell as bad as the bags. It doesn't help that Wolf is off bartering somewhere, leaving Dolly and me to handle it all ourselves. None of the townies offer to help. Instead they completely ignore our presence. Men rest on rocks or lean against nearby buildings in small clumps, carrying on conversations that fall silent when we get close. And it really is all men; the women have disappeared. So have the elderly, and the incapable. Every single person left lingering outside looks like they could give me a thorough ass-kicking if necessary. I can feel their eyes following me when I turn my back.

"This is weird," I say in a low whisper. I glance over at Dolly, who keeps her eyes forward. "Isn't it?"

She gives a minuscule shrug of her shoulders and says nothing. I guess that's as close to an answer as I'm going to get. I sigh and try to ignore the uneasiness creeping up on me. These people did invite us to stay in their town for the night. That alone makes them friendlier than the town I left. Wolf and Dolly would've been shot the second they got within ten paces of the place. These townies are just being reasonably wary of strangers. Probably.

"So, where are you and Wolf headed, anyway?" I ask, trying

to distract myself from my nerves. Neither of them has told me anything about themselves or why they're here. They haven't asked about me, either. Come to think of it, I don't think they've even asked for my name. Maybe I'm supposed to assume those are the rules of our temporary relationship, but my curiosity is getting the better of me.

"Nowhere," Dolly says. I frown.

"So you're just...driving around randomly? Isn't that kind of..." Pointless? Dangerous? A waste of precious gas? I don't even know where to begin. "Are you traders?" Traders are the only people I can think of who would have any reason to wander like that. Well, and myself, but I have my own reasons.

"No," she says. I wait for her to continue. She doesn't.

"Okay," I say. When I was young and my papa left me in our bomb shelter by myself, I used to play a game that involved bouncing a ball off the wall. It always just came bouncing back, but I would keep doing it like I expected something new to happen, or thought a friend might materialize. Trying to carry on a conversation with Dolly feels about as productive as that did.

I shut my mouth and keep walking. I should save my breath, anyway. Even though I'm only carrying half as much as Dolly, the bags are heavy, and the exertion is making me more aware of the hunger in my belly and the tired ache in my bones. Despite that, it's nice to feel helpful. Back in my old town it was always *Get out of the way, girl* and *Don't you know how to do anything right?* One of the many reasons why braving the wastes alone sounded better than staying.

As we pass one of the rickety buildings, the door bangs open. A woman comes out, dragging a young boy behind her. I guess there are children here after all; they must just keep them hidden away when strangers are around. The woman stomps her way over to a group of men sitting on the hood of a rusted, broken-down vehicle. She speaks in hushed whispers to them, saying something that involves a lot of head shakes and hand gestures. She releases the hand of the boy as the conversation seems to grow more heated. The boy's gaze wanders over to us. As our eyes meet I shoot him a friendly smile.

My smile drops as the kid takes that as a sign to start walking over to us.

"Oh, no. No, no, no," I mutter. As much as I like children, somehow I don't think this kid is supposed to be near us. I don't want to give the townies any other reason to distrust us. But it's not easy to wave him away with my hands full, and I don't want to raise my voice and draw attention.

I slow down as he gets closer. It's hard to see the kid around the bulky bags I'm carrying.

"Careful, little guy," I say, stepping around him. "This is heavy stuff."

Apparently he's not the sharpest tool in the shed, because he moves away from me and steps directly into Dolly's path. He stares up at her with wide eyes and doesn't move. Dolly stops in her tracks.

"Can I touch your hair?" the boy asks.

"We're kind of busy here," I say. Dolly doesn't seem like the kid-friendly type, and I don't want to see her go all ice queen on this poor kid. But instead, to my surprise, she drops her bags and crouches down, bringing herself to eye level with the young boy. With several inches between their faces, they scrutinize each other with an apparently shared sense of awe. He raises a hand and touches the ends of her hair with small, chubby fingers. I'm sure his hands are filthy, but Dolly doesn't pull back from his touch. I catch a glimpse of something oddly soft in her face, a crack in her blank expression. She almost looks sad for a moment.

"Mommy said you were bad people," the boy says, "but I think you're nice." He smiles. His two front teeth are missing. Dolly leans close and whispers something in his ear.

A surprised expletive alerts me that the boy's mother has noticed his disappearance. She looks around frantically, homes in on us, and rushes over, her eyes wide and fearful.

"Jimmy," she hisses, grabbing the boy by the hand and yanking him away. She pulls him behind her and backs away from us. Her suspicious eyes flit back and forth between Dolly and me. Once she's apparently decided we're not going to attack her, she turns her back and hurries away, tugging her son along. "What did I tell you about talking to strangers?" she scolds him.

With another loud bang, she disappears into the building she came from. The men near the jeep are watching us with a renewed and obviously unfriendly interest. I frown, and glance at Dolly to see if the interaction bothered her, but her face is back to its usual blank slate. She stands up, takes her bags, and resumes walking. I hurriedly follow, trying to match her long strides.

"You like kids, Dolly?" I ask, not really expecting a response.

"Yes." A straight answer, to my surprise, and when I turn to look at her there's a ghost of a smile on her lips. It disappears immediately when she notices me looking.

"Me, too!" Finally, some shared ground. I smile at her, but she doesn't seem to notice. "What'd you say to him?"

"To listen to his mother."

I nod slowly, automatically assuming it to be good advice before I remember what his mom said.

As the day grows later, the townies invite us to share a meal with them. It's good hospitality, especially for a place this small. The idea would have been laughable where I came from. Even after living there for a couple of years, I wouldn't get fed unless I got enough work done during the day.

I'm grateful for the generosity, and yet something about this place is definitely rubbing me the wrong way. Nobody says anything openly, but everyone gives us these weird sideways glances and dirty looks. It's gotten even worse since this morning. Part of me wonders if it's Wolf and Dolly specifically they're suspicious about, but since I arrived with them and have stuck with them since getting here, it's a little late for me to try to distance myself from them.

Since Dolly is watching the jeep, Wolf and I are alone. The townies light up trash can fire pits, place sheets of metal over the tops, and set aluminum cans of food on top of those. They cluster around the trash cans as the sun sets and the day's warmth slips away. Wolf and I stand apart from them. I can barely feel a hint of heat from this distance, and have to rub at my arms to keep from shivering. However, the smell of the meal cooking reaches us just fine, and my mouth waters at the distant memory of hot food. I haven't eaten anything but cold beans for days.

But the looks from the townies sour my stomach. They all look incredibly pissed off as soon as they catch me looking. I can read the accusations in those stares: *strangers, untrusted, unwelcome.* I'm particularly familiar with the latter. In the wastes, you have to fight for your right to exist.

"Are you sure we were invited?" I ask, turning to Wolf and trying to ignore the stares. My stomach churns with a familiar discomfort. I didn't leave my last town just to become an unwanted mouth to feed again. At least Wolf doesn't seem to mind my presence.

"'Course I am." He continues staring at the food. He pulled his goggles down around his neck when the sun set, and his eyes are sharp and intense without them. I shrug and look down at my boots.

As the townies start passing out cans, clumps of people shift into a messy line. I watch as Wolf walks up and completely ignores them, bypassing the line and snatching a can of food without a moment's hesitation. I attempt to follow in the wake of his bravado, but only make it two steps before someone bumps into me and sends me stumbling.

I look up to see a gaunt-faced townie scowling down at me. His eyes are hard, his lip curling derisively.

"Sorry," I say automatically, as my brain tries to work out where the hell he came from. All of the other townies were by the fire pits, so why was this guy behind us? Was he watching us? My uneasiness deepens, and I swallow hard.

"You ain't supposed to be here," he says.

"Huh? Wolf said—"

"Not him. *You*." He jabs a finger into my chest. I back up, rubbing at the spot and staring at him. "What are you doing with them?" he asks me.

"Umm, well, it's kind of a long story—"

"Scrawny little thing like you," he says, stepping closer and bringing his face down to mine. I'm uncomfortably aware of how much bigger than me he is. Would the other townies step in if he tried to hurt me? I doubt it. "Think you can just wander into town and help yourself to our food?"

"I thought—"

"You thought wrong." He puts a hand on my chest and shoves, sending me stumbling right into Wolf.

"Is there a problem here?" he asks.

I never thought I'd be so happy to see his crazy grin. I scamper behind him and stay there, eager to have a shield from the townie. The man stares at Wolf for a long few seconds. Wolf barely looks at him; he's focused on the can of food in his hands, which he's slowly opening with a knife much too big and sharp for the task. Metal grates harshly on metal as he peels it open. The townie's jaw is clenched, a tic jumping in his cheek. He looks like he's dying to throw a punch. But just when the tension seems taut enough to snap, he shakes his head and walks away.

I let out a low whoosh of breath and step out from behind Wolf.

"Well, I'm sure glad I didn't show up here alone," I say, forcing a laugh. Wolf shrugs nonchalantly, raises his can to his mouth, and takes a big gulp. My mouth fills with drool at the sight, and I realize with a sad twist of my stomach that there's no way I'll be brave enough to get food for myself now. Wolf lowers the can and notices me staring.

"What?" he asks, wiping his mouth with the back of his hand. "What is it? Why aren't you eating?"

"Oh, uh, I'm not that hungry," I say. "I just ate...the day before yesterday."

Wolf rolls his eyes.

"Do I gotta do *everything* for you?" he grumbles.

Before I can protest, he shoves his can into my hands.

"Let me show you somethin', kid," he says. He walks over to the townies and casually cuts into the front of the line again. He grabs a can, grins at the man passing out food, and saunters back to me. "See? It's that simple."

Apparently he doesn't notice the death glares and murmurs that follow. Though, at this point, it's probably more accurate to say that he doesn't give a shit.

"Well, that's easy for you to say. You're—" I pause before the word *scary* leaves my mouth. "Umm. You have a really big knife."

"Oh, this?" He looks down at the knife, which he's currently using to pry open the second can of food, and chuckles. "This ain't nothing. Now eat your damn beans before they get cold."

Of course it had to be beans. I suppress a sigh and take a sludgy gulp of the familiar food. At least they're hot. I scarf them down as quickly as possible and swipe a finger around the can to collect the last remnants.

Once I'm done, I watch Wolf. He eats slowly, which is strange. Most wastelanders eat as quickly as possible, not only because we're starving half the time, but because we're afraid someone might take our food. The way he eats shows that he's not worried about either of those problems. It says a lot about him, and raises more questions, too. I can't help but wonder about him and Dolly. Who are these people? Where are they from, where are they going, and why did they stop to pick me up?

When he finally finishes eating, he notices me looking and exhales an exaggerated sigh.

"What do you want now?" he asks.

"Oh, I, umm." I consider the whirlwind of questions in my head, but bite my tongue. "I just wanted to say thanks. You didn't have to do that. Get me food, I mean."

"'Course I did," he says. "I took your last can, didn't I? Fair's fair." He shrugs. "Anyway, you're with us—for now. And we look out for each other."

I'm not really sure what being "with them" means for me, and the pointed "for now" is a little worrying. Still, I guess it's going pretty well so far, seeing as I've got a belly full of warm food and avoided getting shoved around by that townie.

"Sounds good to me."

"Good. 'Cause you've got first watch tonight."

He turns and walks away. I smile at the back of his head before setting off after him.

III
Sharks

"No idea what you're flapping your gums about."

I awaken to the sound of a voice nearby. It's just past dawn, judging from the light. I'm sprawled out on the ground, twisted up in my papa's blanket, but the spot Wolf slept in is now empty.

"You sayin' this is all coincidence?"

There's another voice. Both are marked by open hostility, and gradually rise in volume.

"Yeah, that's exactly what I'm saying."

Wolf's lazy drawl alternates with the low rumble of the townsman. They must be only a few yards away.

"Stop bullshittin' me."

A heavy silence falls. Even though I'm not involved, I can taste the tension in the air. Several seconds of silence pass, and a new sound fades in: footsteps, headed in my direction. Wolf's face enters my line of vision, his dreadlocked head bending down toward me.

"Eavesdropping?" he asks.

"Well, kind of, I guess." No sense in being dishonest.

"Heh. So you know we're leaving?"

"Now I do."

"Good. Get up." He prods me in the side with one foot.

Apparently I'm along for the ride again. I don't mind at all.

As if yesterday wasn't strange enough, with the atmosphere this hostile, I don't want to be left here alone. While tagging along with these strangers isn't a great option, either, I'd rather be out on the road than stuck here. It's actually nice to have a reason to get up. When I was by myself, it wasn't always so easy. I'd sometimes lie there for hours trying to think of a reason to keep going, and mostly coming up with reasons not to.

Not that it's ever really *easy* to get up. Even now I feel like I could sleep for another week or so. Being run out of town by pissed-off townies is not exactly how I like to start my day. Plus my feet still hurt, I'm down to one day's worth of water, and I have absolutely no idea where I'm headed next.

So?

That's what my papa always said on the long trek across the wastes after we left our bomb shelter, looking for somewhere new to live. "I'm thirsty," I'd say. *So?* "My feet hurt." *So?* And then he'd look at me expectantly.

"So I carry on," I mumble, sitting up. Luckily Wolf isn't paying enough attention to give me shit for talking to myself. Instead he's staring away from me, sucking his bottom lip between his messed-up teeth. He almost looks worried, which makes *me* worried. If the guy with a big-ass knife is concerned, that means it's definitely time to go.

Despite the sense of urgency, I take the time to carefully roll up my dusty blanket and place it into my backpack before I stand. I have to take care not to step on the bags of meat surrounding me.

"So why are we leaving?" I ask.

"Thought you were eavesdropping?"

"Only kind of."

"Well, you did a shit job of it."

"Not a lot of practice," I say with a shrug. Following his lead, I start picking up bags. Today the smell has increased tenfold, and the bags squish against my chest as I lift them. There's no way this stuff is still edible.

"S'pose not," Wolf says. "Well, the gist of it is that there have been an awful lot of disappearances over the last couple weeks, so of course they're inclined to blame us." He rolls his eyes exaggeratedly. "That, and some suspicious strangers showed up a couple days ago. They're convinced we knew 'em or something."

"Oh," I say uncertainly. "Well, *do* we know 'em?"

"And what's more," he continues, "the townsman seems to be implying we not only killed the missing locals"—he pauses as he lifts a particularly full sack—"but *then* we might've come and tried to trade with the very town they came from." He turns and winks at me, grinning devilishly. "But that would be a fucking stupid plan, huh?"

"Uh, yeah," I say. "Yeah, it would be." Wolf seems way too unconcerned, and the whole thing is starting to feel a bit fishy to me. Still, right now, I just want to get the hell out of this town, so I'll keep my mouth shut and roll with it. Anyway, I have to get to work picking up our reeking cargo, because Wolf's arms are already full. He starts walking away as I hurry to finish gathering the rest.

"Get to the jeep when you've got everything," he calls without turning around.

I nod, look over my shoulder, and falter. The townsman is standing only a couple of yards away. He's watching me. His dark arms are folded over his chest, jaw set, body tense. The other townies are gathered in clumps near him. Some of them carry weapons, metal pipes and rusty knives and the like.

Shuddering, I turn around and speed up my efforts. I need to scram, and fast. But without Dolly there's more to carry, and Wolf didn't make up for much of the slack. That leaves me with a hell of a lot to juggle.

I stack up the bags, forcing them into one big pile, and lift it with a grunt. My scrawny arms can barely fit around it all, and my muscles tremble with the effort.

One step. So far, so good, although my eyes water and my arms burn.

I take a second step, and the bag resting on top begins to teeter precariously. I stuff my face into the bags in an attempt to steady them. The stench is overwhelming: rotten and raw.

I take a third step, moving as carefully as I can, and the bag falls. The wet smack of impact stops me. The rest of the pile doesn't follow the first one's tumble, but that doesn't improve the situation much. What the hell am I supposed to do now? If I want to pick up the fallen bag, I have to set down the rest and start over. A second bag falls as I hesitate.

"Need some help?" a voice asks, and a chorus of angels somewhere sings to accompany it. It's the townsman. I crane my neck to see him walking toward me.

"Uhh, sure," I say. Though the sudden kindness from him is strange, I don't really have any alternatives but to accept his help. "Thanks!"

He crouches next to the fallen bags and pauses, hand hovering over one. Suddenly he pulls out a knife and drags the blade down the length of it. The fabric rips loudly and easily. A mass of moist red meat begins to ooze out of the tear, spilling sloppily into the dirt. There's no skin or bone to be seen, just a mound of wet, raw meat.

And, oh God, the *smell*. It hits me like a slap to the face. I choke on the putrid air, gagging.

"What the hell did you do that for?" I ask, my voice squeaky with surprise. Ignoring me, he plunges his hand into the puddle of meat and sifts around. I find myself filled with inexplicable apprehension, and some very explicable disgust, as I watch. He freezes, and gradually withdraws his hand, now in a closed fist. He unfurls his fingers one after another.

Resting in his hand is a bloody human finger.

"Shit," I say.

Oh, holy goddamn *shit*.

"Sharks," he snarls, turning a burning gaze toward me.

Sharks.

People will do a lot to survive. Everyone in the wastes understands that. Scavengers, thieves, whores, raiders…everyone knows they're just trying to stay alive. But even in the desperate, lawless world of the wastelands, sharks are hated by all. They practice the last taboo, the one globally acknowledged evil, the act too immoral and repulsive and unfathomable to be accepted: cannibalism.

The bags tumble from my numb arms, toppling one by one and smacking against the ground. I hold on to the last one, sticking it out in front of me like a shield, but I hastily drop it as I remind myself what's inside. The townsman rises to his feet, knife clutched in his hand.

"Stop the others!" he roars, and the townies scramble to obey. "I'll take care of *him*."

He takes a step toward me.

"Actually, I'm a gi—" The glint of his blade reminds me how very unimportant that is right now. I step back, raising my hands palms out. "Wait, wait, just hold on a second here—" He continues his advance. "I'm no shark! I'm not even with them! I mean, sure, I got here with them and all—" And I was about to leave with them, too. *Shit.* This really does not look good for me.

My foot catches on a rock as I back away. I stumble, pinwheel helplessly, and topple over. I hit the ground hard. The townsman is just a few feet away now, knife raised and face twisted in a righteous fury, ready to avenge all of the crimes against humanity he thinks I've committed. Aw, hell, I always knew I was gonna die over something stupid. I squeeze my eyes shut.

There's a sudden roar, a rush of movement. My eyes fly open just in time to see a familiar jeep hurtling at the townsman.

He dives for safety, arms outstretched, and lands belly-up on the dirt several feet away from me. The jeep flies past. Chest heaving, he rises again. Knife still clutched in his hand, he turns and lunges toward me, but the jeep is already making a sharp turn.

His eyes bulge as he turns to face the oncoming vehicle, and—

Crunch.

The driver, Dolly this time, drives back and forth a few times to ensure he's well and truly dead, while Wolf whoops appreciatively from the passenger seat.

Disgust and gratitude fight for control of my mind. On one hand, I just saw someone die—messily. On the other, he *was* going to kill me. I guess I'm not really sure how I should feel right now, so I save my judgments and stand up.

Wolf extends his hand from the nearby jeep, grinning.

"The hell you waiting for, kid?"

As if this is perfectly ordinary. Then again, it could be for them. I hesitate, letting my gaze drift to the townie's body and then quickly dragging it back to Wolf. Do I really want to stick around two people who could do that to a man and grin about it? Scratch that—two *sharks*? I'm not really sure. Then again, it's either these two sharks or a mob of angry townies at my heels, and the sharks have been quite a lot nicer to me. They even came back for me.

"You saved me," I say, the statement rising at the end into an almost-question. "Umm, thanks." I step forward to grab his hand and pull myself up, but Wolf shakes his head.

"Get the cargo first!"

Or maybe they came back for that. My nose wrinkles, but I stifle my disgust and start heaving sacks into the jeep. If they're my ticket out of here, I'm not complaining.

A few bags into the job, a loud bang nearly makes me jump out of my skin. I whip around to see one of the townies in the distance, pointing a gun at me.

"Aw, calm the hell down, kid. There's no way he can shoot us from that far away," Wolf says.

I nod shakily and toss in another bag.

There's another bang, and then the unmistakable sound of a bullet sinking into the ground just a few feet to my left. I freeze, wide-eyed.

"Then again, I could be wrong," Wolf says. "It happens occasionally. Get in."

I hop into the backseat and burrow into the pile of bags, just moments before the jeep jerks forward and we roar toward freedom.

IV
The Mob

"No, no, not that way!" Wolf is shouting. "We gotta drive through—for fuck's sake, not *toward* the townie with the gun!" He lets out a long string of swear words that don't make much sense when used together, followed by "Oh, shit, they're gonna shoot for our ti—"

The jeep swerves. Bags slide and thud, and I find myself crushed by them. A loud crash, and the jeep shudders with the impact of hitting something heavy. The engine whines with the struggle, a pathetic sound lasting only a few seconds before we jerk to a stop.

My head spins. I gasp for air. Someone grabs me by the shoulder and drags me out of the jeep, only to drop me on the ground again. I pry my eyes open to see Wolf. His lips are moving, but my brain is too jumbled to make any sense of the words or bring myself to move. He gives up on me, rummages through the jeep, and pulls out a ragged duffel bag.

I manage to drag myself to my feet as my ability to think returns. We seem to have crashed inside one of the ruined buildings. A makeshift covering of sheet metal and cloth lies crushed under the jeep's wheels.

"Staircase!" Wolf barks. I turn in a full circle and a half

before locating the barely intact stairs. Wolf is already clambering up them. I take a step forward, skid on loose gravel, and fall flat on my face. Groaning, I rise up to my knees, shaking my still-spinning head in an attempt to clear it. I'm distantly aware of shouts and howls from outside. The townies are closing in. I will myself to move, but with my vision swimming and my legs shaky it's hard to get my body and mind to cooperate.

A hand closes around my arm and yanks me to my feet.

"Come on," Wolf says gruffly. "You lookin' to get torn apart by those townies or something?" He half-carries, half-drags me up the stairs. By the time we reach the top I've regained my sense of balance.

The second level of the building seems on the verge of collapse. The roof is torn off and the wooden floorboards are smashed up and unsteady, with a big chunk caved in to the left of the staircase. The wall across from us gapes with holes, letting sunlight and sound pour in. I dash over to find a relatively safe spot against the wall and peer out. It provides a clear view of the street below.

Townies are swarming the building. They look thirsty for blood, nothing like the hollowed-out, passive folks from yesterday. Their dirty hands are full of weapons—some makeshift, some very real and deadly. One of them aims a gun at my head as he spots me. I duck down to the shelter of the wall.

Wolf searches through his duffel bag, whistling something off-tune. Dolly looks as calm as ever as she scopes out the approaching townspeople.

"Quite a few of them," she says tonelessly.

"Yeah," Wolf says, similarly unaffected.

"Some of them have guns."

"Yeah. Since when do townies have such big-ass guns?"

"Maybe they took them from the others," she says, shrugging.

"If they're not dead already, I'm gonna tear those bastards apart for not showing up."

"What bastards?" I ask. They ignore me. The more I try to make sense of this situation, the more bizarre it gets.

"You can always trust Pretty Boy to screw up a job," Wolf says, shaking his head and grimacing. "Townies closing in?"

Dolly peeks out and quickly recoils. A rock flies through the space her head occupied.

"Yeah," she says, casually flicking a strand of blue hair out of her face. "Armed. Some with guns."

"No worries," Wolf says. That wild grin is back. He pulls a shotgun out of the bag and turns to face the staircase. "Mine's bigger."

The townies announce their arrival in an awful cacophony, raucous howls and shouts bubbling up the staircase. I cringe at the noise. They sound like a pack of starving animals, all shreds of civility gone.

Wolf stands directly in front of the stairs, the barrel of his shotgun aimed at the doorway.

"Dolly," he says, inclining his head toward the duffel bag. "Arm yourself and the kid. I can handle the first few."

Amazingly enough, there isn't a hint of nervousness in his voice. If I stood alone against a pack of angry townies, I'd shit myself. In fact, I'm pretty damn close right now. Yet somehow Wolf doesn't seem concerned.

While Dolly grabs the bag, the first townie stomps up the stairs. He's alone, testing the waters. He's either very brave or very stupid for doing so...or maybe completely mad, which is what it looks like. His eyes are way too big and bright, his teeth clenched in a violent grimace. He looks like the human equivalent of a rabid dog, except he's armed with a gun instead of tooth and claw.

He pauses at the top of the staircase and turns his wild eyes on us. Wolf calmly aims. The man takes one step, pointing his gun at Wolf's head, and the sound of a gunshot drowns out the mob below.

The townie's face shatters and his body tumbles down the stairs. The crowd's yells subside. I blink rapidly, feeling as though the image is imprinted on the back of my eyelids. So fast, so sudden, and a man is dead. Bile rises in my throat, and I swallow it back.

"Have I mentioned how much I love close-range gunfights?" Wolf says cheerfully. "What a mess. A fucking beautiful mess, y'know?"

Actually, I'm kind of wishing I could go back and unsee that happening. Point-blank shotgun blasts to the face aren't really my thing. But there's no time for me to dwell on that gruesome image. Dolly kneels next to me with the bag, head bowed, long hair nearly covering her face. She pulls out two pistols, ensures they're loaded, and stands. One dainty foot nudges the bag toward me in an open invitation. I peek inside.

It's full of weapons. There are guns of all shapes and sizes along with boxes of ammo. No wonder Wolf went out of his way to grab this. Stuff like this is *valuable* nowadays. With a collection this size, it's obvious these two have done a lot of traveling, and a lot of raiding, too.

I let out a low whistle and sift through it all, trying to choose one. This one looks too big, I doubt I could even lift it. And this one looks way too small! Bullets that size couldn't do much damage, could they? Not a single one of these feels right. And how am I supposed to know which ammo to use?

In the background, the roar of the townies is rising again. We don't have much time. I imagine them egging each other on. With the way they've looked at us since our arrival, the hate in their eyes . . . we must be like fresh bait to them. However this ends, it won't be with peace.

Footsteps on the stairs announce the arrival of more townies. I look up from the weapons as three of them burst into the room. One is instantly taken out by Wolf's shotgun, but Wolf has to pull back to reload. The two remaining men home in on me, crouched on the floor and completely unarmed. Their faces light up at the sight of such easy prey. These two don't have guns, but they do have knives. They manage to take about two steps before Dolly shoots from somewhere behind me.

Compared to Wolf her shooting is beautiful. She kills like it's an art: two bullets at once, two clean shots, splitting their skulls open like eggshells and erupting in a mess of brain matter on the other side. They're gone before they hit the ground.

"Nice shooting, Dolly," Wolf says. With his gun loaded again, he moves back to his former position and places one foot on top of a body.

"Yeah!" I agree enthusiastically. It draws Wolf's attention to me, and he frowns.

"And where the hell is *your* gun?"

"Umm . . ." I glance between the bag and his face, smiling awkwardly. "Is this a bad time to mention I've never used one before?"

"Oh, for the love of—" Wolf cuts himself off and scowls. "Just grab a gun! You aim, you pull the trigger, brains go flying. Easy."

Dolly mumbles something.

"Right," Wolf says. "Don't forget the safety thing."

"Safety thing?" I pick up a random gun and stare at it in bewilderment.

"Yeah, you know, the—" A townie comes into sight, and Wolf blows his face off. "The safety thing!"

The townies are getting louder outside. My heart pounds faster and faster as I scrutinize the gun, unable to make any sense of it.

"Goddamn," Wolf says, and for once he seems to feel a flicker of concern. "Dolly, we're going to need some explosives. This kid is obviously useless."

"I'm right here," I mutter under my breath, though I know it's true. Dolly tears her eyes away from the doorway and looks through the bag again. She moves hastily, but her face is still completely blank.

"And by the way, I *do* have a name," I say, raising my voice. "It's—"

Dolly interrupts me by shoving something into my hands, saying something too soft for me to catch. I drop the gun and grab it, surprised. The shape and texture are odd, unlike anything I've ever felt before. I open my hands and stare.

A grenade.

She did *not* just hand me a grenade. I freeze, eyes locked on the explosive, which I'm sure is about to blow my hands off in a matter of seconds. Holy shit, I can't even shoot a gun; how did she *possibly* think I could handle a grenade? I've only ever seen them in pictures, but I know damn well what they can do. Time slows down. My breath quickens and my heart beats a million times per second. Even the yelling of the mob fades into the distance, my breathing somehow louder in my ears. Nothing matters except the grenade resting in my hands. My brain whirs, attempting to come up with a course of action that doesn't involve me splattering into a thousand bloody bits.

After a moment of frozen panic, instinct kicks in. I turn and hurl the thing toward the far wall. Thankfully, it sails out one of the holes rather than bouncing back to me.

I turn around, feeling triumphant, and Dolly's dumbfounded expression tells me I just screwed up. It's the first time I've seen actual emotion on her otherwise impassive face. It changes from shock, to disbelief, to unmistakable anger before returning to a stony, controlled state.

"Did you just throw away our last grenade?" she asks, her voice low and toneless.

"Well, I wasn't going to hang on to it!" I tell her defensively. What did she expect?

"You have to pull the pin before you throw it."

She's still staring at me.

"Pull the...what?"

"It won't work unless you pull the pin."

That would explain the lack of an explosion.

"Where are those explosives?" Wolf yells, turning around to glare. Dolly points at the wall behind us.

"Out there," she says.

"And what the fuck are they doing there?" he snarls. She points at me.

"Kid!" He looks about ready to rip my throat out. "Are you *really* this stupid, or are you just fucking with us?"

"Seriously, I have a name!" I say, pointedly ignoring the rest. "Like I was trying to say, it's—"

I'm drowned out by the sound of townies coming up the stairs. A *lot* of townies. All three of us turn back to the doorway, and the two who aren't miserable failures raise their guns.

A clump of townies spills into the room all at once. A few are taken down by some well-aimed shots by Wolf and Dolly, but they don't have time to reload before others are upon them. I scramble into a back corner and crouch there with the gun I have no idea how to use.

Wolf tackles the closest man and brings him down with a thud. He smashes the butt of the unloaded shotgun into the townie's face, hitting him repeatedly until he goes limp. Two others are on him almost instantly. He disappears beneath them.

A few bodies are already on the floor near Dolly. She has a crowbar and is attempting to hold back the crowd at the doorway, while the mob outside seethes and writhes like water about to boil over.

Despite Dolly's best efforts, it's already too late. Wolf doesn't seem to be faring well with his two attackers, and another man is lunging at me.

I dash for the window on my hands and knees, but a hand closes on my backpack and yanks me back. I scramble for a hold, scraping my nails against splintered wood. It's useless; he has me. As I turn, I recognize him—it's the man from last night, the one who shoved me. His mouth spreads in a gap-toothed grin as he meets my eyes. The hand that doesn't have a viselike grip on my pack is holding a broken bottle, the jagged edges glinting cruelly.

When I reach for the gun, the townie gives another vicious yank, pulling me away from it and closer to the sharp edges of the glass.

An explosion drowns out my screams.

The building shakes. The man lets go. My eardrums nearly burst.

Everyone is disoriented from the blast, stumbling and blinking. Wolf gains his composure first and takes advantage of it, pulling down the two townies he's been tussling with. Spurred into action, my former captor grabs a hold of me again. I kick out desperately. This time I dislodge his grip and crawl away on my hands and knees. As I search for an escape route, Dolly steps between me and the townie. Armed with a crowbar, she looks like the closest thing to a miracle I could expect right now.

I peek around her legs and see the man smirk.

"Pretty thing, ain't ya?" he comments, leering at Dolly. "Come on, little girl, you can't fight me."

One crack to the side of the head is all it takes to prove him wrong. Unsatisfied with that, she bends down and beats the crowbar into his skull until blood pools around him. I can't look away, my eyes wide open and locked on despite the nauseous churn of my stomach. Finally Dolly stops and turns to me, pale face flecked with red. She offers me a bloody hand.

"Thanks," I squeak, pulling myself to my feet. Wolf is up as well now, and looks very satisfied despite the blood streaming from his nose and a gash on his head. The room is still, aside from us. Strangely, gunfire continues down below.

"Phew!" Wolf wipes a hand across his forehead, pushing his matted hair back. "Now *that* was a good fight."

I don't even know what to say to that. Instead I ask, "So... uhh...what exploded?"

"Not the grenade you wasted, that's for sure." I wince at the reminder. "But otherwise...haven't got a clue."

"The jeep?" Dolly suggests.

"Let's hope not."

Wolf leads us down the stairs, which are blackened from the explosion and thoroughly decorated with townie guts. I have to step over detached limbs and disfigured torsos to get down. I feel nothing; numbness stifles the emotional responses struggling to fight their way out of me. I almost feel like I'm watching the scene through someone else's eyes.

At the bottom of the staircase the mob is dispersing. Injured townies are scattered on the ground, howling in pain and nursing wounds. The remainders sprint or limp off to safety. I see the mother and son from yesterday in the distance, hightailing it out of town, and am thankful they didn't end up involved in this mess.

Amid the dead, dying, and deserting stands a single figure, who raises a hand to greet us.

"Pretty Boy!" Wolf exclaims.

And *damn* is he pretty.

V
The Aftermath

I'm not the kind of girl who gets all flustered about boys. But, then again, the wastelands have a serious shortage of boys like this. It's rare enough to find someone who isn't missing a few teeth, or a few fingers, or maybe their sanity. Everyone's missing something or other. For me it's probably wits, and for *this* guy... well, he's not lacking anything in the looks department, that's for sure.

"Pretty Boy," as Wolf referred to him, is dusty and tired-looking and has a smear of blood down the side of his face, but beneath that he's still ridiculously attractive. He has high cheekbones and long eyelashes and beautiful hazel eyes. Sure his nose is a little crooked, most likely from being broken a couple times, and his dark hair is tousled and dirty, but I'll be damned if it doesn't just add a hint of roguish charm to his otherwise perfect looks.

As he walks toward us, he holsters his gun in his belt and winds his way through mangled corpses with an effortless grace. I, on the other hand, trip over a severed arm as I stare.

"Am I late to the party?" he asks with a grin. He shoots me the briefest of glances and I avert my eyes. I'm suddenly aware of my sunburnt face and boyishly short hair.

"Yeah," Wolf says, and spits. "Just a little."

He punches him right in his pretty face.

Pretty Boy reels from the impact, loses his footing, and trips over a nearby body. He falls to the ground hard, holding his face. I gape. Dolly laughs quietly from somewhere behind me.

"What the hell, Wolf?" Pretty Boy wails from the ground, still covering his face with both hands. "Why do you always have to—"

"Where the fuck were you when we showed up? Do you know how much shit you got us in?" Wolf shouts at him. "Do you have to screw up *every* job?"

"I didn't... It wasn't... I swear...!"

"Shut up." Wolf grimaces and turns in a circle, surveying the messy scene around us. "Where the hell is Tank?"

Pretty Boy pulls his hand back from his face, double-checks that his nose isn't bleeding, and stands up. He takes a few steps back, putting some distance and a corpse between himself and Wolf.

"He's coming," he says, his voice sullen. "Slowly."

"Fat bastard," Wolf says with a wry smile. "Ah, I missed him. Dolly isn't much company."

"Is that why you picked up the stray?" Pretty Boy's eyes shift to me. I smile awkwardly. He looks back at Wolf.

"Yeah, well, we needed an extra hand." Wolf looks at me and shakes his head. "Damn near got us killed, though."

"Sorry," I say.

"What? How?"

"The little shit tossed our last grenade out the window."

"Sorry," I repeat sheepishly.

"Well, that explains a lot..." Pretty Boy gives me another, more curious look. "Lucky I was there to find it, then, eh?"

"Very lucky," Wolf says, his tone implying a lot of unfortunate consequences that would have happened otherwise. I try to pretend I'm not terrified.

"Boss, I'm here!" An unfamiliar voice bellows out of nowhere. A few seconds later a dark-skinned stranger comes into view, plowing toward us at a slow jog. When he finally reaches us, he leans over with his hands on his knees, wheezing. "I...made it...sorry...is everyone dead already?"

This guy is *huge.* He must be at least twice my height and width, with broad shoulders and a thick torso. It's difficult to tell whether all of the extra padding is fat or muscle, but either way, it looks like he could snap my spine like a toothpick. His face is scarred and hard, but the smile he shows us seems genuine, teeth whiter than I'd expect.

"Tank!" Wolf's greeting is considerably friendlier than his one to Pretty Boy. He walks over and gives the big man a slap on the back. "Good to see you, buddy. And yeah, everyone worth killing is smeared across the ground, sorry to disappoint."

"Damn," he wheezes out. Only when he finally catches his breath and straightens up does he notice me. "Who's the little one?"

"Hi," I squeak at him nervously. Standing up, he's the biggest man I've ever seen in my life. "I'm—"

"Just some kid we picked up," Wolf finishes with a shrug. "We needed some help."

"So what do we do with him now?" Pretty Boy asks.

"I'm a—"

"Not much meat on the bones, wouldn't make much of a meal," Tank says, his face hard as he looks down at me. I force out a laugh and hope he's joking.

"Might be useful," Wolf says, scrutinizing me. "Or might not. Who can say?"

"I can be useful," I say, desperate to get a word in. I really don't want to end up a meal. And if I *could* make myself useful to these guys, with their jeep and all those guns, well...my days of being afraid and hungry would be over. They might be a little bit crazy, but with them on my side, even I might manage to stay alive out here in the wastes. I stare at Wolf, seeking acceptance, my mouth opening but unable to find the words to convince him.

"I want to keep it." Dolly steps up behind me and lays a hand on top of my head. "Let's keep it."

"It?" I repeat, confused. I guess I should probably be offended she's referring to me like some kind of pet...but, in the end, being a pet is better than getting left behind or becoming dinner.

No one says anything. Tank is hard-eyed, Wolf skeptical, and Pretty Boy, I notice nervously, has his hand on the gun at his hip.

Wolf breaks into a grin and the tension snaps like a twig. Everyone else relaxes the moment they see the all-too-amused look on their leader's face. Tank gives an easygoing smile, followed by a booming laugh.

"Okay, Dolly, fine. We'll keep it," Wolf says. He walks over and punches me in the shoulder. What he probably intends as a light tap sends me reeling. "Welcome to the crew, kiddo!"

"Um, thanks." I rub my shoulder and smile. "And just so we're all on the same page, I'm a girl."

"Whatever," he says. "Someone get the jeep. Let's get out of this shithole."

VI
The Crew

We make camp a few miles out from the massacred town, with a fresh supply of dead townies to chop up and sell as "hog meat." After seeing how terribly awry it went, I wonder how often this plan works, but I figure it's best not to bring that up. At least we now have the gasoline Wolf was looking for, toted by Tank from the town coffers, and plenty of canned food. Listening to the way Wolf boasts and brags, it's as if the mission was a great success.

As for me, I'm most excited by the fact we have ample food, not to mention a fire. Everyone else seems amused by my delight, but I don't care. I've had too many long, dark nights spent shivering because I was too afraid of what flames could bring. When I was with Papa we had to be cautious about fires, and when I was alone they weren't even a remote possibility. Now we make camp out in the open and build a roaring bonfire. When I suggest it could cause trouble, Wolf laughs.

"We *are* the trouble, dumbass," he tells me.

That's when I remember the guns. And I finally feel safe, safer than I ever have before.

I sit close to the warmth of the flames while the others enthusiastically sift through the loot we collected. Wolf finds a new pair of boots that fit him almost-right. Pretty Boy finds a broken but shiny pocket watch, which Dolly promptly steals from him. Tank finds a rusty knife, which he tosses down at my feet.

"Wolf says you can't handle a gun for shit," he explains with a good-humored smile.

"Oh, wow!" I pick it up and turn it over in my hands. Underneath patches of rust, the blade glints in the firelight. It's small, but it's sharp. I tuck it away into the side of one of my scuffed-up boots. "Thanks!"

Soon it's time to eat. I knew it would come eventually. I try to steel myself, but still, it's rough. At least they did the slicing and dicing back in town, so most of it is unrecognizable, but the smell still gives me an odd combination of repulsion and hunger. My brain knows that what they're cooking used to be a person, but really, it just smells like meat. The last time I had real meat was when my papa found a dead rat and attempted to cook it. It didn't turn out well.

This, on the other hand, actually looks really...tasty. After days of beans, the sight and smell make my mouth water.

I look away from the spit on the fire and try to busy myself by sharpening my knife on a rock. It doesn't seem to do much, but it distracts me from my hunger. When I glance up, I see Wolf and Pretty Boy standing together with their heads bowed conspiratorially, both looking in my direction. I quickly look down again and pretend I didn't notice.

Still, when Wolf sits beside me with a chunk of cooked meat in his hands, it's hard not to pay attention. The smell wafts toward me tantalizingly, and out of the corner of my eye I see him tearing into it with a vehement hunger. I slowly turn my head, even as I will myself not to, and see that what he's holding is clearly a human arm.

To my horror, my stomach lets out a loud rumble.

I turn away, face reddening. Wolf laughs.

"Hungry, kiddo?" he asks.

"Nah," I say weakly.

"Like hell you ain't." He leans over and holds it out in offering. "Here, have some."

"Uh," I say. "Um. Well."

He's looking at me expectantly. I fumble with my words, not even sure what I'm trying to say.

"I don't know...if I...I just...uhh." I look back and forth between the meat and Wolf's hideous grin. My hands flutter in some vague gestures that communicate even less than my words do. "This is kinda, uh..."

"Just try it," he suggests, and shoves the meat into my hands.

I glance around nervously and, of course, everyone is watching me. Dolly is blank-faced, Tank grinning broadly, and Pretty Boy curious. A sudden weight descends on my shoulders. I realize that this moment could be important, that I'm being judged by the group.

I turn the meat over in my hands, looking at the way the grease glistens in the firelight. I swallow my excuses and try to smile.

"Well," I say. "Papa always said don't knock it till you try it."

My teeth brush against the meat—and I stop as a wave of revulsion rises up in me. I can't bring myself to bite down. I can't stop thinking about how this hunk of flesh used to be a person.

The silence around the fire thickens as I lower the meat. I hold on to it for a few seconds, trying to decide if I want to change my mind, before I hand it back to Wolf.

"Sorry," I say. I hunch over self-consciously, biting my lip. I wonder if this is the part where they kick me out and leave me behind in the dust. Or, more likely, put a bullet in my head and be done with it.

Wolf looks down and sighs heavily. I watch him, my shoulders tensing nervously, not sure what he's going to do. A moment later he abruptly looks up and grins.

"What'd I tell you guys?" He holds out a hand and gestures to the others. "She didn't eat it. Hand over your shit."

I look up, frowning, and realize that the spotlight is no longer on me. Everyone is looking at him. Tank groans and tosses over a glass jar half-full of what looks like jam, which Wolf hoists triumphantly. Pretty Boy sullenly produces a metal flask from his pack and hands that over as well.

"Not fair," he complains. "You really had to give her an arm?"

"Thanks, guys. Pleasure as always." Wolf stuffs the new goodies into his pack and smirks, giving a mock-gracious bow of his head.

"What's going on?" I look around the circle, trying to make sense of what just happened. "You guys aren't..." Going to kill me? "Upset?"

"Nah," Wolf says. He's chuckling, looking very pleased with himself. "More meat for us. We always bet on whether or not the newbies will eat. And Pretty Boy is always wrong."

"One day someone's gonna do it, and I'll win big," Pretty Boy says.

"Nope. You'll forever be the only one who was fucked-up enough to eat the first time."

I stare at Pretty Boy, surprised. Out of the lot of them, I definitely wouldn't have expected him to be the one who took to cannibalism so easily. He shrugs.

"I thought they would kill me if I didn't," he says by way of explanation, not quite meeting my eyes. I nod. I thought the same thing, but there's no point in saying that.

"And he puked it all up about thirty seconds later," Tank says. "Waste of good meat."

"And you bet that I would eat, too?" I ask, looking over at him—or, rather, at his protruding belly, because it's rather intimidating to stare at his scarred-up face.

"Well, look at you. Scrawny little thing, I figured you must be hungry," he says. Despite losing the bet, he's smiling, his tough face softened by good humor.

"Joke's on you, big guy," Wolf says. "She ate yesterday. I made sure of it."

"So you rigged it," Pretty Boy says. "Asshole."

The three of them devolve into bickering over the fairness of the bet. I watch, half-amused and half-disturbed by how lightly they view the whole issue. A tap on my shoulder startles me out of my thoughts. I look up to see Dolly, who wordlessly hands me a can. The top is already half-opened for me.

"Oh," I say, surprised. "Thanks!"

She stares at me. It seems like she wants to say something, but she merely turns and walks away. I smile at her retreating figure before raising the can and taking a sniff.

Beans.

After everyone finishes eating, the camp settles down and I relax into a state of sleepy contentment. Maybe I shouldn't feel so safe, considering I'm surrounded by cannibals who just decimated the population of a small town, but I do. It's pretty clear they have no interest in killing me at the moment, and it's hard to feel too concerned with a full belly and a warm fire. Matter of fact, I'm starting to nod off as the exhaustion of the day hits me.

A pair of fingers snaps in my face, jolting me awake.

"Hey, you," Wolf says, waving a hand in front of my eyes. "Go to sleep already. You've got second watch."

"Umm, okay." I rub my eyes and yawn. The fire has died down to glowing embers. It looks like Dolly has already fallen asleep, curled up on the ground near where Wolf was sitting. Tank is setting up a spot close by, while Pretty Boy is sitting near the fire and has a peeved expression that tells me he got stuck with first watch. I'm about to dig out my blanket and find a flat spot on the ground when I realize they still haven't bothered to ask for my name. "By the way, I've been trying to tell you, I'm—"

"Nope!" Wolf practically shouts so I have no chance of talking over him. "No names."

"Huh?"

"Most people who join us don't last long," Tank says. He states it like someone might comment on the weather.

"Like Sticks," says Wolf, counting off on his fingers. "Three days, that one. Or Snake Eyes. One week, I think. Or Bluebird—"

"I liked Bluebird," Pretty Boy says, sighing.

"You liked her tits, you mean. Anyway, the point is, we don't use real names."

"Oh," I say. "Okay. So, who should I be?"

Wolf grins.

"That's obvious," he says. "You'll be Kid."

VII
Trouble

I wake up with the barrel of a gun in my face.

It takes my foggy brain a few seconds to register the danger. As soon as it does I snap awake, sitting up and scrambling back in the dirt. The gun follows, never losing sight of its target.

I keep my eyes locked on the gun, and only then think to look at who's holding it. I feel sick to my stomach, thinking I'll look up and see Pretty Boy or Wolf ready to pull the trigger. I slowly raise my eyes, letting my gaze climb from a hand to an arm to a face...a crooked and cruel face I don't recognize. It's almost strange how relieved I feel that it's not one of the crew.

Wolf swears loudly from behind me. Careful not to make any sudden movements, I swivel my eyes from side to side to take in the situation. Dolly and Tank are also being held at gunpoint, Tank on the ground and Dolly crouching like an animal ready to pounce. Pretty Boy is on his knees with his hands behind his head, though nobody is actually pointing a gun at him. And Wolf, I can only suspect, is as tied up as the rest of us.

The fire has burned down to dully glowing embers and the sun is just starting to rise. We almost made it through the night without any trouble. I try to keep in mind that Wolf said we are the trouble, but that's hard to believe right now.

"Who the hell was on watch?" Wolf asks. "'Cause I am going to kick their ass."

"It was you," Dolly says flatly.

"Aw, shit. I take that back about the ass-kicking."

"Shut up," the man above me growls. He's a stooped guy with missing teeth and a face peeling from sunburn. He jabs me in the forehead with the gun. "Nobody move."

He takes a few steps away, still keeping the gun pointed in my direction as he makes his way around our campsite. As his attention shifts to the jeep, I sneak a glance at Wolf. He's on the ground, held down by a hulk of a man with a wide-brimmed hat. Wolf looks over at me and raises his eyebrows. Maybe it's a signal, but I have no idea what he's trying to tell me. I shrug at him helplessly and he rolls his eyes.

"What the fuck is this?" the man checking out our camp asks. I look over to see him drop a bag, chopped-up townies spilling out as it hits the ground. He recoils, covering his mouth. "Well, looks like we caught ourselves some sharks, boys."

"Hey, hey, isn't there a bounty out for sharks?" one of the others asks. "From them guys out by the radio tower?"

"Only if we bring 'em in live, I think."

"What do they want with live sharks?"

"Don't know, but that's how it is. We could take the jeep, but still, too many of 'em."

"So we shoot a couple, bring in the rest."

"Waste of good money."

As the men eagerly discuss their prize, their attention falters. I look back at Dolly and notice her slowly reaching for her boot, eyes locked on the man above her. She's so close—but so is his gun, and if he happens to look down at her . . .

I don't think, I just spring up and barrel toward the man pinning Wolf down. I ram into him at full speed. It has all the effectiveness of a pebble against a boulder. But when I wrap my arms around him, he's forced to let go of Wolf and stand, trying to shake me off. He lets out a furious bellow.

"Keep it under control, Kid!" Wolf says, and he's gone. I can't tell where or why or what's happening. The man has taken to spinning wildly and trying to tear me off him with his huge, clumsy hands. Everything is a blur of motion, and all I can do is cling. My grip slips. I dig my fingers in like claws, but I can feel myself losing my hold bit by bit. When the man stumbles and falls, he flings me off.

I hit the ground like a sack of meat. I'm instantly sprawled out on my back, the breath knocked out of me and the world still spinning. I suck in air and look to the side. The huge man is already stirring, head turning in my direction. I flip onto my stomach and crawl away. I block out all the noise and chaos around me, vision tunneling, searching for anything that can help me—a person, a weapon, anything!

I see the jeep. I propel myself toward it on all fours and worm underneath.

Though the noise rages on nearby, I feel safer in the cramped darkness underneath the vehicle. I allow myself a moment to breathe, closing my eyes and resting my forehead against the cool sand.

Something cold and sharp pokes the side of my throat.

I hold my breath and raise my head agonizingly slowly.

"Pretty Boy?"

"Kid? Ah, hell, you scared the shit out of me." He pulls the knife back, gripping it so tightly his knuckles turn white. He eyes are wide and his chest heaving. "What are you doing?"

"Hiding. There was this big guy...I got away, but...wait, why are *you* hiding? Don't you have a gun?"

"Just get out!"

"What?"

"I'm hiding here, so go somewhere else!"

"But I—"

We shut up as a pair of boots appears next to the jeep. We look at each other, and back at the boots. The man outside falls to a crouch with a grunt. One large hand reaches underneath the jeep, groping around near Pretty Boy.

Don't move, I mouth at him. He's focused entirely on the hand moving closer and closer to him. It brushes his arm.

He lashes out with his knife, severing two fingers. The man yells and recoils the hand, but his other one shoots under and grabs me by the leg.

"Pretty Boy!" I squeak imploringly, reaching for him. He pulls back, his face cold. I'm yanked out from my hiding place, hands full of nothing but sand.

I end up upside down, held by one ankle and swinging helplessly through the air. I catch glimpses of things happening around me as I swing back and forth: Wolf struggling with someone in the dirt, Dolly chasing a wounded man, Tank on the ground and motionless, Pretty Boy wriggling out from beneath the jeep. My heart surges at the latter, but he runs in the opposite direction.

"Help!" I yell, still trying to find something to hold on to as the man carries me away. "Pretty Boy! Someone! Help me!"

No one does. And when I turn my head, it's all too clear where I'm being carried: the fire. Along the way he grabs a container of gasoline.

"Oh shit," I say, mind going blank with panic. "Oh shit oh shit oh shit." I squirm like a worm on a hook. The man looks down at me and grins.

"Into the fire, little monkey," he says, gleefully swinging me.

"I'm not a monkey!" I wail. I latch on to one of his legs and cling there, wrapping both arms around him.

He stops, grunts in annoyance, and swings the gas can at me

in an attempt to dislodge my hold. One glancing blow hits me on the ear and makes my head ring, but I refuse to let go. He drops the can with a curse and grabs one of my arms with his injured hand.

I act instinctively and bite down on the bloody stubs of his fingers.

Howling, he drops me, and I get a face full of sand. I taste dirt and blood. I force myself onto my hands and knees, shaking.

A bang deafens me. The raider stumbles, disbelief spreading across his face as red blossoms on his chest. He almost catches his footing again, but another gunshot goes off and a new wound appears near his heart. He crashes down into our still-smoldering fire pit, and struggles for a few moments before lying still.

Footsteps approach. Wolf prods me in the side with the barrel of a gun.

"Y'all right, Kid?" he asks.

"Yeah. I'm okay." I pat myself down to verify, checking for injuries and finding nothing substantial. I look up at him. "Thanks for saving me."

"Eh, just didn't want you to get all the glory."

I laugh breathlessly and he offers me the barrel of the gun, which I use to pull myself to my feet. My mouth tastes like severed fingers. I spit a couple of times, which doesn't help.

"Damn, that was a mess," Wolf says.

"Yeah…and what was that about a reward for sharks?" I ask.

"Y'know, I've been hearing rumors along those lines for a while now," he says. He pauses for a moment, thinking, and then shrugs. "Eh, well. Sounds like a problem for later."

He walks off, and I look around to survey the damage. Tank is still on the ground, but stirring now. Wolf crouches beside him, laughs, and pats him on the shoulder, so I figure he's all right.

Dolly appears beside me, moving too close like a little kid who doesn't understand what "personal space" means. Her face and clothes are stained with blood. It's hard to tell how much of it is hers. I stare at her. After an awkward moment she holds out her hand, clutching something. It takes me a few moments to recognize the dirty piece of fabric as my beanie. I don't even remember losing it.

"Oh, wow, thanks," I say. I shake it out and put it back on. Dolly says something I don't quite catch.

"What?"

She leans closer. I step forward and wrap my arms around her, automatically assuming she's looking for a hug or something. The way she stiffens up immediately informs me that I was wrong about that. After a brief pause she pats me on the shoulder awkwardly, and I pull back, a little embarrassed. But once I let go, she offers a smile for a brief instant before moving on to inspect the bodies of the raiders. When one moves, she shoots him in the face. I look away, grimacing.

"Anyone seen Pretty Boy?" Wolf yells from Tank's side. I point in the direction I saw him going.

"He ran off," I say.

"'Course he did. Always runs when things get too hairy. Dolly, find him."

Dolly gives the raider's body another kick and dutifully runs off, gun in hand. The sight gives me a flicker of worry for Pretty Boy. I do my best to stifle it, remembering how I almost burned to death while he ran away. Taking a shaky breath, I walk over to the jeep and sit down for a much-needed rest. My heart is still pounding and my hands trembling as if my body hasn't realized I'm out of danger yet. Tank lumbers over and sits next to me. We smile wearily at each other.

"What a way to wake up," I say.

"I've had worse," he says, chuckling.

"I don't even want to know."

"Really, I'm mostly disappointed I got knocked out so early. As soon as the fight broke out the guy hit me over the head with his gun, and then...next thing I remember is waking up to a bunch of dead raiders." He lets out a long sigh. "Missed the whole damn fight. Again."

Before I can respond, Dolly marches back into camp with Pretty Boy in tow, gun in one hand and a fistful of his hair in the other. She shoves him in front of Wolf. He stumbles for a few steps before catching his balance, and slowly raises his eyes to Wolf's face.

"Well, glad to see you're all okay," he says with a flicker of a smile.

"Shut up." Wolf waves at him dismissively before turning to me and Tank. "And you two, get off your lazy asses!"

"Seriously?" Tank groans, hauling himself to his feet. I follow.

Wolf shades his eyes with a hand and looks toward the sun, which is just starting to peek out over the distant mountains.

"Time to move out," he says. "The day's just getting started."

VIII
Heating Up

"Well, the jeep's wrecked."

"How wrecked?"

"Very," Tank says, shutting the hood with a bang. "Looks like it took a gunshot too many."

"Damn." Wolf begins to pace, running his hands through his stringy dreadlocks.

"You can't fix it?" I ask, turning my head from side to side to watch him. I'm in the broken-down vehicle next to Pretty Boy, where we were seated and ready to take off until it failed to start. My hand brushes against his leg and I jerk it away with a whisper of an apology. He doesn't seem to notice.

"What? No. Do I look like a fucking mechanic to you, Kid? Don't be stupid."

"Oh. Sorry," I say sheepishly. He doesn't respond, but Tank ruffles my hair.

"I might be able to if I had the right tools, kiddo, but I don't," he says.

"So what do we do now?" Pretty Boy asks. He only glances at me once, and looks quickly back at Wolf. He hasn't looked me in the eyes since the fight.

"We get a new one, obviously."

"Where from?"

"Ahh…" Wolf stops pacing and stares into the distance. I picture rusty gears turning in his head. After a moment he snaps his fingers, triumphant. "We go see the Queen!"

"And how do we get there?"

"Stop asking stupid questions, Pretty Boy."

"Who's the Queen?"

"Same goes for you, Kid."

Dolly produces a rolled-up piece of paper from a pack and holds it out to Pretty Boy. As he unfurls it, the others gather around him. I join in, peering curiously.

"Is that a map?" I ask. I can't read a word of it, but I recognize the shapes of mountains and roads.

"Again with the stupid questions," Wolf says. "Of course it's a damn map. See, it's got all the towns and shit."

"Wow." This piece of paper holds more of the world than I've ever seen, not that it means much. Before I left town, I knew other places like it existed, but certainly not their locations or names. "You guys made this?"

"Got it off a caravan," Pretty Boy says.

"So you stole it?"

"It doesn't count as stealing if they're dead," Wolf objects.

"I think it still counts if you killed them for the map…"

"I never said *we* killed them," he says. "And no. That would count as looting, ain't that right?"

"Isn't that worse than stealing?"

"Whatever." Wolf silences me with a wave of his hand and gives Pretty Boy a rough nudge. "Where are we off to, then?"

"All right, well we just came from—" Pretty Boy slides his finger over the map and taps a small black mark. "Here. It was called Steelforge. So now we should be just around here." He moves his hand up.

"Is Bramble on there?" I interrupt. He looks up and meets my eyes briefly.

"Yeah. Of course." He points it out. It looks like it's only a stone's throw away from Steelforge. It felt like so much longer when I had to walk most of the way.

"That where you're from, Kid?" Tank asks.

"Well, I—"

"I don't give a shit about Bramble. We want to see the Queen," Wolf urges impatiently. I shut up.

"Right. She's up here." Pretty Boy points.

"Fuck, that's far," Tank groans. "All that on foot?"

"We won't make it," Pretty Boy says. "There's no way. We might have enough food, but definitely not water."

"We have to make it," Wolf says. He regards the map with pursed lips, and then indicates a town sitting between us and our destination. "What's this one?"

"Blackfort," Pretty Boy says. "I've heard of it. Not very friendly."

"So if we raid Blackfort on the way, we can make it to the Queen, yeah?"

"Well, we can follow the road...but, again, there's the water." He shrugs. "Hard to say."

"Great." Wolf claps his hands together and grins. "That's the plan, then."

"Wait, but—"

Despite Pretty Boy's protests, the others begin preparations. As Tank siphons gas out of the jeep and Dolly searches the raiders' corpses, Wolf gathers up some makeshift packs and tosses them out, shouting orders about how to divide up supplies. I rush to follow his directions, and Pretty Boy joins me. Each of us gets a small ration of food, a jug of water, and some stuff worth trading: gasoline, first aid supplies, weapons. I stuff everything into my backpack, my blanket tucked neatly beneath it. This time they even give me a gun, after a lecture from Wolf about how I better keep it pointed far away him. Having a real weapon tucked into my waistband is both exciting and nerve-racking.

"I hope you know what you're doing, Wolf," Pretty Boy says, weighing his portion of water and looking uneasy. "This isn't much."

"Oh, cut the whining. We've made it through worse."

"Yeah, and usually someone ends up dead."

"Well, what a coincidence. I've been looking for an excuse to get rid of you!" Wolf says cheerfully, clapping him on the back. Pretty Boy looks even more nervous. "By the way, Kid, I don't suppose you can read?"

"Nope, sorry."

"Damn shame. Relax, Pretty Boy, we still need you around." Wolf grins at him. "And don't think I didn't notice you pocketing the map. Hand it over. That's way too important for you to carry."

Pretty Boy looks as if he might argue, but another look from Wolf silences him. He purses his lips and pulls out the map. Wolf takes it, gives him a shove that may or may not be playful, and tosses the map to Dolly.

"Well, guess we're as ready as we're gonna get," he says, and we're off.

It doesn't take long for the going to get rough. Everyone sets off in good spirits, talking and joking, but after a few hours the sun is directly overhead and the heat beats us into silence. The light brings the wastelands to life, and soon heat radiates from both above and below us. The cracked asphalt of the road becomes too hot to walk on, so instead we walk alongside it. The sand is hot, too. I can feel it through the thin soles of my boots, and if I pause for more than a second it feels like my feet are being boiled in them.

The landscape remains the same in every direction. There's

nothing but dry, empty sand marked only by the occasional old building. The mountains in the distance never seem to get any closer. It's easy to lose yourself in the wastes. When I was alone I feared they might swallow me, especially with bad memories behind me and Lord-knew-what ahead. I now know why the wastes can make men mad. There are crazies that live in the emptier parts, wild and hungry like packs of dogs. I had a brush with them once with my papa, and I still have nightmares about it.

Traveling is easier with company. The others carry on with determination and purpose, and I follow their lead. I plunge forward, one foot in front of the other. Despite my best efforts, soon I'm panting and sweating and lagging behind, unable to match the pace of Wolf and Dolly. I end up beside Pretty Boy.

He stares ahead without acknowledging my presence. One hand brushes sweaty hair back from his face, and he groans a wordless complaint.

"Umm," I say after a few moments. "I'm not, uh, mad at you or anything. Just so you know."

He looks at me sideways and away again, hesitating before he speaks.

"Why would you be?"

"Well…" I bite my lip. "You did, you know, kind of run off and leave me to die."

"Ah. Right." He pauses again, and I sneak a glance at him, not sure if he intends to continue. He clears his throat, still not looking straight at me. "Yeah. I guess I did. Sorry about that."

"Oh, no big deal."

"It's just kind of how things are, you know?" He doesn't sound sorry at all.

"Yeah, I guess." I think about how Wolf came back to save me in the end, but don't say anything. Wolf is a bit crazy, after all, so maybe Pretty Boy has the right of it.

"Well, I'm glad you didn't end up dead, if it means any-thing," he says, and smiles at me. His smile is slightly crooked and way too charming for a guy who almost let me die earlier today. I blush and promptly feel like an idiot for doing so.

"Uh. You, too?" It comes out an uncertain squeak. I don't know how to deal with a boy who smiles at me like that.

"Thanks," he says dryly. "You're probably the only one."

"That can't be true!" Sure Wolf gives him a lot of shit, but he's still clearly a part of the crew.

"Yeah, Tank might miss me." He looks over his shoulder at Tank, who has fallen even farther behind than us. "Hey, fatty! Would you miss me if I was dead?"

"'Course I would! Who would I make fun of?" Tank shouts back. We slow down and he huffs and puffs to catch up with us. Sweat runs down his face and stains the armpits of his shirt, but he looks cheerful. He cuffs Pretty Boy around the neck, and Pretty Boy yells about the stench before wiggling free.

Having Tank around lifts the tension, and Pretty Boy visibly relaxes.

"So, Kid, how old are you?" he asks.

"Uh, sixteen. I think."

"Oh, wow. You really are a kid, aren't you? Everyone used to call me young, and I'm eighteen."

"Shit, how do you guys keep track?" Tank asks. "I haven't got a damn clue."

"That's 'cause you're an old man," Pretty Boy says, earning himself another cuff.

"Papa told me I was born in the winter, right 'round when it starts getting cold," I say. "That's how I keep track."

"Your papa?" Tank asks. "He still around?"

"Nope," I say. "Dead. For a long time." I didn't see it hap-pen, but I know it to be true. The town took me in and left him out in the wastes. No one makes it long alone. I later wondered if the townies even really let him leave, or if they just shot him when I was gone.

"I was born on April twelfth," says Pretty Boy. "Not that it means anything, most of the time. The Queen knows those kinds of things, though, so I can check up on it from time to time. She usually gives me a present."

There's that name again. Seeing as Wolf isn't around to tell me to shut up and stop asking questions, I try again.

"So who is this Queen person?"

"You've never been?" Pretty Boy asks. I shake my head. "Ah. She's called the Queen of the Wastes. Nobody is really sure how she started off, but now she lives in this big mansion with a ton of guards. She runs this place called the Crossroads. All of the trading routes of the main caravans cross there."

"Why?"

"Water, mainly. She lives right next to a river, and has a way to make the water drinkable. So people trade her for it, and now she has just about everything you could ever need. Traders buy and sell her shit along their routes. And people like us, too. Raiders, I mean. Sharks. No discrimination as long as you have stuff to trade."

"Wow," I say. It sounds big and important, definitely more so than anywhere I've ever been. "I didn't know anyone like that existed. I guess I never thought about where the caravans get their supplies."

"Yeah. She's a powerful lady. And a rich one."

"So you guys go to her a lot?"

"Whenever we get a chance. She has a lot of stuff that's hard to get anywhere else."

"It doesn't hurt that she has a thing for Pretty Boy," Tank butts in.

"Shut it," Pretty Boy says. "She likes Dolly, too. Dolly used to work for her."

"What do you mean, used to work for her?" I ask. They exchange a glance. "Like, a bodyguard?"

"Not exactly," Pretty Boy says. "She was…" He trails off, looking nervous. I follow his gaze to see Dolly staring back at us. She studies each of us for a few long seconds before slowly turning back forward.

"That is just not normal," Pretty Boy mutters under his breath. "God, she's creepy."

"She just doesn't like you," Tank tells him.

"No, no, it's not just me! Once we went into a town as partners, you know, scoping out the place. And it was the one and only time, because nobody wanted a damn thing to do with us. Thought she might be less sketchy than the rest of you, but nope, not even a little. There I was trying to be friendly and get them off their guard and shit, and Dolly would just stand there with that face of hers, just staring and not saying anything and…ugh, it was bad." He shakes his head.

"I think she's nice," I say.

"Well, she likes you," Pretty Boy says. He almost sounds jealous. "For whatever reason."

"She does?"

"Seems like it."

I look ahead at her, scrutinizing the back of her long blue hair. As if on cue she looks over her shoulder again, meeting my gaze. I smile, and she blinks and looks away.

"See? That's about as friendly as she gets," Pretty Boy says, watching with a wry half smile. "If I ever tried to smile at her like that, she'd break my nose."

"Again," Tank says.

"Right. Again."

"She broke your nose?" I ask.

"He deserved it."

"Shut up, Tank."

"But I thought you guys were all friends," I say, confused.

"Friends?" Pretty Boy laughs. "You have a lot to learn, Kid."

I don't understand, but his condescending tone bites enough to make me stop asking questions. We walk along in silence, the only sound our ragged breathing. It hurts to inhale. My mouth and throat are already as dry as the sand we're walking on, and the hot air burns. My tongue feels thick in my mouth, as if even that is coated by dust, and my lips are starting to crack and bleed. I finally cave and pull out my water flask. I take a short gulp and quickly cap it again before I chug the whole thing.

It doesn't even take the edge off my thirst. The water is warm and goes down as thick as paste.

Soon enough even Wolf and Dolly are beaten down by the heat, and they slow enough to allow all five of us to walk side by side.

"You know," Wolf says, "it's days like these that really make me appreciate humanity."

His comment is met with silence. I assume everyone, like me, is trying to work out how that makes any sense.

"The fuck?" Tank finally says, effectively summing up my own thoughts.

"I'm serious. I mean, look at this place. Look at this fucking world we live in." He sweeps his hands in a broad gesture, indicating the expanse of wastelands around us. "It's unlivable. Or at least, it should be, you know? And yet here we are. I bet most of you weren't even alive before the war, huh, Kid? Pretty Boy? Little post-bomb babies raised on radioactive milk, that's what you are. Probably shouldn't even be possible." He lets out a low whistle and shakes his head. "People just do what they have to do, like always. Ain't nothing that can kill us."

"Like cockroaches," I say.

"Right. That's deep, Kid." Wolf laughs and abruptly stops walking, cracking his back. "And this cockroach is about ready for a break. One hour, everybody eat and piss and do whatever else you need to do."

The first day is long and rough. By the time we stop for the night, seeking shelter in the broken-down shell of a house, my water canteen is dangerously close to empty. Judging by the way the others check their flasks and mutter and pore over the map, I'm not the only one. It's frightening how much water I consumed in a day.

Wolf doesn't want to risk a fire after this morning. We eat a quick, cold dinner and I spend the night squeezed between Tank and Dolly, with my blanket wrapped around me and my backpack as a pillow. I have trouble falling asleep with water weighing on my mind.

Still, curled up and staring at the dark sky through the holes in the roof, I think back on all the nights spent on my own and know this is so much better. Ever since my papa was swallowed by the wastes—maybe even at the end of when we were still together—I've felt a constant ache of loneliness. Even though Wolf snores and Tank smells and everyone's a bit crazy, somehow I feel like I belong here. I finally fall asleep with that thought in mind, and it makes everything a little more okay.

IX
Death Sentence

"Wake up, lazy fucks!"

The voice cuts through the fog of sleep and wakes me. I keep my eyes squeezed shut and my blanket wrapped tightly around me.

"No, not yet," I groan and roll onto my side, trying to hide from the sun. Hands yank my blanket off me. "Hey!" I stand up slowly, rubbing my eyes and yawning. Wolf's grinning face steps into my line of sight, and a hand smacks the side of my head and sends me staggering.

"That enough of a wake-up call for you, Kid?" he asks. I shake my head to clear it and give him a weary thumbs-up. At least this is better than waking up to a gun in my face. He returns my blanket, and I pack it up. "Good, good. Let's get going."

Everyone except Wolf looks as tired as I feel, but they all trudge onward so I have no choice but to follow. I shoot Pretty Boy a sleepy-eyed smile. He smiles back, which makes my stomach do a flip and helps me keep going.

I feel more awake after we've been traveling for about an hour, when the last coolness of the night has leaked away and the sun seems intent on roasting us where we stand. Today is windier than yesterday, but the hot air blowing at us gives little relief. Instead it only fills my eyes and mouth with gritty sand. I feel dry and dusty deep down to my core, but resist the temptation of my canteen. I refuse to be the first one to take a drink.

"So..." My voice comes out rough and unfamiliar. I cough and clear my throat and try again. "So, what's the plan once we get to Black...Blackrock?"

"Blackfort," Pretty Boy corrects.

"Yeah, that one."

"Right, a plan," Wolf says, as if it had just occurred to him. "We should reach it today, so I guess that would be a good idea."

"How do you guys usually do this?"

"Eh, well, we send in two people to scout, make sure the townies aren't going to chase us out with pitchforks on sight or nothin', trade some of our shit for their shit..."

"Who does the scouting?" I ask.

"Always Pretty Boy, because he's good at bullshitting if nothing else, and then whoever else has got nothing better to do."

"It'd be better if you let me go alone," Pretty Boy says. "All the rest of you ever do is make my job harder."

"Ha, ha, let you go in alone? So you can fuck us over and leave? No way in hell."

"And after you scout, then what?" I ask, not wanting them to veer off track.

"They meet up with the rest of us, and if it seems like a good target, we raid the place." He shrugs. "Kill some people, take their stuff, you know, the fun part."

"Okay..." It doesn't sound like the most well-thought-out plan, but I figure they've been doing it for a while so I'm in no place to question it. "Wait, so, what happened at that town back there?"

"Well, that time everything got a bit screwy."

"How do you mean?"

"Pretty Boy fucked it up."

"I did not!" He throws his hands up in exasperation, shaking his head. "Tank and I got there to scope it out, and they were suspicious from the start. I don't know, the area was a shithole, maybe we looked too well fed or something. We had to get the hell out and camp nearby. Seriously, I thought they were gonna string us up there and then."

"So why did you and Dolly still go there?" I ask Wolf.

"No choice. The jeep was almost out of gas so we had to just roll with the plan. But hey, it worked out all right."

"Except we ended up losing the jeep for the gasoline," says Pretty Boy, "so we're still fucked."

"Aw, lighten the hell up," Wolf says.

"We probably don't have enough water to make it to Black-fort, and even if we do they'll likely as not shoot us when we get there. We look like a bunch of crazy raiders."

"But we *are* kind of a bunch of crazy raiders, aren't we?" I ask, confused.

"It's usually not so obvious," Pretty Boy says. "It's vital that we trick them into thinking we're harmless. So as long as we look like this, we're screwed."

"Shut up, you're pissing me off," Wolf says.

Pretty Boy falls into a sulky silence. He grabs his flask off his hip and takes a swig of water, which makes my heart surge. Finally, I can take a drink without feeling too guilty about it.

"Hey, don't get all moody on us now," Tank says to Pretty Boy as I break out my canteen. "It's just Wolf being Wolf." He reaches over to clap him on the back.

Allowing myself a tiny sip of water, I'm far too focused to pay attention to anything else. It's only once I've finished my paltry drink that I notice everyone else has stopped walking. I turn around, about to ask what everyone is staring at, but as soon as I look their way I know.

Pretty Boy is standing with an arm outstretched, a look of

shock on his face. On the ground is his water flask, with the last of it draining out into the sand. The dirt takes it in as hungrily as any of us would; just like that, it's gone.

He unfreezes and falls to his knees, snatching up the canteen and placing it upright. As an afterthought he desperately scoops up the wet earth in his hands, as if he could take the water back from its clutches. But as the dirt sifts through his fingers it's already drying, disappearing as if it was never there.

Pretty Boy sits back on his heels and stays there. Everyone is dead silent. I screw the top back onto my canteen, suddenly afraid of it falling from my hands.

"What the hell did you do that for?" Pretty Boy asks after a few seconds, his voice shaky. He glares at Tank with red-rimmed eyes.

"I didn't do anything!"

"You fucking knocked it out of my hands!"

"I didn't—I didn't mean to! Come on, Pretty Boy, you know I would never..." Tank looks horrified.

"Well as it stands, I don't..." Pretty Boy sucks in a deep breath. "There's no way I can make it to..." He looks up at Wolf with his lower lip trembling. "Wolf, please."

"What do you want me to do?" Wolf asks, his face and voice hard. He's more serious than I've ever seen him, both the humor and ferocity absent, and it frightens me.

"I don't—" He gestures despairingly, the words dying in his throat. "I mean, it wasn't like I just *dropped* it—"

"I saw."

Pretty Boy opens his mouth to speak again. Wolf holds up a hand to silence him. He sighs and pushes his goggles up, leaving a streak of sweat and dirt behind. His face is stony as he rubs the bridge of his nose, and after a few seconds he slides the goggles back into place and looks up at Tank.

"Tank, give him your water." The sentence falls as final as a guillotine.

Tank doesn't argue, but I can see his hands shaking as he hands it over. Pretty Boy drops his empty flask and takes the new one from Tank's hand, clutching it against himself.

I stare at my feet. The silence feels thick, and I'm struck by the impression that all of them are strangers again.

Wolf turns back to the road and starts walking again. Dolly follows first, and then Pretty Boy, and then me. When I look back I see Tank picking up Pretty Boy's empty canteen and checking it for any drop of water before tossing it away again. He follows the group even more slowly than before, and nobody but me looks back at him.

As the sun saps our strength and the sand grows hotter, it's impossible not to notice how far Tank is falling behind. Wolf and Dolly exchange meaningful looks. Pretty Boy looks at nothing but the ground and doesn't say a word. His eyes are red, but dry.

I keep glancing back at Tank. He's struggling, sweat streaming down his body and chest heaving.

The next time I look back, he's stopped, his eyes closed. I look frantically at the others.

"Guys, wait, Tank is—" Nobody stops walking or so much as glances at me. "He stopped, shouldn't we wait...?"

"No," Wolf says without turning around.

"No?" I stop, staring at their backs as they continue to move forward.

"He's not gonna make it, Kid," Wolf says. "We keep walking."

Keep walking. Carry on. It's what I have to do, what I've always done.

I will my feet to move, telling myself this is the way things have to be, yet somehow I can't bring myself to. The idea of leaving Tank behind makes me feel sick. I remain motionless, all too aware of the others moving farther away every second.

But I can't continue.

I turn and walk back to Tank. He opens his eyes and gives me a weary half smile.

"Hey, Kid, it's okay," he says.

I offer my canteen to him.

"What are you doing?" he asks.

"Take it."

"No way."

"Come on, it's fine, you can have the last of it," I say. Forcing myself to crack a smile, I add, "It's not like I'm thirsty or anything, anyway."

He chuckles, but still hesitates; I give him an encouraging nod, and only then does he take the canteen and down the rest of it. Even I have enough common sense to know we're both screwed at this point with no water between us. Still, I can't regret it. I couldn't have lived with myself if I left him behind.

"Thanks, kiddo."

"Yeah." I start walking again, and Tank comes with me. "I mean, we're friends, right?" I add.

"Friends," he repeats. He smiles in a sad way and puts an arm around my shoulders, giving them a gentle squeeze before releasing me again. "Yeah, I guess so."

We catch up to the others, and nobody breathes a word to either of us.

It takes a while for it to sink in, but eventually I realize I'm going to die. I mean, I always knew it would happen, and probably sooner than later, but it feels too soon. Maybe it always does. I never thought it would be like this, though. All the rules my papa taught me about survival keep running through my mind. Trust no one. Eat anything edible, even if it's gross. And always bring enough water to get there and back again.

I force myself to keep pressing on, but I feel myself growing weaker. Every step is a little harder, comes a little slower than the one before it. My vision blurs. I do my best to focus on Pretty Boy's back in front of me. I cough, and my breath comes out as dry as sand.

Pretty Boy's silhouette warps. I can't tell if it's a trick of the sunlight or my own hazy vision.

"Guys, I—" I stop to cough again. My voice lowers to a raspy whisper. "I don't know if I can..."

I trail off. Nobody answers or even looks at me, or maybe I didn't even really speak aloud. Maybe my brain is boiling in my head. Maybe this is how people become crazies. Even as my thoughts melt, some survival instinct keeps me plowing forward. *Carry on,* I tell myself. Keep moving. Always.

It's not enough. Whiteness creeps up on the edges of my vision. I feel distant, as if I'm watching everything through a screen that is beginning to blur with static. My head feels hot and heavy.

"I don't feel good," I murmur, or maybe I don't. Everything goes white.

I don't realize I'm on the ground until I hear voices above me. The sand must be hot, but I can't feel it. I can't open my eyes, either.

"Is she dead?" Dolly's soft voice.

"As good as," Wolf says. "Dolly, no, don't poke her. She's out."

"Get up, kiddo." There's Tank's voice, closer than the rest. A hand shakes me and I will myself to move, but I can't.

"It's no use. Come on, Tank," Pretty Boy says. "We should be close now. You can probably make it."

"Then I'll wait for Kid to wake up."

"It's her own fault." Pretty Boy sounds irritated. "You'll both die if you stay."

"We need to get moving," Wolf says, "or we're all dead." A brief pause; a shuffle of feet. Footsteps fade away.

"Don't be stupid, Tank!"

"Tank?" Dolly again, even quieter than before. "They're both staying?"

"Looks like it. Let's go."

"Seriously, man? Seriously? I can't believe this shit." Pretty Boy's voice wanes, farther away. "You're an idiot, you know that? She ain't worth it."

Then there's silence, and a hand on my arm again.

"Get up, Kid," Tank says. "We have to find some shade, at least."

"I'm so tired," I say, the words barely audible. *So?* My papa's voice whispers on the edge of my mind.

"You have to get up," says Papa—no, Tank. But I can't.

I shake my head, and feel my grasp on the world slipping. I find relief in the stillness.

X
Wastelands

I dream of water, and wish I could dream forever, but I don't.

When I wake up again, my thoughts go immediately to the raw, dry pain in my throat, and then to the realization I'm moving. I peel my eyes open. The sunlight hurts. I see only the sky at first, and then, as I move my head, Tank's face. He's carrying me.

"Are we dead?" I ask, voice cracking.

"Don't think so, Kid," he says wearily. "Too thirsty to be dead."

"Makes sense," I say. I cough and run a dry tongue over my cracked lips. "Where are we going?"

"Blackfort."

"We won't make it, they said."

"We're gonna try."

I don't know what to say, and speaking hurts my throat anyway, so I shut up. Tank manages to continue for only a few minutes more before he stops. He carries me into the shade behind a boulder, where the sand isn't quite so hot. He sets me down and sinks to the ground.

"Just a little break," he says, leaning back against the rock and closing his eyes. His breath comes in shallow wheezes. "Wake me up in ten minutes."

I'm ready to pass out again myself, but my instinct screams

no. If I let myself go here, I won't wake up again. I force myself to stand and take a few shaky steps away from the resting spot. It's not like I haven't been here before, this awful dehydration and exhaustion. One of the last days with my papa, I asked for a drink and he told me there was nothing left. I remember that sinking feeling, that fear, that certainty I couldn't go on. And yet, I survived. It's kind of what I do.

I shield my eyes with a hand and survey the wastelands around us. Off in the distance I see the remnants of a building. There isn't anything more promising, so I force myself to stagger in that direction. Wind whistles around me, and I cover my eyes to shield them from the dust.

In the ruins there are a few metal cans lying around. I snatch them up eagerly, but only end up burning my hands on the hot metal to find them empty. I kick the cans aside and continue searching, opening ruined cabinets and drawers. I'm too weak to open some of them myself, and the effort saps my breath. Everything is empty. The place has been ransacked already.

I see movement out of the corner of my eye. The sight makes me gasp and whirl around, nearly falling over in the process. And there it is, sitting on the table: a lizard.

"What the hell?" I mutter, placing a hand on my chest to steady my racing heart. Of course there are still animals running around, but they're rare, like humans. We just have more of a tendency to clump together. I can't remember the last time I saw a little creature like this. My first thought is it's cute enough to keep as a pet. The second is wondering if I could stay alive by drinking its blood. I almost laugh ... and quickly become somber, thinking harder about it. It seems worth a shot.

I inch toward the tiny creature, slowly raising my hands.

"Hey, little guy," I attempt to coo, but it comes out raspy and disturbing. I sound like a creepy old man. "Come here, buddy."

I lurch forward and grab for it. My hands clamp down on

empty air. The lizard is gone in a flash, nimbly skittering away before I'm even close. I stay frozen, and despair flows over me like a wave. I would probably cry if my eyes weren't as dried out as the rest of me.

"Well, this is it," I say aloud. "I'm gonna die."

I sink to the ground and flop onto my back, accepting my fate. My head hits harder than expected. The action is accompanied by a strange clanging noise. I slowly raise my head and bring it down again. *Clang.* It's a hollow, metallic sound, definitely not the kind usually produced by either my head or the sand.

I sit up, feeling only dull curiosity at first but soon filled with realization. Almost afraid of feeling too hopeful, I wipe the sand away and dig down to what's hidden beneath: metal. I recognize this kind of hatch in the floor instantly. It's exactly the kind my own home had. It's a bomb shelter, just like the one I grew up in.

Once I reveal the edges of the hatch I try to pull it open, but it refuses to budge. I uncover more and more, fingers searching for a weakness or opening. Finally I find the latch, and the lock that goes with it. The lock is heavily rusted, but not weak enough to break with my bare hands. I take off my backpack and grab my gun, pointing it toward the lock.

I'm stopped by a vivid mental picture of the bullet ricocheting and killing me. It seems *far* too much like an appropriate ending for my mess of a life, and I lower the gun again. I take the safer option of using the butt of it. I beat at the lock, smashing the gun into the rusty metal as hard as I can. When nothing happens, I hit it again, and again, and again. I carry on until the dry skin on my knuckles cracks and bleeds, and keep going.

"One more time," I mutter to myself when my arms feel too weak to continue. I raise the gun and bring it down again, hard, the contact vibrating up my arms. Nothing. I suck in a breath through my teeth. "One more…" My hands bloodied and stinging, I strike again.

The lock breaks. Panting, I move the broken metal aside. I dig my hands underneath the hatch and pull, struggling to lift the heavy metal. It swings open to reveal a staircase. Only hints of sunlight pierce the depths below, but I don't have time to waste on being scared of the dark. I plunge downward. An awful smell is drifting out, bad enough to make me light-headed, but I hold my sleeve over my mouth and nose and continue downward.

The shelter is small and cramped and dark. I fumble along the wall, unable to see anything but fuzzy silhouettes. My hand catches a switch, and dim fluorescent bulbs flicker to life.

"Oh, wow," I whisper. The place looks a lot like the one I grew up in. If not for the stink, it might feel like home. Better yet, the walls are lined with shelves full of supplies. I see cans of food, bottles of medicine, bandages, soap, and, best of all, *water.* One shelf is full of dusty bottles of it. I rush forward and grab one, hands shaking as I struggle to remove the cap.

I've never tasted anything so good. The water is lukewarm, but still refreshing after the heat. As soon as I've had a taste my body screams for more, and I can't stop. I down an entire bottle in less than a minute, and am reaching for another when I remember Tank. I shove several bottles into my pack and turn to clamber up the stairs.

Then I notice the body.

It's off in a dim corner of the room, sprawled across a cot on the floor and mostly decayed. I've seen corpses rot incredibly fast in the heat, but underground it's cooler, so it's hard to judge how long he's been dead.

I take a few tentative steps toward it, noting the stain of blood on the mattress and the gun hanging limply in the body's hand. Locked up alone down here, it must have been suicide. So many supplies, and he killed himself.

I don't want to admit it to myself, but I can think of plenty of reasons why. My gaze shifts to another cot next to the body.

This one is empty. My brain churns out possibilities. The shelter was locked from the outside, so maybe his companion left intending to return, and never did. And this man could have waited, and waited, and finally got tired of waiting. My stomach twists as I remember long days and nights of wandering alone. Living in town was just as lonely.

I bend down and touch the corpse's hand. The others would probably strip his body for loot, but I can't bring myself to.

"Sorry, friend," I say quietly. "Sorry you got left behind." The loneliness reminds me I have a living friend to get back to. I shake off the sadness and half-run up the stairs.

I find him resting against the boulder with his eyes closed, completely still.

"Tank!"

His eyes open slowly. He smiles, looking tired and half-dead.

"Hey, buddy, we're gonna be okay!" I say. I drop to my knees and let my backpack fall to the ground, bottles of water spilling out. I see disbelief cross Tank's broad face, followed by joy, and he grabs and uncaps a bottle. The water spills across his face and down the front of his body in his eagerness.

"Holy shit," he says once he's finished the bottle, life seeping back into him. "How did you find this?"

"I was trying to catch a lizard," I say. "I found a bomb shelter full of stuff. There's first aid kits and food, too. Oh, and a dead body."

"Damn," he says, shaking his head. "I can't believe ... Where the hell did you *come* from, anyway, you crazy kid?"

"Oh, you know ... around. Same as everyone." I shove the rest of the water bottles into my pack, smile brightly, and stand up. "So, are we going to Blackfort?"

"You still want to meet up with the others?" he asks. He drags his bulky body up with visible effort.

"Of course!"

"They left us to die, you know."

I shrug.

"It's just the way things are, ain't it?"

"But you wouldn't leave me."

"Well…" I kick at the dirt and shrug. "Maybe I'm not as smart as the others, I guess?"

Tank laughs, a great booming laugh that makes me smile.

"Well I like you just the way you are, Kid." He ruffles my hair and grins. "Let's stock up at this bomb shelter of yours, and then we can go find the others."

We spot Blackfort from a distance, and my dread of the place only grows as we approach. It becomes more and more clear this town is no Steelforge, and a far stretch from Bramble or anywhere else I've been. A fence runs along the perimeter, sharp metal spikes reaching toward the sky. Inside it is the usual shamble of poorly made shelters amid a mess of crumbling buildings, but even so, it's off-putting. It looks bigger than other towns, the ragged edges of ruined buildings making intimidating silhouettes against the horizon. I'm not sure if it's the memory of the last town or the one I came from, but the sight makes me uneasy.

"You think we'll find the others here?" I ask Tank, trying to shake my nerves.

"Hope so. 'Course, they could have taken off already."

"And then how will we find them?"

"We won't," he says bluntly.

The town looms closer. The sun is setting, and its dying rays make the fence shine like knives. The wastelands are deceptively friendly at sunset, when the heat is dissipating and the chill of night hasn't set in yet. It almost seems more appealing to stay out in the wastes rather than venture into the unknowable town. I remember what Pretty Boy said about the place: *not very friendly*.

Flickers of light appear within the gated town, fires starting to ward off the night. They grow larger as we approach, until finally we find ourselves at the entrance. There are two armed guards standing outside. My heart starts to pound.

"What if they won't let us in?"

"They'll let us in. Relax."

"What if they only let me in and make you leave?"

"What? Why would they do that?"

"I don't know," I say, even though I definitely do. My chest feels painfully tight. I don't want to be alone again, especially not now, when I've finally found real friends.

"*Relax*. And just in case," Tank mutters as we approach, "if we see the others, pretend we don't know them."

"Why?" I ask, but by then the guards have noticed us. We stop in front of the guards and I resist the instinct to run when one of them points a gun at me.

"What's your business here?" The guard sounds like he's deliberately trying to make his voice deeper. He leans close to me and puffs out his chest, but Tank stands bigger and broader than the two guards combined. I scoot closer to him.

"Trading," Tank says, his voice a growl. It's far from the jovial tone he uses with me. I almost forgot how intimidating he can be. I put my hands on my hips and plaster on a solemn face, trying to be as frightening as I can be at just over five feet tall. The guards smirk, deflating my posturing and my pride.

"And what would two ragged waste-rats have to trade with *us*?" one of them asks, mocking.

I look at Tank. He nods. I remove my backpack and show them the inside, filled to the brim with clean bottles of water. The guards each take a turn peering in, their hard faces revealing nothing, and mutter to each other.

"Might be that there's more where this came from," I say, "if we can work something out."

They confer again, and one of them gives us a sharp nod.

"All right. Are you two armed?"

I look at Tank again.

"Of course we are," he rumbles. "And we're going to stay that way."

"Then keep 'em put away. Act like a threat and you'll be treated like a threat, you hear?"

We both nod.

"In with you, then."

They unlock the gate and allow us in. One of the guards accompanies us. As they shut the gate I nervously realize this is the only way in or out. The gate has closed around us like a bear trap. I swallow hard and stay behind Tank as we follow the guard into the depths of the town.

On the inside, Blackfort looks much like any other town. It's the same collection of ramshackle buildings with their crumbly parts patched up. But torches light our path, and the streets are empty. Not only does the town have a fence, but guards patrol the perimeter and stand watch at the entrances of the bigger buildings. As we pass through the center of town, I see something that strikes dread deep within me: a wooden post with a noose hanging from it.

"We hang troublemakers here," the guard says proudly, noticing my interest. "Ain't worth the ammo of a proper shooting. Matter of fact, we've got a few lined up for an execution tomorrow."

"That so?" I ask, my voice squeaking. I risk a peek at Tank.

"What are they in for?" Tank asks, with considerably more composure than I can muster up.

"Cannibalism," the guard spits out with disgust. "Damn sharks wandered into town earlier today, but we were ready for them. Matter of fact, we were warned specifically about 'em." He looks over his shoulder at us and grins. "Maybe you can come watch the hanging at sunrise."

Oh, shit.

XI
The Rescue

I stay as calm as possible while the guard escorts us to a room for the night. It's tiny and outfitted only with two sleeping cots. He promises we can speak with the mayor in the morning, and informs us that there's a guard right outside. *Just to be safe,* he assures us. Normally I would be giddy over such safety, but not now. The guards, the fence, the capacity to take in strangers: All of it says a lot about Blackfort, and it isn't good news for us. Whoever is in charge has total control over everyone here, visitors included. The idea is terrifying to me. Somehow I imagine the fence isn't only for keeping people out.

Once the door is closed I allow my panic to set in. I sit on one of the hard cots and put my face in my hands.

Tank paces the length of the cramped room, stirring up dust.

"He said they were warned about them," I say, recalling the guard's words. "What does that mean?"

"I don't know," Tank says. "Last town was ready for us, too. Something's going on." He continues to pace. The whole thing gives me a headache just to think about—but more important than that is the problem currently at hand.

"So what are we going to do?" I ask, raising my head to look at him.

"I don't know," he says again. He stops pacing and sinks onto the cot across from me. "I just look scary and kill people, I don't make plans."

"Shit," I say. Plans have never been my strong point, either. I pull my knees to my chest and hug them, trying desperately to think of something. I'm stumped, and evidently so is Tank; we sit in silence as time ticks onward.

"We should eat," Tank suggests. His stomach rumbles as if to second the notion. "Maybe it'll help us think better."

We dump out the contents of our bags. Along with the dry remains of the food we took for traveling, we each gathered a few cans from the bomb shelter. Some of them were labeled, not that it's much use to me. Tank can read at a very basic level, bits and pieces he was in the process of learning before the bombs dropped, but after scrutinizing some of the cans he admits the only word he knows is *beans*. We each take a can.

Without any utensils it's hard to eat, and I have to drink from the metal container. I end up spilling an unfortunate amount down the front of my already-dirty shirt. The beans are cold and bland, but they fill up my stomach. Tank adds some townie-meat for taste, which bothers me less than I'd expect. He gulps down another couple of cans after I'm done.

With my belly full and a bed beneath me, it's difficult to resist the urge to pull out my blanket and sleep my troubles away. My brain is so tired it hurts to think.

"Got any ideas?" Tank asks.

"Not a clue."

"Me neither."

I sigh and lean my head against the wall, picking at the peeling paint with one idle hand. I wish Wolf was here with his wild ideas that always seem to work out in the end.

"You know," Tank says, "maybe we shouldn't do anything."

"What?"

"It might be impossible to save them, and we would just be risking our asses for nothing." He shrugs. "Might be better to just cut our losses."

"No way!"

"You're being stubborn, Kid. They'd do the same."

"I don't think so," I say. "I mean...the water issue was one thing. They would've died if they had waited for us. But, when there's a chance...I think they'd give it a try." I think about it. "Okay, maybe not Pretty Boy."

"Definitely not Pretty Boy," Tank agrees. "I mean, he and I get on all right, but I know he'd never risk his ass for me. For any of us."

"Why does he stay with you guys, anyway?" I ask. "Couldn't he just leave one night?"

"He's..." He pauses and searches for the right words. "He's, you know, one of us. He may not act like it sometimes, but he is. Just like the rest of us, probably too screwed up to make it with everyone else. He's just better at hiding it." His face hardens suddenly. "You remember that, Kid, all right?"

"What do you mean?"

"What I mean is..." He sighs and shrugs. "What I mean is even though he's my friend and all, that doesn't mean I trust him. None of us do, and you shouldn't either. Okay?"

"Okay," I say, though I don't quite get it.

"Anyway, back to the rescue plan, if you're sure about that."

"Ah, yeah." I scratch my head. "Do we even know where they're keeping them?"

"There was a building near the noose with a few guards outside. It *could* be a jail," Tank says.

"How many guards?"

"Two or three."

"Think we could handle them?"

Tank shrugs.

"If we take them by surprise? Probably. But gunshots will bring others running."

"Aw, shit, you're right." I sigh and press my palms against my eyelids, trying to ward off a steadily building headache. "What if we just hit 'em over the head with something?"

"Could do. I think I packed a crowbar."

"And I could get a...a rock or something," I say. "And then..." Then, who knows. I try to picture it: the two of us, knocking out the guards and busting into the jail. We would need a key, but one of the guards would probably have it. We'd grab the key, release the others, and fight our way out. I wouldn't be so scared of taking on the guards with the others on our side. It seems like a decent plan to me.

"Well, do you have any better ideas?" I ask Tank.

"Nope."

"So I guess that'll have to do." We don't have the time to construct anything more concrete. The guard said the hanging would be at dawn, and I'm guessing we should hightail it out of here before the whole town is awake.

"We have to take care of the guard here, first."

"Oh, right. Shit."

"Go distract him, and I'll come do what I do," Tank says. He sifts through his bag and pulls out his crowbar. The metal is stained with rust and what looks like old blood.

"Oh...you mean, like, *right* now?"

"When else?"

I guess he's right. Still, I feel nervous. I try to fight back my fear as I sling my backpack over my shoulder and head over to the doorway.

I glance at Tank, take a deep breath, and walk out.

The guard is leaning against the wall across from the doorway.

He stands at attention as the door opens and fixes a pair of mean eyes on me. I smile nervously.

"Where do you think you're going?" he asks.

"I...gotta piss," I say. I move out of our doorway, leaving it partially open, and take a few steps toward the stairwell leading out of the building. I try to act nonchalant, but my movements feel stiff. The guard turns to follow me, putting his back to our door.

"Oh." He almost loses interest, but regains it after a second glance. "So why are you bringing your bag?"

"Uh," I say. I try to think of something smart, but my mind fails me. "In case of..." I start, and then stumble over my words. "In case of trouble?"

"Won't be any trouble," he says. "We have this place on lockdown."

"Right, well, umm," I say. I can feel my face turning red. "I still need it."

"Why's that?"

I gape like a fish. He stares at me.

"None of your business!" I blurt out, not knowing what else to say.

"Actually, it is," he says. "I'll come keep an eye on you."

"No!" I say quickly. His hand is now resting on the holster of his gun. "It's...I need the bag for..." I pause, stutter, and finally come up with something. "It's...girl stuff, you know?"

"Girl stuff?" he repeats incredulously. We stare at each other in silence. His face changes as he understands, gradually shifting from fierceness to embarrassment. "Oh," he says. "You mean...Oh."

"Yeah," I say. My face is probably purple by now, and his is reddening as well. "So..."

"Fine, fine, off with you then. Hurry up or I'll come looking."

He makes a shooing motion at me. Out of the corner of my eye I see our door sliding open, and Tank's bulky form emerging. Realizing I have to stall a bit longer, I try to grab his attention again.

"Where should I go?"

"Oh. Right. If you leave this building, the latrines are that—" He turns to point, and comes face-to-face with Tank. "Way?"

Tank grabs the guard's head and slams it into the wall. He crumples to the floor without so much as a cry.

"Let's go," Tank says. I nod, exhaling a breath I hadn't known I was holding in, and follow him outside.

We make our way toward the execution square, dodging behind buildings whenever someone approaches. It's hard to shake the feeling we'll be surrounded by guards at any moment. I try to stay calm and follow Tank's lead, moving when he moves and waiting when he waits. Eventually we find ourselves around the corner of the building Tank mentioned.

"Can you tell if it's actually the jail?" I ask. He shrugs. I shrug back.

"As good a bet as any," he says. He fishes his crowbar out of his pack. I search around on the ground until I find a decent-size rock. "I'll take the guard on the left," he says.

"Got it," I say, straightening up. As my arms shake I wonder if I should have picked a smaller rock, but it's too late.

Tank holds up three fingers and counts down as I try to steady my grip. *Three. Two. One.*

Tank turns the corner and charges at the guards. I raise the rock above my head and follow. The guards are too surprised to pull their weapons. Tank plows into one of them and knocks him off his feet, and I fling my rock at the other before he can react.

It falls short of its mark. *Very* short.

The guard turns toward me with an incredulous look, and I curse and fumble for my knife. As soon as I get it out of my boot I run to attack, but it's not fast enough.

"Intruders!" the guard bellows, his voice echoing as loud as a siren in the quiet town. "In the execution square!"

"Sh-shit!" I plunge my knife toward his stomach, but he grabs my arm and twists it, making me cry out. The knife falls. I desperately kick at his shins as he reaches for his gun.

"Heads up!"

I duck. The crowbar whistles through the air above my head and slams into the guard's chest. His grip on my arm goes slack as he falls.

I scramble to pick my knife up and turn to Tank, panting for breath.

"Well, so much for secrecy," he says, and reaches into his pack for a gun. I shove the knife back into my boot and do the same, retrieving the handgun that Wolf gave me. It feels strange and unfamiliar in my hands, and I fumble to find a way to hold it that doesn't seem awkward.

Tank and I bust through the door to the building, guns ready.

We find a small, bare room which is very clearly *not* a jail. There's only a table and a chair, with a lone woman sitting behind it. She's middle-aged and plain-faced, and her expression upon seeing us is more skeptical than afraid.

There's an awkward pause as we all stare at each other. It's hard to say who is more surprised by the situation.

"Who the *fuck* are you?" the woman asks.

"Uh," I say. "This...isn't the jail, huh?"

She stares at me.

"'Fraid not, hon," she says. "This is the mayor's office."

The door opens behind us and the room floods with guards. I look around and count three, seven, *nine* guns total pointed at us.

Tank and I simultaneously let our weapons drop and raise our hands in surrender.

The woman, who I now assume is the mayor, lets out a derisive chuckle at our expense.

"Oops," she says, grinning. "Looks like someone made a mistake."

"We really should've thought this out better," I whisper to Tank.

"Tell me about it," he mutters back.

"Now, let's get you two to that jail you were looking for." The mayor motions to the guards. "Take 'em in with the others, boys."

The jail, as it turns out, is the place *next to* the mayor's office. It's a stout building that smells like sweat and piss. The guards jeer at us as we're marched down a row of cells. Many of them are full. Some prisoners beg for release as we pass by, some rattle the bars and shout vulgarities, and others stare at us with dead eyes. I've never seen a jail this full. The town I came from shot troublemakers on sight, so the jail only held the occasional drunk who needed to cool off. Chaining people like this somehow feels worse. The sight of so many prisoners makes me angry in a way that surprises me. I suddenly find myself wishing we had taken down a few more guards before ending up here, and hoping we'll have another chance to crack some heads.

They lead us back to the very end of the row, a dark and lonely corner where most of the cells are empty. One, however, is very much not so.

"*Please* let me out of here!" a familiar voice says. An arm reaches through the bars, clutching at a guard's leg. "I don't belong with these psychopaths, I swear, this is all just a big—" Pretty Boy turns his pretty, pleading eyes to us and cuts off abruptly. "Oh, fuck."

"Hey to you, too," Tank says grimly.

"Mayor's right," one of the guards says. "Looks like this is the big guy who was supposed to be with them."

"What about this one?" Another one of them points to me.

"Dunno. The broadcast didn't say anything about an ugly little boy, did it?"

I sigh.

"Nope. Ah, well, might as well toss 'im in. If he knows them, reckon he deserves a hanging."

They open the door and shove us inside. Wolf, Dolly, and Pretty Boy are all sitting on the dirty floor, the latter as far from the others as he can manage to be. With Tank there, the five of us can barely fit. As the door slams behind us I squeeze into the corner next to Pretty Boy.

"Oh, it's a miracle, you guys are alive," Wolf deadpans. "Thank the Lord, we're saved."

"Don't start," Tank says. He sits with a groan. "We tried."

"No, really. I'm thrilled. Now we can die together, a big fucking happy family."

I sigh and let my head rest on the cold metal bars, staring up at the ceiling.

So much for our big rescue.

XII
Prisoners

When I wake up, sunlight is streaming through the bars on the window.

I blink at the light and slowly regain my bearings. I realize I'm slumped against Pretty Boy's shoulder and quickly sit up. He looks at me with hollow eyes.

"You drooled on me," he says.

"Sorry," I whisper, my face heating up. "On the bright side, we're not dead yet."

"Clearly," he says. He squints at the window. "I stayed up all night, thinking they would be here any second."

"You didn't sleep at all?"

"No. I figured if I was about to die…" He chokes on the word, his eyes watering. "I want to at least be awake for my final moments."

"Yeah…" I say, trying to think of something meaningful enough to redeem myself for drooling. Nothing comes to mind. I attempt a joke instead. "Wouldn't want to wake up dead, right?" He gives me a completely unamused look. I sigh. Something about Pretty Boy always turns me into a bigger idiot than usual. And some stupid part of me still desperately wants him to like me, despite his issues and the fact we hardly know each other.

"Say, Pretty Boy," I say as that sparks a thought. "Would you mind telling me your real name?" If there was ever a time for it, it'd be now.

He looks over at me, stares silently for a long moment, and shakes his head.

"What's the point?" he asks dully.

Before I can respond, the door to the jail opens and the mayor enters with a handful of armed guards. They come down the dim and cramped hallway directly to our cell. Pretty Boy sits up straighter next to me, and Dolly awakens at the sound of footsteps. Wolf stirs soon after her, and wakes Tank with a kick. I find myself scooting closer to Dolly for protection.

The mayor glares down at us behind the bars.

"Well, looks like it's your lucky day, sharks," she says. "Your execution has been postponed."

Nobody speaks. I hold my breath, unsure if I should be grateful or if this will be a new, worse development.

"Turns out you're wanted at the radio tower," she says. "Alive."

"Where the hell is that?" Wolf asks.

"You're not in a position to be asking questions," she says coldly. "All you need to know is that you're being transported."

"Why?" he asks.

"I said you're not—"

"And who wants us?"

"You—"

"How are we getting there?" he asks. "How long will it take?"

The mayor stares at him, unblinking. Wolf breaks into a grin.

"Aw, I'm just fucking with you. Let's get going, I'm tired of sitting around."

She turns a stiffened back toward us and gestures to the guards. They unlock the door with a creak. I recoil, but there isn't enough room to make it far. A man grabs my arm and pulls me to my feet.

"Tie them up," the mayor commands.

The guard forces my wrists behind my back and binds them with rope, pulling it so tightly I can barely wriggle my fingers. The others get the same treatment. Pretty Boy whimpers pathetically as they tie him. At least I'm holding it together better than him.

They push us along in front of them, a line trailing out of the cell and through town. A small crowd has gathered around the execution square. Disappointed by the lack of a hanging, they jeer and throw things at us as we're herded past. Wolf shouts insults back at them, far too entertained by the entire situation.

Just outside the gate, a truck waits. It's a bulky, durable-looking vehicle with a sizable back compartment, probably used for transporting goods.

"Well, hell, looks like we got ourselves first-class treatment," Wolf says. "Mighty kind of you. It'll be nice not having to walk everywhere."

The guards ignore him. They push us forward and into the back. I'm not tall enough to climb in without the use of my arms, so one of the guards lifts me up and tosses me inside. Once we're all in, they shut the doors. It's nearly pitch-black inside. I can only see silhouettes of the others.

When my eyes adjust, I see the compartment is filled with crates of supplies: food, water, and other goods. I guess that includes us. If Blackfort is willing to comply, they must be trading for something valuable. The thought gnaws on the corners of my mind, and I think back to when we were attacked by raiders. They mentioned a reward, too. Someone's definitely out to get us, but who? And how is it that wandering raiders and the town of Blackfort both know about it?

"I don't understand what's going on," I mumble, looking at Wolf for answers.

"Don't look at me," he says with a shrug.

"Has this happened before?"

"What, facing imminent death? Yeah, all the time."

"No, I mean being transported like this."

"Oh, right." He pauses to think. "Nope, don't think so."

"Well, what do you think about it?"

"I'm just glad not to have a noose around my neck, ain't you?"

"I guess." I lean against a crate, letting my head loll back.

My efforts to rest are undermined when the truck starts moving. The engine makes a god-awful roaring sound as it starts up, and continues to growl unpleasantly. The compartment shakes and shifts as we move, making me slide around on the floor. So, no sleep for me. I sit up and look around at the others.

"So...what are we gonna do?" I ask. Nobody answers. I sigh and shift, stretching out my legs and trying to better position myself so I won't slide so much. When I look down at my outstretched boots, a realization hits me.

When they put us in jail, they took away our weapons and my backpack, but they didn't search me very thoroughly. Perhaps because I don't seem like much of a threat—which is a valid assessment—they didn't bother to check inside my boots... which means I still have my knife.

I squirm around in vain attempts to dislodge it. As it turns out, it's not such an easy task without being able to use my hands. I awkwardly wiggle one way, and another, and stick my foot in the air and shake it, but nothing happens.

"You gotta piss or something, Kid?" Wolf asks. When I look up, everyone is staring at me. I blush.

"Err, no," I say. "It's my knife. I think I still have it."

"Well, shit, get it out then!" Wolf says.

"That's what I'm trying to do!" A frustrated sigh escapes my lips. I abandon all dignity and stick both feet in the air, flailing them with all the effort I can muster up. *Finally* the knife falls out, and narrowly misses hitting me in the face. It clatters onto the floor just beside my head.

"Nice technique," Wolf says. I ignore him, and push myself up to a sitting position. I slide closer to the knife, trying to grab it with my bound hands.

Just when I'm finally close, the truck makes a sharp turn. I topple over and slide across the floor to slam against the opposite wall. The knife slides, as well—and ends up just beside Pretty Boy.

I look at the knife and up at him. A look I can't identify flashes through his eyes, and I remember what Tank said about not trusting him. If he got free, would he even help the rest of us?

"Aw hell no," Wolf says from the other side of the truck. "Don't even think about it, Pretty Boy." He starts to scoot over, fixing him with a hard gaze. "Slide the knife to me."

Pretty Boy bends over, reaching for the knife. Wolf scoots faster, face screwed up in determination. Just as Pretty Boy is about to grab the knife, Wolf launches himself at him, head-butting him in the chest. The air goes out of Pretty Boy with an audible *oof* and he collapses with Wolf on top of him. The knife skitters away.

"Get off of me!" Pretty Boy yells, attempting to wiggle free.

"Give me the knife!"

"I don't even have it!"

"You guys are both being idiots," Tank says. "Calm your shit and stop making so much noise."

Rather than heed his advice, Wolf does his best to beat the crap out of Pretty Boy despite his lack of hands.

The truck swerves suddenly and sends everyone tumbling. I crash into the side of the compartment once more, slide back the other way as the truck swerves again, and end up sprawled across Dolly's lap. She looks down at me with a slightly alarmed expression as I wiggle helplessly. The others are similarly entangled in a heap of limbs. The truck stops.

"The hell just happened?" Wolf asks, still half on top of Pretty Boy. The latter tries to say something, but with his face pressed against the floor of the truck it's hard to decipher it.

"The truck stopped," I say.

"Very helpful, Kid, as always."

The growl of the engine cuts off, and so does our conversation. In the silence I hear doors slamming as the guards exit the truck, followed by the crunch of footsteps.

The truck doors swing open and sunlight pours in.

"What are you idiots doing?" the guard asks, scrutinizing us.

I notice the knife glinting conspicuously a few feet away. I try to slide a foot over to cover it, but unfortunately the movement only captures his attention. He climbs into the compartment and snatches up the weapon.

"Ah, trying to escape, eh?" he asks, smirking and dangling it from one hand. "No such luck, sharkies." He turns around and yells to his partner. "Found the problem yet?"

"Tires are blown. We got spares?" a voice answers from outside.

"Yeah, I'll get 'em. Find out what we hit, would you?"

"Got it."

Meanwhile, the guard uses my knife to cut a length of rope off the supply crates.

"Just so you lot don't get any ideas..." He reaches down, forcibly pushing and pulling the pile of us apart. It's hard for anyone to retaliate much, bound as we are. I squirm around until I manage to flip onto my stomach and crane my neck, trying to see what he's doing to the others. I can't tell what's happening, but it sounds like a struggle.

I can finally see when the guard moves: He's used the rope to bind Wolf and Pretty Boy back-to-back.

"No fucking way," Wolf growls. Pretty Boy looks horrified.

"Good luck escaping now," the guard says, grinning. He's about to give the same treatment to Tank and Dolly when his partner returns.

"We have a problem," he says.

"Yeah?"

"A big problem."

He turns to him.

"What is it?"

The guard outside holds something up. I see the glint of sun off of metal, blades sharp as fangs. My stomach twists as I realize what it is: a strip of road spikes.

"This wasn't an accident," he says, his face paling.

"Shit." The guard lets the rope drop and stands, reaching for his gun. "Raiders on the trade route. We need to get the hell out of here, and—"

Gunfire interrupts his sentence, and the guard standing outside falls with a choked cry. The man inside stares, slack-jawed. In the distance I hear whoops and catcalls and shouts, growing closer by the second. It doesn't just sound like raiders. It sounds like crazies.

"Untie us," Pretty Boy begs. "Please. Please. Don't let me die tied to this maniac!"

"For once I agree. It would be fucking embarrassing," Wolf says.

The guard ignores them. He runs to the back of the truck and grabs his injured companion, hoisting him up. He slams the doors shut behind him and bends down to assess the damage.

"I'm fine," the wounded man gasps, while the blood leaking from him says otherwise.

"I can treat his wound," Pretty Boy says. "I can help. Untie me."

"Shut up!" the uninjured guard yells. He rips off part of his shirt and ties it around the bullet hole, his sloppiness revealing he has no idea what he's doing.

Outside, the noise draws closer every second. Soon it's clear they're just outside, and there are a lot of them. Fists and weapons rain down on the sides of the truck, the sound exploding like gunfire inside. I flinch as something hits the wall just beside my head. Since the truck doors open from the outside, I know they're messing with us, toying with their prey before they go for the kill.

"Just listen to me. *Listen*. There's no way you can fight all of them," Pretty Boy says, speaking like he's trying to coax an animal out of hiding. "If you untie us, we can help. We won't tell anyone you let us free."

The guard hesitates. As his ailing friend loses strength and consciousness, he seems to consider the offer. He reaches into his pocket for the knife.

The doors to the truck burst open. Noise rushes inside, cackling and jeering filling the truck. There's a mob outside. Faces swim in my vision as they clamber to get inside. I scoot away and press my back against the crates. The guard pulls out his gun and fires wildly into the crowd outside. Few of them react, and they cackle madly as their companions fall. For every one that goes down, another two spring up. They look wild, faces crusted with dried blood, skin peeling from sunburn, scraps of clothing hanging off their lean and scarred bodies.

These aren't raiders like Wolf's crew. They're madmen who know nothing but mindless violence. Sometimes the wastelands swallow men up and they don't come out the same. Whether it's the radiation or the heat or something else, their minds are just broken.

Panic surges in my gut as a memory hits me: hiding in an abandoned building with my papa, a pack of crazies right outside. I never saw them, but I heard them as they screamed and jeered. Papa held one hand over my mouth. The other held a gun, and it shook. I had never seen him shake like that.

They didn't find us, but another traveler wasn't so lucky. She screamed all night, just yards away from our hiding spot. Papa had to put her down himself, after the crazies had left her writhing in the dust.

I drag my mind back to the present as the mob surges forward and into the truck, a swarming mass of crazed faces and reaching arms. The fallen guard goes first, swallowed by greedy hands. The second guard is next. He tries to fight back, gun firing several times. It doesn't make a difference. He disappears with a scream.

I catch a glint of something on the floor and recognize my knife, forgotten again. I wriggle my way toward it. Luckily, the mob seems to be temporarily distracted with their new playthings. I can hear the guards screaming, and try to ignore my rising panic as I grab the knife. I saw frantically at the ropes on my wrists. The knife is slippery in my sweaty palms, but the rope gradually thins.

I can only hope it will be fast enough. The mob's bloodthirst won't be sated for long.

"Pass the knife, Kid!" Pretty Boy hisses from behind me. "Hurry!"

"It's hard," I huff out, struggling with my nearly numb fingers. Finally, the knife saws through and the ropes go slack. Blood rushes back into my hands.

I get on my hands and knees and crawl to the closest person: Dolly. I hack at the ropes binding her, ignoring the pins-and-needles sting as feeling returns to my fingers. I'm not fast enough.

A hand closes on my leg, and I'm yanked backward too quickly to scream. The knife clatters out of my hands, and I catch a glimpse of the horrified faces of the others as the crazies drag me away.

XIII
Crazies

I'm in a sea of writing bodies. I find myself pulled and pushed, choked by the reek of blood and sweat. Hands tug at my clothes, my hair, my skin. Nails like claws drag across my arms and leave bloody trails. I open my mouth to scream, but can't even hear it through the noise around me. It's a huge pack of crazies, at least a couple dozen from what I can see.

I use my bony elbows to jab around me. It's enough to grant me open air. I try to run, but a leg catches me in the knees and sends me tumbling. My face hits the dirt. The mob cackles as they drag me back.

Fists and feet pummel me, but never steel. They don't want to kill me yet, they just want to play with me. The thought is not reassuring.

I notice a flash of Dolly's blue hair amid the chaos and fight my way in her direction. I shove my way through the crowd until she's within sight, and struggle to stay there as the mob surges around me.

"Pretty, pretty," a man says, leering at her. He runs a hand down the front of her shirt and tugs, ripping the fabric. Dolly's eyes flash dangerously.

A second later, a knife is buried deep into the man's eye. He screams and Dolly yanks it back out, slashing at others nearby.

The man stumbles into the crowd and they laugh at him, shove him to the dirt, excited by the sight of his blood. Several jump on the weakened man, tearing into him with knives and teeth.

I try to move closer to Dolly, but someone grabs me by the hair and yanks me back. Another hand clamps on to my arm and pulls me in the opposite direction. A vicious tug-of-war ensues. They tug me one way and then the other until it feels like I'm going to be ripped in half. Finally the hand on my head loses its grip, pulling out some hair in the process, and I stumble forward. The hand releases me, and I fall to my knees. Dolly is gone. I'm surrounded by grinning, mad faces.

A creature barely recognizable as a woman crouches next to me, serrated knife in hand. I stop struggling as she lightly presses the tip of the blade against my wrist. The steel ghosts its way up my arm and neck while I cringe. She rests the flat of it against my face.

"Eyes or tongue?" she asks, breath reeking of rotten meat.

"Um, neither, please," I squeak out, trying to breathe as little as possible.

She smiles too wide, showing a nearly toothless mouth.

"Tongue it is," she says. She shoves her free hand into my mouth, and I choke on the taste of blood and dirt. Before she can grab my tongue, I bite down as hard as I can. My teeth break the skin and she screeches wildly. She yanks her hand back and the knife swings down toward me.

I catch her wrist with my free hand with the knife just inches from my face. We strain, unmoving, neither of us strong enough to overpower the other. The woman is stick-thin, but her anger and savagery lend her strength. The knife inches closer to my face; soon it's just a centimeter away from my nose.

I wrench my other hand free just in time. With her knife about to sink into my skin, I instinctively jut my hand out to stop it. The steel cuts deep into my palm, and pain shoots all the way up to my elbow. I force her back, she yanks the knife away with a snarl—and the blade catches my little finger, slicing it clean off.

I stare at the stump where my finger used to be as blood begins to gush out. Luckily the woman with the knife is just as distracted as I am, though by something else: Tank charging into the fray. With his hands tied behind his back, he barrels into the crowd, knocking people down left and right. He goes down quickly but takes several others with him, crushing them beneath his weight.

I take advantage of the distraction and scramble to my feet, holding my injured hand against me and shoving people aside as I make my way back to the truck.

Wolf and Pretty Boy are in the crowd as well. They're still tied back-to-back. Wolf seems intent on following Tank's lead and rushing into the mob, while Pretty Boy is trying to run in the opposite direction. They lurch back and forth, neither of them able to get anywhere.

I force my way through the mob of crazies, weaving between them and darting under their legs. Everyone is distracted enough by the others that I can slip by and reach the truck. I pull myself into the back, panting, and crouch beside the boxes. My hand has gone numb, but blood is still spurting. And my finger...my finger is gone. Where my pinky used to be is just a bloody stub. I stare at it, wiggling my other fingers. It's strange, as though I can *feel* it still there, but it's gone.

And the others are still out in that awful mob. I have to do something. I refuse to run away and hide like Pretty Boy would. But what can I do? My knife is gone. I have nothing.

My heart sinks as I hear the crazies approach, their loud and barely human voices signaling their arrival. The crazies don't even speak properly, only using guttural noises and broken phrases to communicate. I hear "the small one" and "blood" and "kill" as they approach. Everything else is unintelligible, but none of it sounds pretty. I squeeze between two boxes, trying to hide without losing my view of the outside. Three of them are approaching. Luckily, none of them are armed; unluckily, they could easily kill me bare-handed. Desperate, I grab some cans of food out of a box, cradling them in one arm and poising to throw with my uninjured hand. As soon as one of the men climbs into the truck, I send a metal can flying at him.

It sails right past his head. He looks surprised, then cackles madly. The next can catches him right in the teeth and sends him stumbling backward. He falls.

Not waiting for the next one, I take my ammo and run, jumping out of the truck and past them. I stagger precariously for a few steps before catching my balance, and take a look behind me at the three men. They stare at me. I throw a can at them, catching one in the shoulder, and take off running. Shouts and howls follow me.

I run as fast as my scrawny legs can move. My path loops around the perimeter of the truck, marked with an occasional pause to launch a can of food behind me. I run around the truck once, twice, three times, gasping for breath and wondering how I haven't been caught yet—and a man steps into my vision, growling like a dog. I skid to a stop, turn in the other direction, and collide with one of the guys who were chasing me. I stumble and fall. The remaining cans spill from my hands.

One of the men grabs at me, but I dodge his grip and roll sideways—and keep rolling, until I reach the truck. Not the most graceful exit, but it'll do. I tumble under and crawl into the darkness, panting for breath.

I'm not alone down here. For one moment I expect it to be Pretty Boy hiding again. Instead I find one of the guards. It's the one who was shot, and apparently he isn't quite dead yet. He raises his head, eyes dull, and points a gun in my direction, but it's halfhearted. After a moment he lets his head and weapon fall again, and sighs wearily. His head droops back, as if he exhaled the last of his energy.

I crawl closer and ensure his eyes are closed. When he doesn't respond, I snatch the gun out of his hand. His eyes flutter open and he looks at me again, but does nothing.

I retreat, half-dragging the gun. It's a huge, heavy assault rifle, not at all like my handgun. When I crawl out from beneath the truck, I try to hold it like I know how to use it.

The three crazies from before are still there, waiting. One of them grins at the sight of me.

"Gun?" he says, jerking closer. "Ha. Ha, ha. Too big for the little boy."

"As if," I say, trying to sound confident. I pull the trigger.

Bullets spray wildly, mostly hitting sand as I stumble from the recoil. Somehow, miraculously, I manage to hit the man. He falls with a snarl, blood streaming from multiple bullet holes.

I try to keep my tough face on despite the growing pain in my injured hand. My hand and the gun are slick with blood. Breathing heavily, I point the barrel at the other two slack-jawed crazies. They take off running. I give chase, blood pumping, giddy to be the hunter for once.

I stop as I spot the huge mob of crazies. I *could* point the gun into the crowd and go wild, maybe mow down every last one of them, but the thought makes me queasy. And with my luck I'd probably gun down my friends, too.

"All right!" I yell, trying to make my small voice carry over the noise. It doesn't work. "All right!" I try once more, still to no avail. Frustrated, I raise the gun and fire into the air.

This captures their attention. The crowd quiets down, hungry eyes on me.

"I just want my friends," I say, "please."

The crazies jeer and hiss. Someone throws a bottle that narrowly misses me.

"Dolly?" I search the mob for signs of her shocking blue hair. "Dolly!"

She shoves her way out of the crowd. She's limping, blood running down her leg, with her clothes torn and her hair in wild disarray. She's still clutching my knife.

"Are you okay?" I ask, although clearly neither of us is. She silently hands my knife back. I wipe it off, put it back into my boot, and place the gun into her more capable hands. For a moment she stares at it, looking even more dazed and distant than usual. She slowly looks back at the mob of crazies. Some of them are circling closer to us now that I haven't opened fire immediately. A frightening look comes over Dolly.

"Wait," I say. "We need to make sure the others are—"

The burst of gunfire is shockingly loud. I drop to my knees and clap my hands over my ears. A mess of blood and horrible screaming follows. The mob falls one after another. They don't even attempt escape. Some of them lunge at us; they drop like flies. Bodies pile up. After a few seconds, I squeeze my eyes shut.

When the gunfire dies, it leaves a hollow silence. Dolly is still jamming the trigger, producing dull clicks. I hesitantly open my eyes.

There are bodies everywhere, mounds of them, and *messy* bodies. Sometimes it's hard to tell where one ends and another begins. I fight the urge to vomit. There's no time, because there are still others left, more than I expected.

As the remnants realize we're out of ammo, they grow bold again. They approach us, grabbing weapons from their fallen comrades. One of them beats two metal bars together, the harsh sound ringing out louder and louder as he draws closer.

"Shit," I say. *Clank.*

Dolly holds out a hand. *Clank.*

"Knife." *Clank.*

I hand it over, shakily rising to my feet again.

Clank.
Clank.
Clank.

"Stay close," Dolly says, and they're on us.

She slits the first man's throat before he can touch her. Blood gushes out like a fountain, splattering all over my face. A kick forces the next one back, followed by a swift elbow to one behind her.

The man with the crowbars comes for me, grinning with bloody teeth.

"Dolly!" I squeak as the first crowbar whistles toward my head. I barely duck. Dolly reaches over me and stabs him in the chest before he can use the second. Two men grab her from behind as she yanks it out again. They pull her backward and separate us.

I drop to the ground, grab a crowbar from the dying man, and swing at the nearest pair of legs. With a resounding *crack* to his knees, he falls. I rise to my feet and flail wildly with my weapon, keeping them at bay. My injured hand is slick with blood and it hurts to clutch the crowbar so tightly, but I ignore it.

I swing at one of the men holding Dolly and he stumbles back, howling. She shakes off the other and we stand back-to-back, both gasping for breath. There's still a ring of crazies around us. They seem endless, coming one after another.

"Too many," Dolly says, echoing my own thoughts.

"What do we do?"

"Get the others." She jerks her head at the pile of bodies.

"And if they're already dead?"

She shrugs.

Crazies lunge at us from all directions. Dolly darts forward, cutting down one man and breaking through the gap in the closing circle. I run after her, the mob on my heels.

"Tank! Wolf! Pretty Boy!" I yell, frantically searching for any sign of them. Someone groans to my left. As I turn my foot catches on a body. I fall hard, coming face-to-mangled-face with a corpse.

I squeak and sit up again, only to feel my head hit warm flesh. I look up to find a man standing over me with a bloody meat cleaver.

Shit. I spin around and bring up my crowbar. His blade collides with the bar, metal screeching. He pulls the knife back and I scramble away before he can swing again. I crawl over bodies, trying to ignore the wet squish and discomfiting warmth of them. When my hand hits something moving, I recoil in surprise.

The mound of bodies shifts and swells. A familiar face pokes out from the mass.

"Tank!" He doesn't look good. There's a gash on his forehead and his torso is covered in knife wounds. At least he's still conscious, though, and it looks like he wasn't shot when Dolly went trigger-happy.

"Kid! Get me the fuck out of these ropes!"

"Right, right," I say, looking around for something sharp. I set my crowbar down in favor of a piece of broken glass. I accidentally grab it with my injured hand and grimace at the immediate sting. I pass it to my other hand and start sawing at Tank's bindings. My grip on the knife keeps slipping, hands shaking and slick with blood.

"Watch out!" Tank yells before I can finish. I throw myself to the ground and hear something *swoosh* through the air above my head. Looking up, I see the man with the cleaver has caught up to me. I reach for the crowbar, but he kicks it aside.

As he comes at me again, I dive between his legs and scramble behind him. He whirls around to follow. Behind him, Tank strains at his ropes. After a few seconds of struggle, he breaks free. He grabs the crowbar and looms up behind the unsuspecting man.

Before the crazed man can slash at me with his knife again,

Tank grabs his scrawny arm with one hand and twists it. The cleaver falls to the ground. A few cracks and crunches later, the man falls, lifeless. Tank grabs my hand and pulls me to my feet.

"You all right?" he asks.

"Mostly." My hands are still shaking. I try to steady them. "Are you?"

"I'll be fine."

"The others…?"

He points behind me. I turn to see Wolf, Dolly, and Pretty Boy, all thoroughly beaten up but mostly intact. Dolly and Wolf are armed now, and making short work of the remaining crazies. Pretty Boy isn't helping much, but the other two are doing just fine on their own. The crazies may have numbers and crude weapons, but they're no match for my friends.

"Looks like we're okay," I say.

"We're lucky it was crazies. Real raiders would've sliced us up before we got untied."

"Looks like the crazies sliced you up pretty good."

"Eh, nothing serious," he says nonchalantly. Behind me, I hear a particularly loud *thud* of impact, followed by a nasty squish. I try not to imagine what's happening. Tank continues, apparently oblivious. "Shallow cuts, mostly. They were just trying to fuck with us. Thought we were easy prey."

"Big mistake."

"Damn right." He looks down at his torn-up body and grins. "I'll have some good scars. Think I'll look scary?"

"You already do!"

He laughs heartily.

"How 'bout you, any good battle wounds?"

"Well, umm…" I hold up my hand and wiggle it, displaying my missing finger.

"Holy shit, Kid!" Tank exclaims, staring.

"It's pretty ugly, huh?" I stare at it for a second, then let my hand fall to my side. As the thrill of the fight dies off the pain is growing, a throbbing pain that shoots up my whole arm.

"I can't believe that bitch cut my finger off," I say.

Tank chuckles and slaps me on the back.

"You're gonna be fine, Kid."

He turns to watch Wolf and Dolly at work, his expression unchanging. I do the same, wincing at the brutality in the way they pick off the last of the crazies.

When that's done Wolf props a baseball bat up like a walking stick and leans against it, breathing heavily.

"All right, guys," he says loudly.

"You okay, Wolf?" Tank asks as we walk over to them. Dolly moves among the dead, hunting for weapons.

"All right," Wolf repeats. He looks more disheveled than usual. He's covered in blood, dripping from his dreadlocks and down the front of his shirt. It's hard to tell how much of it is his own. He pushes up his goggles and glares at us. *"All right.* You know what? I am *sick* of this. I am sick of being pushed around and tied up and all of that shit! Come on, people, we're supposed to be the bad guys! What the fuck is going on here?"

He casts a furious look around at the lot of us. Nobody speaks. Pretty Boy abruptly bends over and vomits. Wolf shoots him a disapproving glance and continues ranting.

"Well, I'll tell you what. It ain't gonna happen again. No fucking way. We are gonna find out who the hell these assholes trying to get us captured are, we are gonna find the fuckers, and we're gonna kill 'em. You got that?"

"Got it, boss," Tank says. I give a thumbs-up, and Dolly nods, looking very pleased with a pistol she found. Pretty Boy says nothing.

"Good," Wolf says. He slides his goggles down and gives the nearest body a kick for emphasis. "Now, are either of those Blackfort guards still breathing?"

Dolly locates one of them crumpled on the ground nearby. He never made it far from the truck. She walks over and kicks him. When he groans, she shoots him.

"No," she says.

"God damn it, Dolly, I wanted him alive."

"Oh."

"Fucking hell, nothing ever goes according to plan." Wolf sighs and pushes his dirty hair out of his face. He looks genuinely irritated for a moment, but soon breaks into his usual grin. "Fine. We'll follow the original idea and head to the Queen. Load up the bodies; she's never opposed to buying some meat." He gestures to the truck with his bat. "And I get to drive."

With the tires changed, the bodies sliced up and piled in the back, and my injured hand half-assedly bandaged, we all squeeze into the seats up front. I'm squashed between Tank and the door, with my backpack on my lap—we found it stored in the back with all the other stuff.

Wolf, using the key taken off the dead guard, starts the truck. He grins at the obnoxious rumble of the engine.

"This is a big-ass truck," he says, looking satisfied. "*Almost* as good as killing people."

He slams his heel on the gas and the truck lurches forward, nearly throwing me out of my seat. The tires bump as if going over something heavy, and only then do I recall the guard beneath it. *Oops.* Probably best not to mention that.

Despite my exhaustion, it's impossible to sleep with the engine snarling and Wolf driving like a madman. The truck threatens to topple at every sharp turn, which only excites Wolf. I hold on for dear life and stare out the window, watching the wastelands go by.

XIV
The Queen of the Wastes

After we've been driving for a while I notice something strange: other vehicles. It's rare to see even one on the road, with gasoline so scarce, let alone this many. They come from all directions as smaller roads merge with ours. Some are big supply trucks like ours, while others are smaller jeeps and transports. A few are bulky, scary-looking war machines, crudely adorned with spiked tires and built-on weapons. One has a rotting body tied to the hood, a gruesome warning to all who see them coming.

"This is the crossroads," Wolf yells above the engine. "All roads lead to the Queen, they say."

As the road thins, the vehicles are forced into a single-file line. Progress slows until we stop, forming a winding line outside of a gate. We end up boxed in by gigantic raider trucks.

"Couldn't someone attack us and steal all our stuff?" I ask, peering at the truck in front. I can barely see through their blood-streaked window, but I think someone turns to look back. I duck down quickly.

"I guess," Tank says. "Queen's protection doesn't apply until we're inside the gates." Seeing the look on my face, he adds, "You'd have to be crazy to try it, though."

"Well, I've considered it," Wolf says, "so keep your guns ready, boys."

So we do, and I keep a wary eye out the window, but nothing happens. The line inches forward until we reach the gate.

Wolf attempts to roll the window down; it jams, not budging. He hits it. Nothing happens. After a few tries, he shatters the window with his bat.

The gatekeeper barely blinks as glass rains down around him. He's an older man with a shaved head, a missing eye, and a big gun. He wears all black, with the emblem of a golden crown stitched messily onto the front of his shirt.

"Wolf," he says, his expression souring.

"Been a while, eh?"

The man nods stonily.

"No trouble," he says. "You know the rules."

"Yeah, yeah, and you know me..."

"No trouble. I mean it." He waves us through.

Wolf drives considerably more carefully as we pass the gate. The Queen's place looms up ahead, growing steadily until I find myself in awe of its size. It's a giant building, one of the largest mostly intact ones I've ever seen. It must have been someplace fancy and important before the bombs dropped. Now chunks of it are crumbling, with sections of walls missing, windows broken, and paint coated in dust and rust. Old glamor still shines through in glints of gold and careful architecture. It's somehow both awe-inspiring and horribly sad. It also gives me a hint of the same nervousness Blackfort gave me, but I try to quash it with the reassurance that Wolf and the others trust this woman.

Wolf pulls into a vast expanse of space designated for vehicles. There are rows and rows of them lined up. The Queen's men wait on the edges of the lot, waving people in to organized rows and keeping an eye on everything. Wolf parks under the directions of one of them, and gives another truck a bump to the side that seems entirely intentional. The Queen's man scowls and flips us off. Wolf goes to talk to him as the rest of us wait.

"Wow," I say, staring up at the monster of a truck parked next to us. "Don't people worry about these getting stolen?"

"The Queen's men keep everything under control," Tank says. "They look after the vehicles and tally up your goods. If anything goes missing, the guards are responsible."

"And what if the Queen steals 'em?"

"She can't," he says. "If she did, the whole system would fall apart. She needs people's trust."

"I guess that makes sense." The whole thing seems awfully organized for the wastelands, but I suppose the Queen has the power to do it. "What's she like, anyway?"

"Oh, you'll see soon enough," Tank says with a chuckle.

Pretty Boy sighs exaggeratedly, his face twisting in distaste. I wait for an explanation, but before they can speak, Wolf is back.

"All right," he says. "Business taken care of. Let's go see the Queen. Hopefully she has some nice presents for her old friends." He grins and sweeps a look over us, pausing on Pretty Boy. "You keep her nice and happy for me, got it?"

"As always." Pretty Boy sighs, shakes his head, and walks toward the building. "Lord, I need a bath and a woman…"

"And a meal," Tank adds as the rest of us follow Pretty Boy's lead. "And some whiskey."

"Some better bandages would be nice," I say wistfully, looking down at my injured hand.

"You whiny bastards," Wolf says, and laughs. "Don't worry, we'll get everything we need. Safest place in the wastes, this is."

We enter the building after the guards' approval. They don't allow the larger weapons into the building, but we're able to keep our knives and smaller handguns.

The room we step into is huge and mostly empty, with tall ceilings that make me feel very small. A massive set of double doors is directly ahead, with other doors to either side.

Everything is very white, though that changes when we come in trekking dirt and blood. I'm painfully aware of how out of place we are in the clean room. We're all wearing torn, dirt-ied clothes and nursing multiple wounds. We look terrible, and probably smell worse.

And this place is trying so hard to be fancy. There are paintings on the walls, delicate-looking vases, even a few semi-crumbled statues. It's attempting to look elegant, but the decorations look strange with armed guards everywhere and dirty wasteland folk heading in and out of the building.

"Wait here," says a guard. "The Queen is coming to greet you."

"Well, shit, makes me feel pretty special," Wolf says.

"Doubt it's for you," Tank says, and glances at Pretty Boy.

"Don't even start."

"No need to get shy, lover boy."

"I'm not her fucking—" Pretty Boy cuts off abruptly as the double doors swing open, and replaces his scowl with a very wide, very fake smile. "Ah, the Queen herself. What a surprise!"

The Queen swoops in elegantly. She has a guard on either arm, both ruggedly handsome men with the crown icon stitched onto their clothes. I can't help but stare. She looks like someone who was once beautiful, and hasn't yet realized that beauty has long since faded. The wastelands age people fast, making their skin sun-spot and shrivel—but still, she looks *really* old. An overly lavish, too-long black dress hangs awkwardly on her thin frame. Heaps of gaudy jewelry adorn her neck and wrists, glinting and clanking as she walks, and her face is slath-ered with makeup. Her hard eyes remind me of the power she holds. As she draws closer I straighten up and smile politely with the others.

She throws her arms around Pretty Boy and plants a wet kiss on his cheek, leaving a red smear. The smile melts off his face and his lip curls in disgust, but he fakes another smile in the time it takes her to pull back and look at him again.

"Ahh, Wolf and the crew," she says in a croaky voice. She speaks oddly, with some kind of lilting accent that sounds over-the-top and forced. She pats Pretty Boy on the shoulder before scrutinizing the rest of us. After a moment she erupts in an overly loud cackle, a sound that clashes with her pseudo-elegant appearance. The laugh soon descends into a coughing fit that lasts several seconds. Everyone waits for it to pass. "It's been too long, darlings," she says finally. "Though I've been hearing an awful lot about you recently."

"That so?" Wolf asks, pleased with himself.

"Sounds like you've been quite busy."

"As always. Spreading joy and goodness around the wastes."

"I bet you have." She laugh-coughs again, and the sound grates on my ears. As if locking in on my discomfort, she turns her shrewd eyes to me. "And this must be the new one I've been hearing such *interesting* rumors about."

"Kid," I introduce myself, trying not to crumple under the attention. "And, umm, despite what you've probably heard, I'm a girl."

"So you are." She doesn't take her eyes off my face, and I squirm under the scrutiny. I scuff the heel of one boot across the floor, leaving a streak of dirt behind. "Well, I can see why there was a misunderstanding," she says, and cackles some more. I blush. "A bath would do you some good. All of you, actually."

She touches Dolly lightly on the arm. I expect Dolly to give her typical blank stare in return, but instead she smiles. Tank and Wolf receive only customary nods, and the Queen turns around with a swish of her dress.

She walks back the way she came, her bony hips swaying and her dress dragging on the tile.

"Clean yourselves up," she says over her shoulder, with a

wink at Pretty Boy, "and I'll treat you to dinner. We can catch up then."

The sound of the doors closing booms in the quiet room.

As soon as she's gone, Pretty Boy leans against the wall with a groan. Tank laughs and claps him on the shoulder. I feel a little overwhelmed. She swept in and out so quickly it was hard to get a read on her.

"She seemed even weirder than usual," Pretty Boy says, shaking his head.

"Yeah, seems like the ol' hag is losing her marbles a bit," Wolf says. "But we need the supplies, so be a good boy and keep her happy. If that means spending the night with her, do it."

"Let's hope it doesn't come to that." He looks sickened by the thought. I sincerely hope it's not an actual possibility. Even with her age aside, the Queen seemed a little *off* somehow.

Wolf lets out a hearty guffaw and turns around. He sets off down one of the hallways leading out of the room.

"Well, you heard the lady. Let's go, boys. Kid, you go with Dolly. See you at dinner."

I turn to Dolly to ask where we're going, but she's already walking away in the opposite direction of Wolf. I hurry to catch her. She walks quickly, so I have some trouble keeping up.

"So you know the Queen?" I ask. She glances sideways at me and doesn't say anything. "You used to work for her or something, right?"

In response, she only speeds up. I fall behind despite my best efforts.

"Nice talking to you, too," I grumble under my breath. I follow her around the corner and into one of the rooms.

Suddenly there are naked women everywhere.

And I do mean everywhere. There are at least a dozen people stuffed into this room, and not a single one aside from me and Dolly is fully clothed. The air is warm and steamy, but it doesn't actually conceal anything. I'm not sure if I should cover my eyes or run out of the room or what. Did we take a wrong turn? I freeze in place and stare down at my boots. Somehow no one else seems the least bit fazed by this, least of all Dolly.

She notices I'm not following her after a few steps, and turns to give me a confused look.

"Why isn't anyone wearing clothes?" I ask, dumbfounded.

"Bathing room," she says, as if that explains everything. Now that I've gotten over the initial shock of excessive nudity, I can see the baths set up around the room. Still, it seems weird that everyone is so comfortable being naked.

Before I can ask any more questions, some of the other women notice Dolly. To my surprise, a lady with long red hair squeals and throws her arms around her like they're old friends. Two blondes who look like twins come over to say hello as well. Dolly smiles.

"Dolly! It's been ages!"

She nods silently, still smiling, her icy exterior thawing in their presence. The redhead's eyes slide to me.

"And is this your little friend?"

Dolly nods again.

"This is Kid," she says quietly. "Do not be alarmed, she is a girl."

"Of course she is." The woman walks over and tweaks my nose, which I would be more comfortable with if she was wearing a shirt. I try to keep my eyes on her face. She grins, showing a gap between her front teeth. "I'm Ruby. And I don't see how anyone could mistake you for a boy, you're far too cute!"

"Really?" I've been mistaken for a boy so many times it almost feels odd to be called a girl.

"Of course! Not that I blame you for hiding; it's dangerous to be a girl in the wastes. But not here!"

She grabs my hand to pull me, and jostles my stubby once-finger. I yelp. She lets go instantly, an apology on her lips.

"Sorry," I blurt out before she can say anything. "I, umm, hurt my hand." I hold it up to show her. She gently takes my hand for a closer look, murmuring sympathetic words.

"We can find help with that, too," she says. "But first, clean up."

I don't really have a choice in the matter. The ladies strip me and dunk me into a big metal tub of water. I cover as much of my body as I can with my hands, but nobody even seems to pay attention to it. It seems it really is no big deal here, and after a few minutes I manage to stop feeling so self-conscious.

The baths are filled with river water heated by a fire. It's too hot at first, and I feel like I'm being boiled in it. Warm baths are an oddity to me. Both in the bomb shelter and in town, I made do with the occasional cold sponge bath. I find an actual bath less pleasant than expected. The sting of soap reminds me of every scrape and cut I had forgotten about, and many of my old scabs bleed freshly afterward.

After scrubbing my skin raw, the Queen's ladies give me fresh clothes: a dress. It's plain and nothing too frilly, but still painfully feminine for me. I can't even remember the last time my legs were bare. It makes me feel vulnerable to show my prickly stick-legs and scabby knees to the world. Dolly is coaxed into a dress, as well. Hers is even worse than mine, a white and puffy thing with a big bow on it. She really does look like a doll. Actually, she looks far more natural in it than I do.

Despite my discomfort, it's hard to complain when everyone is being so nice. Even when they take my familiar beanie and clothes, with the promise to return them after a wash, I keep my mouth shut. I don't let them take my backpack, though.

"So do you all work for the Queen?" I ask, uncomfortable while the blondes fuss over my hair and the redhead bandages my injured hand.

"That's right, miss," Ruby says.

"What do you do?" I ask. She glances at Dolly and doesn't say anything.

"Look pretty," one of the blondes deadpans.

"And sweet-talk," her twin says.

"And *entertain*," the other one adds.

Ruby winks. As it dawns on me, I feel my face heat up. They all burst into laughter, except for Dolly, who remains stoic.

As I walk with her to dinner, feeling weirdly clean, it hits me that Pretty Boy said Dolly used to work for the Queen. And she *knew* those women. And if they sell their bodies for a living, then…

My thoughts whir and tumble with that idea, and I have to force myself to act normal and keep my mouth shut as we walk to meet up with the others.

The boys are freshly washed and dressed as well, although it appears Wolf hasn't let anyone touch his dreadlocked hair. I resist the urge to swoon over Pretty Boy, with his hair still dripping wet and all the dirt washed off his handsome features. For once he notices me as well, doing a double take when he sees me.

"Wow, Kid," he says. "You almost look like a real girl."

"Uh, thanks," I say with a blush. It's pretty close to a compliment. He leans closer, smiling slightly, and I stare up at him with wide eyes.

"So, you had some freckles under all that dirt," he says. "Cute." He raises a hand as if to touch my face, and I'm bright red between that and the fact he called me *cute*, but then Dolly walks directly between us and shatters the moment. Pretty Boy steps back, and so do I, and by the time she passes through it's gone. I blink uncertainly at the back of Pretty Boy's head as he turns to talk to Wolf.

There isn't time to dwell on that, though. I wait for the others to distance themselves and grab Tank's arm. Taking the hint, he slows down so the two of us fall behind the rest of the crew as we walk through the Queen's dwelling. The overly fancy decorations and endless doorways pass by in a blur.

"A while ago, Pretty Boy said Dolly worked for the Queen once?" I ask in a low voice. He nods. "So when he said...did he mean Dolly used to be a...a...?"

"Yeah," he says in a quiet voice, not needing to say the word. My eyes go wide.

"B-But, that's so...*she's* so..." I glance up at Dolly, who is oblivious to our conversation, and shake my head in disbelief.

"Weird, yeah. She's different now."

"How did she go from that to *this*? Why'd she quit?"

"She, uh, got pregnant."

"Dolly has a *kid*?" It takes serious effort to keep my voice down.

"No," Tank says. "Not anymore."

It takes a few seconds to sink in. When it does, I let my grip on Tank's arm go slack. He pats me on the back and moves ahead to join the others. I lag behind, head reeling as I sort this new information into place.

I'm not given much time to process, because there's already new material flying my way. The room we enter next is huge and lavishly decorated and very, very white. The walls are painted white and adorned with paintings, the tile is white and clean, and the long dining table is covered in a lacy white tablecloth. I feel guilty entering the room. My very presence must dirty the place, even after having my first bath in months. I stick close to the others so I feel less out of place. They all look bored, but I stare around in amazement.

"This place always makes me want to break something," Wolf mutters.

"Please don't," says Pretty Boy.

"Aw, shut up."

Moments later the Queen enters, wearing a new dress, this one a ridiculously puffy and lacy monstrosity that matches the red of her lips. She sweeps across the room with two guards shadowing her every step. One pulls her chair out. The Queen even sits in a grandiose way, gracefully falling into the chair and crossing one leg over the other. Wolf and the others sit across from her, and I hurry to follow suit. I catch myself sitting with my legs open, remember I'm wearing a dress, and hastily squeeze my knees together.

"I'm so happy you came to join me today," the Queen says, batting absurdly long eyelashes.

"'Course we made it," Wolf says. "It's free food, ain't it?"

"And we're *very* grateful," Pretty Boy adds quickly, coaxing a smile out of the Queen.

Silent men set food before us, so much food I can hardly believe my eyes. I thought the crew had it pretty nice as far as food goes, but this is a *feast*. Along with heaps of white rice, there's a colorful selection of corn, peas, and other stuff I don't recognize. I avoid the beans and mix a variety of stuff together on my plate before digging in. I even try a weird little fish that Tank calls a sardine.

I notice out of the corner of my eye that the Queen makes one of her men taste everything before she eats it. Odd, considering it's her own food, but I'm too busy stuffing my face to care. The food is just too good, and there's so much of it.

The meal even comes with real plates and utensils. The plates are cracked and stained, but they look like they could have been nice once upon a time. I try eating with a fork, but when that gets too frustrating I grab two spoons instead and stuff my face like a starving animal.

"So," Wolf says through a mouthful of food, "I've got some questions."

"Yes?" The Queen stops eating and raises her eyebrows at him. No doubt she notices that he's eating with his hands and making quite a mess of the fancy tablecloth, but she doesn't say anything.

"What the *fuck* is happening around here?"

Silence falls as the Queen stares at Wolf. I become very fascinated by my plate.

"I'm afraid I'm going to need more clarification."

"Why's everyone out to get us all of a sudden? We were at, uh, one of those towns—"

"Blackfort," Pretty Boy supplies.

"Right-o, that one, and they fuckin' arrested us the second we walked into town. And *then*, instead of hanging us, they said they was gonna transport us somewhere." Wolf stuffs another bite of food into his mouth and leans back in his chair so it threatens to topple over. He points his slightly bent fork at the Queen, gesturing for her to speak. "So...what the fuck?"

"Ah," she says. She delicately sets down her utensils and folds her hands on the table, her long nails stark red against the white tablecloth. "Yes. I'm surprised you haven't heard yet. There's been a bit of an...upheaval, so to speak. Times are changing, Wolf."

"Changing how?" His voice lowers to a growl, as if he's offended that anything could change without his explicit permission.

"The return of law, and order, and authority," she says. "Or so he says." Her lips twist, something dark flashing across her expression.

"*Who?*"

"He calls himself Saint."

"Pff," Wolf scoffs. "Sounds like an asshole."

"Law in the wastelands?" Pretty Boy asks. "How?"

I keep eating and pretend not to pay too much attention to

the conversation, but my interest is caught. I steal glances at the three of them between bites. Dolly and Tank seem content to stay out of it.

"Saint has secured a radio tower," the Queen says, looking at Pretty Boy rather than Wolf. "And from there he's managed to spread his message and solidify his control."

"So he talks to the towns that way," Pretty Boy says, and nods thoughtfully. "That's why everyone's ready for us."

"Yes, there's a description of your little crew out on the radio waves, and a hefty price on your heads. He's after sharks, and you're well-known enough for him to target you specifically."

"But not to kill us?" Pretty Boy asks. "They've been trying to capture us alive."

"Yes, yes, for a reward. That's another part of what he's trying to do: trials and all, just like the old days, rather than shooting anyone straightaway."

"And what's your take on all this?" Wolf asks, pointing again with his fork. The Queen turns to him, her thin lips pinched together. She glances at the utensil, then at his face, and smiles insincerely.

"You know me, Wolf. I stay neutral."

"Well, we can't afford that." He drops his fork and leans back in his seat again, placing his boots on the table. "So what do we do then, eh?"

"What *can* we do?" I ask, unable to keep myself out of the conversation any longer. "This seems bigger than us." My place in the world has improved significantly since I started tagging along with Wolf and the crew, but the idea of going against someone like Saint still seems overwhelming.

"Nothing's too big when you've got enough explosives, Kid." Wolf grins, suddenly confident and fierce.

"You want to blow the place up?" Pretty Boy asks, his eyebrows drawing together.

"Damn straight I do. I'll explode the shit out of it."

"You want to blow up a radio tower," he repeats slowly. "That's your plan?"

"Seems like the most obvious solution," Wolf says. Tank and Dolly nod along with him.

"Well, count me out." Pretty Boy throws his hands up. "I've signed up for a lot of crazy shit with you, but I'm not along for this."

"Like shit you ain't," Wolf says. I look back and forth between the two of them, a spoonful of food held halfway to my mouth.

"Who says it's such a bad thing, anyway? A little law in the wastelands? A world where our lives aren't threatened on a daily basis?" Pretty Boy shrugs. "What's wrong with that?"

"People like us ain't got no place in a world like that."

"People like *you*."

"Oh, fuck you. You and your uppity bullshit. Just because you can play nice and pretend you ain't like—"

The Queen slams her silverware against her plate. The loud clang silences everyone. When she has our attention, she plasters on a sickly sweet smile.

"As lovely as it is to listen to you bicker," she says, "I'd prefer if you did not do it *here*."

"Whatever, I'm done." Wolf takes his feet off the table, and his chair comes down on the tile with a heavy thud. He stands, stretches, and sends the Queen a lazy mock salute.

"I'll expect compensation for what I've told you," the Queen says coldly.

"Right, right. I've got a truck full of shit to trade. We'll work it out."

He leaves, the sound of his footsteps echoing in the silence left behind him. When he slams the door shut, Pretty Boy quickly smiles at the Queen.

"Thank you for your hospitality," he says, his politeness an abrupt change. "Really, we appreciate it, though Wolf is too crude to say as much."

The Queen waves a hand dismissively, still frowning. I glance at Pretty Boy and detect a hint of nervousness. If his sweet-talking isn't enough to win back the Queen's good mood, that can't be good.

"We'll be off to our rooms, then," Pretty Boy says. "No need to bother you any further."

He stands up and pushes his chair in, and the others hastily follow suit. I scarf down a few more mouthfuls of food and scamper after them. As we leave the room I cast one last glance back at the Queen. She's still seated at the table, hands folded in front of her, head bowed so her face is obscured.

When the door shuts, we stop and look at each other.

"Well," Tank says, "let's hope Wolf is in a good enough mood to buy us some liquor."

XV
Alcohol

Wolf is in a decent enough mood by the time we find him. He has plans to meet with the Queen soon, but tells us we're welcome to help ourselves to some booze in the meantime. The cost will be subtracted from whatever deal he works out with the Queen.

"None of the girls, though," Wolf says, pointing a finger at Pretty Boy. "They're expensive as shit, and we can't afford it right now."

"Seriously?" Pretty Boy asks, looking pained.

"I mean it. We need the credit for big-ass explosives."

Pretty Boy lets out a long sigh. Tank, I can't help but notice, looks similarly disappointed. I look away from both of them and try to push back my discomfort. I really don't want to think about either of them with the Queen's ladies... though for very different reasons.

Everyone cheers up soon enough when we get our hands on the booze. It's a big, plastic container with no label. The liquid inside is a deep red-brown.

"Ahh, cheap-as-shit whiskey, just the way I like it," Tank says. He takes a hearty drink and passes it to me. Just a whiff of it is enough to make my eyes water, so I pass it on to Pretty Boy, who plugs his nose and takes a swig. As soon as he swallows he starts coughing.

"Holy shit, worse than I remember," he chokes out, and hands the bottle to Wolf with a grimace.

"As tempting as that is," Wolf says, giving the bottle a sniff, "I'm about to meet with the Queen, so..."

"Sounds like a good excuse to drink," Tank says.

"Yeah, actually." Wolf grins, raises the bottle in a cheers, and takes a long gulp. "That's fucking disgusting," he says, still grinning, and hands it back to Tank.

"You drinking, Kid?" Tank asks.

"Um, I don't think so." From what I've seen, drunkenness never leads to anything good.

"Aw, why not?" Wolf asks. "Loosen up."

"I've never really drank before." The bottle ends up in my hands again, and I stare into it uneasily.

"I bet you'd never hung around sharks or shot someone before, either," says Wolf. "And look how far you've come!"

"Well, if you put it like that..." It still doesn't sound appealing at all. But everyone is staring at me, so I figure it's worth a try. I raise the bottle and take a tiny sip.

The taste hits me like a truck. It's god-awful, and the burn in my throat is worse. I start choking as soon as it goes down and nearly drop the bottle. Pretty Boy grabs it out of my hand while Wolf slaps me on the back.

"Good girl, taking it like a champ," Wolf says. I'm coughing too hard to answer. Eyes tearing up and throat burning, I wonder why the hell anyone would put themselves through this torture. Even when the burning recedes, I'm left with a nasty aftertaste. The heat in my belly is nice, though.

"Well, I better be off," Wolf says. He snatches the bottle out of Pretty Boy's hands, takes another long swig, and lightly punches me on the shoulder. "Have fun, guys. But not too much fun." He pauses to whisper something in Dolly's ear, and he's gone.

"So now what?" Pretty Boy asks. He holds on to the bottle, taking small but frequent sips.

"Now we have fun," Tank says, putting an arm around his shoulders and stealing the bottle from his hand.

We wander the Queen's mansion until we find a promising room. It's a big dining hall, but not as stiflingly luxurious as the one where we dined with the Queen. This room is more understated, with wooden tables and chairs adorned with crude carvings and stains. It's full of traders and raiders and other wasteland wanderers, many carrying bottles of liquor like us. It seems like this is the place to mingle. Some sit in small groups and speak in lowered voices, having the kind of conversations that stop whenever someone draws too close. Others seem much more relaxed. Cards and dice are strewn over the tables, with rowdy groups playing games and shouting at each other. Often it's hard to tell if they're having fun or about to break into a fight, but since there are no weapons out I assume the former.

We attach ourselves to one of the groups, which is playing some sort of card game. The guys play while I watch and try my best to follow. Dolly stands behind my chair and dutifully watches our surroundings. One man attempts to speak with her, and she responds with utter silence and a devastatingly cold glare. No one else tries to be friendly to her.

A whirl of noise surrounds me. I watch the game go by without understanding it, and listen to Pretty Boy chat with traders. He has a gift for striking up conversations, talking with strangers as if they're old friends.

"Hey, weren't you one of Big Ben's crew?" he asks the man to his left, a thick-necked, red-faced guy with a shaved head and facial piercings. "Whatever happened to him?"

"Saint," he says, spitting the word like a curse. "Got a hold of him and most of the others a few weeks back."

"Really? Damn."

"Radio said they were all executed a few days later," the man says, shaking his head. "Fuckin' Saint. We can't touch anything as far up as Sniper's Gorge."

"Well, shit. It's the same out in Blackfort," Pretty Boy says. He pauses, looking thoughtful, and then lowers his voice. "He's expanding fast. The Queen isn't threatened by it?"

"Maybe, maybe not," the raider says. "But between you and me, she ain't really in a position to do anything about it. Old bitch isn't doing so well. Especially with that cough she's got, and the way she's been acting...she's pretty fucked."

Pretty Boy looks suddenly nervous, glancing around the room.

"Few months ago, one of her men might've shot you for saying shit like that," he says finally, relaxing when it's clear nothing is going to happen.

"Heh, yeah. Few months is a long time."

I hang on to the conversation, but when their talk turns to the game they're playing, I lose interest. With nothing else to do, I take small drinks from the bottle whenever it's passed my way. It never tastes *good*, exactly, but it seems a little less awful with each sip. Maybe I'm getting used to it, or maybe it's slowly killing my taste buds. Either way, I keep drinking and keep to myself.

It's interesting to observe what's happening around me when there's such a strange variety of people in the room. There are traders trying to sell their goods, men and women selling their services as bodyguards or bounty hunters, raiders like us enjoying a danger-free day. The Queen's women slip among them selling *their* wares, and from what I see, they're a hot commodity. I'm in no place to judge; everyone is trying to get by.

It feels so nice not to have to worry about danger or dehydration or where I'm going to sleep. The Queen's palace really does feel like a safe haven. I'm happy to sit and drink and let sleepy contentment wash over me.

I'm startled out of my little bubble when one of the men playing slams his fists down on the table. The illusion of peace shatters like glass. Conversation ceases as he rises from his chair. It's the man Pretty Boy was talking to earlier, and he's even more intimidating standing up, towering over everyone at the table.

He points a beefy and accusatory finger at Pretty Boy.

"You goddamn cheat!" he shouts, causing heads all around the room to turn. The circle of card players is tense and motionless aside from him.

"What are you talking about?" Pretty Boy asks. He doesn't cower away like I'd expect, instead staying in his chair and tilting his chin up to look the man in the eye. Maybe the liquor lent him some courage. The raider stares down at him, scowling, his face turning nearly purple with anger.

Behind us, I notice Dolly is holding a knife that I'm *sure* wasn't in her hand until a few seconds ago. She doesn't even raise her eyes to the standing man, but casually twirls it in her hand, a clear threat. He notices, and begins to sink back into his seat.

And then there's a gun in his hand. I can't even tell where he pulled it from. As my head jerks toward him, the world takes a few seconds to catch up. I may have had a bit more to drink than I thought. Maybe for that reason, it's hard to keep up with what's happening. All I know is within a few seconds, literally everyone has a gun in hand... except me.

I clutch my bottle tightly and shrink down in my seat, wondering if I should slip under the table and hide.

"I didn't *cheat*," Pretty Boy insists. Though he has a gun in hand, he's halfway out of his chair, as if he has yet to decide whether he wants to fight or run. He teeters, eyes flicking around the circle. "And even if I did, what would it matter? We're just playing for fun, aren't we?"

Even with alcohol slurring his words, his go-to reaction is to try to talk himself out of trouble. I glance around to see if anyone is convinced, and find only unreadable faces. Aside from my friends, the other four men playing cards don't even seem to be together, and nobody is sure where to point their guns. One of them, looking absolutely baffled by the situation, rapidly switches the barrel of his gun between Pretty Boy and the other man.

The humor in the situation strikes me and, to my horror, I feel laughter bubble up within me. I can't fight it; no matter how serious the situation may be, it looks pretty ridiculous. I let out a loud laugh before I can stop myself, and slap a hand over my mouth.

Everyone's eyes move to me. Again I wish I could disappear.

The pierced man who started it all starts to grin, and then to guffaw. He slides his gun into the back of his pants and sits, gesturing for the game to continue. Everybody relaxes and the weapons disappear. The game resumes. In the aftermath I notice Pretty Boy surreptitiously slide a card into his sleeve. Tank reaches over and ruffles my hair, giving me his big, good-natured grin as he takes the bottle from my hands.

"Well, this feels lighter…how much you been drinking, Kid?"

"Enough," I say with a smile, and he laughs.

Soon I start to think perhaps it was more than enough. I grow more and more nauseous as the alcohol hits me. It's hard to focus on anything or talk to anyone. My vision blurs and spins, and everything looks hazy.

"I think I'm gonna go to bed," I say eventually, not even sure who I'm telling. If I'm going to be sick, I don't want it to be here.

I push out my chair and stand, only to immediately stagger as the world tries to slide out from beneath my feet.

"Whoa." I grab on to the nearest solid object for support. It turns out to be Dolly, who shoots me a confused look. "Ah, sorry."

"You all right, Kid?" Tank asks. He grabs my arm and steadies me.

"I'm fine. Just, uh…"

"Drunk," Tank says.

"Yeah, maybe that."

"How many fingers am I holding up?" he asks, raising a hand. I squint as my vision blurs.

"Is that a trick question?"

Tank chuckles.

"Really though, Kid, you can't just wander around here alone. It's not safe."

I wave him away, shaking my head.

"I'm fine, I'm fine, I'm fine." My nausea hasn't receded, and upchucking seems like a serious threat. "I really gotta go." I shake off his grip and slip away, making my unsteady way through the crowd. I accidentally bump into several people. Unfamiliar faces swim in the air around me, some angry and some amused. I wander through a cloud of sweet-smelling smoke that almost makes me gag. It feels like I'll never find the door with the whole room tilting and spinning. I can't even remember which direction I'm heading and where I came from.

Finally I find the door. I fumble with the knob before bursting into the open hallway outside.

As the door shuts behind me, it's like turning off all the sound with a switch. The quiet is instantly relieving. I pause to take a few deep breaths of air that isn't laden with the smell of sweat and alcohol and smoke. I want to curl up on the floor here, but the thought of a bed keeps me going. I only make it halfway down the hall.

"Hey, Kid, wait up!"

I turn toward the voice sluggishly, trying to find its source as the hallway lurches in my vision. It's a struggle just to stay on my feet. To my surprise, it's Pretty Boy coming toward me. His feet are almost as unsteady as mine.

"Hi?"

"Hi," he replies with a crooked smile. He stands strangely close to me, his hand resting on my lower back. I don't understand. My mouth opens and shuts uncertainly.

I don't realize I'm moving backward until I hit the wall. I think maybe I stumbled, but then understand he must have pushed me there. His hands are on my hips all of a sudden, bunching up the fabric of my dress and exposing more of my legs. His face is very close to mine, his breath warm and heavy with liquor.

"What—" I start to say, and his mouth covers mine.

Getting kissed by him is not at all like I thought it would be. I've never been much for romance, but I know this is wrong. It feels wrong. It's too much, his tongue in my mouth and his hands all over me, his touch sloppy and rough. He tastes like that awful booze and it makes me nauseous all over again. His body presses hard against mine, but it doesn't make me excited like I'd expect. I feel like throwing up.

I stand there stiffly for a few seconds, not sure how to react, before placing my hands on his chest and pushing him away.

"What's wrong?" he asks, hands catching my wrists.

"Umm," I say. I try to form an answer, but it's hard to even form thoughts. My brain feels hazy and my tongue clumsier than normal.

"I've seen the way you look at me," he says, slurring his words. "I know you want this." He smiles, his eyes crawling down my body.

"I don't feel good." I try to turn away, but his hold on my wrists prevents me from escaping. Nausea bubbles up through my stomach and into my throat. He leans close, letting go of my wrists and putting his hands on my body again.

I vomit all over him.

He releases me instantly, taking a step back and looking down in horror at the chunky mess.

"Holy fucking shit," he says, his voice filled with disgust.

"I'm sorry," I say. I just want to sit down and maybe cry. I turn away from him and walk in the direction I hope my room is in, but Pretty Boy grabs my shoulder and spins me around. I nearly fall over.

"I just want to go to bed," I say, struggling to break free of his grip. "Please, I don't—"

He shoves me back against the wall with a frightening force, knocking the wind out of me.

"S-Stop it!" I yell.

"You little bitch, you think you can—"

He stops. There's a knife at his throat. Moving very slowly, he takes his hands off me. He raises them in the air and the knife retracts.

It's Dolly. I'm not even sure when she got here, but I'm relieved she did.

"Don't touch her again," Dolly says, giving Pretty Boy an icy look.

"I wasn't—" He gestures wildly, taking a step back. "She was coming on to *me*—"

"Don't. Touch. Her."

Dolly slashes near him with the knife. He stumbles and falls on his ass.

"This is bullshit," he says. "I didn't do anything."

Dolly takes a step toward him and he scrambles backward on the floor. She turns to me next, and I try not to flinch under the coldness of her gaze even though it's not meant for me.

"Thanks," I say, my voice shaky. "I'm . . . going to go to bed now." I resume walking. After a moment Dolly falls in step beside me and taps me on the shoulder. She jerks a thumb in

the opposite direction. I nod and turn. Dolly follows, and neither of us looks back at Pretty Boy as we head to our room.

As soon as we arrive, I go for my backpack and pull out my
papa's blanket. Clutching it tightly and inhaling the familiar
smell, I flop onto the bed face-first. I still feel sick and confused
and upset, but I try to stifle it. When I look up, I find Dolly staring at me.

"Are you okay?" she asks.

"Yeah," I say. "Better since throwing up." It's true, the world
isn't spinning so much.

"That's not what I meant," she says quietly.

"I'm fine."

She blinks at me.

"Okay."

"Okay," I repeat, and turn away from her. Exhaustion swallows my whirring thoughts, and I fall asleep with my face
pressed into my blanket.

XVI
Betrayal

When I wake up, my head is pounding and my whole body hurts. I taste old vomit in the back of my throat. A groan escapes me and I raise my blanket over my head, trying to will myself back to sleep. It takes me a while to realize the pounding sound isn't coming from inside my skull. Someone's knocking at the door.

Bleary-eyed, I lower the blanket and look around. The sunlight coming through the room's sole window is nearly blinding. I can barely see Dolly standing beside the doorway, a knife in her hand. I stare at her.

"What are you doing?" I ask croakily. It is way too early for her to have a knife already.

"Trouble," she says.

"What? Why?" I sit up, wincing as my stomach rolls. "Already?"

"Wolf isn't here. That means trouble."

"How do you know he's not with—"

"He said he'd be here," Dolly says, cutting me off. "And he's not. Trouble."

I'm really not in the mood to deal with trouble right now, but the knocking is insistent and Dolly seems pretty confident that some bad shit is about to go down. I drag myself out of bed, roll up my blanket, and grab my pack. I fumble around until I find my gun, and place the blanket inside.

"What kind of trouble?" I ask, glancing over my shoulder. Dolly shrugs. I stand up, reach to put my gun into the back of my pants, and stop as I realize I'm still wearing a dress. "Aw, shit. There's no way I can fight in this." I search around for my old clothes, but there's no sign of them.

"No choice," she says.

I heave a sigh and nod. When she places a hand on the door, I hold the gun behind my back in what I hope is a subtle way.

The door opens.

Rather than a host of armed guards like I was expecting, I find myself greeted by the face of the red-headed woman I met yesterday: Ruby. She's wearing clothes this time, albeit scanty ones that strongly accentuate her womanly features. She shows her gap-toothed smile and holds up a tarnished silver tray.

"Brought you ladies some fresh water," she says cheerfully, "and your old clothes. Though you look much cuter in that, miss!"

I'm too tired to respond. Dolly puts her knife away and steps out from her hiding place behind the door. The redhead squeaks at her sudden appearance, but quickly covers her surprise with a smile.

"Hey there, Dolly." She glances from her to me. "You okay, miss? You look sick."

"Hangover," I answer hoarsely. I may not have experienced it before, but I've seen the symptoms enough times to be familiar with them. Now I understand why my papa hated being woken up in the morning.

"Well, drink up, that should at least help a little." She sets the tray on the bed and gestures to the water. I pick one up. My mouth is as dry as the wastes, and the water looks tantalizing.

"Don't drink that," Dolly says. She shuts and locks the door behind her.

"What? Why?"

Dolly doesn't answer, and advances toward the red-haired woman. The knife is in her hand again. Ruby retreats, raising her hands palms out.

"Whoa, Dolly! What are you—" She cuts off with a squeal as Dolly holds the knife to her throat.

"Where's Wolf?"

"I don't know what you're—" Dolly presses the knife closer, drawing blood and a whimper. The woman loses her composure, eyes filling with tears. "T-The Queen has him! That's all I know!"

I gape dumbly, still holding the glass of water.

"What do you mean she has him? What's going on?"

"She betrayed us," Dolly says.

"But she can't do that! Isn't she...what do you call it? Neutral?"

"She's supposed to be." Dolly glares at the woman. Her furious eyes are all the more frightening in her icy face. "Why is she betraying us?"

"I don't know!" When Dolly's expression darkens, Ruby starts to cry. Her tears leave gunky black trails down her face. "I swear, that's all she told me! I was just supposed to come here, a-and act like everything was normal—"

"Please tell me there's not something wrong with the water," I say, looking longingly at the glass in my hand. Ruby bites her lip and looks away. I sigh. "Aww, man, I'm really thirsty..."

"Why?" Dolly asks.

"She didn't tell me!" She can barely speak through her tears.

"I think she's telling the truth," I say, feeling a pang of sympathy. "You're not going to kill her, are you?"

Dolly looks over to me, back at her captive, and pulls the knife away. The woman sinks to the floor, whimpering.

"No," Dolly says. "We need a hostage."

"You really think that'll work?"

"Ruby is very valuable."

"Dolly, you can't do this to me!" Ruby wails. "This is crazy! Do you know how many guards the Queen has?"

"It doesn't matter."

Ruby stares at her with wide eyes.

"What the hell happened to you?" she whispers. "How did you end up like this? With *them*?"

Dolly ignores her. She turns and tosses a stack of clothes to me.

"Oh…right." I turn my back to them and change into my normal clothes, trying not to think about them watching me. It's a huge relief to feel covered up again. Still, I shove the dress into my backpack in case I need it later.

"Dolly, you don't have to do this," Ruby pleads. "Just go to the Queen, I'm sure she'll take you back. And she can protect you from this…this…crazy shit!"

Dolly looks down at her, eyes ice-cold and pistol in hand.

"I don't need protecting anymore," she says, and points the gun at Ruby's head. "Stand up, hostage."

When the woman doesn't comply, Dolly grabs a fistful of her hair and pulls her to her feet.

"Stop crying," she commands. Ruby takes a few moments to compose herself, wipes her face with an already-dirty handkerchief pulled from the front of her shirt, and blows her nose. "You will lead us to the boys' room," Dolly says. "And I will stay very close to you with my gun. You will not yell or raise any alarm."

Ruby nods. Her lower lip trembles, but her eyes don't spill over again.

"Good," Dolly says. She hesitates, and adds, "I don't want to hurt you, but I will."

Ruby says nothing. Dolly presses the barrel of the gun against her back, keeping it held low by her own hip so that it will be hard to spot. Ruby takes a deep breath and stands up straighter. She picks up the tray. Though the rest of her is well controlled, her hands shake, making ice clink against glass. The sound makes my mouth feel drier than ever.

Dolly nudges her with the gun and she starts walking. I shove my gun into the back of my pants, grab my pack, and follow them.

We make our way down the first hallway without trouble. But when we round the corner, we run into two guards standing in front of the doorway to the main hall. They exchange a glance and stare pointedly at Ruby. She slows as she approaches them.

"Good morning," Ruby says. I can't see her face from where I'm standing, but I imagine it as fake-cheerful as her voice.

"Morning," one says. "Where you taking these two?"

"To see the Queen."

"Why's that?"

"Her orders."

They glance at each other again.

"Last I heard, her orders were—"

"They've changed," Ruby interjects. I notice her make an effort to steady her hands on the tray.

A few tense moments pass. Finally one guard nods and opens the door, waving us through. Dolly carefully angles the gun to hide it from their sight as we pass. I smile at the man holding the door, and he squints at me suspiciously.

There are more guards in the main entrance, more than yesterday, and they all stare as we pass. Thankfully, none of them stop us. I'm sweating, perspiration spreading across my brow and beneath my arms. I try very hard to act normal as we cross the room, and find it increasingly difficult. It's like I forget how to walk normally as soon as I start paying attention to it, and awkwardly shuffle along behind Dolly, smiling weakly at every guard we pass.

We cross into another hallway. This one is empty of everything but a few paintings on the wall.

"Calm down," Dolly tells me.

"Calm? I am calm."

"Then why are you making that face?"

I drop my attempt at a smile and wipe a hand across my forehead.

"Did you see all those guards?" I whisper to her. "We're so screwed."

"We'll be fine."

"How do you know?"

"We have a hostage. And the guards won't want to kill us."

"They won't?"

"The Queen wants the reward. So, she wants us alive. Yes, Ruby?"

Ruby says nothing. Dolly pushes her forward and we resume walking. She stops in front of one of the last doors.

"Here," she says. Dolly jerks her head in my direction. I nod, sidle up beside them, and knock on the door.

"Yeah?" Tank's voice comes from within. Relieved, I push through the door. Dolly and Ruby slide in behind me, and we shut the door behind us.

The first thing I notice is Pretty Boy, kneeling on the floor over a bucket. He doesn't look up, and continues retching into it with an unpleasantly wet noise. He seems to have cleaned the vomit off his shirt, at least. Tank is crouching beside him and patting him on the back. He looks bleary-eyed, but not ill like Pretty Boy.

My cheeks color as broken memories of last night dart

through my mind. My stomach churns, and I try not to let my eyes linger on Pretty Boy for too long.

"What's going on?" Tank asks, noticing Dolly's gun and Ruby's terrified expression. He straightens up and puts on his tough face. "Who's that? Where's Wolf?"

"We're in trouble," Dolly says flatly, ignoring his questions. Tank stops asking them. With a resigned and entirely unsurprised expression, he leaves Pretty Boy's side and lifts his heavy-looking bag onto the bed. He starts pulling out weapons and laying them on the bed: a crowbar, a gun, and a few knives of various sizes.

"So what are we gonna do?" I ask. "We can't actually fight them, can we?"

"Not much of a choice," Tank says.

"You've got to be kidding me," Ruby says. "Do you know how many guards the Queen has?"

"A lot, I'd bet," Tank says. He shoves the gun into the side of his pants and a sheathed knife through one of his belt loops.

"You people are insane."

"We get that a lot," Tank says cheerfully.

Someone knocks on the door.

Everybody freezes in place, even Pretty Boy leaning over his bucket.

"Yeah?" Tank calls out after a second.

"A message from the Queen," a man's voice comes from outside.

Tank and I draw our guns. Then there's a lot of nudging and whispering and meaningful glances as we try to decide who should open the door. Eventually Dolly pushes Ruby forward. She hesitates, gives Dolly a long, searching look, and slowly swings the door open.

"Ruby?" The man outside, a broad-shouldered and grim-faced guy wearing the Queen's emblem, looks confused. "What are you—" His eyes slide past her and spot the rest of us. He reaches for his gun.

The second his hand is on the holster, Dolly and Tank fire simultaneously, reacting faster than I would have thought possible. The bullets whiz just past Ruby's head and bury into the guard. One only skims him, but the other, likely Dolly's, goes through his left eye.

The body falls. Ruby screams, loud and horrified like someone who's never seen a man die before. The quiet that follows makes me realize how loud the gunshots and screaming must have been.

"So much for subtlety," Tank says. He bends down, grabs Pretty Boy, and throws him over his shoulder like a sack of meat. "Gotta move, now!"

"No," Pretty Boy says, struggling frantically. "No no no no, just leave me here, I'll meet up with you guys later and…"

Tank neither acknowledges his words nor makes any move to set him down.

"What's the plan?" I ask. Dolly grabs Tank's pack and the gun off the dead man.

"Find Wolf," Dolly says. "Kill everyone in our way."

"I like that plan," Tank says. "Shoot anything that looks dangerous. Don't hold back, Kid."

"Me?" I gulp and nod. "Got it!"

"Good. Let's go."

We move out, guns ready. Tank carries a complaining Pretty Boy over his shoulder. No guards are in this hallway yet, although the curious faces of other guests poke out of rooms to see who's shooting who. A few guns point at us out of narrowly cracked doors. We rush past them and through the door to the main entrance room.

There are six guards here, all of them armed, and they stop abruptly when they see us.

Dolly holds her gun to Ruby's head, yanking the woman against her so she can't escape. She says nothing, but her hard stare communicates the message well enough.

"Where the hell is Wolf?" Tank asks, his face hard.

The guards hesitate for a split second. Then one raises his gun, and Tank opens fire. I take his cue and do the same, firing wildly in the general direction of the guards. The sound of gunfire booms in the huge, empty space of the room, filling it all the way up to its sky-high ceilings. One guard stumbles into a wall and slides down, leaving a streak of red on the white surface. Another goes down with a bullet to the chest, and a third is incapacitated by a hit to the leg. Three down, but we're not fast enough to kill the others in time.

Our group scatters as they return fire. I dive behind the nearest statue and crouch there. Bullets bite into the already-crumbling marble, sending chunks crashing to the floor. Dolly shoves Ruby aside and drops to the ground, firing back at the man with his gun trained on her. Her bullet splits his forehead before he can loose another round. Tank drops Pretty Boy on the floor and charges the remaining two guards. He rips the gun out of one's hands and smashes him over the head with it. The guard reels and falls; Dolly shoots him the second he moves to stand.

One left. I level my sights on his head. Our eyes meet for a moment, and his mirror the fear I'm feeling. I hesitate. Before I can react, the man turns and fires at Tank. Tank jolts and stumbles, obviously hit—but runs forward again, heedless. He grabs the last standing guard by the throat and lifts him up with terrifying ease. He slams the man into a nearby statue, and his skull hits marble with a *crack*. The sound echoes sharply. Tank smashes the man's head against the statue once, twice, three times, and lets the body slump to the floor.

The last remaining guard is still on the floor and clutching his leg with one hand. He points his gun in Tank's direction, his hand trembling. After only a moment he lets it drop and raises both hands in surrender.

The room is still.

I creep out from behind the statue, which is now missing half its head. The one Tank was using as a weapon is dripping blood, and all the paintings are splattered with red and bullet holes. The white tile shows every splotch of blood and brains. A pool is leaking out from the man with the bashed-in head, collecting in the cracks between the tiles and slowly spreading across the floor.

Dolly climbs to her feet, brushing herself off. She points her gun at Ruby without even glancing in her direction. She freezes where she is. Tank leans against a wall, breathing heavily.

"I am way too hungover for this," Pretty Boy groans from the floor, clutching his head. He doesn't seem to have moved since Tank dropped him.

"Are you okay, Tank?" I ask. I step over a couple of bodies on my way over to him and pause to take the gun from the still-living guard, who cringes away and makes no move to stop me. "You got shot, didn't you?" My stomach knots with guilt. If I had taken that shot, I could've prevented it.

"No big deal," he says. "Guy was scared, missed anything vital." He holds up his arm and shows me the hole in it, up near his shoulder. I wince. "Clean through, no problem."

"Wow," I say earnestly. "You're so brave."

"Nah, just been shot a lot." He smiles at me, but his face hardens again instantly as he turns to the remaining man. He walks over and shoves the barrel of his gun into the cowering man's face. "Where's Wolf?"

"W-With the Queen," the man answers quickly, not even trying to act tough.

"*Where?*"

He doesn't answer, but looks at the huge set of double doors directly across from the entrance door.

"Okay," Tank says. He shoots the man in the head.

Ruby lets out a loud sob. I realize with a guilty twist in my gut that I'm not even bothered by things like that anymore. I've grown used to it, mostly. Maybe I couldn't shoot a man while looking him in the eyes yet, but a random death no longer has any effect on me. I guess I really am becoming one of them: a raider, a shark. For a second I feel conflicted, but a swell of pride overwhelms the uncertainty.

Tank turns to the big set of double doors. He yanks on the handle, but of course it's locked. He raises one leg and gives it a hard kick. The room booms with the noise, but the door barely moves. He stops and stares at it contemplatively, scratching his head.

"Well, I'm out of ideas," he says.

"What do we do?" I ask. I catch myself looking around for Wolf before remembering he's not here.

"Move," Dolly says from behind me. I take one look at her and scamper out of her way. Tank doesn't take long to follow.

She opens fire the second we've moved, an assault rifle jetting out a stream of bullets. I instinctively duck behind one of the barely intact statues. I peek out at the door from my hiding place, watching as bullets pepper the wood. At first they don't seem to have much effect, but as Dolly unloads relentlessly, holes start popping up. Soon bullets shred the wood like paper, making the doors look more and more flimsy. She doesn't stop until she runs out of bullets. The doors look worn down, but they're still standing. She reaches for a second gun. Tank stops her.

"I got this," he says. He walks over to a statue, crouches down low, and lifts it off the ground with a grunt of effort. Obviously straining, he waddles over to the doors. He plants his feet, pulls the statue back, and swings it forward like a battering ram. It blows through a whole chunk of the already-weakened wood. A second blow makes half of one door fall, leaving an entrance big enough for any of us. Tank drops the statue, and bits and pieces of marble break off as it thuds to the floor.

"There we go," Tank says triumphantly. I creep out and peek through the hole, but not much of the room is visible. All I can see is an expanse of empty white tile. I'm too afraid to actually stick my head through.

The others seem similarly hesitant about stepping in, but soon we don't have a choice. The sound of footsteps and voices comes from first one, and then the other door, and then from the entrance as well. Guards are coming, and a lot of them. The only way out is forward. Tank drags an unwilling Pretty Boy up from the floor and pushes him through, and the rest of us file in one by one, Dolly dragging Ruby along at the rear.

We step into the Queen's throne room.

It looks like a much, much larger version of the entrance room, with the same stark white tile and pompous decorations. I notice, with a sense of baffled amusement, that all of the decorations here are obviously modeled after the Queen. The numerous statues and busts bear a striking resemblance to her, minus the wrinkles and other not-so-appealing parts, and the paintings depict her posing dramatically and dressed in her over-the-top fashion. Several of them are done in a crude mockery of older styles, mimicking other paintings I've seen in the building. Even I can tell they're pretty poorly done. They're embarrassing to look at.

"Well, well, well," comes the Queen's voice, and I tear my eyes off a disturbing half-naked portrait of her to face the real thing. She's seated on her throne at the head of the room. There's a huge painting behind her, showing a younger version of her swathed in a fancy dress and sitting on a golden throne much larger than life. The real Queen seated on her real throne, a rickety old wooden chair, looks sad in comparison, like a balloon with all of the air squeezed out.

Next to her, suspended upside down, is Wolf. He's all tied up, ropes holding his wrists and ankles together, and another keeping him swinging a couple of feet off the ground. The rope is attached to a hook on the wall that must have been made for this very purpose. There's a huge bruise across his cheekbone and dried blood around his nose, but he doesn't seem seriously injured. He groans when he sees us.

"You idiots *would* barge right in here," he says. "And what the hell is the plan now, dumbasses?"

As if on cue, a ring of guards surrounds us. They emerge from behind plants and statues, from the corners of the room where the dim lighting made them hard to notice, from everywhere. I turn back to where we came from, but within seconds the room behind us is full of more guards. They step through the hole we made and force us into the empty space in the middle of the room, right in front of the Queen and her throne. There are dozens of them, all with guns trained on us, and most of them have weapons bigger than ours. Pretty Boy immediately raises his hands in surrender. The rest of us hesitate, turning around and trying to figure out where to point our weapons. There are too many targets to choose from. I finally settle on one man directly ahead of me and aim at the center of his forehead. My hands don't shake, though my heart is pounding.

This time, I won't hesitate.

"Give it up," the Queen says. Her lips are curled to the side in a smirk, her long fingernails tapping against the armrest of her throne. "You know you don't have a chance." She folds her hands on her lap and smiles an irritatingly self-satisfied smile.

"You betrayed us," Dolly says. I glance at her; her fingers are clutching her gun so tightly that her knuckles are turning white. The Queen turns to her, still smiling.

"Of course I did," she says. "Saint's new world is coming whether you like it or not, and I intend to survive in it. A partnership with him is exactly what I need to start my new life."

Wolf starts to laugh.

"Start your new life," he says mockingly between laughs. "I think you mean desperately attempt to stay relevant." He grins at her. "And if you think you can take us in alive," he says, "you seriously fucking underestimate us, bitch." One of the Queen's men hits him across the face with his gun. It looks and sounds like it hurts, but Wolf only continues to laugh.

"He's right," Tank says. "You can let us go, or you can kill us. We ain't gonna let anything else happen."

"Wait a second," Pretty Boy says. "I didn't agree to—"

Tank elbows him to shut him up. The Queen locks her eyes on Pretty Boy and smiles.

"Oh, darling," she says in a voice that makes my skin crawl. "I don't intend to lump you in with the rest of them, you poor thing. Come here, I'll keep you safe." She spreads her arms wide and beckons to him.

Cold dread grows in my belly. I can't bring myself to look at Pretty Boy. He'll take the deal, I know he will. Anything to save his own skin, as he's demonstrated time and time again. Everything is falling apart. The Queen has Wolf, and soon she'll have Pretty Boy, and then what do we have left?

Not a chance.

"Don't do it, man," Tank says quietly. I finally dare a glance at Pretty Boy. He looks like someone who was staring down a shotgun barrel and just realized it's out of bullets.

"Well," he says, "your highness, I've always..." He takes a step forward. Tank reaches out to grab his arm. Pretty Boy pauses for a second, the two of them exchange a look, and Tank lets him go. He takes another step toward the Queen.

An explosion shakes the building. Silence falls, and everyone freezes in place. This room is still intact, but it sounded close.

"What the actual *fuck* was that?" the Queen asks in a low growl, dropping both her dramatic flair and her accent. She gestures impatiently to her closest guards, who rush out through the double doors we destroyed. The rest of her men stir uneasily. The Queen only sits up straighter and glares at us, her composure returning. "Whatever you sharks are trying to pull, it's not going to work."

"What are we trying to pull?" I whisper to Tank. He shrugs. I look at Dolly, who also shrugs. "Did we do that?" More shrugs.

Wolf is laughing again.

"I tried to tell you, your *highness*," he says mockingly, "that this would backfire on you. Everyone knows you've been losing it, and the second you turned on us, broke your own rules, you were bound to—"

"Shut up," she snaps. "And secure the rest of them. What are you idiots doing?"

The Queen's men close in around us. We pull into a tighter knot, all back-to-back. Dolly yanks Ruby closer to her and jams her gun into the side of her head. Ruby closes her eyes, trembling.

"Don't move any closer," Dolly says.

"Oh, Dolly, sweetie," the Queen says with a grating, half-coughing laugh. She lazily waves a hand at her men. Two of them immediately open fire. Before anyone can react, Ruby's body is littered with bullet holes. Her body goes limp in Dolly's grip. When she lets go, Ruby falls to the floor. Dolly stares down at her, shock evident on her normally blank face. I realize she must have never actually intended to kill Ruby, let alone get her killed by the Queen. It's enough to crack her usual cool composure.

Dolly's expression turns to sheer, naked rage and she lunges forward. She fires three bullets with deadly precision, taking down the guards in front of her so she can burst out of the circle. She dodges another man who tries to grab her, slips between two coming at her from opposite directions, shoots another guard in the hand so he drops his gun. The barrel of her gun points directly at the Queen's shocked face. But before she can fire, two guards take her down. One wrestles the gun out of her hand and the other keeps her pinned to the floor.

Dolly screams. It's a wordless sound of pure hate and rage. The room magnifies it so the sound hurts my ears and echoes disturbingly in the quiet that follows.

The Queen's eyes are wide, her mouth slightly open—but she recomposes herself.

"Hold her," she says to the guards, flapping a hand at them. "And get the others."

Tank rushes forward at the line of the Queen's men, trying to shove past them and get to Dolly. They latch on to him on every side and take him down. I try to cling to Pretty Boy's arm, knowing the Queen's men won't hurt him, but they yank me away. A man takes my gun and holds my arms behind my back. All I can do is wriggle helplessly.

"M-My Queen!" I turn my head to see that one of the men who left to investigate the explosion has returned. He's clutching his side. A trail of blood snakes out the door behind him. "They're rioting! T-They're killing us, taking the girls, looting the place... You need to send more men! A lot more!"

"Who?" the Queen asks, her eyes blazing and her fists clenched. "Who dares—"

"Everyone!"

XVII
The Escape

Noise floods the room. The Queen shouts orders and her men rush to obey, some running out to rein in the chaos outside and others fortifying the doors we busted down. The Queen's orders are followed without question, but her men look nervous. There's a hesitancy to their movements, an uncertainty in their expressions. It's obvious they haven't dealt with anything like this before.

The guard holding me is distracted by the mass confusion. His grip on my arms slackens, and as he turns to look at the door I wriggle out of his grip and dart away. He shouts, but no one pays attention. They have much bigger problems; namely, the rioting is already overflowing into this room. I hear shouting at the entrance, and gunfire, but catch only glimpses of the action. Mercenaries, raiders, townies, traders, wastelanders of all sorts are fighting, taking down the Queen's men. It's no organized attack. I see raiders attacking other raiders, and the Queen's men fleeing or ripping off their incriminating emblems. Soon everyone is fighting everyone. I see the pierced-up man from last night deep in the fray, along with plenty I don't recognize. The guard really meant it when he said *everyone*. Rioting must have swept through the building like a wave as soon as people heard and saw us fighting the Queen's men.

It's the nature of the wastelands: If you smell blood, it's time to fight.

Gunfire and shouting and dying surround me. A bullet narrowly misses my head and pings into the wall. I duck behind a fake potted plant for shelter. Within seconds, a burly man picks it up and walks away with it, leaving me without cover again. I crouch down and scoot along the wall. Luckily, most people are too busy shooting someone or getting shot to notice me. I don't even have a gun, but I do have my trusty knife, which I take out for comfort's sake if nothing else.

Unable to spot the others, I move toward where Wolf was hanging. I find the Queen standing beside him. She looks remarkably out of place in her flowing dress and excessive makeup, and she doesn't have the usual gaggle of guards around her. Most of her men are already immersed in the fight. I creep closer, scuttling between potted plants and statues.

The Queen is still yelling orders like "Contain this mess" and "Kill them already" and "Do something, you idiot," but nobody seems to be listening anymore. Wolf, meanwhile, is swinging from side to side and wiggling like a very determined worm. It doesn't seem to be accomplishing much. Neither of them notices me.

The Queen starts to pace, wringing her hands.

"Idiots, idiots, all of them," she says. There's a crazy gleam in her eyes, breaking through her grandiose attitude. "I merely ask them to secure a few sharks, and then this mess..."

"Instant karma!" Wolf says cheerfully, still swinging.

"Shut up. Just 'cause I can't kill you doesn't mean I won't maim you."

"Likely get a price reduction for missing parts, though, eh?"

"I can think of a few that shouldn't be necessary."

I attempt a somersault to a nearby potted plant, and accidentally smack my face into the clay pot instead. I freeze there, feeling like an idiot and sure someone must've heard the noise, but nobody reacts. I duck behind the pot with a hand over my smarting nose. Once I determine I'm not bleeding, I peer through the rubbery leaves of the fake plant. The Queen's back is turned to me. None of her men are looking toward me, either. Everyone is too focused on the brawl.

I crawl out from behind the plant and toward Wolf. He finally notices me as I draw closer. He stops swinging, glances at the Queen's back and then at me again.

I check to make sure I still haven't captured the attention of the Queen's men and find them distracted by a new problem: Dolly, who somehow broke free and gained a gun again. As the nearby guards rush to stop her, I stand and use my knife to saw at Wolf's bindings. I manage to free his hands and am trying to figure out the best way to cut him down when the Queen notices me. Her eyes go wide, her thin upper lip curling back into a snarl.

"What the fuck do you think you're doing?" she shrieks. I frantically saw at the ropes holding Wolf, but before I can finish, the Queen shoves me. I stumble away from Wolf and fall to the floor. "You little bitch. Don't interfere—"

I lunge forward and stab my knife into the trailing fabric of her dress. I expect to just tear through it and hit the floor, but instead my blade sinks into flesh.

The Queen screams. I scream, too, in surprise, and yank my knife back to find it covered in blood. Oh God, I just stabbed her in the foot.

"Guards!" she screeches.

Two men disentangle themselves from the rioting and turn to come after me. I scoot away as fast as I can on all fours and duck behind my trusty plant again, only to turn around and realize both guards are already dead.

Dolly makes her determined way toward the Queen, gun

raised. The Queen, swearing and hobbling, melts back into a crowd of guards.

Dolly takes a step forward, ready to plunge in after her.

"Wait!" I yell, stepping out from behind the plant. "Wolf needs help!" She stops, still staring after the Queen. Finally Dolly turns to face me. Her face is once again a blank slate. She looks up at Wolf and raises her gun, aiming at the rope holding him.

"Hold up," Wolf says. "Hold on one goddamned—"

She shoots through it, and he falls to the floor with a heavy thud. He groans and sits up, rubbing his head.

"God damn it, I hate you guys sometimes."

I help untie his wrists. He does his ankles himself, stands up, cracks his neck, and stretches his arms. Dolly hands him a gun as he checks out the chaos around us.

"This all makes a lot more sense when I'm not looking at it upside down," he says. "Now, where are the others?"

Dolly raises an arm and points. Tank is clearly visible in the middle of the chaos, towering above everyone. He has a metal pipe in hand and is swinging it wildly, taking people out left and right, guards and rioters alike.

"And Pretty Boy?" I ask. I don't see him anywhere.

"Screw Pretty Boy, let's leave 'im. He was about to finally stab us in the back anyway," Wolf says.

"But—"

"We need him," Dolly says. Both Wolf and I stare at her in surprise. A lightbulb seems to go off for Wolf.

"Ahh," he says. "I see."

"See what?" My lightbulb remains dim. They ignore me and move in Tank's direction. Dolly pauses to shoot a few guards who take notice of us, and soon enough we're safely immersed in the insanity. I stick close behind Wolf while Dolly covers us. We don't attract too much attention. Everyone is too focused on their own goals. I see a pair of raiders playing tug-of-war with a blood-splattered painting, and a mob surrounding a screaming man who is probably one of the Queen's men, and plenty of other nasty things. There seems to be an attitude of general revelry among the rioters, while the guards are all terrified.

We hack our way through the crowd to Tank, who looks a bit too happy to be smashing some poor raider woman's head in. When Wolf grabs his arm, Tank whips around and raises his crowbar. He narrowly stops himself from hitting Wolf.

"Oh, hey there, guys," he says, his scary war face relaxing into a smile. "Come to join the fun?"

"Not this time. We're getting out of here."

"Aww…"

"I know, I'm disappointed, too," Wolf says. "This is a hell of a brawl. But we gotta do the smart thing for once."

"All right," Tank says with a sigh. "But…where's Pretty Boy?"

We all pause to look around. Unsurprisingly, there's no sign of him amid all the action. He could've run to the Queen for safety, but seeing as we just came from that direction, it doesn't seem likely. Finally Dolly raises a hand and points. He's in a corner of the room outside the thick of the brawl, cowering and half-hidden behind a broken statue. When he sees us approaching, he shrinks back.

"Get the fuck away from me!"

"No can do," Wolf says. He grabs him by the arm and drags him out. Pretty Boy fights as much as he can, trying to dig his heels into the tile and yank his arm free, but it barely slows Wolf. We head for the entrance room and have nearly made it out when a small group of guards intercepts us. There are five of them, their uniforms torn and bloodied.

"Don't move!" one says. He keeps his gun trained on Wolf. "Didn't think we'd lose track of you, did you?"

"Nah," Wolf says. Looking completely composed, he holds his gun to Pretty Boy's head. He stops struggling and sucks in a startled breath. "But you're gonna let us past, or I'll blow his brains out."

My lightbulb finally crackles to life. Of course we need Pretty Boy; the Queen wants him. The guards must be well aware of that, because they look worried.

"Not even a shark would kill his own," one says, but his voice wavers uncertainly.

"Oh yes he would," Pretty Boy says quickly, his voice high-pitched with nervousness. "He definitely would, he'd love to, please don't give him an excuse!"

Seeing the guards' hesitance, Wolf takes the opportunity to move past them. Tank shoulders a few guards out of the way as he moves by, and I stick close behind him. The Queen's men look at each other uncertainly, clearly at a loss about what to do without orders. Before they can decide, we rush by and into the entrance room. Wolf lowers his gun but keeps a tight grip on Pretty Boy's shirt.

Dolly opens the front doors to find a line of guards standing right outside. They open fire without bothering to check who's coming out, and she slams the door shut. Bullets *thunk* against the other side.

"Goddamn," Wolf says. "Guess we'll have to use the back way."

"And then what? We don't have the truck anymore!" Pretty Boy says.

"Yeah, well, we'll have to figure something out."

"But," Dolly says, "the only thing out the back way is—"

"Shh!" Wolf holds up a hand and everyone shuts up. From the throne room I hear the Queen's voice yelling orders to come after us. Either she's starting to gain control of the situation again, or she's decided to drop all else and follow us.

"Run," Wolf says. He shoves Pretty Boy at Tank, throws

open the door to one of the hallways, and starts sprinting. Dolly takes off after him, and Tank is soon next with Pretty Boy in tow. I follow along doggedly.

The hallway we run through looks completely different than it did last night. The place is utterly destroyed. Most doors are hanging open or ripped off their hinges. Others are closed, and horrible screaming comes from inside one of them. We run past the room where we all played cards and drank, and inside is a complete bloodbath. I narrowly dodge a bottle that flies out of the doorway, and don't pause to see who threw it. I trip over the body of a poor half-dressed woman and nearly gag when I see her mutilated face. We ignore any jeering challenges or cries for help, and just keep running.

At the end of the hallway, Wolf throws open a door and we find ourselves outside. We're behind the building now. It's completely empty, just an expanse of flat ground and then ... a cliff.

"The only thing back here is the river," Dolly says.

"Well, shit, you couldn't have said that earlier?" Wolf says. He curses, looks around, scratches his head, and turns back to go through the door. The second he opens it, we can see the hallway inside flooding with guards. He hastily closes it again and backs toward the edge of the cliff. "Fuck. We're fucked."

They shoot down the first few guards to exit, but soon a crowd of them rushes through and there are too many targets. We keep backing up as they approach. Tank releases Pretty Boy to focus on shooting. After a moment's hesitation, he stays with us.

Soon we're at the very edge of the cliff. The river roars below as the Queen's men approach from the front.

Wolf swings his gun from side to side, unable to decide where to aim. I have only my knife, which I brandish uselessly. Next to me, Pretty Boy is getting the panicked look that usually means he's about to take off running. This time he has nowhere to go.

He takes a step back and the ground beneath him crumbles. As earth starts sliding down the cliffside he pinwheels his arms frantically, trying not to meet the same fate.

I drop my knife and grab his arm with both hands.

"Got you," I say, only to feel my own feet start to slip. I sit down in a desperate attempt to ground myself, and keep sliding. "Oh shit—" I try to dig my feet in, but the dirt slips out from under me. As Pretty Boy's feet go over the edge his weight yanks me forward. Not a second too late, Tank's strong arms grab my waist and hold me up.

"D-Don't let go!" Pretty Boy yells, his feet dangling off the edge. He looks down at the river far below, and his eyes grow even wider. "Holy shit!" I cling to him as best as I can, but I can feel his hand slipping out of mine. My injured hand hurts like hell, and the bandages make it hard to get a good grip.

"No! Pretty Boy!" I'm losing my hold. He closes his eyes, whispering what might be a prayer under his breath. "I can't—"

A hand shoots out from beside me and grabs Pretty Boy's arm.

"I've got ya. Fucking idiot."

I look up to see Wolf. When he nods, I gratefully release my grip and let Tank pull me back to solid ground. Panting for breath, I hurriedly pick up my knife again when I remember the Queen's men are still there. Tank and I keep them at bay while the others pull Pretty Boy to safety.

"Be *careful*," the Queen says, looking immensely relieved to see her favorite pet unharmed. She wields a shotgun as she approaches. "No need to panic, I'm not going to kill you."

"'Course not. Then you wouldn't get the reward, ain't that right?" Wolf asks. "Fucking hell, so much for you being an impartial trader."

"I told you before, Wolf. Times are changing," she says. "Saint is a reasonable man. Maybe he won't even kill you. I'm sure you can work out some sort of deal."

But Wolf has stopped listening. He turns his head to look back at the river, and a thoughtful look passes over his face.

Next to him, Pretty Boy stands up, chest still heaving after his near fall.

"Thanks, Wolf," he says breathlessly.

"No problem, buddy," Wolf says, and shoves him off the cliff.

Silence. Everyone stares at Wolf, who looks remarkably pleased with himself.

"Man, that felt good," he says.

"W-What just...?" I ask, stunned. "What did you—"

"After that whole mess, *now* you decide to kill Pretty Boy?" Tank says, his voice shaking. "Jesus, Wolf, that's *fucked-up*!"

The Queen, recovering from her shock, howls in anger. Her men hesitate, awaiting a command.

I turn and peer over the cliff's edge, searching the roaring waters for any sign of him. There's nothing but water, churning white and frothy as it rushes by. Yet after a few moments, I see something: a head, bobbing downstream.

"Hey!" I shout, watching the figure flail and fight in the rapidly moving river. "He's okay!"

"'Course he is," Wolf says. When I look up at him he has a smug grin, and the realization hits me.

"Oh, no," I say.

"Oh, yes," he replies. "Here's our escape route. Hold on to your guns, guys."

The Queen's forces, realizing our plan, begin to tighten around us.

"*Get them!*" the Queen screeches, her composure dissolving. Her men are more hesitant than she, seeing as we have weapons and a cliff to shove them over.

I move backward until I find myself on the edge. Just looking over makes my legs go wobbly. I shove my knife into my boot, taking deep breaths to fight back my panic.

"I can't," I say. "Wolf, I can't swim."

The Queen smacks one of her subordinates with her shotgun in fury, and turns the barrel on us.

"Tough shit, Kid," Wolf says, keeping a wary eye on her. "Time to go."

"I can't!"

"Learn," he says, "or die."

He pushes me over the edge.

I scream the whole way down, though the sound is swallowed by the roar of rushing air. I remember to close my mouth just before I hit the water—and hit it *hard.* The surface smacks me harder than a thousand hands and leaves my skin screaming, but then I'm submerged and the cold water numbs me. It churns and roars, the current stronger than I could have imagined. I tumble like a rag doll. The surface is impossible to reach. I can't even tell which direction the surface *is* anymore, and when I open my eyes all I can see is murky water. Panic blooms. I flail wildly.

By some miracle, one of my hands breaches the surface and finds open air. I fight in that direction. My lungs are about to burst. I finally heave my way up to the surface and stick my head out. One gasp of air, and I'm sucked under again.

I have to struggle not to lose my sense of direction again. A few times I find my way back to air, but it's always brief and never satisfying. In my bursts of open air I try to spot the others, but all I can see is frothing water all around me. I try to yell for help, but instead I get a mouthful of water and go under again.

The cycle continues for what feels like hours. My strength wanes away. It becomes harder and harder for me to reach the surface each time, and I feel like I'm getting less and less air. It's difficult to thrash my way upward with my arms growing heavy and my body going numb. My backpack weighs me down, but it's tangled around me so I can't cut it loose. Eventually I can't do it anymore; I have no choice but to drift underwater, letting the current carry me, fighting the urge to open my mouth and breathe in.

Just when I think I'm done for, a hand closes on my arm and pulls me upward. I open my eyes sluggishly and find, to my surprise, my head is above water—if only barely. I breathe in panicked gasps and the pain in my lungs lessens.

"I see the learning isn't going well for you," Wolf says, grinning. His goggles are still on and his dreadlocks are slicked down with water. He treads water while keeping one hand firmly around me, holding me up with him.

I try to say something and choke up some water instead.

"How 'bout you just keep your mouth shut for a while?"

Sounds like a good plan to me. I focus on just breathing, and trying to imitate Wolf's motions to help keep us afloat. The water isn't roaring by so quickly anymore; it's mellowed out to a slower stream, which makes it much easier to stay above the surface.

As we drift downstream, the river slows even more, and becomes shallower. Finally it reaches a point where Wolf's feet touch the ground and the current is reduced to a gentle pull. He drops me, and I splash around clumsily before realizing I can stand up on my tiptoes.

"What do you know," Wolf says. "We made it."

"And the others?"

"Well, if you survived by flailing around like a fucking idiot, I'm sure they'll be just fine."

"It's not my fault I—"

Wolf shoves me before I can finish and sends me underwater again. I come up a few feet downstream.

"What was that for?" I ask, spitting out river water that tastes like sewage.

"Get to shore."

"Shore?"

He points, and I follow his finger. The sight of land makes my heart swell. There's an embankment here where the river gets shallow, a reprieve from the rapids. I struggle my way toward it at a painfully slow rate. Even this weak current is enough to make it hard to keep my balance. It doesn't help that my backpack is still wrapped around me and constricting my motion, either. Really, though, I'm just glad it didn't get lost in the river, even though the straps seem intent on strangling me. Wolf plows through the river at a much quicker rate. As soon as he catches up he grabs my backpack and drags me along behind him.

He shoves me onto land and I stumble and fall to my knees, grateful to have solid earth beneath me.

Pretty Boy is already sprawled out on the ground, looking as bedraggled as I feel. He looks at us, coughing up water, wet hair plastered across his face.

"Have a nice swim?" Wolf asks.

"Fuck you. You could've killed me."

"Well, I didn't," Wolf says. "Though I probably should have." He ignores the other insults Pretty Boy spits out and looks at the river. I do the same, and see Tank bobbing along. He doesn't seem to have much trouble staying afloat.

"Hey, big boy! Over here!" Wolf yells, waving a hand. Tank swims in our direction. Dolly comes right after him, moving smoothly and gracefully through the water. It looks like I'm the only one who had much trouble with the river, which makes me feel a bit ridiculous.

I struggle to disentangle my pack and squeeze water out of my clothes as the others make their way to land. I feel like a drowned rat with my clothes plastered slick against my body and my hair flattened. My beanie must have been lost in the river. I feel almost naked without it. It's something I've worn for years now. But I don't have time to feel sad.

When Dolly emerges from the water, I notice she's missing something as well: her hair.

I stare at her. Where her long, sleek, vibrant blue locks used to be is a plain black bob.

"Dolly...you..." I point at her as she comes closer. "Your hair...is gone?"

She gives me a quizzical look and raises a hand to her head.

"Oh. My wig."

"Your wig?"

"Of course," Wolf says, giving me an odd look. "You didn't think her hair was *actually* blue, did you?"

"Umm."

Wolf laughs, shaking his head.

"Oh, Kid. You never fail to fucking amaze me." I duck my head and blush. Thankfully he shifts his attention to Dolly. "So, time for a new color?"

She nods and bends down, opening her bag, which was tied securely to her waist, unlike mine. She pulls out, to my surprise, three wigs of varying lengths and colors. She eyes each of them critically, and holds up a bright red one.

"This?" she asks, looking at Wolf. He shrugs, and she looks at me instead. Her eyes bore into me with an intimidating intensity, as if this is an incredibly important decision. I gulp and nod quickly.

"It's a nice color," I say, not really sure what she wants from me. She nods, satisfied, and pins her hair up. When she places the new wig over it, the combination of that and the dress makes her look like a new person.

"Are you changing out of that?" Wolf asks, gesturing at her dress. She glances down at it impassively.

"Should I?"

"It's a little bit...well..." He actually sounds awkward, maybe even embarrassed, which is something I've never heard out of Wolf before. I scrutinize the dress to see what he's so bothered about, and find that the soak in the river has made the white material practically transparent. Apparently, Dolly doesn't wear a bra. I blush. Wolf looks away, and glares at Pretty Boy when he notices him staring.

"I'll change," Dolly says, though she doesn't seem overly bothered. She unpacks her old clothing and disappears behind some nearby rocks.

Wolf clears his throat and looks around. "Where the hell is Tank?"

"Here, boss!" a strained voice calls back. I turn to see Tank still struggling to reach land. He's practically waddling through the shallow water. When he finally reaches shore he flops down on his belly, wheezing.

"Glad you made it, fat-ass," Wolf says.

"'Course, we're all probably gonna die in a few days anyway," Pretty Boy says. "Seeing as we've all been soaking in radiated sewage water."

"Aw, shut up. We've been soaking in radiation since birth. A bullet'll probably get us before that does, anyway."

"Or an angry townie," I say.

"Yeah, or an explosion," Wolf says. "See, that's the kind of attitude I'm looking for. With all of this shit to worry about, what's the chance the radiation will get us first?"

"Is that supposed to be comforting?" Pretty Boy asks, looking queasy.

"No, it's supposed to get you to shut your damn mouth." Wolf grins and looks around at the lot of us, still sprawled across the ground and trying to catch our bearings. Dolly emerges from the rocks wearing her old wasteland garb. "So, we ready to go?"

"Are you kidding?" Tank asks.

"Not a bit," Wolf says. He looks up at the cliffs on either side.

"The Queen will be after us soon, and we need to find a way out of this damn canyon."

"Just shoot me now," Tank groans.

"Ten minutes to rest, and then we're off," Wolf says. He sits down and starts pulling guns out of his pack, inspecting them for damage.

My backpack—I almost forgot to check it. I sit up and disentangle myself from the straps, dropping the pack into the dirt in front of me. The first thing I notice is that the zipper is open. My chest tightens. I dump out the contents, claw at the inside to make sure there isn't anything stuck, and then sit back and stare. The only thing left is my dress from the Queen's, which only survived because it tangled and caught on the zipper. My rations are gone, and my water, and...

"Shit," I say, my voice coming out flat despite the hot feeling behind my eyes. "I lost my blanket."

"So?" Wolf asks without looking over. *So?* My chest aches. I suck in a deep breath and slowly let it leak out of me again.

"It was from my papa," I say, squeezing the words out of my tightened throat. I press the back of my hand against my eyes, willing myself not to cry. I feel like a child. I don't want the crew to see me like this. "It was the only thing from him I had left."

I lower my hand. Wolf is looking at me, his expression inscrutable. I sit silently, waiting for him to tell me to stop acting like a baby, or that we don't have time for this shit right now. He sets aside the gun he's holding, sighs, and stands up.

"Five minutes," he says gruffly. I stare up at him. "What are you waiting for? Get off your ass and look. Maybe it got caught on some rocks or somethin'."

I wipe my eyes, nod, and scramble onto my feet. Wolf is already wading into the water by the time I'm up. I splash after him and straight over to the nearest clump of rocks. I crouch down and search around with my hands, prodding into every nook and cranny where my blanket could have possibly gotten stuck. I know it's a long shot. The blanket could have ended up anywhere, but that doesn't stop me from hoping. As soon as I'm positive it's not here, I move to the next possible place, and then the next. I find a crumpled tin can, and some plastic, and a soggy piece of wood, but no blanket.

My heart sinks the longer I look, as my optimism gradually fades. Eventually I'm forced to admit I'm not going to find it. I stop my search and stand still, staring at the water rushing by. It's gone. My beanie is gone. My blanket is gone. The last piece of my papa, gone.

When I look up, I see that both Dolly and Tank have come to help look as well. Pretty Boy is sitting on the shore with his head in his hands, but at the very least he isn't complaining about the waste of time. The others are all searching diligently, spread across the width of the river. The tight feeling in my chest loosens.

Maybe I don't need memories to keep me going anymore.

"I think it's been five minutes." I cup my hands around my mouth and shout to make sure they can all hear me, because Wolf has wandered pretty far downriver. He turns back and cocks his head to one side. "It's... it's gone." I sigh out a breath and wade back to land. The others follow as I return to my backpack, shove my dress back in, and zip it up. By the time I straighten up, my eyes are dry.

Dolly's small hand squeezes my shoulder as she passes by, and Tank stops beside me as he reaches land.

"Sorry, Kid. You all right?" he asks, looking down at me. I tilt my head up and manage a smile.

"Yeah, actually. Yeah, I think I am." I look around for Wolf, and find him back with his guns, wordlessly shoving them into his pack. "Let's carry on, then."

Wolf slings his pack over one shoulder and nods at me.

"Right," he says. "You guys heard Kid. Let's get going."

XVIII
The Plan

We soon realize escaping isn't as easy as we thought. The river is at the bottom of a canyon, so cliffs rise up on either side of the water, with only a few rocky outcroppings on the way up.

"There's no way I'm climbing that," Tank says, staring up at the cliffside.

"Me neither," Pretty Boy says.

"Don't be babies. It looks easy." Wolf climbs up on a rock to demonstrate. He grabs at the lowest outcropping for leverage, but his grasping fingers fall just short. "You just—you just gotta—aww, hell!" He loses his balance and stumbles off the rock. Narrowly managing to catch his balance again, he folds his arms over his chest, disgruntled.

Pretty Boy lets out a snort of laughter, and Wolf rounds on him.

"What the fuck are you laughing at? You have any better ideas?" he asks, giving him a shove that sends him stumbling. "Yeah. No. Didn't think so. But I have another one." He jabs a finger in Pretty Boy's chest. "Get on the ground."

"What?"

"On the ground. Now."

When Pretty Boy still hesitates, Wolf smacks him upside the head.

"You think I'm fucking kidding?"

"All right, all right! Ow, really, you don't—" Pretty Boy clamps his mouth shut as Wolf draws his hand back again, and obediently drops to the ground.

"On your hands and knees. There ya go. Now a bit to the right…" Wolf positions an unhappy-looking Pretty Boy to his liking and climbs onto his back. His arms start to tremble the moment Wolf steps on. Wolf bounces up and down a few times. Pretty Boy grits his teeth, arms shaking violently.

"*Wolf!* Come on!"

"Eh, fine, fine." Wolf grabs the rocky ledge, grasping it easily from his new height. With a grunt of effort he hoists himself onto the outcropping. It's narrow, but he manages to crouch there, leaning against the cliff wall. "See? Easy!"

Tank, Dolly, and I glance at each other.

"Yeah, that ain't gonna work out for me," Tank says. Dolly silently walks away, heading downriver.

"Where are you going?" Wolf shouts after her. She doesn't turn around. "Whatever. Your turn, Kid, get up here."

"Me?" I look up the cliff uneasily. "I don't know about that…"

"Shut up and get over here."

I nervously tighten the straps of my bag and walk over. I'm about to place a foot on Pretty Boy's back, then think twice about it. Indecisive, I end up hopping awkwardly on one foot.

"Here, Kid, let me hoist you up," Tank says, noticing my predicament.

"Nah, Pretty Boy's got it," Wolf insists. I look up at him and he grins deviously. "Go on, kiddo. Step on up."

I hesitantly place one boot on Pretty Boy's back, and then the other. I pinwheel my arms before finding my balance.

"Sorry," I mutter. He doesn't respond. I bite my lip and look up at Wolf.

"Can you reach?"

I stand up on my tiptoes and grab for the edge. My fingers scrabble at the cliff just a few centimeters beneath it.

"Uh, almost—" I try to stretch taller and lose my balance. One foot slips and lands on Pretty Boy's head.

"Ow!"

"I'm sorry!" I cringe and move my foot back over.

"Here, Kid." Wolf extends a hand down to me. I grab a hold of it with both of mine, wincing at the pressure on my bandaged injury, and we both struggle to lift my weight. I scramble against the cliff wall for a foothold, showering dirt and rocks down. Finally I manage to reach the ledge and crouch beside Wolf, panting. I look down to see Pretty Boy covered in dirt from my ascent. He glowers up at me. Wolf is smirking. To my surprise, I feel a glimmer of amusement myself. Biting back a smile, I look away from both of them and stare at the stretch of cliff above us.

"So now what?"

"We find another ledge."

"How does this solve anything? The rest of us still can't get up," Pretty Boy says from below, dusting himself off.

"We'll figure it out," Wolf says.

The next ledge isn't any easier to reach than this one was. Wolf has to help me again, giving me a boost so I can reach. Even then, I only barely manage to clamber up.

"Now help me up," Wolf says.

"What? How?"

"Grab my hand." He reaches out for me. I look around for something to steady myself, and grab onto a sturdy-looking rock jutting out of the cliff. I reach down with my free hand to clasp Wolf's and strain to pull him up. It's no easy task, even with him doing most of the work. Soon my arm is burning and my palms are slick with sweat. My injured hand, the one grasping the rock, starts to hurt pretty badly. It feels like the wound is tearing open again. My eyes water at the pain.

"I-I can't do this!"

"You got it. I'm almost there." His free hand grabs the ledge, finally—and it crumbles right out from underneath us. I lose my grip on Wolf's hand and he slides downward, scrambling for a hold.

"Shit! Shit, shit!" I try to hold on to the rock as the rest of the ledge crumbles away, but I soon lose my hold and my footing and I'm free-falling. I scream, eyes closed, desperately hoping I won't break my neck when I hit the ground.

And then—*thud.* I freeze, expecting pain, but none comes. I tentatively open one eye, then the other, and find myself resting safely in Tank's arm. He grins at me.

"Caught ya."

"Oh…thanks." I let out a shaky breath. He sets me upright on the ground, and I look around for Wolf. He's sprawled across the ground on top of Pretty Boy. They're both covered in dirt but look relatively unharmed.

"So. That didn't work out well." Wolf stands up with a grunt, leaving a groaning Pretty Boy on the ground. He turns to survey the cliff, shielding his eyes as he looks up. "Yeah…that wasn't even halfway up, was it? Damn."

"It wasn't?" I follow his eyes. He's right. And it felt so high already…

"Well, let's give it another go," Wolf says.

"No!" Pretty Boy and I exclaim simultaneously. I notice him glance at me and refuse to look over. Wolf looks taken aback.

"Well, we ain't got any other plans, guys."

"We could try riding the river downstream—" Tank starts, but I quickly interject.

"I am *not* going back in that water!"

"Then, how 'bout Wolf climbs up, gets a rope, and—"

"There ain't no way I can lift you up, fat-ass."

"Well…" Tank tries to think of something else, fails, and shrugs. "I guess that *is* our only option."

"That's what I'm sayin', dumbasses. Now let's try this again, and try not to screw it up this—" Wolf stares up at the cliff and pauses, his mouth hanging open.

I follow his gaze. Dolly is standing at the top of the cliff, peering down at us as if confused why we aren't up yet.

"What the hell? How did you get up there?" Wolf shouts up to her. In response she points downriver.

We follow her direction to find, not very far at all, a much easier path up the cliff. It's narrow and winding and the thought of climbing it makes my legs wobble, but it's still a hell of a lot better than Wolf's plan.

"Well, shit," Wolf says. "I guess that works just as well."

From there, it doesn't take much time to reach the top. Soon enough we find a road and we're back on track as if the ordeal with the Queen never happened.

As the heat of the day sets in, the sun soaks up the moisture from my clothes and body—all except for my boots. My feet still feel damp and clammy while the rest of me is way too hot. My feet squish noisily with every step, painfully loud in the near silence. I feel more and more ridiculous, though nobody says anything. Everyone seems subdued, or maybe just exhausted. Pretty Boy walks with his head down and his shoulders slumped, Tank is lagging behind as usual, and Dolly stays a few yards ahead and doesn't say a word. I want to speak to her, but I have no idea what to say. The atmosphere is grim; even Wolf is dragging his feet.

"So what's the plan, then?" I ask eventually, unable to take the dreary silence any longer.

"Same as before," Wolf says. "This Saint asshole's got Lord

knows how many sharks locked up already, and we sure as hell ain't gonna join them. So we find that radio tower and explode the shit out of it." He says it matter-of-factly, without his usual excitement.

"Really?" Pretty Boy asks, lifting his head. "How the hell are we supposed to do that?"

"In the usual way, dumbass. With explosives."

"Wolf, we don't *have* any explosives."

"So we get some."

"Oh? Just like that? We can't use the Queen anymore."

"This is the fucking wastelands, Pretty Boy, everyone has explosives. We just need to find a town."

"A town that will know we're coming, thanks to that broad-cast."

"Shit, you're right." Wolf pauses for a second. "Guess we'll need disguises, then."

"Disguises?" I ask. "Does that actually work?"

"'Course it does. This one time, we dressed Pretty Boy up as a girl and—"

"I am *not* doing that again. No way."

"It worked way too well," Tank says, looking disturbed.

"Yeah, it did. He looked more like a girl than you do, Kid."

Somehow, I don't find that hard to believe.

"Actually, that could work. We dress *Kid* up as a girl," Wolf says, face lighting like he just came up with something brilliant.

"Uh, Wolf, I am a girl."

"Yeah, but hardly. It still counts as a disguise."

"What, so we send Kid in as a scout? You really think that's a good idea?" Tank asks. He says it without malice, but it stings a little.

"Yeah. Kid and Pretty Boy."

Pretty Boy and I glance at each other simultaneously. He looks away first. I try not to let my mind wander. It makes me feel sick to think about last night, and there's something hard and bitter inside me that grows with every reminder.

"She'll fuck it up," Pretty Boy says bluntly.

"We ain't got any other options," Wolf says. "I'm too easy to recognize, Tank is too scary, and Dolly is too . . . you know."

"She'll fuck it up," he repeats.

"Shut up. That's my decision and we're sticking with it."

I glance at Pretty Boy again to find him adamantly avoiding my gaze, his jaw set. It takes me a moment to realize what's happening here. Pretty Boy might not trust me to do the job right, but Wolf actually does. I smile down at my boots, but at the same time my stomach flutters nervously. I hope his faith in me isn't misplaced.

"So what do we . . . do?" I ask.

"Just go in, test the waters, don't blow your cover. If things look bad, you get the hell out. If all goes well, you wait for the rest of us."

"Why not just go in together?"

"'Cause if they're gonna shoot us up the moment we step into town, then . . ."

Wolf trails off and abruptly stops walking. The others do the same. I run right into Tank and stumble back.

"What is it?" I ask, seeing nothing.

"You hear that?" Wolf asks, looking at Dolly. She tilts her head, pauses, and nods.

"What? What?" I ask, looking back and forth between them. Wolf turns to the stretch of road behind us, raising his goggles and squinting. He points.

I turn around and see it: a cloud of dust speeding down the road toward us.

"Someone's coming."

I squint at the cloud, confused.

"Vehicles. Big ones," Dolly says.

"The Queen?" I ask.

"Let's hope not. Binoculars?" Wolf asks. Dolly produces some from her pack and hands them to him, and he scopes out the fast-approaching dust.

"Doesn't look like the Queen," he says. "Or raiders. Looks like a trade caravan."

"How do you know?" Pretty Boy asks.

"Just got a feeling."

"Last time you said that, we ended up tied up in that crazy old woman's basement and—"

"This time will be different." Wolf lowers the binoculars and shows that crazy grin of his. "And screw the scouting plan, I've got something else in mind."

XIX
The New Plan

So then I end up standing in the middle of the road and flailing my arms around as the vehicles roar toward me.

There's three of them: an open-top jeep, a big supply truck, and a pickup truck. There are a few car lengths of space in between them. They're moving at a relatively slow speed, but my heart still pounds as they bear down on me. Wolf promised they would stop. He insisted that these guys are "bleeding-heart traders." Probably.

As they come closer I raise my hands as high as I can get them, waving wildly to ensure they see me. A gust of wind whips my dress up, and I hastily pin my arms to my sides. Damn dress is such a pain, but Wolf insisted on it. *They ain't gonna stop for some ugly boy,* he said. *But if they see the dress before your ugly face, maybe you'll have a chance.*

They don't seem to see me. Or, if they do, they don't care that I'm here. The head jeep keeps roaring toward me without any sign of stopping. I suck in a deep breath and feel my knees start to tremble. Still, I hold my ground. I close my eyes and grit my teeth, expecting to be splattered across the road at any second.

The jeep roars past, a gust of wind buffeting me as it does so. I stumble and cringe, knowing the supply truck is next. There's no way it can pass by on this narrow road. It'll either stop or hit me head-on. I peek open one eye, unable to help myself.

And, to my amazement, the truck is stopping. It gradually slows as it approaches, brakes squealing, and stops just a few feet ahead of me. The thing is *huge*. It towers over me, making me feel like a bug about to be squished. The engine sounds like some angry beast growling and ready to swallow me whole. Legs still shaking, I manage a timid wave and a shaky smile. I can't see anything through the windshield.

A door slams. Footsteps approach. Against the sunlight, all I see is a vast silhouette getting closer. I shrink back nervously. I know the others are nearby, hidden behind a crumbling wall on the side of the road, but I still feel alone.

"Umm...hi...c-can I get a ride?" I squeak out, still taking tiny steps backward as the silhouette approaches.

The figure swings close, thick shoulders blocking out the direct sun so I can see. It's...not exactly what I expected.

"Well, howdy!"

The driver, it turns out, is a broad woman with a near-blinding grin of what look like fake teeth. She wears a wide-brimmed hat and is fatter than Tank, with rolls on her arms and multiple chins. Her eyes are set a little too far apart, and her round face is all smiles. She doesn't look very bright or all that threatening. I almost feel bad about what's going to happen to her, but I stifle it. This is something I need to do for my crew.

"Umm." I have no idea what to say.

"What's a little girl like you doing wandering around all by your lonesome?" she asks.

"Oh. I got separated from my family." I try to pull my face into some semblance of sadness. My facial features don't want to cooperate, though, and I just grimace awkwardly.

"Aww, poor little thing." She yanks me into a hug. I find myself with my face squished into her chest. My entire body stiffens. I can't remember the last time someone hugged me, let alone a stranger. It's...squishy, and uncomfortably warm and damp, and suffocating. I hold my head back as far as I can.

"Yeah—there were raiders, and—I don't know if they're—I...can't breathe..." She finally releases me. I stumble back, blinking, and gasp for air. "Can I get a ride to the nearest town, please?"

"Well of course, sweetie! I'd be happy to give you a lift!"

"Great!" My reply comes out a little too eager. I try to tone it down, and ask, "Where, uh...where is the nearest town, anyway?"

"Just a bit up the road from here. Ain't far, hun, don't worry. Maybe your family will meet you there, if they escaped."

"Huh?...Oh. Right. Yeah." My response comes a little late, but she only grins wider.

I hear the rumble of a vehicle at my back, and turn to see the jeep has circled around. There are two men in it, each with a bandana over his head. One has a gun, which he aims at me. His eyes are dark and shrewd.

"What's the holdup, ma?" the driver shouts at us.

"Found this little one just standin' in the road!" The woman places a fleshy arm around my shoulders, squeezing me a little too hard. "She's lost her family, poor little doll."

"And?" the man responds. I look back and forth between him and the woman with a growing sense of unease. It's hard to tell which of them is in charge here.

"And...just look at her!" She beams down at me. I can feel the man's eyes on me as well, and stare down at my feet.

"I'm looking."

"She's a little girl, Frankie!"

"And?"

"Do you know how much some people will *pay* for little girls?"

I'm already nodding along with her, agreeing with my defense, when her words hit me.

"Uh, pay?" I ask.

"An ugly little thing like her? Don't think so," Frankie says, ignoring me.

"They always pay more for girls!"

"You sure we can even sell her 'round here, with this Saint guy running things?" he asks.

"Saint ain't gonna bother us. It's not like we're sharks or somethin'."

"Still, I'm pretty sure his 'law and order' spiel don't involve sellin' people…"

"We'll find a way," the woman says. "There's always some-one willing to do business." I try to wrench free from her grip, but she clutches me tighter. "Oh, calm down, sweetie. If your family is there, we'll try an' sell you to them first!" she says cheerfully. "Only if they can pay the price, though. How much should we charge, Frankie?"

"Dunno. What do you think, Freddie?" He looks at the man with the gun, who shrugs without comment. "Ehh, we'll figure it out. Fine, fine, ma, just throw 'er in with the rest of the loot."

"No!" I struggle to break free, but the woman lifts me up off my feet. I cast a frantic glance toward where the others are hiding. No one emerges. "Don't do that! I'm not loot!" I raise my voice pointedly. "It would be really nice to *not become loot!*"

The woman looks down at me, raising her eyebrows and pursing her lips.

"Help! Somebody! Please! Help *now!*"

"Crazy little girl. Ain't nobody that's gonna help you," she says with a chuckle.

"Hold up. Why's she keep looking over there?" the driver asks. I avert my eyes, feeling my cheeks redden. "Something ain't right about this." He reaches over and nudges the passenger. "Go check it out, Freddie."

The man nods silently and gets out, gun in his hands. He stalks past the woman and me, heading straight for the wall the others are hiding behind. I freeze, not even remembering to struggle. *Shit.* Oh man, Wolf is going to kill me for blowing their cover like this. But they should be fine. Just three of them here, and...my heart sinks as I remember there was another truck behind them. I can't even see how many guys are in that one, since it's hidden behind the supply truck. *Shit, shit.* My stomach sinks. I really screwed up this time.

I watch as Freddie approaches the wall, gun held ready, walking slowly and steadily. He pauses for a moment.

He jumps behind the wall and lets loose a spray of gunfire in one smooth motion. I squeak and renew my struggling. There's no way they could have avoided those shots! And there's no sound of return fire. The others...

Freddie stops, looking perplexed. He looks from the wall to me.

"Nobody here," he calls out.

"What?" I ask, dumbfounded.

The woman lets out a snort of laughter.

"Guess she really is just slow in the head," she says. "Now, be a good girl and keep still."

She walks toward the back of the truck, humming to herself as she carries me. I thrash around, starting to get seriously worried. Where the hell could they be?

"This isn't fair! I'm not loot! Definitely not loot!"

"You are now," she says, cackling. "And you are gonna fetch me a pretty penny, oh yes you are. A bit too scrawny and ugly, but so long as you got the right parts I'm sure someone can put you to good use—"

She rounds the back of the truck and stops when she sees the pickup truck.

The former driver is slumped in the seat, her head utterly pulverized by some blunt object. The two others aren't in much better shape. One is already lying on the side of the road, his seat stolen by a grinning Tank with a crowbar. The other is in the truck bed, and is currently having his throat slit by Dolly while Pretty Boy keeps his mouth covered.

Wolf stands triumphantly on the truck's hood, an assault rifle pointed at us.

"Hey there," he says. "These are some nice guns. Thanks."

He opens fire.

The woman shrieks and drops me. I fall to the ground and roll away, wincing at the too-close gunfire, which thankfully only hit the woman's legs.

"You could've shot me!" I yell at him, climbing to my feet.

"Well, I didn't," he says.

"And you didn't kill her, either," I point out. The woman is still rolling around on the cracked asphalt, howling, her legs full of bullet holes and leaking everywhere. As I watch, she reaches down to a sheath on her waist and whips out a knife. She waves it wildly in the air. Wolf and I merely stare at her.

"You can do the honors." Wolf reaches into the back of his pants, pulls out a pistol, and tosses it to me. I fumble, and it hits me in the chest with a painful *thud* and clatters to the ground. I retrieve it, rubbing at my sore chest, and only then do I realize what he said.

"Oh," I say. "You want...me to...?"

"Yeah, yeah." He gestures impatiently to the still-shrieking woman. I look from the gun to her face, with her mouth wide open and tears streaming down her round cheeks.

"I don't know—"

"She was gonna *sell* you, Kid," he says. "Probably to some pervy old man."

I chew my bottom lip and nod. He's right. She deserves it.

Back when I was alone, if I had gotten picked up by these people instead of Wolf, I would be dead or worse by now.

I point the gun at her head, remembering to pull back the safety. I carefully aim the sights at the center of her forehead.

"Umm." I hesitate, trying to think of something witty to say like Wolf always does. "...I'm not loot."

Close enough.

And I blow her brains out.

It's easier than I thought. One shot, no recoil from a tiny gun like this. One shot, and her screaming stops. She stops flailing and lies very still. I can see the light go out of her wide-set eyes.

I stare at the body. My stomach churns, and I swallow back bile. My hands are shaking, the gun suddenly heavy in my hands. It shook up something in my core, seeing someone die like that. And yet, I don't feel guilty. Not at all. She deserved to die, and I killed her.

"Not bad," Wolf says. I turn to him, a smile growing on my face. It's silly to think about at a time like this, but I'm pretty sure this is the first time Wolf has ever praised me.

"Gee, Wolf, tha—" I cut off with a shrill scream as a bullet whizzes past my head. I drop to the ground and crawl on my hands and knees to the pickup truck, seeking shelter behind one of its big tires. The sound of gunfire explodes from multiple places around me, thankfully no longer aimed at me.

Once I'm safely behind a tire I peek out. The two guys from the jeep, Frankie and Freddie, are exchanging fire with Wolf. Their bullets ping against the hood of the truck. Wolf topples off. He hits the asphalt hard, and the gun clatters out of his hand.

As the two men aim at him, I point my pistol in their direction and unload. A bullet hits one in the shoulder, and the rest of my shots miss. At least I've captured their attention. They turn their guns on me instead of Wolf. I duck behind the tire just in time as they both open fire.

The tire bursts, and the truck groans as it leans off-balance. I scramble farther underneath the now-slanted truck, clutching my now-empty gun. I frantically try to think up some way to help—but, thankfully, I don't have to. Gunfire erupts above me, coming from the bed of the truck. I wait for it to stop and crawl out from my hiding spot.

Frankie and Freddie are down. I can tell at a glance they won't be getting up again. Wolf is still lying on the asphalt.

I stand up and walk toward him, peering from side to side to make sure no other armed men are approaching us. Once I'm satisfied we're safe, I focus on Wolf and notice the blood soaking his shirt. My heart leaps into my throat and I rush over to his side. His eyes are closed.

"Oh, shit," I breathe. The red stain is spreading from his shoulder. "Guys, Wolf is bleeding! It looks like he got shot! Somebody hel—"

A hand pulls on my leg and sends me tumbling to the ground. I fall on my ass with a surprised squeak.

Wolf glares at me from where he's lying, and releases my leg to press a hand to his wound.

"Shut the fuck up, Kid. I'm fine."

"You got *shot*!"

"Nothing vital." He sits up with a grunt and a grimace, and looks down at the wound. "It's hardly even bleeding. Jeez, don't be so dramatic."

"Well, excuse me for being concerned!" I snap, the words jumping out before I even think about them. Wolf gives me a taken-aback look, and I feel my cheeks flush, but bite back an apology.

He stares at me for a second longer, and then looks around at the messy scene we've created. There are bodies strewn all around us, along with blood and brains and bullets. He stands up, hand pressed to his shoulder, and heaves a sigh.

"Well, time to get back on the road," he says. "But first, let's eat."

XX
Disguises

We build a small fire using wooden crates from the traders' truck. There are a lot of goods in there, food and medical supplies and such, but Wolf insists we have to save most of it to trade. Still, he lets Pretty Boy find some canned fruit as a treat. We pass the cans around the circle, eating with our hands, while Tank roasts the meat on spits of splintered wood. The reek of fresh blood makes me nauseous, but the smell of cooking meat chases that away. I watch one of the pieces slowly turning, dripping grease into the fire. My mouth waters. I swallow hard, trying to stifle the thought of meat, and resign myself to beans again.

"Mmm-mmm," Tank says. "Nice and fatty."

"Which is why we'd eat you first if it ever came down to it," Pretty Boy says. He tosses a slice of canned peach to Tank, who catches it in his mouth.

"You could try," he says, grinning as he chews. "Who's gonna take me down, huh? I'll take all of ya."

"No way, you're too slow," Pretty Boy says. Wolf, sitting between him and myself, pretends to fire a shotgun at Tank with sound effects included. He hasn't let us clean his wound yet, but it hasn't put a damper on his mood.

"All I'm saying is it would be easier to kill someone else," Tank says, and nods not so subtly in Pretty Boy's direction.

"Well, Kid would be the easiest to kill," Wolf says, "but she ain't got no meat on her."

I glance down at my skinny legs and shrug. He reaches over and grabs my face with one hand, pulling on my cheek to stretch it out.

"We-ell, maybe a bit here . . ."

I slap his hand away and stick my tongue out at him.

"She'd taste terrible," Pretty Boy says matter-of-factly.

"Hey, what's *that* supposed to mean?" I ask. Somehow I find it genuinely offensive.

"Shame we couldn't find that finger she lost, could've had a taste," Tank says.

"Oh, jeez, no!" I say, horrified but laughing despite myself. "Wouldn't want to tempt you or anything!"

"Y'know, good point," Wolf says. "The real question is who would taste the best." He squints thoughtfully around the circle.

"Dolly," Pretty Boy says without missing a beat. She stares at him, unamused.

"Whoa, that was quick," Wolf says. "You've already thought about this, haven't you, ya sick fuck?"

"I'm the sick fuck? You brought it up!"

Wolf ignores him, and continues staring at each of us in turn.

"Yep," he says eventually. "It's gotta be Pretty Boy."

"Why me?"

"Trader raised. Always taste best."

"What?" I say, looking back and forth between them. "Pretty Boy was a trader?" I address Wolf instead of talking directly to him.

"'Course he was, look at him. He can read and he can lie, certainly ain't no dumb townie."

Curiosity overcomes my desire to avoid him. I swallow a lump in my throat and lean forward to meet Pretty Boy's eyes.

"So you were raised in a caravan?"

"Yeah," he says. "Trader's son. I was only there until I was about ten years old."

"Why?"

"Oh, here we go," Wolf groans.

"Don't encourage him, Kid, he *loves* to talk about himself," Tank says.

Heedless, I climb over Wolf's lap and squeeze in between them so I'm next to Pretty Boy. It makes me uncomfortable to be so close to him, but I try to push it away. It can't be all awkward glances and ignoring each other forever. I raise my eyes to his face, and resist the impulse to look away. When I swallow, it feels like there's a lump of dust in my throat.

Pretty Boy looks down at me, eyes partially closed so his long eyelashes stand out more than ever. Seeing him close up, with his beautifully crafted cheekbones and jawline, makes the old swooning instinct swell up again. I fight it down. No, no, no, I'm not going to forgive him just because he's pretty on the outside. He hurt me. He probably would've hurt me worse if Dolly hadn't shown up. I set my jaw, hold his gaze, and don't smile.

"Well, my mother owned a store before this place was a wasteland," he begins. He says it like he's already told the story a thousand times. Judging by the groans from Tank and Wolf, he probably has. He ignores them. "So, post-bombs, our family went on the road as a trader caravan with the goods she saved. My mom taught me to read so I could help with inventories, to use maps so I could navigate, to talk to people and make them listen, to barter and lie if I needed to..." He shrugs. "She was grooming me to be head of the caravan."

"And then what?" I ask, enthralled despite myself.

"And then—"

"Watch out, guys, this is the tearjerker part," Wolf interjects. I glance around to notice all the others are watching us. Pretty Boy glares at Wolf before continuing.

"And then, raiders," he says simply. "This was back before the wastes got real crazy, before it had really sunk in that there was no more government or law or order, so we weren't ready. The raiders killed everyone, my mom included." His voice is tinged with sadness, as if the incident is still raw and painful for him. I stare, wide-eyed, my resentment toward him melting.

"Except for you?" I ask, my voice softening. He smirks, and the sadness is gone in an instant. *He's pretending*, I tell myself, frustrated at being hooked in so easily.

"Except for me. I was just a kid."

"Why didn't they kill you?"

"Because I was useful." I try to rack my brains for ways a ten-year-old could be useful to a band of raiders, and come up with nothing. He continues before I have to ask. "I was bait. It'd usually be something like what you just did. Stand on the side of the road and wait for someone to stop. Then we'd jump 'em. I was cleanup crew, too."

"Right," I say. "You didn't run away?"

"Nowhere to go," he says. "Anyway, I wasn't with the ones who killed my family for long. They got killed off by another crew of raiders. They kept me around when I explained what I could do. It happened like that a few times, just getting passed around over the years."

"And that's how you got with Wolf, too?"

"Pretty much."

"Actually his crew captured us. We cut a deal with him while he was on watch duty, and he let us slit their throats in their sleep," Wolf says cheerfully.

"They were a bunch of assholes anyway," Pretty Boy says without a hint of remorse. I never questioned the fact the crew didn't trust him, especially considering his cowardice, but now it makes even more sense.

"And now he's our resident scapegoat and navigator-slave," Wolf says. "Touching story, right?"

"Does it bother you?" I ask. Pretty Boy turns away from Wolf and looks down at me, brow creasing.

"What?"

"To kill people like your family was killed."

The question strikes him off guard. I see the way his eyes widen before he controls them again. He purses his lips and studies my face.

"I don't need you judging me, Kid," he says, his voice suddenly soft and dangerous.

"I'm not!" Face heating up, I backpedal. "I didn't mean it like that."

"Does it bother *you* to kill townies?"

"What makes you think I'm a townie?"

"You're far too stupid to be a trader, for one."

"We-e-ell, time to eat!" Tank says overly loudly, in a painfully obvious attempt to break the tension. I stare at Pretty Boy for a moment longer, refusing to show that his comment hurt me, before turning to Tank and smiling. "Kill was yours, so first serving goes to you, Kid," Tank says, "if you want it."

My stomach flips at the thought, and I'm not sure it's a strictly unpleasant flip. Tank holds out a stick of skewered meat. I stare at it, observing how glistening fat clings to muscle and grease drips from the end. It doesn't look human; it just looks like meat. Juicy, rich, tantalizing meat that sure sounds a lot better than beans right now.

"Okay," I say, the word practically spilling out of my mouth before I have time to consider. I reach out and take the skewer from him, twirling it in my hands and trying to pretend I can't feel everyone's eyes watching me.

Agreeing was easy, but now that it's actually in my hands

I find myself hesitating. Am I really going to cross this line? Take the final step to join the rest of the crew? After the first bite, there's no turning back. Even if this is the one and only time, it'll change me forever. Brand me. I'll be a shark—the most hated thing in the wastes. Most wastelanders don't even believe in good, but they'd agree that this is evil.

I slowly raise the skewer to my mouth, inhaling the smell of warm meat. An image of the woman in her floppy hat springs to mind for a moment.

I take a bite.

Though juicy as expected, the meat is still tougher than anything else I've eaten in a while. I tear off a chunk with my teeth and chew for a full five seconds before I can swallow it. The lump feels thick as it worms its way down my throat. I suck in a deep breath.

And I take another bite. And another.

It may be chewy and thick and wrong, but holy shit does it taste good. Once I start I can't stop, eating with a relish that surprises me. It feels warm and satisfying in my belly. It's not just taking the edge off my hunger but making me actually feel *full*, something I haven't had in forever.

Only when it's halfway gone do I remember everyone is watching me. I look up, juices running down my chin, and smile.

"I cannot believe," I say, "I spent so long eating goddamn beans."

Tank laughs, Dolly smiles, and Wolf shoots me a thumbs-up and his usual fierce grin.

"You really are one of us, Kid," he says. My smile widens. "Now, stop hogging all the damn meat." He leans over and steals a bite before I can stop him.

"Hey!" I yank it away, laughing. Tank chuckles, reaching to grab another skewer off the fire.

"Plenty to go around, guys."

And there is. By the time we're done everyone is full and content—except for Pretty Boy, who remains unsmiling the whole time.

Dolly ends up driving the supply truck while the rest of us pile into the jeep. We leave the truck with its blown-out tire and hood full of holes. Tank drives the jeep and the rest of us sit in the back. Pretty Boy and I are given the job of patching up Wolf's wound. Or, rather, Pretty Boy is supposed to patch him up while I hold him down, but it doesn't prove so easy.

"You better keep him down this time," Pretty Boy says through clenched teeth, his eye already starting to swell from our last attempt. Turns out, Wolf instinctively lashes out when it hurts. Either that, or he just likes hitting Pretty Boy, even when he's trying to dig a bullet out of him. Hard to say.

I focus on holding Wolf's arms down. Trying to, at least, my skinny arms wrapped around his muscular ones.

"Okay, got him," I say. Wolf flexes his arms and chuckles. Pretty Boy looks nervous.

"Seriously, Wolf," he warns, "if you hit me again, I'm done."

"Shut up. You're done when I say you're done."

"Well, you'll be stuck with a bullet in you until you let me do my job!"

Wolf sighs and nods grudgingly.

"Yeah. Fine. Get to it already."

Pretty Boy bites his lip and raises the knife again. I look away as he moves it toward Wolf's wounded shoulder. The knife is the sharpest, thinnest one we have, and it's been sanitized with alcohol, but it's sure as hell no medical tool, and Pretty Boy is no doctor.

Still, I guess it's the best we can manage.

"Hold him *tight*," Pretty Boy tells me. I squeeze my eyes shut and clutch Wolf's arms as tightly as I can, putting all of my strength into keeping them pinned.

Wolf doesn't scream when the knife goes in, but his whole body goes rigid. His muscles bulge with the tension, straining against mine, although he doesn't pull free this time. I hold on tightly, wary of what he'll do the second he gets a chance.

"Fuck," Wolf says. "Fucking shit God damn *hurry up, Pretty Boy*!"

"Almost got it," he says. "Try to relax."

"You're digging around in my shoulder with a fucking *knife*," Wolf snarls. "Tell me to relax one more time, and I'll—"

He cuts off with a low grunt. A jolt goes through his body, and his arms tremble.

"Got it," Pretty Boy says.

Wolf hisses in a breath and lets it out in a long sigh. The tension drains out of him along with the air.

"You can let go now, Kid," he says after a pause. I release him and scoot back, worried he's going to hit me.

Instead he cracks his neck and stretches his arms, careful not to jostle his shoulder too badly. Once I'm convinced he doesn't intend on punching me, I turn to Pretty Boy. He's holding up a small bullet, its silver surface coated with blood.

"That's it?" I ask. "It's so small!"

"You ever been shot, Kid?" Wolf asks. I shake my head. "Damn right you haven't. So shut up. And where the hell are my bandages, Pretty Boy?"

"Do I at least get a thank-you?"

"So now you want me to thank you for letting you knife me? Finish your job, idiot."

Pretty Boy grabs the bottle of alcohol and douses Wolf's shoulder without warning. Wolf lets out a shout before clamping his mouth shut to stifle the noise. The sharp smell of alcohol reminds me of vomiting and other unpleasant things.

When I glance at Pretty Boy, I see the corner of his mouth

tugging upward. Wolf notices it as well. Intermingled blood and alcohol drip from his arm.

He punches Pretty Boy in the jaw, the blow hitting hard enough to wipe the smirk off his face and twist his head to the side. I don't feel sorry for him at all.

"Stop looking so fucking happy!" Wolf yells.

"Lay off, Wolf," Tank rumbles from up front. He doesn't turn away from the road, but his voice is loud enough to carry back to us.

Wolf looks rather miffed about being scolded. Nonetheless, he pulls back from Pretty Boy and drops his still-raised fist.

"Now bandage this. I'm leaking all over the place."

Pretty Boy cradles his face, staying back.

"I *told* you if you hit me one more time—"

"Oh, stop whining and get—"

I grab the first aid kit and pull out the gauze myself, half because I want them to stop arguing and half because Wolf's still-bleeding shoulder is making me nauseous. I wrap the wound as best as I can with my clumsy hands. Wolf stubbornly sets his jaw and doesn't say anything.

"Is that all right?" I ask when I'm finished. It looks like a mess, but at least it's bandaged.

"Good enough," Wolf says tersely. I know better than to expect a thanks. As Wolf rises to move up to the passenger seat, he smacks me on the side of the head. I look up at him, wondering what I did wrong this time, but instead he grins at me. It looks about as close to affectionate as Wolf can get. I smile back.

"Wake me up when we're getting close," Wolf says, slumping down in the passenger seat. I silently agree and curl up in my own seat for a nap.

I wake up to a hand shaking me and an unfamiliar face.

I let out a nervous shriek and lash out, smacking the face

away as hard as I can. He recoils immediately, letting out a curse, and only then do I realize it's Pretty Boy.

Suffice to say, he's not looking so pretty right now. He has a black eye, a split and bloody lip, and his jaw is red and puffy—not to mention the fresh mark from my slap. Wolf's punches really did a number on him.

"Oh, shit, I'm so sorry!" I say.

"What the hell was that for?"

"I just...didn't recognize you for a second!"

Wolf is cackling in the front of the jeep. Pretty Boy's shocked expression gradually changes to an indignant one.

"It's that bad?" he asks.

"No, well, it's not..." I scramble, trying to think of something nice to say before remembering I have no reason to be nice to him. "Yeah, you look awful."

He rubs at the swollen part of his jaw, looking miffed.

"Told you it was a good enough disguise," Wolf says, turning around to give us a thumbs-up.

"Yeah," I say. "I mean you certainly don't look *pretty*, so that means—"

Wolf cuts me off with a burst of wild laughter, and Pretty Boy looks even more affronted.

"So it means it's a good disguise," I say.

He shoots me a cold look and I stifle a smile.

"Anyway, we're almost there," Wolf says, "so we're workin' out our disguises and the bullshit we're gonna tell the townies."

"We're a trade caravan," Pretty Boy explains without looking at me. "We fought off a group of raiders on the way over, which is why we're so banged up."

I nod. Sounds easy enough.

"And where's your disguise, Wolf?" I ask.

"I don't need one."

"Like hell. Everyone knows what you look like," Pretty Boy says. "You need *something*."

"I ain't wearing no wig or anything."

"Then you at least need a messed-up face like me."

"No!"

"Wolf, it's one or the other." Pretty Boy grins at the idea. Wolf grits his teeth.

"Fine, then. The face."

Pretty Boy leans forward eagerly, but Wolf shoves him away.

"I ain't giving you the satisfaction. Kid, you do it."

I stare at him.

"You want me to...hit you?"

"Yeah."

"In the face?"

"Yeah."

We stare at each other. I clench one fist and stare at it, trying to imagine hitting Wolf. I can't even conjure up a mental picture of that. It seems absurd.

"I don't know if I can do that."

"I can," Pretty Boy says.

"Shut your mouth. Kid, man the hell up."

I grit my teeth and nod. Balling up both fists, I try to conjure up anger against Wolf. I draw back a fist, start to swing...and stop a few inches from his face.

"I can't," I confess, letting my hands drop to my sides.

"God damn it, Kid."

"What the *hell* are you guys doing?" Tank asks, turning away from the road to look at us.

"Beating Wolf up so no one will recognize him," Pretty Boy says smugly.

"You guys are idiots. Nobody pays attention to Wolf's face, it's the hair and the goggles people will know him by."

We all pause to mull that over.

"What do you mean, nobody pays attention to my face?" Wolf asks. Tank doesn't answer, watching the road again. "What the hell is wrong with my face?" He turns to me and grins frighteningly with his full set of crooked, yellowing teeth.

I gulp.

"Umm. Nothing. Nothing's wrong with your face."

"Damn straight."

"Well, you heard Tank. You have to wear a wig," Pretty Boy says.

"No."

"Or cut it."

"No!"

"Wolf, if you blow our cover because—"

"I'm in charge here, I'll blow our cover if I want to!" Wolf says. Pretty Boy gives him an incredulous look. Eventually Wolf sighs, resigned, and turns to me.

"You still got your old shirt?"

"Umm...yeah?" I dig in my pack and pull it out, presenting the dust-colored fabric to him.

"Thanks," he says, and rips it in half. I stare, heart sinking as I realize I'm now trapped in this dress. I press my knobby knees closer together and try to fight back self-consciousness. I watch as he tears the shirt apart and wraps the ragged remains around his head, tucking his dreadlocks beneath it. Soon his head is cocooned, with only his eyes, mouth, and a few slivers of dirty face peeking through.

"How do I look?" he asks, and smiles. The effect is disturbing.

"Scary enough to reduce children to tears," Pretty Boy says dryly.

"Good, that's what I always aim for."

"What about Tank?" I ask.

"I'm not that easy to disguise. I'll just lie low and hope for the best," Tank says. "Heads up, here's the town."

It's a small, barely inhabited place, all crumbling buildings and crudely done repairs. Three surprisingly tall buildings stick up among the humble little squats. They're towers of garbage, with car doors and wire mesh and other scrap metal filling the holes. The mere fact they're still standing seems to defy some law of the universe, and they look ready to topple at any second. Heaps of scrap metal and old, rusty cars decorate the town. As Tank winds between them to get inside, I stare up at the towers apprehensively. Several heads peek out from different heights on the buildings. Just the thought of being up there makes my knees quake.

"Remember," Wolf says as the jeep stops in the center of town, "don't call each other by the usual names."

I glance around and notice at least three guns pointed at us from the tower windows. I gulp.

"What do we call each other, then?" I ask in a whisper.

"Huh," Wolf says. "I didn't think of that."

But it's too late to solidify our plans, because we're already here and the townies are approaching. They crawl out of every nook and cranny, emerging from rusty cars and shady corners and the three towering buildings.

"Just wing it, Kid," Wolf says, noticing my apprehension. He smiles at me, eyes glinting between folds of fabric. "And don't fuck it up."

XXI
Towers

Townies swarm our jeep like flies on a carcass. We're surrounded in minutes. Men, women, and children alike arrive to greet us. They don't seem afraid, not even of Wolf and his wrapped-up head, or big ol' Tank with his scary face on. It's almost strange how friendly they are. Some hold up little trinkets and trash-treasures, hoping to trade. I guess the towns this close to the Queen are more peaceful, less wary of outsiders.

Then again, maybe they're just well protected. I'm all too aware of the snipers up in those towers, as much as I'm trying not to stare at them. Instead I stare at the crowd. The amount of them is intimidating, no matter how friendly they seem.

A little girl with a dirty face holds something up toward me: a pocket watch on a rusty chain, its surface cracked. I reach out to take it, but Wolf slaps my hand away.

"No, no, no," he says. "Don't take anything. Then they'll want something in return."

"Oh," I say sheepishly. I give an apologetic smile to the girl, who blinks up at me with wide eyes. She offers the watch to Wolf instead, but he shakes his head. She sticks it out farther, insistent. The other townies are pressing in closer, too, all trying to speak at once in an indecipherable flood of noise.

All of the sound and motion surrounding me suddenly

reminds me of the mob of crazies. Nervousness hits me in a flash, and a jolt of pain goes through my missing finger. I shrink back closer to Pretty Boy and swallow hard, telling myself that these are friendly townies, not madmen. But their smiling faces now look like bared teeth, and I feel like they could turn on us in an instant and—

A hand lands on my shoulder and I jump. I turn to face Pretty Boy.

"It's okay," he says. His face looks softer than usual, his head tilted in an annoyingly charming way, but I'm not going to fall for his bullshit.

"I'm fine," I say, and brush the hand off. Still, I keep my distance from the townies leaning over the jeep's sides.

"Hello, hello, hello," a very loud voice booms out. The townies abruptly stop talking and all turn in the same direction. I swivel around to do the same. They're looking at a pile of old, run-down vehicles nearby, stacked three cars high. On top is a man, only his silhouette visible against the sun. He jumps down from car to car in a series of loud crashes. When he stops a few yards away from our jeep, I realize that he's actually quite tiny. The height and his loud voice created an illusion of greatness.

The voice was an illusion, too, I see, as he lowers a megaphone.

He smiles at us. It's a slimy smile on a ratlike face.

"Welcome to Towers," he says.

"These townies," Wolf mutters under his breath, "always so clever with their names." I stifle a laugh.

The rat-man notices Wolf speaking and promptly raises the megaphone again.

"We are always very pleased to have visitors," his voice booms obnoxiously, "especially traders."

He clicks the megaphone off and lowers it, face still oozing friendliness.

"But you aren't traders we're familiar with." He speaks in a conversational tone, and makes his slow way toward us. "And we are familiar with many traders. Where are you from, strangers?"

"Across the wastes," Wolf says. The lie comes smoothly and easily. "Things are bad where we came from, real bad, so we decided to find new grounds closer to the Queen." Wolf mirrors the man's unnerving grin. "And this Saint guy. Love what he's trying to do."

The man squints at him as if trying to decide if he's joking.

"Saint is a very ambitious man," he says after a pause, "and I admire his work to make the wastes a safer place."

"Ain't working so well this far," Wolf says. "We got jumped by raiders on the way over. Look what they did to our poor friend's face, the savages." He points at Pretty Boy, who looks like he's trying very hard not to roll his eyes.

"Savage indeed," the rat-man says, his eyes never leaving Wolf. "It's a good thing we're all civilized people here, now isn't it?"

"Right, right. Now, about that trading business. I assume you're in charge here?"

"You assume right."

"Let's have a chat, then."

Wolf climbs over the side of the jeep and approaches the man. He gives him an overenthusiastic handshake and the two walk over to the supply truck, talking in low voices. I glance around at the others.

"What are *we* supposed to do?" I ask.

"Keep an eye on the townies," Pretty Boy murmurs. I eye the crowd of townsfolk. They're no longer clustered around our jeep, but are spread out and loitering around, stealing glances at us.

"Keep an eye out for what?"

"Anything suspicious," he says, and pointedly looks upward.

I follow his gaze to one of the towers, where a sniper rifle is still aimed in our direction. It's too far away to tell for sure, but I have a nervous feeling his sights are on my head.

After a few minutes Wolf and the man return, along with Dolly, looking as porcelain as ever in her red wig. It stands out starkly in this dusty town, where almost everything, people included, is in shades of brown or gray.

"Yes, yes, we'll work something out," the rat-man is saying. "What are you looking for, exactly?"

"Guns," Wolf says. "Big guns. And explosives."

Rat-face's forehead furrows, and his eyes narrow.

"And why is *that*, exactly? Surely traders like yourselves—"

"—have a very pressing need for self-defense," Pretty Boy finishes from beside me. Both heads turn toward him; he smiles. "Not to mention, there's a high demand for explosives right now."

"Right," says Wolf. "Come talk to the man, Tobias, tell 'im all about this high demand."

Tobias? It takes me a second to remember we have to use fake names. *Tobias. Right. Tobias.* I try to engrave that in my memory as Pretty Boy goes over to speak to the man.

"With Saint gaining influence and collecting sharks, raiders are getting worried that they're next. That fear makes them desperate, which makes them more dangerous than ever. People have to fortify..." The words become muffled as he and the townsman turn away from us. Wolf walks over and leans on the side of the jeep.

"All right," he says. "We're gonna stay here for the night."

"Really?" I ask nervously. "You remember what happened in that last town? And the Queen—"

"Ain't got a choice," he says. "We'll smooth over negotiations and get out of here early tomorrow. It'll be fine. Promise."

*   *   *

We're given a room on the fifth floor of a tower, which is high up enough to make me avoid looking out the window at all costs. It's a cramped room, especially since Wolf insisted all five of us stay together. There's no furniture aside from three ratty cots on the floor. One is covered with stains that look suspiciously like dried blood, another is littered with cigarette burns, and the third smells like someone died on it and nobody noticed for a few days. Each of them has a blanket in an equally undesirable state, and two have lumpy pillows. Despite their condition, everyone jumps to claim one.

"Murder scene is mine," Wolf says, indicating the blood-stained one with one hand while he removes his head-wrap. "No arguments."

Tank says nothing, and flops down on the burnt one with a weary groan. Sprawled out, his thick body doesn't even fit on the mattress. He lies there, eyes closed, as if daring someone to try to move him. No one does.

And so the stinky cot is left to Dolly, Pretty Boy, and me. I step away from it, raising my hands in surrender. It's not worth fighting over...not that I'd be able to get it if I tried. Dolly and Pretty Boy glare at each other.

"Oh, come *on*," Pretty Boy whines. "I was puking my lungs out all night at the Queen's, and—"

"Don't care," Dolly says flatly.

"—and then Wolf did *this* to my face, and—"

Dolly shakes her head.

"—you *always* get the nice things, Dolly. I never get anything. And I'm a part of this crew, too. I talked to that townie for all of you today..."

"No," Dolly says.

"I deserve it! It's mine!" Realizing his wheedling isn't getting him anywhere, Pretty Boy defiantly sits down on the cot. Dolly walks over, shoves him off, and takes his place.

Pretty Boy scoots away on the floor. He seems to consider challenging her again, but thinks better of it.

"Assholes," he says, and retreats to a corner to lean against the wall.

Tank starts to snore. Apparently he fell asleep mid-argument.

"Think he's got the right idea," Wolf said. "Dunno what you all are complaining about. I'm the one who spent the night bein' kidnapped and shit." He places his hands behind his head and yawns. "Someone else take first watch. And by someone I mean Pretty Boy."

Pretty Boy sighs but doesn't protest. Dolly walks over and hands me the pillow and blanket from her bed.

"Oh, wow, thanks," I say with a smile. She returns to her cot.

I'm about to set up my own makeshift bed when a thought stops me. Pretty Boy *has* had a rough time lately...and more importantly, he came very close to abandoning us in favor of the Queen. Is it really the best idea to give him first watch? He could screw us over far too easily here. I hesitate, and then walk over to his corner and offer him the sleeping supplies.

"How 'bout I take first watch?" I say, holding out the folded blanket and pillow. He stares up at me, surprised and a bit suspicious, as if he's expecting some kind of trick. Our eyes meet, and it doesn't make me want to blush out of either attraction or embarrassment. I hold his gaze steadily, and after a moment or two he's the one to drop his eyes. He takes the offering.

"Thanks," he says without looking up, and curls up in his corner.

I sit under the window, keep an eye and an ear out for trouble, and try not to let my mind wander to dark places. The room becomes eerie real fast once the others are asleep. The window doesn't have any glass, and the wind whistling through it reminds me how high up we are. I swear the whole tower creaks every time the wind blows, and I hear whispers and footsteps from the room above us.

I hug my knees to my chest and look over at my sleeping friends for comfort. Tank is snoring loudly, Wolf is sleeping with his mouth open and has a string of drool trailing onto his pillow, and Pretty Boy shifts and mutters in his sleep. Dolly, I realize with a jolt, isn't actually sleeping at all. She's wide-awake, and staring at the ceiling.

"Dolly?" I whisper. She's across the room, in the cot closest to the door, but her head turns toward me. "Is everything all right?" She nods. "Why aren't you sleeping?" No response. She turns and stares at the ceiling again.

I move over, stepping over Wolf, and crouch beside Dolly's cot. Something must be bothering her. I search my brain for what it could be, and guiltily remember Ruby's death. That's right—I wanted to ask if she was all right, but we've been so busy it slipped my mind. Somehow it never seemed appropriate to say in front of the others, anyway.

"Umm," I say timidly, "I'm sorry about, um, your friend."

"Friend?" she asks, her face a mask.

"Ruby."

"Oh. Yes."

I pause.

"She was your friend back from when you worked for the Queen, right?" She nods. "So . . . that must suck. Sorry." I'm no good at this whole comforting thing. She falls silent again, and I wonder if maybe I should stop prying—maybe she doesn't want to talk about it, and I'm just being a nuisance. But just when I open my mouth to apologize, she speaks up again.

"I didn't think the Queen would kill her," she says quietly.

"Yeah. Me neither." I stare down at my ragged boots. "So . . . it wasn't your fault or anything."

"I know," she says.

"But it must suck, still."

"Yes."

We lapse into silence. The wind whistles and the tower groans around us. I can't tell if Dolly welcomes the chance to talk or resents it, but at least she seems to be opening up a little. It stirs my curiosity, and I can't help but try to get more out of her. It's such a rare opportunity to speak to Dolly like this.

"So, umm." I try to think of the most tactful way to continue. "Someone told me about . . . when you worked for the Queen."

"Hm."

"And why you stopped."

She doesn't respond. I steal a glance at her and notice that she has, seemingly without noticing, placed a hand on her stomach.

"I had a baby," she says after a long pause. She stops again.

"Yeah?" I say. Trying to get information from her is like pulling teeth, but somehow I get the impression she does want to talk about it. Maybe she just doesn't know how. Or maybe I'm reading her completely wrong . . . It's hard to tell with Dolly.

"She died," she says bluntly.

"How?"

"Don't know. She was sick," she says. Another long pause. "Since she was born. And born too early."

"Oh . . ."

"Radiation. She wasn't strong enough for it."

"I heard that happens a lot," I say. It happened all the time back in town. Lots of times the pregnancy went wrong, or the baby was born dead, or wrong, or died real young. Healthy post-bomb babies are rare. But I was born after the bombs fell, and so were plenty of others, and we lived and grew just fine. Nobody really knows why we survive while others die.

"It's strange," Dolly says. Her voice stays as quiet and unemotional as ever. "When it first happened I was scared. Couldn't work like that. I wanted to get rid of it. But then...I couldn't. The Queen let me keep the baby. She was nicer then."

I try to picture that: the crazy old Queen supporting Dolly, letting her take off work, prepared to let her raise her child there. I can't make that idea match with the woman who shot Ruby in cold blood. I guess people change. The wastelands warp them.

"One day I woke up and she was cold," Dolly says.

"I'm sorry," I say.

"I never even thought I wanted her. And then she was gone and I knew I did."

I bite back another *sorry*. It's all I can think of saying, but I feel like repeating it just makes it feel empty.

"And then you left the Queen's?"

"Yes."

"Alone?"

"Yes."

"So how'd you get all wrapped up in...this?"

"Wolf found me," she says. "He saved my life. I wanted to be like him."

I know trying to get the full details on *that* story would be near to impossible, so I'm not even going to try. My imagination can fill in the blank spaces.

"Wow," I say. "And now you're so cool."

"Cool?"

"Yeah. Like..." I scuff one boot across the floorboards. "Like I want to be like you, the same way you wanted to be like Wolf." It sounds so lame when I say it. I can feel myself turning red. When I look over at Dolly, though, she's smiling.

"Thank you," she says.

"Umm, you're welcome."

"Holy shit." Wolf's voice nearly makes me jump out of my skin. "This is the most awkward conversation I've ever eavesdropped on. Can you two shut up and go to sleep already?"

Embarrassed at being overheard, I clamp my mouth shut and rise to move to the window. Dolly sits up and grabs my arm before I can get there.

"Can't sleep. I'll watch," she says. When I hesitate, she stands up and nods to the cot.

"Are you sure?" I ask. She nods. "Oh...all right." I *am* feeling awfully tired, so it's hard to resist. I lie down on the offered cot. It's definitely not as nice as the bed at the Queen's, and the reek is pretty awful, but I'm so exhausted I hardly care. "Good night, Dolly."

"Good night."

I'm asleep within minutes.

XXII
The Queen's Return

When I wake up, sunlight streams through the window. It's not the gentle glow of early morning, but the harsh light of midday. The cozy room has become a furnace; I'm covered in sweat. That discomfort, and the realization I'm alone, wakes me up.

Blinking away a sleepy haze, I notice I'm on a different cot as well. I somehow swapped to the bloodstained one—the prize formerly claimed by Wolf—and picked up a pillow and blanket. No wonder I slept so damn long. I disentangle myself from the sticky blanket and rush to the window, hesitating a moment before I stick my head out. The height makes my head swim, but I ignore the shaky feeling in my knees and search the town below. Our huge supply truck stands out among the squats and smaller vehicles. When I squint, I can make out the others clustered around it, unloading with the assistance of some townies. I spot Dolly's bright hair, Wolf's ridiculous head-wrap, and Tank carrying a hefty-looking box on each arm. Soon I see Pretty Boy as well, standing nearby and talking to the rat-faced townsman.

Hurt pricks me. I hate being left behind like this. Wolf must have really been worried I would screw things up for everyone, but like hell am I going to sit around in this room all day. I have to go out there and show them I can keep up. I head for the door, nearly tripping over a pile of stuff on the way.

Upon closer look, I realize it must be meant for me. There's a bottle of water, a tin can of food, and a pile of clothes too small to fit anyone else. I unfold them. It's a new outfit: a T-shirt and an old pair of jeans.

I change out of my god-awful dress in favor of the new clothing. The shirt is baggy and dusty, and the jeans have various multicolor patches crudely sewn on to cover holes, but it's a lot more comfy than that girly thing I was wearing. I take a gulp of water, grab the can of food, and leave to meet up with the others.

As I reach the bottom of the stairwell I use my knife to pry open the can of food, and eye the red insides before taking a cautious slurp. It turns out to be cold and slightly chunky tomato soup, not bad at all.

Outside, the town is full of midday hustle and bustle. Towns-folk are everywhere, carrying boxes of supplies to and from our truck. Everyone seems to be in good spirits, and the townies chat happily as they investigate crates of food and water and other supplies. They smile at me as I pass. My friends are smiling, too, and as I get closer I can see why: As they empty the truck of other goods, it's slowly filling up with guns and explosives. They sure have a lot of shit for such a small town. I guess towns close to the Queen really are lucky.

Even rat-face is smiling as he talks to Pretty Boy. Either his suspicions have been dismissed, or he stopped caring so much when he saw the goods we brought. I avoid the two of them and head for Tank. He's setting down two crates in front of a group of townies, who all crowd in to peer at what's inside. I nearly yell out his name, but stop myself as I remember we're using other aliases here.

"Hey!" I yell instead, and stand on my tiptoes to tap him on the shoulder. He turns around and grins at me.

"Oh hey, what's up?" He squeezes the breath out of me in a one-armed hug. "Sleep well?"

I squirm out of the iron vise of his arm.

"Well, yeah...but why'd you guys leave me? I wanted to help!"

He notices my disgruntled face and laughs.

"Oh, kiddo. We just figured we'd let you sleep. You've been through a lot."

"Yeah, but..." It's hard to keep feeling crabby in the face of Tank's easygoing warmth. "But so have all of us!"

"Yeah, but you're, y'know, the baby of the group."

"I am not a baby!"

Tank laughs and heads back to the truck. I doggedly follow on his heels. The back compartment is wide open and surrounded by a crowd of people. A few men inside, including Wolf, hand off crates to the waiting townies. Every time a new box is delivered into the truck, Wolf rushes to look inside, as giddy as a little kid with sweets.

"Well, these will come in handy," he says to one, gives the townie a thumbs-up, and dashes over to check another one. "Is that a *bazooka*? Holy shit, I love you townies."

I line up behind Tank, waiting for Wolf to stop drooling over his new toys and keep the line going. As soon as Tank walks off with a crate in each arm, I step up, hold out my own arms, and wait.

Wolf walks over with a box. He bends down to hand it to me, and looks surprised when he sees my face.

"You should, uh, maybe let someone else handle this one," he says.

"No, no, I got it!" I stand on my tiptoes and reach for it.

"If you say so." He hands it off to me and straightens up.

It's...a lot heavier than I expected. The wooden crate is wider around than I thought, too, and I find it difficult to get a good grip. I take a few shaky steps away from the truck, gradually leaning backward from the weight. Someone puts a hand on my shoulder to steady me.

I pause to regain my footing. Once I feel like I can stand on my own, I readjust my hold on the crate. My injured hand slips. Pain shoots through my stumpy finger. I hurriedly shift my hand, and feel the crate sliding out of my grasp.

I try to fix my hold again, narrowly avoid dropping the whole thing—and find myself falling backward. I topple over before I can even react, and land flat on my back on the hard dirt. The crate spills out its content of bandages and first aid supplies onto my face. I lie there, reeling. I can hear Wolf howling with laughter from the truck. Some things never change, I guess.

I'm too embarrassed to stand and face the stares and laughter, so instead I try to muster up some inkling of dignity. After a few seconds, Pretty Boy's bruised face pokes into my line of sight, his expression oddly caring.

"You all right, sis?"

"Eh?"

"Are you all right?" he asks, and adds with more emphasis, "*Sis?*"

Sis? It takes me a second to process. Another part of our act I have to remember. Reacting a little late, I nod. He lifts the crate off me and offers a hand. I ignore it and stand up on my own.

"I'm fine, I'm fine," I say, brushing myself off. A wad of gauze sticks to my boot, and I try to inconspicuously peel it off with my other foot.

"Maybe you should help out with some, uh, less strenuous stuff," he says, and laughs charmingly. It doesn't have its old effect. I can tell now he's only pretending, and it grates on my nerves to have him keep trying it on me. So I don't return his smile, and stare at my feet instead.

Unperturbed, he reaches over and grabs my arm. Before I

can shake him off he turns over my injured hand and gently examines it.

"Looks like you could use some new bandages. Does it still hurt?"

Of course it still hurts. I'm missing a *finger*. I bite my lip and nod.

"Come sit down, let me have a look."

"I can do it myself," I say quietly.

"Whoa, somebody's stubborn today. Come on."

He grabs my arm a little too roughly and leads me away before I can protest. We sit on a pair of overturned crates and he obtains some first aid supplies.

I can't help but be impressed by how well he can act. The kindness he feigns is so completely different than the real Pretty Boy. If I didn't know him any better, he'd have fooled me easily. But I set my jaw and refuse to react as he tends to my wound. He unwraps the old bandages as gently as possible, and I wince at the ugly injury it reveals. There's a lot of dried blood and scabbing, and it hurts somewhere deeper than physical pain to see my finger missing.

"Well, it doesn't look infected," Pretty Boy says. "That's good." He douses it in water to wash away the caked-on blood, and then in alcohol to sanitize it. My eyes tear up from the sting, and I lower my head in an effort to hide it. "Sorry...it should only hurt for a second." He touches my shoulder, squeezing lightly. I'm about to shake him off when I notice Mayor Rat-Face standing nearby and scrutinizing us. Being forced into playing this out just makes me more embarrassed, but my pride isn't worth blowing our cover.

I stare at my boots as Pretty Boy all too tenderly applies some antibiotic ointment and new bandages to my hand.

"That all right?" he asks, holding my freshly wrapped hand between his own.

"Yep." I yank my hand away and stand. "Thanks."

From the side, I hear rat-face laugh. Pretty Boy and I turn to him.

"Siblings, eh?" he asks, taking a step toward us. Up close and personal, he's only a bit taller than I am, and has to look up at Pretty Boy.

"Yeah?" Pretty Boy says. His arm slithers around my shoulders. "And?"

"You two don't seem like siblings."

"I don't understand what you mean," Pretty Boy says. I decide it's best to keep my mouth shut, but the townsman turns his sharp eyes to me.

"What's your brother's name again, little one?"

I open my mouth—and freeze, racking my brains.

"Uhh," I say. "Well...it's..." I can feel color creeping into my face.

Pretty Boy grimaces.

"She's, uh, the special sibling," he says.

"Oh, cut the crap," the townsman says. "I know you're not siblings, and you're not traders, either. You're a good actor, kid, but she's definitely not." Pretty Boy starts to say something, but he cuts him off. "Did you really think those disguises were fooling anyone? It's obvious you all are trying to hide something, and I'm not so stupid I can't put two and two together, especially not after that transmission about your escape yesterday."

Pretty Boy is starting to look trapped. I notice him glancing around, making sure no other townies are closing in on us. His hand sneaks toward his gun.

"Uh-uh. Wouldn't do that if I were you." Rat-face juts his chin at the towers. "Snipers all over town." He takes another step toward us and grins his slimy grin. "If I wanted you dead, you'd already be dead."

"Then what are you waiting for, exactly?" Pretty Boy asks. "You trying to cut some kind of deal with us?"

"Oh, no, no." The townsman shrugs. "I don't care about Saint, or the Queen, or any of this political bullshit. You're trading us essential supplies, and that's all I really give a rat's ass about. I'm a businessman. I'm not interested in making friends or enemies."

We both stand there, not sure what to say, and the townsman laughs.

"Just don't cause us any trouble, or I really will kill you."

"We won't, sir."

"Good. Then I have no problem doing business with sharks." He gives one final unnerving smile and walks away.

I unconsciously hold my breath as he leaves, expecting the snipers to start shooting any second, but nothing happens. The townsfolk all seem as friendly and helpful as before, and continue carrying goods back and forth.

"You trust him?" I ask Pretty Boy.

"Not a bit," he says. "We need to get out of here. I'm gonna go talk to Wolf. You make sure we didn't leave anything in the room."

I hate taking orders from Pretty Boy, but it's a good idea. I run back to the tower, dodging townies and trying not to attract too much attention. I slow down every time someone seems to be staring at me, and speed up again when I'm alone. Once I'm inside the tower, I try to sprint up the stairwell but run out of breath after a couple of floors. I know it didn't seem *that* urgent for us to leave, but still. If something happens, I don't want to be split up.

Once I reach the room, I hurriedly gather the stray belongings. There's nothing much, just a few cans of food, my backpack, and some half-empty bottles of water, but anything is worth saving. I shove it into my pack and, on second thought, also grab one of the blankets we used. Before heading back down I peek out the window—and notice, with a feeling of dread, a stream of vehicles approaching the town. They're all painted black and have a design painted on the side. I squint; it's a crown.

I take off running again. The staircase moves by in a blur as I stumble down. All I can think about is how I have to warn the others before the Queen's men arrive. They'll recognize everyone instantly, and I doubt this seedy mayor is going to help us. Maybe he even called her here...

As I round the corner and start down the last stretch of steps, I plow right into someone heading up. He falls backward and we both tumble down a few steps before coming to a rest at the bottom. I find myself on top of Pretty Boy, both of us wide-eyed and breathing hard.

"Kid," he says in between breaths. "The—"

"The Queen is coming!" I blurt out as soon as I get my own breath back.

"Yeah. We saw."

"So where are you going?"

"To hide."

"Pretty Boy!" Of course he would run and hide. I try to get up, but he grabs my arm and holds me there.

"No, no, listen. We can't go out there; if she sees our faces it's over. Dolly's moving the truck, and Wolf said he had some kind of plan, so..."

I keep struggling for a few seconds as his words sink in. Wolf has a plan. I hesitate.

"Is it a *good* plan? Is it going to actually work?"

"I don't know. He looked pretty excited, though."

"So...explosives?"

"Presumably."

He releases my arm, and I scoot off as I realize I'm still on top of him. We move on our hands and knees over to the nearby window and poke our heads up to get a better view.

The Queen's squad of vehicles is pulling into the town. There are four big trucks, all with the Queen's obnoxious and rather poorly painted golden crown on the hood and sides. Guards pour out of the trucks, dozens of them, all with guns at the ready. And then the Queen herself emerges. Her leg has a fresh cast. Despite the injury, she moves as grandiosely as possible.

Our truck is gone, and Dolly and Tank with it. Wolf, however, is standing right out in the open, arms folded across his chest. The town's mayor is beside him, twitching nervously. Everyone else has vacated the area. I suck in a sharp breath.

"What is he doing?" I ask. "The Queen is gonna see right through that disguise!"

"No idea," Pretty Boy says in a low voice. "But it *is* Wolf. He must have something batshit crazy up his sleeve. And, against all logic, his plans usually work."

"Usually?" That's not very comforting.

"Usually," he says firmly, and I notice sweat running down the side of his face.

I tense at the sight of the Queen approaching Wolf. All my instincts scream at me to do something, but I repeatedly assure myself Wolf wouldn't do something *this* suicidal without a plan.

I can't hear what they're saying to each other from this distance. All I can do is watch the Queen's extensive hand gesturing. The mayor talks to her, while Wolf stays where he is.

"What's happening?" I hiss at Pretty Boy.

"How the hell am I supposed to know?" He studies the scene, biting his bottom lip. I turn away from the window and creep toward the doorway.

"I'm gonna get a closer look," I whisper. He notices me moving away and his eyes widen.

"No, Kid, just stay here—" He reaches out to grab me, but I scamper away on my hands and knees.

"I got it, don't worry!"

I rise to a crouch once I'm in the doorway. I can't see Wolf and the townsman from this angle, but I can see the Queen's escort of vehicles and several guards. I scoot out of the door-way and move toward the building across from me in a slow, awkward shuffle. About halfway there I realize there's really no benefit in doing this when no one's even looking this way, and break into a sprint. I reach the doorway and find it locked. My heart sinks, but to the side I spot a window. It has no glass, just a thin blanket covering it. It's a low window, about even with my chest, so it's easy enough to squeeze myself through it.

But the makeshift curtains wrap around me, and I end up fumbling and falling to the floor. With a loud rip of fabric, I land on my back. Only when I've managed to sit up and escape from the blanket do I realize I'm not alone.

Sitting in the corner of the dim, dingy room are two chil-dren, a boy and a girl. They're tiny and thin with eyes too big for their gaunt faces, and they're both staring at me in sheer terror. I completely forgot this little squat was probably some-one's home.

I wave at them tentatively, but they only shrink farther back into the corner.

"Umm, hi," I say, keeping my voice as quiet and soothing as possible. "I'm not here to hurt you, so—"

Something hard and metal slams into my skull. I stumble and fall, ears ringing and brains all shook up.

"Ow! What the—" I turn around just in time to see the fry-ing pan swing toward me a second time. I duck out of the way and scramble across the floor. The woman is skinnier than her kids, practically skin and bones, but there's a fire in her eyes that makes her scarier than Tank at his worst. She advances on me, frying pan held above her head. She pauses at a thump behind her, and we both turn to see Pretty Boy climbing through the window.

"What are you doing here?" I hiss at him. The woman looks

back and forth between us, quickly determines who the bigger threat is, and flies at him.

He grabs her wrists before she can hit him and struggles to get the makeshift weapon out of her grip. Seeing their mother in potential trouble, the two kids run to her aid. The boy attaches himself to one of Pretty Boy's legs while the girl beats on him with tiny fists.

"Uh, Kid, a little help?" he says, struggling to keep them all off of him.

As amusing as it is to watch him get beaten on by little kids, I'm worried about the children getting hurt by all of his flailing around. I grab the girl under the armpits and pick her up. She struggles and yells in my grasp, so I hold her as far away from me as possible and deposit her in a corner. By the time I run back to grab the boy she's already back again, this time attacking *me* with her pitifully weak punches. I ignore her and grab the boy, prying his tiny fingers off Pretty Boy's leg. The boy reattaches to my arm and bites me, hard. I yell and recoil, but he clings to me. Meanwhile, the girl grabs me by the legs and pulls. I flail for a moment before dropping to the floor. Both of them jump on me, hitting and scratching and biting.

A loud *clang* echoes through the room, and everything stops. The mother stumbles and falls to the floor. Pretty Boy stands there, breathing hard, frying pan in hand.

"Mommy!" the girl wails, rushing to her mother's side. "You killed her!" She starts to sob.

"Mommy?" The little boy lets go of me and sits there, open-mouthed.

"*Pretty Boy!* You killed their mommy?!" I yell at him, horrified.

"I didn't kill her!" He looks baffled by the reactions. "She's just knocked out; calm down. And what the hell are *you* freaking out about, Kid?" He walks over, pulls me up from the floor, and drags me over to a window on the other side of the room.

"We're here to see what's happening, aren't we? So stop wasting time."

"Stop trying to yank me around!" I slap his hands away, but I know he's right. I stay low, pull the ratty curtains aside, and look out. We're a handful of yards away from Wolf now, and I can hear bits and pieces of their conversation. I can see some of the guards, too, standing around and surveying the area. As one looks my way, I duck down lower.

"Then take off the head-wrap," the Queen says demandingly. She has her hands on her hips and looks seriously displeased. The townsman is shaking his head; he takes a few steps back from the two of them. Wolf gives a big, theatrical shrug and raises both hands to the cloth wrap. He pauses for a moment—then raises one hand and waves wildly. I'm confused for a second before realizing it must be a signal.

The Queen backs toward her guards, who are instantly up in arms. They all look around wildly, trying to find whoever Wolf is waving at.

Nothing happens.

Wolf drops the hand, then raises it and does it again, this time making the gesture even more over-the-top.

"Seriously?" he yells. "You tryin' to make me look stupid or something?"

"Are we supposed to do something?" I whisper to Pretty Boy.

"No clue," he whispers back.

Then I hear it: a sound like rushing air, growing louder. Those outside all hear it, too. Wolf and the townsman back away from the Queen and her guards. Some of the guards panic and run, while the rest rush to cover the Queen.

"What *is* that?" I ask, and just *barely* see something hit in the middle of the cluster of the Queen's men before Pretty Boy tackles me to the floor, just in time for the explosion.

XXIII
Queen's Gambit

The roar of the explosion is deafening. Heat leaks in through the window, followed by smoke. I pull my shirt up and cover my mouth with it. My ears buzz.

"What was that?" Pretty Boy asks between coughs.

"A bazooka, I think," I say, remembering Wolf's excitement over finding it.

"Of course. A bazooka. Should've known."

I look over at the two children and their unconscious mother. I can barely see them through the smoke.

"You two should stay here, okay?" I say, and move toward the door.

"*We* should stay here!" Pretty Boy protests. Nonetheless, he follows me. I push aside the dresser barricading the door, inch it open, and warily peek out the crack.

At first only the cries of the injured come from the smoke, rising up like the eerie howls of ghosts. But gradually the smoke clears away to reveal the carnage. The explosion took quite a chunk out of the Queen's escort, leaving bodies everywhere, although there's still a handful left unharmed. Mayor Rat-Face is gone, likely hightailed it out of here the second he realized a fight was erupting in his town square. The Queen seems unhurt, thanks to a few of her men shielding her. She pushes them away and straightens up. Her expression shifts from fear to simmering rage as she sees the explosion's aftermath.

With the last wisps of smoke clearing away, Wolf finally emerges. He's laughing, of course. He tears off his head-wrap and points at the Queen.

"*Yeah!*" he says triumphantly. "Motherfucking bazooka! That's what I'm talking about!"

The Queen turns to him, face contorted in rage, and pulls out a gun.

Before he can even open his mouth, she shoots him in the chest.

For a second I'm too stunned to move or speak. Then Wolf hits the ground, and I lurch forward.

"Wolf!" I try to run to him, but Pretty Boy holds me back.

"No, Kid, no—you'll get yourself killed."

"She's gonna kill Wolf!"

"He's dead already, Kid! Point-blank to the chest, there's no way—"

I ignore him and try to squirm free. I break out of his hold and dash forward, only to be tackled into the dust after two steps.

"Why are you being like this?" he hisses as we fumble on the ground.

"Why are you always like *this*?"

"I'm trying to save our asses!"

"Well, you're *not* helping!"

I backhand him. He lets out a low hiss of frustration and grabs both of my wrists.

"Is this about me kissing you?" he asks, contemptuous. "Because if it is, get the fuck over it. It was nothing."

Even in my frantic state, that stings. Not just that he's downplaying the whole incident, but that he thinks being kissed is what I'd be upset about. I didn't even *want* to be kissed. I furiously blink back tears.

"Like I give a shit about that! This isn't *about* you! Let me go!"

After some more back-and-forth scuffling around in the dust, we realize at the same time how quiet it is. I look up to find the Queen staring at us from a few yards away. Her eyes light up upon sight of Pretty Boy.

"Get them!" she screeches. She's lost all semblance of composure and elegance. Her eyes are wild in a sweaty face, her white dress torn and dirtied. She looks crazy, and her scowl deepens when her torn-apart group of guards fails to respond immediately. She heads toward us in long, determined strides. A handful of her men straggle after her.

Pretty Boy and I scramble to our feet, tripping over each other in our hurry to get up, and run in the opposite direction. We squeeze through a narrow alleyway between two buildings, Pretty Boy shoving me forward and frantically whispering at me to hurry up, and keep running. The town is empty, all the townies holed up in their dens. We weave between buildings and piles of garbage and scrap metal. The Queen's shouting and her men's footsteps gradually fade away as we lose them. We find a small, doorless hovel and dash inside.

I drop to a crouch, panting. Pretty Boy stands near the doorway and steals worried glances outside, but it seems we've lost them for now. Even as the immediate danger wanes, I feel a deeper fear growing inside me. Thinking of Wolf brings up a raw, painful flood of emotion, but I force it down and clench my shaking hands at my sides.

"What are we going to do?" I ask, staring at Pretty Boy. Of course, out of everyone to be stuck with, it had to be him. He'll probably just run off and leave me alone, and then . . . and then, what will I do?

"I don't know." Pretty Boy looks even more frightened than I feel, and checks every few seconds to make sure no one is outside. He fiddles nervously with his gun.

"Well, you said they had a plan, right? Wolf must have something—"

"Wolf got *shot!*" he says. I ignore him and keep babbling in an attempt to calm myself down.

"And someone had to shoot that bazooka, Dolly and Tank must be around—"

"We don't know that! And even if they are...with all the Queen's men, there's no way the townies will help us..." Pretty Boy finally stops checking out the doorway. He slumps down to the floor with his back against the wall. "Maybe we should turn ourselves in to the Queen."

"Don't be stupid, she'll hand us over to Saint!"

"So we should run."

"Of *course* you would say that," I say. My voice comes out harsher than expected. "That's all you ever do."

"Kid...Kid, listen." He leans toward me, eyes wide and earnest. "You and me, we aren't like them. You know that. We'll just get ourselves killed if we keep doing this. There's nothing wrong with running away."

"There ain't nowhere to go, Pretty Boy," I say. "And we'd never last in the wastes on our own."

"We'll figure something out!"

"No!" I take a deep breath and push my fear back, forcing up anger and determination instead. "You know, you've had plenty of opportunities to run off. Every night, every town, the Queen...and you haven't!"

"That's because—"

"It's because you're too scared to even do that!" I'm practically yelling now, but I can't stop myself. "Because you've never actually *been* on your own! You've always had a family or a crew or somebody to take care of you!"

He doesn't try to interrupt me this time, but just stares.

"You're scared of being alone because you've never been

that way," I say, "and I'm scared of being alone because I have. So we can't run. We have to stay and find the others. We *need* them. Both of us."

I stop, chest heaving, and realize my eyes are watering. I wipe at them impatiently and turn away from him, trying to get myself under control. A lot of feelings are stirring up all of a sudden, and I can't deal with them right now. Most of all, I'm afraid. Afraid that he'll run off and leave me, afraid that he'll stay and my choice will get us both killed.

Pretty Boy is silent. When I turn back to him, he's staring at the floor. He runs a hand through his hair, swallows hard, squeezes his eyes shut for a moment, and opens them again.

"I'm not cut out for this," he says. "I was never meant for this life."

"You can learn. Even I am."

He sighs, and is about to respond when something stops him. He raises a hand to silence me and peeks out the door. When he jerks his head back his face is pale.

"Shit, they heard us. They're coming."

"What do we do?" I ask. He hesitates, eyes rapidly searching the room.

"Got it," he says. "Take this." He throws something to me. I fumble and nearly drop it: his gun.

"What—"

"Give me your knife."

"But why—"

"Just do it!"

I hand it over. I have no idea what he's thinking, but he seems to have some kind of plan and that's better than I can say for myself. He nods, brow furrowed.

"Now shoot the gun."

"Huh?"

"At the ceiling. Now."

I fire upward. A chunk of plaster falls to the ground, making me jump. I look at Pretty Boy for further instruction, but he isn't paying attention to me. Without warning, he slashes the blade across his own stomach, ripping his shirt and slicing a shallow-but-wide gash. I stare as blood starts to well up. Before I can even voice a question, he abruptly drops to the floor, clutches his stomach, and screams. I stare, baffled.

"What the hell are you—"

Guards are in the room before I finish my question. There are three of them, one nursing a wound, all with weapons on me. I drop the gun. The Queen is right behind her men, entering the room with a dramatic flourish despite her condition. She glares at me, but the look softens as she turns to Pretty Boy.

"Darling, what happened?" she coos, swooping down on him like a vulture.

"She shot me!" I hear him say as a guard grabs my arm and twists it behind my back. I stare over at Pretty Boy, my mouth hanging open, and see him looking up at the Queen with a face wet with tears. He's actually *crying*. "I said I was going to run and she . . . she tried to kill me!"

"Oh, you poor thing. Don't worry, I'm here now." The Queen helps him up, her hand lingering on his arm. He keeps one hand pressed to his stomach, his face contorted with nonexistent pain. He smiles weakly at her, and she doesn't see the fakeness.

The Queen's guard turns me away so I can't see what's happening anymore. He roughly searches me.

"Wh-What—" I say, flabbergasted. "But, I . . ." This is his plan? He's going to betray me and run to the Queen with his tail between his legs? My stomach twists. I never should've trusted him, never should've listened to what he said. I had him figured out at this point, I should have *known . . .*

"Let her go," Pretty Boy says. It takes a second to sink in. I turn to find him holding my knife to the Queen's throat. He has a fistful of her hair and is holding her in front of him, a meat shield between himself and the guards. The man holding my arm lets go and turns his gun on Pretty Boy, but hesitates. All three guards are obviously too afraid to fire.

"Darling," the Queen says, her voice strained but still somehow coddling, "what do you think you're doing?"

Pretty Boy yanks her toward the door.

"You heard me," he says loudly. "Let Kid go and no one has to get—" He flinches as one man takes a step toward him, and slouches down so more of his body is hidden behind the Queen. "—hurt," he finishes more quietly, bravado cracking.

I stare at him, then at the Queen's men. They all look to her, but she's too shocked to give orders. Nobody moves.

I take a timid step away from the guards.

"Umm, so, I'm just gonna go ahead and—" Before I can finish my sentence, the nearest guard lunges at me. I jump backward to avoid him, slip, and fall to the floor hard. As soon as I hit I crawl for the door. Somebody fires a gun, and the bullet whizzes right past my head.

At the first sound of gunfire, Pretty Boy immediately loses his composure. He shoves the Queen forward and takes off, running out the door and leaving me in the dust. I scramble to my feet and follow, the Queen's furious screech sounding off behind me.

I can't see where Pretty Boy went; he got out of here way too fast. I run blindly, avoiding open ground, instead climbing fences and squeezing through tight alleyways I hope they can't follow me through. My heartbeat fills my ears. I can't tell if I'm being chased, and I'm too scared to turn and find out. The streets are all empty of life. I don't even know where I'm going or what my plan is. I just run until I can't run anymore.

Finally I stop in a narrow space between two hovels and crouch there. My chest and legs burn.

When my wheezing breath finally quiets down, I strain to hear any voices or footsteps. The town is dead quiet. Either I lost them, or they found someone else to chase. I catch a whiff of smoke and look up to see a cloud of it growing above the town. It's impossible to tell where it's coming from. I wonder who's setting fires: the Queen's men trying to smoke us out, or one of my friends spreading chaos?

Movement catches my eye. The cloth covering a window above me shifts, and a pair of sunken eyes stares out suspiciously. As soon as I look up, they disappear.

I have to keep moving. The mayor claimed he's not on anyone's side, but I wouldn't put it past him to give us up, especially with his town getting wrecked. I force myself to my feet, choose a random direction, and start moving. Once I reach the edge of the building I peer out. There's no one in sight. I hesitate, unsure what to do next, when I hear a gunshot from somewhere to my right. I instinctively head that way. I could be walking toward all the Queen's men . . . but then again, if there's gunfire, it means at least one of my friends is there.

I dash from building to building on my way, ducking behind houses and rusty piles of metal and garbage. I pass a few burning buildings on the way. The fire moves quickly, spreading around town, eating through cloth and wood and anything it touches. I pause to marvel at the blaze before continuing, and use the smoke as cover. I'm painfully careful to make sure no one sees me, sometimes crawling on all fours between shelters. I don't encounter a single person on the way. By the time I get closer to where the gunshot came from, I'm completely out of breath and feeling pretty silly about my efforts to be sneaky. Around the corner I hear voices. None are familiar, which makes my stomach turn to knots.

I make my half-crouching way over to the rusty remains of an old car and duck behind it. I hide there for a few seconds, making sure there's no change in the voices I hear, and rise up to peer over the hood.

On the other side is a wide open strip of land between two of the towers. A handful of the Queen's men are there, a ragged bunch clustered in a circle. The shadow of one tower falls across them. They look torn up already, nursing wounds and dripping blood in the dust. One's gun hand seems to be dead, but he's dutifully clutching it in the other one, limp arm hanging at his side.

At the center of their circle, tied up and blindfolded, is Pretty Boy. He's slumped onto his side on the ground, with one side of his head bloodied.

"We've got one here," a guard says into a walkie-talkie. The response is too full of static for me to understand. "No, he's by himself. Any sign of the others?" More static. "Dunno where they are, but they're giving us hell."

All I can think about is Pretty Boy trying to save me back there. I know there's not much I can do, and I really should turn my back and run... but how can I leave him? Even with all of the confused feelings I have about him, he's a member of our crew. Seeing him like this melts away my anger. I can't turn my back on him.

I duck behind the car again and pat down my pockets, searching for anything useful. I have no gun, no explosives, not even my trusty knife. There aren't any big rocks around to throw. All I have is my backpack, which contains a half-empty canteen and little else.

"Shit, shit, shit," I hiss under my breath, desperately trying to think of something. I bite my lip and stand up, looking over at the guards.

As I watch, Pretty Boy rolls onto his back and groans. A

guard responds with a sharp kick to the side, making me wince. Pretty Boy rolls over and tries to crawl away, but another man pins him down with a boot on his back. The circle laughs.

My stomach tightens and my fists clench at my sides. I can't just sit here and watch, not even if it's Pretty Boy. Chastising myself all the while for being such an idiot, I move out into the open.

"Hey!" I yell at the guards, hands still balled into fists. I move toward them with absolutely no idea what I intend to do. "Stop it!"

They turn to me, guns raised in an instant. There's a confused pause as they try to figure out who the hell I am. One of them finally recognizes me.

"We-ell, you sharks are even dumber than we thought," he says, grinning and advancing toward me. "Just gonna walk up and surrender, huh?" The rest of the guards leave Pretty Boy where he lies and fan out, moving toward me as a unit. They close around me in a half circle, the car at my back. I hold my ground.

"We've got the little girl," another guard says into his walkie-talkie. Smirking, he takes a few steps toward me and reaches for my arm. "Now c'mere, and don't try anything stupid…"

His hand closes around my arm as I'm still trying to figure out how to react. He drags me forward and—*swoosh*. An odd sound, like rushing air.

I freeze. The hand on my arm goes slack, and I step to the side just in time as the man falls forward. He hits the ground, a chunk of skull missing. Blood and brains ooze from the back of his head.

Everybody stares.

"What the hell?" The Queen's men look as baffled I am. One opens his mouth, and before he can speak there's another soft *whoosh* and a bullet hole appears in his forehead. As the second body falls, panic breaks loose among the rest of them. One man turns in a circle, wildly firing his guns at both of the nearby towers. Another points his gun at me. The latter goes down in a second, before he even has a chance to voice a threat.

The last two promptly lose their shit. One falls to the ground and cowers, and the other, the man with the injured arm, sprints away. He falls before he makes it to the shelter of the next building.

"Please," the last man begs, crouched in the dirt with both hands over his head. "Please don't kill me!"

I'm the only person left standing. Bodies litter the ground around me. The only other living people are Pretty Boy and the begging guard, both cringing on the ground.

"I, uhh...don't really have any control over it. Sorry?" I say.

He stays on the ground, whimpering, while I stand there awkwardly. After a few seconds of nothing happening, I walk over to Pretty Boy. He's still tied up and blindfolded and is valiantly trying to squirm away from the action. When I touch his arm he flinches.

"It's me," I say, and slip the blindfold off. He blinks up at me, breathing hard, and looks around at the bodies of the Queen's men.

"Kid?" he says, taken aback. "What...what did you do?"

"Umm," I say. "Nothing?"

"Uhh, you sure?" He chokes out a nervous laugh. "Thanks, I guess?"

"You're welcome, I guess," I say, imitating his dry tone.

The whimpering of the man behind me stops abruptly. I turn around, expecting to see one of my friends finishing him off.

Instead I find the Queen.

She's an absolute mess. Her hair is in disarray, her face smeared with dirt, her fancy dress ripped and stained. She's completely alone, her usual gaggle of guards nowhere to be found. She looks more like a crazy than a queen, trailing blood and dirt in her ridiculous getup, but the shotgun in her hands demands that I take her seriously. The gun looks too big for her, and her skinny arms are shaking, but I have no doubt she could and would kill me in an instant.

"My Queen!" the man says. He crawls toward her, groveling. "Thank God you're here, they were—"

"Shut up," she says, and shoots him in the face. I try very hard not to look at the messy body as it falls. Instead I keep my eyes locked on the Queen as she approaches, reloading the gun.

"Well, well," she says, in a cracked and lilting voice that makes it pretty clear she's completely lost it. I swallow hard. "I've finally caught up with you two."

She aims the shotgun at my head.

XXIV
Long Live the Queen

I slowly raise my hands in surrender and otherwise stay as still as possible.

"You dumb little bitch," the Queen says. "Do you know how *embarrassing* it is to chase a bunch of fuckup sharks like you around? This is beneath me. So beneath me." She chews her lip and glances around the empty area. "And where are all my men? Where? All dead? And fuck if I know how. This isn't how any of this was supposed to happen."

"You didn't have to come here," I say. "And you don't have to—"

"Shut up!" she snarls. I clamp my mouth shut. Her lips twist to the side in a scowl. "My mansion is in ruins because of you fuckers. Now the last of my men are dead. I'm not about to let you go, not when you're my last shot at securing a partnership with Saint."

I'm really wishing my mystery sniper would step in right now, but no gunshots come. The town is silent and empty: There's just me, the Queen, and Pretty Boy, and the latter is useless. I meet his eyes and wonder if I look as scared as he does.

"Your highness," he says, and shifts his gaze from me to the Queen. "Why don't you just calm down for a second? She's worth nothing dead."

The Queen whirls on him and her face contorts. She shoves the barrel of the gun in his face, pushing him flat on the ground.

"W-We!" he squeaks out. "*We're* worth nothing to you dead!"

"And *you*," she says through gritted teeth, "after everything I offered you, this is how you repay me?" She leans close. Spit flies out of her mouth, peppering his face. He tries to cringe away, but he's stuck between her gun and the ground. "I could have saved you from all this."

Her fingers twitch and tighten around the gun, moving as if to pull the trigger, then releasing again.

"But maybe," she says, and licks her lips, smearing red lipstick around her mouth, "maybe I should keep you around. A pretty face always has its uses…"

Her eyes are locked on Pretty Boy, or maybe staring through him, with the strange glazed look of someone falling apart. She seems to have forgotten I'm still here, crouched right beside the two of them.

"Or maybe I should just kill you," she says, and her mouth stretches out into a too-wide, creepy smile. "Yes, that would be much more satisfying." Her fingers start to tighten on the trigger.

I tackle her to the ground. She screams, kicks, and flails, while I use both my hands just to keep the gun pointed away from me. It's a pretty pathetic fight, a ragged old woman versus a skinny little girl. We're stuck for a few seconds, her desperately trying to get a clean shot at my face and me desperately trying to stop that from happening. When she realizes neither of us is budging, she drops the gun and lashes out with her hands. Her long nails rake my face like claws. I scream, and her other hand closes around my throat and cuts off the cry. I grab two handfuls of her long hair and yank as hard as I can. We're stuck for a few seconds, both tightening our grips—she lets go before I do. But with a loud shriek and one big push, she topples me off of her. I get a face full of dirt and scramble away, kicking up a cloud of dust around us.

Through the haze I see it: the shotgun, lying in the dirt. I grab it and jump to my feet, swinging around to point it at the Queen. She's on her hands and knees still, coughing from the dust. As the cloud clears, I raise the barrel to her head.

She grins up at me. Her dress is ripped further from our fight, and her knees look bloody through the torn cloth.

"Look at you," she says, rising to her feet. I follow her with the gun, but hesitate to shoot. "We both know you won't pull that trigger, little girl. You're not like the others." She walks toward me, coming just a few inches away from the gun, not a hint of fear on her face. I stumble backward, but she keeps coming closer.

"You really didn't have to come here," I whisper.

Her chest presses against the barrel, daring me.

"You're not going to shoot me," she says. She starts to laugh, that awful high-pitched cackle.

A few days ago, she might have been right. But not today. I close my eyes and pull the trigger.

The recoil takes me by surprise. So does the blood, a ridiculous amount of it erupting all over me. I end up on my back in the dust, ears ringing, drenched. The gun drops from my hands. I feel numb. After a few seconds of shock, I peel open my eyes. Mistake: The Queen's body is right in front of me, and it's not pretty. I squeeze my eyes shut, turn away, and take a deep breath before opening them again.

My face is warm and wet and sticky. I raise my hands to try to wipe it off and realize my hands are covered in blood as well. The smell is so thick I can taste it on the back of my tongue.

I had to kill her. She made the choice to come after us, and to try to kill me. I'm not going to feel bad about it . . . but my hands are shaking. Taking deep breaths, I scoot over to Pretty Boy and untie his hands.

He sits up and rubs his chafed wrists, with only a slight, wordless nod of acknowledgment. He recovers a lot faster than I do. He gets up, walks over to the closest body, and starts rummaging around in its pockets.

I sit down heavily. If Pretty Boy is relaxed enough to start looting, that means it's over. I strain to hear any gunshots or commotion, but there's nothing to hear. The townies are all still holed up in their homes, and the Queen's men must be either dead, hiding, or gone. Judging from the state of things, Dolly and Tank must have been busy picking them off. And Wolf...

Thinking about him getting shot makes me feel like something cold and sharp is poking into my chest. I suck in a breath through my teeth, let it out slowly, and force myself to my feet again. His body must be nearby. Not far away, I can see the scorched earth where the bazooka's rocket exploded, surrounded by pieces of charred bodies. But as for Wolf, there's no sign of him. I walk over just to make sure, and ignore how the smell of the burnt bodies makes me a little hungry. Wolf's body is gone. I saw the Queen shoot him right here—did the guards take the body? Or...

Just on cue, I hear a familiar low whistle from behind me.

"Wow, what a fuckin' mess. You do all this yourself, Kid?"

I turn around and there he is, as alive as ever.

"Wolf!" A surge of relief fills me and overflows, and I can't stop myself from running over. I slam into him, making him stumble back a few steps, and wrap my arms around him in a tight hug. He pauses, looking baffled, and roughly shoves me off. I fall on my ass in the dirt and scramble up again, still grinning. "You're alive!"

"Of course I am, dumbass," he says. "You think I would go into a situation like that without a plan?" He rips off the remnants of his tattered shirt, displaying a black vest underneath, and grins. "Bulletproof vest, motherfuckers."

He does a double take at me, and his triumphant grin fades slightly.

"You look like you massacred a small village with your bare hands. What the hell happened?"

"Yeah, umm. I killed the Queen. With a shotgun." I rub the side of my head self-consciously. "It was a little messy."

"We-ell, look at you, Kid." His grin is back in full force. "Killin' people and runnin' around covered in blood. A lil' baby shark, eh?"

The baby comment chafes a little, but I still smile. He takes a look at all the dead men spread across the ground and the bloody remains of the Queen.

"I'm not even gonna ask what happened," he says. "'Cause I'm not sure I wanna know. But I'm proud of you, kiddo." He punches me in the shoulder. And as silly as it may be, I feel happiness welling up at his words, covering up all my shaky feelings over killing the Queen. He's *proud* of me. Hell, even more than that, I'm proud of myself. For once, I did something on my own. I smile like an idiot and can't stop, even after Wolf has walked away and started checking the bodies for weapons and valuables.

A hand claps me on the shoulder, and I turn to see Pretty Boy. In his outstretched hand is my trusty old knife. I take it.

"Forgive me yet?" he asks.

"Ain't that easy," I say, "but it's a start."

He smiles a little, but then turns serious.

"I'm, uh...I'm sorry. About, you know, what happened. I shouldn't have done that."

"Nope, you shouldn't have." I stare down at my feet, my smile fading away.

"I've been a real shithead to you, and you've treated me way better than I deserve. I mean, you came and saved me even after everything, and that's really..." He trails off, and when I look up at him his cheeks are turning red. "You're a good kid, is what I'm trying to say."

"Thanks." I don't know what else to say. "You…um… you've got potential to be a good guy someday. Maybe."

He laughs, and for once it doesn't sound fake or mean.

"Thanks," he says. He's about to say something else when he's interrupted by a very loud and distinctly Tank-like whoop of excitement.

He and Dolly emerge from one of the nearby towers. He's lugging the bazooka with him, and Dolly is carrying an impressive-looking sniper rifle with all the delicateness of holding a child.

"Did you see me with that bazooka? Did you see?" Tank asks Wolf excitedly. "Damn, that was fun."

"Told you the plan would work," Wolf says. "We didn't even fuck anything up for once."

"*You* guys didn't!" I butt in. "Pretty Boy and I spent the whole time running away!"

"And getting the shit kicked out of me," he adds. "And you guys get to have fun with your fancy guns, what the fuck?"

"And I thought you were *dead*!" I say to Wolf.

"Aww, Kid, that's insulting. Should've known better."

"Well, you could've let us know!" Pretty Boy nods in agreement.

"No time. You two are both pretty useless, anyway," Wolf says.

"Hey, don't lump Kid in with Pretty Boy. That ain't fair," Tank says with a laugh. Pretty Boy attempts to shove him, which has absolutely no effect on Tank's girth.

Meanwhile, Dolly comes up beside me.

"You have blood all over your face," she informs me quietly.

"Uh, yeah, I know. The Queen's."

"I saw."

"Thanks for shooting those guards."

"I ran out of bullets."

"That's okay. I handled the rest."

"Yes, you did," she says. She walks over to the Queen's body and stares down at it. Her face not showing any reaction, she sets down her sniper rifle, pulls out a pistol, and points it at what's left of the Queen's head. I look away just before she starts shooting, and keep my gaze averted until she finishes unloading the clip. I hear her sigh quietly before walking away.

The others have started looting the bodies already. Wolf goes straight for their weapons, collecting himself quite a pile despite the fact we already have a truck full of guns and explosives. Pretty Boy is smart enough to take their walkie-talkies, which even Wolf admits is a good idea.

"All right," Wolf says, trying to juggle a few too many guns in his arms. "Now let's get the fuck out of here before the townies realize *I* set those houses on fire."

For the first time in what feels like ages, we aren't running from anyone. Everyone is in high spirits as we set off, leaving Towers behind with a mess of bullet holes and blackened buildings to remember us by. I wonder if the mayor will rethink his policy on dealings with sharks.

I ride in the jeep with Wolf and Dolly, while Tank drives the big truck with Pretty Boy riding along. Pretty Boy and Wolf each have a walkie-talkie so we can communicate between vehicles. Wolf takes advantage of this by spewing vulgarities and insults at Pretty Boy whenever he gets bored. Dolly spends almost an hour meticulously cleaning her new sniper rifle, and I do my best to clean the blood off myself. Pretty Boy navigates with the help of a map from the townies, and we drive straight through the day. I drift in and out of sleep, relaxed by the movement and the warm air.

When the sun goes down we pull onto the side of the road to rest for the night. Since we didn't see any other cars and Pretty Boy judges we aren't *too* close to Saint's territory yet, Wolf lets us have a fire. There aren't any people to fry up this time, but we bust out a generous amount of canned food. There's soup, beans, and fruits. Pretty Boy reads off labels and divvies it out to whoever claims it first. I end up with some sliced pineapple and a can of chili. Fruit is always a treat. I save it for last and eat very slowly, savoring each bite with its almost overwhelming sweetness.

I sit cross-legged next to Dolly on the ground. She's proving, as usual, to be the only person in existence who can eat straight out of a can without making any kind of mess. By the time I'm done with my meal I have sauce and pineapple juice covering my hands and all down the front of my shirt. My clothes are still caked with blood, and I'm sure my combined smell of that and sweat and pineapples is pretty rank. I find myself wishing for a bath like I had back at the Queen's, but I guess that's out of the question.

Normally I wouldn't waste the water, but since we have excess right now, I use some of it to rewash my hands and face after the meal. It's quiet. Everyone is stuffed and tired and content. For a while nobody speaks, and we all sit around watching the fire and basking in the calmness. It's too dark to see anything beyond the reach of the firelight, but the wastelands don't scare me anymore. I feel safe within our bubble of light and warmth.

Pretty Boy stretches out on the ground and soon dozes off. Tank, still sitting, nods off intermittently. Dolly cleans her fingernails with a knife, and Wolf pores over one of the maps he bought. I don't know how he could be getting much out of it when he can't even read, but judging from his furrowed brows he's doing some serious thinking.

"So we're really gonna do this, Wolf?" I ask, pulling my knees to my chest and hugging them. He squints at me.

"Do what?"

"Blow up the radio tower."

"Well, yeah."

"But…" I scuff one boot in the dirt. "I mean, why?"

"Ain't got much of a choice, Kid, this Saint guy's after us."

"Well, we could always run or something," I say. "And, I mean, from an outside perspective, isn't what he's doing kind of…good?"

The silence around the fire suddenly feels uncomfortably thick. I feel the tension growing with each second that passes. Wolf scrutinizes me from across the flames, and Tank and Dolly both watch him and await his response.

"Let me ask you something, Kid," Wolf says with a hard edge to his voice. "Do you know what happens when you give one person too much power?"

"Not really?"

"Nuclear wastelands, that's what happens." He spreads his arms wide to show the empty stretch of desert around us. In the silence after his response, I realize how quiet it is out here. There's only the crackle of flames and the sound of my breathing. "You know, there used to be plants here. There used to be animals. There used to be people. You think any of them had a say in starting the war? No way. But they paid the price all the same."

"But you don't know if Saint would be like that, he—"

"*Everybody* is like that when they get too much power. Look at the Queen: She used to be all right. She stayed neutral, her mansion was a safe place for travelers, and she treated her own people well. But once she got all big and powerful, she got addicted to it. And the second that power started to slip out from under her, she fuckin' threw away *everything* to try and get it back. She was willing to betray us, to kill Ruby. She broke all her own rules. And that's what all people are like. They'll do anything to gain power, and to keep it once they have it." He shakes his head, grimacing. "You post-bombers all think the world before was some kind of utopia. It wasn't. People still killed each other, and assholes didn't get the punishment they deserved. We had people in charge worse than the Queen, and the whole 'justice' thing was a lot slower and a lot less reliable than putting a bullet in someone's head."

Tank lets out an impressed whistle.

"And here I was thinking we were doing it just for fun!"

"Well, that too," Wolf says, the corner of his mouth curving upward.

"I thought you were just a kid when the bombs fell? How do you know all this kinda stuff?" I ask.

"My parents talked about it when I was growing up. They were real smart, so it's gotta be true." He nods to himself. "My mom was a cop back before, y'know."

That raises a lot of questions, like if they were so smart how did Wolf turn out so messed up, but I figure now isn't the right time to bring that up.

"A cop? Those were like town guards, right?"

"Ehh, kind of. It just means she must've been right."

"Oh. Okay." I trust Wolf, so I accept it. "My papa used to say some of the same stuff, actually."

"Oh yeah?" Wolf looks barely interested.

"Your papa?" Tank asks, looking considerably more so. "Y'know, you've never said...where did you come from, anyway? How'd you end up alone?"

"Well..." It feels so far away now. Wolf and the crew have become my life. It's like I shrugged off the past and have been ignoring it ever since I got into that jeep. "I used to live in this town...Bramble, it was called."

"So you were a townie?"

"No. Well, kind of." I never considered myself one, but I guess I did live there for a number of years. "I mean... I grew up in a shelter. One of the underground ones. My papa and me."

"What about your mom?"

"Oh, she died when I was young. Got sick or something. So it was just me and my papa for a long time." I fiddle with my empty can, uncomfortable with everyone's eyes on me. "But he started getting... sick. Not, um, physically." I don't have the proper words to describe it. I still remember the way he looked, his eyes so distant and strange all the time, but I don't really know how to explain that. "I think he was lonely. And we were running out of food. So we had to leave." I force myself to set down the can, but then I don't know what to do with my hands. I pick at a hole in my jeans. "I had never been out of the shelter. My papa was scared about radiation; he used to wear a gas mask whenever he went out. I had no idea what it was like out there, and he had no clue where to go."

"How old were you?" Tank asks.

"Umm, twelve, I guess."

"So where'd you go?"

"We just wandered for a while. Lucky we didn't meet any raiders or anything. We had enough food and water to survive, if barely. Finally we found a town. It was built into what my papa said used to be a school."

"And they took you guys in?"

"They took *me* in," I say. The answer sits there, heavy. I don't need to say anything else. Towns are wary, were warier still back then. They were all just scared, desperate survivors. They didn't trust outsiders, and only agreed to take me in because I was too young to be a threat. I remember my papa's big arms engulfing me when we said good-bye. I didn't understand why he had to go. Part of me hated that he was abandoning me; the rest of me was just grateful to have food, water, and a roof over my head.

I don't have to explain any of that. Good thing, because my tongue feels too thick to voice it.

"Sorry," Tank says gently.

"It wasn't too bad," I say, trying to shrug off the sadness. "They kept me safe and fed. There were some other kids I played with. 'Course, they both died from radiation poisoning, but nothing anyone can do 'bout that…"

"Wow, Kid, way to dampen the mood," Wolf says.

"Sorry," I say. "Anyway, it never really felt like home, so eventually I left and I found you guys. The end." My reasons for leaving run deeper than that, but I'm not quite sure how to explain them—the unwelcome glances, the constant feeling of not belonging, the fear they shot my papa years ago—so I leave it at that. I sit nervously, hands folded on my lap, feeling awfully exposed.

"Naw, Kid," Wolf says. "The beginning."

XXV
Target Practice

When I wake up, the boys are still asleep. Tank is sleeping upright with his head leaning against a box, snoring loudly. Each of us got a couple of pillows, which Wolf was kind enough to grab along with the explosives, but Tank gave his to me. Wolf is sprawled across the open space, leaving only a tiny corner where Pretty Boy is curled up. He looks innocent when he's sleeping, handsome features relaxed and open. I don't feel an uncomfortable attraction to him like I used to, nor do I feel embarrassed or hurt or spiteful. I just feel sort of neutral, which is nice.

I sit up and stretch, cracking my shoulders and back. The crates didn't make the most comfortable bed even with a few pillows stacked on top, and there's a weird kink in my side, but I feel rested. Dolly's absence makes me curious enough to forgo more sleep. The doors are opened a tiny crack, and I can't see where she is. I slide off my crates and carefully step over Wolf. It's a challenge getting to the doors without stomping on some part of him, and I have to hop from space to space to reach the exit. I squeeze through and shut them behind me.

Dolly is just outside the truck, beside the ashes of last night's fire. Guns and boxes of ammo are spread out on the ground. She's kneeling in the middle of it all, inspecting a small handgun. As I jump down from the truck, the small sound of impact makes her instantly turn the gun toward me. I freeze and she lowers it again.

"Morning," I say cheerfully, and take a few steps closer. I place my hands on my hips and look down at all the weapons. "Wow, that's a lot of guns."

"It's enough," she says.

I crouch next to one and pick it up, handling it delicately and making sure not to point it at myself or Dolly.

"Do you know how to shoot yet?" she asks.

"Well, I mean…" I shrug. "Kind of?"

She nods, stands, and holds out the handgun she was inspecting. "Let's practice."

"Practice?" I repeat. "You mean practice shooting things? I don't know, that seems a little…" *Dangerous* is the first word to come to mind. *Embarrassing* is the second. I'm not exactly the best with guns. Hell, the Queen was right next to me and I still managed to goof it up, getting knocked over like that. I hesitate. Dolly doesn't budge or react whatsoever. She simply stands there, gun held out to me, until I give in and take it.

She smiles.

"Good," she says, and grabs a pistol for herself.

We find a spot several yards away from the truck where there's only open wasteland and no danger of me accidentally shooting anyone. Dolly sets up the target: a pyramid of empty tin cans, the remains of our meal last night.

"So should I try to shoot it from…what, here?" I ask, standing a few yards away. Dolly shakes her head, places a hand on my elbow, and leads me back quite a bit more. "Seriously? There's no way I can hit that!"

"Try."

I look doubtfully at the gun in my hand and back at Dolly.

When she doesn't say anything, I sigh and plant my feet, assuming what I think is a good shooting pose. Behind me, Dolly laughs quietly.

"What?" I ask, turning around.

"Nothing. Go."

"Right, right..." I turn back to the target and raise the gun. I suck in a deep breath, blow it out, do my best to steady my shaking hands as I focus on the target. Ready, and...pull the trigger.

Nothing happens.

"Safety," Dolly says.

"Oh, shit." I'm turning red already and I haven't even managed to fire yet. Silently cursing myself, I click the safety off and raise the gun again. I'm already frazzled, heart thumping nervously. I don't know why it's so important to me to impress Dolly, but it is.

I fire.

I'm not sure where the bullet goes, but it's definitely nowhere near the target. A defeated sigh leaks out of me, and my arms fall slack at my sides.

"It's useless," I say. "I'm never gonna—" Before I can finish, Dolly places her hand on my lower back and steers me forward a few paces.

"Again," she says. When I raise the gun, she reaches over and grabs my hands, repositioning them slightly. "Like this."

"Oh. Thanks." I shoot again. The bullet dings off one of the outside cans and ricochets into the dirt.

She takes me closer, and closer. She corrects my grip and helps me aim again and again until, *finally*, I manage to knock a can off the pyramid. I let out a triumphant yell—and am promptly surprised by the sound of smattering applause behind me.

I turn around and find Wolf, Tank, and Pretty Boy sitting on the ground nearby. All the blood rushes to my face as I wonder how long they've been watching me shoot at nothing. Wolf looks thoroughly amused. I'm too flustered to say anything.

"Nice shot," Tank says.

"Yeah, you killed the *shit* out of that can!" Wolf says, not quite as sincerely. Pretty Boy says nothing, but smirks.

Dolly pats me on the head. It makes me feel a bit better, but I'm still embarrassed. I hand the gun back to her.

"I'm done," I tell her. Louder, to the boys, I say, "Show's over, get outta here!"

After I stand there for a while and make it clear I won't be shooting again, they lose interest and find something else to do. I sigh, push sweaty hair out of my face, and go to pick up the can I knocked over. When it's in my hands I inspect where the bullet hit. A knot forms in my stomach. If I had this much trouble hitting an unmoving can, there's no way I'm going to hit someone trying their damnedest to kill me. I've been trying to feel optimistic about this radio tower plan, but anxiety is creeping up on me. I can't leave the others on their own, no matter how little help I may be, but I'm starting to realize the chances of me making it out are slim. I mean, hell, they're slim for all of us, but most of all for me.

"Are you okay?" Dolly asks, jolting me out of my thoughts.

"Ahh, yeah," I say. "Just a little worried, I guess."

"You'll be fine," she says. I nod halfheartedly. "I'll make sure of it," she says, and places the gun back in my hand. "Practice more. I'll watch for the boys."

I bite my lip and look down at the gun.

"All right, all right..." I take a few paces away from the target and stop. "But I'm starting from here this time."

We practice for at least an hour or two. I get better, but not by much. We take a break when the others announce it's time for breakfast, and after that Wolf decides he wants to help, too.

"If you don't hit it this time, I'm gonna hit you," he says, leaning up too close behind me.

"What? No!" I lower the gun and turn to him. "That's *not* helpful, Wolf!"

" 'Course it is. I learned like this. C'mon, just shoot."

"Well, now I don't want to . . ."

"You have five seconds before I hit you."

"Wolf!"

"Four . . . three . . . two . . ."

I raise the gun frantically and fire. It misses. I try to duck, but Wolf smacks the side of my head before I can get out of the way.

"Ow!" It didn't really hurt that much, but it's still annoying. I frown and rub the side of my head. "I don't want to do this anymore."

"Aww come on, don't be a pussy. I'm tryin' to help you out here."

I fold my arms over my chest and shake my head.

"Fine, fine. How about something a little more realistic?" He leaves my side and walks over to the stacked cans.

"What do you mean a little more—" A can flies through the air toward my face. I narrowly dodge it. "What the hell?!"

"Moving target! Shoot it!" he yells back, throwing another. It hits my shoulder this time.

"Ow! Wolf! Stop it!" I look around frantically. "Where's Dolly? I want Dolly's training back!"

"Fuck you, I'm way better at this!"

The next can hits me in the head and sends me reeling, and I decide it's about time to change tactics. I drop my gun in the dirt, turn away, and start running.

"Get the fuck back here, Kid! That's cheating!" Another can whizzes past me. I run back to the truck and climb inside. The others are sitting there, having a conversation that stops the second I arrive. I duck behind Tank, panting.

"So I'm guessing training didn't go well?" he asks, smiling down at me.

"No. He's throwing things. He's crazy. Hide me."

Wolf clambers noisily into the truck a few seconds later, breathing heavily. He leans one hand against the wall and spits on the floor. The spittle lands dangerously close to Pretty Boy, who wrinkles his nose and scoots away.

"Fast little fucker, ain't ya?" Wolf says. "Knew there was a reason your dumb ass managed to stay alive for so long." I poke my head out from behind Tank and grin at him.

"You must be getting out of shape, Wolf," Pretty Boy says. "Or maybe just old?"

"Shut up!" Wolf aims a halfhearted kick in his direction, but Pretty Boy dodges it. "The only reason *you're* in shape is you're always runnin' from the fight."

"Maybe you only stay because you can't run fast enough."

"I said shut up. I don't need your shit right now."

Pretty Boy shuts up, and Wolf sits down.

"All right, enough fucking around, we gotta get going soon." Wolf takes out one of his maps and smooths the crinkled paper against his knee. "So, there's a road leading straight up to the radio tower...but we ain't gonna use that, 'cause we ain't *that* stupid." He uses one finger to circle something on the map. Wanting a better look, I come out from my hiding spot behind Tank and sit between him and Dolly. Wolf has the map angled so all of us can see it. "Instead, we're gonna go around here." He draws a path leading to the tower from behind.

"Right, they'll *never* expect that," Pretty Boy says dryly. Wolf ignores him.

"Problem is, we got no idea if there are roads back there, or what the terrain is like. Might not be able to bring the big truck o' explosives around this way, which would be shitty because it's hard to blow stuff up without explosives. So, a few of us will go ahead in the jeep and scout it out first, and the rest will follow a ways back in the big truck."

"And what if the truck can't make it?" Tank asks.

"We load the jeep up with everything we can take and pile in."

"That sounds shitty."

"I dunno, it would make a pretty fuckin' good entrance to charge in there in a jeep full of guns and explosives..."

"We'd probably blow ourselves up," Pretty Boy says. "Nothing ever goes right for us."

"Yeah, why the fuck *is* that?" Wolf asks.

"I blame you. You're in charge."

"Shut up, Pretty Boy." Wolf folds up the map and shoves it back into his pocket. "So, who wants to go in the jeep?"

"I guess I will," I offer. "I like the jeep."

"And I'll drive," Wolf says. "Pretty Boy, you come navigate for me."

"Ugh, fine."

"Did I say you could talk?"

"Fuck you."

Wolf only laughs.

"Tank, Dolly, you two get the truck then. One of you stay on the radio in case anything goes wrong, and watch out for other cars. We don't know if Saint has patrols in the area, and we can't get ourselves spotted." They nod. "All right, let's get going."

It doesn't take long for the ride to get bumpy. Off-road, the ground is uneven and rocky. The jeep can handle it, but after a few big bumps send me a couple inches out of my seat, I decide to put on my seat belt. Wolf's driving makes it worse. I swear he's hitting big holes on purpose, not to mention ramping off uneven ground and trying to catch air. Pretty Boy keeps yelling at him to drive more carefully, but eventually he gives up and fastens his seat belt as well. If our route is so rough, I can only imagine how the big truck is faring behind us. I keep turning around to make sure they're still following us. They manage, albeit slowly. I stay in contact with them via walkie-talkie, since I don't have anything else to do.

After a few rolling hills, we reach a stretch of land that's open and flat.

"Thank God," Pretty Boy says, relaxing in his seat.

"This should be easier," I say into the radio.

"Aww, this is no fun at all," Wolf says, immediately looking bored. He jams his foot down on the gas and the jeep jerks forward. After the rocky hills, this speed feels like we're flying. The wind whips through my hair and drowns out the sound of Wolf and Pretty Boy yelling at each other. I close my eyes and smile at the familiar sensation. It reminds me of the first time I was in the jeep with Wolf and Dolly, how I didn't know where I was going but was just happy to be going *somewhere* and—

An explosion.

My eyes fly open as the jeep jerks violently. My head slams into the headrest, and my body lifts from the seat. A chaos of noise and movement surrounds me, and I squeeze my eyes shut again. I lose sense of all direction as the jeep tumbles sideways, rolling over once before coming to a stop upside down. The frame of the windshield held, miraculously, and manages to prop the jeep up—the only reason we weren't crushed.

I stay with my eyes shut and my hands clenched tightly on my seat belt. I smell gasoline, hear it dripping. I force myself to take a few deep breaths and slowly open my eyes again. The world is confusing upside down. I slide my eyes from side to side.

"Wolf? Pretty Boy?" I croak out. My clumsy fingers fumble with the seat belt for a few seconds before I manage to escape and fall to the ground. I crawl out from beneath the wrecked jeep, my whole body shaking. I try to stay calm despite how disoriented I am. Once I make it a few yards from the jeep, I stop and look back. I can see Pretty Boy, just now unfastening his seat belt. Wolf isn't in the jeep or anywhere near it. I sit up and look around, and see him lying on the ground a ways away. He must have been flung from the jeep when it rolled.

"Wolf! Wolf, are you okay?" I slowly get to my feet, legs trembling, and move toward him. The walkie-talkie is sitting in the dirt nearby, and I scoop it up on the way.

"Kid, stop!" Pretty Boy yells from the jeep. I stop and turn.

"What is it?"

"Don't move," he says. His voice is getting tight and anxious, his eyes darting all over the place as he crawls out from beneath the toppled vehicle.

"Why?" I ask, but Wolf catches my attention with a groan. I look over and see him sitting up groggily, holding a hand to his head. There's a gash on the side of his face, and he looks pretty out of it, but I'm just glad he's still in one piece, somehow.

"I really can't fucking afford to lose any more brain cells," he says loudly, wincing. "What the *fuck* was that?"

"A mine!" Pretty Boy says. He steps closer to me, frantically looking around in every direction as if expecting another one to jump out at him. "This is a minefield. We are *so* fucked."

"Oh, shit," I breathe. I plant my feet and slowly raise the radio to my mouth while shifting my body as little as possible. "Guys, don't come any closer," I say into it. "We hit a minefield."

"That Saint fucker is way too clever," Wolf says. "Why isn't this on my map? Goddamn townies. We should go back and blow the place up for this." He clambers to his feet, and I cringe at every careless movement he makes.

"What the hell are we supposed to do?" Pretty Boy asks, edging on panicky. He stands so close that he's practically on top of me, his elbows and feet invading my personal space. I'm too nervous to either move or push him off, and keep trying to stay as still as possible.

"We can go back the way we came before we hit the mine. That should be safe, right?" I say.

"Do you remember the path we took? The *exact* path?"

We all pause to look around. The silence speaks for itself.

"So what do we do?" Pretty Boy asks again.

"Why the hell are you both looking at *me*?" Wolf asks, glowering at us. His hands clench and unclench at his sides. He looks almost…nervous. My stomach tightens as I realize he has no idea what to do. If even Wolf is scared, that's bad news for us.

"You're supposed to be the boss!" Pretty Boy practically shouts.

"Well, fuck, I don't know nothing about no fuckin' minefield."

"Wolf, please, *focus*," Pretty Boy says, looking like he's desperately trying to keep a level head. "What are we supposed to do now?"

I stand where I am and stare around me, also awaiting his answer. Wolf takes his sweet time wiping blood off his face and brushing off his clothes.

"Well…we gotta make it back to the truck."

"Obviously."

"And I guess someone will have to go first and check it out."

"Who, exactly?"

"Not me. I'm clearly the most useful person here."

I stare down at my feet. Out of the three of us, I know it has to be me. I'm the weakest link in the group, everyone knows it. I open my mouth to volunteer, but before I can make a sound Pretty Boy speaks again.

"Right, of course, it's me. It's always me. Who gives a shit if *I* get thrown under the bus, right?"

"Pretty Boy—" I say.

"No big deal, there shouldn't be *too* many mines in one area, right?" Pretty Boy continues, not even noticing my attempt to talk to him. I fall silent and meet Wolf's eyes. Neither of us says anything. I look back at Pretty Boy, who is chewing his lip nervously and looking at the stretch of land between us and the safety of the truck.

"What's happening?" Tank's voice crackles over the radio.

"Pretty Boy's gonna try and find a safe path to you guys," I say.

"Tell him to be careful."

"Tank says be careful," I say. I bite my lip. "And I second that."

"Right, I'll keep that in mind." Pretty Boy lets out a long breath and runs his hands through his hair. "All right, all right. I'll be fine. Easy."

He starts to walk in the direction of the truck. At first he moves at a snail's pace, taking laughably small steps and pausing to verify his safety after each and every one. Eventually Wolf shouts at him to hurry the hell up and he moves faster, pausing every so often to search the ground in front of him. I'm not sure if the mines are even visible, or if they're buried deep enough that this is all a matter of luck. I chew my dirty fingernails and try to commit his path to memory so I'll know where to go when it's my turn. It's a little difficult, because he does some strange snaking route that seems pretty random.

Every step makes me wince. Every pause lasts minutes. Every time he stops I'm *sure* something is wrong. Maybe he sees a mine; maybe he heard a telltale click of warning beneath his foot. My heart is already racing; I can't imagine how I'm going to cope with trying to cross the field myself. My eyes stay glued on Pretty Boy as he makes his agonizingly slow way toward the truck.

Something cracks. Pretty Boy and I both nearly jump out of our skins, and he freezes in place.

"My bad," Wolf says. "Just cracked my back. S'nothing. Go on, Pretty Boy, you're almost there."

Pretty Boy lets out a shaky laugh.

"Okay," he says. "Okay." I think he's trying to reassure himself more than anything. He's still frozen, nerves all riled up again.

"You're doing fine," I yell out to him. "You're almost there!"

With visible effort, he forces himself to take a step forward. And another. Another. The truck isn't far now. He starts to regain confidence, walking at a near-normal pace. I can see how eager he is to get back to safety, keeping his eyes on the truck ahead of him.

"Holy shit," he says, looking over his shoulder at us. "I hope you guys watched me, because I am not trying this aga—"

Boom.

I scream.

XXVI
Carry On

"Kid, look at me."

There's a buzzing in my ears and a tightness in my chest and I can't take my eyes off the chunks of flesh that used to be Pretty Boy.

"C'mon, snap out of it."

I've seen plenty of people die, but not like this. I guess I didn't realize that people could die so sudden, here one moment and gone the next. I didn't realize they could end up in so many pieces so quickly. I didn't realize how hard it could be to tell which pieces are which.

"Kid!"

I finally turn to look at Wolf. I stare at him, my eyes wide and watering. I realize my mouth is hanging open and snap it shut. I take a deep breath and shakily raise the radio to my mouth.

"Pretty Boy is dead," I say. The words come out weird, flat. There's a burst of something choked and unintelligible on the other end, followed by silence.

"That stupid piece of shit," Wolf whispers, staring out at the minefield. "He was almost there. Why'd he have to take his eyes off of—" He cuts himself off, shaking his head. "Fuck. *Fuck.* Fuck everything about this."

My hands are shaking. I clamp them around the walkie-talkie and hold it against my chest, trying to make myself still.

"What do we do?" I ask, looking out at the minefield alongside Wolf. I can't bring myself to look at his face. "Wolf?"

The radio crackles to life, startling me.

"I'm coming to get you guys." It's Dolly now, not Tank.

Wolf rips the device out of my hands in an instant.

"No," he says sharply into it. "You two stay put. We'll make it out." He looks at me, his face back to its usual hardness, all trace of emotion gone. "We're gonna go together."

"Okay," I say weakly.

"And we're gonna be fine." He reaches out, grabs my shoulder, and gives it a brief squeeze before letting go. "Don't lose your shit on me now, all right?"

"Okay," I repeat more firmly. I let out a breath and nod at him.

"There we go. Now watch where I step, and follow me. Not too close, in case—" He pauses. "Just stay back a few feet. And don't look at the mess."

I nod again, trying not to think too hard about those last parts. Wolf sets out without anything further, his steps surprisingly confident given the situation. He glances back and gestures at me to follow, and I will my feet to step forward into the space he occupied a few seconds ago.

I move without thinking about it. It feels like my brain has shut down, things like sadness and fear pushed to the side. All that passes through my mind is where to step next, my eyes tracking Wolf's movements and my feet imitating them while my brain remains empty. Step, wait, step. I can do this. Soon we're halfway there, and it almost feels easy.

Then I see the arm.

Suddenly my feet won't move and neither will my eyes,

staying glued on the scorched limb just a few feet to my right. It simultaneously reminds me of the arm Wolf once offered me to eat, and the first time I saw Pretty Boy. The meat I did eat, and Pretty Boy's smile.

I slap a hand across my mouth and lean over, my stomach heaving violently. Bile burns the back of my throat.

"Hey," Wolf says from up ahead. "What'd I tell you? Keep your eyes on me."

I slowly remove my hand from my mouth and swallow hard. I still can't take my eyes off the arm.

"Are we just going to leave him here?" I ask, my voice coming out thick.

"We don't have a choice. Get your shit together and keep moving."

I wipe my eyes and take a shuddery breath. I take a step closer to the arm, off of the safe path.

"What the hell are you doing?"

"Just one piece," I say, my voice wavering. "Then we can have a funeral."

"It's not fucking worth it!" Wolf shouts at me. The genuine alarm in his tone gives me pause, but I take another step before I can lose my resolve. One more, and I'm able to bend down and gingerly snatch the arm out of the dirt. Ignoring the blood and the discomfiting limpness of it, I clutch it against my chest.

"Got it," I say, making my way back to the path Wolf took.

"Good for you, you got the bloody fucking arm. Now get your ass over here before you blow yourself up."

Through a combination of luck and attempting to follow the path Pretty Boy took, Wolf and I make it back to the truck safely. Tank is sitting on the ground in tears when we arrive. Wolf talks to him quietly while I sit with Dolly, my head resting on her shoulder. It takes me a while to remember I'm still holding the arm. Tank wants to go back for more of him, but Wolf says it's too dangerous.

We debate about leaving some sort of headstone until we realize none of us can write, and the hard-packed earth defeats our idea of a partial burial. So we settle for just the arm, a hunk of flesh that will soon be melted away by time and heat and leave nothing but dusty bones. I hope they'll serve as a warning to travelers about to cross into the minefield.

We form a half circle around the makeshift grave, and nobody knows what to do next. Tank's bulky shoulders heave with sobs. He doesn't even attempt to hide the tears flowing down his dark face. I find myself crying, too, albeit more quietly. I can't bring myself to think of the wrongs Pretty Boy did or the worse ones he might've done if he had a chance. No matter what, his loss leaves an emptiness behind.

The other two are stony-faced. Dolly's expression remains unchanged, not a flicker of emotion crossing her features as she stares at what's left of Pretty Boy. Wolf's face is unreadable, but he pats Tank on the shoulder a few times. The big man's loud sobs are the only noise besides the wind for several minutes. My mind keeps replaying the explosion over and over again, the way Pretty Boy was gone in an instant and left only a mess of guts and scattered limbs behind. A person one second, meat the next. That's the nature of the wastes.

Eventually Wolf clears his throat, looking uncomfortable.

"Well, I guess we should say something," he says. Nobody answers. After an awkward stretch of silence, he looks over at Tank. "You go first, big guy."

Tank nods and takes a shaky breath. He stifles his sobs and controls himself before speaking.

"He was my friend," he says. "And maybe he wasn't always the most reliable friend, but he was the best I had for a long time." He looks down at the pile and clenches his jaw, fighting back a fresh wave of tears. "I would've taken the fall for you if I could, buddy. And I'm sorry there wasn't anything I could do."

He stops and glances at me as if to signal that he's done. I swallow hard, trying to dislodge a lump in my throat.

There's a lot I want to say, but I don't really know how. I want to talk about how I think he tried a lot harder than anyone gave him credit for, and how he probably did the best he could to deal with a life he never wanted. I want to say he might've been a great guy in another world, but was never really cut out for this one. I want to express how unfair it is that he got blown up just when we were finally becoming friends. But the words stick on my tongue and I can't quite bring myself to say them. I don't think there's really a point in saying them, anyway. It's no good now.

"We didn't always get along," I say, "but you were nice, um, toward the end. So thanks I guess. And sorry for throwing up on you that one time, though you kind of deserved it."

I shut my mouth and cross my arms over my chest. Wolf coughs in the quiet that follows, and when I glance over at him it almost looks like he's smirking.

The silence goes on for a while before we all look at Dolly.

"I have nothing to say," she says flatly when she notices us staring.

"Aww, c'mon, Dolly. Say *something*," Wolf says.

"I didn't like him."

"No, something nice."

She pauses and stares into the distance, apparently deep in thought.

"He was…" she says haltingly. "Not so bad to look at."

Wolf lets out a sound like he's choking. I slowly turn my head in his direction and find, to my amazement, he's trying to stifle a laugh. When he notices all of us looking at him, he loses it.

The laughter explodes out of him like it was tired of being cooped up for so long.

"Look at this," he says, laughing so hard his whole body shakes, "look at this fucking mess. It's a goddamn *arm*. What kind of sick fucking funeral is this?" He pauses to gasp for breath and laugh some more.

I'm shocked by his sudden mirth, offended by the idea that he would laugh with a freshly dead friend in front of us. I don't even know what to say, and stare at him with my mouth gaping open.

But then I look at the gory arm in front of us, the meat that used to be Pretty Boy, and, oddly enough, I feel it bubbling up within me: a laugh. It bursts out before I can suppress it, the laughter coming guiltily at first but then rising in volume and shamelessness. Soon even Tank is laughing, despite the tears running down his face. Dolly gives a small smile, as if not quite sure what the joke is but sharing in our amusement anyway. We stay like that, laughing in front of a makeshift grave, for a while. And in the end, drained of my tears and laughter, I feel lighter.

"Rest in pieces," Wolf says almost affectionately, "you mother-fucker."

The ride is quiet without Pretty Boy. Occasionally someone tries to say something, but it's too weird. There are awkward pauses where everyone waits for one of his dry comments or jabs at Wolf, empty moments where he should be but he isn't anymore. Despite the fact he got blown to pieces right in front of me, his death doesn't hit me right away. It's like at first I don't realize he's really gone—gone forever. But as time goes on, it sinks in. I find myself expecting him to say something, and each time have to remind myself that he isn't there, and he's never going to be there again. And even though we had our issues, and even though he wasn't exactly a good guy, I find myself still missing him. I guess that's the best definition I have for death: You miss them being there, and you miss it forever.

It was the same with my papa. Losing someone doesn't hit you straight-on, it creeps up on you. Just when you think you're done feeling like a part of your life is missing, it hits you again out of nowhere and the grief is like a fresh wound. I know how it is, and I think everyone else does, too. I know Dolly has been through loss, and judging from the looks on Wolf's and Tank's faces they have as well.

But when it comes down to it, we don't have time to grieve. The wastelands aren't going to sit and wait for us to suck it up, and neither is Saint. Every passing hour is another hour he gets to prepare for our arrival, and we really can't afford that. Before too long Wolf starts pulling out his maps again and talking strategy in a low voice with Dolly, and Tank and I start killing time by playing "I Spy." It's a damn slow game out in the middle of nowhere, but at least it's a distraction.

Eventually I build up the courage to speak to Wolf.

"So, uh...what's our plan now?" I ask. We've unanimously decided that taking a back route isn't an option anymore. We don't know how far the minefield extends, or if any other traps lay waiting for us.

"We-ell..." The look on his face clearly says he has no idea. But of course Wolf would never admit that, so instead he wings it. "We're gonna charge in from the front after all."

"Seriously?"

"Yeah," he says, voice growing more confident as he plunges ahead. "We drive the big truck right in through their front door, and start tossin' out grenades. They'll never see it coming."

"Didn't you say we couldn't do that 'cause it's too dumb?"

"Well, yeah, but that's the genius. It's so fuckin' *dumb* they're never gonna expect us to actually do it. Element of surprise."

This is where Pretty Boy would say this sounds like a bad idea, or declare there's no way in hell he's going on this mission. Everyone is probably thinking the same thing, because nobody says anything for a while. Or maybe everyone's just thinking about what a shitty plan this is.

"Okay," I say finally, unable to take the silence any longer. "I guess we've done stupider things before."

"Damn right we have!" Wolf says cheerfully. He claps me on the shoulder. "We'll need to stop soon, divvy up the guns and grenades and other goodies. All of us load up, go in guns blazing."

It sounds like the kind of idea that could get us all killed, but I'm not gonna be the one to say that. We don't have a lot of options, anyway.

Wolf soon declares it's time to stop and prep for arrival. We pull onto the side of the road and everyone crams into the back compartment with all of the boxes.

Wolf has sorted most of the goods into helpful piles, including guns, big guns, and "really fuckin' huge" guns. The explosives have also been lumped together in one very dangerous-looking pile. I sit as far away from it as possible.

Wolf gives each of us a bulletproof vest and some guns to start with. My vest is way too big and looks ridiculous, but I have it better than Tank, who can barely squeeze into his. His big belly protrudes from underneath, so it doesn't really look like it's protecting anything.

Everyone else gets some big, hefty, deadly-looking guns, and I get a pistol. Wolf says he doesn't trust me with anything bigger, and I'd probably shoot myself or one of the others with anything automatic. Honestly, I'm just happy to have a gun in my hands. He gives me a new knife, too: a big and scary-looking one that looks sharp enough to slice through bone. It's definitely a lot more intimidating than my old one, but I keep that, too, just in case. It's gotten me out of a few tight spots.

"All right, so," Wolf says. He unfurls a piece of paper with a very crude drawing on it. "I mapped out the place so we can—"

"Wait, where's the *actual* map?"

"You insulting my handiwork, Kid?"

"Umm, no . . ." I scrutinize the so-called map for another few seconds, and still can't make any sense out of the wobbly circles and squares. It looks like something a kid with too much radiation to the brain would draw. "I mean, I just . . . you didn't get one from the townies?"

"They didn't have any of the inside, but they knew the basics. Are you sayin' there's something wrong with my map?"

"Er, no. It's, uh, great."

"Damn right it is. Now keep your dumb mouth shut, I'm explainin' a plan here." He clears his throat and points a long and dirty fingernail at a big circle. "Now this here is the radio tower. It's not actually a circle, it's a big fuckin' tall metal thing. And, according to the townies, it's a little harder to blow up than I first imagined. So-o, with that in mind, we're not gonna go right for that one. Instead . . ." He circles his finger around slowly and stops it on a square next to the circle. "We're gonna go here."

A moment of silence falls. I stare at the map, struggling to keep my mouth shut like Wolf said, until finally Tank speaks up instead.

"And what the hell is that supposed to be?"

"It's the control room, ya big dumb fuck. It's the place they've actually got all the equipment and shit for their brainwashin'." He taps the square a few times, nodding thoughtfully. "So we get in here, we shoot some guys, we blow the shit up. Most importantly, we kill the *fuck* out of Saint." He looks up at us, his expression sobering for a moment. "That's the most important bit. Remember what I said about people with power, and all the 'law and order' bullshit this asshole is trying to pull. This is our entire way of life at stake. The guy's gotta go down, no matter what happens."

"Right, boss," Tank says, while Dolly nods. After a moment's hesitation, I nod my agreement as well. Wolf is right: Saint has to die. Especially with the Queen gone, he'll have far too much rein here if we don't pull this off.

"So what's the rest of the plan?" I ask.

"Uh…that's it. Then we get out. Easy." He grins triumphantly, rolls his map up, and sticks it into his back pocket. He looks around at us as if expecting applause. Everyone stares at him.

"Well," I say, trying to sound enthusiastic, "I guess that doesn't sound too hard."

"Child's play," Wolf says confidently.

"And we're just gonna drive the truck right into the place?"

"Yup. I figure someone drives, the rest of us hide in the back, we crash through the front of the building, and—bam! All pile out and give 'em a hell of a surprise."

"And what if we accidentally blow ourselves up?"

"Well that would be fuckin' unfortunate, wouldn't it, Kid?" Wolf grins, as unconcerned as always. He looks between me and Tank, who both look a little dubious. "Aww, come on. Why can't you guys just be nice and quiet and follow along with the whole thing like Dolly does?"

Dolly glances up at the mention of her name, and then returns to scrutinizing guns, which seems much more important to her.

"So this is really happening," I say. It still doesn't feel real to me. Looting towns and the like is one thing, but this is something else entirely.

"Yep," Wolf says. "Don't worry, Kid. It'll be fun."

"Yeah, fun," Tank says, and not sarcastically. "Plenty of

people to shoot. And look how big our guns are! No way they have bigger guns than these."

"Yeah, no way we can lose with guns this big."

I shake my head at them, but can't help but laugh.

"Seriously, though," Tank says. "Don't worry, Kid. I'll be looking out for you."

"Me, too," Dolly says quietly behind me.

"I'll be way too busy killing people, but I'm sure you'll be fine," Wolf says.

XXVII
The Radio Tower

Next thing I know, I'm in a truck full of explosives barreling straight at a brick building. Tank, Dolly, and I are in the back of the truck, clinging desperately to boxes for support. The truck sways and shudders. It's clearly not built to drive this fast. I'm half-worried the thing will fall apart before we hit the building, half-worried it won't. Judging from the nauseous look on Tank's face, he shares the sentiment. Dolly's face is blank. With one gun in her hand, another strapped to her back, and a belt stocked with grenades and extra ammo, she looks ready for anything. I imagine Wolf is having the time of his life up front, pushing the pedal to the floor and not giving a shit about the consequences.

"Here it comes!" Wolf shouts over the walkie-talkie. I squeeze myself in between two stacks of boxes, close my eyes, and hold on for dear life.

We slam into the building.

I feel the impact go through the truck like a wave. There's an awful crashing sound, and I can tell from the noise that we made it through the wall. Boxes topple over around me and something falls on top of my head—a can of food, I think. I ignore it and stay crouched down. The truck keeps going for a short while and slams into something else.

The engine whines like a dying animal. Everything else is silent as we all attempt to regain our bearings.

"You all right, ladies?" Tank asks.

"Fine," Dolly says.

"I'm okay." I realize my eyes are still closed and force them open. The back of the truck is an absolute mess, the boxes now scattered all over the floor. I stand up and brush myself off.

"All right," Tank says. He steps over fallen boxes and supplies and makes his way to the back doors. He places a hand on the latch and turns to look back. "Kid, you run up front and make sure Wolf's crazy ass is still alive. Dolly and I will cover you."

"Got it."

Tank opens the latch and pushes one door open. He pauses for a second behind the other door, waiting for gunfire, but none comes. He nods at us and steps outside. Dolly slips out after him. I follow with my pistol held ready.

The room outside is full of dust. I wave a hand as I step out, trying to get a clear look at anything, but it's impossible. I can't even tell how big the room is. I pull part of my shirt over my face to avoid breathing in dust and inch along the side of the truck, using touch to guide me. I keep my gun out. By the time I reach the front of the truck, the dust is starting to settle. The vehicle is a wreck, the hood dented in where it smashed into the wall, and the windshield is shattered. I struggle to pry open the door, and it falls off completely.

Wolf is in the driver's seat and looks relatively unharmed, which means his ridiculous plan actually worked. He's covered from the neck down in pillows. Pillows of various shapes and colors, all strapped to his torso and limbs for protection. It makes him look like a giant, fluffy scarecrow. He has a blanket over his head, too, which kept all the broken glass off him. He got pissed at us for laughing at him while he was tying them on, so I try to refrain from laughing now, but it's hard.

He's struggling to undo his seat belt. He can barely even move around in his seat, and the seat belt is stretched as tight as it can go across him.

I reach over to undo the seat belt and grab one of his pillow-arms, half-dragging him out of the truck. Once he steps down, he stumbles for a second before falling flat on his padded stomach. It releases a soft *fffshh* of air as the pillows beneath him deflate slightly. He shakes off the blanket covering his head, dispatching shards of glass with it, and I can no longer stop myself from laughing.

"Fuckin' told you it would work!" Wolf says gleefully. He sits up with visible effort, and needs my help to stand.

"Yeah, it's...genius," I say, laughing again at the sight of him. His arms and legs look ludicrously thick, and the padding on his stomach makes him look fatter than Tank.

With the dust all settled down, the room we destroyed becomes visible. It's small, some sort of entrance lobby. It's plain aside from a few paintings on the wall, one of which is now dangling crookedly and about to fall off. It looks like our truck smashed right through the front desk, and there are at least two mangled bodies in the wake of the tires. There's no sign of anyone alive. After sweeping the room and checking all the corners, Tank and Dolly return to us.

"This is a bit of a letdown, honestly," Wolf says. "I was expecting a gunfight right off the bat."

"Yeah, what a shame, that getup would have been real intimidating," Tank says.

"Fuck you. Safety first." Wolf waddles over to the truck, which is releasing an alarming amount of smoke from under its hood. He grabs a sawed-off shotgun and a metal baseball bat for himself, and a heavy-looking backpack, which he tosses at me. I scramble to catch it, but it hits the ground. I bend down to pick it up.

"Whoa, Kid, watch it. That thing is full of grenades an' shit."

"W-What!?" I nearly drop it again. "Well don't be throwing it around like that! And why do *I* have to carry it?"

"'Cause everyone else has big-ass guns to worry about. Just remember, you mess up and you'll blow us all to hell."

"Gee, thanks." I secure the straps around my shoulders. It isn't as heavy as I expected, but I feel nervous with it on my back. "I feel like a suicide bomber."

"Don't worry, that's only our last-resort plan," Wolf says. He starts removing his pillows one by one. Before I can figure out how serious he is, or he can finish de-pillowing himself, a door near us bursts open. The three others immediately turn their guns toward it, and I fumble to get my pistol out of my belt.

A man's head pokes out of the doorway. A burst of gunfire follows as Tank, Dolly, and Wolf all open fire. The man retreats hastily, leaving a door riddled with bullet holes.

"Oh hell no," Wolf says. "You ain't gettin' away so easy." He runs toward the door, heedless of the pillows still covering most of him, and busts through. Dolly and Tank follow, and I do the same after a slight pause. But before I can even make it to the doorway, all three of them turn and run back outside, pushing me along with them. The sound of gunfire explodes from behind them.

"Fuck, that's a lot of them!" Tank says.

"We're so fucked," Wolf says. "We need to find another door."

Dolly grabs a grenade off her belt, pulls the pin, and tosses it through the open door. Everyone pulls to one side. The grenade goes off, and silence follows. We all look at each other uncertainly.

"Someone check," Wolf says.

"Why are you looking at me?" Tank asks. "Just 'cause I'm big don't mean I'm bulletproof. You go, pillow man."

"Do you think pillows will help against gunfire?" I ask, doubtful.

"Shut up, Kid. You go. As the most useful member of the crew, that's your duty."

"W-What? What about that other door, we can—"

Before I can finish, Wolf grabs me by the backpack, nearly lifting me off my feet, and shoves me through the doorway. I stumble for a few steps and then freeze, looking around warily. The remains of a few bodies are splattered on the floor and walls, but otherwise the hallway is empty. The whole building looks like it's falling apart, too. I thought Saint's headquarters would have the same kind of fancy looks as the Queen's, but it's all very plain and simple.

"Nobody's here," I call back to the others. Wolf creeps through the door cautiously, as if expecting I'm lying, with Dolly and Tank on his heels. Dolly stays facing backward, watching the door behind us as we come to a halt in the middle of the hallway.

"Well, shit," Wolf says. "Guess we scared 'em off, huh?"

The door behind us opens and in pours a crowd of armed men and women. They're a ragtag bunch dressed in scrappy wasteland clothing, each with a red bandana tied to their left arm. Other than that, they look more like well-equipped townies than the trained army I was expecting, but there are a *lot* of them. Dolly and the others open fire immediately, gunning them down as they try to funnel through the doorway. I panic and run forward, heading straight for another door. Just as I'm about to grab the handle, it opens to reveal another group of Saint's soldiers. I scream and slam the door shut before they can react. There's no way to lock the door, and I know I only bought myself a few seconds, so I run back to the others.

"Behind us! More of them!" I yell.

"Which behind us?" Wolf asks, turning my way. I point. The other two stay focused on trying to push back the crowd coming at us from the other side.

"Kid, you have a gun, fucking use it!"

"Right!" I steady my shaking hands on the pistol and plant myself next to Wolf. With a face of steely determination, he points his sawed-off shotgun and fires. It takes out chunks of all three men in the front of the group. While he reloads, I fire my pistol desperately, catching one man twice in the gut and another in the shoulder. It doesn't take either of them down, but it slows them enough for Wolf to be ready to fire again. But I can tell we're not nearly fast or efficient enough, and so can Wolf.

"We need to move!" he says. "Can't be tryin' to fight in two directions!" He gestures to Tank and Dolly, and they move closer to us. Back-to-back, we make our way down the hallway and toward the door ahead of us. We start by taking it slow and steady, until I hear the dull *click-click-click* behind me that indicates someone's out of ammo. Tank abruptly turns and shoves past me and Wolf. He takes off running down the hallway and bashes into the group of Saint's men like a battering ram. Wolf jumps in after him, swinging his baseball bat and cracking skulls left and right. After a few more seconds, Dolly and I drop our attempt to hold off the ones behind us and start running as well. It's hard with this bulky backpack, but I move as fast as I can. She tosses a grenade behind us, and neither of us turns to check the result. Our crew plows through the group of men, carving a bloody path.

A bullet hits me in the back. There's a moment of blinding panic where I think I'm done for. The initial hit feels like being punched, hard, by someone a lot bigger than me—I close my eyes and wait for the worse pain to follow, but nothing comes. I look down at myself and remember the bulletproof vest. Still, being shot *hurts*. The next bullet hits me in the chest, forcing all the air from my lungs. I stumble and almost fall, but Dolly grabs my arm and pulls me up at the last second. She half-drags me along as I struggle to breathe normally again.

The hallway is lined with identical doors, no way of telling what's behind any of them. Wolf dashes to the closest one and tries it: locked. The next, also locked. Finally he finds one that opens and darts inside. He waves the rest of us in before shutting and locking the door. It's a tiny supply closet, barely big enough to fit all of us.

I sink to the floor, trying to catch my breath. It's hard forcing myself to breathe calmly when there's so much shouting and ruckus just outside the door. Trying to ignore it, I start pulling bullets out of my vest. Dolly helps with the one lodged in the back. I check myself for wounds, but it looks like I made it out fine.

The others weren't quite so lucky. Wolf's nose is bleeding heavily, making a mess of all his pillows, and as I watch he spits out a tooth. The old wound on his shoulder seems to have reopened. It amazes me that he could swing a bat with that injury. One of Dolly's arms is dripping blood, though it looks like the shot went clean through. Tank is bleeding from multiple wounds and must have at least a couple bullets in him, though he seems unconcerned.

"So," Wolf says, wiping blood off his face, "I'm starting to think this was a pretty fuckin' bad idea."

"You think?" Tank says with a strained laugh.

"And we crashed our only means of escape, didn't we?"

"Pretty much," I say.

"'Course we did." Wolf spits again, leaving a red splatter on the tile. "Hand me that bag, Kid." I'm eager to be rid of it. He unzips it and searches through the insides. "Well, guess everyone should take a couple grenades. If you're gonna go down, at least take a handful of 'em down with you, right, guys?"

"Would you expect anything less?" Tank asks, taking his. Wolf shoves a couple into my hands and I stare at them nervously. I still remember that time I accidentally threw one away without pulling the pin. I'm not likely to make *that* mistake again, but I'm sure I can find a hundred other ways to fuck it up.

"So what's the plan now?" I ask, putting one grenade into my pocket and moving the other from hand to hand. Tank watches me apprehensively.

"Kill the bastards," Wolf says.

"Yeah, well, how?"

"Still workin' on that part." Wolf is just buying time, and I can tell. As I wait for a real answer, the noise outside grows louder. The soldiers are pounding on the door and yelling at us to come out so they can blow our heads off. I guess Saint's ideal of nonviolence doesn't apply to people who drive trucks into his base of operations.

"All right," Wolf says. "We're gonna need to split up."

"How is that gonna help anything?" I ask. The others are already nodding, but I feel anxiety creeping up on me. I don't want to split up. If I end up alone, I'm done for.

"We're too outnumbered, can't fight 'em head-on," Wolf says. It still doesn't make sense to me; wouldn't breaking up the group just make the odds *less* in our favor? I'm pretty sure it's a bad idea, but now isn't the time to start questioning Wolf.

"So we split up, and then what?" I ask, still nervously toying with my grenade.

"Well, we'll blast our way out of here and scatter. Try to stay alive, try to pick 'em off, and try to move *up*." He points at the ceiling.

"Why up?"

"The control room's gotta be somewhere up there. The building is three stories high, and I reckon it's on the top one. If one of us makes it there, blow the shit out of it and kill Saint."

"And what if none of us make it there?" Tank asks.

"One of us has to," Wolf says.

Whoever ends up making it, I doubt it will be me. That

means my role here has been reduced to a distraction. Once I accept that, my nervousness fades. Now *that* I can do. If I can run fast enough to stay alive for a while and get some soldiers to chase me, I'll consider it a job well done. There's a lot less pressure thinking about it that way.

"Okay," I say. I stand up, clutching the grenade in my right hand. "Let's do this."

"I like that attitude, Kid." Wolf gives me a high five. "How 'bout everyone else?"

"Gotta die sometime," Tank says. "This ain't the worst way to go, I guess."

"I won't fail you," Dolly says.

Everyone has a look of grim determination. I can tell they must have gone through the same thought process I did. There's no way we're gonna make it out, but at least we should accomplish what we came for. We followed Wolf here, and we'll follow him to the end.

Still, it feels strange to look around and realize this might be the last time I see one of them, or even all of them. Even though I haven't been with the crew for that long, and even though things have been crazy, I wouldn't have done it any other way. Living alone isn't really living, and they're the first people I grew to love since my papa died.

"Umm," I say, looking up at them. "I just wanted to say . . . it's been fun, guys."

Tank smiles.

"Wouldn't have been the same without you, Kid."

"Yeah, things would've gone a lot smoother," Wolf says. "And don't go gettin' all sentimental on us, we're not dead yet."

"Yet," I repeat. "Good vote of confidence, boss." I grin at him and turn to the door.

"Now let's bash some fucking heads in!" Wolf says. He throws open the door and tosses a grenade into the crowd outside.

XXVIII
Alone in the Tower

The grenade blows a hole in the mob outside, and scatters them enough for us to burst through the door. Not even watching where the others go, I dash between two startled men and down the hall. A burst of gunfire follows me, but I dart around a corner before they can get a good shot at me. Footsteps come soon after, loud on the building's cracked tile floor. I keep running down the unfamiliar hallway. The long hall is deserted; the soldiers must have clustered around us, so there are none waiting here. I try to open a door as I hear them gaining on me. The first one is locked. *Shit.* The second also locked. *Double shit!*

They're getting closer. I refuse to look back and see just how close. I can't let myself panic; I don't have my friends here to watch my back this time. If I panic, I'm dead.

The next door is unlocked, but it's so rusty I have to struggle and waste precious time opening it. I glance behind me to see three soldiers only seconds away, two men and one woman. One has a gun, one a knife, and the last a metal pipe. Any of them would be enough to kill me.

I run inside and immediately ram into something. I stagger, catch my balance, and get a better look at the room. It's dimly lit, the only light filtering in from a broken window in the back. Desks and chairs are scattered around the room, and many of the desks have computers on them, some intact but most smashed up.

Once I have a decent map of the room in my head, I dive behind one of the desks and crawl on my hands and knees toward the back window. It's low enough for me to escape through if I need to, though the jagged, broken glass makes me hope I won't. Furthermore, the dim lighting and ample hiding spots tilt the odds slightly in my favor. It's a good spot for me to fight. The best I can hope for, at least.

I wait behind a desk and listen. I hear the three soldiers enter the room, their footsteps loud in the small space. I hear distant gunshots and the sounds of fighting elsewhere in the building, but this room is quiet besides my breathing and their footsteps.

"The little bitch is here somewhere," a deep voice says. I can't help but be pleased people are finally getting my gender right.

"Could've gone out the window." This one sounds female, though still gruff.

"Not enough time. She's here. Spread out, don't let her get away."

I lean back against the desk, keeping hidden and silent. I try to quiet my breathing to hear better. I hear the crunch of glass as one moves on the other side of the room. Another bumps into something and grunts, just a few yards away.

Bang! A gunshot deafens me. I nearly bolt before realizing it wasn't actually aimed at me; they still don't know where I am. *Crash. Crunch.* More noises filling the room, coming from various directions. They're trying to scare me out. I stay where I am, my hands curling into fists. After a few moments the noise quiets down again. I listen intently and hear footsteps coming toward me. The others sound farther away. Guessing I still have a few seconds before the footsteps reach me, I look around for something I can use to my advantage. My eyes land on a nearby computer cord. I reach out and pull on it, testing. It feels almost like rope, and an idea hits me. I draw the big knife Wolf gave me out of its sheath and saw through the cord, cutting off a section about two feet long. I slide the knife back into its sheath and coil an end of the cord around each hand, drawing it tight as I crawl back over to the desk. I slip into the alcove under it and wait. The footsteps are close, very close.

I hold my breath as the soldier steps around the corner of the desk and pauses. I can just barely see his feet and legs. I imagine him scouring the area—and he moves on, apparently not seeing me. I scoot out from under the desk and creep up behind him, moving slowly and quietly. As something else in the room catches his attention, I jump on him. One hand scrabbling for a hold on his shoulder, I bring the cord over his head and around his neck. A yank draws it tight and forces his head back. A choked cry escapes him. He stumbles around, trying to dislodge me as I pull tighter and tighter. He stumbles into a wall, and then a computer. I hang on doggedly as he bangs me around. Finally he trips on another cord and goes down; I drop to the floor and scramble out of the way. His head strikes the corner of a desk and he hits the ground. His gun clatters to the floor. I snatch it up and run for the door.

The other soldiers cut off my exit. The woman blocks the doorway, waiting with a cleaver in hand. The other heads right for me, wielding an iron pipe. He shoves one of the desks, sending it clattering to the floor right in my path. I freeze, trapped against the wall. Fear almost drives me into a panic, but I hold my ground and draw out the knife again. The man steps over the fallen desk and advances toward me. I glance around and find the guard I felled earlier isn't getting up. Good for me.

While I'm distracted, the closer man swings at me with his pipe. I narrowly dodge, feeling the air from its passage, and lunge forward with my knife. The blade sinks into his thigh, deeper than I expected—seconds later I realize I could've easily hit someplace more vital, but it's too late for that. The man howls with pain and stumbles back. My hands still wrapped around the knife's handle, I stumble with him, and attempt to yank the blade out. It's sunk too deep. I'm not strong enough, and the gushing blood makes the handle too slippery for me to grip properly. I let go and he falls backward over the fallen desk.

That leaves me and the woman with the cleaver. She's still standing in the doorway, and grins at me when she sees me looking. She has a dyed-red Mohawk and a face like a pig, broad and mean and ugly. I stand a few yards away from her, eye her, and pull out my gun from the back of my pants. I aim at her and she stands there, unblinking—then charges at me with a yell. Caught by surprise, I fire wildly and catch her in the shoulder right before she barrels into me. The impact sends me flying backward to slam into a desk. The air leaves my lungs. I lean against the desk for support, panting, but I only have a second to recover before she swings wildly with the cleaver. I drop to the floor and it hits the desk with a heavy *thunk*. Before she can swing again, I tackle her at the knees. She crashes down. Her head slams into the floor.

I leap to my feet, dash for the door again—and trip on a computer cord. I twist and try to right myself, but land awkwardly with my arm crushed beneath me. A jolt of pain shoots up from my wrist. Behind me, I hear the scrape of the cleaver against the ground as the woman gets on her feet. I crawl for the door on my hands and knees and force myself not to look back as heavy footsteps follow me. My heartbeat pounds in my ears. I tune out everything else, ignoring the swiftly approaching footsteps and the cries of the injured men. The door is the only thing that matters. I'm so close to escape, so close—

And I'm out the door. I scramble to my feet, turn to run, and slam into someone a lot bigger than me.

I stumble backward and into the woman who was pursuing

me. She grabs my arm before I can escape, and when I look up at the other person I ran into, I find a gun in my face.

To my surprise, the soldier doesn't shoot. I stay there, trembling, waiting to die... but nothing happens.

"I'll kill the bitch," the woman growls. She shoves me against the wall and grabs my throat, pinning me there. "Fucking pain in my ass. I'll chop her into little bits."

"Not yet," the man with the gun says. He's a tall, lean guy with a face full of piercings and an arm covered in crude tattoos. I look at him desperately, choking. "Saint wants her."

"You sure? This one?" Her hold loosens slightly and I can breathe again.

"He wants 'em all. Been trying to grab 'em for a while now." He licks his thin lips and shrugs.

"And they was dumb enough to show up for us. Heh."

The pressure eases up as the woman backs off. I try to run, but she yanks me back and throws me to the ground. I fall on my ass and stay there, subdued. I let out a long, slow breath that makes it feel like I'm deflating. My heart slows as if accepting its fate, and I become aware of the distant shouting and gunshots elsewhere in the building. It sounds like the rest of the crew is giving them a hell of a time, which makes me smile despite my own predicament. I did what I could. It wasn't like anyone expected much of me, anyway.

A realization comes to me. The piercings, the tattoos, the scars... these soldiers don't seem like townies. They're too big, too dangerous, too obviously familiar with their weapons. Everything about them reeks of brutal efficiency. It reeks of raiders. But why would Saint have raiders as his guards?

Instinct tells me something is wrong here. Mostly, though, I'm relieved I'm not dead yet.

"What do we do with her?"

"Take her up, I guess."

"Take me up where?" I look from one to the other, but neither of them spares me so much as a glance.

"Knock her out, Ben," the woman says.

"Wait wait wait—"

A sharp pain, followed by darkness.

I wake up groggy and confused. I look around blearily and my confused thoughts thicken as I find only unfamiliar surroundings. I'm in a dimly lit room, sitting on a rather dilapidated couch that sags beneath my weight. The walls are bare except for the off-white, peeling wallpaper. I'm alone.

Something moves behind me. Scratch the alone part. I whip around and somehow manage to fall off the couch. The tile hurts my knees, but I ignore it and crawl to hide next to the couch, as if it were all a part of the plan.

Hiding there, I can't see who or what is moving.

"She's awake," a deep voice says. I stay where I am, heart racing as my memories catch up with me. Where did the guards take me? Where are my friends? I peek around the couch to see a rather rotund soldier opening the door. I scramble toward it and slip between his legs. He grunts in surprise and tries to grab me, but I slide under him and take off running. The hallway is unfamiliar and lined with closed doors. I try a few of them, but they're all locked. The fat soldier runs after me, huffing and puffing along as he tries to catch up. I spot the stairwell and run for it. I open the door and run into the biggest man I've ever seen in my life.

My mouth hangs open. I take a step back.

He's a monster of a man, even bigger than Tank, and made of solid muscle. Each of his arms looks as wide around as my waist, his legs thicker than tree trunks. Unlike Tank he doesn't have a big belly. In fact, it doesn't seem like he has an ounce of fat on his body. He doesn't have much of a neck, either, just a strong jaw meeting ridiculously muscular shoulders. His face is unremarkable aside from a thick scar that runs from his temple down to the corner of his mouth. His head is shaved except for a thin strip down the middle. There's a huge ring through the front of his nose, like bulls I've seen in picture books.

I stare at him, meanwhile noting the soldiers on either side. They flood out of the stairwell after him, surrounding me and cutting off my escape. The huge man folds his arms over his chest and grins, showing yellowed teeth.

"You must be the Kid," he says, his voice a slow and pleasant rumble. The kind of voice people would trust. The kind of voice they'd listen to.

"Um. Just Kid," I squeak, not sure how else to respond. The man laughs, a sound that echoes through the empty hall.

"Nice to meet you, Kid," he says. "I'm Saint."

XXIX
Saints and Sinners

I gape at the proffered hand and back up at his face.

"*You're* Saint?" I ask, terrified. "*You're* the guy we're trying to kill? Aw, hell!" If I ever had a slim hope of taking this guy down, it's gone now. This guy is *huge.* I kind of pictured him as a nice old man in a suit or something, not this. If I ever ran into him in the wastes, I'd think he was a mercenary, the kind of guy who would crack some skulls and eat townies for breakfast.

"That's what they call me," he says, with a rumble of laughter at the look on my face. He lays a hand on my shoulder, turns me around, and marches me back to the room I just escaped from. I don't even try to struggle. There's no point; he's at least ten times bigger than I am. I remain helpless as he not so gently pushes me back onto the couch. He takes a chair across from it, an armchair that would be big for me but looks ludicrously small for him.

"Leave us," he says to the soldiers behind me. I hear receding footsteps and the click of the door shutting, and gulp. I'm alone with Saint, the guy I came here to kill, the guy who looks like he could crush my skull between two fingers. He studies me and I avert my gaze, my eyes skittering around the room.

"So, Kid. Why do you think you're here?" he asks.

"Umm, because we drove a truck into the building?" My answer comes out like a question.

"No, I mean here, in this room."

"Because your guards brought me here," I say slowly.

He sighs. I blink at him.

"And why did they do that instead of killing you?"

"I don't know. You tell me. You're the guy in charge." I force a smile. He looks utterly unamused.

He cracks his fingers and I'm reminded again of the power those hands hold.

"Well, umm, I guess you bring people here so you can have a trial and shit before you kill them," I say uncertainly, and then realize "kill" doesn't sound quite right. "Execute them? Is that the word?"

"That's why everyone outside thinks you're here. What do you think?"

"I'm not really the thinking sort of person," I say. "Usually I kind of dive headfirst into things and hope it works out for the best. It, uh, doesn't seem to be going so well right now." He waits silently. I keep looking around the room, eyes flicking back to his face every few seconds. His expression doesn't change.

What do *I* think? I haven't exactly figured it out myself. Something is pulling on the edges of my mind, some realization I have yet to uncover. The radio tower, the soldiers who look so much like raiders, Saint himself...it doesn't fit with the mental image I had of the man trying to unite and protect the wastelands.

"You're not who everyone thinks you are," I say.

"What makes you say that?" He leans forward, placing his hands on his knees.

"Your men are all raiders," I say. "Or were." I study his face. "You look like a raider, too."

He smiles.

"There we go."

"But why would you have raiders?" I ask. "I thought you were wiping out the bad guys."

"Now that would be noble." He laughs, the sound filling the room to the brim.

"So...you're not going to kill us?" I ask hopefully.

"No, Kid. I'm trying to recruit you."

"Recruit us?" I repeat, not understanding at first. Something finally clicks in my mind. "All the raiders the townies bring you..."

"Exactly. I'm building an army, and the townies are helping me do it." His smile oozes smugness. "By the time they realize it, I'll be too strong for them to stop me."

"That's..." Pretty smart, actually. "What's in it for the raiders?"

"Safety in numbers," he says. "All the reward without the risk. All the power. The only thing I ask for is loyalty, and a cut of their loot."

My head is spinning with the idea. This is huge—and no one outside of here has any clue what he's doing. All of the towns we've been to have trusted him, listened to him, delivered him raiders like he asked them to. Everyone knows Saint's plan is to change the wastes, but it's definitely not in the way they think. I'm not sure how to feel about it.

"So what are you talking to me for?" I ask.

"Well, Kid, you pose an interesting problem for me." Saint leans back in the chair and folds his arms over his chest, looking down at me. I shift in my seat and find my back sticky with sweat. "I've been tracking Wolf and his crew for a while now. They're infamous. Wolf has been wreaking havoc since he emerged from whatever hellhole he came from. Tank was one of the best mercs in the business before he went raider. Some of the fringe towns still tell ghost stories about a blue-haired woman called 'the man killer.' And Pretty Boy has been with various crews since he was a child." He scrutinizes me. "Where exactly is Pretty Boy?"

If Saint doesn't know he's dead, he might think we still have some trick up our sleeve. I stare back at him silently, putting on my best poker face. After a few moments he sighs.

"So he's dead, then. That's a pity. He would have been useful."

He would have been useful. He says it so crisply, without a scrap of emotion in his voice. It makes my blood boil to hear him talk about a dead friend in such a calculated way. That's how he sees all of us; we're nothing more than assets to him.

"So," he continues, "then you show up out of nowhere. Who are you? Where do you come from? Nobody knows." He scrutinizes me. "And yet you survive, so clearly you're not as useless as you appear."

Obviously, he hasn't spoken to the rest of the crew yet. I may not be the brightest girl in the wastes, but I'm smart enough to know he's measuring my value right now. I sure as hell better trick him into thinking I'm worth recruiting.

"Well, obviously," I say, puffing out my chest and trying to act confident. "It's not like I could've made it this far without offing a few people." Despite my attempt at bravado, my hands are starting to sweat. I clench them into fists to stop them from shaking.

"How did you end up with Wolf's crew?"

I pause, unsuccessfully trying to come up with a good reason.

"Why should I tell you?" I retort. He lets out a snort of laughter, the corner of his lips curling upward.

"Let's not play games, little girl." He leans forward in his chair, and I sink down in mine. "I'll be frank with you: If I decide not to recruit you, I'll kill you. And right now, you don't seem very useful to me. So, go on. Change my mind."

I swallow hard. My tongue feels thick and clumsy in my

mouth, and the words won't come to me. I've never been very good at lying.

But then again, I'm not the person I used to be.

I'm not some helpless little girl missing her papa. I'm not the kind of girl who throws a grenade out the window without pulling the pin—I mean, not anymore. I'm a part of the crew. A raider. A killer. I've made it through a lot of shit, and like hell am I going to die like this.

"Well that's the thing, isn't it?" I start, speaking slowly. I think of my friends: Wolf's swagger, Tank's strength, Dolly's quiet badassery, Pretty Boy's silver tongue. "I don't seem very useful. I don't look big or tough or strong. And yet here I am, in the middle of your fancy base." I gesture to the room around me, and feel the shaking in my hands subside. "Before I even met these guys, I was wandering the wastes alone. Completely *alone*. Do you even know what that's like?"

Saint is silent, studying my face. I swallow and continue. "Not a lot of people do. 'Cause most people who end up alone just die, and that's the end of that. But not me. I joined a crew of goddamn sharks. I ate human flesh to survive. I learned to shoot. To kill. I blew the Queen's head off. I watched a friend die yesterday and I still came here to kick some ass." I take a deep breath, feel my chest rise and fall, the words nearly tumbling out of my mouth now. "And you think I'm not good enough for your mess of an army? Just 'cause I'm a little girl? Well *fuck* you. I'm worth two of your guards, and tomorrow I'll be worth four of 'em, and eventually the whole lot. Because that's who I am, and that's what I do. I survive."

I feel the silence, tense and thick, like a noose around my neck.

"Are you done?" he asks eventually.

"Yeah, I think so." The bravado seeps out of me, and I self-consciously raise a hand to scratch at the back of my head. "Was that, uh, too much?"

Saint sighs deeply and shifts in his seat. He looks down on me with thoughtful eyes.

"Well, Kid—"

He cuts off. I look around, confused, before I hear what he hears: gunshots outside. Saint stands, gesturing at me to stay seated.

"Wait here," he says, moving to the door.

I jump to my feet the second the door shuts. If I'm lucky, my friends are here to kill Saint and rescue me. But I'm rarely lucky, so I need to be ready when he gets back.

I walk along the edges of the room, searching for anything that could possibly be used as a weapon or escape route. The room is bare but for the furniture and an excessive amount of cobwebs. Still, I stubbornly circle the perimeter of the room, checking every inch. I pause by the window and look down. I'm on the third floor, so that's no good. Most of the windowpane is gone, but ragged shards of glass still cling to the edges like broken teeth. I lightly touch the edge of one. It's not as sharp as I would've hoped, but it's still the closest thing to a weapon in the room. I grab a long, thin sliver and determinedly wiggle it around, careful not to let the edges touch my skin. It's already weakened by age and abuse, and soon cracks start to form. I'm as careful as possible; I already have one injured hand, it would just be embarrassing to mess them both up.

But, hearing a scuffle outside, I wiggle more frantically. In my haste I slip, and an edge digs into my palm. It draws a line of blood and stings something fierce, but beyond the pain I feel triumphant—if it's good enough to cut me, it's good enough to cut someone else. I grit my teeth and give a final wrench to jerk it free. Flipping it in my hand so the sharpest edge is facing out, I rush to the door and press myself against the wall beside it.

Outside, the sound of a fight continues. A gunshot rings through the air. Silence follows. I wait, holding my breath as the door slowly opens. Someone steps inside.

I launch myself at the person, bellowing out a war cry, and sink the glass shard into soft flesh. It doesn't cut deeply or easily, but it does its job. I feel the skin break and the glass sink in another few centimeters. It gives me a thrill of victory—until I realize the person I just stabbed wasn't Saint at all.

He yells.

I scream.

"Did you just fucking stab me, Kid?!" Wolf shouts, looking down at the shard of glass sticking out of his arm.

"I thought you were Saint!" I say, still frozen in my just-stabbed-a-guy stance.

"How fucking dumb are you?"

"How the hell was I supposed to know it was you?" I shoot back, refusing to back down.

"Fucking shit God damn—" He grits his teeth, growls under his breath, and yanks out the glass. A gush of blood rushes to escape. Luckily it doesn't seem like I hit anything important. Wolf presses a dirty hand to the wound to stem the flow, glaring at me like he wishes it was my throat he was constricting. "You're lucky I didn't blow your head off."

Considering he's wielding a shotgun, I do consider myself pretty damn lucky. I give Wolf a once-over. He's looking pretty worse for wear. The pillows are gone and his shirt has been torn to shreds, leaving only the ragged-looking bulletproof vest. Scrapes and bruises decorate his arms, and there's an ugly gash across his forehead.

"You look like shit," I say.

"So do you, but that's normal." He scans the bare room with growing confusion. "What the hell were you doing in here?"

"Some guards brought me up. Saint wanted to talk to me."

"Saint? He was here?" He turns in a circle rapidly, pointing the barrel of his gun at each corner of the room as if expecting to find him hiding.

"Yeah, he left a couple minutes ago and—wait, Wolf, listen!" I grab his arm as he turns to leave again. "This guy, Saint, he's not at all like he's pretending to be. He's trying to recruit us for some big raider army of his."

"Raider army?" Wolf stops and squints at me, processing the information. "And that's why he's taking people. Huh." He nods slowly. "That makes sense. I *knew* one of the assholes I killed looked just like this guy Big Ben. So Saint is just tricking everyone into thinking he's the good guy?"

"Yeah."

"Man, that's fucked-up. Knew he was an asshole." He chews on his lip. A second or two passes, and his eyes widen, as if some big realization just hit him. "Wait...so Saint is actually the bad guy." He presses his lips into a firm line, nose wrinkling in distaste. "Does that make *us* the good guys?"

I pause, mulling it over, and slowly nod.

"Yeah, I guess it kind of does?"

"*Damn.*" He shakes his head, looking seriously annoyed. "When this is over and done with, we better ransack the shit out of all the nearby towns so no one gets the wrong impression."

"Good plan. But first, let's kill this guy."

"Took the words right out of my mouth."

Part of me wants to ask if he knows where the others are, but I know the answer will be more of a distraction than anything. If we lost someone...I don't want to find out now. I want to hear it later, when I have time to grieve. If I'm the only one that made it this far, Wolf needs me, and I'm not going to let him down.

XXX
The Good Guys

The building is surprisingly quiet except for the occasional muffled gunshot from below. Aside from a few bodies, presumably Wolf's handiwork, this floor is empty. It's almost eerie to be so alone after all the chaos. My body is still convinced it should be in fighting mode, my senses at their peak and my heart pounding despite the lack of action. I jump at every sound and check every corner for danger. Meanwhile, Wolf strides ahead with his typical lack of fear. We reach the stairwell without incident and start the climb to the top floor.

"You really think we can take him?" I ask. My whole body is sore, but I have to keep pushing forward. If I stop to rest, I'll crash. I can't afford to be tired or hurt right now. I wait for an answer, but none comes. "Wolf?"

"'Course we can," he says finally. He stops and turns to face me, and I see what delayed his answer. He's breathing hard—really hard, each deep breath punctuated with a wince. Beads of sweat run down his grimy face.

"Are you okay?" I ask, knowing he's not.

"Fucking fantastic." He clambers up the last stretch of stairs. I frown and follow more slowly. One foot slips on the stair he stopped on. I grab the handrail and look down to see a pool of blood. My gaze drifts up the stairs, following the red trail Wolf's leaving behind him.

"Wolf..." I follow him to the top. He leans against the wall, struggling to catch his breath. "You're hurt."

"No shit. I was stabbed by a small, ugly girl about five minutes ago."

I feel a twinge of guilt, but it's easy to see that the wound on his arm isn't the real problem here.

"You got shot," I say. "Where?"

He looks as if he wants to argue, but stops himself. He lifts up his shirt, wincing as the fabric peels off the wound. Breath hisses through my teeth. It's a bullet hole all right, and an ugly one, right through the fleshy part just above his hip.

"That bad?" he asks.

"Pretty bad."

"Well, can't do nothin' about it now." He lowers his shirt and steps closer to the door, resting a hand on the knob. "You coming?"

I raise my eyes to his face, now recognizing the pain beneath the hard set of his jaw.

"I think you should stay behind," I say, the words popping out before I have much time to think about them. He lets out a startled laugh, the sound echoing off the walls of the stairwell.

"You're screwing with me, right?"

"No. I'm serious. You're hurt." I bite my lip, struggling to maintain my newfound confidence. "And I can do it on my own."

"We don't even know what's in there." Despite the words, he takes his hand off the door handle and turns to face me. My heart jumps—he's listening. He's taking me seriously.

"When have we ever? And we've done pretty good up till this point."

"That was different."

"I can do this," I say. "On my own. Let me prove it." He

doesn't look convinced. "Come on, give me a chance to be the hero for once." I pause. "Or...the villain? I'm still a little confused about where we stand as far as that goes?"

"Don't think about it too hard, you'll hurt yourself," he says. But he isn't saying no. He takes a deep breath and wipes the back of one hand across his forehead. "Look, Kid, you don't have to do this. Me, Tank, Dolly, we wouldn't make it in a normal world. We ain't never gonna settle down in some town and live a peaceful life. We're too fucked-up. That's why we're here, see? It's our way of life at stake here. Good guy, fake good guy, whatever he is, this Saint wants to change the wastes, and that would mean we're done for. But not you, Kid. You're different. You can still make it."

"And just leave you guys?"

"Why the hell not?"

"You still don't get it, do you?" I ask. "I haven't had a home in a long time. But you guys, you're..."

"Don't you get all choked up on me," Wolf says, but without the usual biting tone.

"Sorry," I say, wiping my eyes with the back of my hand. "It's just...I wouldn't want to live in a world without you or Dolly or Tank, even if it means my life is a whole lot shorter because I'm with you. I know I don't have to do this, but I want to." Ignoring the burning feeling behind my eyes, I try to shape my face into a fierce expression. "And I'm one of you now. I got this, Wolf."

Wolf scrutinizes me silently. I do my best to hold it together. I know Wolf hates this kind of emotional talk, but I can't think of any other way to get through to him.

"Fine," he says finally. "But it ain't 'cause of that sappy shit you said. It's just 'cause I know you'll charge in like an idiot even if I say no."

"Thanks," I say, smiling despite my best attempt to conceal

my emotions. Unable to help myself, I step forward and wrap my arms around Wolf in a hug. He stiffens, but rather than pulling away, pats me awkwardly on the back.

"Yeah, yeah. Don't go thanking me yet, you'll probably get shot up the second you go in there," he says. I step back and nod, readying myself with my gun again.

"Time to go kick some ass," I say cheerfully.

"Not with that gun," he says. "Give me that."

I hesitantly hand over my pistol. He pushes his sawed-off shotgun into my hands.

"Much better," he says, although I feel a bit ridiculous carrying it. "If anything's gonna get your skinny ass through this, it'll be that baby. But remember, only two shots, all right? So make 'em count."

"Got it," I say. "Thanks, Wolf."

"Go give 'em hell."

He opens the door for me and I step through. As the door swings shut behind me, I feel utterly alone.

The top floor is as silent and empty as the last one. As soon as I step out of the safety of the stairwell, all of my senses are on alert. Blood pumps overzealously through my veins. My hands shake, making the barrel of my gun wobble. Just because I'm willing to die doesn't mean I particularly *want* to, and despite my big words I'm scared. This is it: the final showdown. All the fighting, all the struggle, all of it has led up to this. Despite my anxiousness, I don't let my steps falter. Teeth clenched and gun raised, I swing into the first doorway—and stop. It's empty.

I break through another two doors and find both as empty as the first. The floor doesn't seem to hold anything other than old furniture and cobwebs. It makes me wonder if Saint is even up here. That's when I notice the room at the end of the hallway. The door is open, and it looks like there's a light on inside.

I guess I probably should have checked that one first. There's a very high possibility that it's a trap—but what am I supposed to do, back off? No way, not after giving that cheesy speech. I'm not gonna run back to Wolf with my tail between my legs.

I walk toward the room, barrel pointed at the doorway, and step inside.

Saint is waiting for me. He's surrounded with some kind of machinery I've never seen in my life, all alive with light and sound. Like I noticed, he even has a light on. Real electricity. I've heard some towns have it, but I've never seen it before. It's like magic. I find it hard not to gawk at the sight, but remind myself why I'm here and focus on Saint instead, keeping my gun trained on him.

To my surprise, he's unarmed, holding his hands palms out to display his lack of a weapon.

"You?" he asks, his eyebrows drawing together. "Well, I certainly wasn't expecting you to walk in here alone," he says. "But that's fine. I want to talk. Work out a deal. Decimating each other's forces doesn't do any good for either of us. Look: no guards, no guns. Just me, ready to be reasonable."

I sweep my eyes around the room, searching for any good hiding spots. I don't see any.

"Okay," I say, not lowering my gun. The situation seems safe for the moment, but I don't want to let my guard down. "So, say we join you. What exactly does that look like for us?"

He eyes the gun, looks like he's considering saying something about it, but then smiles instead. He leans back in his chair, arms folded over his chest, his posture relaxed.

"You'll continue working together as your own individual crew," he says. "Only thing that changes is that Wolf answers to me. I'll tell you what towns to hit. Sometimes you'll work alone, sometimes with other groups. You carry out raids like usual, and then give me a percentage of the loot."

"A big percentage?"

"A fair percentage. And you can trade supplies with me or the other crews if you need something."

I turn my attention back to his plan, and try to envision the world he proposes. An army of raiders would sweep through the wastelands easily. With the Queen gone, Saint is the only powerhouse left; maybe he even planned on her dying. The townies won't stand a chance.

"So, your army takes over," I say slowly. "And then you're in charge of everything."

"That's the plan," Saint says. "In a way, I really will be bringing peace to the wastelands."

"Okay, one last question," I say. "Is the rest of my crew okay?"

Saint leans forward, hands on his knees, and smiles broadly.

"They're all perfectly intact and alive last I heard. Now, about our deal—"

Bang.

Saint's face slowly changes from surprised to baffled to angry. He looks down at himself as a red stain spreads across his chest. I lower the barrel of my gun.

"That's all I needed to know," I say. "Thanks!"

His eyes are still wide open and full of hate. He opens his mouth to say something, but the attempt produces nothing more than a bloody gurgle. I wince.

"Umm, this is awkward. I thought for sure that would kill you." I raise the gun again, point it right at his extremely pissed-off face this time. "Well, here we go again."

Bang.

"And that's it?" Wolf asks as we head down the stairs. His wound slows him down, and I walk ahead of him with a bounce in my step.

"Well, yeah. Then I banged up the radio equipment as best

I could and left. I thought about using the explosives, but it looked pretty broken already." I grin and whirl to look at him. "Seriously, though, you should've seen the look on Saint's face."

"No epic speech, no nothing?" Wolf asks, frowning. I sigh, disappointed by his lack of enthusiasm.

"Nah, I already got the speech out of my system. Figured I should just end it quickly."

"Honestly, I'm kind of disappointed." He shakes his head. "All of that buildup for nothing."

I sigh as we reach the bottom of the stairwell. Regardless of what Wolf thinks, *I* think I did a damn good job. I reach for the door, pull it open—and nearly jump out of my skin as a burst of gunfire comes from the other side. I slam the door shut, pressing my body against it to hold it closed.

"Oh shit," I say, my eyes wide. "I kind of forgot there's still the whole 'army of raiders' issue."

"Yep," Wolf says, looking more resigned than startled. "I don't really have a plan for this part." After a moment's consideration, he yanks his shotgun out of my hands, hands me my pistol, and leans against the wall beside the doorway.

"Saint said Dolly and Tank are fine, so maybe if we meet up with them..." I trail off, realizing it still seems unlikely that this turns out well for us. Even with Saint gone, there are so many raiders remaining. My gut twists. Could this really be the end of the line? After we came all this way, took care of Saint and his radio, did the job we came here to do—are we just gonna die like this?

"Well," Wolf says. "At least we'll go out with a bang." He faces the door with his shotgun. "On the count of three, you open it and we go in, guns blazing. Got it?"

"Got it." I swallow back nerves and grab the door handle with one hand, my gun in the other. I look at Wolf.

"One," he says. "T—"

"Wait, on three or after three?" I blurt out. Wolf sighs, lowering his gun.

"On three, dumbass. C'mon, you're killing my adrenaline rush here."

"Okay. On three. Right."

"One...two...th—"

The door slams open from the other side, smacking me in the face and sending me stumbling backward. I hit the floor on my ass. The door separates me from Wolf for a moment, and when it closes again I see three of Saint's raiders on him.

Cursing, I scramble to my feet and throw myself at the only one with a gun, sending both of us crashing to the floor in a heap. I end up on top of him—and my pistol skitters across the floor, out of reach. *Shit.* I grapple with him for his gun, struggling to keep the barrel aimed away from me. When it becomes clear I'm never going to overpower him, I free one hand and jab him in the eye with a finger. He howls in pain, and I successfully yank the gun out of his grip and turn it on him.

An arm wraps around my neck from behind. My captor lifts me up, away from the man beneath me. I struggle to break free, my feet barely scraping the ground as he pulls me off my feet, and fire the gun wildly in an attempt to hit whoever's holding me. He lets out a grunt of pain, but the arm around my neck only pulls tighter. My breath is cut off; stars dance in my vision. Desperate, I aim at the man still on the floor below us. If I can at least take out one of them, then maybe—

"Hold up!" Wolf shouts, and I stop, my finger freezing where it was about to pull the trigger. I can't move my head, but I shift my eyes to the side to get a glimpse of Wolf. He's face-to-face with the third raider. I now recognize her as the woman who captured me before, the one with the Mohawk and meat cleaver—which is currently raised above her head like she was just about to strike. Wolf is staring at her intently; she's staring at the shotgun in his hands, currently pointed right at her face. "Aren't you Betty?" he asks. "From Big Ben's crew?"

The woman starts, raising her eyes to Wolf's face and squinting.

"Wolf?" She pauses for a moment before grinning toothily and lowering her weapon. "Ahh, I remember you. So *you're* the asshole crazy enough to attack Saint's headquarters. I should've guessed."

They grin at each other, shotgun and meat cleaver both lowering. I let out a choked gurgle, since they seem to have forgotten I'm still being strangled over here. Betty glances over and jerks a hand. The pressure eases up as the man releases me. I take a deep gulp of air and glance at the guy, satisfied to see that my wildly fired bullet has taken a chunk out of his ear. I shoot one last glare at him and grab my pistol from the floor before moving over to Wolf's side.

"So," Betty says. "I'm hoping you guys have realized that Saint's not really Mr. Law-and-Order?"

"Yeah, we got that much," Wolf says.

"We've been trying to tell that red-haired one that Saint just wants to recruit you guys," the man I shot says, holding one hand to his ear and speaking a little too loudly. "But she kills anyone who comes near her."

"Sounds about right," Wolf says with a grin.

"So what do you say?" Betty asks. "Your crew gonna join up with him?"

Wolf and I exchange a glance.

"Well," he says. "We—"

"Saint's dead," I say bluntly. "I killed him."

All eyes are on me the moment the words leave my mouth. I look back and forth between Wolf and Betty. The former looks a little concerned, his eyes flashing at the other raiders and his grip on his gun tightening once again. My own fingers twitch on the trigger of my pistol, ready in case this turns into another gunfight.

But Betty laughs, giving me a look that seems almost impressed.

"Well," she says. "That's that, I guess. Time to pack it up and head out, boys." She glances at Wolf. "You seen Ben around?"

"Nope," he says quickly, shooting me a sharp look that I assume means to keep my mouth shut. I bite back a smile.

The other raiders grumble a bit as Betty barks orders at them to prepare to leave, and soon they trickle out of the room and leave Wolf and me behind. Outside, I hear Betty shouting the news about Saint's death to the other raiders. A chorus of groans and complaints answers her, but overall no one seems overly upset—or surprised—by the news.

Once it's clear no one is planning on hunting us down and shooting us for taking down Saint, Wolf and I walk out of the stairwell and over to the main lobby. None of the raiders we pass pay much attention to us, all prepping to head out, a rowdy mess of them taking anything they can find in the building and separating into individual crews again. There are a few tussles over weapons and other supplies, but we stay out of the fighting for once, searching for the rest of our crew instead.

We find Tank laughing and joking with a group of strangers, showing off a few new wounds he must've earned in the fighting. The moment he sees us, he lets out a whoop of joy and sweeps me up in a bone-crushing bear hug, spinning me around. I'm breathless and dizzy by the time he sets me down.

"Goddamn," he says, grinning from ear to ear. "I can't believe we actually pulled this off."

"I knew it would work out the whole time," Wolf says with a dismissive wave of his hand. "The plan was foolproof."

"Pretty sure it was mostly dumb luck," Tank says. "Plus the fact that hardly any of these raiders were actually loyal to Saint.

A bunch of 'em took off the second trouble started, and a bunch of the others decided to start looting the place since Saint was busy trying to deal with us."

Wolf lets out a snort of laughter.

"'Course they did," he says. "Don't know why assholes like him think they'd ever be able to control us wastelanders." He grins, fierce and proud. "Ain't nobody gonna tame these wastes."

We find Dolly waiting for us near the wreckage of our truck, bodies strewn across the floor around her. She's covered in an astounding amount of blood, none of which seems to be hers, and is carrying more weapons than seems like should be humanly possible.

Her face reveals no surprise whatsoever at seeing us, but she does smile—and I smile back as she squeezes my arm, and ignore the fact that it leaves behind a smear of half-dried blood. When Wolf explains the Saint situation and his death, she merely shrugs, as if it doesn't really matter to her either way.

We leave Saint's former headquarters battered, bruised, and bleeding, but pretty damn pleased with ourselves. I can't stop smiling and feeling like a big damn hero. It doesn't last long, though. Exhaustion comes creeping up fast once the nervous energy drains out of me. Soon I can feel every little scrape and bruise and find myself wishing more than anything for a comfortable bed to sleep in for a few weeks or so. The others are quiet aside from the occasional groan or muttered curse, so I assume they're feeling much the same.

Once we make it a good distance away from the building and the rest of the straggling raiders, we stop to gather ourselves.

"So, what's the plan, Wolf?" I ask. Tank sits down heavily on the ground, and I resist the urge to join him. If I sit now, it'll just be ten times harder to get myself back up. Dolly stands next to me, quietly sorting through her various new weapons.

"Well…" Wolf spits on the ground and looks around. Outside

of Saint's grounds, there's nothing but the same old wastelands. In the distance I can see a few of the other raider crews, some on foot and some in vehicles, gradually vanishing into the wastes. "It's gonna be a shitfest around here with all these other crews heading out again, but I've got a whole lot of killin', lootin', and eatin' to get out of my system after that whole mess." He shakes his head, his face sour. "Can't believe we turned out to be the goddamn good guys. What a fuckin' embarrassment."

No more vehicle, no more goal, and possibly not even enough supplies to make it to the next town, wherever that might be. Sounds about right. Maybe the thought should be daunting, but a grin spreads across my face.

"Well, no point hanging around doing nothing," I say. "Let's go!"

So we carry on.

Acknowledgments

There are some people without whom this book would've never existed, so I'm going to try my best to articulate how much they mean to me. Many thanks to:

Matthew Scrivener, the best teacher I ever had, and the first person who made me truly believe in my writing.

My agent, Emmanuelle Morgen, for having faith in *Bite* ever since it was just a messy draft, and being incredible every step of the way.

Jess Rosen, for being awesome and boundlessly enthusiastic.

Susan Barnes, my fantastic editor, who fought for this book and pushed to make it the best it could be. Lindsey Hall, for being so helpful throughout the publishing process and putting up with how bad I am at answering e-mails (sorry Lindsey!). Lauren Panepinto, who designed the super kickass cover. And the rest of the amazing team at Orbit: Thank you all for working so hard to make this book a reality.

And, of course, my family. Gramma, Memere, and Pepere, who hopefully weren't too scarred by this book, for endless love and support. My mom, who made me fall in love with reading and always encouraged me to pursue my passion. My dad, to whom I suspect I owe much of my weird sense of humor. And my brothers, Todd and Lucas, whose quick wit keeps me constantly on my toes. You make my life interesting. Love you all.

RAID

For nasty women

I
Hunters and Prey

Raiders always think they're the top of the food chain until I come along.

This one hasn't even noticed me following him for the past week. It probably never crossed his mind that he was being hunted until this very moment. I take out his legs first, a bullet in each kneecap before he can react. He falls forward, bleeding and snarling, rusty meat cleaver clutched tightly in hand. He still manages to crawl in my direction and brandish the knife, his ugly face contorted with pain and rage and hatred. I shoot him in the shoulder, twice for insurance, and he falls flat on his face and stays there.

I study the man, lying still in the dirt, and take a few steps closer with my gun trained on him.

His cleaver swings at my ankle. I step aside and slam my boot down on his hand. I grind my heel into his fingers until he stops struggling, then lift it and kick the knife out of his reach. The fight bleeds out of him quickly after that. I wait a few seconds before flipping him onto his back, where he lies dusty and bloody and struggling for consciousness.

"Bitch," he spits at me, his eyes half-shut. I ignore him and pull a crumpled wanted poster out of my pocket, smoothing it out before comparing the hand-drawn face on it to this ugly motherfucker. The picture was clearly drawn by some half-brain-dead townie, making it hard to compare, but that huge knife is easy to recognize.

"Beau the Butcher," I say. Probably came up with the name himself; he looks like the type.

"You know who I am," he wheezes out. "Means you know who I work for. Means you know you're dead if you kill me."

I crouch down beside him, grabbing a handful of his stringy hair and yanking his face up, closer to mine. His eyes find the burnt skin that twists up the left side of my face and widen in recognition.

"Clementine," he says, his breath quickening, and I grin. "You bi—"

Two hits are all it takes to knock him out.

I drop his limp body in the dust and grab his knife. It's a famous thing, this knife, both the namesake of this asshole and better known to people than his ugly face. I admire it before tucking it into my pack with my own weapons.

Embers still smolder nearby, the remnants of the campfire that allowed me to find him last night. Idiot was too stupid and drunk on power to head somewhere safer to sleep, making him easy pickings for me this morning. I dump sand on the fire, smothering the last of it, and search through his small collection of belongings. I find a couple bottles of water and a can of food, which I stuff into my pack. There's also some dried meat, but I toss that aside; there's only one kind of meat to be had around here, and I refuse to partake.

Once I'm done ransacking his camp, I grab the unconscious raider by the feet and drag him to my truck. I tie his hands and feet, gag him in case he wakes up, and throw him into the backseat.

With that done, I allow myself a moment to breathe, and re-tie my dark hair back into a neat ponytail. Then I climb into the driver's side, and smile at the roar of my truck coming to life. No matter how many times I hunt down a raider, it always gives me a special pleasure to make prey out of them.

I throw the Butcher facedown in the dirt. The townies scatter as if expecting him to jump up and grab them, staring goggle-eyed first at him and then at me. Several of them back away, their eyes wide.

My mistake. I forgot I was dealing with *civilized* folks. At least, that's what they fancy themselves, hiding in their walls and ram-shackle communities and clinging to scraps of what life was like before the bombs fell. They're not like raiders, who fully embrace the mayhem of the world and make their livings killing and loot-ing. Townies would rather rely on scavenged canned food, rather stay half-starved than eat human flesh like the sharks do. I admire the way they stick to some semblance of morality, even in a world like this. I try to do the same, though I'm no townie—not any-more. Of course, I'm not a goddamn shark, either. I exist some-where in between the two ways of life, apart from all of them.

The townies don't let me forget it, either. Right now, they're staring at me like I'm some kind of monster that wandered into their midst.

The two dozen standing in a half circle around me comprise the bulk of the population of Sunrise, a dingy little town on the edge of what we call the eastern wastes. The buildings of Sunrise are all stout and cramped together, not one above a single story high. It's like they're crouched in the dirt, afraid to lose their hold on the earth. Beau the Butcher lies still in the middle of the dusty ring the people of Sunrise call the "town square."

"Is he dead?" one man asks, after several moments of silence. He cautiously cranes his neck and then retracts it, like he simul-taneously wants to get a better look and fears what he'll see if he does.

"Well, no," I say, my eyebrows drawing together. "Figured you'd want to do it yourselves."

They ogle at me some more. One man clears his throat. Nobody meets my eyes.

"But he's one of…" A townie starts, and stops. He licks his lips and drops his voice to a loud whisper. "Jedediah Johnson's men."

"Yes," I say, not sure what that has to do with anything. "And he killed your sheriff over a card game. So you wanted him dead. What am I missing here?"

There's another long stretch of silence, in which all the townies glance at each other and shuffle their feet and refuse to look at me. Finally, a woman steps forward. She's a solidly built, middle-aged woman, dusty and stout like the buildings of her town. The top of her head barely reaches my chin, but then again, my height rivals that of a decent amount of the men in town as well. I recognize her as the woman who made the initial deal with me—the wife of the recently murdered sheriff, who seems to be taking on the role of her dead husband.

"Well, there's a reason we hired you to do it," she says. "If word got out that we killed one of Jedediah's men, he'd burn this place to the ground." She pauses, her eyes sliding across the scarred and burnt section of my face, the angry red skin that stretches across the entire left side. With my hair tied back, my burns are on full display. I'm not afraid to show them off, but if this woman thinks she can bring them into an argument, I'll blow her damn head off. "We know what happened to Old Creek," she says, and leaves it at that.

My lip curls in disgust. So they're willing to hire someone to kill a man, but not to get their hands dirty themselves. I knew that they hired me because they didn't have the means to take Beau out themselves, but it seems they also don't have the guts when the opportunity presents itself. I thought they'd relish the chance to deal out their own justice, especially this woman who lost her husband... but I guess I overestimated them.

In the dirt between me and the woman, Beau the Butcher starts to stir, lifting his head and looking around through the one eye that isn't swollen shut. When his eye lands on me, he chuckles, spitting out a glob of saliva and dust.

"Knew you wouldn't have the balls to kill me," he says. "Now, if you'll just untie me, we can talk about—"

I un-holster my pistol, shoot him three times in the head, and re-holster it.

"All right," I say flatly. "Pay up."

The townies gasp and blink and step back. Some of them gag. But, to her credit, the new sheriff holds her ground and her stomach. When she gestures to a couple of the men, they manage to stop staring and disappear into one of the closest buildings. They return with armloads of canned food and bottled water. I make no move to take it from them, so they dump it all in a pile at my feet and retreat to the rest of the gathered townsfolk.

I separate the pile with my boot. All laid out, they've given me three bottles of water and four cans of food. I count again, ticking them off on my fingers, and fix the sheriff with my hardest stare.

"You said four and six."

The woman doesn't flinch. She even raises her chin at me, though her lower lip wobbles as she does it.

"Ain't got six to spare," she says. "Still got to pay the tax this month."

I sigh. Part of me admires the gutsiness, but I don't have time for this shit. Damn townies always use the tax as an excuse when it comes time to pay out. Sure, it sucks for them, giving up a share of hard-earned goods to the self-proclaimed ruler of the eastern wastes. But they know damn well that it comes every month, and they know damn well that they should take it into account when we make the deal, not when it comes time to pay me.

I know better than to try to talk sense into townies. Instead, I take my pistol out of its holster again and let it hang by my side.

"You'll find the rest," I say. The sheriff hesitates. I press my lips into a firm line, tapping my gun against my leg. Finally she nods and gestures to her men again. We wait in silence until they return with two more cans of food and one more bottle of water, and dump them on the dusty pile in front of me. I wait until they step back to join the others, count the payment once more, and slide my pistol back into its holster. I swear I hear a collective *whoosh* of the townies releasing breath, but maybe that's my imagination.

I keep an eye out in case they get any stupid ideas, but none of the townies move or even look at me as I stuff the goods into my pack. When I finish and straighten up, only the sheriff meets my eyes. The wobble in her lip is gone, and she stands with her posture stiff and her jaw set, looking up at me like she's waiting for me to demand more.

"I'm a fair woman," I say. "Just want what I'm owed."

The townies stare at the ground with pinched faces, and I tighten my grip on my bag.

I wish I could say this kind of treatment is unexpected. It sure hurt the first time it happened, when I had just lost my home and I was so hopeful for a new one. I was sure the town would take me in after I helped them with their raider problem. After I got my reward, I stood there waiting for the inevitable *You know, we could use a woman like you around here*... Instead, the sheriff said, *You've got what we owed you*, and the townies all stared at me like these ones are staring at me now.

As it turns out, towns aren't so eager to trust strangers. That's especially true when a stranger with a burnt face shows up after a local town is burned to the ground, and that stranger turns out to be particularly good at killing people. Towns do see me as an asset, but not the kind they want to invite in for dinner. Makes it hard to find a home when people view you as a necessary evil.

At this point I know better than to expect the townies to be welcoming, or even understanding, but they could at least stop acting like I've done something horrible by taking what they promised me.

I turn my back and walk away without another word. I keep my ears pricked and my eyes searching, just in case, but of course none of them have the spine to say or do anything. As I reach the edge of town I sigh, relax my shoulders, and reach into my pocket for my keys. Just as my fingers close around them, something on the horizon catches my eye and my blood runs cold.

Cars. Black cars, coming this way fast. And black cars mean only one thing out here.

"Oh, fuck me," I breathe. For one moment, I consider running for my truck and booking it out of here. But instead I turn, run back into town, and skid to a dusty stop near the cluster of townies. They cluster more tightly together at the sight of me, wild-eyed with my hand on my gun.

"Incoming," I say. "Jedediah Johnson's men."

II
The Reign of Jedediah Johnson

Once, Jedediah Johnson was just the leader of another crew of raiders carving their bloody way across the wastes. They were known as the toughest and the meanest raiders around, the scum among scum, but the scariest thing about them was their leader. People said he was some kind of mad genius, more wily than any raider before him; he was the reason why nobody saw them coming, and why no town stood a chance against them.

Of course, people also said that he could hear his name every time someone spoke it, that he could change his face every day, and that he gained the knowledge of every man he killed and ate. Rumors still run wild; nobody knows what the guy looks like, even now. But the genius part I believe. He and his men cut through the wastes in a way that had never been seen before.

One day, that infamous leader decided he'd rather be a dictator than a raider. He settled down in an old mansion in the town of Wormwood, told everyone he was in charge now, and started calling his raiding "collecting taxes."

At first, people laughed at him. When he actually showed up to collect, they fought him. Soon, those who laughed and those who fought were all dead. Everybody left didn't dare do anything but obey the self-declared king.

Even I know better than to fuck with Jedediah and his men.

I'll pick off a stray if he's off on his own with a good price on his head, like the man I just killed, but that's risky enough, and it's as far as I dare to go. I've been killing raiders my whole life, but Jedediah's crew are a breed of their own. Better fed, better equipped, better organized. There's a reason they've been able to hold down this corner of the wastes for years, keeping townies under their thumb and fending off wandering raider crews as well. Jedediah holds all the power here.

So predictably, the townies lose their shit at my announcement. Most of them panic and flee to their houses. A few of the smarter ones remember the dead man lying in the middle of their town square—a dead man who worked for the very same dictator they're so afraid of. If Jedediah's men find that body here, they'll massacre these townies and burn their town to the ground.

"Just tax collectors," the sheriff shouts, struggling to be heard above the general clamor. "They don't know nothin', they're just here for the tax. Get what we owe, and hide the damn body."

Two townies go to move the corpse, but I shoulder one of them out of the way and grab its feet myself. The sheriff hesitates, as if ready to tell me to leave, but thinks better of it.

"Get it inside and cover it up," she says. We drag it to one of the nearby ramshackle homes, throw it onto the cot in the corner, pull a blanket over him—all the way over the head, since the multiple bullet holes in the face aren't exactly subtle.

A small collection of townies stays in the town square, including the sheriff and a handful of the bigger men. They surround her, which mostly just makes their leader look dwarfed and nervous. The rest of them cower inside their homes. They shut doors if they have them, cover windows with boards and blankets, and stay out of sight. When the townies move to cover the window of the house I'm in, I wave them off before they can finish, keeping a corner of it uncovered. None of them question me; they're too busy running to find their hiding spots. I crouch down next to the open spot, staying between the window and closed door, my gun in my hand.

I force myself to breathe deeply, trying to keep the wild beating of my heart under control. I've always heard about Jedediah's tax collectors, and seen the aftermath of their visits, but I've never been present for one.

Living out of my truck and never spending a night in any town means that I never get surprised. I engage with Jedediah's men on my terms only, like I do everyone else. But this... this is unexpected, and I'm unprepared. I could take out one of Jedediah's men with the element of surprise, *maybe* two if I'm lucky, but any more than that and I'm fucked. And even if I can handle them, killing them here when they're out collecting taxes would make it far too easy to trace them to Sunrise, and then to me.

I need to lay low. Now is not the time to fight Jedediah's men, though it's hard to hold myself back. After all, killing raiders is what I'm best at. I've been doing it since I was eight years old.

The first was a huge brute of a man with a squashed face and a hissing voice. He was alone, but our town was young, many of us barely out of our bomb shelters, and we weren't prepared. One armed raider was enough to send everyone cowering. Ours was the third house he broke into, and nobody had dared raise a hand to stop him. Even at eight, I knew what would happen: He'd take everything we had, and probably kill us too. I was stupefied to see my parents cowering on the floor in front of this man. They looked at him and their brains told them *Cower, hide, let him take it, just let us live.* Behind his back, I looked at him, and I looked at the gun he had seemingly forgotten on the table, and my brain said: *Kill.*

I was proud that night, and so was everyone else. Afterward, the sheriff started giving me shooting lessons, and my pa gave me first pick of weapons whenever we found a new haul. I would strut around town with a pistol on my hip and people would smile at me when I passed by. "The little hero," they called me. But, as I eventually learned the hard way, there's a time and place to be a hero.

Right now, right here, is not it.

Outside, the town is dead silent. I lift myself up to steal a glance out of the peephole just in time to see Jedediah's men arrive. They're unmistakable, with their heavy black clothes and huge guns. One of them is a massive man, six foot four at least, and made of muscle. He's middle-aged, with a bushy beard and hard eyes that are constantly roaming the area around him. The top of his companion's head barely reaches his shoulder, but he's solidly built as well, with a mess of wavy blond hair and a shaggy beard. His face is nearly covered by hair, his eyes barely visible, and the skin that pokes out is ruddy and sunburnt. They approach the town square and stop a few feet in front of the sheriff. The men around her draw back as Jedediah's men get close. The sheriff stands alone, straight-backed, her chin raised.

"We've got your tax," she says. "Don't want no trouble."

The two men study the sheriff and the pile of goods at her feet. It's easily three times what the townies paid me for the job, and I feel a stab of resentment at them for trying to hold back the extra goods they owed me.

"You're not the sheriff of Sunrise," the shaggy raider says. He brushes his hair out of his eyes and squints at her. "Where's what's-his-name? With the goatee?"

The big man mumbles something in a surprisingly soft voice, so quiet I can't make out the words.

"Yeah," the shaggy one says. "Sheriff Daniels."

The new sheriff hesitates, considering how to answer. *Don't mention Beau*, I think. *Whatever you say to them—*

"He was killed last week by one of your men," she says. "Called himself the Butcher."

Damn stupid townies.

"Oh," the shaggy man says, letting his hair fall back into his face. "Alrighty then." Without further ado, he crouches down and starts counting the goods for Jedediah's tax.

The townie woman's face turns red, and then purple, while Jedediah's men pay no attention whatsoever to her. I grit my teeth, willing her to keep her mouth shut. She may have already fucked her people over by mentioning Beau. When he shows up missing, Jedediah's men are likely to remember this conversation.

"He killed him over a card game," she bursts out finally. "Beau hacked his head off. It took him five hits." The words pour out of her, like she can't help herself. "There was no reason for it. Just cruelty."

"Well, there's your reason," the shaggy raider says, still counting. "I don't need the details. Was just curious."

"Aren't you going to do something about it?" the sheriff asks, her voice rising to a near shout. I wince, tightening my grip on my gun. Jedediah's men have killed people for less than raising their voice.

The shaggy raider pauses, then shrugs and keeps counting.

"Not my job," he says. "My job is collecting taxes...which you're short on. Need four more bottles of water and three food."

The sheriff, still red in the face, looks ready to argue more, but the massive, quiet raider shifts his grip on his gun. She looks at him, and her shoulders slump.

"This is the amount it's always been," she says, sounding more tired than argumentative.

"We need more this month."

The townie woman says nothing, but doesn't move to collect the extra goods either. The rest of the townspeople shuffle their feet behind her, none of them looking at either her or the raiders. After a moment, the shaggy man sighs, straightens up, and raises his gun. He steps forward until the barrel rests against the side of the sheriff's nose, and taps it against her face.

"All right, I've had about enough of this shit," he says. "Get what you owe us. Now."

The sheriff doesn't move or speak, just stares down the barrel of the gun at the raider. But the men behind her immediately scramble to do his bidding, disappearing into a nearby building for a minute before rushing back with the extra cans and bottles. They dump them hurriedly in front of the tax collectors and retreat, none of them daring to help their leader.

The shaggy raider is still staring at the sheriff's defiant face, his own expression impossible to read with his hair in front of his eyes. After a long few seconds, he lowers the gun.

"See? Not so hard," he says, and gestures to his big companion. The huge man bends down and scoops up the goods. The pile looks small and paltry in his arms, but I can tell by the stricken look of the townies that it's a fortune to them. Still, they don't make so much as a whisper of protest as the men turn to go. I sink down, resting my back against the wall, and sigh out a long breath.

I wait until I hear the sounds of their vehicles starting up, and then wait a few minutes more, staying inside even after the townies have trickled out of their houses to gather in the square. Finally, when I'm sure that Jedediah's men are gone, I stand up, holster my gun, and head outside with the others.

The townies stand in a tight, worried knot in the middle of the square, speaking in lowered voices. They turn to stare at me as I emerge, and I pause. I can feel their eyes on the bag I carry, their minds no doubt on the food and water they handed over before the tax collectors came. I pull the bag tighter against my body and rest my hand on my gun.

"Thanks for the business," I say. The townies say nothing, but continue to stare at me, hollow eyed, like I'm the one who did this to them. After a few moments, I turn my back on them and head for my truck.

Truth be told, if they asked nicely, I might hand over what they paid me. If they showed an ounce of compassion or understanding or trust in me, I might help them out. But they won't ask, and I won't give, because this place and these people aren't right. I need to save my supplies for when I do find my new home, or at least for the journey there.

Still, I pause for just a moment on the edge of town, as if I'm waiting for something. Gratitude is a long shot, but they could show some recognition for what I've done for them. At the very least, they could stop looking at me like I'm a goddamn monster just for taking what they owed me.

But it's been a long time since anyone looked at me like anything else, and I should know better by now.

III
The Collector

I drive until my truck is long out of sight of Sunrise or any other town. Once I'm secluded enough, I pull over and dig a can of food out of my bag, prying it open with my knife and slurping it down in a matter of seconds. I almost open up a second one, but stop myself.

Pickings have been slim lately. The more Jedediah solidifies his hold on the east, the more dangerous it gets to take out one of his men, and the stray raiders and thieves are few and far between out here. It's been harder and harder to find work bounty hunting. It took me a week to catch Beau somewhere secluded enough to take him down. I had to ration the last of my food, and even now that I've gotten paid, I doubt it'll last me until the next cash-out. Maybe I'll get lucky, but I know better than to count on that. For now, though, I'll allow myself a moment to relax.

Back when I started, when I was just a sixteen-year-old townie girl with a pistol, cashing in a bounty was always a grand affair. I'd claim my reward, head home and hand it over to the sheriff, and we'd all celebrate. There'd be claps on the back and smiles and thanks. *Our little hero.*

Now, I look forward to eating in my truck alone. It is what it is. Being alone isn't so bad, especially when I'm all wound up from talking with those townies. Dealing with people always proves to be more frustrating and more disappointing than I expect. They don't understand me, I don't understand them, and altogether it's never a good experience for anyone involved. After I lost my hometown, I quickly realized that all strangers see is a tall woman with a burnt face, a gun, and some rather unsavory skills. I soon learned it was better for me to keep my distance, spending nights in my truck and staying focused on my job.

I thought maybe my job was the key, and that building up a reputation for myself would help people see the real me. I've built up respect, to be sure—but it's respect out of fear, not out of liking. Still, the only thing to do is keep trying, and keep saving. Maybe one day I'll have a chance to prove myself; a town in need of supplies or protection, a person who asks me for help, an opportunity to show that I can be more than just a killer... or maybe I'll just have to wait until I save up enough supplies to go somewhere new and get a fresh start.

But there's no time to dwell on that. There's still work to do. I left Beau's body with the townies, not wanting to lug it around after a near brush with Jedediah's men, but I still have his knife. So after a few minutes of soaking up the silence, I start my truck.

There are several bounty collectors in the area, all of whom have a price set for any member of Jedediah's crew, especially one as blatantly vicious as Beau the Butcher. But Alex the Collector is the closest, and one of my favorites, so I head to him.

His place is small but sturdy, a lone, stout building in the middle of nowhere, surrounded by a wire fence. It looks like another abandoned ruin to someone who doesn't know better, but I've been here many times before. The guard at the fence barely glances at me before waving me through. But Alex himself squints out from a barely cracked door, scrutinizing me thoroughly as if there's some trick involved. I bite my cheek and wait as he finishes his inspection and checks behind me twice before letting me inside.

With all the windows covered, the room is dim even with the sun still up. The place reeks of some kind of chemical— or maybe that's just Alex. The Collector is a squat, jiggly, nervous man with thinning hair. He's deathly afraid of the outside world, and I suspect it's been a long, long time since he's set foot out there. But once the door is shut and locked and it's just the two of us, his nerves give way to barely contained excitement. He trembles with it, barely able to restrain himself from immediately demanding to see what I've brought. I make him wait, taking my time looking around.

His center of operations is, if possible, weirder than the man himself. Alex is a collector not just of bounties, but of souvenirs. The walls are lined with dusty wooden shelves, the shelves lined with his mementos. I don't mind the weirdness; I appreciate the fact that Alex is a freak, because it means he doesn't look at me like I'm one. Dealing with him is much better than dealing with townies.

Still, staring at his souvenirs too long makes me uncomfortable. Some are fairly normal, like a boot sitting on a low shelf, or a sniper rifle hung high on the wall. But most venture far past the limit of the reasonable and into the land of the grotesque. A scorched femur, a skull split down the middle, an eyeball floating in a vat of murky liquid. Each one has a wanted poster framed next to it, announcing who the item once belonged to. Several of them came from my own collected marks.

"So," Alex says, rubbing his hands together, his eyes bright. "What've you got for me today?"

I dig the knife out of my bag, hold it up until I see recognition light his face, and deliver it hilt-first into his waiting hands. He turns the weapon slowly, admiring the rusty and bloodstained blade. His fingers find the small initials B. B. carved into the hilt and tap against them.

"Beau the Butcher," he says, a smile splitting his face. I allow myself to smile back. He's one of the few people who appreciates my line of work, unlike the damn townies who treat me like I'm barely better than a raider. "But no body?"

"You think I'm going to lug around one of Jedediah's men?" I ask, rolling my eyes. "You recognize the knife. That's enough."

"But how do I know that he's dead?" Alex asks, still admiring the knife. I stare at him until he glances up. As soon as he sees the look on my face, he blanches and lets out a nervous laugh. "Right," he says. "Never mind. Will be a reduced payment, though, and I can't help that."

"Fine," I say. It's not worth the effort of arguing, especially when I'm already double-dipping for the reward—first the townies and now a collector. "How much, then?"

"Hmm," he says. "Well, considering it's just the knife . . ." His eyes flick upward as he no doubt considers how much of the bounty he can weasel out of paying. After a moment, his eyes flick back to me. "Four and six."

I frown, digging the crumpled wanted poster out of my pocket to double-check the listed reward. I hold it up for him to see.

"That's less than half."

"Well, there's no body."

I glare at him, and he takes a step back.

"Five and seven," I say.

"Fine," he says, so quickly I mentally kick myself for not asking for more. Before I can say anything he's already scrambling to the back room, the knife clutched in his greedy hands. He returns soon after with the goods wrapped in a plastic bag. I take them out to count.

"By the way," Alex says, "I've got an informant in Buzzard's

Beak looking for you. I've worked with her a few times, she's never steered me wrong."

I pause, and then resume counting, double-checking to ensure he gave me the right amount before returning my attention to him.

"She's looking for me specifically?" I ask, wary. That rarely means anything good.

"She's looking for the best of the best," Alex says with a smile. I give him a dead stare, and he drops it. "Well, looking for someone who isn't afraid of a hard job and won't let any personal feelings get in the way."

"Fair enough. You send anyone else her way?"

"Only you," he says, which I take to mean, *So far.* Alex is a cunning bastard, and he never places everything on one gamble. "Huge payment, I hear."

"For who?"

"She didn't specify. Just said it was a big job, a dangerous job, and a huge payout. I'd get there quick."

"I'll see what I can do," I say. "Got a lot on my plate right now."

I count my reward for a third time, gather it up, and head out.

Buzzard's Beak isn't far, and I reach it by sundown. It's a dull little town full of dull little people, and tonight it seems even more dreary than usual. The townspeople are scuttling into their homes now that the sun's going down, and they all avoid eye contact and scoot out of my way as I walk down the street. Some of them must recognize me—I've done business here before—but nobody says a word of greeting. Judging by the mood, I'd guess Jedediah's men have been here. I wonder if they upped the tax here as well as in Sunrise, but don't care quite enough to ask one of the dead-eyed men or women trying to ignore my existence.

There's only one place in this town that stays alive after sundown: the saloon. In this case, "alive" means there are two flickering lanterns keeping the room lit, and a whopping five people occupying the rickety chairs and stools. I sweep my eyes around the room, and it doesn't take long for me to find who I'm looking for. There's only one person out of place, one person who meets my eyes and isn't coated with three layers of dust and sorrow: a woman sitting in a corner with a half-empty bottle of water on the table in front of her.

I size up the dusty handful of townies in the room and scope out the dark corners, but it doesn't look like there are any surprises waiting for me. Once I'm confident that nothing looks suspicious, I walk over to the woman's table and take a seat on the slanted wooden stool across from her. She studies my face, idly toying with her bottle of water.

"I know you," she says. "Clementine, right?"

"Mhm." I can't deny that it pleases me to be recognized, though *tall woman with a burnt face* isn't so difficult to remember. At least we can skip the part where I convince her I'm trustworthy.

"I've heard good things about your work."

I almost smile, but suppress it. She's just trying to butter me up.

"Tell me about the job," I say. "Who's the mark?"

She hesitates, and my frown deepens.

"Are you a risk taker, Clementine?"

Though her face and voice show nothing, one of her hands taps out a nervous beat on the table. I stare at the hand, and she stops.

"I am if I'm paid enough," I say, folding my arms across my chest. "What, is it one of Jedediah's men?" I should be wary, but it's hard to keep the hunger out of my voice. I lean forward, and she leans with me, allowing me to drop my voice. "I've taken out almost a dozen of them over the years."

She studies my face, showing no hint of surprise at my words.

"So I've heard," she says. "But this isn't one of Jedediah's men."

I lean back again, disappointed despite myself. There's a certain thrill to hunting down the scum who work for our not-so-benevolent overlord—the risk, the challenge, the sense of justice, and of course the more personal thirst for revenge. But I push those thoughts aside. A job is a job…and more importantly, I'm starting to wonder what mark would make the job such a challenge, if it's not one of Jedediah's underlings. There isn't anyone else who poses a threat around here; Jedediah's made damn sure of it.

The informant glances around the room, licks her lips, and gestures for me to lean forward again. I sigh, but oblige, and she leans in even farther so our faces are a mere half foot apart.

"The mark is Jedediah Johnson himself."

My head snaps back. I'm shocked into silence for a moment— and burst out in a harsh bark of laughter that causes every head in the room to turn toward us. The informant sinks down in her chair, her cheeks growing red. By the time I finish laughing, all but one passed-out townie in the corner have fled the room. In the silence following my laughter, the townie snores quietly.

"Well," the informant says. "Now that you've succeeded in drawing far too much attention to us, I think we're done here." She stands up and moves to leave, but I grab her arm before she makes it far, yanking her back. She stares down at me, and I stare right back.

"What is this?" I ask. "Some kind of convoluted scam? An ambush? What's the point of telling such a stupid lie?"

"I'm not a liar," she says. "I'm sure Alex told you as much, or you wouldn't even have showed up."

I chew that over, relaxing my grip on her arm just a bit. While I wouldn't go so far as to say I trust Alex, he doesn't have any reason to waste my time. I bring in a lot of business, and a lot of his beloved souvenirs.

"Getting to Jedediah is impossible," I say. "He never leaves the Wormwood mansion, and he's surrounded by his goons." I've looked into it, hunted for information that could lead me to him, even risked scoping out the place myself a couple times. I've wanted to kill him for years, but it's just not feasible. There are guards at every door of his mansion, armed patrols, impenetrable defenses. The place is a fortress.

The informant sighs. She pulls her arm back, and I let go after a moment, gesturing to the seat across from me. She slowly sits down.

"There's new information," she says. "From someone on the inside."

My eyebrows shoot up.

"Why would one of his men betray him?" It doesn't make sense. Jedediah's men have it made, and they'd be dead if they went against him in any way.

"They say he's been acting strange," she says. "Upping the taxes, tightening his noose a little too snugly. The townies are pissed, and his men are taking the blame. There's been talk of dissent in the ranks, maybe even an uprising. Maybe they think they're jumping off a sinking ship."

I've heard no such rumors of an uprising—but then again, why would townies tell me? They've made it pretty damn clear that they trust me just a hair more than they trust the raiders. And I know the part about raising taxes is true. I gesture at her to continue.

"Whatever the reason, this person came to me. And they told me there's something hardly anyone knows about the place. Something that, if you knew, would make it easy to get into the Wormwood mansion, right to Jedediah himself."

She stops there. I know she wants me to ask more, but I'm still wary. I want to believe—want to believe so badly that I'm try-ing very hard to hold myself back. My mind keeps flashing to what a job like this would mean for me. Jedediah Johnson is the reason that my home is now a pile of ashes. He's the reason my family is dead and my face is burnt and my life is the way it is.

But taking him down would be about more than revenge, or honoring the memory of my people...It would be a chance to show, once and for all, that I'm on the good side. I could liber-ate the eastern towns, get rid of a tyrant, save people from this oppression. People would love me for it. No more unwelcoming stares, no more mistrust, no more looking at me like I'm some kind of monster. They would let me in with open arms.

I'd be a hero. I'd have a home.

But I'm getting carried away here. No matter how much this would mean for me, and how badly I want it to be true, I can't let that blind me. It's still highly unlikely that this is true, and far more likely that I'd be wandering into a trap.

"Fine. Give me the information and maybe I'll consider checking it out," I say, even as I will myself to walk away.

The informant looks far too satisfied for my liking. She knows she's caught my interest. I plaster on a scowl, waiting for her to stop looking so smug and continue.

"Near the mansion is a scrapyard," she says. "Bunch of rusty, good-for-nothing old cars, all the good parts stripped. But beneath one of them—a red truck—is a hidden trapdoor."

"Seriously?" I ask, rolling my eyes. This sounds more and more like another urban legend about Jedediah.

"Inside is a tunnel. A tunnel leading right under the Worm-wood mansion, that opens up right in Jedediah's bedroom."

I stare at her.

"There's no way it can be that simple."

"Jedediah's a smart man. He knows he needs a way out in case shit ever goes down. But hardly anyone is allowed into his room, and nobody's going to bother to check under rusty old cars. Very, *very* few people know about this, as far as I understand."

"And you're sure there are no guards waiting on the other side?"

"Like I said. Hardly anyone knows the tunnel exists, including his own men."

I tap my fingers on the table. I still have so many questions, and so many doubts. And yet, I want so badly to believe it could be true, want so badly for there to be a chance to take out Jedediah. If there was even a half-believable shot, I would be willing to take it. And yet...

"What a load of bullshit." I shove out my chair and stand up, shaking my head at her. "Thanks for wasting my time," I say dryly, and head for the door.

"Clementine!" she calls after me. I don't turn around, but she continues anyway. "If you get him, get him alive. No one will believe you otherwise."

I pause at the door, scowling over my shoulder at her.

"I'm not chasing some fairy tale," I say, and leave without another glance back. I head to my truck, start her up, and hesitate for just a moment, my hands gripping the steering wheel tightly. The information has to be fake...it has to be. All signs point to this "job" being absolute bullshit. And yet...what if it's not?

I jam my heel on the gas and head straight for Wormwood.

IV
The Tunnel

The tunnel is real.

I sit back on my heels, staring at it. It was waiting beneath a rusty old red truck in the middle of a scrapyard, exactly where the informant said it would be. The metal trapdoor was coated with dirt, making it virtually invisible unless you were looking for it, but it was here. The darkness of the tunnel stares back at me, an awful smell drifting out of its open mouth.

Goddamn do I wish the tunnel wasn't real. Would've made things a whole lot easier if I could've just dismissed the whole thing as bullshit. I could've laughed at myself for being stupid enough to believe it for even a second, for risking my life coming out to Jedediah's headquarters in Wormwood, hiding my truck, and sneaking past his patrols into this abandoned scrapyard. I could've walked away kicking myself about nearly falling for such a stupid trick.

But the tunnel is real. So now what?

I chew my bottom lip, keeping my gun aimed at the open tunnel just in case something comes crawling out of it, but inside it's still and silent. There's no hint of what's within, aside from the smell, and no hint about what's waiting on the other end. It could be an ambush. It could be a dead end. Or maybe, just maybe, it could be the self-declared king of the eastern wastes.

It seems far more likely that it's a trick...but if I don't find out for sure, I'll wonder about this moment forever.

"Fuck it," I mutter. I scoot under the car and lower myself into the darkness.

Inside, it's cramped and earthy, and I have to crouch to prevent my head from hitting the ceiling. The terrible smell is ten times worse than it was outside. I cough, and cover my mouth with one hand to stifle any further noise, the other keeping my gun aimed at the darkness in front of me. It's impossible to see anything ahead.

I remove my hand from my mouth and grope along the wall, pressing forward. After a couple minutes, the dim moonlight from the entrance is barely visible. Muffled sounds come from above—voices and footsteps. I must be directly underneath the Wormwood mansion. I pause, looking up and imagining Jedediah's men right above me. The ceiling of the tunnel trembles, raining dust whenever it gets too loud above. It's easy to picture the whole thing collapsing on me, burying me as punishment for my stupidity, but I brush the concern away. Clearly the tunnel has stood for this long, and it will continue standing tonight. I push forward, half-listening to the sounds above, just in case there's a clamor that means they may have found my truck, or the disturbed trapdoor, or some other sign of an intruder. None comes.

After a few minutes longer, I bump up against something. I step back, so startled I almost make the grave mistake of firing my gun, but it's just another wall. My stomach sinks at the thought that I've hit a dead end. Is this it? The end to my fantasy of killing Jedediah?

The ceiling groans, and I look up. There are footsteps above, and barely visible in the darkness, another metal trapdoor. I reach up to run my fingers over it, and my heart thuds wildly in my chest. I haven't hit a dead end after all. This is it: the exit, and the moment of truth.

Someone is right above me, in the room this trapdoor opens into. I listen carefully for a couple minutes, but I can only hear one set of footsteps. Perhaps not an ambush, then. But could it really be him? The raider king himself, Jedediah Johnson? Is this the moment where I prove myself an idiot for believing what the informant told me, or the moment where I prove myself a hero?

Time to find out.

Gun held ready, I push open the trapdoor, grab the edge with my free hand, and pull myself up to the other side.

V
The Capture of Jedediah Johnson

"Oh, hello," Jedediah Johnson says, going slightly cross-eyed as he stares down the barrel of my gun.

I've imagined this moment a thousand times, in a thousand different ways, but it never played out quite like this. I thought the infamous Jedediah would be angry about being captured, or afraid, maybe even impressed. At the very least, I thought he'd be surprised. But instead, he just seems curious and progressively more cross-eyed.

He doesn't look the way I'd expected, either. Rumors abounded about his appearance, of course, mostly involving hideous scars and jewelry made of human teeth. I was more realistic; I knew he was the brains of his crew, with more than enough brawn eager to do his dirty work, and he wouldn't have to be huge and intimidating like his made-of-muscle tax collectors. But still, this guy looks like I could deck him with one good punch.

And he has a very punchable face, with a mouth that seems on the verge of smirking, even at this moment. He's surprisingly close to my own age, and has no scars, burns, tattoos, piercings, or any marks of the life of violence and depravity I know he leads. And he's *shorter* than I am. It's not unusual, but still, I would've assumed a man with such a towering reputation would top five foot ten. In a room full of strangers, I never would have picked this man as the infamous raider-turned-ruler. In fact, I wouldn't spare him a second glance for any reason.

But this is him. It must be. Against all odds, everything else the informant told me has been correct—and why else would there be a secret tunnel into Jedediah's headquarters, if not as an emergency escape route for the man himself?

"Get on your knees," I say, gesturing impatiently when the gun in his face doesn't seem like enough of a clue for him. "Put your hands behind your head."

"Yes, ma'am," he says, sinking to his knees on the carpet. I can't believe the bastard actually has carpet in his bedroom, plush and beige and offensively clean before my boots smeared a trail of dirt across it. He also has a real bed, with real sheets, and a closet full of clothes that look like they've been barely worn. It's exactly the life of luxury I would've expected an evil, conniving dictator to lead. At least that makes sense about this situation.

But his attitude is really throwing me off. He seems completely unconcerned, even with a gun to his head, even when I roughly jerk his hands down and tie them behind his back. He doesn't struggle, doesn't yell for help, just sits there patiently waiting for me to finish. Once his hands are secure, I circle around to the front of him, jabbing the gun in his face again. This time he doesn't go cross-eyed, but looks right past the gun and meets my eyes. One corner of his lips curls up.

"You don't have anything to say?" I ask. I know it's a bad idea to engage an extremely dangerous prisoner, but I can't resist.

"Oh, is this the part where I'm supposed to beg for my life?" he asks. "Or ask how you got in here?" His eyes swivel to the trapdoor. "I mean, that one is pretty obvious. I suppose a more appropriate question would be 'Which traitorous ass-hole told you about the secret entrance?' but that's a mystery easily solved. There are a very limited number of people who know about it. It shouldn't take the crew long to figure out who spilled the beans, find them, and kill them." He says it very matter-of-factly, and smiles as he turns back to me.

I stare at him. Maybe there's nothing fishy going on here after all; maybe he's just this damn arrogant.

"I thought about yelling for a guard," he continues, "but I figured you'd likely shoot me if I did that, and I'd prefer not to get shot."

"So you think I'm not going to shoot you?" I ask, keeping my voice even and flat.

"Don't think so. I'm worth more alive, right, Clementine?"

I jerk at the sound of my name.

"How do you know who I am?" I ask, trying to hide how much it rattles me to hear my name from his mouth. I never thought the raider king himself would know about me. I thought he'd have his goons worry about things like bounty hunters, while he stayed holed up in this pretty little room.

"Oh, please," Jedediah says. His eyes slide across the burnt half of my face, his gaze so penetrating I can practically feel its touch. His eyes reach the twisted corner of my mouth, pause, and shift up to meet my stare. "You're prettier than I thought you'd be."

I stuff my handkerchief into his mouth to make sure he's thoroughly silenced. He waggles his eyebrows at me, the corners of his eyes crinkling in amusement.

I have yet to decide if he's utterly insane or just ridiculously confident, but either way, I need to keep this job professional. Clean. The way I always do things. It doesn't matter that this is goddamn Jedediah Johnson I'm dealing with, and it doesn't matter that I've been dreaming of taking him down for years, and it doesn't matter that this could change my entire life. For now, all that matters is getting the job done, and getting it done right.

Collecting a mark usually means a lot of struggling and fighting and yelling, at least until I knock them out. I certainly wouldn't mind landing a couple of good punches on this bastard, but he's behaving himself remarkably well, and I'd rather avoid dragging him all the way to my truck if I can help it. Still, I'm not gentle as I shove him into the tunnel, my gun aimed at the back of his head. I jump down and pull the trapdoor shut behind us. When it closes, it's just him and me and the darkness of the tunnel. I can barely make out his shape ahead.

"Move," I say. Jedediah balks, hesitant for the first time. I wonder if it's the sudden realization of his own helplessness, or that he's leaving the safety of his headquarters, or maybe just the fact that his secret escape tunnel smells like something died in it a while ago and was never discovered. Regardless, a sharp jab with the barrel of my gun gets him moving again.

I move slowly, quietly, listening for any sound of a disturbance above or company joining us in the cramped tunnel. But I hear nothing; no one approaching, no sign that anyone has noticed my presence or Jedediah's absence. I'm listening so carefully that a sudden noise makes me jump. It takes me a few moments to realize what it is. Jedediah is...humming. Humming cheerfully under his breath like this is a pleasant stroll.

"Stop that," I hiss once I've shaken off my surprise, poking him in the back of the neck with my gun. He shuts up, but I swear I hear muffled chuckling.

At the end of the tunnel, I make him wait behind. I pause, my hands on the trapdoor, listening for any voices or footsteps outside. When I hear nothing, I push it open—first just a few inches so I can peer around, and fully when the area appears deserted.

The trapdoor scrapes against the bottom of the car above as I open it. I climb out and reach back to help Jedediah up. Thankfully he's a scrawny bastard, and easy enough to pull upward. I move on my hands and knees to the other side of the vehicle, and glance around once more before dragging Jedediah out and pulling him to his feet. He coughs on dust, frowning, unable to wipe himself off after the drag through the dirt. I almost smile at the look on his face, but stifle it, reminding myself I'm still not in the clear.

Outside of Jedediah's mansion, which towers like a lone giant among the other buildings, Wormwood is much like every other town—dreary, dusty, on the verge of falling apart. It's quiet, perhaps a little too quiet, the doors all shut and the people sealed away. I guess Jedediah's crew keeps a tight watch over this place. I'm careful to keep quiet myself, creeping along with Jedediah ahead of me. He trips over a discarded car door, and a loud *clang* echoes through the scrapyard. I pull him back and freeze, but the town remains silent around us.

My truck is parked a few minutes' walk away, hidden behind a decrepit building on the outskirts of town. I'm careful to stay behind crumbling walls and old buildings that seem unoccupied. The goal is to secure Jedediah and be out of Wormwood before his crew notices anything is wrong. But if I fail, I'll have dozens of angry, heavily armed raiders hot on my trail.

Thankfully Jedediah is quiet at the moment, and still cooperating. Probably a smart move, because right now I'm so jumpy that I very well might shoot him, intentionally or not, if he startled me. The night is still and calm, no sound other than our footsteps and my own heartbeat in my ears. I push Jedediah forward, gun never leaving his head. I know better than to underestimate him, despite how accommodating he's being about his own kidnapping.

Voices ahead.

I grab Jedediah's arm, yanking him back and dropping to a crouch. He lands on his ass beside me with a thump, a burst of dust, and a muffled groan of complaint. When he notices the voices, he turns sharply in that direction. There are at least two men, and they're moving this way.

Pulling Jedediah with me, I straighten up and move to a nearby building, pressing myself against it. I wait, holding my breath, wondering if the men heard us. But their conversation sounds casual, their pace leisurely. They don't seem to suspect that anything is wrong; they're just patrolling the area.

Ordinarily I wouldn't hesitate to take down two unsuspecting men, but I can't afford to raise a ruckus. And if I try to sneak by, I don't trust that Jedediah's compliant attitude will hold up with help just a shout away. Is this why he's been so smug and unconcerned? Did he know we would run into one of his patrols on the way out? I turn to him, my lips pressed into a firm line. He's staring in the direction of his men, his eyes narrowed as if carefully considering something, his muscles tense. He looks ready...for something. To run, to fight, to make a sound to attract their attention.

He looks over at me as he notices I'm staring, and his eyes widen, as if he can see my intention. He tries to say something, his words unintelligible through the gag.

I deck him with one good punch.

VI
The Sale of Jedediah Johnson

Halfway through the process of dragging an unconscious Jedediah to my truck, I almost regret my decision to knock him out. But, if I'm being honest, the satisfaction of my fist hitting his face was more than enough to make up for the annoyance. I really do try my best not to be overly sadistic while working, but this is Jedediah Johnson. Even setting the personal vendetta aside, I've heard more than enough stories about the things he's done. If I hadn't personally witnessed the results of his dictatorship, I would've thought he was an urban legend. But portions of hard-earned goods disappearing every month, people stolen in the middle of the night, rebellious towns burned to the ground—those are real, and they all have one name whispered in their wake: *Jedediah Johnson.*

I have about a thousand reasons to put a bullet in this man's head. Luckily for him, there's one very important reason not to. Like the informant said, no one will believe me if I lug in a body and claim it's Jedediah Johnson, considering no one knows his face. His men could easily cover up the death, since he spends his time holed up here anyway—and even if the information did eventually get out, by that time my name would be long forgotten. I'm staking everything on this. I need people to know it was me. I need to be the woman who freed the eastern wastes.

And with Jedediah unconscious, there's no one to stop me from getting away with it. The patrol is relaxed, noisy, and easy to avoid even when I'm weighed down by a body. I make it to my truck without trouble, tie Jedediah up, and throw him in the backseat.

"Damn easy job," I mutter to myself with a smile, and start up my truck.

With that done, I ride toward freedom. First slow and steady, so I don't attract unwanted attention from the residents of Wormwood. But as soon as I pass the outskirts of town, I pick up speed, gradually and then suddenly, and grin at the roar of my truck's engine and the thought of what's to come. Soon, very soon, everything is going to change for me.

I'd be hard-pressed to find someone that *doesn't* want Jedediah's head, but Alex the Collector is where I started this journey, so I show up at his door. It's the middle of the night, and his guard seems wary about seeing me again so soon, but they let me in when I show them I'm bringing in a mark.

Alex holds a lantern up to the crack in the door, providing a sliver of flickering light in the darkness. His thinning hair is in disarray, his eyes bloodshot.

"Well, well, Clementine. Back so soon?" He eyes me, and then the unconscious man I'm dragging behind me, raising his lantern to get a better look. "Who's this?"

"Open up and I'll tell you," I say. He licks his lips, peers around for any sign of someone following me, and lets me inside.

I drag Jedediah into the room, past the shelves of souvenirs. I note Beau the Butcher's knife already displayed in all its rusty glory. Next to it is another new souvenir, a freshly severed hand from a raider named Left-Hand. It makes me wonder what he'll take from Jedediah. I smile slightly at the thought.

I drop Jedediah and continue to the far wall. This one doesn't have collectibles, but is instead covered in current wanted posters. The lantern light flickers across names and sketched faces.

"So, who have you brought me?" Alex asks as he locks the door behind us. "I don't recognize him."

"Few people would," I say. I can feel his questioning eyes on the back of my head. I find the poster I'm looking for, the one that has nothing but a silhouette and a question mark where a sketch would normally be. I'm not the best reader, but this name is so imprinted in my brain that I recognize it immediately. I rip the poster off the wall and turn around, holding it up for Alex, a broad grin on my face.

Alex raises the lantern to get a better look. He stares at the poster for a long few moments, and then at me, and then at the unconscious, dusty man sprawled out on his floor.

"Jedediah Johnson?" he asks. He takes several hasty steps away from the man, and shakes his head so violently I swear I hear his jowls flapping. "No," he says. "No way."

"It's him, all right," I say. "Your informant's tip sent me right to him."

Jedediah stirs. The timing is so convenient that it occurs to me maybe he wasn't actually unconscious, but just waiting for the proper moment to step into the conversation. Alex jumps back like the man is a snake uncoiling on his floor. Jedediah's eyes open slowly. They land first on Alex, who stares back in utter terror. One eyebrow rises. When his gaze sweeps over the shelves of souvenirs, the other eyebrow rises to join it. Then he sees me, and both eyebrows lower again.

"Mmmpfff," he says, wiggling.

"What's he saying?" Alex asks in a loud whisper, refusing to take his eyes off him. His usual excitement over a bounty has shifted into the deep fear he normally reserves for the world outside. It seems I've brought a piece of the wastes a little too big for him to handle. "Was that . . . a threat?"

"I don't know or care," I say. Jedediah shoots me an offended look, which I ignore. "Look, do we have a deal or not?"

Alex chews his fingernails, finally tearing his eyes away from Jedediah and turning to me. He sizes me up and makes a non-committal noise in the back of his throat.

"I want to hear what he has to say," Alex says.

"I doubt that," I say.

"Gag off, or no deal. I want to know what I'm getting myself into."

I know this is a bad idea, but I can't do much when my customer is making a demand. I sigh, step closer to Jedediah, and yank my handkerchief out of his mouth, letting it fall to the ground. He sighs contentedly and leans his head back to look up at me.

"Wow," he says, his voice earnestly impressed. "You throw a hell of a punch."

"More where that came from," I say, eyeing him in case he decides to try something. But he seems as mellow as before, apparently unconcerned by where he is and what's happening. He grins at me, but as he turns toward Alex, the smile disappears. The Collector takes a step back. Jedediah stares silently.

"What's he doing?" Alex whispers, looking to me for answers. I shrug.

"I'm deciding how I'll kill you when I'm free," Jedediah says brightly. "Alex the Collector. I've heard of you. And now I'll know exactly how to find—" I step forward and give him a swift kick to the gut to stop him from saying anything else, but the damage is done. Alex lets out a sound like a wounded animal, his hand-wringing accelerating to light speed. I sigh and brush hair out of my face.

"Alex, he's—"

"No," he says. "No, no, no. I can't do it. He's too dangerous."

"You're the one who sent me to the informant," I remind him. "Now you're saying you're not going to pay out?"

"I didn't know she would send you to Jedediah fucking Johnson! I was just the middleman!"

"You—"

"I can't, Clementine." He throws up a hand to stop me from continuing, his voice growing firm. "Think about what you're asking me. You're asking me to take *Jedediah Johnson* off your hands, in an area ruled by the *crew* of Jedediah Johnson. Do you see the problem?"

"Yes," I say, grudgingly. "I'm not an idiot." I take a long look at Jedediah, who is still groaning after my kick, and back at Alex. "What if I only take half the bounty, to make up for potential trouble?"

"Not happening."

"A third."

"I'm not getting anywhere near this, Clementine," he says. "I wouldn't do it if *you* paid *me*."

I pinch the bridge of my nose. My dreams of adoration for this catch are quickly slipping out from between my fingers.

"Why offer a bounty if I can't cash it in?" I ask.

"No one thought it was possible to just waltz in and take him!" Alex says, throwing his hands up. "I thought the only way this would happen was if his whole crew was taken out, or he lost his position, or... I... I don't know. But I didn't expect... *this.*"

My heart sinks. Alex is right to be concerned about Jedediah's crew showing up on his doorstep, whether it be before or after we deal with Jedediah for good. Still, I never thought a collector would be so afraid that they'd turn him down. I think back to the way the townies stared at me when I asked if they wanted to kill Beau the Butcher, and shake my head. Every time I start to think I understand people, they surprise me with new depths of cowardice.

I look down at Jedediah, who has recovered from the kick and is now humming under his breath while waiting for us to finish talking. I sigh, shift from foot to foot, put my hand on the gun at my hip. The feel of it beneath my hand is reassuring. But I see Alex eyeing me nervously as he notices me gripping it, and force myself to remove my hand and place it on my hip instead.

"So what am I supposed to do with him, then?" I ask, finally admitting to him as well as to myself that I have absolutely no idea where to go from here. I doubt I'll have luck with any other collectors. With anyone other than Alex, it'd be a real pain in the ass just to prove that this is the man I claim it is—and even if they believed me, they could turn me away. I can't just keep dragging Jedediah around. His crew will catch up to me eventually. Do I kill him, cut my losses, and be done with it? It would be satisfying, sure, but... I'd get nothing out of it. I'm not sure I could live with the knowledge I was so close to everything I'd ever wanted, and let it slip away.

Alex looks like he wants to throw me out in the dust here and now. But maybe he sees the desperation in my expression, because a few moments later his face softens.

"Look, Clementine," he says. "It's suicide for me to get involved in this, and you're not gonna have any more luck with anyone else in the area. But maybe you could reach a little further, past where people are so afraid of this guy."

I drum my fingers on the butt of my gun.

"Turn in his bounty somewhere else?" I ask. "All my contacts are here."

Alex licks his lips, looking at Jedediah and back at me. I wait silently. After a few moments, he sighs and nods.

"Follow me," he says, and walks into the back room. I make sure Jedediah's bonds are secure before following.

The back room is small, musty, and windowless. I've never

been allowed back here before, but there's not much to look at. Just a ratty cot in the corner, where the Collector must sleep, and a wooden, half-broken desk and chair. The desk is piled with outdated wanted posters and other papers. I'm not a strong enough reader to get any information out of them at a glance, and a glance is all I get before Alex steps between me and the desk. He sets the lantern down on it, leans over, and rummages through one of the drawers. He plucks something out and places it atop the mess on the desk.

"A radio?" I ask, glancing over at him. "Didn't know anyone used these anymore."

"They usually don't," he says. "I'd just fiddle with it occasionally, for fun. But then I started picking up something." He scrounges around on his desk until he finds a particular piece of paper, and holds it up. "A broadcast. A real one, a nightly one, always the same guy, who calls himself 'Saint.' It was a long spiel, mostly a lot of blah-blah-blah about justice and taking the wastes back. He's got a radio tower, and the towns love him. He's been gaining a lot of power off to the west of us."

"The western wastes?" I ask incredulously. "He wants to take back the *western* wastes?" I doubt that's even possible, but more importantly... "What the hell does this have to do with me?" Alex can go over-the-top with the theatrics sometimes, and I'm painfully aware of every passing minute, another minute that Jedediah's crew could be coming for me.

"Well," Alex says. "His whole deal is that he's capturing sharks. Er, getting other people to capture them, really—the townies and such bring them to him, and he gives out rewards in return. The idea is to clean up his area of the wastes, but I'm sure he wouldn't complain about getting a famous raider from over here either."

"Huh," I say, processing the information. Sounds like the same idea as bounties, but on a larger scale. Jedediah probably isn't the type of person this Saint guy is expecting to get. He and his crew aren't like raiders in the rest of the wastes. They were once the same—loose cannons making a living off raiding towns, killing and looting, preying on the weak. Now Jedediah and his men have moved on to organized tyranny. No point in random raids when the towns are all under the thumb of the self-proclaimed ruler. But, though the west has never seen anything like him, Jedediah *is* a shark, and a raider, and most definitely a menace. If Saint is really trying to do some good for the wastes, surely he won't turn me away.

"What does he do with the sharks?" I ask.

"Supposedly, he holds trials, and executes the ones he finds guilty."

I let out a huff of air.

"Trials," I say. "What's the point?"

Alex shrugs, setting the paper down on his desk.

"Dunno, but that isn't your problem, is it? You hand over Jedediah, you get a nice reward, and the business is over with."

I rub my thumb over the handle of my gun, considering. The reward would have to be a pretty damn sizeable one to make it worth a trip to the western wastes. Things are shitty here, with a madman in charge demanding monthly tithes, and public executions of everyone who defies him, and his crew doing whatever the hell they want. But at least we have safe trade routes, and a reasonable attempt at a currency system, and rules—even if those rules are defined by a dictator. When people are killed, it's usually for a purpose: profit, or punishment, or power. The townies get the roughest of it, but for someone like me who's skilled enough to live outside of the rules, life isn't so bad.

From what I've heard, the west has none of the structure we have out here. They say it's completely out of control, a cluster-fuck of mindless violence. It's so overrun with raiders and crazies that whenever a bounty runs that way, we usually just check them off as dead and gone. Still, I've always admired the place. It may be utter chaos, but it's also utter freedom. A place where you have a chance to be anything you want. Where you fight tooth and nail to survive, but at least you have a chance to fight.

A place without the tyranny of Jedediah...yet also without any aspect of the life I've always known. Things may not be great here, but at least they're familiar. Without bounties to hunt and towns I know, who would I become? Part of me has always wanted to find out, and part of me has always feared it. Either way, there's always been too much work to be done over here. Bounties to collect, raiders to hunt, townies to save. Since I lost everything five years ago, I've let my life revolve around my job. Hatred and hunger are enough to keep me pushing forward. I've tried to keep everything else at bay, including that distant but nagging desire to be something more than an outsider again.

But now...if I could save the eastern wastes *and* take a shot at someplace new, all in one...there's so much possibility. And maybe the west could be better for me. Maybe it's a place I'd actually fit in, a place where people wouldn't stare at me with fear in their eyes. Especially if I show up to hand an infamous dictator over to this Saint man, whom all the towns love...

"You're sure this is legit?" I ask.

"I've got mostly rumors and word of mouth to go by, but all the news from the west says he's either a good guy, or doing a damn good job of pretending to be." He shrugs. "At the very least, you can be confident that you'll get paid."

I nod, folding my arms over my chest.

"So. Heading west," I say. "I'm going to need a map, gasoline, some basic supplies."

"I've got whatever you need," Alex says. "But what will you trade?"

I can see his greedy little eyes light up, probably already imagining one of my precious guns hanging on his wall. The mere thought makes me sick to my stomach, and anyway, my guns and ammo are essentials. You never know how much you're going to need for a trip like this, especially since I'm going to be traveling through the crazy-ass western wastes.

Unfortunately, though, I only have one other thing to give him.

VII
Across the Wastes

The truck is a liability, I tell myself as I hand the keys over to
Alex. Anyone looking for me could recognize it, and such a
nice vehicle sticks out like a sore thumb in the wastes. I push
away memories of years spent behind that wheel, of nights
spent sleeping in the backseat, and instead focus on the stash of
goods I'm getting in return: a map to Saint, water and canned
food, some gasoline, and a new vehicle.

The car I'm downgrading to is a small, shoddy thing, its
chipped brown paint barely distinguishable from the rust. It
looks like it won't make it five miles, but Alex swears up and
down that it will get me where I need to go. I'm not too keen
on trusting people, but I don't have much of a choice here. So
I transfer my stuff from the truck bed to the trunk of the new
car—water, food, bandages, and all of my guns and ammo.
Grabbing the last armful of goods, I give my truck a pat on the
hood, the only sentimental gesture I allow myself. After I dump
the goods into the trunk and slam it shut, I head back inside.

Jedediah is lying on the floor where I left him, now resting
on his side and snoring loudly. He looks way more comfortable
than he has any right to be. I resist the urge to kick him again,
find a spot against the wall for myself, and doze off.

I catch a few hours of sleep on Alex's floor, just enough to keep me going, and wake up automatically at the crack of dawn. I re-gag a still-mostly-asleep Jedediah with my handkerchief, drag him out to the passenger seat of the new car, and start it up.

The engine comes to life with a pitiful whine, and the entire vehicle shakes and shudders and rattles like it's going to come apart at any second. Wind whistles through a crack in the window, and the interior smells faintly of piss. But despite all appearances, the thing *does* run. So, with a wave at Alex's guard, I take to the road.

The first few hours pass without incident. I'm enjoying the feeling of being on the open road, and reveling in the knowledge that every mile of wasteland is a mile between me and Jedediah's crew. I know that I'm heading into lands full of their own danger. Surely though, it'll be different for me. I'm a bounty hunter. A professional. I've spent my whole life killing raiders. There may be more of them in the west, but they can't be any worse than they are here.

For the start of the ride, Jedediah dozes in his seat, head resting against the window. When he finally wakes up, I have a sinking feeling that my peaceful morning is about to be over. He soon proves me right. He starts with some muffled noises and squirming in his seat, which is easy enough to disregard. Then he progresses to kicking the windshield, which I can't afford to ignore. Sighing, I turn sharply—throwing him half out of his seat—and pull over. I get out, march over to his side, and yank his door open. He tumbles into the dirt.

"What's your problem?" I ask, placing a boot on his chest. He lets out a string of words that are entirely unintelligible through the gag. I grimace and grudgingly remove the handkerchief from his mouth.

Jedediah stretches his jaw, licks his lips, and clears his throat.

"I'd like," he says in a raspy voice, "a drink of water."

I roll my eyes, removing my boot from his chest.

"That's it?" I ask. I thought he had finally realized his life was in danger, and intended to do something about it, but this is much better. I leave him in the dirt and grab my canteen from the trunk. Luckily I have a few big jugs of water left—I would never be stupid enough to travel the wastes without them—so I don't have to be *too* frugal.

I'm not entirely sure what the west will bring, or how long it will last, but I'm as prepared as possible. Alex said it would take about two days of travel to get to Saint's tower, but that's assuming I don't hit any major obstacles along the way, like angry townies, or raiders, or crazies. But whatever comes along, I'll be ready. I have enough food and water for more than a week, and plenty of ammo to mow down anyone who gets in my way.

I take a swig of water before walking over to Jedediah and pressing the container to his lips. He takes several big, greedy gulps, and I tear the canteen away.

"A little more?" he asks, licking the remnants off his lips.

"That's more than enough to last you the whole day," I say, screwing the top onto the canteen and tossing it into my seat. Clearly, this guy has grown accustomed to a life of luxury. He might've once been a raider, but he's had goods hand delivered to him for years now. Guess he's forgotten what it's like to be out in the wastes.

I move to place the gag back in his mouth, but he ducks aside. I smack him upside the head and try to gag him again, but he shifts the other way. I sigh. "Oh, come on," I say. "Don't tell me you decided to be difficult *now.*"

"Is the gag really necessary?" he asks, his neck craned to keep his face as far from me as possible. "It's gonna be a long ride. We can talk!"

"I have no desire to talk to you."

"I'd be a lot happier without the gag," he says.

"I don't c—"

"And a lot more likely to continue cooperating," he adds. When I scrutinize him, he smiles.

I suppose a drive with Jedediah occasionally speaking *would* be much better than a drive with him trying to escape. I could always tie him up and throw him in the back, but I'd rather keep him in my sight. He may be mostly acting like a cheeky little shit, but I'm not going to underestimate him. There's a mad genius in there, somewhere beneath the smiles and the sass. It's impossible to tell what he's thinking, but at least I can keep an eye on him.

"Fine," I say. "But I won't hesitate to knock your ass out again. Got it?"

"Crystal clear."

Jedediah seems content to look out the window and hum under his breath, occasionally asking a question, which I respond to with short, clipped answers while keeping my eyes on the road. He stretches himself out in his seat, putting his shoes up on the dashboard and leaning his seat back, getting about as comfortable as a man with his wrists bound in front of him can get.

"My crew didn't kill your father or something, did they?" he asks, after staring out the window for a while.

"What?" I ask, startled by the question.

"Brother? Sister? Mother? Oh, jeez, I really hope we didn't kill your mom. That would be awkward," he says. He pauses while I struggle to process what he's asking me. "...Husband?"

"No," I lie, keeping my eyes fixed on the road ahead.

"Do you even have a husband to kill? Er...that came out wrong. Ignore everything after 'husband.'" He pauses, but continues after I open my mouth and shut it again. "Or wife. Life partner? Anything like—"

"That's really none of your business," I say once I've finally gathered myself. I catch myself grinding my jaw and force myself to stop. I can't let him get to me.

"Right. Anyway. Very relieved to hear that I haven't killed anyone close to you," he says, looking out the window again. "We get a few of those every so often, showing up at the Wormwood mansion. Lots of yelling and tears. 'You killed my mother! Prepare to die!' Etcetera. Very dramatic."

"I think that comes with the territory," I say dryly.

"What territory?"

"Being a complete fucking psychopath."

"Hey now," he says, in a voice like I've offended him terribly. "You kill people too."

My back stiffens at the gratingly familiar words. I've seen the way townies look at me, heard the things they say. Sometimes it seems like they don't think I'm any better than the people I'm killing. And they have no idea how many people I choose *not* to kill—how many I'd really like to, if not for my personal rules.

"It's different," I say eventually.

"How so?"

"I only kill assholes like you," I say. For a moment I flash back to words my old sheriff once said about me—*She's a weapon. We've just got to make sure she's pointed in the right direction.* But, like I did back then, I tell myself that's not an issue. I know the difference between good people and bad.

"Ah," he says. "So it's okay as long as they're a worse person than you are?" He says it almost teasingly. I tighten my grip on the steering wheel.

"I'm not going to discuss morals with a cannibalistic tyrant," I say. That shuts him up, giving me several seconds of blissful silence. Then he starts mumbling under his breath.

I know I shouldn't ask, but I can't help myself. I take my eyes off the road to glance over, and find him with a deeply thoughtful expression.

"What are you muttering about?"

"Tyrannical cannibal," he says, answering overly quickly,

like he's been waiting impatiently for me to ask. "You should've gone with that over 'cannibalistic tyrant.' Sounds a lot better, doesn't it? Tyrannical cannibal. Rolls nicely off the tongue."

I sigh. Whatever goes on in that fucked-up brain of his, clearly nothing I say is going to get past the layer of crazy. Not that it matters; he'll be dead soon, and I'll be a hero, and these pointless conversations will fade from my mind.

I stay silent while he repeats "tyrannical cannibal" to himself several more times, in varying tones and pitches, before finally shutting up.

I shoot down his further attempts at conversation, and we drive through the day in silence, aside from the rattling of the car and Jedediah's humming, which comes and goes every couple of minutes. At first, we pass by a town every few hours, which makes it easy to check our progress on the map. These are all the towns under Jedediah's reign, and he perks up at the sight of each one, loudly announcing its name as if I wouldn't know. "That's Sunrise!" "Buzzard's Beak!" "Last Stand!" He's like a little kid seeing his first meal in a week. Then again, I guess the towns *are* pretty much meals to the man who demands a tithe from each one.

As we get farther out, the sky gets darker, and the towns get sparser, and Jedediah gets even more excited to see each new one.

"Hey, there's Old Creek!" he says happily as he sees the latest one—one of the last before we hit the somewhat official border of the eastern wastes, the end of the area claimed by Jedediah and his crew. "There was never a creek there. I don't know why they named it that."

The name sends an immediate and involuntary shudder through my body. I don't need to look to know what I'll find, but I do it anyway. There's no town—not anymore. Just the husks of old buildings, melted and blackened by the fire that scorched the place to the ground almost five years ago. As with most tragedies, there was one name whispered in the aftermath. Unlike others, this one I don't need to rely on rumors to know about.

"Shut the fuck up," I say, struggling to keep my voice level as a wave of revulsion rises inside me. "Right now." He looks at me, eyebrows rising as if surprised by the reaction. I turn to glare at him, and in doing so, show the left side of my face again. His eyes land on the burns, and he pauses.

"Oh," he says.

One of my hands automatically moves from the wheel to my gun, and for a moment I can clearly imagine pulling it out and putting a bullet between Jedediah's eyes. Or maybe in his knees first—something slow and painful, something I could really relish.

But no. I can't. Killing him now would get me nothing; personal satisfaction isn't good enough.

I take a deep breath and slowly remove my hand from the gun, forcing myself to tear my eyes away from the man nonchalantly talking about the town he burned to the ground. At least he has the good sense to be quiet now, watching the burnt remains of Old Creek fade into the distance.

When I look away from him and glance at the mirror to my side, I notice it: a cloud of dust on the horizon. Behind us, and gaining fast. I squint at the rearview mirror, watch it getting closer. It could be a dust storm...a very fast, very deliberately moving dust storm. But I know it's not.

We're being followed.

"What's that?" Jedediah asks, noticing the approaching cloud at about the same time I do. My pulse rising, I press harder on the pedal. It coaxes a little more speed out of this shitty car, but not enough. Not nearly enough.

"Shut up," I say. "Stay low." I don't check to see if he's obeying, too busy glancing between the road ahead and the road behind. I can't see the vehicle clearly enough yet. Is it Jedediah's crew behind me, on my trail already? But *how*? Surely they couldn't have already determined that I left the area and headed this way. Unless Alex sold me out...

I grit my teeth and keep driving.

"Bet you're missing your truck right about now," Jedediah says.

"Shut. Up."

I press the pedal to the floor. The car shudders violently, rattling every bone in my body, and chugs along at a slightly faster rate. It's enough to pull ahead for just a few moments, so our pursuer disappears from sight. And I see something else that sparks an idea: a heap of junk alongside the road, what looks to be the remains of two cars after a wreck.

I swerve off the road, drawing a startled yelp out of Jedediah, and drive right up alongside the metal carcasses. I kill the engine and yank Jedediah down with me.

Without the grumbling of the engine and the rattling of the car's frame, it's very quiet. I sit, silent, listening. I hold my breath as I hear the vehicle approaching, wondering if the ploy will work. It's a gamble: a gamble that whoever is following me will be looking for my big truck rather than this shitty car, and a gamble that this piece of junk will pass off as a literal piece of junk.

The roar of the engine becomes nearly overwhelming, until I'm sure our pursuer is about to smash into us. My hand seeks the handle of my gun, and I grip it tightly, my eyes fixed on the window though I can see nothing outside. Then comes the blinding shine of headlights, growing brighter and brighter and then—gone. Past us.

I let out a long, slow breath as the roar of the vehicle recedes. Once the sound is completely gone I sit up, releasing my gun.

"Phew," Jedediah says, struggling to sit up himself. "That was a close one, huh? Who do you think it was?"

Ignoring him, I drum my fingers on the wheel. I could keep

driving, but I'd run the risk of encountering whomever that was again, and it's definitely not worth the risk of using headlights in the dark now that I know we're not alone out here. Better to stop now, catch a few hours of sleep. Hopefully, by then, that car will be long gone.

Sleeping with a prisoner in tow is a new experience for me. I never hang on to a mark longer than necessary. Usually I'd keep working right through the night, but the journey ahead is too long for that. Which brings up a new issue: what to do with Jedediah overnight.

I could leave him in the passenger seat, but that would run the risk of him escaping his binds and killing me in my sleep. I could throw him outside, but he might try to run. We're in the awkward no-man's-land between the eastern and western towns, so there's nothing but empty wastes for miles all around, but he hasn't shown much of a sense of self-preservation so far. So, I can't let him kill me or get himself killed. That leaves only one option.

After a lot of squirming and pleading, Jedediah is safely tied, gagged, blindfolded, and stuffed into the trunk. I made sure to tie him up even more tightly than before, wrists and arms and ankles, just to make sure he doesn't get any bright ideas. I move my gun bag from the trunk to the backseat to make doubly sure. After I lock him in, there's some jostling and bumping for about ten minutes, but finally he quiets down. I curl up in the backseat, taking my gun out of its holster and cradling it against my chest.

It's unsettling, knowing that an infamous killer will be just a few yards away while I sleep. But it doesn't matter. I'm not afraid, I tell myself. Jedediah Johnson may be a different breed, but he's still a raider, and I'm not afraid of raiders.

VIII
Poachers

A sound wakes me before dawn. My gun is in my hand before I even open my eyes. I swing it one way and then the other, searching for the source of the mysterious thumping, and then realize it's coming from the trunk. Right—Jedediah. Not danger, just an inconvenience. I sigh, placing my gun back in its holster, and rub my eyes. I could've used another hour of sleep, but I'm awake now, so I might as well get an early start.

It's tempting to leave Jedediah in the trunk, where I don't have to deal with the constant stream of shit coming out of his mouth, but I'm sure he'll find some way to get free or injure himself if I continue to leave him unsupervised. In fact, it's possible that he's already done so, so I take out my gun again as I head to the trunk. But Jedediah is still tied up neatly, and looking very unhappy about having spent the night crammed into the small space. I check to make sure the ropes on his wrists haven't loosened, and drag him up to the front seat. I remove the gag to give him a quick drink of water, and put it back again despite his protests.

"Give me an hour to wake up," I say. "If you behave yourself, I'll take the gag out then."

He nods—surprisingly agreeable, but given the dark rings under his eyes, he's probably just too tired to put up much resistance. Pleased with that, I get into my seat and start driving. Jedediah soon nods off, his head lolling against the back of the seat. I resist the petty urge to make him less comfortable, reminding myself that him sleeping means I get peace and quiet.

The road is still dark, but not too dark to see, the wastes tinged with the bluish light of almost-dawn. I relax as I drive, expecting a good few hours of nothingness before we hit the western towns and the day really begins.

That peace is quickly ruined as I see something on the horizon. I slow down, squinting at the column of smoke. My stomach clenches at the thought of fire, but I force myself to move closer. It soon becomes clear that it's not a wildfire, or a burning town, but a small, personal blaze. A campfire. No one in their right mind sets a campfire, unless they're fully confident that they can kill anyone who sees it, so I'm wary as I approach. I kill the engine and roll to a stop a good distance away, make sure Jedediah is still asleep, and rustle through my bag in the backseat. I fish out a pair of binoculars and study the camp.

There are two figures by the fire. One is stretched out on the ground, likely sleeping. The other is sitting upright, but looks relaxed, not fully alert. I watch them for several long moments, trying to gauge who they are and what they want—and then I spot their vehicle parked nearby. A rusty old truck, that was once green from the look of it. Not black, like the ones Jedediah's raiders drive.

This must be the vehicle that was following me. Very few people have reason to travel on these open roads, the stretch of nothingness between Jedediah's lands and the wild towns in the west. It's rare that anyone has the means or a strong enough reason to travel from one to the other, and there's absolutely nothing of interest in between. The only reason for somebody to be out here is if they're on the run, or looking for someone... and I have a sneaking suspicion that these people are looking for me. But if they're not working for Jedediah, why are they after me?

Now is a good opportunity to find out.

I check on Jedediah again—still sleeping—and gather my weapons. My brain is already forming a plan of attack, the old instinct bubbling up: *Kill.* The thought rises to a clamor as I load my guns, making sure my trusty pistol is full of ammo, slinging a rifle over my back, and grabbing an extra pistol just in case.

There are only two of them, not expecting trouble. They must still think they're following me, and won't expect me to come from behind. It would be easy to kill them both, no matter how prepared they think they are. But it's not that simple. I have rules, rules that set me apart from the people I hunt.

My ma and I made them together when I was ten. I had killed five and a half people by that time, and the "half" was the reason the rules came to be. He was a man who came to town half-dead, begging for water. I couldn't decide if he looked like a raider or not in the sorry state he was in, but he was a stranger looking to take what was ours, so I opted for caution. I beat his head in with a cast-iron pot we used to make stew. When my ma asked why I did that, I said, "I didn't have my gun on me."

That night, when they thought I was asleep, I overheard her talking with the sheriff when he stopped by to visit.

"She's a little girl," my mom said.

"She's not *just* a little girl," the sheriff said. "She's a weapon. We've just got to make sure she's pointed in the right direction."

That miffed me more than anything—the idea that I didn't know who to kill and who not to kill. Of course I knew. I didn't kill the sheriff when he shouted at me for eating too much, or old lady Brenda when she pinched my cheeks, though I couldn't say the idea hadn't occurred to me once or twice. I only killed the bad people. Raiders. Men and women who made a living preying on townies like us, who would come into town waving big guns and take whatever food and water they could find. That's what made me a hero. Everyone in town said so.

The next day, my ma sat me down with a pencil and dirty scrap of napkin and said, "Let's make a list."

I was never much good at reading and writing, but I was excited to practice back then, so it seemed like a good exercise. I asked what kind of list it would be, and my ma said it was a "No-Kill List." A list of people I would never kill, she explained. Even though I was good at killing people, and I never seemed to feel too bad about it, there had to be some people I didn't want to kill ever, right?

Right. I wrote "Ma" immediately. Under it I wrote "Pa." But, after a moment's thought, I erased that one.

"What'd you do that for?" Ma asked, her smile growing strained.

"Well," I said. "I'd never *want* to kill Pa, but I think I might, if I had to. If it was you or him, or me or him, I'd probably have to do it."

It seemed reasonable to me, so I smiled and handed back the paper with only one name, but my ma seemed concerned. So, she tore up the list and proposed a new plan: We would make rules about killing, just to make sure I didn't kill the wrong people by accident. I would only kill for necessity, and for profit.

It took me a lot of time, and one very big mistake, to realize why the rules were so important. After that, I vowed to never break them again.

Which is why, despite all my instincts screaming at me to do so, I don't ram my car into the camp, or snipe them from a distance, or charge in with my guns blazing. Instead, I approach the camp with the intention to talk.

Of course, I approach it as quietly and stealthily as possible, because getting shot on sight isn't conducive to having a decent conversation. And I'm not a goddamn idiot, so I still pull out my two pistols as I approach, keeping one leveled at each of their heads. By the time they notice me, I have them at my mercy.

And I realize, upon getting a better look, that I know exactly who these people are.

There are a lot of *off* folks in my line of work. Loners, weirdos, probably even a few psychopaths. I have no delusions about it, I know I'm definitely at home among them. But these two... these two are top-of-the-line freaks.

Cat and Bird. I'm sure at one point they must've had real names, but that's all anyone calls them anymore. Cat is tall and willowy, her skin so dark it's nearly black, her hair twisted into tight braids. She has stiff-as-a-board posture, a proud tilt to her chin. Despite a slender build, there's nothing delicate about her; she's all hard angles and lean muscle. Even in the act of standing up when she notices me, each movement is precise and controlled and deliberate, no energy or time wasted. She seems almost normal at first glance—pretty, even—until she smiles, displaying a pair of canines sharpened into points. From what I've heard, she likes to use them.

Bird, on the other hand, does some ungainly flailing and scrambling in the dust before climbing to her feet. She stands stone-still, except for a twitch every few seconds—first a tremble up her arm, then an odd jolt of her head, then a shift in her foot, like a bug is jumping around beneath her skin. Her body is wrapped in cloth, layers and layers of it stacked on top of one another and sewn together haphazardly, with flaps and scraps of fabric hanging off and fluttering around her. The top layer is a tattered, hooded brown cloak. Her patched-together outfit is all in shades of gray and brown, with an occasional deep red stain. She never seems to take off a layer, even when it's filthy or torn. Instead, she just sews up the tears and throws on more clothes to cover it. She wears dirty gloves, at least two scarves wrapped tightly around her neck, and a pair of oversized, bright red rain boots.

But the truly strange thing about her outfit is the mask. It's a gas mask, black and too big for her body. She peers at me now through the darkly tinted goggles, her head jerking one way and then the other.

Of all the people for me to run into, it had to be these creepy motherfuckers. Not only are the two unsettling, but their reputation is questionable at best...even among bounty hunters, which says a lot. Worse than that, we have history.

"Don't touch those guns," I say.

Cat meets my gaze steadily.

"Hi, Clementine," she says, staying very still. Out of the corner of my eye I see Bird shift. I turn to her, and she freezes, one hand halfway to a knife strapped to her leg. She jerks her head toward Cat, as if seeking guidance, jerks it back toward me, and flutters a hand at me in an awkward wave.

"Hands up," I say, and she immediately throws them skyward, her fingers twitching one by one. I keep my eye on her for a few seconds before slowly turning back to Cat. She meets my eyes and runs a tongue across her sharpened teeth.

"What are you doing out here?" I ask. Normally, seeing two fellow bounty hunters wouldn't be such a terrible thing. "Friendly" would be a stretch, but it's not like we're trying to kill each other...without reason.

"Nice to see you too," Cat says. "You're not still mad, are you?"

"No," I say flatly. If I was still mad, I would've gunned them down the moment I recognized them.

"Good," Cat says. "Because that was all a terribly unfortunate accident."

"Accident," Bird repeats in her muffled, high-pitched voice, mask bobbing up and down in a nod.

"Uh-huh." A terribly unfortunate accident where they stole a mark I had spent three *weeks* hunting down. While I was cutting through the bounty's men, they yanked her away and claimed the reward for themselves, later arguing that they just happened to be after the same person. "Now tell me what the fuck you're doing here."

Silence answers me. I lower my gun to point at Cat's leg.

"We're hunting," she says quickly. "Just like you, right? We're on the same side." She grins at me; it's a grin I don't like, too wide and toothy, made threatening by her sharpened teeth.

"Why are you following me?" I ask, not buying the bullshit excuse. There's no reason for them to be hunting this far out. I guess if anyone would be willing to chase bounties west it'd be these two assholes, but my gut tells me there's something else going on here. Or maybe I am still a little resentful about the last time they stole from me.

"Following you? Like I said, we're chasing a bounty," Cat says, with a casual shrug. "He fled this way."

I eye her, mentally chewing that answer. It's not completely unreasonable. Sometimes a bounty will run west if they know there's a price on their head and hunters on their heels. But still...

"Whose bounty?"

"Why should I tell you?" she asks, her eyes narrowing. "You'll just try to steal him."

"I'd say you've got bigger things to worry about right now," I say, gesturing with my gun. Cat exchanges a long look with Bird, who stares at her silently.

"Fine," she says. "We're after Left-Hand. Heard he fled this way."

"Oh," I say. "Left-Hand." I relax, rolling my shoulders back. "Well, that's a relief. I was almost worried you were going to say something feasible, and I'd have to think a little harder about what to do with you."

Too bad for her. I saw that name recently—right next to his famous, freshly severed hand on Alex's shelf. So I know it's a lie, and I know what a lie means: The only bounty she's after is the one I'm trying to claim. These two are damn poachers, trying to take my hard-earned reward for Jedediah. I don't know why Alex told them, or why they thought they could get the best of me, but none of that matters right now.

Cat's eyes widen, her mouth opening. I shoot before she gets a word out.

The bullet sinks into her leg, and she goes down with a shout. Bird flings herself at me. She slams into me with a surprising amount of force for her small size, and we both hit the dirt, my back slamming against the ground. I lose my hold on one of my guns, and quickly raise the other, but she pins my arm beneath her knee and renders it useless. I grab at her with my free hand, but my fingers come away with a scrap of filthy fabric. I can't get a good grip, or a good hit, with every inch of her protected by cloth or mask.

Bird grabs the knife off her leg and raises it. She brings it down, and I jerk aside. The blade sinks into the dirt just an inch from my head. She yanks it out and raises it again, and I grab her wrist with my free hand, grappling with her, my hand slipping on rotting cloth. I dig my nails in, trying desperately to get a hold—and when she jerks her hand away, her glove rips.

Bird freezes. She stares down at her hand, at the torn glove and the slivers of pale flesh showing through, as if she can't believe what she's seeing. Then she screams. She leaps off me, clutching her wrist like her hand has been severed. She runs across the camp, emitting a loud, high-pitched wail like a siren.

I climb to my feet, pointing my gun at Cat again. She has a gun in hand, but lowers it when she sees me aiming at her. She's swaying on her injured leg, a sheen of sweat on her forehead.

"Stop," I say, trying to hide my own shortness of breath. I

wait for her to move her hand away from her gun, then turn to Bird. The masked woman is kneeling in the dirt and has produced a roll of duct tape from her bag. As I watch, she wraps the tape around her hand, again and again and again. She continues until her skin is thoroughly hidden, and keeps going, rocking back and forth as she does it.

I return my aim to Cat, keeping my gun trained on her as I move to retrieve my other pistol from the ground. I keep that one pointed at Bird, though she doesn't even glance up. "In the spirit of respect among bounty hunters, I'm not going to kill you," I say. "But if you keep following me, you'll force my hand. Got it?" I look from one to the other. *"Got it?"* I prompt again, gesturing with both guns. Cat, her teeth bared, nods. Bird clutches her freshly taped-up hand to her chest and trembles.

Guess that's as good an answer as I'm going to get. I back away from the two poachers, keeping my eyes trained on them. Once I'm far enough away, I turn and walk briskly back to my car. I hop in, shut the door, and sigh with satisfaction. Letting people live always makes me feel so benevolent. I pause for a moment, basking in the feeling and listening to Jedediah snore, before starting up the car again.

IX
The Western Wastes

There's not much to see on the ride, just empty wastelands and a seemingly endless road, the monotony occasionally broken by a broken-down building or car. There are no signs of life in any of them, nor do I see anyone traveling by foot. Jedediah dozes in the passenger seat, still recovering from his night in the trunk. By the end of the day we're far from Jedediah's towns, and we should arrive at Saint's tower sometime tomorrow. Just one more day having to deal with this piece of shit.

Just when I'm starting to get excited about how close we are, we hit a roadblock. I slow as we approach. The road is covered by junk, heaps of trash and twisted metal covering the entire width of it, forming an almost-solid barrier about six feet high. I roll to a stop. These kinds of blocks can easily be traps. With my truck I would ram right through, and hopefully take out a couple waiting raiders in the process, but there's no way this shitty little car can handle it.

As I'm thinking, the gunfire starts.

Raiders pour out from behind the barrier, three on each side. Only two of them have guns, which they fire wildly at the car; the rest run straight at us, shouting and swinging blunt weapons. I duck my head, slam on the gas, and turn the wheel sharply. The car rams right into two of the approaching raiders, sending one of them rolling over the windshield and crushing the other beneath my tires. The car whines and shudders, but keeps going. I drive out into the wastes, leaving the raiders and their guns behind.

I'm not sure whether this thing is equipped to handle off-roading, but I don't have a choice. There's no way to know how much of the road those raiders have claimed as theirs, so it's best to avoid it. Luckily, the wastes here are flat and empty. The car rumbles along; it's a bumpy ride, but it holds together, and seems undamaged other than some bullet holes in the windshield.

"Ooh," Jedediah says, sitting up in the passenger seat with his eyes bright. "What an adventure."

I suppress a sigh. As if I didn't have enough to deal with.

Our path is much more difficult to trace without a road to follow on the map. After driving for a couple hours, and taking additional detours to avoid possibly occupied buildings and trash heaps, I find myself uncertain of our location. I keep the map stretched out across the dashboard and continue glancing at it, but there are no landmarks to look for. Just flat, empty wastes, nothing but occasional shells of buildings.

After almost an hour of total uncertainty, I see a town on the horizon. I slow down, tracing a finger across the map. Based on our approximate location, there are two options: This town is either Lefton or Bramble. I gnaw my lower lip, considering my options—but really, there aren't any feasible ones other than stopping. I've heard towns around here can be rough, wary, even worse than the east. But I'm sure it's nothing I can't handle.

"What's this?" Jedediah asks when we stop, craning his neck to look out the window one way and then the other, finally focusing on the town ahead. "Are we here?"

I ignore him, shutting off the engine.

"We're stopping?" he asks. For the first time, something like alarm crosses his face. "Here? A town? Are you sure that's a good idea?"

I'm not. I've heard that western towns can be just as dangerous as raider crews. But I need to find out where we are, make sure we're headed in the right direction.

I get out of the car and move around to grab Jedediah. I'm tempted to throw him into the trunk while I'm in town, but I'll probably need to get in there for supplies if the townies want to trade. Bringing him along still tied up could lead to some unwanted attention… but I definitely don't trust him free. I settle for gagging him again, despite his protests. He digs his heels into the dirt, but I'm more than strong enough to drag him along behind me.

"The townies will stone you to death if they know who you are," I say as we approach. "So I'd suggest laying low."

At the edge of town, we're greeted by three men armed with shotguns. I resist the urge to grab my own gun, though my mind is busily calculating how to survive this if it comes to a gunfight. I could always use Jedediah as a meat shield, though that would make the whole trip here pointless. Better to avoid violence, if possible.

I stop and raise both hands in the air. It's almost physically painful to move my hand away from my gun, but I do it, banking on the bet that the townies won't shoot me unprompted. It's a risky bet, especially in the western wastes, but I don't have many choices.

"Who're you?" one man barks at us. "What d'you want?"

"We're lost," I say. "Want to know where we are."

The townies look at each other, exchanging shrugs, but nobody lowers their gun.

"Got no business with strangers," one says, gesturing with the barrel of his shotgun back at my car. "Get goin'."

I sigh, lowering my hands and rolling back my shoulders. I guess townies are the same no matter where you are.

"Tell me one thing and I'll go. Is this Bramble or Lefton?"

They continue scowling at me, not relaxing their holds on their guns.

Goddamn townies and their fear of outsiders. I can't blame them, especially in this area of the wastes, but this is ridiculous. My pride won't allow me to turn and leave without getting *something*. But how can I get them to trust an outsider?

That's when it hits me.

"You guys heard of a man named Saint?" I ask. Hopefully Alex's information was good, and this place isn't too backwater and isolated to know who he is. The three men squint at me, but the one in the middle lowers his gun just a little.

"What about him?" he asks.

"I'm headed his way," I say. I grab Jedediah by the arm and haul him forward. He tries to scoot backward, but I hold him in place, and his feet scramble uselessly in the sand. "Following the broadcast. Got a present for him."

There's a long pause. I wonder if maybe I made a mistake telling them this. Maybe not all the towns support Saint, or maybe they'll get the notion to take him in themselves. I almost reach for my gun, but one man lowers his weapon to his side, and the other two follow.

"Well, if you're doing Saint's business, you can't be too bad," the man in the middle says, almost grudgingly. "You got anything to trade?"

I have to stop myself from scoffing at the idea. As if these townies have anything that would be worth my precious food and water. I've got enough—which is more than a lot of people in the wastes can say—but barely so.

"No," I say. "I just wanna know where I am."

Their scowls are back in an instant, though thankfully their guns stay lowered.

"Surely you've got something to make it worth our while,"

one of them says. "Seeing as you're heading across the wastes to Saint an' all, and got them nice guns."

Noticing their hungry eyes on the pistol at my hip, it takes all of my resolve not to draw it on them. I take a deep breath and let it out. Goddamn townies... I really don't want to hand over any supplies, but I guess I don't have a choice.

"Fine," I say. "Might be able to spare a couple cans of food."

Just one more day till Saint, I tell myself as I grudgingly hand two cans of food in exchange for a bottle of dirty water. Once I reach him and claim my reward, I'll have everything I need and plenty more. Still, I hate wasting supplies, and will likely have to throw this water out rather than drink it. But these townies are stubborn as hell about trading. At least they finally give me what I'm really here for: the name "Lefton." I dodge the question about where I'm coming from, avoid giving a name, and make *damn* sure not to breathe the name Jedediah Johnson. I'm not so dumb as to think that I'm not recognizable if someone is looking for me, but once I reach the safety of Saint's tower it won't be an issue.

Just one more day. Then Jedediah will be out of my hands, and this whole business will be over and done with. I keep telling myself that as I finish haggling with the townies, letting the conversation drag just long enough that I hopefully won't offend them. Once we reach a deal, I head back toward where I left Jedediah with some townies to watch him, ready to get out of here.

But Jedediah isn't there. I pause, staring at the spot in the dirt where I left him.

Alarm bells ring in my head. Maybe I was right before, in thinking that telling these townies too much was a bad idea. Or maybe one of them had the bright idea of removing Jedediah's gag, and he convinced them to free him...

Heat spreads through my chest and simmers there. My hand finds my gun. I grip it tightly and turn to look at the townies.

I don't want to hurt these people, but if they've turned against me, I have no choice.

I'll take the armed men first. Then I can use one of the younger women as a hostage. Hopefully, that will minimize the casualties and allow me to get out of here with Jedediah.

"Somethin' wrong?" one of the men asks, nervously eyeing my gun.

"Where," I ask in a soft, dangerous voice, "is my prisoner?"

I survey the townies, looking for signs of guilt. One young woman turns an alarming shade of red. I focus on her, taking a step closer so I tower over her.

"He asked for a drink of water," she says, twirling a strand of hair around her finger and shrinking down. "So, um, we took him inside to give him some and—"

"Where?" I ask. She jumps, and points a finger at the nearest building. I shove her out of the way and step inside. I try to stay calm, but my pulse is racing as I think of all the things Jedediah could have gotten into. I guess these townies haven't intentionally turned against me, but they *are* apparently dumb as rocks, which is almost worse. Clearly they don't know what Jedediah is capable of. This is the man who conquered the eastern wastes, kept an iron grip on the towns there; the man who burned down an entire town for one act of rebellion. He could have gotten free, found a weapon. He could've taken out half the town and been long gone by now. He could've . . .

Been sitting on the floor of a house, surrounded by a ring of children. I stop as I catch sight of him. The first thing I notice is that some idiot *did* have the bright idea of removing his gag, which he's taking full advantage of at the moment, telling some kind of ridiculous story that involves a rocket launcher and mutant bears to the small collection of townie children. He gestures wildly—an impressive feat considering his wrists are, thankfully, still bound—and the kids around him squeal with laughter. Frowning, I make my way closer. A couple of the children turn to me as I approach, and the laughter dies out quickly as they see my scowling, burnt face. Jedediah is the last one to notice me. He pauses midsentence, looks up at me, and grins.

"Oh, hi, Clementine," he says, using his limited hand motion for a small wave.

"What are you doing?" I ask, folding my arms over my chest and glaring down at him. I'm trying very hard to restrain my temper right now, both at him and at the townies who were dumb enough to let their kids near him. Not that I'm much a fan of children—I find them kind of creepy, really—but still. It's the principle of the matter.

"Telling them a story," he says, all smiles and innocence. As if he's the kind of person who genuinely enjoys sitting around telling stories to small children.

"The legend of Jedediah Johnson!" a young boy says. I stare at him. Though he's dirty and stick thin, his eyes are wide and sparkling at the moment. "He's a really famous hero!"

"Really famous," Jedediah agrees, nodding. "Also very smart, and strong, and handsome."

"And born from radio garbage!"

"Radioactive waste, actually, but close," Jedediah says.

The children all nod excitedly, and I relax a bit. Clearly, they know nothing about the real Jedediah Johnson, only the bullshit that the man is currently spewing about himself.

"Finish telling the story," a young girl pipes up. "I wanna hear about how he saved all the towns!"

"We-ell," Jedediah says. "First he—"

"Where I come from," I say, cutting him off, "they say Jedediah Johnson eats children who trust strangers too much."

The children all turn away from Jedediah to stare at me, their eyes huge in their little faces, mouths gaping. Jedediah gapes along with them, as if he's also shocked by the news that

Jedediah Johnson is a horrible person. I nod, struggling to keep a straight face. "Then he wears their teeth as a necklace."

This stuns them all into silence for a solid few seconds. Jedediah is the first to recover, his expression shifting from shocked to affronted.

"*That*," he says, "is simply not true. How dare you slander the name of Jedediah Johnson—"

I grab him by the front of his shirt and haul him up before he can continue. I yank him toward the door, but he turns to do one last final wave at the children, many of whom look on the verge of tears now.

"Bye!" he says cheerfully, and I pull him out the door.

"What the hell was that?" I hiss at him, ignoring the good-byes of the townies as we march back to the car. "What did I tell you about laying low?"

"Oh, come on," Jedediah says. "I was just having a little fun." He eyes me, still smiling in the face of my wrath. "Got a lot more fun when you made the kiddos cry, though."

"I just gave them a dose of reality."

"Me eating children is *not* a reality!" he says, seeming offended by the notion. "Not enough meat on them, anyway. I don't see what the point would be . . ."

"More tender, I'd imagine," I say without thinking about it. Jedediah's head turns sharply in my direction, his eyebrows rising. I open my mouth to say something to defend myself, but before I can, he lets out a delighted laugh.

"Did you actually just make a joke, Clementine?" he asks. "Or was it just a creepy slip of the tongue? Either way, I support it."

I grit my teeth. I shouldn't be engaging with a prisoner. It's a slippery slope, associating with people like him. It's already fucking with the way I think.

Just one more day, I tell myself. One more day, and I'll be rid of him.

X
Saint's Tower

Though I want nothing more than to speed to Saint's radio tower the next day, I force myself to be patient and careful. The area nearby is treacherous; there are some larger towns I'd prefer to avoid, as well as a minefield I need to drive around, according to the map Alex gave me. I'm painstakingly careful to ensure that I'm taking the right roads, heading the right direction. I'm not going to come all this way just to die thanks to a goddamn mine.

Jedediah is quiet in the passenger seat. Maybe he realizes how close we're getting, how near at hand his judgment is. If this Saint does hold trials, I have no doubt Jedediah will be deemed guilty. Hell, if Saint wants me to, maybe I'll even stay awhile and testify against him myself, and stay to watch him hang too. Jedediah may not be the man I thought he'd be—he's awfully cheerful and *very* talkative for a ruthless dictator—but it changes nothing about what he's done.

Finally, the radio tower appears on the horizon. It's a sight to behold, tall and prominent, shiny metal in a dusty world. Saint's headquarters are in the building beside it, according to the map, but I can't see it from where I currently am, heading up the side of a hill. I jam the pedal, eager to have the end in sight, and the car huffs and puffs its way up the rest of the hill.

Once we reach the top, Saint's headquarters come into sight—and I slam on the brakes. Jedediah yelps as he's thrown forward, but I ignore him, completely fixated on the sight ahead.

Someone drove a fucking truck into Saint's headquarters.

One wall of the building is completely destroyed, a huge semi-truck sticking half out of it. Smoke still rises from the wreckage.

"What the fuck?" I ask the air. I reverse down the back side of the hill, stopping the car in a spot where it shouldn't be visible from Saint's headquarters. I reach into the back for one of my bags, grab my binoculars, and climb out of the car. As an afterthought, I drag Jedediah out as well, and haul him behind me as we head for the top of the hill.

There, I fall to a crouch, pulling Jedediah down beside me, and scope out the building below. I scan it, searching for any signs of what's going on down there. It's easy enough to see that this was an attack. But more importantly, who's winning? Should I get down there and try to help Saint, or will it be suicide?

Soon enough, my question is answered.

They pour out of the building—or rather crash out of it, violent and sudden, like a wave with a grudge against the shore. Raider, after raider, after raider emerges from the doors. They keep coming until it becomes a mob, huge and boisterous and rowdy. I don't think I've ever seen so many people together in one place, let alone *raiders*. I never imagined it would be possible for so many of them to get together without killing each other.

And these aren't the kinds of raiders I'm used to, not the well-equipped, well-trained, purposeful ones that make up Jedediah's crew. These are scarred and pierced and tatted, clothes shredded and bloodstained, armed with rusty knives and baseball bats and iron pipes. They boil and seethe with restless energy. Some are busy—loading up vehicles, arguing with each other, prepping for some kind of journey—while others stand around. But all of them are angry, restless, ready for something, radiating bloodlust. The air brims with the promise of violence. It's only a matter of time before it erupts.

I don't understand what's happening here, why there are so many raiders or where they came from, but I know a bad situation when I see one. Fuck the Saint plan. Even a huge bounty for Jedediah, and the life-changing effects it could have on my reputation, is *not* worth getting caught in this crossfire. Especially out here in the west, raiders are wild, and ruthlessly violent. I'm sure they'll tear us apart if they find us, just for kicks.

I lower my binoculars and take a deep breath. In, out. Panic surges in my chest, but I force it down. Now is not the time to lose control. I think I'm doing a decent job of covering it up, but Jedediah is looking at me out of the corner of his eye, very still and very quiet, like he expects any sudden motion or sound will make me snap.

"We need to go," I say after a moment of collecting myself. There's no time to waste. Some of those raiders have vehicles, and vehicles a hell of a lot bigger and more powerful than the piece of shit I'm driving. We need as much of a head start as possible if we want any hope of making it to safety. Thankfully, Jedediah nods and keeps his mouth shut.

I edge backward down the hill before climbing to my feet, and stay crouched even then, moving slowly. When I pull Jedediah off the ground, he follows my lead. He's quiet for once. I'm grateful for that, though it's also concerning. Considering his cheerful, blasé attitude even when he was being kidnapped and had a gun to his head, the fact that he's taking this so seriously means that we're in some real deep shit.

Once we're on our feet and out of sight of the tower, I break into a sprint, dragging a slightly lagging Jedediah with me. He struggles to keep up, nearly tripping several times, but I force him to keep running. Though it looks like I won't be able to turn him in to Saint after all, he's still my bounty, and I'm not going to lose the reason I came all the way to this hellhole. No time to figure the situation out now, but somehow I'll make it work.

I yank open the car door as we reach it, throw Jedediah in, and slam it shut before running to my own seat.

My brain is a blur of thoughts, and my body struggles to keep up with a flurry of actions in response—starting the car, spreading the map across the dashboard, putting on my seat-belt, starting to drive. Behind it all, one thought pushes me: *Get out. Get out. Get out.* I saw those raiders—*so many raiders*—and I need to get the hell out of here before they see me. I drive reck-lessly, wildly, trying to get as far away from the radio tower as possible. But where do I go? Where the hell can I possibly go, that I'll be safe from that mob?

I glance frantically between my map and the road, knowing the raider vehicles could be bearing down on me with every second. There's no way I'll make it all the way back to the east without getting run down by one of their war machines. I'm not even sure I have the gas to make it. I barely had enough supplies to last the journey here.

Maybe if I can make it to one of the bigger western towns, I could hole up there, wait for this to blow over. But will any of the towns around here actually hold against the onslaught of raiders? *Maybe* Blackfort—I've heard that place is a safe haven, and knows how to kick some raider ass—but I wouldn't gamble on it, and it's too far away for us to reach. We'll never make it there before being overtaken. I don't think we can make it to *any* town in time.

"We've got company," Jedediah says. Swearing under my breath, I shove the map aside and take a look in the rear-view mirror. The "company" he refers to is a huge truck, already close enough for me to make out some of the finer details, includ-ing spikes on the tires and a grinning skull painted on the front.

It's an ugly thing, a killing machine, made of mismatched parts all stuck together. It's massive, and intimidating, and definitely fast enough to catch us. It's too late to hide like we did from the poachers, and there's nothing but empty wastelands all around us. No room to pull a maneuver or a clever trick; we're out in the open, being run down by an enemy we can't hope to match.

"Untie me," Jedediah says. "Give me a gun. I'll shoot while you drive, take out their tires—"

"Not happening."

"You're going to get us both killed!" he says, his voice rising to a shout. Every bit of his cheerful attitude is gone. "Let me *go*!"

His plan would make sense, if he wasn't an insane tyrant and I could trust him not to put a bullet in my head the second I gave him half a chance. Unfortunately, that is not the case. Even if we both die, I'm completely willing to let him die tied up and helpless, rather than giving him a chance at taking me down and surviving himself.

I slam my foot on the gas pedal. The car struggles and rattles and whines, gaining a pathetic amount of speed. Despite the vehicle's best efforts, soon the truck is right on our tail.

It hovers behind us for an instant or two, while I swear and Jedediah yells. Then it rams us, slamming hard against our fender. We skid out of control, tires screeching. The truck falls back while I struggle to straighten us out. They're fucking with us, I realize. They could have easily run us off the road, or slammed into us hard enough to send the car rolling, but they don't want to. No need to rush—it's not like we're going anywhere.

I hate being toyed with, and I especially hate that there's nothing I can do about it. I grind my teeth and keep driving, trying to coax more speed out of this goddamn piece of junk car. Jedediah screams something from the passenger seat, over and over again. It takes three times for me to process the word he's shouting at me: "gun!" I duck my head just as a bullet whizzes past me and through the windshield. I hunch over the steering wheel, while Jedediah shrinks down as far as he can in his seat, eyes shut tightly, letting out a constant stream of swear words.

More bullets pepper the car, none doing any serious damage— just continuing to fuck with us, I'm sure—and then the truck gains speed suddenly, roaring its way up beside us. There it slows again, keeping pace. I look over to see a raider grinning at me. The scarred man hangs half out the window, holding a revolver with both hands, the gun pointed right at me. Heart hammering, I slam on the brakes, and the truck pulls ahead. A moment later it reverses, and I shoot forward again. I stay ahead only for a moment or two before the truck is back at our side.

Desperate, I ram our tiny car sideways, right into their huge truck. The raider nearly topples out the window, and the gun falls from his hands, lost to the road. He scrambles for a handhold, his face utterly shocked. Once the man regains his balance he scowls at me, and shouts something over his shoulder at the driver. Before I can react, the truck rams us back.

We skid sideways, nearly off the road, and I fight to keep control of the car. At least I don't have a gun pointed at my face now...but unfortunately, I've introduced the raiders to a fun new game. They ram us again, and again. When they're close, I can hear the laughter drifting out of their open window. As soon as I recover, they hit us once more—and this time stay locked to our side, metal grinding against metal, their truck pushing against us.

I grit my teeth and turn the wheel sharply, trying to break away, but the truck sticks to us. It edges us toward the side of the road. The car whines pitifully, engine struggling. I push it harder, harder, knowing I have to get away. I pick up speed, but the truck easily keeps up.

Too late, I see the crumbling building ahead. Too late, I realize the raiders' plan. I jam my heel against the brake in an attempt to slow down, but all it does is make me lose control. With a screech of tires, the raider truck shoves me off the road and the car rams straight into the side of the building.

Car hits wall. Forehead hits steering wheel.

For a moment everything goes black. I fight it. I force my eyes open, will myself to move, to stay conscious. But my brain is hazy, uncooperative. It takes all my effort to lift my head, shaking it in an attempt to clear it while the world spins around me. Jedediah is crumpled in his seat, groaning.

Gradually, my head clears, and adrenaline sparks me into action. I shift the car into reverse and rev the engine. It only makes a horrible screeching noise, producing no actual movement. Judging from the smoke coming from the hood, this poor piece of shit has finally rumbled its final rumble. The good news is that the raiders have rammed their big-ass truck into the building as well, and despite its size it doesn't look like the thing won its battle with the wall.

The bad news is that the raiders are now jumping out of their vehicle and coming for us. I curse, scramble to open the door, and climb out. I stumble in my hurry, my legs shaky beneath me after the crash, but I force myself to keep going. I rush to the trunk, prop it open, and grab the first gun I find: an assault rifle. Jedediah yells at me from the passenger seat, but I ignore him and turn to face the raiders. There are four of them, one with a gun, the others with hand weapons. I immediately release a spray of bullets at the armed one, and he falls with a shout. Before I can aim again, another raider is on me, swinging a knife at my face.

My gunfire goes wild as I jump back to avoid the blade. I try to level my weapon at the man with a knife, but he dives at me, shoving my arm so the barrel of the gun jerks upward. He shoves me back against the same wall my car crashed into.

We struggle. I block his wild swings with my gun, unable to get a shot off as I try to prevent my nose from being sliced in half. He grabs the barrel of the gun with his free hand, yanking it out of my grip; I let go immediately, so his own momentum sends him stumbling.

I grab a loose brick from the wall behind me and launch it at him. It catches him in the side of the head, and he shouts, clutching his ear. I grab another before he can recover and tackle him to the ground. The gun slips out of his hands and clatters into the dust. He holds on to the knife and slashes at me, but I block it with the brick and shove his hand to the side, leaving his face wide open. His eyes widen as he realizes what's about to happen, and his mouth opens, but I bring the brick down before he can say anything. Once, twice, three times, and his face is reduced to a bloody mess. I hold on to the bloody brick, panting.

I have a mere second to recover before I see another raider diving for my fallen gun. I lunge at her, and smash the brick onto her hand as soon as she grips it. She snarls, trying to snatch her hand back, but I keep it pinned. With my free hand, I grab her arm and yank her down into the dirt with me. We tumble on the ground, both losing our weapons and resorting to hits and kicks and bites and scratches. She's smaller than me, scrawnier, and eventually I get a good grip on her hair and pin her facedown in the dirt. I find her companion's fallen knife on the ground nearby, and jam it hilt deep into the back of her exposed neck. She jolts and goes limp, and I slowly pull the blade free.

I climb to my feet with the knife in hand, breath hard, blood pumping, veins full of the half-fear, half-excitement muddle that a fight always brings out in me. I focus on the last raider still standing. The huge man has dragged Jedediah out of the passenger seat. As I watch, he lifts the wriggling smaller man and slams him down on the hood of the car. Jedediah stops moving.

No. Not my bounty. If he dies here, all of this was pointless.

I run at the raider, a shout tearing out of my throat. He turns toward me, and I sink the blade of the knife deep into his shoulder, just missing his neck. He grunts and grabs me by the arm. He starts to lift me off the ground, but I aim a swift kick at his groin, and he loses his grip. I smash a knee into his face as he leans over, and shove him backward. He stumbles into the car, his back slamming against it, and drops to one knee with a grunt of pain. Before he can recover from the flurry of attacks, I find my gun and release a hail of bullets on both him and the car. Bullets ping against metal, and his body jerks and convulses with the force. Finally the gunfire dies, and the body falls to the ground.

I lower my gun, gasping for breath. My whole body is trembling from the rush. Nearby I can hear at least one of the raiders still groaning, but a quick glance confirms that he's not going to be a threat. I march over to Jedediah instead. He's facedown on the hood of the car, not moving. I nudge him, and when I get no response, flip him over. Blood trickles down the side of his face.

His eyes flutter open and focus on me.

"I'm okay," he says dazedly. "I'm good. Don't you worry about me."

I check him over. The blood looks bad, but the gash on his forehead is superficial. Judging from the look on his face he probably took a couple good slams to the head, but he's still intact enough for my purposes.

"I wasn't," I say curtly. I leave him there and head to the trunk of the car. We don't have much time to spare, especially since we're on foot now. I glance at the map, noting the towns nearest to where we are, before shoving it into my pocket. I fill a duffel bag with supplies—food, water, bandages, ammo, and as many guns as I can fit. It hurts me to leave any behind, but overburdening myself will slow me down, and slowing down could get me killed, considering there's a fuckload of raiders hot on our trail. I'm not going to die for a couple of guns, no matter how nice they are. With that done, I return to Jedediah and grab him by the arm, hauling him to his feet. He sways, nearly falling over backward again. I sigh and slip an arm around his midriff to keep him upright.

"You're not very durable for a raider," I say.

"Well, you're not very…uh…" He trails off as he notices the scene around us, his head tilting side to side as he surveys the carnage. "Woah," he says, blinking. "You killed them all." He turns to look at me. I expect him to be frightened, like people normally are when they see what I can do, but instead he breaks into a wide grin. "Well, damn. Nice work."

I glance sideways at him, surprised—and, though I'd never admit it, a little bit pleased at the compliment. If he had any lick of sense he'd be terrified after that display, but instead he looks impressed.

"It was necessary," I say. I half-carry, half-drag Jedediah through the aftermath of the fight, sidestepping bodies and dying men. I put Saint's radio tower behind us, and set off into the wastes.

I wander in the direction of the next town, but my heart tells me there's no way we're going to make it. We have to stop and duck down every time a vehicle passes, though none of them notice us, or if they do, they don't care enough to stop for two pathetic wanderers. Jedediah gradually recovers from the fight, and soon we're walking side by side, though he needs some prodding to keep up.

I'm just trying to put as much distance as possible between us and the raiders, but something unexpected soon looms on the horizon: a town. I frown, slowing down; this is way too soon to hit the place we were heading toward.

"Oh, hell yeah," Jedediah says, picking up his pace. I let him stumble on ahead as I pause and check the map.

Unless I'm horribly lost, this place isn't on it. Once we get a little closer, it's not hard to see why. The town is tiny, just a cluster of tilted, haphazard buildings that seem like they're drunk and struggling to stay upright. But there are signs of life here and there: blankets covering windows, the faint smell of fire, whispers of conversation carried on the wind. Normally I would never stop here, knowing I'd only find desperate people, and desperate people are likely to do desperate things when they see someone better off than they are. But for now, it's the only thing breaking up the endless emptiness of the wastes, and we need to get out of open ground. I follow Jedediah, checking my guns just in case violence does break out.

As we draw closer, I find that the town is dead silent. There's no movement or sound, nobody around as far as I can see. Maybe I was wrong, and the signs I saw before were just wishful thinking. Maybe it's a ghost town, abandoned or never really occupied. I'm already considering whether it's a smart idea to hide in the abandoned buildings or keep going when I hear conversation nearby. I grab Jedediah's arm and pull him against me, pointing a hand in the direction the noise is coming from. He nods, pressing his lips firmly closed. I draw my gun and we creep around the corner together.

A small cluster of townies gathers in the street we enter. They're dirty, thin people, and all turn to stare at us with wide, reproachful eyes. One man has a gun, but he doesn't raise it as he sees us, just stares with a look of resignation. After a moment

I lower my weapon, and the armed man steps forward, holstering his own gun.

"Who're you?" he asks. He's a ragged man with a moustache and a head of scraggly brown hair, eyes squinting out from a wrinkled and sun-spotted face. I holster my gun, keeping my hand on it just in case, but he makes no move to draw on me. The rest of the townsfolk clump together and peer at me fearfully from behind their apparent leader.

"Stranger looking for a place to stay," I say.

"Friendly?"

"Sure."

He eyes me for a moment longer, gaze lingering on my burnt face and the gun at my hip, and nods. He must gather that I'm not a raider, based on the fact that I haven't tried to shoot anyone up yet. Either that, or he's accepted his fate already.

"Fine," he says. "We've got bigger problems to deal with anyway." He steps forward and juts out a hand. I shake it firmly. "I'm the sheriff here," he says, "for what it's worth."

"Place got a name?"

"Nope," he says. "We just settled here 'bout a week ago. We were nomads before. When we heard about what Saint was doing, thought it was finally safe enough to settle down. Picked up some stragglers along the way, found a spot nice and close to Saint's tower, and...well, here we are now."

"Shit luck," I say. He nods shortly, his face grim, and then eyes Jedediah. He takes in the ropes around his wrists and the state of him, as well as the fact that I'm toting several large guns.

"Guess it's shit luck for you too," he says.

"Yep." I shrug, as if it doesn't matter. Better to keep up a brave face around people like this, not show them that I'm scared shitless just like them. "You hear what happened? Raiders storm the tower?"

"Oh, no," he says, his face sagging. "No word for sure what went down, but those raiders didn't all come from outside the tower. They came from inside." He folds his arms over his chest. "People brought him so many raiders...he must've not really been killin' them like he said."

It doesn't surprise me. Not many good men left nowadays, and those that do exist usually don't last long. This isn't a place for good men. Isn't a world for good men.

"Well," I say. "No use wasting time chitchatting. You've got a fuckload of raiders coming this way fast. Let's figure out how to survive this."

XI
The Truth

The sheriff leads us into a building nearby. They seem to have tried very hard to patch it up, and haven't quite succeeded. The windows are boarded up, the door is attached by only one hinge, and the entire place has a very sad, dusty look about it. The interior isn't much better, just a bunch of half-broken furniture scattered in a dim room.

Most of the townsfolk are huddled here. There's a surprising number of them. Every chair and stool is occupied, as well as much of the floor space, making it hard to walk. The atmosphere is grim, the people mostly silent aside from the occasional murmured conversation or person weeping. Clearly these people know what they're up against, and they're not liking their odds. I want to tell the sheriff that it's a bad idea to have everyone clustered in the same building, where they could easily be mowed down by a machine gun or a couple grenades, but I don't see the point. These people aren't going to survive.

The first few groups of raiders, the ones with vehicles, will likely pass right by this place; they're not interested in such slim pickings when there are much better things on the horizon. But the straggling groups, the ones who know they won't make it to the real towns before they're already ransacked...those are the ones who will see this place as an easy target.

A few of the townspeople perk up as I walk in, likely noting the gun I'm carrying, the absence of the scared-shitless look that everyone else is wearing, and the fact I'm accompanying the sheriff. I'm careful not to meet their eyes. I don't want to give anyone the impression I'm here to save them. I follow the sheriff through the room, struggling not to step on anyone. Jedediah shuffles along behind me, and I hear him consistently bumping into objects and people and muttering apologies.

The sheriff leads us through the room and down an empty hallway to a small supply closet in the back. He shuts the door behind us, and I eye the cramped room. It's full of shelves and wooden crates, most of them empty. These people don't have much other than a couple jugs of water and a handful of cans of food. I grab one of the empty crates, turn it over, and use it as a seat. The sheriff does the same. When Jedediah moves to sit beside me, I shove him to the floor. He sighs and sits cross-legged there instead. The room is dark and dusty, the sole window boarded up, only shreds of sunlight peeking in.

"So," the sheriff says. "Who are you, exactly?"

"My name is Clementine," I say. No point in lying here. It'd be difficult to get in deeper shit than I already am, and this man will be dead tomorrow anyway. "Bounty hunter. Was taking this to Saint." I jerk my chin at Jedediah.

"So you worked for Saint?" he asks, eyes narrowing.

"I work for no one. Just heard the broadcast."

"Ah," he says, nodding to himself. "So, then...this is a raider?" He eyes Jedediah, his eyebrows slightly raised. Jedediah waggles his fingers at him in a wave. I'm ready to kick him if he opens his big mouth, but thankfully he keeps it shut.

"This," I say, keeping my eyes on Jedediah, who smiles up at me like an idiot, "is Jedediah Johnson."

A long silence follows. Jedediah's eyes flick from me to the townsman, and I slowly raise my eyes to him as well when he doesn't answer. I expect him to be startled by the news, or afraid, but instead he just looks very, very confused.

"Do you not know who that is?" I ask, uncertain. These towns are small and unorganized out here. Maybe they have no idea what's happening over in my area of the wastes. "He's a—"

"I know exactly who he is," the townsman says, interrupting me. I fall silent, waiting for him to continue. He clears his throat, looking like he's struggling to find the words. "It's just... ah... that's *not* him."

Now that takes me by surprise. My eyebrows draw together in confusion, and my jaw works for a moment, trying to locate the right words.

I settle on, "What the fuck are you talking about?"

The townsman turns red. He looks back and forth between me and Jedediah, who is no longer smiling and has assumed a guarded, unreadable expression. The sheriff clears his throat, scratches the back of his head.

"Well," he says. "Of course we've heard about Jedediah Johnson. Matter of fact, we've been hearing a lot about him lately. Just got news on the radio this morning that he's headed this way from the east." He points his thumb in a direction I'm fairly certain is north, and continues. "Him 'n' his crew just wiped a town called Lefton off the map. Says they're coming to get back one of their crewmates who was stolen."

We both turn to look at Jedediah—or whoever the hell he really is. He hesitates, looking back and forth between the two of us, and smiles nervously.

"Well, this is awkward," he says.

I slowly lean back, tapping one hand across my arm. I stare at Not-Jedediah, and then at the floor, and then at the sheriff.

"Give us a few minutes alone," I say.

"Or not," Not-Jedediah says quickly.

"Sure," the townsman says, ignoring Not-Jedediah. He leaps

to his feet, looking more than eager to get away from this conversation. He glances back at us as he shuts the door behind him, leaving just me and Not-Jedediah in the cramped room.

I stay silent for a long moment, which turns into several moments, which turns into minutes. Jedediah says nothing, either, though he keeps opening and closing his mouth like he desperately wants to. After a long deliberation, I sigh, crack my neck, and shove one leg of my pants up above my ankle. Strapped there is my favorite knife, a long, sharp, cruel thing I reserve for especially personal kills. I slide it out of its sheath, let the pant leg fall back down, and toss the knife from hand to hand while staring at the ceiling. My gaze slides to Jedediah, whose eyes are following the movements of the knife.

"Er, so," he says, clearing his throat, "clearly we've got a lot to talk about."

"Not really," I say. I rise to my feet and move over to where he sits. He scoots frantically away, moving until he bashes into a wooden box. He tries to stand, but can't quite manage to do it with his hands tied together. I stand above him, looking down.

I don't even feel angry. The usual hot rage is missing. I just feel . . . cold. Purposeful.

"So you're not Jedediah Johnson," I say slowly.

"You know, technically, I never said I was," he says, his eyes flicking from the knife to my face. Whatever he sees in the latter, he doesn't like it. A drop of sweat paints a line through the dust on his forehead. "You just kind of assumed—"

I crouch down and grab him by the shirt with one hand, the other bringing my knife up to his face. He freezes.

"Tell me who you really are," I say, deadly calm. "And the story better make sense, if you want to keep this." I press the blade against the back of his ear, just enough for him to feel the edge. He sucks in a sharp breath, though he has the good sense not to squirm.

"Okay," he says quickly. "Okay, okay. Well. My name *is* actually Jedediah Johnson." I apply more pressure, enough to draw a thin line of blood, and he squeaks and shuts his eyes tightly. "T-the Second, that is!"

I pause and draw the knife back, frowning.

"What?" I ask.

He peeks one eye open.

"Well, they usually call me Jed," he says. "Jed the Second."

I don't like the sound of that at all.

"So the real Jedediah Johnson is..."

"Good ol' Dad," he says, forcing a weak smile. I stare at him as the words sink in. The son of Jedediah Johnson. I have the son of Jedediah Johnson in my possession. It sounds ridiculous. I've never heard so much as a rumor that Jedediah even has a son...but then again, it would be in his best interest to keep that hidden, wouldn't it? A son would be a weakness. A vulnerability.

Of course Jedediah would hide his son's existence. And of course he would keep him in a plush room in his headquarters, with an escape tunnel. And of course his son wouldn't look much like a hardened raider, and of course he would be a crazy little fucker...

The more I think about it, the more it clicks into place. Everything lines up with this explanation...and it all points to me being in some very, very deep shit right now.

"Fuck," I say. I sit back on my heels. With his ear no longer at my knife's mercy, Jed relaxes and sits up.

"Yeah," he says. "I can imagine this is a bit of a sticky situation for you now."

"Sticky situation" is an understatement. Not only do I *not* have my hands on Jedediah Johnson, nor any hope of using him to start a new, better life for myself, but now I'm stranded in the western wastes with someone useless, worthless, and yet *very* dangerous on my hands. Nobody's going to be impressed by me capturing Jedediah's son, especially since the world doesn't know he exists. And now I've got the real Jedediah Johnson, who is surely incredibly pissed off, coming for me. Not to mention the fact I went on a wild-goose chase into this godforsaken area of the wastes, and I was never going to get anything out of it in the first place, because this piece of shit isn't the bounty I thought I had.

I've taken all the risk, and I'm not getting any goddamn reward.

"You let me believe you were your father this whole time," I say in a low, seething voice. "You wasted my time, you risked your life... *Why?*"

"I didn't know what else to do," he says, his eyes wide and earnest. "When you first showed up, I thought you'd probably shoot me if you didn't think I was worth something. And then, once we got all the way out here, I was *sure* you would shoot me if you found out I wasn't who you thought I was, so..." He shrugs helplessly. "I didn't want to get shot."

"So you said nothing," I say. "You said nothing and let me come all the way out to this godforsaken hellhole for *nothing*. And now I'm going to die out here, for *nothing*." My voice gradually rises. I stand and grab him by the collar, dragging him up with me. "Do you even realize what you've done?"

"Well," he says hesitantly, like he hasn't fully figured out where the sentence is going yet. His eyes dart around the room. "As far as I can tell, I've led us on a journey together that has actually, thus far, been pretty—" He cuts off as I shove him against the wall. "Well, it's n-not the worst thing that's ever happened, right?" he says, forcing a half smile. "We've had some good times, some good conversations—"

My knife is at his throat in an instant. He tilts his head away from it, wincing.

"You don't have to do this," he says. His eyes search my face, find it hard and cold. His chest starts to heave a little harder. "Look, I know—" I pull the knife back, raising it, and he flinches, real fear in his eyes for once. "Look, I'm sorry I lied. I'm sorry I'm not worth anything, but you don't have to—" He cuts off in a yelp, squeezing his eyes shut as I bring the knife down.

He stays with his body braced for a couple seconds, and then slowly opens his eyes and looks down at the severed ropes in a pile at his feet. He looks from them, to the knife, to me, to his chafed-raw but now freed wrists, and flexes his hands wonderingly.

"Oh," he says. "Well. This is a nice turn of events." He looks up at me and smiles, immediately back to his old self. "All right," he says cheerfully as I place my knife back in its sheath. "Now that we've established you're not going to kill me, step two is probably—"

My fist catches him right in the nose, hard, with a sound like I may have broken it. The back of his head smacks the wall behind him, and he gasps sharply. He pauses, his head leaning back, and raises a hand to wipe at the trickle of blood from his nose.

"Um," he says, his voice coming out thick. He wipes his bloody hand on his shirt. "Okay. Right. Should have expected that. Anyway, moving on to step three: We make up and figure out what to do next."

I give him a disgusted look. I can't believe, after everything that's happened, he's expecting us to just *make up*, as he says.

"No," I say. "*This* is step three." I grab him by the collar again and pull him out the door. He protests all the way down the hall and through the building full of townies; they all turn to stare at us as we pass by. I ignore them, and drag Jed right out of the building, down the street, and to the outskirts of town. I shove him ahead of me, and he stumbles and falls to the ground on his side. I stay where I am while he struggles in the dust. He rolls onto his back and looks up at me, his expression almost hurt.

"You're free to go," I say, and turn away. No point in dragging this situation out further. I need to talk to the townsfolk and figure out what the hell I'm going to do about this situation. I only make it a few steps before I hear Jed scrambling to his feet and following me.

"Wait, wait," he says, running to catch up and falling into step beside me. "That's it? You're just going to let me go?"

"You're useless to me now," I say. "And I only kill when I have to." I speed up, but he stays beside me, chewing his bottom lip.

"Why can't I stay with you?" he asks, sounding genuinely confused. I stop walking and turn to face him. He has the good sense to back out of punching range. "Where else am I supposed to go?"

"Go back to your daddy and his crew, dipshit. Or die out in the wastes somewhere. I don't care." I whirl around and start walking again. No footsteps follow me, and for one blissful moment I think I've lost him. But soon enough he follows again, clinging to my heels like a stray dog hoping for scraps.

"How will I get back to the east?" he asks plaintively.

"I'm sure you'll figure it out," I say. "Or you won't, and you'll die. Once again: I. Do. Not. Care."

"But Clementine, I—"

I pivot to face him again and shove him, hard. He stumbles, barely stops himself from falling, and looks at me with wide eyes.

"Listen up, you fucking dumbass," I say. "I'm trying very hard to be nice right now." My voice is low, anger simmering just under its surface. "And trying very, very hard to forget that *you* are the reason I'm stranded out in the middle of butt-fucking nowhere, with no car, caught up in a townie-raider war that will probably get me killed. I would suggest getting out of here before I decide to stop trying, and make an exception to my kill-only-for-profit rule."

He's still looking at me with confused-puppy eyes, making no move to walk away. I growl under my breath and whip my gun out of its holster, pointing it right between his eyes.

"What exactly is hard to understand about this?" I ask, my voice rising. I don't know what it is about this guy that pushes my buttons so hard. Maybe the fact that he can't understand I'm trying to do him a goddamn favor and let him get out of here before shit hits the fan, when by all rights I should be putting a bullet in his head. "I'm done dealing with you, I'm done being responsible for you, I'm done looking at that stupid goddamn look on your face. Just get out of here, Jed. Fucking *go.*"

Even with a gun in his face, he still just stands there looking at me with that pathetic, dumb-ass expression. I guess I shouldn't be surprised at this point; the man clearly has no sense of self-preservation. The idea of pulling the trigger becomes more and more tempting. After a few seconds, I force myself to lower the barrel. When I walk away this time, Jed doesn't follow.

Back inside, I find the sheriff talking to his people. I must've missed some kind of inspiring speech, because people are smiling and clapping all of a sudden, and he's saying something about defending their home and putting up a fight when no one expects them to. My mood only further sours. I stand apart from the townies, leaning against the wall, and grind my teeth as I watch the sheriff deal out weapons and rations. Townsfolk smile and thank him as they get their share.

Don't these people realize that they don't have a chance? Do they really think these weapons will do anything for them when the raiders get here, or that rationing the food and water will make any difference? As if they need to save it... As if any of them will be alive to use it past tomorrow. This level of delusion is pitiful, and the sheriff's cheeriness is only making it worse.

I wait until the sheriff is alone, his people sated, before approaching him. As soon as he sees me coming, he jerks his head at the back room, and I follow him there.

"Surprised you aren't long gone," he says.

Me too, to be honest. But I'm not going to leave without attempting to get the reality of this situation through the man's thick skull.

"You're going to get your people killed," I say bluntly. He regards me silently, with no visible reaction. "I'm being straight up with you because you seem like a decent man," I continue. "You and your people will die here. You have no chance. You'd be lucky to handle one raider crew, let alone a dozen of them."

The sheriff doesn't look surprised at what I say, or defiant, or anything much at all. Instead he just looks weary. Out of the view of his people, he seems suddenly deflated, the shadows around his eyes darker, his shoulders slumping.

"You think I don't know that?" he asks. "You think I honestly believe we're going to win this fight?" He shakes his head slowly. "I'm not an idiot. But what else am I supposed to do?"

"Run," I say. "Now's not the time for pride, or sentiment about this place, or whatever the fuck is holding you here. Just run."

He shakes his head again.

"Me and my people have spent less time in this town than we spent walking here," he says. "We still haven't recovered from the journey. We're tired. I'm tired. And we have children, and elderly, and sick. We don't have the supplies to make it anywhere in time, and even if we did, we'd be run down before getting there."

"Leave anyone who can't travel, then," I say. It seems obvious to me. "No point in everyone dying. If a few can be saved, then save them."

"We're a community," he says, gently, like he doesn't expect me to really understand. "It doesn't work like that."

I wish I didn't understand, but I do. It stirs up memories of a time when I had a town to call home, and people who I never would've left behind. As much as I hate to admit it, I know that's something worth fighting for, even if it's stupid to do so. I let out an irritated huff, fold my arms over my chest, and glare at him.

"So what?" I ask. "You're just going to give up?"

"No. I wasn't completely bullshitting out there. We're going to make a last stand. We're gonna take out as many of the bastards as we can, and we're gonna die with dignity." He raises his chin, defiant, like he's daring me to tell him that it's pointless. It *is* pointless, but I know that telling him that won't get me anywhere.

"You're lucky if you take out one raider for every three of you," I grumble. But there's no real venom behind the words, and the sheriff relaxes.

"I'm not asking you to stay, lady," he says.

"Yeah, yeah," I say, with a long sigh. "Tell me what your plan is."

XII
Defense of the Nameless Town

The sheriff's plan, as it turns out, is a halfway decent one. We do disagree on some points—he thinks the elderly, children, and anyone else unable to fight should hide, while I think that's pointless—but ultimately, the man is sharper than I would've guessed. He and his people construct a wall at the side of town facing Saint's former headquarters. There's plenty of junk lying around town, and the townies drag out all the furniture they have as well. Chairs, beds, all of it—there's no point in keeping any of this stuff, because if the wall falls, they won't have much use for it anyway. I spend some time constructing the wall, meanwhile concocting my own plan in my head. After an idea hits me, I grab the first person in my line of sight: a gangly, awkward-looking teenage boy with a tuft of messy hair. He jumps when I grab his arm, and stares at me all wide-eyed and pale faced.

"You. What's your name?" I ask. He looks around wildly, as if I could be talking to someone else, and gulps.

"Wyatt," he says, his voice halfway to a whimper.

"Okay, Wyatt." I toss him my ammo bag, which he barely manages to catch. "Help me find a good spot to shoot people from."

Despite all of his stuttering and blushing and struggling to form a coherent sentence, Wyatt ultimately pulls through. He leads me to the roof of a nearby one-story building to set up. I can already see the mob of raiders on the horizon, approaching slowly, all on foot.

I recruit townsfolk to help me drag up the junk they can spare. Some splintered boards, a rusty car door, and a couple blankets become my makeshift barricade. I set it up on the edge of the roof and deposit my supplies behind it. The townsfolk ogle my guns and ammo supply, practically drooling at the sight of how much ammunition I have. Luckily they have the common sense not to ask about using any of it. I may be here to help, but I sure as hell am not sacrificing any of my guns in the process. I fought, sweat, and bled for each and every one of them, and there's no way I'm letting a single piece out of my sight.

From my spot on the roof, I have a good view of both the townies below and the raiders approaching town. The townies are lined up behind their wall. Every able-bodied man and woman is there, armed with whatever they could find. About half of them have guns—better than I would've expected— while the others are using knives, metal pipes, broken bottles, and a variety of other objects that could potentially kill someone. They all look nervous, as they should. But the sheriff, to his credit, is doing his very best to hold it together. He doesn't cry, doesn't complain, doesn't despair, and does his best to keep his people from doing those things too. I can see the way he bolsters their morale. No wonder these people followed him across the wastes to settle here. He could've been a great leader, and this place a great town, if not for their shit luck. Maybe I could've settled here, if things had been different. Maybe this could've been home. The thought makes a lump rise in my throat, and I clear it, trying to focus my thoughts on the fight to come.

"Your sheriff is a good man," I murmur, glancing over at Wyatt. The wiry boy is crouched beside me near the makeshift barricade, looking through my ammo bag. I gave him a quick rundown of the basics, and told him to stay up here to hand me ammo and keep me shooting as much as possible. He seemed more than happy to do the job, especially since it meant he didn't have to be down there with the other townies on the front line.

"Yup," he says. "Saved all our asses more'n a few times." He stands up, peeking around the barricade at the wastes. On the horizon, I can see them coming—a wave of raiders, unhurried but unrelenting. Wyatt looks at them for a long few seconds before turning to me. "Reckon we can survive this?"

I don't answer. I may be many things, but I'm not a liar.

Chatter from the townsfolk below drifts up to us, but it gradually dies off as the raiders draw closer. My heart sinks as I stare at them. There are so *many*—just over a hundred, I'd guess. Raiders never work in groups this big. Even Jedediah Johnson's crew doesn't have these numbers. But if they were all holed up in that radio tower together, and this was the only direction with towns to loot, I guess they've made some kind of truce.

I had hoped the majority of the mob would be long gone by now, having procured vehicles for themselves or wandered off in other directions, but a good portion of the crowd I saw earlier is coming straight at us. Every time I think the steady stream of them has to stop, more come. They're in small clusters, their own individual crews, but they move together, all toward one target: this little town, too small and fresh to even have a name for itself.

The raiders have to know that this town won't have much for them, but I'm guessing they don't have a choice. The crews with vehicles have the time to skip over this little place in favor of bigger conquests, but the rest of the raiders need to take what they can get as they cross the wastes.

The town is silent. I can hear my heartbeat thudding in my

ears, but soon enough that is drowned out by a different sound—
the shouting and heckling of the raiders. They're psyching
themselves up for the assault, bloodlust rising to a frenzy as they
approach.

"Holy shit," Wyatt says, peering around the barricade beside
me. "There are so many of them." He looks at me, the whites of
his eyes showing. "We ain't got a chance. We should run."

"Too late." I grab my sniper rifle and set the barrel atop the
barrier. Once it's steady, I place the first of the raiders in my
sights.

"We're gonna die here," Wyatt says.

"Make it worth something," I say, and fire.

I take down a dozen raiders before they get close enough to
start firing back. When they do get in range, I duck down and
ditch the sniper rifle, swapping it out for an assault rifle. I shout
out quick instructions to Wyatt, who looks on the verge of puking or pissing himself, but he follows my orders nonetheless.
Despite my warnings, he can't seem to help but keep peering
around the barricade, watching the approaching raiders with
growing panic.

As soon as the new gun is in my hands and loaded, I start firing again. I mow down raiders, but it hardly seems to make a
dent in their ranks—there are so *many*, and they never seem to
stop coming. Despite my best efforts, the wave of raiders soon
crashes against the barrier the townies have set up. With crowbars and pipes and hands, they make short work of tearing it
apart, and the battle starts for real.

It's a bloody fight, a desperate one for the townies, and
quickly devolves into a free-for-all. I fire into the mess, doing my
best to handle the worst of the threats. Any raider with a gun I
instantly take out, or anyone who tries to climb up to me. But
soon they realize I'm the biggest threat here. More and more of

them notice me up above, and anyone with a gun starts shooting my way. Bullets ping against the makeshift barricade, or zing through weak spots—it really is a shoddy thing, not sturdy enough to hold up long in a gunfight. I'm forced to crouch down, keeping myself behind the rusty door, and peek around the side to take shots.

"Need more ammo," I say, keeping my eyes on the messy fight below. When one raider sets his sights on me, I send my last bullet through his face. "Now, Wyatt." I hold my hand out for it, still watching below for any signs of imminent danger. A few seconds pass, but my hand remains empty. I tear my eyes away from the fight with a hiss of frustration. "Wyatt, what the fuck are you—" I start, and stop. Wyatt is down, a bullet hole through his throat and a whole lot of blood around him. I didn't even hear him hit the ground.

"Fuck," I mutter under my breath. "What a mess."

I pry the blood-splattered ammo pack out of his stiff fingers and haul it over in front of me, searching through and reloading my gun myself. When I'm not staring down my sights, the battle seems a lot louder, a lot closer, a lot scarier. I'm suddenly aware of all the sounds of people fighting, the cries of the dying. The air smells like gunpowder and death. With adrenaline flooding my body, my senses are all kicked into overdrive, and the battle overwhelms them. But somehow, through everything else, I pick up on one thing: footsteps behind me.

No time to finish reloading. I turn immediately, swinging my rifle in an arc, and catch the approaching man in the side of the head. He lets out a grunt of pain, stumbles, and lands on his ass.

"Oof," he says, shaking his head. "Ouch."

"*Jed?*" I stare at him. I can hardly believe it, but there he is. "What the fuck are you doing here?"

"You really ruined my entrance." He squints up at me, clutching his head. "But, uh, figured you'd be missing me right about now. And you know me, people pleaser an' all."

A lot of emotions fight for control of my head and my heart, pulling me back and forth between anger and relief and utter bewilderment. Jed should be long gone by now. He should be someone else's problem . . . or someone else's rescue, or whatever is happening right now.

But there's no time to figure out that mess right now, or argue with Jed about why he didn't hightail it out of town long ago, so I shut off my thoughts. I turn around, finish reloading, and use one foot to shove the ammo bag in his direction.

"You're on ammo duty," I shout without turning around, and set my sights on a new target.

"Yes, ma'am," Jed says. Out of the corner of my eye I see him kick Wyatt's body out of the way and grab the ammo bag.

I take raiders down, one after another after another. Each shot is a kill. Jed is quick with the ammo, much quicker than Wyatt, already moving to resupply me before the words are out of my mouth—he must be counting my shots just like I am. He watches the kills, too, shrewd eyes moving over the battlefield. He stays quiet, but every time I glance at his face as he hands me more ammo, he looks more grim.

Despite my best efforts, the town is being overrun. There are too many raiders to handle, and no one other than me is doing much to impede the assault. The townies below go down one at a time. The sheriff is the last to fall. He fights tooth and nail as he goes down, wild and animalistic in his will to live, but he goes down nonetheless. With no one left to stop them, the raiders swarm into town, right into the buildings where the townies who couldn't fight sought shelter.

Then the screaming begins.

I lower my gun, taking a deep breath. With the front-line gone, there's no hope of defending this place. The battle is lost.

I let that sink in for a few moments, and then raise my gun and resume firing.

"Give me a gun," Jed says from beside me.

"No," I say. "No point, we're leaving."

"You know as well as I do that we're going to fight our way out," he says. "Give me a *gun*." His voice is edging on desperate now.

"So you can shoot me in the back? I don't think so!" I shout without looking at him, too busy taking out as many raiders as I can. When I run out of ammo, I drop the rifle into the bag and grab one of my pistols. I have a feeling this fight is about to become very short-range; the raiders are flooding the town, and soon they'll find a way to me. Sure enough, I hear footsteps on the back stairs. I turn to face them, steadying the barrel of my gun.

"You try to fight this on your own, you're dead anyway," Jed shouts at me. "At least together we have a chance!"

Even if there were five more people with guns, or ten, or twenty, "we have a chance" would be a long shot. But at this point, he's right—we're probably both going to die here anyway. I stare at him for a moment, studying his face. When it comes down to it, really, I don't know much about who this man is at all. I spent most of our journey assuming he was the man who burned down my home and killed my family. It was an easy thing, a simple thing, to hate him. But now, things are a lot less simple. He's the son of one of the worst raiders the wastes have ever seen . . . but does that mean he inherited his father's character? His father's guilt? I don't know. But I do know that a gun in his hand could slightly up our chances of survival.

"Are you even a good shot?" I ask.

He grins. With chaos all around us and very probably impending death, he grins.

Part of me is certain that this is a bad decision, but even so,

I grit my teeth and force myself to hand over a pistol. He takes it and turns to face the stairs just as three raiders burst onto the roof.

With a gun in his hand, Jed transforms. It's like the weapon becomes an extension of his arm, and the rest of his body shapes itself around it. My eyes suddenly find taut muscles in his arm, a hard set in his jaw, a shrewd gleam in his eye, things I swear weren't there a few minutes ago. When he raises the gun, it's easy to see the raider in him, the bloodline of a devilish tyrant, the instincts of a killer. For a moment, I'm certain I made a grave mistake putting that gun in his hand.

His first shot rings out a half second before mine, his second shot just afterward. All three raiders topple over lifelessly. Jed lets out a whoop of excitement, and in that moment returns to the ridiculous human being I became acquainted with on our journey here, the one who hums when he's being kidnapped and tells absurd stories to townie children. I guess I can add "smiling while shooting people" to that list of hobbies now.

"Right in the nose! Did you see that? That was disgusting!" he says happily, firing another two shots in the time it takes him to get the words out. I'm about to tell him to shut up and focus, but when I see a body on the ground for each bullet he's loosed, I figure I'll let him do his thing.

People have a tendency to surprise me, but it's almost never in a good way. Jed is different. He's a damn good shot—almost as good as me—and we fall into a surprisingly easy rhythm. Between the two of us, we take raiders down as fast as they swarm us. I've fought side by side with others before, and I've always found it uncomfortable. I can never focus knowing there's another person so close, with a gun they could turn and fire at me at any instant.

But this feels almost natural. There's a wordless synergy between us—choosing different targets without calling them out, unconsciously planning our timing so we don't need to reload at the same time, covering each other without needing to ask. It feels like we're a two-man army, shooting down raiders as fast as they come, and I find myself smiling amidst the bloodshed. This is what I'm good at, the only time I feel *right*, like I'm exactly where I need to be—blood pumping in my veins, heartbeat thudding in my ears, bullets flying from my gun, walking that fine line between fear and joy, danger and triumph.

And Jed smiles too—smiles and laughs. He feels the rush just like I do; has the same ability to thrive in the chaos rather than surviving it.

Then, as I pause to reload, he turns his gun on me.

I stare at him, my eyes going wide and time slowing around me as I realize there's no way for me to react before he can get a shot off. His smile vanishes, his mouth becoming a tight line as he fires.

I gasp and jerk as the bullet flies right past my head. After a moment's pause, I turn to glance behind me, and see the body of a raider facedown just a few feet away, a crowbar still clutched in his dead hand. I blink at the body and look back at Jed.

"Whew, that was close," he says, an easy grin splitting his face again.

"Guess they found a way up on that side," I mutter, not sure what else to say. Without another word, we place our backs to each other so we cover all directions.

We manage to keep the raiders at bay for longer than I would've thought possible, taking out each one as they come up the stairs—three at a time, and then four, and then more, and then...too many. The buzz of a good fight fades as I remember this is still a losing battle. We've held our ground, but the raiders keep coming, and we're steadily running out of ammo. Next time I pause to reload and look into the bag, my heart sinks.

"Jed," I say, finishing reloading and covering for him as he does the same. "We have to go."

"What?" he asks, moments before peering into the ammo bag. "Oh." He looks like a kid whose dog just died, being told the fight is over, but he heaves a sigh and slings the ammo bag over his shoulder. He jerks his head at the side of the building. "Follow me," he says, and takes off before I can voice my disagreement.

I hesitate. He may not have shot me the second he got a gun in his hands, but that doesn't mean I trust him. He's not the man who burned down my home and killed my family, but I don't have a damn clue who he really is either. But there's no time to figure it out right now. Jed is already gone with my guns and ammo, so I don't have any choice except to follow. I fire off one last shot, directly through the eye of a man running at me, before following Jed.

I have to sprint to keep up, dashing across the rooftop and following as he shimmies down a rusty pipe on the side of the building. He's running again the moment he hits the ground. I rush to match his pace, my steps quickened by the roar of the mob behind me. Thankfully not all of the raiders are on our heels. Most are too preoccupied picking off the last of the townies and pillaging the town. Still, a few stragglers hunt us. I catch glimpses of them as I follow Jed through the ruined buildings.

He dashes through alleyways, climbs through windows, smashes through flimsy barriers. The town isn't even very large, so we must be backtracking and running in circles, but he seems determined to follow this nonsensical path. I want to shout at him to hold up, but I can't spare the breath, so all I can do is follow. Twice I'm afraid that I've lost him, but I always manage to catch him at the last moment, a glimpse of my ammo bag disappearing around a corner or a straggling shoe disappearing through a window.

Finally, we emerge into open ground on the other side of town. I glance behind us, but we've lost the raiders who were chasing us—apparently Jed knew what he was doing with his ridiculous path.

Out in the wastes, I turn to take one last look at the nameless town we've left behind. It's quiet now; without Jed and me, it seems there's no one left to shoot or be shot. Smoke rises from one building, blackening the sky above. I give it one last, searching look, and then harden my heart and turn my back on it—to find Jed standing with his hands up and a gun pointed at his head, and another gun aimed right at me.

"Well, well," Cat says, smiling her sharpened smile from behind the gun. "Look who we have here."

XIII
The Capture

They subdue Jed and take my weapons. Bird pats me down roughly while her companion keeps a gun trained on my head. Cat glares at me, and I glare back, while Bird removes my gun from my holster, and my knife from its strap on my leg, and my other knife from inside my boot. She takes the bag from Jed as well, and lets out a low whistle after a peek inside, slinging it over her shoulder.

"You followed me all the way here," I say, still not really believing it. I don't fight as they take my weapons, knowing it'll just make things worse.

"For *him*, we'd follow you anywhere," Cat says, jerking her thumb at Jed and looking immensely pleased with herself.

"He's worthless," I say.

"I think you mean priceless."

Clearly, they're still under the impression that this man is the real raider king. I hesitate, unsure if I should correct them.

"You can't even claim the bounty," I say. "No one will take him."

"No one sane, nope," Cat says. "Luckily, we have several less-than-sane contacts who will gladly pay out for him."

It could be bullshit, greed, or plain old wishful thinking, but she's not going to believe anything I say; she'll just think

I'm trying to scam her out of the reward. I know because I'd think the same in her position. I take a deep breath and change tactics.

"You don't have to do this," I say, trying to keep my voice calm. "There are bigger issues than a bounty here. There's an angry mob of raiders right behind us."

"Oh, we saw 'em. And they'll spend at least a few hours combing that town and deciding where to go next," Cat says. "We'll be long gone by the time they get moving."

I flex my hands, resisting the urge to take a swing at her. If I want any hope of getting out of this situation alive, I have to get on her good side somehow.

"You're really going to kill a fellow bounty hunter?" I ask. "Won't do good things to your reputation." An already-shitty reputation, but I keep that to myself.

"Who's gonna tell?" Bird asks in her high voice.

"Anyway," Cat says, "we're not going to kill you."

I turn to look at her.

"You're not?" I ask warily, sure there must be a trick.

"Oh, no." I don't like the way she smiles at me at all. It's playful in a nasty way, like she's toying with her food. "You were *kind* enough not to kill us when you had us at your mercy. So, we're going to return the favor. But like you said, there's a lot of angry raiders around here, and we've got a long journey back home." She shrugs. "So I'm afraid we're going to need to take your guns, your ammo, and, uh…just about everything else, really. I'm sure you understand."

"I see," I say, my voice deadly calm. "So you're not going to kill me, you're just going to leave me to die."

"Bingo!" Bird says.

My eyes flick to Jed, who has been absolutely silent this entire time. He's staring at me, his eyes wide and troubled, and hasn't moved an inch from his original position. There's only one

other card I can pull here—the fact that Jed isn't who I thought
he was, and who they still think he is. I could tell them that taking him is useless, because there's no bounty to claim. Maybe
they'd just leave us both here to rot, then...or maybe they'd
shoot him in the head for causing all this trouble. Considering
how vindictive these two seem, I'd guess the latter.

And I find, to my immense surprise and puzzlement, that I'd
rather Jed stay alive. So I say nothing.

"Okay, well, I think we're done here," Cat says. "You're going
to stay right here, and not lift a single finger, or we're going to
shoot you. Got it?"

I stay still and silent as Cat grabs Jed and drags him along,
Bird walks away with my weapons, and the three of them head
to their truck. Jed looks back at me twice, as if waiting for me to
do something, but I stand and watch and do nothing. The truck
starts up with a roar and takes off, leaving me alone in the wastes.

I take a deep breath, and then another one, trying to force
back the tightness in my chest and the panic buzzing in my
ears. Now is not the time for panic. Now is the time to figure
out how to survive.

First things first: I take stock of what I have, searching myself
just in case Bird missed one of the weapons hidden on my body.
She didn't. Nor was I smart enough to store any food or water
somewhere clever in case I got myself into a situation like this.
So, in short, I have absolutely fucking nothing other than the
clothes on my back and the boots on my feet. I suppose they
could have taken the latter if they were really feeling cruel, so
maybe I should be grateful, but mostly I'm just feeling thoroughly, utterly fucked. I don't even have my map, though I've
looked at it enough times that I have a shaky sketch of it in
my head, just enough to know that there are zero towns close
enough for me to reach without any rations.

Still, I'm not the type to sit and accept my fate. I'm not going to wait for raiders to catch up to me, or for the thirst to take me. I force my feet to start moving, walking in the direction that I saw the poachers take Jed, because I have no other goal to aim for.

It's almost strange, being alone now. I was used to it before, but over the days with Jed, I must've gotten accustomed to his constant chatter and inane questions. He always had something to say, questions to ask. I found it…interesting, if I'm being honest. If nothing else, it kept me distracted. Now there's nothing to keep my mind off the tired aches of my body and the reality of this awful situation. At one point I catch myself humming under my breath to fill the silence and stop myself.

The wastelands are silent, hot, and utterly unhelpful, stretching out all around me with nothing to break the monotony. Perhaps I should be grateful that there's nothing to see, because whatever it is would probably try to kill me. But a slow, passive death is much worse. At this point, there's nothing I can do except keep walking. And walking. And walking.

After a while, my brain shuts down.

One by one, I tune things out: the sun bearing down from overheard, the blisters forming on my feet, the sense that I can feel my skin frying. Soon, all that's left is walking.

One foot forward, then the other, then the first again. I do it mechanically, unthinkingly, because that's the only way I can keep going. I'm especially careful to tune out any thoughts about how long I've been walking, or how much farther I have to go, or how long I can possibly go on like this.

I stop when it gets dark, sleep curled up in the dirt with shivers racking my body. When the sun rises, I walk again. More tired, more thirsty, more hopeless than yesterday, but I walk, because the only other option is to stop and wait to die.

I tell myself lies to keep going. I've only been walking for an hour. I only have another hour until I'm done. I know where I am going. There is someone waiting for me there.

When driving, I sometimes forget just how *huge* the wastes are. In a car, with a destination in mind, the flat expanse of wasteland is just something to tolerate for a brief while. But out here, on foot, alone, not knowing where I'm headed, the wastes are everything: vast, empty, and unchanging. I travel all day, and see nothing but sand. Then suddenly, just before sunset, I do find something: a broken-down truck.

And it's not just any truck, I realize as I draw closer. It's the very same truck that was driven by the poachers who took Jed and left me for dead. I'm incredulous at first, certain that I'm hallucinating at this point. I reach out to touch the vehicle, and immediately pull back my finger with a hiss as the hot metal burns me. It's real. And it's easy to see why the truck stopped when it did: A tire's been slashed. Nearby, the cracked earth is splashed with blood. Not too much of it—not a lethal amount— but definitely blood, dried to a muddy red brown. I stare at it for a moment, and then search through the car, every inch, hoping for a forgotten scrap of *anything* left behind for me. But there's nothing; the poachers made sure not to leave anything potentially helpful for whomever found this. I wonder if they suspect I'm on their trail.

I spend the night in the backseat. It may not be my own truck, but it's still a familiar place to sleep, and warmer than the ground. When I wake, my body is more tired than ever, but my mind is invigorated.

I walk briskly now, and with purpose, despite the fact that I can feel my body wasting away.

After a couple hours, I make a new discovery: the sun glinting off metal, which turns out to be a few aluminum cans lying in the dirt. I pick up each one and check for scraps. To my surprise, one still has a few mouthfuls left. Cold beans, mixed with a not-inconsiderable amount of dust, but I scarf them down anyway. Only afterward do I realize it may have been a trap, because what idiot would possibly leave actual, edible food lying out in the wastes?

At least one idiot, it seems, after I've walked another couple hours without dying. I think I know exactly who that idiot is... and how this move might not actually be so idiotic, if he knows that I'm following in his footsteps.

Humming under my breath, I keep walking, with a new energy to my steps. The sun may still be hot, my skin still burning, my feet still aching, but that all seems much less important than before. I have it now: a destination. Someone counting on me. Something to aim for.

As I walk, I alternate between thinking of my guns and fantasizing about my hands around the poachers' throats, slowly squeezing the breath out of both of them in turn. I may have spared them once, but that was before they stole my guns and my bounty and left me to die. Now, it's personal. I want to hear them beg for their lives.

After another hour of brisk walking and thinking about that begging, I think I'm imagining it when I catch a whisper of voices carried on the wind. I stop and look around. Nothing to see yet, but after another moment, I'm *sure* I hear a snatch of conversation. My heart jumps as I recognize Jed's voice—and then Cat's. My hand moves to my gun, only to grasp at empty air. A good reminder that I need to be cautious, no matter how badly I want to sprint toward the voices and smash my fist into someone's face until I feel better. I move carefully, crouching low, sweeping my eyes over the wastes around me. There's nowhere to hide out here, and nowhere to run. It's very important that I see the poachers before they see me.

But after a few minutes of walking and straining to hear, I

have yet to see them or hear more voices. I pick up my pace, frowning, wondering if they managed to lose me somehow or if I really did imagine it. After a couple more minutes and still no sign of them, I walk even more briskly. I should've caught up with them by this point, but there's nothing but the wastes.

Just when I start to panic, I see a lone building ahead. It barely stands, missing its roof and one wall, but it will provide some shelter. I half-jog toward it, and to my relief, catch a snippet of voices as I approach. I press myself against one of the walls.

"But I'm *tired*," Jed's distinctive voice complains just on the other side. "Can't we rest for ten more minutes? And can I get some more water?"

I grin, and a surge of something dangerously close to affection rises inside of me. The truck's slashed tire, the food left behind, and now this. Jed must have orchestrated it all, giving me the time I needed to catch up to the poachers. I would never have made it without him helping. Thanks to him, both of us have a chance.

"We've wasted enough time," Cat snaps. Judging by the tone, I'm guessing she's had more than enough of Jed's shit at this point. "And keep it down. We don't know who else is out here."

"Ten more minutes," Jed insists, followed by the sound of a scuffle.

"No, you—" Cat says. "Don't lie down! We're leaving!" A long pause, and then a sigh. "I *know* you're not sleeping. Closing your eyes isn't going to fool me. Get the fuck up."

It's far too easy to imagine the irritated look on Cat's face, listening to her exasperated groans as she presumably tries to get Jed off the ground. No wonder I was able to catch up to them, if he's being this difficult. He may be completely out of his mind, and damn lucky that the poachers haven't given up and shot him, but I have to admit I'm impressed.

"Fucking hell," Cat says finally. "We're going to have to drag him."

The sound of more scuffling comes toward me. I duck to the side and crouch down. After a few moments, the trio emerges. The poachers are dragging Jed along the ground behind them, each holding one of his arms. He's lying completely limp with his eyes shut, making it as difficult as possible for them.

I follow from a distance. I have to stay quite a ways back in order to stay hidden. Luckily, they make it easy enough to follow. Jed's dragging body leaves distinct marks in the dirt, and he complains loudly every few minutes, his voice carrying across the empty wastes. Honestly, I'm surprised they haven't attracted more attention than just me. The raiders must have stayed in the Nameless Town for a little while, like Cat guessed they would, but they can't be too far behind.

As I follow the poachers, my brain works to come up with a plan. Finding them was the easy part. Now I have to take them out and get my guns back. If I had even a single weapon, it'd be easy. But without one, I can't stand up against two armed hunters. Maybe I can sneak into their camp at night...but even then, it's risky.

I keep following, turning the situation over in my mind. No matter which angle I approach it from, I can't see a way to win this fight, even if I have Jed on my side. He's tied up, I'm running on fumes, and we have zero weapons between us. The only advantage I have is the element of surprise, since they don't even know I'm still alive, but that can only do so much.

My excitement over stumbling upon the group gradually fades. I can follow them all I want, and Jed can do his damnedest to slow them down, but there's not much either of us can do aside from that. Even with the scraps of food that Jed left for me, my body is running down, each step harder than the last. I'm weak, definitely not in any state to fight. While there may be a goal in sight, it's starting to seem like an unobtainable one, and I'm not sure how much longer I can carry on like this.

I find myself lagging farther and farther behind the poachers and Jed. *Maybe this is foolish*, I think. Maybe I should give up on this chase and try to find a town to resupply in. Cut my losses, focus on staying alive. Jed's efforts could be enough to help me survive the journey, and maybe that's the best I can hope for.

When I first hear the voices, I'm too distracted to process them. I'm used to catching snippets of conversation from the poachers. But eventually, it dawns on me that the voices I'm hearing are not familiar ones, nor are they coming from ahead. I stop, turn, and squint at the wastes behind me. I can't see anyone—but there, again, voices. The words are unintelligible, but they're definitely men's voices, coming from behind me.

My fingers once again grasp at the air where my gun should be. My pulse quickens. I force myself to take a deep breath, let it out, and resume walking. I'm in a delicate situation now; I can't walk too slowly and let whomever is following catch up, and I can't walk too quickly and stumble into the poachers. At this point, I have to assume that running into either party will result in a bullet in my brain. As I keep walking, with nothing but empty wastes all around, panic creeps up on me. How long can I keep this up? How long until I get too tired to continue, or at least too tired to keep this pace? How long until one of them realizes I'm here? So many ways this could all go to shit.

But soon comes a reprieve in the form of a small cluster of buildings. It's not a town; these buildings are falling apart, long abandoned. There are no signs that anyone tried to make the place livable, not even any attempts at patching up the holes in the walls. Still, the buildings provide shelter, and I gratefully duck into the closest one. Using crumbling walls and narrow alleys to stay hidden, I can relax my pace. The poachers and Jed are up ahead, still noisy and easy to follow. If I'm bold enough, I realize, I can even wait and see who's behind me.

And with swiftly waning strength and no end to this journey in sight, I don't have much to lose. I find a perch atop a wall, with a good view of the streets between buildings. It's a risky move, but I can't resist the urge to get a look at whomever is coming. If I'm lucky, it could be a group of townies, fleeing the onslaught of raiders; possibly even a group I could join up with.

The approaching voices get louder and louder, and I fight with the urge to run. Finally, the group comes into sight as they walk between two buildings on the edge of town.

Raiders. It's obvious at a glance. They're big and bulky, wielding rusty, bloodstained weapons. I don't see any guns, but their shitty pipes and knives are still more than I have. They're a small group, only six of them. They must have split off from the rest of the army. Either they fell behind those who went ahead in vehicles, or they pulled ahead of the mob behind, leaving them isolated. I could probably handle them myself, if I had my guns. Since I don't, I jump down to the ground and quickly, quietly move to the edge of the ghost town, taking great care not to be spotted.

Defenseless or not, I think I know a way to deal with those raiders. Slowly, carefully, I begin to construct a plan.

When night falls, I'm ready. I follow the poachers until they make camp. They're smart enough to go without a fire now, and stay quiet in the darkness, but I make sure I know exactly where they are.

I leave them and head for the raider camp. Contrary to the poachers, the raiders are loud and rowdy, with a crackling fire much larger than necessary. They have no fear of the wastes surrounding them—and why should they? They're bigger and meaner than anyone in the area, myself included. Well, they're bigger at least, and I'm not much of a threat without my guns.

Yet here I am, creeping closer to their camp, using darkness as my cover. Clutched in my hand is a tin can—left behind by Jed, licked clean by me, and now the only weapon I have.

My heart pounds as I approach, but I won't let myself panic. *I have a plan*, I tell myself. *This isn't suicide.*

The raiders don't even check the surrounding area for threats. They're drowning in overconfidence, and currently wrapped up in a meal: meat, judging by the smell. They eat and talk among themselves, completely at ease.

I get as close as I dare, and push myself to get even closer, so close that my mouth waters at the smell of meat and I can hear one of them chewing with his mouth open. Close enough that, if he were quick enough, one could grab me if he noticed me— but lucky for me, none of them do. I take a deep breath and slowly stand. Still, no one notices me in the darkness. I wind back my arm, and send the can flying.

It smacks right into the side of a man's head. He grunts and drops his hunk of meat in the dirt.

"What the fuck?!" the raider shouts, rising to his feet. He turns to glower at his companions. "Which one of you idiots did that?" The others match his confusion, staring at the can on the ground. After a few moments something clicks, and the man's gaze travels from the fallen can, to the edge of camp, to me, probably barely visible by their fire. The raider's eyes widen. "Who the hell are *you*?"

I run. Shouts and footsteps follow me. *Good.* If they were a little smarter, they might be more wary about following a lone stranger into the darkness. Then again, they probably think I'm just a desperate scavenger trying to steal some food. Either way, their pride won't let them sit back and wait for me to escape. So, they follow.

I run as hard as I can, but my body is weak from lack of food and water, and soon I'm stumbling and panting for breath. If any of the raiders had guns, I'd be dead right now, but luckily they don't. I just have to stay a few paces ahead, far enough that they can't reach me with their fists or weapons. I force my shaking legs to keep moving—just a little farther. A little farther. I'm almost there.

As I see my target I gain a final burst of adrenaline, and hurtle right into the heart of the poachers' camp.

They turn their guns on me in an instant. Cat bares her teeth in a snarl. Bird turns her head one way and another, scrutinizing me through her goggles like she doesn't quite believe what she's seeing. Jed, tied up on the ground and looking like he just woke up from a nap, smiles.

"Clementine!" he says cheerfully, apparently unconcerned by the fact I now have two very big guns pointed at me.

"What the *fuck* are you doing here?" Cat shouts, while I pant for breath. "Guess you really do have a death wish. And I'm more than happy to—"

She cuts off as a half dozen raiders charge in behind me.

For a moment there's a pause—a long pause, as the raiders and the poachers stare at one another across the camp, mirroring the others' bewilderment. As they stare, I drop to the ground. A moment later, the shooting begins.

I crawl on my hands and knees across the camp while the fight rages. I flinch and duck at every gunshot and clang of metal and thud of flesh, but none of it is aimed at me. The raiders are more concerned about the ones with guns, the poachers too busy handling three angry raiders each to pay attention to me, but Jed's eyes never leave me.

"I knew you'd come for me," he says, grinning, as I draw closer.

I crawl right past him, my eyes homing in on one thing: my

bag of guns. I scoop it up and unzip it, quickly sifting through to verify my guns and ammo are inside. I check that my pistol is loaded, take that, and sling the bag over my shoulder. I find two bottles of water as well, tossing those in with my weapons. Unfortunately, there's no food to be found. But despite that, a deep calm settles over me. With a gun in my hand, it feels like I just might make it through this alive.

"Clementine," Jed says, attempting to wriggle in my direction. "Hey! You *are* here for me, right?"

I pause, glancing over the fight still raging between the poachers and raiders. As much as I'd love to be the one who kills those damn poachers, I don't think it's worth getting involved.

"C'mon! I left that food for you. I saved your life!" Jed is saying. I finally look at him. He's a bit battered, with a split lip and a swollen eye. His good eye is very wide and locked on me. "You know I can be useful. We're better off together."

"Yeah, yeah," I mutter, crouching beside him. Getting my guns was more important, but I never planned on leaving him here either. He's right that he's saved my life more than once now: first in the Nameless Town, and later when he left food behind. And while he's probably going to run back to his father as soon as he gets a chance, for now, we are better off together. Can't say that I'm not eager for companionship out here in the wastes, either, as much as the realization of that surprises me. The long days of wandering alone have changed my perspective a little, and given how weak I am right now, it won't hurt to have someone else around.

I work at the bindings around his ankles first, and then those around his wrists. I glance over him as I do so. Aside from the minor wounds on his face, he seems mostly unharmed. Considering the way he was acting, he's pretty damn lucky to still be in one piece.

We're going to need a little more of that luck to get out of here alive. The raiders and poachers may be too busy dealing with one another to pay much attention to us, but there are still bullets and limbs flying everywhere. Cat stumbles right toward us, entangled with a raider twice her size. Jed sticks out a leg to trip the man and they both go down. Cat's pinned beneath the man, trapped—but a moment later, the raider screams as her sharpened teeth rip into his throat.

I keep one eye on the fight as I finish untying Jed's wrists. Right now it's a total bloodbath, and it's hard to tell who's winning. We need to get out of here before that changes and they suddenly remember we exist. Once I get Jed free, I stand and yank him to his feet beside me.

Nearby, Cat is grappling with two men now, a third lifeless nearby, blood still spurting from his torn throat. Bird has another raider on the ground, and is currently straddling his chest and driving a knife repeatedly into his face. Her head jerks up as Jed and I stand, her mask whipping toward me, goggles shining in the darkness. Another raider tackles her to the ground before she can do anything about it.

"Whew," Jed says. "Like I said. Knew you'd come for me."

I glance sideways at him, suppressing a smile.

"Oh, shut up," I say. "Let's get out of here."

Together, we run into the wastes.

XIV
The Council of Fort Cain

We run until we can't hear the sounds of shouting or gunfire any longer, and then slow to a walk, side by side. Neither of us talks. Not enough breath, and nothing to say, at least on my part. We're back together, for better or for worse.

After a while, it feels like we've put some good distance between us and the poachers. My weakened body is exhausted, and stumbling around blindly in the dark becomes more trouble than it's worth. I point out a cluster of rocks nearby, which seems like the best shelter we're going to get, and we curl up against the biggest one. I down most of a bottle of water, rest my hand on my gun, and drift into sleep beside Jed.

We wake up at the crack of dawn and start walking again. I'm more tired than ever, my body wearing down quickly from the lack of food, but I force myself to keep moving. The wastes are quiet around us. No poachers, no raiders. Maybe they killed each other off, though I doubt we're that lucky. I'd be willing to bet that Bird and Cat made it through. It's more likely that they just don't know where we are, or have temporarily pulled back to lick their wounds. Either way, we're safe for now. Better yet, Jed says the poachers spoke of a town while he was with them, and he knows what direction to head in, though he doesn't know how far it is. It's possible we'll run into the two assholes on the way there, but it's still our best bet.

"Wait," Jed says, jerking to such a sudden stop that I quickly look around for some kind of threat. There's nothing but empty wastes around us, so I turn back to Jed, who is staring off into the distance and frowning. "Wrong way," he says, turns to the left, and starts walking again.

Within the next hour, he does the same thing twice more. I have to admit I was relieved to be reunited with him and have some decent company out here, but that relief dwindles as my stomach growls. We may have gotten enough water to keep me from collapsing, but I'm still weak from exhaustion and hunger.

"Do you actually know where we're going or not?" I ask, grinding my teeth and trying to refrain from snapping at him. Jed stops walking again, placing his hands on his hips and tapping one foot.

"Good question," he says. He pauses, gnawing his bottom lip while he thinks, and then his eyes light up. "Wait—got it!" He licks one of his fingers and thrusts it up in the air above him. He holds it there, the rest of his body stock-still.

"What the fuck are you doing?" I ask, after several seconds of this.

"Checking the wind," he says without moving. I stare at him, bewildered. A solid thirty seconds pass without any change. Finally, he lowers his finger. "There's no wind," he says, regretfully.

"Yeah, no shit," I say. "This isn't the time to fuck around, Jed." I know at this point that he's certainly no idiot, but he *is* wasting our time right now, and we don't have much to spare. My legs feel like they're going to give out at any second.

"Just trying to lighten the mood," he says, shrugging. "It's getting kind of grim around here."

I sigh and resume walking in the latest direction he's chosen, beginning to wonder how the hell Jed has survived this far, and how I could've ever missed having him around. After a few moments, he trudges after me.

After seeing nothing but empty wastes for a few hours, I start to think Jed might have no idea what he's talking about. Even if there's a town somewhere around here, I'm not sure if I can make it. My legs are starting to shake, threatening to give out every few steps, and my head feels light. Progress is agonizingly slow, and I can feel my already-paltry strength waning by the minute. My throat and eyes burn, every blink and breath harder than the last one. Soon Jed ends up walking ahead of me, while I lag behind. Jed shoots worried glances over his shoulder and stops humming and making his stupid jokes.

"Can't be much longer," he says. His voice is quieter than normal, almost coaxing, his face etched with a frown that makes him look older.

Of course it can be, I think, half-delirious, looking out at the expanse of endless wastelands around us. It could be forever. The town we're looking for might not even exist anymore. It could've been swallowed by the wastes, and soon we will be too. But I say nothing, and force myself to keep moving.

And against all odds, after a second hour passes, a town emerges on the horizon.

"There it is," Jed yells, pointing toward the looming buildings and turning to me, as if there's any way I could possibly have missed them. "I told you so!"

"Quiet down," I say, eyeing the place. "We don't know if they're friendly."

"Well, it's not like we're gonna sneak up on them," Jed says. Still, he quiets as we draw closer.

This place is certainly bigger than the Nameless Town. It may not have been on the map I had, but it's clearly an established town nonetheless, not something shoddily thrown together. A wall constructed of scrap metal and spare car parts surrounds the place, topped with barbed wire. The only break in the fence is the front gate, a huge and impenetrable-looking sheet of rusty metal. Jed and I stop a few feet away from it. I scrutinize the gate, searching for a way to open it.

"Move along, strangers," a voice calls from above. I lean back and look up to see a woman scowling down at me from a lookout perch. It sticks out just above the wall and is tilted slightly, as if it's on the verge of falling over. The woman wears a helmet and wields an impressive sniper rifle. I raise both my hands, and elbow Jed in the side, prompting him to do the same.

"We mean no harm," I shout up to the woman. "Just need a place to stay for a night or two."

She says nothing, but gestures with her gun for us to leave. My gut tightens. If this town turns us away, I'm done for. I need food badly. Without it, I don't think I'll be able to get up tomorrow. But talking to people has never been a strong point of mine, and it's harder still with my head swimming from fatigue and hunger.

"Do something," I whisper to Jed.

He blinks at me, and looks up at the guard above.

"Please," he says, with as much desperation as he can channel into a shout. "We've got nowhere else to go. We won't make it to the next town."

"Not my problem," she says, and leans back in her perch, a clear dismissal. Jed and I exchange another glance, and I shrug.

"All right, strategy number two," Jed mumbles under his breath, and clears his throat. "We've got guns to trade," he shouts up to her. "And ammo."

"I don't—"

"You're gonna need 'em," he adds, "for what's coming this way."

She leans forward, looking down at us.

"The raiders?" she asks. "We got word from out there, but..."

"We've faced it ourselves," I shout up to her. "Barely made it out."

She stares down at us, clearly thinking about something. I have no idea what it could be, but Jed's face sharpens with realization.

"Let us in and we'll tell you all about it," he says. "We faced them once and lived. We'll help you do the same."

She pauses for a long moment. Then she stands up, looks down at the other side of the gate, and gestures to someone. A moment later, with a screech of metal, the gate starts to rise. It does so slowly, full of creaking complaints, like it's tired of doing its job and wants the world to know.

"Nice job," I say to Jed, glancing sideways at him.

"Told you I could be useful," he says, grinning.

Jed and I stay where we are with our hands in the air. Gradually, the rising gate reveals the town within, including a man manually working the crank, and a half dozen armed townies waiting on the other side. I resist the urge to grab my gun. When they gesture at us to enter, we step inside, and the gate slams shut behind our backs.

The townies welcome us by shoving guns in our faces and shouting commands.

"Get on the ground!" one man yells, at the same time another says, "Don't fucking move!"

Jed and I look at each other in confusion.

"Uh," Jed says. "Which do you want us to—"

One man circles around to Jed's back and jabs him forward with the gun, and another promptly shoves him back. He stumbles, struggling to stay on his feet. It takes all my willpower to keep my hands in the air.

"Give us your weapons," a man in front of us says. I reach for my pistol, and immediately another townie screams at me not to touch my gun. I stop moving and take a deep breath, desperately trying to keep my shit together, while the townies push us this way and that, shouting a variety of commands.

Jed keeps his hands held skyward. I very slowly pluck my gun out of its holster, lower it to the ground, and raise my hands again. Thankfully none of the idiot townies mistake that for aggression, and once it becomes clear we're not going to resist, the shouting gradually dies down. Despite our cooperation, they still insist on holding us at gunpoint while others pat us down, removing each and every thing that could remotely constitute a weapon from our bodies. I force myself to bite my tongue as they take my guns, no matter how much I hate it. I just got the damn things back, and already they're gone.

Despite the treatment, part of me is glad to see that the townies are so wary. It means they haven't given up yet. They are, however, very afraid. They're tightly wound and jerky in their movements, eyes skittering around, three lookouts keeping an eye on the wastes outside like they expect us to have armed friends charging in behind us. I'm half-certain they're going to take our weapons and throw us out in the wastes again, which would be a death sentence. But thankfully, after we've made a great show of being cooperative and peaceful, they relax a bit—though they keep our weapons.

The town looked imposing and organized from the outside, but on the other side of the wall, we're merely the newest addition to a cluster-fuck of activity. Townspeople are running everywhere, carrying personal belongings and supplies to and fro, arguing over what belongs to whom, fighting over what should be saved and what should be left behind. We pass two men playing tug-of-war with a half-broken chair, yelling about whether it's better to burn it for cooking or add it to the defenses. If there's someone in charge here, they're not showing their face. I guess they have bigger things to worry about than a tussle over furniture.

A group of five of the men and women who were guarding the front wall escort us through town, completely ignoring the chaos around us, guns pointed at our heads the whole time. Jed lowers his hands and walks at a leisurely pace, glancing around at the various ridiculous scenes around us. He looks like he's trying very hard not to smile. I shoot him a glare for that. We're already walking on thin ice; the townies don't need to see him being amused by their trouble. Thankfully, none of the townies notice his mirth.

They lead us to a building in the back, away from the chaos at the heart of town. After muttering among themselves, the group accompanying us disperses, leaving only the woman from the lookout perch behind. She silently escorts us into the building.

The room we enter is quiet. It holds only a run-down, stained wooden table, with two women and a man seated at it. Spread across the surface between them is a frayed, yellowed piece of paper with curled edges. As soon as we enter, the three grab it and turn it facedown, hiding its contents from our sight. I catch only a glimpse of what seems to be a diagram of the town.

"What's this?" one of the women asks sharply. She's middle-aged, with pinched lips and olive skin. She scrutinizes Jed and me and glares at the guard accompanying us. "I thought we agreed not to let any strangers into town. We've got enough to worry about already."

"I know, I know," the guard says. She takes off her helmet, runs a hand through her sweaty hair, and shrugs. "But these two say they've seen the raiders. Thought we should hear what they have to say."

The woman at the table looks back at us, her eyes narrowing.

"They've been disarmed, at least?"

"Of course," the guard says. "And I gotta say, there was a lot of disarming to be done. The two were packing. Her especially." She jerks her chin at me. I keep my face neutral, meeting the eyes of the woman at the table. Her lips twist to one side, and she nods at the guard.

"Got it. You can go now."

The guard leaves us. When the door shuts behind her, the room is quiet. The three townies at the table eye us warily. Jed, beside me, shifts from foot to foot and clears his throat. I shoot him a warning glare, just to make sure he doesn't get any stupid ideas, but he stays quiet.

"So which of you is in charge here?" I ask finally, looking from one to another.

"All of us," the single man says. He has hard eyes and a scruffy black goatee. "We're the council of Fort Cain." He says it with a proudly raised chin, like I should recognize the name of their backwater little western town. I look at Jed, wondering if I should have heard of the place, but he shrugs back at me, as lost as I am.

"All right," I say. "Well, we—"

"So you saw the raiders?" the woman who spoke before asks. "We've had a few people fleeing this way, talking about some massive army coming this way, but no details. You actually saw them?"

I take a deep breath, trying to stifle my annoyance at being interrupted, reminding myself that we're currently at these people's mercy.

"We did," I say. "They overtook the last town we stayed in."

"How many of them were there?" the man asks. I know what he's really asking: *Do we have a chance?* I don't think he really wants to know the answer, but is it really better to lie to him, set up false hopes? I exchange another look with Jed.

"A lot of them," I say. "It's hard to get an exact number." It's the best I can do, I figure, without causing a panic. But the council, of course, isn't pleased with that response—or maybe the implied answer behind it: *Too many.*

"It's possible some of them have split off from the main group by now," Jed adds, finally speaking up. "But yeah, last time we saw, I'd say...about a hundred of them, at least."

Clearly he hasn't taken the hint to be vague. The council members murmur among themselves, their expressions troubled. I stay silent, waiting for them to speak again. Whatever damage Jed has done with the truth, it can't be undone at this point.

"We appreciate the honesty," the third council member says, speaking for the first time. She has a plain and open face, lined with age and experience. "Is there anything else you can tell us?"

I pause, considering. I know what she wants to hear is good news, something that will help them, or at least boost morale, but there's not much to give. There isn't some big secret that's going to change the fact that they're completely fucked. But I'm not going to be the person to tell them that, especially not when I'm looking to stay here for a night or two, utilize their shelter and supplies for as long as they last.

"They don't have any vehicles," I say after a moment. "The ones who did already went ahead. These are...the strays, I guess. They don't have the best weapons, and they're disorganized. Not a singular army, but a bunch of crews who happen to be headed the same way. They'll work together, but only to a certain extent."

Of course, the council looks disappointed. I know they wanted more, but I can't give anything else without lying blatantly to their faces.

"Thank you," the older woman says. While the other two are sullen, she at least seems to be holding it together. "I have one last question. Is it true the raiders came from Saint's tower?"

I hesitate for a long moment. I don't want to break these people, but so far this woman, at least, seems to have genuinely appreciated the honesty.

"Yes," I say finally. "That's what it seems like. The sheriff of a nearby town said most of them came from inside the tower, that they'd been there all along."

I've barely finished speaking when the other woman suddenly slams a fist on the table. The man and the elderly woman turn to face her with startled expressions.

"He fucked us," she says through gritted teeth. "Do you know how many raiders we brought to him? And this whole time, he was lying about killing them. Jesus *fuck*. He's no better than that Jedediah Johnson in the east."

"Jedediah Johnson would've been better," the man mutters. "At least he's upfront about what he's doing."

I try to suppress my reaction, and refuse to look at Jed, though I see him glance at me. I clear my throat, collecting myself before speaking.

"You know of Jedediah Johnson?" I ask, very carefully.

"Heard of him recently," the older woman says, speaking before the other two have a chance to. She's still maintaining her composure. I respect that. "Other towns sent warning that he's headed this way, stopping at each and every town, looking for someone. I guess a couple of them have sworn their loyalty to him already, hoping he'll protect them from the raider army. Word is he'll be here within the week."

I feel a cold prickle of fear at that. Within the week? As if we didn't have enough to worry about with the raider army. Even if this town miraculously holds against that onslaught, I still won't be safe from Jed's father here. There's no way the town can keep him out, especially not when they'll be worn down from their encounter with the raiders.

"Dunno why he's bothering with this area," the other woman says. "It's enough of a shitfest already."

"Maybe that's the point," the man says with a shrug. "This place is ripe for the picking, ain't it? And maybe it wouldn't be so bad. Maybe we should consider swearing to him when he gets here. *If* we make it that long."

"Jedediah Johnson is a monster," I spit out, unable to help myself. The council turns to me, surprised by the interjection, and I take a breath to calm myself. "I've been to the eastern wastes. People live awful lives. Whatever you may have heard, he's nothing but a dictator. And not a benevolent one."

Beside me, Jed shifts and makes some noise that sounds almost like protest under his breath. I shoot him a dark look, and he presses his lips together, saying nothing.

"Well, at least they live," the man says. "Better to be under his control than to be wiped out by raiders, ain't it?"

The two women exchange a glance, drop their eyes, and say nothing. I keep my mouth shut as well and, to my own shock, feel a glimmer of uncertainty about whether he's right.

The conversation may not have gone too smoothly, but in the end the council agrees to let us stay in town. They let us loose without a guard, though I suspect that's less of a sign of trust and more of a sign that they can't spare anyone to babysit us. They do, however, refuse to give us our guns back, which leaves me feeling itchy and vulnerable.

This place is certainly better equipped than the Nameless Town. They have real defenses set up, real guns to arm their townies with, real plans on how to hold out against the flood of raiders headed this way. If I hadn't witnessed the massacre at the Nameless Town, I might've let myself have a shred of hope. I might've thought they could at least hold well enough that the raiders would get bored and move on to an easier target. But as it is, all I can think of is the march of raiders on the Nameless Town, the seemingly-endless amount of them, the sheer vicious- ness of the mob as they tore their way through the people there. Plus, by now the raiders will be hungry. I can't help but feel that, no matter what defenses and plans they have, these people don't understand what's coming for them. It's all too easy to imagine the wall coming down and these people being slaughtered.

But Jed and I are in no position to be on the run again so soon. We need this time to rest, prepare ourselves for more travel ahead. We have little choice but to stay here—for as long as we can, at least. I'll be happy if we get one good night's sleep under a roof instead of out in the open wastes. I know better than to expect more than that. After Jed speaks to the townies and gets us a tiny serving of water and canned food to share, I keep to myself in town, sitting quietly in the shade of a building and watching the townies go about their defensive preparations.

Jed, apparently, is not on the same page as I am. He's unnat- urally quiet for the first hour or so, probably exhausted and shell-shocked from our bumpy journey here. But after a brief nap—during which I keep watch, because I don't fully trust these people—he's back to his old self again, but in hyperdrive. I have no idea where he finds the energy or the spirit, but soon he's flitting around and chatting up just about anyone who will listen. I sit by myself and watch him, half-annoyed and half- puzzled, as he talks the ear off every townie he can find.

It's easy to write him and his constant chatter off as ridic- ulous, but he's remarkably skilled at getting on people's good sides. The townies seem mistrustful of him at first, but soon he's earning himself smiles, and then laughs, and soon enough they're treating him like one of their own. Meanwhile, I sit alone, and townies shoot me nervous glances and give me a wide berth as they pass by. I don't understand how he does it...

but I have to admit that I respect his ability to earn people's trust. Not just respect—part of me envies it. No one has looked at me the way people look at him since Old Creek burned.

Still, I don't see the point of getting to know these townies when they're basically dead already. This is not the time or the place to get friendly with the locals, and it irritates me that Jed is wasting time working his charms on them right now.

"Hi," a quiet voice says. I look up to find a townie girl standing a couple feet away. She's young, barely a teenager from the look of her, with mousy hair pulled back in a ragged braid and a pair of buck teeth.

"What do you want?" I ask, a little more harshly than I intended, and the girl blushes.

"Um, well, I heard that you and your partner got into a scrape with some raiders," she says, and I suppress an eye roll at the word "partner." Goddamn Jed. "I thought you might be hurt, so I brought some bandages." She holds up a bag for me to see, gauze poking out from within.

"I'm fine," I say. Again, the words come out unnecessarily hard, but the girl doesn't back away like I'm half-hoping she will. I glance around for Jed. He's busy talking with a small crowd of men nearby, and doesn't notice me looking.

"Are you sure?" the girl asks, her forehead creasing. "You've got a cut on your cheek, and—"

"I said I'm fine, girl." My voice is intentionally sharp this time. "Now shoo."

The girl's eyes widen, and she scurries away without another word. Sighing, I let my head fall back against the cool bricks behind me. My brain flashes an unwanted image of that townie kid, Wyatt, who helped me in the Nameless Town, and I grimace. I don't need any more faces haunting my thoughts. If things were different, maybe I could make an effort, try to settle down here. But this place is practically dust and ash already.

While I want to find a new home, I don't think I can take losing one again.

After a few minutes, footsteps approach. I raise my head again, bristling, ready to tell off whatever townie is disturbing me this time, but it's only Jed. He looks down at me with his head tilted to one side, and then drops to a seat beside me. He hands over a bottle of water. It's much more than the townies initially gave us; at least Jed's socializing has gained us that benefit.

"What are you up to over here?" he asks, while I take several greedy gulps.

"Keeping my distance," I say, lowering the bottle and wiping my mouth with the back of my hand. I eye him as I hand the bottle back. "What are *you* doing?"

"Well, I was over there telling Dan and Bert about our journey here, but Mary came by and said—"

"Stop it," I snap. "For fuck's sake, Jed. I don't want to know these people's names."

"Why's that?" he asks, frowning.

"Don't play dumb," I say. "You know as well as I do that these people will be dead come tomorrow. This stay is *very* temporary."

He's quiet for a moment.

"Yeah, I know," he says finally, without any of the casual joviality from before. "Still, can't hurt to figure out how many people are in town, how many will be armed when the raiders come, what kind of defenses they're setting up..."

I stare wordlessly at him. I never would have expected that, with all of his joking around and casual chatting with the townies, he's getting important information. Once again, it seems I've underestimated him. I give him an appraising look. He's a damn good shot, charming as all hell, clearly much smarter than his constant joking suggests...What else lurks beneath that ridiculous exterior?

"I'm getting a feel for our options," he says, when I don't comment.

"What's that supposed to mean?"

He smiles. After one more sip of water, he hands me the last of it and stands up.

"Don't worry about it," he says, brushing dust off his pants. "Just...y'know, you do you, and I'll do me."

With that he's gone, back to talking with the townies and helping with the hustle and bustle around town. I watch him, frowning, still trying to puzzle him out and decide whether I trust him. He may not be the infamous raider I thought he was, but he's still a raider, and his father's infamous blood flows through his veins. I have yet to figure out how I feel about him, but I do know that I don't understand him at all.

Plus, I think, watching him dramatically reenact our journey here for a group of townies, *I'm still not convinced he's entirely sane.*

As night falls, the townies retreat into their saloon. Despite its worn appearance and half-broken door, it isn't too bad inside. The floorboards are scuffed up but mostly intact, and there's even some makeshift furniture: tables and mismatched chairs, a bar with a couple of rickety stools. The bar doesn't actually serve anything other than water, but still. A few townies stay outside on the wall to keep watch, and the rest crowd inside of the small building.

I stand in a corner, waiting to grab the attention of someone important and ask where Jed and I can spend the night, but anyone with any semblance of authority seems to be dealing with a steady stream of worried townies. As I wait, Jed brings me a warm can of beans. I slurp it down, and he leans against the wall beside me, looking out at the townies with an oddly shrewd face. I stay quiet, watching alongside him.

"Wait a second," he says, his face lighting up as his eyes find something in the corner. "Is that what I think it is?"

"Oh, no," I say under my breath, following his gaze. I reach out to grab his arm and stop him, but he's already weaving his way through the crowd on the way over.

What he finds, stuffed into the corner of the room and half-covered with a ragged blanket, is a piano. He drags the blanket off, revealing a dusty and cobwebbed but still mostly intact instrument. The townies make room for him on the bench without him even asking. He slides onto it between two townie women and brushes his fingertips over the keys. He blows off some dust, cleans a spot of grime with his shirt, and prods a few keys to test it out, his head tilted to one side and his expression deeply thoughtful. A satisfied smile spreads across his face, and he starts to play.

"You've got to be fucking kidding me," I mutter to myself, still leaning against the wall where he left me. Of course Jed actually knows how to play a goddamn piano. There are some missing keys and the thing is clearly not in the best state of repair, but he still manages to play a song that sounds almost correct. I recognize it as the one he hums all the time—and he hums still as he plays, fingers dancing over the keys. The townies are absolutely delighted by the unexpected entertainment, their faces lighting up, gathering around Jed as he plays. Some attempt to clap along, though it's clear none of them actually know the tune.

"Of all the useless skills to have," I mutter to myself, shaking my head. What person nowadays actually knows how to play an instrument? Who would spend their time learning that, of all things? And how would someone even manage it? It's absurd. Then again, I suppose if anyone had the time and resources to learn a useless skill, it would be the son of a crazy dictator. I guess when you don't have to constantly worry about how to survive, you can spend your time on other things.

The "why" of the matter is a bit harder to grasp, but it always seems to be with Jed. Spending time with him is basically a long series of me repeatedly wondering *why*. I don't think he even knows the answer half the time.

Though the "why" of learning the piano is hard to gauge, the "why" of playing it now is evident: the townies absolutely adore him for it. The tension melts away, and the townies treat him like an old friend, laughing and joking and clapping him on the back. Jed invites me to join him on the bench a few times, but I shake my head and keep my distance.

It's strange, watching how easily Jed interacts with people. I've never had his easy charm and way of speaking to strangers like they're friends. Actually, I seem to have the opposite effect on most people. People respect me, fear me, occasionally trust me, but I'm well aware that most people don't particularly *like* me. Nobody has, ever since Old Creek. Except…Jed, perhaps.

But people look at Jed like he's a torch in the darkness. They listen to every word he says, laugh at every joke out of his mouth—some of which are *definitely* not funny. The men trust him easily, and the women blush when he looks at them. It's puzzling, and a bit aggravating, especially when I know his father's legacy. Jed's skills with both guns and people must have come from him, I realize. It's a disquieting thought. And I think I'm beginning to see how Jedediah Johnson came into power.

Later, when most of the townies have dispersed and we've finally managed to get someone's attention for long enough to ask about a place to stay, we leave the saloon. Jed is cheerful, still humming his song under his breath, though I don't understand how he has any energy at all left after the events of today.

He follows as I trudge ahead, finding the building on the outskirts of town. It must be the living quarters for the townies as well, because we pass several others headed to bed, many of whom greet Jed as they recognize him. I ignore them and follow the directions we were given to a room in the back corner.

We step inside, shutting the door behind us—and thankfully it has an actual, functional door—and Jed raises the lantern we were given to get a better look at the place. It's a dim room, with a single window that's been boarded up, bare except for a single cot in one corner.

"Wow," I say. "They actually gave us a cot. With a blanket and everything." It's more generosity than I'm used to getting, though I'm sure it has more to do with Jed than with me. Still, Jed immediately finds a spot against the wall near the foot of the cot, leaving it to me without a moment's hesitation.

I inspect the cot for any overly concerning stains or marks and, finding nothing, lower myself onto it. My body creaks as I stretch out, and I sigh with relief, pulling the blanket over me.

I know I should just try to get some sleep, but while my body is exhausted, my mind is a-whir with the events of the day. After a few minutes of tossing and turning and attempting to sleep, curiosity gets the better of me.

"So where did you learn that?" I ask, staring up at the ceiling.

"What?" Jed asks from the foot of the cot, his voice groggy and half-asleep.

"Music," I say. "I've only known a couple of people who could play it, and they learned it before." Before the bombs, when people had all the time in the world to spend on silly things like that.

There's a moment's pause. Jed sits up and scoots closer, all hints of sleepiness gone.

"Clementine?" he asks, his voice *far* too excited. "You're

asking about me? A personal question? You want to get to know me?"

"Jed—"

"This is it," he gushes, his eyes sparkling. "A bonding moment. It's finally happening. You. And me. Forming a lasting friendship."

Noticing that he's scooting a little too close for comfort, I sit up and shove him. He falls back with a thud and immediately scrambles up again, sitting cross-legged just beyond the foot of the cot.

"Forget I asked," I say, rolling my eyes, and fighting back embarrassment because he's right—I *did* want to know more about him. Because, while Jed is strange and difficult to understand and frequently irritating, I can't help but find him interesting. I want to figure him out, though I'd be hard-pressed to explain why that is.

But, as earnest as he seems, I'm guessing that obnoxious response was his own crazy way of derailing the conversation and brushing me off. I guess he doesn't want to tell me the truth, which is fine. It was probably a mistake to bring it up. We're together out of necessity, not anything else; I can't let myself forget that. Jed may be friendly toward me, but he's friendly to anyone. It was stupid to think there was any other reason for it. I pull my blanket tighter around myself and try to get comfortable again. But just when I think Jed is about to go back to sleep, he speaks up again.

"My mom taught me," he says. He speaks quietly now, the over-the-top excited act totally gone. I pause, letting the words sink in, and resume curling myself up in a nest on my cot. Clearly, the question was even more personal than I intended it to be. "She taught me when I was a kid. Before she, uh, died."

"I see." No point in expressing condolences. It sounds like it happened a long time ago, and anyway, it isn't anything special to lose one's parents. Pretty much everyone's parents are dead at this point; it's just a fact of life. The wastelands aren't a place where people lead long, healthy lives.

"Was killed, I mean," Jed says. "By my dad. My dad killed her. When I was a kid."

"Oh." Now that is a more unique scenario, and I'm feeling even more deeply uncomfortable. It's been years since I had a conversation this personal, and I don't think I ever really mastered how to handle them. Again, speaking condolences seems wrong, but what else can I say? We both fall silent, the only sound our breathing in the dark room. After a moment, barely even knowing what I'm doing, I sit up and reach out to him. My hand finds one of his, and I squeeze it briefly. When I try to pull back, Jed holds on to me.

"Clementine," he says quietly.

"Yeah?"

"I have to confess something," he says. I stay silent, still gripping his hand, all too aware of the small amount of space between us. "I got caught on purpose."

"What?" It takes me a few moments to realize what he's talking about. We've been through so much at this point that the start of our journey seems impossibly long ago.

"I could've called for a guard. There was one right down the hall," he says. "And I could've told you I wasn't who you thought I was too. But I didn't."

"Why?" Again, with him, the eternal "why." Why would he do that? Why is he telling me? Why now?

"Because I couldn't stand being there any longer," he says. "And I don't want to go back now." He loops his fingers through mine, squeezes more tightly. "Can I stay with you?"

It's been a long time since I've been asked something like that. A long time since I kept company that wasn't for necessity or profit. I was half-convinced nobody ever would again after I lost my home. I'm not sure how to react to it now. I open and shut my mouth a couple times, trying to come up with an answer, and de-tangle my fingers from his.

"Let's just worry about surviving for now," I say finally. "We'll work the rest out later."

"Okay," he says, his tone hard to read. He curls up on the floor again, his head resting on the edge of the cot now. I sigh quietly, and after a moment, I lie back and try to sleep.

XV
Preparations

I wake to the sound of shouting. I jolt upright, untangling myself from my blanket and standing up. The commotion is coming from outside, not within our room, so the danger isn't immediate...and it's lucky that's the case, because Jed hasn't moved an inch. I stare down at him, still fast asleep despite my movement and all the noise outside, and wonder how the hell he's managed to survive for this long.

He finally wakes up when I kick him, and blinks at me from the floor.

"What is...What? Is something happening?" he asks, rubbing at his eyes with one hand. I ignore him and go to grab my gun from its holster, only to realize that it's empty. No guns, not even a knife; the townies stripped us bare and helpless when we walked into town.

"Damn it," I say, looking down at a still-groggy Jed. For a moment I feel a flicker of discomfort, remembering our way-too-personal conversation last night, but I stifle it. There's no time to dwell on that. I grab him by the arm and haul him to his feet, pulling him toward the door without giving him a chance to protest. "C'mon, Jed. Time to be useful again."

By the time we've left our room, the chaos has died down

somewhat. A handful of townies are still running around, moving supplies and checking defenses, but the majority of them have already taken their places on the wall. From the way they're talking and moving, it's easy to guess what caused the ruckus: The raiders are coming.

Despite the still-obvious fear, the townies seem to know what they're doing. They have a strong front line, some good vantage points, even a couple snipers set up on the rooftops. The elderly and children hover just behind the fighting folk, carrying ammo, water, and first aid supplies. They're preparing themselves for a long siege.

It's far more organized than I would've expected from a shitty little western town. Jed and I exchange a glance as we head to the wall, and I imagine he's thinking the same thing I am: *Is it possible these townies actually stand a chance?*

As much as I want to charge in and demand my guns, I hang back as Jed goes to talk to one of the town's council members. After a few minutes of conversation, Jed shoots me an overly enthusiastic thumbs-up before disappearing with the man. A few minutes later, he returns with our weapons.

The moment I see the bag, I'm itching to have my hands on it and fill the hole its absence left. I suppress the urge to run over and rip it out of Jed's grasp. The townies already eye me like they think I might be a mass murderer on the verge of snapping. It won't help my case if I act like a psycho who's in love with her guns, whether or not that may be true. Still, when Jed hands over the bag, and I find my pistol sitting right on top, I hold it to my chest like a long-lost child.

"Gee, thanks, Jed," Jed says, after a moment or two of me cradling the gun. "Good work, buddy. I like you at least half as much as I like my guns. Maybe one day it will be three-quarters as much."

I smirk and tuck the gun into its holster.

"Never gonna happen," I say, grabbing my knife and slipping it into its strap on my leg. I'm about to sling the assault rifle over my shoulder, but pause, hesitating briefly before handing it to Jed. His jaw drops.

"You're giving me the big gun?" he asks, hugging the weapon against him. I eye it in his hands, wondering if I've made a mistake.

"You know how to use it?"

"Of course I do!" He shifts the gun so he's holding it properly, and turns in a quick half circle, making sound effects under his breath as he pretends to fire at invisible enemies. I watch him warily, but despite the ridiculous attitude, it does look like he knows what he's doing. I nod at him, sling the now-mostly-empty weapons bag over my shoulder, and head to the wall. I find one of the council members nearby, the older woman. Relief flickers across her face when she sees us. Guess she thought we were going to take off, which isn't an unreasonable concern. I'm still not convinced that staying is the best option, but it's a little late now.

"Glad to see you two," she says, and gestures to the wall. "You can take a place on any of the towers, or wherever else. I'll trust your judgment."

I nod to the councilwoman, Jed shoots her an obnoxiously over-the-top salute, and the two of us head to a nearby watchtower. From there, we should have a good view of the front gate, the direction the raiders will be coming from. I climb the ladder propped up to allow access, and Jed follows close on my heels.

The townies already waiting in the tower are all smiles once they see us and the guns in our hands. Jed strikes up a conversation with the man to our left, but I stay silent, busying myself with checking my ammo supply. It's wearing thin. I'll have to make sure every bullet is worth it.

I look up again only when I hear a gasp beside me—a gasp quickly joined by a surge of murmurs and whispers from the townies, which then dies down to a total, complete silence. My eyes find the horizon.

They're here.

XVI
The Fight for Fort Cain

The raider mob is even bigger than I remember. For one moment of pure terror I wonder if their numbers have grown— but that's impossible. If anything they must have lost men, between the assaults on previous towns, the long trek across the wastes, and the fights that surely broke out among them, but it doesn't seem that way.

They don't shout and jeer and tussle among themselves as they approach the town. They're not treating it like a game this time. I wonder if they've grown, become more organized… But when I get a better look at them, it's easy to see the truth: They're getting desperate. They can't have looted much of value from the Nameless Town, or any other small groups they came across. After traveling all this way, they must be tired, hungry, thirsty. I'm not sure if the raids before were out of necessity, or fun, or just a general sense of sticking with their vicious way of life, but now they need supplies if they're going to survive. They've already come so far, and it's a long journey to the next town worth looting.

I steal a glance at the townies on either side of me, wondering how they'll fare now that they've seen what they're up against. Their faces are grim, but not terrified. This isn't like the Nameless Town. These people may be afraid, but they're not helpless, and they certainly haven't given up. I can feel their determination, even the most nervous of the townies steeling themselves as they see the raiders approaching. They stay in position along the wall, weapons at the ready. Not a single one of them turns and flees in the face of the approaching enemies. No one breaks down or breaks rank. They're ready to fight, no matter what the odds may be.

A townie fires off the first bullet, the sound of a gunshot ringing across the quiet space between the raiders and the town. It goes wild, sinking into the sand, but the sound of gunfire incites both sides to a frenzy. More shots ring out, and a shout goes up from the raiders. The mob breaks into a run, swiftly closing the distance to the wall. Hands and weapons batter at the front gate. The metal shudders and screeches but holds firm, not showing any sign of weakening. Other raiders, seeing the futility, start hoisting one another up to scale the wall.

The council members, spread out along the wall, shout out orders and targets, prioritizing the biggest threats: raiders with guns, or those nearing the top of the wall. Most of the townies are pretty shit with their weapons, but each target goes down eventually. I follow orders as well, taking down raiders as I'm told, counting down bullets in my head.

Amazingly, the townies actually seem to have the advantage here. The wall is holding, and so is the front gate, and between the two, the raiders have no way of getting inside. Townies fall here and there, taken down by well-placed shots, but most of the raiders don't have guns, and anyone who doesn't is entirely useless in this fight. Soon enough, the raiders are forced to retreat. They seem baffled by the turn of events, looking at one another with uncertainty. There's no organization among them, no one shouting orders for anyone other than their individual crews. They're starting to fall apart. Some crews fall back, and others run forward, indecision ripping their ranks apart.

Maybe this place really can win, or at least hold out long enough that the raiders will lose interest and find easier prey. I turn, opening my mouth to comment to Jed, and pause. He's gone.

"Jed?" I ask, looking one way and the other, unable to find him anywhere. "What the hell?" Frowning, I holster my gun and head for the ladder, dropping down to the ground below. Where the hell could he have gotten to? Why would he have left without telling me?

The ground level of town is quiet and mostly empty, and Jed is still nowhere to be found. I search the area with a growing confusion. Finally, I spot him running toward me from the heart of town. He skids to a stop in front of me, panting for breath and red in the face.

"Where the fuck were you?" I snap, my worry quickly turning to annoyance now that I see him safe. He leans over with his hands on his knees, trying to catch his breath.

"Danger," he says between gasps for air. "I saw some raiders sneaking around back and ... We need to move ... Need to—"

"What are you talking about?" I ask, frowning. Of course there's danger, but as far as I could tell, the townies are holding up pretty well. "What's—"

Then I smell the smoke.

My head whips up, searching the town behind Jed for the source. The mere smell is enough to send my senses into overdrive; the sight of the cloud rising above town freezes me in place. My eyes follow it down to the source, and find flames flickering over a building in the back end of town. With the dryness of the air and the already-shoddy structure of the house, the place is ablaze in seconds, fire hungrily eating its way up the building and spreading to the next one.

As I stare in silent horror, a townie screams.

"Fire!"

The shout ignites a panic that spreads as quickly as the flames. The townies' attention shifts immediately from the raiders to the threat inside their town. One of the council members shouts to throw sand on the fire, but everyone is already busily scrambling to escape from the blaze. The townies abandon their posts all at once, flooding down from their watchtowers and rushing toward the front gate.

The fear is palpable, all consuming. In the wastes, fire means total destruction. With so little water to spare, it's practically impossible to contain. It can easily eat through entire towns. And here, we're trapped with it. The wall surrounds us, and there's only one entrance, an entrance that's currently shut, with raiders waiting just on the other side. The panicked townies will just clog it up on this side, making it impossible for anyone to get either in or out. And all the while the fire blazes closer, *closer*—

It takes me a few seconds to realize Jed is shaking me. I forcibly tear my gaze away from the fire and focus on his pale, alarmed face. He's shouting my name. I only know because I can read his lips; the sound is swallowed by the growing chaos around us. For a moment my mind flashes to another fire, another town—to the skin on my hands blistering as I tried to clear a path into the bonfire that used to be Old Creek, desperately trying to reach the screams inside; and the crack of the building collapsing, flaming wood falling right on top of me—

I wrench my thoughts away and force myself to breathe deeply, in through the nose, out through the mouth. This isn't the time to panic, especially not with everyone around me already panicking. The town's defense is crumbling, and the fire is still spreading, buildings falling one by one to the flames.

The only thing not catching is the wall, huge and metal and imposing. Suddenly it seems that it's not keeping the raiders out, but keeping us in, trapped with the fire.

"Clementine," Jed shouts in my ear. "Snap out of it!"

I pull out of his grip and shake my head to clear it. Jed looks from me to the growing blaze behind him, his face lit by the flames. Unlike everyone around him, he doesn't look afraid. His face is sharp and calculating. For a moment, I think of Old Creek, the town burned to the ground, and wonder if his father looked at the fire there in the same way. I banish the thought from my mind.

"This place is done for," I say. Jed's attention snaps back to me.

"Well," he says, "I think it's about time to try things my way."

"What?" I ask, frowning—but he turns and takes off without answering, pushing through the flood of townies around us. I cast one last look at the growing fire and follow him. I keep pace with him as he runs, thankfully away from the fire and toward the front gate. "What do you mean? Where are we going?"

"Well, Clem, so far on this little escapade we've done things your way," he says, half-shouting to be heard above the terror and confusion all around us. "By 'your way' I mean mostly shooting people and making everyone hate us. And, no offense, but your way kind of sucks and has nearly gotten us killed several times now."

That successfully renders me speechless. My first instinct is to punch him, but I manage to restrain that and consider what he's saying. Ever since I lost my home, *my way* has been the only option for staying alive. But Jed is different. He's good with people. He proved it by getting us into this town in the first place, which I'm not sure I could've managed on my own. Maybe he sees an option I don't. Because between this town crumbling, the mob of raiders outside, Jed's father and his crew coming for us, and the poachers likely still on our trail, I'm not really seeing a way out of this.

"So your plan is what, exactly?" I ask, slowing as we approach the front gate—and the heart of the chaos. Some townies are trying to raise the gate to escape from the fire, while others staunchly defend it, wanting to keep the raiders out. I tighten my grip on my gun. This situation is right on the verge of boiling over. I'm sure Jed sees it too, but instead of backing off, he turns and grins at me.

"The plan is…we make some friends!" he says, splaying his hands wide and looking far too pleased with himself. I stare at him, so baffled by the words that I momentarily forget everything else going on around us.

"What the fuck are you talking about?" I ask, but a moment later, he walks into the mob of townies at the front gate.

Swearing under my breath, I shove my way through right behind him. A half circle of terrified townies has formed around the crank for the front gate. Amazingly, the gate still holds. I have to get closer before I can tell why: The crank is being guarded by a councilwoman. It's the elderly woman, the one who seemed to truly be in charge, and even in the midst of this uproar she seems level-headed. By her side is the guard woman who initially let us into town. She stands with a gun in her hand, not actually firing, but swinging it around whenever anyone gets too close. The mere threat of it seems to be enough to keep the townies at bay. Her face is pale, her hand shaking, but she manages to keep everyone away from the crank.

"We need to stay calm," the councilwoman yells, her voice barely audible above the other noise. There's shouting from the townies, gunfire from the watchtowers, banging on the metal gate from the raiders outside. Even I'm barely able to keep my cool in this situation. My senses are all wrought out and singed, and my trigger finger itches, especially with a noisy mob pressed in so close around me and the constant threat of the fire. I want to shoot, to kill, to escape from here—but I hold my bullets, for now.

Jed stands beside me, one hand gripping my arm to make

sure neither of us is pulled away by the movement of the mob around us.

"I know things are bad in here," the councilwoman says, "but if we open the gate we'll be slaughtered. If we wait for the guards to thin out the mob, then—"

"If we wait we die!" a woman wails from beside me.

The townies shout and press inward in response. But the councilwoman stays where she is, planting her feet and setting her jaw. She shows no sign of being intimidated, and that seems to give the townies pause. Despite the chaos and panic, they still recognize this woman as their leader.

"Give us a chance to fight!"

It takes me a moment to realize that shout came from Jed. It's followed by more shouts and cheers of agreement. Encouraged by the support of the townies, Jed presses forward, moving through the mob and over to the councilwoman. I follow in his wake, elbowing and shoving townies aside. I don't know what he's trying to do right now, but I have no choice but to trust him. I stop on the edge of the crowd, but he moves farther still, until he's just a couple feet from the woman, face-to-face, eye-to-eye.

"I'd rather die fighting than helpless in here," Jed continues, with the support of the mob at his back.

"We can handle the fire," the woman says. Her voice is composed despite the situation, and she meets Jed's eyes with her own level gaze. "We just need to stay calm. If we let panic take hold—"

"*Handle* it?" Jed asks, cutting her off. "Have you *seen* the fire? A blaze like this will destroy the whole town. It's out of control."

"We have precautions for—"

"For what? A simultaneous raider attack and fire in the town? I don't fucking think so!" Jed says. The mob is eating his words up, their energy hardly contained. They still don't move forward, not yet ready to commit a total uprising against their leader, but they're clearly on the verge of doing so. "Let us out before it's too late! Let us out!"

The mob roars in response. But the woman seems to hardly notice them. Instead, her eyes search Jed's face, her expression growing puzzled.

"What are you doing?" she asks. Her voice is softer now, so I doubt many people other than Jed and me can hear her. "You're not this dumb. You know you're advocating suicide."

"Nope," Jed says, very cheerfully. "I'm not dumb at all."

The woman's eyes widen suddenly.

"Traitor," she says in a harsh, low voice, and my skin prickles with alarm. Whatever Jed is trying to do, if this woman announces that he's a traitor, the townies aren't too far gone to listen to her. The councilwoman raises her voice to a shout. "This man is trying to—"

In one smooth motion, I un-holster my gun, raise it, and fire a bullet right between her eyes.

Jed turns to face me, his mouth forming an "o" of surprise, as the woman's body falls. For a moment it seems there's only him and me, our eyes locked. He looks at me—a long, searching look—the same way he looked at the fire as it consumed the town. I stare back at him, utterly shocked at myself for what I just did, and how easy the decision felt in the moment.

Then the townies surge around us, full of noise and movement. For a moment I think they'll come for me, but instead they swarm over the body of the councilwoman, overtake her guard, and fight for control of the crank. Jed pushes past them, and they let him take hold of it. I stop beside him. My hands are shaking, my heart pounding in my chest, as I replay that bullet sinking into the townie woman's forehead again and again. *Necessary*, I tell myself. I have to believe that.

"This is your idea of making friends?" I ask Jed, still unsure what he's trying to do. I don't see how opening this gate can do anything good—but nonetheless, I don't stop him. "That woman was right. You just ruined whatever chance this place had left."

"I didn't say we were making friends with the townies," Jed says, and pulls the crank.

Slowly, haltingly, the front gate begins to rise. I find myself holding my breath. The townies push toward it before it's even high enough for anyone to get through, rushing the gate in a mad frenzy to escape. As soon as it rises high enough, they surge forward—and surge back as they find the raiders waiting right on the other side.

Complete madness follows. Both sides fight—one to get in, one to get out. People fall, crawl, get trampled; they fight and die; they struggle against the flow, one way or another. The raiders and the townies are soon one indistinguishable mob of people tearing and clawing at one another, most quickly becoming too immersed in the flood of people to remember which way they're trying to go. I grab Jed's arm and yank him back, away from the thick of the mob. We stare at it wordlessly. I feel sick to my stomach.

Next to me, Jed lets out a low whistle.

"Well," he says, "this is a shitfest."

"Were you planning on turning on the townies the whole time?" I ask, dreading the answer.

"No," he says quickly, and I suppress a sigh of relief. "This was the backup plan, in case the town's fall seemed inevitable. Which it did, with that fire adding to the confusion." He glances over at me, tensing slightly as he searches my face for a reaction. After a moment, I nod, and he relaxes. "I'm sorry I didn't tell you before," he says. "I just...I didn't really want to do this, unless we had to. It was our only option."

I nod again. Part of me is still angry at him; he's the one

who pushed me to kill that townie woman, which is something I know will haunt me. But as long as this is part of some plan that will help us survive, I think I can call it necessary and live with myself.

"So what do we do now?" I ask, assuming there's a next step to this "making friends" idea.

"Let's find somewhere safe to talk," he says. "This place is going to hell real fast."

He's right. I can't believe how quickly the town fell apart when it came down to it, and this was a place I almost believed had a real chance against the raiders. The fire certainly made things worse—but that must've been something the raiders planned somehow, proving their army is more capable than I thought. And Jed's little plan to "make friends" may have helped with Fort Cain's destruction, but like he said, it was inevitable at that point.

I'm still feeling queasy about our part in this, and about the fact that Jed sprung it on me without warning, but I keep telling myself that all he did was speed it along and prevent us from being swallowed by the madness. And now I know the truth: No one can stand against the raiders. The western wastes as we knew them are done for.

Still, I hesitate. Part of me wants to stay here and try to help, to rage against this raider army even if it costs my life, but I know my death will ultimately do nothing. The best thing to do now is just survive, and hope that later I'll have a chance to make up for turning my back on these people who took us in and kept us alive.

I find a cellar nearby, an old bomb shelter that won't be in any danger of catching fire. We head inside and down a flight of stairs, finding the cellar empty but for a few empty wooden crates and some broken pieces of furniture. Jed attempts to keep a wooden stool with a broken leg upright, fails miserably, and sits cross-legged on the floor instead. I lean against a wall, staring at the floor and listening to the fight rage on above us.

"So what's the plan, exactly?" I ask, after several moments of silence. I'm still reeling from what I've done, and what I've allowed Jed to do in the opening of that gate. I need to focus, figure out where we go from here.

"Like I said, we make friends," Jed says. "This time with the winning side. We'll pretend to be raiders—well, you'll pretend, I mean. Seems like the crews have some kind of truce right now, so as long as they think we're just fellow raiders, we should be safe."

"So then, what, we travel with the army?" I ask, raising my eyebrows. "That's insane." The mere thought of surrounding myself with my hated enemies makes my stomach flip.

"No, it's not," Jed says, all too confident. "It's our best bet. You heard the council. My dad and his crew are coming for us. Even if we escape from the raider mob now, we've still got that to deal with. But they won't think to look for us with the raiders. Neither will the poachers, if they're still alive and on our trail. This solves all our problems."

I tap my fingers against the butt of my gun, processing his words. It's definitely a risky plan, but it does make sense. The only problem is whether I can pull off fitting in with the raiders. If they realize I'm really a bounty hunter who makes a living off killing their kind, they'll shoot me in a second. And if I *am* going to pull off the ruse, how far will I have to go?

"I'm not going to become one of them," I say. "I can't. I won't."

"No, no, of course not," Jed says. "It's just until we get out of this bind. When it's safe, we'll escape."

I chew my lip, looking down at my feet.

"I'm sure they lost a lot of raiders in this assault," I say. "They should keep thinning out. By the time they reach somewhere like Blackfort, the townies will have a chance. We can turn on them then."

"There we go!" Jed says, snapping his fingers and grinning. "We've got our plan."

I still think it's tenuous at best, but I keep my mouth shut. No matter how crazy it is, it's the only plan we've got. Another brief silence stretches out, and I try to stay calm and composed. *This is the only way to stay alive*, I tell myself.

"Anyway, you okay?" Jed asks.

"Hmm?" I look down at myself, unsure if the adrenaline surge made me oblivious to some injury, but I find none.

"I mean the fire," he says. "You looked kind of…" He trails off.

Right. That. My nerves still feel jagged and raw after the rush of terror I felt before, and bad memories stir uneasily in the back of my mind. The flames, the screams—they were a little too close to when Old Creek burned. But I'm calmer now, down here in the shelter and away from the chaos.

"I feel better here," I say, and mean it. The shelter feels safe, secure, isolated from everything going on up above. I can still hear it distantly, but it feels very far away.

"Really?" Jed asks. "Being trapped like this makes me feel caged."

"In the early days, when trouble came to Old Creek, we'd hide in one of these under our sheriff's house," I say, remembering. The shelter was dark and cold, and a couple times we spent a full night or longer there before we were sure the danger had passed. I'm not sure why I'm telling Jed. Maybe home is just too fresh in my mind right now, but at least this memory isn't of the town burning.

"Ugh," Jed says. "Weren't you scared in there?"

"No," I say honestly.

"Fearless Clementine," Jed says, smiling. I don't offer up the truth: that I felt safe because my parents told me we were untouchable there, and I blindly believed them. Better to let him think I'm fearless.

All this dredging up of old memories makes me uncomfortable—but it also makes me curious. Jed and I have been stuck together for a while now, but we've barely spoken about our pasts. To my surprise, I find myself wanting to know more about his.

"What was it like growing up with...your father?" I ask, stopping myself from using less kind words. He blinks at me, startled by the question, and then smiles.

"We were always on the road," he says. "He never tried to hide what he was—what *we* were—even when I was young. He explained that this was what the world was like, that raiding was the best way to survive in the wastes. I started getting in on raids when I was about twelve."

No wonder Jed thrives in chaos; he was born and raised in it. He was killing and looting when he was just a child. He must've believed in his dad the same way I believed in my parents when they told me we were safe in our shelter. If I had grown up like he did, who would I be now? The thought makes me shudder.

"How old were you when you first killed someone?" I ask, the question popping out before I've fully decided to ask it. It's one of those questions you just don't ask people, but I have a sudden, desperate need to hear the answer. I've never been close enough to anyone to ask; I was afraid to ask my parents and my old sheriff. Somehow, in all of this, Jed has become the closest thing I've had to a friend—and I have to know. Is it possible he's just as fucked up as me? That I'm not the only one who took to killing so easily?

Jed hesitates. Before he can answer, a sound comes from above. Not from the town, but closer. Someone is in the building above us. Several someones, actually, judging from the cluster of heavy footsteps.

Jed and I turn toward the stairs in anticipation of company. I move away from the wall, pulling out my gun. Jed stays seated on the floor, but pulls his assault rifle off his back and places it in his lap.

A few moments later, a group of townies comes down the stairs. There's a good dozen of them, wielding pipes and bats and other blunt weapons. They're all looking pretty worse for wear after the fight above, coated in dust and soot and blood. One of them is being carried by two of the others. After a moment, I recognize him as the councilman.

My eyes shift quickly from one townie to another, sizing each of them up. Individually, they're not a threat, but all of them together is a different story.

The townies stop when they see us, fanning out at the bottom of the stairs and neatly cutting us off from the only exit. They set the councilman down, and he looks at us with a puckered expression, like he's thinking very hard about something and doesn't like where his train of thought is headed.

"Well, fancy seeing you here," Jed says, cracking a grin. With all eyes on him, he slowly, lazily rises to his feet and stretches out his arms, his rifle still clutched in one hand.

"What are you two doing down here?" the councilman asks, his voice sharp and accusatory. He's leaning against the shoulder of one of the other men, keeping his weight off one leg. "Shouldn't you be out fighting?"

"Well, yeah, about that," Jed says. "Clementine is, uh…She's injured," he says, gesturing to me.

The councilman looks at me, and I look back. After a moment I realize Jed probably meant for me to fake an injury…but I'm not much one for faking, and it's too late now.

"She looks fine to me," the councilman says.

"Yeah, she's a trooper," Jed says, with an awkward half laugh.

"Must be," the townie says. "Because clearly you two wouldn't be hiding out down here, abandoning the people who took you in, right?" His eyes shift back and forth between Jed and me. Jed says nothing, and I tighten my grip on my gun. One of the townies adjusts his hold on his baseball bat, his eyes locked on Jed.

"Well, of course not!" Jed says in an affronted tone. "We would never do such a thing. We're just, uh."

In an instant, Jed's gun is pointed right at the man's face. The townie barely has a moment to open his mouth in shock before Jed pulls the trigger and—

Nothing happens.

I'm not sure which of the men is more surprised that the townie's face remains intact. They stare at each other. Jed jams the trigger a few more times—still nothing.

"Well, shit," Jed says, and the townies lunge toward him.

XVII
Making Friends

I take out two townies before they can reach Jed. It's an automatic response, a thoughtless one, and only afterward do I realize those were my last two bullets... and firing them has drawn attention to myself. Three townies quickly prove more than enough to take down Jed, which leaves plenty to focus on me.

I throw my gun at the first man who comes at me, and reach into my weapon bag for a replacement. Two townies grab ahold of the bag before I can get one. We struggle with it briefly, and the bag rips, sending ammo scattering across the floor. Cursing, I look around frantically for another weapon. My gaze finds an empty wooden crate on the floor. I grab it and smash it over the head of the next townie. She hits the floor, but the box shatters into splintered boards. I grab two of them. The rough wood digs into my hands, but I only tighten my grip, swinging one at a woman coming from my left, and the other at a man coming from my right.

"Clementine!"

Jed's voice cuts through the rest of the noise, and my head instinctively jerks toward the sound. The moment my attention shifts, a townie's fist strikes the side of my head and sends me stumbling. Before I can recover, another swings a metal bar at me. I block it with one of my wooden boards, which shatters when the bar hits it. I drop the useless splinters and swing the remaining board at the townies in an attempt to fend them off, the blow finding no one within striking distance. I'm forced to back up, which only puts more distance between Jed and me— a distance that is quickly filled with more townies. I curse, eyeing the circle of them around me and digging my fingers into the barely useful wooden board.

"Clementine, *help!*"

I wish the growing panic in Jed's voice didn't affect me as much as it does. Normally he's more than capable of handling himself in a fight, so something must be wrong; he must be in serious danger. Adrenaline floods my veins, and a deadly murmur in the back of my head grows to a clamor. All thoughts of my rules, and of morals, and of being a hero fade from my mind. As a townie swings a bat at me, my instincts shift from *defend* to *kill*.

I raise my arms and twist, so the blow glances off my forearms. It should hurt like a motherfucker, but I barely feel the sting through my adrenaline spike. The townie is taken off guard by my choice to take the hit, and I take full advantage of it by bringing my wooden board down on his head. He crumples to the floor. I grab the bat from his hands as he goes limp, and swing it at the next townie with a satisfying *crack*. Something hits one of my legs, and I fall to one knee, but keep swinging.

I send another townie to the floor with a hit to the knees, and the next stumbling backward with a blow to the stomach. The successes barely register through the sound of Jed screaming from across the room. I rise to my feet, half-dragging my injured leg, and swing my way through the crowd of townies toward him.

Finally, I'm able to get a glimpse of Jed—on the floor, crawling on his hands and knees away from a townie woman with a knife. As I watch, one of the men grabs him and hauls him back, dragging him to his feet and pinning his hands behind his back as he struggles. The townies close in like a noose around him, and the woman steps forward, raising the knife. A moment later I'm on top of her, digging a thumb into one of her eye sockets. She's screaming—and then she's not, as I slam her head against the concrete. I grab her knife, slash at the first hand that grabs at me, and lurch to my feet, toward the man still holding Jed. Eyes going wide, the townie jerks the smaller man in front of him like a shield.

I don't hesitate, stepping forward and thrusting my knife right through the narrow space between Jed's arm and torso. He lets out a rather undignified squeal as the blade grazes his side, just before it sinks deep into the gut of the townie. The man releases Jed, who scoots quickly aside, and I rip the knife back out. The townie falls to his knees.

I take a deep breath, and turn to see a crowbar swinging toward the back of Jed's oblivious head. I yank him toward me, and the bar *swooshes* right through the space where his head was a moment before. I slash the throat of the townie holding it, spraying blood out in a wide arc. Jed promptly slips in the resulting puddle and crashes to the floor, nearly taking me down with him. My own feet slip and slide. When I finally catch my balance, I plant myself there, standing over the ungainly pile of limbs as he tries—and fails—to get up. I lash and hack at every townie that comes near us—slashing at an arm, cutting off a finger, slicing through an ear. One by one, I cut them down.

And finally, they stop coming.

I stay braced, knife held ready, my body tense. I look around, taking in the room and the bodies strewn across the floor. It's a bloody mess. Nothing moves, except for me and Jed, who's still on the floor, his chest heaving.

It's over.

I force myself to relax, consciously loosening each muscle, letting my arms fall to my side and the knife clatter to the floor. It's hard to make myself stop after a fight like that, to let the adrenaline and rage drain out of me. I shut my eyes, breathing deeply, and the roar of blood in my ears gradually fades. When I open my eyes again and look down at myself, I realize that I'm utterly drenched in blood. My hair has come loose from its ponytail and hangs in messy waves around my shoulders. I push it out of my face with a bloody hand, and look down at Jed again.

He's staring up at me like he's never seen me before, his eyes very wide in a blood-splattered face. I reach out a hand to help him up. He hesitates a moment before taking it, and carefully climbs to his feet again. We study each other; me trying to gauge his reaction to what he just witnessed, him presumably deciding that I'm a complete psychopath.

I'm starting to feel sick to my stomach now that I see what I've done. These were townies...just townies. I've never killed townies before today. A lump rises in my throat, and I swallow hard.

Jed's spent his whole life around ruthless raiders, and even he looks shocked after that display. I'm all too aware of his gaze traveling from my face to my blood-soaked clothes to the utter mess of my hair. He's silent for a few seconds.

"My hero," he says softly, and smiles.

The words sent a jolt of shock through me. I stare at him, my mouth opening slightly, some warm and unfamiliar feeling bursting in my chest. I never thought anyone could ever look at me like—

Someone clears their throat.

I automatically step between Jed and the intruder and grab my gun off the floor, holding it tight despite the lack of ammo.

Standing at the bottom of the stairs is a girl, wielding a shotgun that looks far too big for her. She looks from us, to the bloody mess surrounding us, and back to us, her eyebrows slowly rising.

"What the fuck?" the raider says, each word punctuated with an incredulous pause. At least, I think she's a raider. She's dressed like a raider, and carries herself like a raider. She's just a very small raider, fresh faced and knobby-kneed, who would not be intimidating at all if not for the shotgun in her hands, which is currently aimed right at my face.

"Woah, relax," Jed says. "We're on the same side, here."

The girl immediately turns her gun to him, and then back at me when she realizes I still have my gun trained on her, and then back to Jed as she realizes he too has a gun.

"You two are with the raiders?" she asks, forehead creasing.

"Of course we are," Jed says. "I mean, do we *look* like townies?" I hear him move closer, almost beside me at this point, but I don't take my eyes off the girl and her gun. She frowns, probably processing the fact we're both drenched in blood and surrounded by dead townies.

"Dunno," she says after a few seconds. "I'm not much in the habit of judging people based on looks."

"Smart," Jed says. "But I can assure you, we're not townies. About as far from townies as you can get, really."

She narrows her eyes, sizing him up. Jed is usually good at talking to people, but right now his charm doesn't seem to have its intended effect. Quite the opposite, in fact. Seems like the more he talks, the more this girl suspects something is wrong.

"Our crew came from the eastern wastes," I say, before Jed can speak again. I ignore his questioning glance and think back to the plan he laid out earlier. "We got brought in to Saint, and then...well...you know how that whole fiasco went."

The girl eyes me up and down.

"So where's the rest of your crew?" she asks. Still wary, but not with the open distaste she treated Jed with.

"Dead, probably," I say. "We got separated. It's just me and this jackass now."

"*Hey*," Jed protests, but the girl's expression softens just a bit. Taking a gamble, I lower my gun. After a moment's hesitation, she does the same.

"Sorry you lost your crew," she says. "Maybe you can come along with mine."

"Thanks," I say. "I'm Cl—" I pause, realizing abruptly that I don't have a fake name at the ready. "Uh...Cled," I say. "And this is...Jem."

I groan inwardly, but try to look confident. I've never been much of a liar. The little raider's face wrinkles at my words, and she shakes her head.

"They've got some real ugly names in the eastern towns," she mutters, half under her breath. "But that's okay. We don't use real names around here anyway."

"So what should we call you?" Jed asks. I don't miss the slight twist of her mouth when he speaks; for some reason, he really rubs this girl the wrong way. She turns her back to us, heading for the door.

"I'm Kid," she says over her shoulder. "Come meet the others."

XVIII
The Crew

The town is completely overrun by raiders. They swarm unimpeded through the streets, ransacking every building and every box for anything useful. As I walk through town, raiders are everywhere, causing trouble wherever I look. They fight over objects I'm sure none of them really need, smash windows for fun, throw townies' bodies aside like they're garbage. My body is a tightly wound spring; I jump at every shout and every gunshot. The fire still rages, but nobody pays attention to the blaze. They're much more concerned about clearing out the remaining buildings before the fire reaches them.

Every time I make eye contact with a raider, or pass too close to one, I'm sure they're about to call me out. Surely one of them must recognize me by my burns, or at least catch the scent of an outsider. I feel like every movement screams that I don't belong here, like my face is broadcasting all of my fear and disgust and hatred. Especially the hatred, which seems to fill me to the brim and leak out of every pore—a hatred so intense my chest feels like it's filled with fire, each breath singeing my lungs.

"All right," Jed whispers to me, and I nearly jump out of my skin. "You remember the plan?"

I glance ahead at the tiny raider, who is too preoccupied with finding her crew to pay much attention to us.

"Yes," I say quietly. The plan is that I pretend to be one of them. We blend in until it's safe to leave. "But I don't know if I can do it. I have no idea how to act like one of them." My chest feels tight. There are raiders everywhere—raiders looting, killing, celebrating their victory. My gun hand is twitching, my pistol seeming to burn a hole in its holster. I have only a handful of ammo left, salvaged from the floor of the bomb shelter and tucked into my now-tattered duffel bag. But if I could take out a raider with each bullet, perhaps it would be worth it.

"You'll be fine," Jed says, and I force myself to look at him instead of planning a suicidal attack on the raiders. "The best lies have a little bit of truth in them. So, just…be yourself. Kind of. But more raider-y."

I put my hand on my gun.

"But not too much yourself," he says hastily, glancing around at the raiders we're passing to make sure they're not watching us. "Actually, scratch that idea. Just act like you think a raider should act. But, uh, don't try *too* hard. If you're exactly what they expect you to be, they'll be suspicious."

"Jed," I say through gritted teeth, "this isn't helpful at all."

Jed sighs and runs a hand through his tangle of hair, flecked with blood from the fight. He looks tense, but a moment later he shines his usual grin.

"Just stay quiet and look tough," he says. "I'll do the rest. Trust me."

Trust me, he says, as if I have any choice at this point. He's the closest thing I have to an ally in the middle of a mob of raiders.

Raiders. They've been the enemy since I was old enough to know there was evil in the world. Since they threatened my home, they were the people I was allowed to kill—the people I was *encouraged* to kill—and so I did. By now, it's basically a trained response: See raider, kill raider. To see so many of them, so close and yet so untouchable, makes me want to rip out my own hair. I need to fight. Hurt. Kill.

I imagine gunning them down, or slicing their throats, or bashing their faces in with my fists. I imagine a bitter, violent end for each and every raider I see, my mental body count piling higher and higher as I walk. I start calculating how many of them I could take out before their numbers would overwhelm me. And how is it possible that none of them see that written on my face? Surely someone must suspect that every time I look at them, I'm imagining a brutal death.

I clench my fists at my sides, my breath quickening. It's almost physically painful to refrain from drawing a weapon, especially when every step feels like a step further into danger, a step further past enemy lines. Surely someone will see through the ruse ... And yet, they don't. Most of them don't even spare me a second glance.

Jed saunters along behind me, humming cheerfully, completely unconcerned. But of course, he doesn't have anything to be concerned about. He has nothing to fake. He may be a different breed of raider from this lot, but he *is* a raider, and a son of a raider, and has been around raiders his whole life. He probably feels more at home here than he did with me. It's not a reassuring thought.

Almost as if he can sense what's going through my head, Jed steps up beside me, reaches out, and squeezes my arm. Just the briefest touch, but in that moment it seems to imply a lot. *I'm here*, it seems to say. And I find myself relaxing my tightened shoulders, letting my hands go slack at my sides. When Jed falls back, I take a deep breath and hold my head high. Nobody knows. Nobody will find out. I have to keep believing that. I'm more concerned about keeping a lid on my anger, which simmers like an itch beneath my skin.

I steel myself as Kid leads us through town—and then back

the way we came, muttering under her breath. She searches for several more minutes, peeking into buildings and apologizing when other raiders glare and shout at her to butt out of their "looting turf." It seems ridiculous to me, that they could claim certain areas of a town they all worked to take down, but apparently that's the way of things. Kid doesn't seem to be looking for a fight, anyway, and briskly moves on to check other places. We search building after building after building, but whoever she's looking for isn't anywhere to be found.

I'm starting to wonder if we made a poor choice of a "friend"; this girl doesn't seem to have a clue what's going on, and I'm getting impatient. After all this buildup, I'm getting real tired of waiting to see if we can pull off our ruse, and convince these people that we're raiders just like them.

"Fucking *shit*!"

The shout cuts through the quiet on the edge of town we've wandered to, an abandoned area dangerously close to the still-smoldering fire. Kid breaks into a grin.

"Oh! There they are," she says, and heads right toward the noise. I exchange a glance with Jed, who shrugs back at me, and we follow the girl. She leads us right into a building that seems to be partially on fire, and *very* on the verge of collapsing. Kid walks in without any apparent concern. Jed hesitates at the doorway, but follows.

Like hell am I going to be the one too scared to go in. I swallow my fear, brace my shoulders, and walk into the building.

Inside, a small cluster of people is waiting. Aside from Kid and Jed, there are three others: a stoic Asian woman with bright red hair; a huge, scarred black man; and a white man with long dreadlocks who is currently swearing up a storm for no apparent reason. Kid is looking to the latter, so I look at him as well. He's a lean man with a pair of goggles pushed up on his forehead and a mouth full of absolutely disgusting teeth.

There's a bandage wrapped around his torso, with a bit of red leaking through on one side, though the injury isn't holding him back from a lot of animate swearing and hand gesturing. Only when he's finished spitting out curses does he finally turn to scrutinize Jed and me. He stares at us for a few moments, then wordlessly gestures toward me and looks at Kid.

"Found them killing some townies," she says with a shrug. "They lost their crew. Told them they could travel with us for a while."

"Oh, is it your fucking job to recruit new members now?" he asks. The ferocious tone takes me aback, but Kid just shrugs again, completely unbothered. Getting no response from her, the man grumbles and eyes me up and down.

"You look like a woman who knows how to use a gun," he says. I nod. His gaze shifts to Jed, who smiles. "And you look fucking useless," he says dismissively. While Jed makes a startled noise of protest, the man looks back at me. I hesitate, and then nod again, and he grins. "Well, whatever. Maybe bigger numbers will keep those bigger crews from trying to fuck with us." He looks at the large man, who nods his agreement, and the red-haired woman, who stares at me with an unreadable expression. He seems to take that as agreement. "Alright, fine. You can keep with us for a while. But do anything shady, and I won't hesitate to blow your fucking heads off, got it?"

"Right," I say, since Jed seems at a loss for words for once. I clear my throat, and pointedly glance around the room. "Well, now that that's settled...you do realize this building is on fire, right?" This floor seems fine for now, but I can hear the building creak and groan above us. Everyone looks up at the ceiling as if they just noticed the danger.

"I'm not a goddamn idiot," the dreadlocked man says. "I picked this one specifically."

"You picked the one that's...on fire?"

"Yeah," he says without hesitation. "'Cause none of the other assholes are gonna be crazy enough to loot this one, yeah? So I figured we'd grab some good shit."

"Huh," I say, and leave it at that. I guess he has a point… a crazy, barely understandable one that puts all of our lives at serious risk.

"Unfortunately," he says, "this place doesn't have shit."

"At least these townies are partially cooked already," Kid offers.

"At least there's that," he says. "Anyway, on to the next one."

He walks out, and the rest of the crew follows. Jed and I linger behind in the slowly burning building. I glance at him, raising my eyebrows, wondering what the fuck we've gotten ourselves into. Jed grins back, and we both trudge after the bickering raiders ahead of us.

XIX
Fitting In

We trail after the odd crew until sundown. By that time, the town has quieted down as raiders retreat with their prizes. Over the hours, the fire has mostly died out, though it still smolders quietly here and there, grudging embers that refuse to admit defeat. We pick through the burnt buildings, following our new crew's leader—Wolf—as he grumbles and curses and shouts that "The good shit has gotta be around here somewhere."

As it turns out, the "good shit" was either taken by other raiders, lost in the fire, or never was here in the first place. I'm not sure what they were expecting, really. These western towns are small and poor. I'm sure one town's loot would be plenty for a single crew of raiders to live on, but a horde of them? No way there's going to be enough to go around. Then again, Kid seems to carry an unlikely amount of optimism with her, and maybe it's enough to infect the rest of the crew as well.

Optimistic or not, by the time the sun is setting, we're forced to retire for the night. Not even this madman raider is crazy enough to keep searching through questionably stable buildings without light to guide us. We've collected a small, pathetic pile of loot: tattered blankets, some ammo, a few bottles of murky water. It's a sad haul, especially considering we put in a few hours of work after most of the other crews retreated for the night. Nobody is happy with it, but nobody seems willing to say anything. Instead, the group seethes quietly as we leave town.

The remnants of town are unstable and ripe with death, so we head out into the wastes to make camp. Most of the other crews are already set up. Small fires dot the wastes surrounding the thoroughly looted town. The raiders seem to be celebrating, the camps lively and rowdy, full of shouting and singing. The air is thick with the smell of cooking flesh and the occasional whiff of alcohol. None of them pay much attention to us as we pass through, keeping to whatever temporary truce is holding this mob together.

I keep shooting Jed long, angry looks. I know it isn't really his fault, but I need someone to direct my frustration toward, and I'm not going to take the chance of pissing off any raiders. Of all the goddamn raider crews, we just had to pick this bunch of misfits, the only ones who seem to have gotten nothing of worth.

Aside from the bodies, of course. The big man carries one over each shoulder, looking quite cheerful about the task, and Wolf drags one with much greater difficulty through the dirt behind us. He huffs and puffs with the effort, hampered by his injury, but snaps at anyone who offers help. The two women of the group carry the loot that isn't dead flesh, while Jed and I trail behind, carrying armfuls of blankets, since that's all they would trust us with.

Throughout the day, I worked on picking up the names they use for one another. They were difficult to distinguish from the insults Wolf throws around, but I got them eventually. The girl, as we already learned, is Kid. The odd, quiet woman is Dolly, the big guy is Tank, and, of course, their foul-mouthed leader is Wolf. It's all very western-wastes in nature, not having real names, but I try to accustom myself to it. After all, we could be stuck with these people for a while. Thinking about exactly *how* long puts a knot in my stomach. How long will it be until I have to raid with them? How long until I get hungry enough to become a shark? How much will I have to sacrifice in order to survive?

In the midst of the revelry all around us, Wolf and the others quietly make camp and start their own fire. I sit beside it—but not too close, the sight of the flames devouring Fort Cain still vivid in my mind, mixing with my memories of Old Creek burning to the ground—and sift through my duffel bag. On the edge of camp I hear Wolf and Tank hacking up the bodies we brought out with us. I try very hard not to look, but the sound of knives hitting flesh is evocative enough without the visual. It reminds me of death, and violence, and I feel like I'm going to be sick. I force myself to breathe deeply and calmly, keep my face cold and stone-like, and force my attention onto cleaning my guns.

I've always known there was cannibalism in the wastes. It's the final taboo, the hard line drawn between sharks and other wastelanders. The thought has always sickened me, always brought up my burning hatred for the raiders and made me feel justified in it. Everyone in the wastes does horrible things to live. We all kill, we all make sacrifices. But this? This is too much. This is the one thing that truly separates them from the rest of mankind. They're not people anymore; they're just sharks.

And now, for the first time, I have to sit here and face it.

I may have imagined these things, but it's a different matter entirely to watch them reduce a human being to meat. At least it doesn't look so obviously human by the time they've put it over the fire to cook, but the sizzle of skin still makes my stomach roll. It smells deceptively like real food, like any other meat, but nonetheless revulsion rises in my throat. It's even worse how *casual* they are about it. There's no grim recognition of how horrible this is, no solemnity about the process. They're even cheerful, talking unabashedly about how hungry they are and how good it smells, no shame in their eagerness to consume what was a living person just earlier today.

At least I feel a little safer with a gun in my hands. It quiets my wailing nerves and the vengeful murmuring of my mind. Being here, in the middle of a raider camp, surrounded by enemies and doing nothing about it, is a betrayal of everything I've ever said and done. I'm a coward. I'm a traitor. My head feels hot, my hands tremble, my vision blurs. I need to hit something. To *kill* something.

As I busy myself cleaning guns and counting ammo, I gradually settle my nerves to a tolerable level. *I'm just doing what I need to do*, I tell myself. Just tolerating this to stay alive. Now is not the time to be a hero.

After prowling around and chatting with the others for a while, Jed sits beside me. He's quiet for once. I wonder if he's concerned for me. I glance at him, but he's staring into the fire, his face impossible to read. I should know better than to attempt guessing at his thoughts. I may have grown closer to him, even to the point where I trust him to some extent, but that doesn't mean I understand what happens inside that weird head of his. He remains an enigma to me. I hope I'm the same to him.

I manage to avoid attention from the rest of the crew for a while. They're busy with their own tasks, and tired from the raid. But once the meat is done cooking and they start doling it out, I can't remain overlooked anymore.

When Tank offers me a slice of meat, my stomach clenches. If they think I'm a raider, they'll expect me to eat it. It's normal for them. If I turn it down, I'll stick out like a sore thumb. But can I go so far? I raise a hand, reaching for the meat—and then draw it back. Tank's forehead creases, still extending the meat like he expects me to grab it at any moment.

"Not eating?" he asks. "Plenty to go around. It's not charity or anything; you're with us now."

"I'm not—" I start, and hesitate. No way are they going to believe I'm not hungry. As Jed said, the best lies have a bit of truth hidden in them. But what can I say that won't completely give me away? "I don't eat meat."

"Eh?" If possible, Tank looks more confused than before. "You serious? A raider who doesn't eat meat?" He looks at Wolf. The leader of the crew scrutinizes me.

"You don't seem like the squeamish type," he says. "What kind of half-ass raider doesn't eat meat?"

"They're not from around here," Kid volunteers. "Maybe it's different where they come from."

I almost nod, but notice everyone's eyes shift. I follow their looks to see Jed eagerly digging into a piece of meat, so gleefully invested that he's totally oblivious to the conversation. It takes him a couple seconds to notice the stares. He pauses, hunk of meat halfway to his slightly open mouth. He tentatively takes another bite, chews it, and swallows. "What?" he asks, finally, his eyes locking with mine.

I swallow hard, disturbed by the image of him eating human flesh just like the others. Before we met up with these raiders, it was easy to forget who he was. Now I'm suddenly finding myself wondering if he's really still on my side, or if it was just convenient. He could throw me to the raiders right now, and carry on his way.

"Looks like you're wrong," Wolf says to Kid. "Surprising no one."

And then everyone's looking back at me, awaiting explanation. I clear my throat, trying desperately to think of something reasonable to say and finding nothing. The tension rises with every silent second. I'm itching to grab my gun just for the comfort of having it in my hand, but I have a feeling that would incite an all-out brawl right now, and I'd rather avoid that if I can help it. I keep my eyes on Wolf, assuming the others will take their cues from him.

If he reaches for a weapon, it's over.

"She's a vegetarian," Jed says, abruptly breaking the silence. Everyone, including me, turns to stare at him.

"What?" Wolf says incredulously, while I try to wipe the dumbfounded look off my face before anyone sees it.

"Weak stomach. She's actually allergic to meat," Jed says. Though I'm grateful that he's trying to argue for me, I bite back a groan. *That's* the best explanation he can come up with? But he keeps a straight face, nodding solemnly.

"Is that a real thing?" Kid asks, looking over at Wolf, who seems about as baffled as she is. She frowns. "It doesn't sound like a real thing."

"Oh, it's real, all right," Jed says in a very grave voice. "I've seen it in action. Real ugly. She'll break out in hives if she even touches the stuff."

As the crew turns back to me, I fold my arms over my chest and force myself to nod. The moment they turn away, I give Jed the most intense glare I can muster up. His lips twist to hide a smile.

"Oh, not to mention she gets the shits," he adds. "You don't even wanna hear about *those.*"

There's a pause. Then Wolf and Tank burst into laughter, while Kid turns red and Dolly looks on, unruffled.

"Shut the fuck up," I say.

"Sorry. Didn't mean to embarrass you," Jed says, chuckling.

"Idiot," I mutter, dropping my eyes to my boots. But, despite my words, I know better than to think Jed is anything close to an idiot at this point. Embarrassing as that exchange was, he did successfully de-escalate the situation. The crew doesn't question it again, and Kid is happy to hand over a can of beans.

I pry it open with my knife and inhale the food in seconds. I notice the big guy—Tank—staring at me, and glare at him out of habit, but he looks more impressed than anything. Still, I maintain the scowl. I'm not going to let my guard down around these people, and definitely don't plan on being friendly.

Once I've finished my meal, I toss the can aside and make myself comfortable by the fire. I try not to think about the fact that I'm surrounded by raiders, or the sound of Jed gnawing the last of the meat off a bone. The rest of the crew chats idly among themselves, and Jed is more than eager to join in, but I stay quiet and tune it out. I catch occasional bits of conversation, mostly about where they're going and what their plan is, which all seems up in the air right now.

Honestly, I'm not sure how this crew made it this far. I haven't seen them in action yet, but they already seem barely competent. They have hardly any loot from this raid, and hardly any idea where they're headed. Perhaps my standards for raiders are too high. Crews like Jedediah Johnson's don't exist out here; if they did, the western wastes wouldn't be the way they are. Still, I expected better than *this*.

"You guys aren't worried about Jedediah Johnson?" Jed asks out of nowhere, jerking me away from my thoughts and into the conversation. I shoot him a warning look. Surely it's better to stay away from subjects like that, which could lead to hints that we're not who we say we are, but apparently Jed has other ideas.

"Who the fuck is Jedediah Johnson?" Wolf asks without looking up from his meal. Jed lets out an exaggerated gasp of surprise, pressing a hand to his chest.

"You don't know?" he asks, appalled. I sneak a glance at the crew, but luckily they don't seem suspicious about how personally he takes the lack of knowledge. Instead, they're just giving him blank stares. "The *legend* of Jedediah Johnson? The one, the only?" He pauses, as if expecting that to ring any bells, and sighs loudly. "They say he was the son of an assassin and a whore—his father being the whore, that is, and also the source of his overwhelming charm and good looks—"

"Skip to the important part," Wolf says, while I resist the urge to roll my eyes at Jed's ridiculous dramatization of his own father.

"Well, it's all important, but yeah, okay. He's a famous raider, king of the eastern wastes—"

"Oh," Wolf says. "Well, that explains that. I don't give a single fuck about the eastern wastes."

Jed, shocked into silence, only stares at him.

"Well, you should," I say. "The eastern wastes are what happen when you let a psychopath take charge." Jed certainly isn't doing the story justice, so I guess I have to step up. "He's a tyrant. You westerners are lucky you killed Saint before he got a chance to do that here."

"I don't know if that's fair," Jed says. I look at him, eyebrows rising. I know Jedediah Johnson is his father and all, but I can't believe that he'd suggest his rule is anything but tyrannical. "You really think life is better here than there?" he asks. I open my mouth to answer, but before I can, he continues, "Not for people like you—people like *us*." He gestures not just at himself, but also at Wolf's crew. "People like you and I are fine out here, obviously. But for other people? Normal people?"

His usual playfulness is all gone, his tone serious and his stare intent. I open my mouth again, ready to argue, but falter. I don't think I realized it until this very moment, but he could be right. People like me, and Jed, and these raiders thrive in the chaos of the wastes, but other people—townies like Wyatt, or that girl who tried to help bandage my wounds in Fort Cain— don't stand a chance on their own. All the townies we've met out here are dead. Under Jedediah Johnson's rule, they'd probably still be alive right now.

"Everyone hates Jedediah Johnson," I say, well aware that it's not an answer to his question.

"Sure, but they're safe," he says. "They're alive. Probably leading longer, fuller lives than the townies out here."

I open my mouth and shut it again, unable to come up with an answer. I'm left feeling shaken. Jed glances around at the raiders, as if suddenly reminded that we have an audience.

"I mean, it's shitty for people like us out in the east," he says. "Just saying, I can respect the guy for what he's doing. Begrudgingly."

There's a long pause, and I look around, worried that he might have ignited suspicion in the raiders. Tank and Dolly have clearly stopped following the conversation, though Kid is giving Jed an oddly piercing look, and Wolf looks thoughtful.

"Fucking eastern wastes," the crew leader says, shaking his head. "Who knew anything interesting was happening out there?"

"Uh," Jed says. "Mostly everybody."

"Next you're gonna tell me shit's going down in the southern wastes or somethin'."

"Wait," Jed says. "You don't know about the southern wastes? Are you serious? They're—"

"No, no, no," Wolf says, waving a hand at him. "I don't wanna know. Got enough shit to worry about already."

Jed sighs, but says nothing.

"You know, I think I have actually heard the name," Tank says, scratching his chin. "Some of the other crews were talking about some guy coming from the east. Some famous raider king, yeah, I remember now. They say he's getting real close to us. We could cross paths with his crew any day now, and no one is sure what will happen."

"Well, he sounds like an asshole to me, calling himself a king," Wolf says. "If we run into the guy, I say we kill him."

I bite back a curse. I knew Jedediah's crew was drawing near to this area, but I didn't know he was quite that close, and didn't think the raiders might intentionally start shit with him. If that happens, our plan of hiding among the army will fall apart. And if it comes down to that, I wonder, will Jed side with me, or his father? I glance at him, trying to gauge his reaction to Wolf's words, but he shows none except for a small twist of his mouth.

"Anyway," Tank says, "if I can make a suggestion to lighten the mood..." He reaches into his bag, pulls out a plastic bottle, and holds it up triumphantly. "Got a surprise in town."

"Oh, damn," Wolf says. "Is that what I think it is?"

"Pretty sure it's vodka," Tank says, squinting at the unlabeled bottle. "Or moonshine. I dunno. Something that smells like rubbing alcohol. I bashed a guy's head in to grab it."

Wolf whistles under his breath and holds out his hands. Tank tosses the bottle to him.

"Ugh," Kid says, her nose wrinkling. "I'm not touching that stuff again."

"Suit yourself, kiddo," Wolf says, unscrewing the top. "More for me."

What he should've said is "more for Jed," as it turns out. Soon enough, my companion is unsteady in his seat and talking much too loudly, with plenty of over-the-top hand gestures that throw him further off-balance. He spouts off story after story, spinning some ridiculous yarn about how we ended up here. The crew doesn't seem to suspect it's a lie, or if they do, they don't care. Tank and Wolf laugh uproariously at each of his stories, and he even earns himself one small smile from Dolly, though Kid still seems wary of him.

As for me, I keep a careful eye on Jed. I didn't expect him to actually get drunk. I haven't taken a sip myself. I'm not usually one to turn down a drink or two if the opportunity arises, but it seems too risky in this situation, surrounded by people who would kill both of us if they knew the truth. But Jed seems to have no reservations, taking eager swigs every time he gets ahold of the bottle, getting progressively drunker and messier. I don't like the way he's letting his guard down, or the way he's talking so much as a result. It seems like it's only a matter of time before some little lie causes suspicion—or even worse, he lets out something true.

I try to act like I'm just relaxing by the fire, but I listen very carefully to every word out of his mouth. More than anything I want to knock the bottle out of his hands, or drag him away to shut him up, but I know that will only arouse suspicion. We have to keep acting like we have nothing to hide. And Jed's constant chatter does do that job . . . as long as he can keep pulling it off.

"Really, though," he says, holding his hands up to get everyone's attention, which he clearly already has. "Let's talk about Jedediah Johnson. The man, the king, the *legend*—"

"All right, well, I think my partner here has had more than enough," I say, cutting him off. He's spewed out a lot of bullshit tonight, but we definitely don't need another conversation along those lines. I grab Jed's arm and haul him upright. He sways on his feet, murmuring slurred protests. "It's time for bed," I tell him firmly. He pouts at me, but he shuts up, and doesn't resist as I pull him away from the fire. I grab the blankets we looted from Fort Cain and throw them over my shoulder as we head for the edge of camp.

"Not gonna sleep by the fire?" Tank shouts after us.

"Nope," I yell back. My skin is still crawling from the blaze earlier, and I have no desire to sleep anywhere near flames. Plus, it's risky being around the crew with Jed like this. As we leave the warm glow of the fire he pulls back, digging his heels into the sand.

"But it's cold out there!"

"Should've thought of that before you downed half a bottle of moonshine and started running your mouth," I say. "I knew your scrawny ass couldn't handle the liquor."

"I'm handling it fine," he protests, right before tripping on a rock. I turn and grab him with both arms to yank him back upright, and we end up face-to-face. It's dark now that we're not by the fire, too dark to see him clearly. He sways toward me, and I place a hand on his chest. The plan was to push him away, but instead I end up resting it there.

We stand still in the darkness for a few moments, breathing quietly, and eventually something dawns on me. I frown and pull Jed closer by the shirt; he initially leans in, and then back when I give a loud sniff.

"Uh, Clementine? What the hell?" he asks, startled. I scowl at him, and release the handful of shirt I was clutching. He stumbles back and falls to the ground.

"Woah there," he says. "Be kind to the poor drunk man."

I fold my arms over my chest and glare down at him.

"You're not drunk," I say.

"What?"

"Not a whiff of alcohol on you." With the amount he supposedly drank, he should've reeked of the stuff. Yet just a few inches away from him, I couldn't smell even a hint of it on his breath.

Jed throws back his head and laughs.

"All right, you caught me," he says, holding up his hands to admit surrender. "I had you fooled for a while though, didn't I?"

"Hmph." I silently watch him climb to his feet. Once upright, he spreads his arms and bows, gesturing with one hand as if to encourage applause. But the only audience he has is me, standing with my arms folded and a scowl on my face. After a moment he peeks up at me, grins, and straightens back to his full height.

"I can't tell if that's your genuinely-pissed-off scowl or your I'm-secretly-pleased scowl," he says thoughtfully, squinting at me. "It's a little too dark."

"I only have one. It's my shut-the-fuck-up-Jed scowl."

He laughs, and I roll my eyes and turn away from him, spreading a blanket on the ground. I toss three of them to Jed and arrange my own two into a makeshift bed. I have a sinking suspicion even two blankets won't do much to ward off the cold. I'm still not used to sleeping out in the open...but even knowing that Jed isn't drunk, I refuse to sleep near the fire, surrounded by raiders. Just the distant crackle of their fire and murmur of conversation is enough to make me feel uncomfortably vulnerable.

I settle into my blankets, and turn to see Jed setting up his own several feet away on the ground.

"What are you doing over there?" I ask, my brow furrowing. He pauses, looking up at me with a blanket clutched in his hands.

"Huh?" he asks. I sigh, and point at the ground beside my own nest of bedding.

"Get over here," I say. He stares at me for a moment longer, and slowly his face splits in a grin.

"Oh," he says, dragging the sound out with a ridiculous waggle of his hips. "What's this, hmm? I thought you'd never a—"

"Don't be an idiot," I say, cutting him off. "I'd just rather not freeze my ass off. We need the body heat." Before this trip to the west, it had been a long time since I slept outdoors. The blistering heat of the wastes can make it easy to forget how bitterly cold it gets when it's dark, but the nights where I was trailing the poachers were a good reminder. I'm not planning on spending another night racked by shivers.

"Oh, right," Jed says, his obnoxious grin fading. But it doesn't faze him for long; soon enough, he's right at my side.

He pulls his blankets on top of us both and burrows himself snugly against me. I grumble at the touch of cold skin and the uncomfortable closeness, attempting to find a comfortable position. It doesn't prove easy, especially since Jed seems to be made of pointy elbows and knees. The worst, though, is his face, looming up way too close. His breath is warm on my cheek.

"Turn around," I say gruffly.

Jed laughs.

"No need to be shy."

"I'm *not* being shy," I say. "I just don't want you breathing on my face."

I firmly grab him by the shoulders and turn him over. He doesn't fight it. I pull him against me, curving my body around his, one arm ending up wrapped around his torso because it doesn't make sense to put it anywhere else. We finally settle into a position that doesn't involve being awkwardly tangled in each other, or elbowing each other in the stomach. Finally, I admit to myself that this *is* actually pretty comfortable, and definitely warmer. I relax, listening to the sound of our quiet breathing, glad that the crackling of the fire is far away.

"Knew you'd wanna be the big spoon," Jed mutters, and I jab him in the side.

"Shut up, I'm sleeping," I mumble against his ear.

"Good night, Clementine."

"Good night, Jed."

XX
Crewmates

In the morning, Jed and I sleepily untangle ourselves from the blankets and each other at first light. We pack up camp quickly and quietly with the raiders, and set off.

We move with the horde.

Wolf's crew keeps their distance from the others, but they keep pace with them and move in the same direction. I wonder if there's a plan, a reason they're headed this way, or if they all just follow the first crew to move.

Alone, the wastes always seem endless, empty of anything but a huge and vaguely threatening silence. Alone, it's easy to remember that this isn't what the world is supposed to be like; this is what happens after the world ends. We're merely survivors who weren't meant to be, clinging to life when we rightly shouldn't. Maybe this world is so harsh because it's trying to get rid of us, the last of the infestation. Those are the kinds of thoughts that creep up on you when you're by yourself. They're the kind of thoughts that can kill.

With company it's different. The wastes seem much less empty, much less dead, much less threatening. But perhaps that's because I'm surrounded by much louder and more immediate threats.

Jed certainly seems at ease among the raiders, talking and

humming as he walks, once even breaking into song, though that's quickly silenced by a chorus of groans and boos and a smack to the head from Wolf. After that he quiets down for a few minutes, but he's back to his cheerful self soon enough. It all seems so easy for him. Maybe that's just the way he is. He adapts, and charms, and weasels his way into peoples' hearts with his smiles and disarming small talk.

Talk that never seems to end, especially with an audience. After last night, I'm not worried about him slipping up and revealing that we're lying to them. Despite his antics, he's not an idiot, and I trust him now to handle himself. I'm content to tune out his chatter and retreat to my own thoughts.

But my thoughts aren't exactly a welcome retreat right now. Surrounded by raiders, hatred still seethes and boils at the back of my mind—and I know that's the real enemy to our façade, not Jed's chatter. I just have to hope that I can keep myself from snapping until we reach safety.

Now that I think about it, maybe it won't be quite so long after all. The close proximity of Jedediah Johnson's crew could be a blessing in disguise. If we pass each other soon *without* violence erupting, Jed and I will be free to go wherever we please, with his father still searching for us closer to Saint's tower. We could steal some supplies, sneak away at night—maybe even head back east, if Jedediah's crew is busy over here.

Stewing on that, I glance around at the other raider crews around us. Though Wolf doesn't seem concerned, I'm not so stupid as to believe there's any real honor code among raiders. Cat and Bird proved there's sure as hell not one among bounty hunters, and raiders are even less scrupulous. Though they seem peaceful for now, I know any of them could turn on us the moment we show weakness. There's a particularly nasty-looking group of men about a dozen yards to our left. They don't seem to be paying attention to us, but I catch occasional snippets of their conversation, usually revolving around their dwindling food supplies. I keep an eye on them, just in case.

I'm so focused on the nearby crew that it takes me several seconds to realize someone is walking beside me. When I do I jolt to attention, my hand moves to my gun. Her hand does the same, and we end up staring at each other, both on the verge of drawing. It's Dolly, with the red hair and the strange staring. After a tense moment, I slowly remove my hand from my weapon. She does the same, and keeps on staring at me.

"Nice gun," she says, her eyes wandering there. I scowl automatically, unsure if the statement is some kind of threat, but she says nothing else.

"Yeah," I say. I eye her. The pistol on her belt is nothing special, but the sniper rifle she carries on her back—which I've seen her holding like a child—is possibly the nicest gun I've seen aside from my own. I'm almost jealous of the thing. I nod my head toward it and let my scowl soften. "Yours too."

She nods.

"You're a good shot?" she asks. At least, I think it's a question; it's hard to tell, sometimes, with the monotony of her voice.

"Yeah," I say.

"Me too," she says.

I hesitate. That statement could be a brag, a threat, or a simple attempt to build rapport. Her face gives no hints. I decide to say nothing in response. We walk next to each other for a couple minutes, both silent after the quick exchange, before she pulls forward to walk alongside their leader. I watch them, trying to see if she's saying something to him, but she's as silent as usual.

Jed pulls back from the rest of the crew to walk alongside me.

"She's a weird one, for sure," he says quietly, jerking his head at Dolly. She glances back at us, as if she could hear the comment, and Jed gives her a bright smile that she doesn't return.

"I dunno," I say, watching her and half-smiling myself. "I think I like her."

After a long day of travel, we make camp again. It's a much quieter affair than last night, with none of the yelling and post-raid revelry from the mob. There wasn't much to loot from the half-burnt Fort Cain, so the dwindling water supply leaves little to celebrate. At least there's plenty of food to go around—for anyone but a "vegetarian" like me, that is. There's only one can of normal food left. They reluctantly hand it over to me, and I make myself eat slowly for once. I'm not sure when I'll eat again. And I wonder, if it comes to starvation, how long will I be able to keep turning down the meat? Honestly, I don't want to find out.

After eating, I'm content to sit cross-legged beside the fire, my shoulders sagging, letting weariness overtake me. I'm thirsty, dusty, and worn-out, but it feels good to rest my bones for a while, as the heat of the day gradually wanes.

I'm not aware that I've dozed off until a loud sound wakes me again. I sit up, reaching for my gun, my heart racing—but it's only a disgruntled-looking Wolf dropping a bag on the ground near me. I shake off my grogginess, mentally kicking myself for letting my guard down.

"Well," Wolf says. "The bad news is that nobody wants to trade for meat, 'cause everyone's already got plenty."

"What a surprise," I mutter under my breath.

"The good news," he continues, "is that everyone's sayin' we're gonna hit the next town tomorrow."

My stomach flips.

"So that means—" Kid starts.

"That means it's raiding time!" Wolf says, cutting her off. His formerly somber attitude disappears in favor of a fierce grin. "And we're gonna do better this time. Gonna get some good loot, not be the poor stragglers pickin' up scraps. You got that?" He points at Kid, who nods, and Tank, who gives him a thumbs-up. He seems content to see Dolly cleaning one of her guns, and then looks at Jed and me. "Are you two in?"

"Of course we are," Jed says—thankfully, since my own tongue seems to be tied up in my thoughts. I swallow, and muster up a nod and a stoic expression when Wolf glances my way.

"Fuck yeah," he says. "Two more bodies will be nice to have."

"Bodies?" Jed repeats.

"He doesn't mean it like that," Kid says, though Wolf ignores him. "Two more guns. That's what he means. Right, Wolf?"

"Meant what I said," he says, grabbing a hunk of meat for himself.

"Well, that's slightly concerning," Jed says. He does a double take upon seeing my face, and scrutinizes me. "What's wrong?"

My insides are a mess of feelings right now—fear, anger, nausea. These people are talking so nonchalantly about raiding a town tomorrow. Do they understand that they're destroying peoples' homes? Their lives? And they talk about it with such *excitement.* Not that I don't feel the same urges—every wastelander knows those urges, that drive to steal, fight, kill, do *anything* to stay alive another day—but at least I try to control them.

Our little hero, I think, and suppress the harsh, manic laughter that bubbles up inside me at the thought. What would my townspeople say if they could see me here with these raiders?

"Clementine?" Jed asks, reaching for my arm. I flinch away from the touch.

"Nothing," I say. When Jed opens his mouth, getting ready to argue, I grit my teeth. "Later."

He nods and drops it.

I spend the rest of the evening stewing in my thoughts. After a couple attempts to draw me into the conversation, the crew gets the message that I'm not in the mood to talk. Jed keeps glancing at me, but he leaves me alone as well.

Eventually, the conversation dies down and the others prepare for bed. Like last night, Jed and I grab our blankets and leave camp to find our own spot out in the wastes.

"You nervous about the raid tomorrow?" Jed asks, once we're a fair distance away. I glance back at the others, just to make sure they're not within hearing range.

"No," I say.

"Well, you don't need to be," Jed says, in a soothing voice, as if my answer was the opposite. I glare at him, but he blathers on. "I'll be with you the whole time, and anyway, should be a piece of cake for you. They're just a bunch of dumb townies."

I stay quiet for a few moments. I want badly to agree with or just ignore him, yet instead I find a confession rising up inside of me. I try to fight it back, but it claws its way out of my throat.

"I don't know if I can do it," I say, each word forced through gritted teeth.

Jed stops walking. I continue for a few paces, but he grabs my arm. I turn to him, raising my eyes to his face.

"What do you mean?" he asks, frowning. "Of course you can handle a few townies."

"I don't mean it like that," I say. "I guess I mean…I don't know if I *should* do it." He tilts his head questioningly. I let out a long breath. "I don't know if I can live with myself after doing it."

"Live with…?" Jed repeats, not getting it. "Clementine, you kill people all the time."

I take a deep breath and push a strand of hair behind my ear, trying to form coherent thoughts and words.

"But it's different," I say. "I have these…rules. I only kill for profit, or out of necessity. That's it." I guess a raid is for profit, but that's just a technicality and I know it. And of course, I can't bring myself to add that "protecting Jed" seems to fall in the "necessity" category now, as proven by Fort Cain.

"Or else what?" Jed asks, and I shake my head, unable to

find the words. "I feel like there's something you're not telling me. There's a story there, yeah?"

My stomach twists and turns.

"I killed for the first time when I was eight years old. A raider." His eyebrows rise slightly. "And I kept killing them, whenever they came to town. I was good at it. *Really* good at it."

"Okay," he says, when I pause. "So you were defending yourself and your people. Nothing wrong with that."

"Sure," I say, thinking of beating that half-dead man's head in with a metal pot. "The town loved me for it. They used to call me a hero. But it got out of hand." Jed is quiet, waiting for me to continue. "One day a man came to stay for a night. I was in town, freshly back from the latest hunt." I take a deep breath. "He was an older guy. Pretty charming, actually. Polite. Funny. Everyone liked him, except for me."

"He was a raider," Jed says. There's an odd look on his face, some emotion I can't discern, even though I haven't finished the story yet.

"Yeah. He had these tattoos, and this look about him, and he carried a huge gun with him even though he never threatened to use it. I knew what he was, and I hated that the townsfolk seemed to accept him despite it. This was in the early days of J—" I pause, remembering who I'm speaking to. "Of your father's rule, I mean, so things were tense and confusing and everyone was still figuring out what it all meant. But I was angry. I wanted to fight. I wanted to protect my people. I thought I understood things, and that it was worth breaking the rules."

"How did you kill him?" Jedediah asks. He stares down at the ground, not looking at me, and the emotion is gone from his face.

"I slit his throat in his sleep," I say, remembering it as I say the words. He woke up halfway through, and fought me, but it was too late and he was losing too much blood already. I can still picture the light dying from his eyes. "I burned the body, but I was an idiot. I kept the gun. So when Jedediah Johnson's crew came looking for the man they lost, they found it stashed under my pillow, and they knew.

"They didn't think it was me. I was just an eighteen-year-old townie girl to them—I had already been hunting bounties for two years, but they didn't know that. They thought it was my father, and while they questioned him, I ran. I thought they would figure it out, that they would come for me and leave the town alone, but... they were dumber than I expected, I guess." That was one time of many that I found myself wrong in my assessment of people. But that time, it was brutally punished. "Later that night I saw the smoke. I went back, and tried to get in to save my family, but..." I trail off, absently raising a hand to touch the burns on my face. The blaze at Fort Cain has the memory vivid in my mind: the intense heat, the hungry flames, the screams. I take a deep breath. "That's why I need to follow the rules. I need to... make sure I stay aimed in the right direction. Make sure I stay on the right side. Like my people would've wanted me to."

Several long seconds pass, and Jed says nothing. I glance at his face, uncertain. Maybe sharing this much was a mistake. But he's not even looking at me, still staring at the ground with his eyes distant, like he's lost in thought.

"Jed?" I ask. His head jerks up. He blinks at me, like he'd forgotten I was there, and his face stays guarded.

"Let's get some sleep," he says. That's it. I take a deep breath, and hope the hurt doesn't show on my face.

"Okay," I say, my voice coming out flat. I set up my blankets, and he sets up his a few feet away. I fight the cold, and my thoughts, for hours before I finally fall asleep.

XXI
The Raid

I wake early. The sun isn't up yet, the wastes still dark and blessedly quiet. I stand and stretch, shrugging off the sluggishness of sleep. It's quickly replaced by nerves, my entire body buzzing with a static energy that hisses up my spine and down each of my limbs.

Today's the day.

There's too much to think about right now—the raid, my rules, my conversation with Jed and its uncomfortable ending. I can't let myself worry about any of it right now. If I'm distracted today, I'll get myself killed. For now, I just need to push it all to the back of my mind.

I mechanically sort through my weapons, mostly as an excuse not to think. Pistol at my hip, knife strapped to my leg, one spare revolver with a few bullets left. Not much ammo left for my pistol either. When I came here, I had so many beautiful weapons, and no end to ammo in sight. But the last several days have had a hell of a lot of shooting in them, more than I'm used to—and that's saying a lot, since I make my living shooting. But back in the east, it's all about the careful balance of power, and purposeful killings, and goods changing hands. Here, it's just charging into the fray, guns blazing, and hoping for the best. For someone like me, the chaos has proved to be livable—but not so much for all the dead townies in our wake.

By the time I've finished my routine, I'm not the only one awake. Dolly is up and watching me, carefully handling her own weapons, going through a process similar to my own. She and I exchange a nod across the open space between us. Near her, Kid and Wolf are starting to stir as well, and Tank is soon woken by a kick from the latter. Jed is still snoring. I let him; I want to enjoy the silence while I can.

Only when the sun is rising and the crew is packing up do I finally wake Jed, prodding him in the side with my boot until he opens one eye. I grab his hand and pull him to his feet, and together we fold up the blankets and stuff them into my bag alongside my paltry supply of remaining ammo. He says nothing about last night—nothing at all, actually, which is odd for him. I mirror his silence. When we're done packing, we set off.

I expected a serious atmosphere on the dawn of a raid, or a ferociously excited one, but instead the crew meanders along and chats among themselves as if this is any other day. I guess it might be, for them. While this is huge for me—my first raid, the day I could easily lose my life or a far more integral part of myself—it's not the same for them. This is what they do, how they make their living. And even though that "living" revolves around killing and stealing from helpless townies, I guess it's just another job to them. Maybe it's as easy for them as bounty hunting is for me.

But the atmosphere changes once the town looms on the horizon. First a hush falls over the raiders—not just Wolf's crew but all of them, chatter and complaints alike dying down to a complete silence. Then someone shouts, and the horde roars back in response. The mob draws together, individual crews dissolving into the singular, terrifying mass that I've seen before.

It feels unnatural looking at a raid from the other side. The mob swells around me, psyching themselves up for the attack. The typical shouts and war cries of raiders, usually a herald of danger, come from all around me now. My whole body is so tightly coiled that it feels like part of me will snap off. I try to keep my face cold and hard, like I'm used to doing this, but my heart is pounding. I can't stop thinking about the concerns I voiced to Jed, and how he hasn't spoken to me since I spilled them.

This thing inside me, gnawing and tearing, it's always hungry for more. If I feed it, it will only grow stronger. Already I can feel it clamoring inside me, making me feel equal parts excited and afraid. Soon the two become indistinguishable, one dizzying rush of adrenaline so intense that my hands shake. Bloodlust is thick and infectious in the air around me.

When a raider from another crew bumps into me, I snap at him, my gun instantly in my hand. It's a decision that could mean disaster, but luckily, he just slinks back with his head down. Jed glances sideways at me, but I refuse to look at him. I'm having a hard enough time keeping myself in check right now without thinking about him. I force myself to place my gun back in its holster, restless hands clenching and unclenching.

As we draw closer, I imagine watching the horde appear from the town. I know from experience what it feels like to see the raider mob for the first time—the awe, the fear, the helplessness. I feel none of that, staring down the town. Instead, I feel predatory. The closer we get, the more my nervousness dissipates, replaced by steely resolve.

This place is no Fort Cain. There's no metal gate, no huge wall, just a cluster of barely stable buildings patched together with scraps, a true western-wastes town. And the townies are nowhere to be seen. Unlike Cain, and the Nameless Town before it, there's no front line of armed townies waiting to meet us, no attempt at defense. The place just looks empty. The raider mob slows as it approaches. I slow with everyone else, frowning, my eyes scanning the town and finding no signs of life.

"Fuckers ran with their tails between their legs," Wolf complains from ahead.

"Probably took all the supplies first too," Tank says glumly.

The other raiders walk right in, eager to scour the buildings for anything left behind. I pause on the edge of town. Wolf's assessment does seem like the most likely case. It's not farfetched that this town, hearing how the others before it fell, would flee instead of standing their ground. And yet something gives me pause. I've learned to trust my instincts, and right now they're telling me that something isn't right.

But the crew is moving forward without me, Jed included. So I grit my teeth, try to subdue the rising urge to run, and advance into the town.

It's eerily quiet, made more so by the fact my senses are all on high alert, straining to find signs of danger in the seemingly dead town. My eyes dart around and my gun is ready. I'm careful to search every dark corner, not put my back to open space. After a few minutes, the effort starts to feel ridiculous. There's no one here. Every noise and movement I jump at turns out to be one of the raiders. They've diffused throughout the town, spreading out to cover as much ground as possible. And yet, my uneasiness only grows. These buildings aren't just empty of people, they're *completely* empty. I would have expected the townies to take all the food, and water, and weapons...but the furniture? The silverware? Every blanket, every article of clothing? It's all gone. I guess it could be some kind of over-zealous, burn-it-all method to ensure there was absolutely nothing the raiders could use to their advantage, but still. It's odd. I don't like odd, and I don't trust it.

After scanning a building to find it just as cleaned out as all the rest, I hurry forward to catch up to Jed. He turns and looks over his shoulder at me.

"What do you think?" he calls out to me. It's alarmingly loud in the quiet town, echoing off the buildings around us. I crouch down automatically, expecting some kind of response, but nothing happens. I slowly straighten up.

"Something's—"

Not right would be the next words out of my mouth, but I cut off at the sound of an explosion nearby. Jed and I both turn toward the sound. There's nothing to see other than a plume of smoke rising above the buildings. Shouts echo around the empty streets, the words unintelligible. I hesitate, torn; do we run toward the chaos, or away from it?

Before I can decide, there's another explosion, this time from the opposite direction. I turn that way instead, but once again, I can't see what happened. The shouts come from all around us now—and then, gunfire. Not a steady unloading of ammo, but short bursts, and no returning fire. I frown at Jed, who's staring in the direction of the latest explosion. He takes off in that direction. Cursing under my breath but with nothing better to do, I follow.

I turn the corner and slam into him. He staggers forward a few steps before coming to a stop again, and continues staring.

Ahead is the aftermath of the blast. From the looks of it, it must've been a grenade, and one that landed right in the midst of a raider crew. Not the one we were traveling with, which gives me a surprising sense of relief.

A few of the unfortunate raiders are splattered across the dusty ground, a couple have been flung away and lie unconscious, and one is holding the bloody stub of a leg and groaning. While Jed seems entranced by the gory sight, I tear my eyes away and scan the town around us. Was it another raider crew that did this? Or was it townies after all? There are plenty of windows in the surrounding buildings, good vantage points to throw an explosive from, but they're empty now.

On the other side of the carnage, a second raider crew turns the corner. They scrutinize the bloody remains and mutter among themselves, before their gazes find Jed and me. We stare at one another across the mess of dead and dying.

"You do this?" one of the men shouts at us, his words echoing up and down the street.

"Of course not," I snap. "We're with you."

"Well, someone took 'em out," the man growls. "And ain't no townies to be found."

We glare at each other. None of us move, but I size up his crew. There are only four of them, a mangy group aside from the bulky, red-faced man who's been shouting at us. Jed and I could probably take them, especially if we shot first, but I'm not eager to start a raider civil war right now. I know what these people are like. If they see a fight erupting, they'll join in, even if they don't know why it's happening. One little misunderstanding like this could rip the entire raider army apart.

Just when I'm starting to wonder if that's such a bad idea, Jed decides to open his mouth.

"Well, let's not get too hasty here," he says, raising his hands in a 'stop' motion.

Out of all of the things that have come out of Jed's mouth, that's possibly the most reasonable sentence yet. But somehow, it incites a murderous rage in the other raiders. The leader lets out a shout as if Jed personally insulted him, and comes flying in our direction. The rest of them follow, their feet skidding and sliding across the bloody mess they have to cross to reach us, one of them stepping right on the stomach of the man who lost his leg.

I hesitate—unsure if I want to run or shoot—but Jed grabs my arm and yanks me back, making the decision for me. We tear down the street, the shouts of the raiders echoing after us.

"What did I say wrong?" Jed asks between pants for breath, casting a look over his shoulder at our pursuers. They're still coming, still yelling, and the situation still doesn't make much sense. Other raider crews are emerging from side streets and poking their heads out of buildings to see what the hell is going on. They all stare as we pass.

I don't answer him—partially because I have no fucking idea, and partially because I'm trying to figure out what the hell to do about the situation. Secretly, part of me is pleased at the turn of events; the immediate danger leaves no room for moral concerns, and the weirdness between Jed and me is gone, replaced by the camaraderie that comes with fighting for our lives together.

I'm guessing our best bet is to find the others. We may not really be part of the crew, but Wolf seems like the type who's always looking for an excuse to fight, and I'm sure he'd gladly jump in. Problem is, I'm not sure where he went. This town seems much bigger now that we're inside of it, a confusing maze of streets and broken buildings. I have no idea where to find them, though every other goddamn raider crew seems intent on gaping at us.

As I'm searching for the crew, I make a critical mistake, a wrong turn. Jed and I skid to a stop at a dead end. A brick wall looms up ahead, cutting off our escape. I scan the area, but there's no other exit, and the crew in pursuit of us has already reached the mouth of the alleyway. They stop there, completely severing our only escape route, while we stand with the wall at our backs. The red-faced leader's face splits into a grin.

"Got ya," he says. "Fuckin' cowards."

The plus side to fighting in an alleyway is that they can't all come at us at once. The downside is that if any of them get a good hold on us, there's no way to escape. My pulse rises to a steady hammer as I raise my gun, Jed doing the same at my side. He opens his mouth, and shuts it again; maybe he's too afraid to talk, now that his previous harmless phrase sent these men into a mad frenzy.

"Calm the fuck down," I say, hoping that speaking "raider" might get the message through their thick skulls. "We don't have time for this shit right now."

Once again, that somehow seems to be the exact wrong thing to say. The man lets out a howl like an incensed animal— but before he can run at us, something falls from the sky and lands right in front of him. His howl cuts off abruptly as he looks down at it.

A grenade.

I yank Jed backward, sending both of us crashing to the end of the alleyway in a heap, just half a moment before the explosion. I press myself against the ground so hard I choke on dust. I wait a couple moments, and cautiously raise my head. Jed is coughing, his eyes watering, but he looks unharmed.

The raiders at the mouth of the alleyway didn't fare as well as us. The scene is almost hilariously reminiscent of the one we found earlier. With all of them packed so tightly around the entrance to the alleyway, not one of them managed to escape unscathed, all four raiders downed and bloody. I climb to my feet, helping Jed up, and we make our way out of the alleyway. Only once we're out do I realize how many eyes have watched this go down—at least a half dozen raider crews are all staring at us from different directions.

"It wasn't us!" Jed shouts immediately. He throws up his hands in surrender, looking from one group of raiders to another. "I don't know what happened, but it was *not* us!"

I can tell from the muttering that not a single one of them believes that. And why should they? There's been no sign of anyone but raiders here, and they've thoroughly combed the town by now.

And yet... someone did throw a grenade. Someone who definitely wasn't us.

Remembering the image of the grenade falling from above, I raise my eyes to the open sky. I sweep them left, and sweep them right, and catch just the slightest hint of movement... something that could be a pale face disappearing over the edge of a rooftop. My head snaps in that direction, and I stare hard at the building. Nothing now, and I can't be certain what I saw.

But somehow I am certain, and I think I'm finally catching on to what my instincts have been trying to tell me this whole time.

"Townies," I say, my voice coming out quiet and dry, choked with dust. I cough to clear my throat, and raise my voice. "Townies! On the rooftops!"

The eyes of all the raiders, formerly on us, rise upward. There's a moment of silence—a moment when I'm sure all of them are trying to decide whether I'm telling the truth, or just trying to shake off suspicion.

Then dozens of faces appear at the edges of the rooftops. A moment later, they begin to pelt us. A fork *dings* off a building to my left, a pot crashes into a raider in front of me, and an empty tin can smacks into the side of my head. I jerk back, my head ringing, and raise my arms to cover myself. The rain of various everyday objects continues, and I retreat back into the alleyway and press against the wall. Jed, caught out in the open, staggers left and right in an effort to avoid falling objects, and finally stumbles after me, yelping as a broken chair leg catches him on his way over.

Most of the other raiders are still caught out in the open streets. They seem baffled about how to handle this situation, some stumbling around in an attempt to dodge, others ducking into buildings, still more holding their ground and trying to shoot at the townies up above. None of it seems very effective.

With the raiders too confused to fight back, the steady fall of objects only grows heavier. When one group of raiders clusters together back-to-back, trying to cover one another, one of the townies hurls another grenade.

Boom. Another bloody mess on the dusty streets.

"Spread out!" Jed yells, struggling to be heard above the constant clatters and thuds and dings of various things hitting the ground, and townies shouting in triumph, and raiders screaming in frustration and pain. With chaos all around us, Jed is staring out at the mess of a fight like it's a puzzle he's trying to solve. "Spread out and find shelter!"

Clearly at a loss for what else to do, the raiders listen to him. The streets empty as raiders hide in buildings and other shelters, leaving only the dead and dying out in the open streets. The rain of objects from above gradually dies down, and the streets become silent and dead once again. I, along with the others, wait to see what will come next—and what Jed will tell us to do. My head is still spinning from that blow from the can.

So what else do the townies have up their sleeves? If we're lucky, maybe it's nothing. Townies are simple things, after all. Maybe they didn't think any further than this clever little ploy. Maybe they thought they'd be able to pick off more of us before we realized what was happening. Though, judging from an explosion on the other side of town, some of the other crews haven't caught on yet. If we're lucky, maybe the townies will just focus their attentions elsewhere.

But luck is rarely on my side lately.

Before I can even catch my breath, the door to a nearby building bursts open, and townies pour out. There are more than I would've expected. Few of them are armed properly, but those that aren't still carry things like wooden boards and broken chair legs and metal pots. There's no fear, no hesitation—they flood out and run, yelling, at the closest raiders. A pack of them swarms Jed and me.

I thought it would be hard to kill townies. I thought—perhaps *hoped*—that some shred of my conscience would awaken and make me hesitate about pulling the trigger on people who are just trying to defend their homes. But, as it turns out, there isn't much time for conscience when the townies are running at me with weapons in hand. It's not even a matter of right or wrong. It's a matter of staying alive. A choice between them and me. A matter of necessity.

Without conscience hindering me, the raid becomes nothing more than a very easy fight. See target, pull trigger, body hits ground. Most of the townies don't have guns, and those who do hardly know how to use them. To a professional like me, they might as well not have any weapons at all. I shoot them down, one by one, before they're even close enough to endanger me. Quick and easy. Almost too easy, actually, and I start to get bored after a while. I put my gun away and grab my knife from its sheath on my leg, using that to take care of the next man who comes at me.

I laugh—and immediately sober as I catch myself doing it. I'm *enjoying* this, I realize; I'm enjoying slaughtering these mostly defenseless townies in their own home. I look around me, at the town swiftly being overrun by raiders. I see raiders killing people, torturing people, looting bodies and buildings, lighting fires and destroying things for the fun of it. Some of them are laughing, just like I was a moment ago. I lower my knife to my side, guilt creeping up on me as I look around at the chaos being wrought.

I search for Jed in the fight, and find him gleefully wrapped up in it, wielding two pistols he must have looted from some- one. I try to catch his eye, but the sight of him taking out two townies at once and whooping excitedly stops me in my tracks. For him, this is just the same as killing raiders in the Nameless Town. I can't let that be the case for me; I have to keep myself under control. I turn away from Jed and head deeper into town, away from the worst of the fighting.

I can't handle being deep in the fray anymore, but I know that the raiders will be suspicious if I'm not doing something helpful. So I decide to search for loot, heading up to the roof-tops where I suspect the townies have hidden their goods.

There isn't much to find; most of it was thrown down at the raiders, and what's left isn't useful. I pick my way among smashed furniture and tattered blankets. Some children hide among the wreckage, staying out of the fight below, but I ignore them and keep looking. Even though I've escaped the fight, the sound of gunfire and shouting is constantly on the edge of my consciousness, and it's almost physically painful to keep myself away. The outcome is obvious; these townies took out an impressive number of raiders, maybe enough to save the next town the army hits, but they're severely outmatched.

I walk to the edge of the building and look down on the town below. The ground is strewn with the remains of the townies' hail of junk, along with bodies from both sides. The fight rages on atop the wreckage. I search for Jed, but I can't find him in the midst of everything, not from this distance.

Instead, I see something else—and my body goes rigid, a sharp breath hissing through my teeth.

Vehicles are approaching. Five of them altogether, and they're not the shoddy, pieced-together scrap metal that people call cars out here in the west. They're big, intimidating trucks, all shiny and painted black. My heart sinks down into my stomach as I get a better look at them. I've seen these kinds of cars before. Everyone in the east has, and everyone knows that they can only mean one thing.

And evidently, people here are learning it too. Before long, people notice them coming, and a whisper starts up. It ripples through the town, even through the chaos, and the fighting comes to a pause. It stops townies and raiders alike, the eyes of both turning toward the east. The vehicles pull up to the front of town and stop there, engines growling loudly, the town quiet in their presence. One by one, the engines shut off, and silence falls. The whole town is hushed.

Then someone shouts it.

"Jedediah Johnson is here!"

XXII
The Raid Gone Wrong

Some of the raiders turn tail and run, while others rush toward the vehicles, shouting and brandishing their weapons. Townies flee, or fight with renewed vigor. Just moments ago there were two sides to this fight, but it soon dissolves into one very confused mess.

On the rooftop, I stand completely still. My hand is on my gun, my face turned toward the black vehicles that I've always known as a portent of death and loss. These are the cars that come when things are about to go terribly wrong. They show up to steal your supplies, to punish your resistance. They show up to drag people away kicking and screaming, people who will never be seen again. Now they've come so far from home, and they've come all this way for me, and for Jed.

Jed. I need to find him. We need to run. Not only is this town about to turn into a massacre of townies and western raiders alike, but if they see Jed, it's all over. Our only hope is that with everything happening around us, we can escape without his father's crew noticing us. They can't know for sure that we're here, so if we manage to disappear quickly enough, maybe we'll have a shot.

I force away the childish fear that the sight of those vehicles ignited in me, and finally break my paralysis. I run for the rusty staircase I climbed to reach the rooftop, clamber down to the street, and keep running. I'm not even sure where I'm running, other than *away*, desperately hoping that Jed will have the same idea and head in the same direction…and desperately hoping that he was telling the truth when he said he didn't want to go back to his father.

But I don't see him anywhere as I run through town, searching every corner and hiding place. I find an elderly couple hidden away in a building on the edge of town, an injured raider dragging himself into an alleyway, a dying townie holding her hands to the sky and begging for Jedediah Johnson to save her. Jed isn't with them, or the mob of raiders racing to meet the eastern crew, or the stragglers fleeing town.

Among those stragglers I find Wolf's crew. The leader seems seriously displeased about leaving the fight, with Tank at one elbow prodding him forward and Dolly at the other, keeping an eye out for trouble. Kid, lagging behind the others, is the one who spots me. She slows down, raising a hand.

"We're getting out of here. You coming?" she asks. I hesitate, and shake my head. She looks over my shoulder at the town. "He was right in the thick of the fight when they got here," she says. "Didn't see where he went afterward." I nod again, a silent thanks. She bites her lip, hesitating for a moment before blurting out, "I don't trust the guy. Talks too pretty."

I'm not surprised. I remember the way Kid distrusted him from the beginning. And maybe she's right; Jed has lied before, after all, and he's pretty damn good at it. But still…

"I know," I say. "But I can't leave him."

She sighs to herself, but doesn't argue.

"Good luck," she says.

"You too."

I stay on the edge of town, watching the crew disappearing into the vast expanse of the wastes before turning back to the town consumed by chaos. This could be my only chance to run. I glance at the wastes again, imagining myself shouting for Wolf and his crew to wait, imagining myself fleeing with them and leaving Jed behind. I imagine a life for myself with them as my family, my home. Then I curse and run back into the heart of town.

Jed could have turned against me the moment his father showed up...or he could be injured, or trapped, or captured. He could need me. And if there's a chance of that, I can't leave him behind. So I ignore my pounding heart and all my instincts screaming at me to run, and head right toward Jedediah Johnson's crew.

The infamous raiders are cutting their way through town, mowing down townies and western raiders alike. Some try to fight, but they don't stand a chance. Jedediah's crew is no unruly band of outlaws; they're professionals, better fed and better trained and much better armed than anyone around here. These western wastelands must be a joke to them. Even for me, a bounty hunter used to dealing with them, Jedediah's crew is a challenge. I might be able to take down a few of them, but I don't like my chances against the whole lot, especially when I'm alone.

Though I know that logically I don't stand a chance, hatred bubbles through my veins at the mere thought of Jedediah's crew, and having them so close at hand nearly makes me forget my goal. I know almost every one of them, by name and by face—and every crime they've committed, every town they've wronged. Some of them are faces that have haunted my nightmares for years; others are newer, but no less awful. I'd gladly kill each and every one of them, and do it slowly and with relish, without a shred of moral uncertainty to weigh on my conscience.

I try to push aside anger and fear alike, to not think, to let my body move mechanically. All that matters right now is finding Jed. But he's nowhere to be found. It's like he vanished as soon as his father's crew appeared. But did he go toward them, or away? Impossible to tell.

I scour streets and buildings. I find raiders, and townies, and plenty of bodies belonging to both sides, but not Jed. I carry on, my search growing more frantic. Then I round the corner and run into a familiar face.

Not a face I know personally, but one I've seen on wanted posters all over the eastern wastes. One of Jedediah Johnson's crew members—Maria Heartless, they call her. A revolver is in her hand and pointed at me; I can tell she knows my face as well. We end up at a standstill, each staring down the barrel of the other's gun.

"Well, well, what a surprise," she says. Then, she raises her voice to a shout, turning her head so the sound carries behind her. "I found the bounty hunter! He's here somewhere!"

The moment her attention shifts, I slam into her. She fires her gun, but the shot goes wild. I slam her back against the closest building. She grunts as she hits crumbling brick, but it doesn't faze her. She slams the butt of her pistol up against my chin, and then into my face as I jerk back. I gasp, blood gushing from my likely broken nose, and keep grappling with her. A close-quarters fight is my best bet, but she's not easy prey. She's lean with muscle and full of fire, matching me blow for blow.

We fight hard and dirty. She yanks my hair, and I spit blood in her face; I knee her in the stomach, and she hits me in my broken nose again, sending a jolt of agony all the way down my spine. I pull a brick free from the wall behind her, and send it crashing toward her face—but she's quick, too quick, and ducks her head to the side just in time to avoid the blow. The contact with the wall sends pain up my arm, my knuckles scraping excruciatingly against the brick and my own momentum throwing me off balance. She slips from my grasp, and I whirl around to find her with her gun aimed at my head.

She laughs, clucking her tongue at me like I'm a disobedient child. Fury threatens to make me do something stupid, but I force it down. My body is already shaking from the brief struggle. The days with scarce food and water have not been kind to me, and I'm at a disadvantage with that gun in her hands. I know when I've lost.

I lower my hands to my sides, ready to admit defeat and let her drag me off to who-knows-where. At least this way, I can buy Jed some time to escape.

She laughs and smashes the butt of the gun right into my nose once more. I stumble back, and before I can recover she hits me again in the forehead, this time causing my head to smack back against the bricks. I drop to my knees, my head spinning, the taste of blood in my mouth.

The woman grabs a fistful of my hair and drags me down the street. I struggle and fight and claw at her hand, but I'm weak and hazy minded, my vision obscured by blood running down my face, my feet scrabbling against the ground. I find myself helpless as she drags me, past fleeing raiders and townies and straight into the arms of her crew.

She throws me on the ground, and I land heavily on my hands and knees. I turn my face upwards to see a huge man towering above me. He's broad shouldered, arms knotted with muscle, with a shaggy beard and hard eyes.

I realize, with a jolt, that I recognize him. He was one of the tax collectors I saw in Sunrise, the giant one who hardly spoke. I wouldn't have guessed that Jedediah Johnson would have the guts to go collect taxes himself, but I suppose it makes sense. And he's exactly what I expected Jedediah Johnson to be: tough, intimidating, emotionless. This is the face of my real enemy, and now I'm at his mercy.

He raises a gun to my forehead, cold steel pressing against my skin. I swallow my fear and meet his eyes.

"Where is he?" he asks. His voice is gravelly and quiet, barely audible above the sounds of the fight.

"He's dead," I say calmly. "Died in the fire at Fort Cain."

His face betrays nothing, but one booted foot shoves me so I land on my back in the dirt. He places the boot on my chest, squeezing the breath out of me, gun still aimed at my head.

"Last chance," he says, his voice as soft and stoic as before. "Where is he?"

"Like I said." I turn my head to the side, spit blood, and turn back to him. "Jed's dead."

His finger tightens on the trigger.

"*Stop.*"

Both of our heads whip toward the familiar voice. I'm not sure which of us is more surprised to see Jed standing there, pointing a gun at the man above me. My heart sinks. The rest of the crew—those who aren't immersed in the fighting, at least—all turn to Jed as well, gasps and murmurs running through their ranks.

"You idiot," I say, struggling for breath with a boot crushing my chest. I try to shove it off, but the huge man doesn't budge. "You're supposed to run!"

Jed doesn't even look at me. His eyes stay locked on the man above me—on his father. Jedediah Johnson.

"Back up," Jed says, his gun hand steady.

You idiot, I think again, though I don't have the breath to speak anymore. This will only get both of us killed. Does he really think he can help me? That his word will sway his father not to kill the bounty hunter who kidnapped his son?

And yet, Jedediah Johnson steps away from me and lowers his gun to his side without a hint of hesitation. I scramble away in the dust, panting for breath and trying to process what's happening. Did he just take an order from Jed? I stare at the man, trying to understand. After a moment, he smiles, an expression that looks strange and foreign on his formerly serious face.

"Hey, boss," he says.

XXIII
A Snake by Any Other Name

At first, I don't understand. The word "boss," the way the raiders snap to attention, the utter adoration in their expressions. To say the crew is happy to see Jed would be a massive understatement. They look at him like a god descended from heaven in front of them. They seem to have forgotten about me entirely. I slowly get to my knees, but my legs give out when I try to rise any farther than that. So I stay down, my eyes locked on the man I thought I knew. The blow to my head is still making things murky for me, and this feels surreal, dreamlike.

"Ah, hello, boys," Jed says, in a voice that's unfamiliar—odd and lilting, smooth on the surface with something dangerous lurking just beneath. He walks into the midst of the crew. The raiders eagerly gather around, but keep a respectful distance. He smiles at them, making eye contact with each and every one of them—and completely ignoring me. My whole body is numb, my brain full of static.

"It's so good to be back together," Jed says. More of the crew members are breaking off from the fight in the town, drawn to him like a magnet. They form a loose circle, all eyes on him. He pauses briefly, stepping up to the big man who nearly shot me. He bumps knuckles with him amiably before continuing.

"And wow, jeez guys, I am *so* touched that you all followed me across the wastes to this hellhole."

"As if we had a choice, Jedediah," a woman says with a half smile.

Jedediah. And there it is, finally, making its way into my shell-shocked brain. Not Jed, but Jedediah. Not the son of a ruthless dictator, but...

"No," I breathe. It isn't possible. There's no way it was really him the whole time, no way I fell for a stupid trick and became *friendly* with the man who burned down my home. No way I saved the life of the man who murdered my family.

But the evidence is right in front of me. "Jed" was a lie. He never existed. All along, there's only ever been Jedediah Johnson.

The one and only, as he said himself not too long ago. All of his long-winded stories, stories I thought he was telling about his father... He's been rubbing the truth in my face this whole time.

He drops his old identity like a snake shedding its skin. His posture straightens, his eyes sharpen, his smile becomes unfamiliar. He rolls his shoulders back and cracks his neck and, in the time it takes me to blink twice, he has become a stranger. I saw glimpses of this man at times. I saw him when I first put a gun in his hands, and when he looked at the fire at Fort Cain— a fire, I finally realize with a growing horror, he must have started himself. He orchestrated the fall of Fort Cain, leading us to the raiders, and eventually... right here.

And I helped him. How many times did I save his life? Risk *my* life for his? How many times did I propel him toward this very moment?

Jedediah frowns at the woman who interrupted him.

"Sh, I'm talking right now," he says in a hushed whisper, waving his hand to silence her, and then grins again. "Anyway, welcome to the western wastes, I guess. What a shitfest, right?" He spreads his hands wide, inviting commentary now, and earns a few chuckles from his crew.

It's ridiculous, how they pander to him. I don't understand. What power does this small, ridiculous man have over a crew of the best raiders in the wastes? I'm barely aware of the next couple minutes of Jedediah's speech; I spend it watching him, studying his face and the faces of his crew. By the time he finishes, and his crew cheers for him, I feel like I'm even further from understanding him than when I started out.

"So," Jedediah says in a conversational tone, turning in a circle and looking at his crew. "We're all reunited, then. Good. I think there's just one more thing to address before we all have a well-earned rest." He un-holsters his gun and spins it around his hand. "Which one of you had the bright idea of pretending to be me?"

Silence falls. Jedediah looks from one face to another, and everyone avoids his gaze. He frowns at the lack of an answer, and raises his hands wide open, gun dangling haphazardly from his fingers like he's forgotten he's still holding it. Everyone's eyes are trained on that weapon, my own included.

"C'mon guys, it's a simple question," he says. "All the towns said Jedediah Johnson was coming through with his crew. Clearly, one of you was claiming to be me." No one responds. Jedediah sighs, lowering his hands to his sides. He twirls his gun around one finger, looking down at his shoes. He stays like that for a long few moments, his expression pensive, and then his head jerks up. "*Oh*, I see. You guys think I'm going to be mad, is that it?" He laughs, a little too loudly, and shrugs his shoulders. "I'm not mad, guys. I mean, I get it. You couldn't exactly admit that I was missing, right? Would really fuck up our reputation. So instead someone had to step up, make it look like we had everything under control, right? And it worked! It totally worked."

I stay quiet as I watch the scene unfold, moving only my eyes to take in the lowered heads and overly stiff statures of Jedediah's crew, so at odds with their leader's smooth and casual movements. I have the distinct impression that everyone knows something I don't.

Finally, someone steps forward, separating himself from the rest of the crew. He's a thick-necked man with his face almost entirely concealed by his hair. I've seen him before, I realize. He's the other tax collector I saw, way back in Sunrise.

"Er, boss," he says, brushing hair out of his eyes, only to have it fall back into place the moment he lowers his hand.

"Yes, Mop?"

The man cocks his head to one side.

"Boss?" he says uncertainly. "My name is—"

"I know, I know," Jedediah says, waving his words aside. "We're doing nicknames now. That's what they do out here in the west. Isn't it cool?"

"Oh," the newly deemed Mop says, brushing hair out of his eyes and frowning. "Do I have to be Mop?"

"What's wrong with Mop?"

"Well, it's just—" he starts, and then halts abruptly as Jedediah stops spinning his gun. The weapon falls perfectly into place in his palm, and he taps it against the side of his leg. Mop swallows. "Never mind," he says.

"Anyway, what were you saying?" Jedediah asks, smiling.

"It was Frank that did it." He pauses and licks his lip. "We thought no one would take us seriously if they knew our leader got 'imself kidnapped an' such. So, uh, Frank decided to say he was you."

"Oh? Frank?" Jedediah turns, scans his gathered crew, and

points with his gun. A few people step aside to avoid the end of the barrel, but one steps forward. It's the huge, quiet-voiced man from before, the one who I initially mistook for Jedediah. He's as stoic as before, his shoulders braced and his face stone-like. "Is this true?" Jedediah asks, leaning his head back and squinting up at the big man. Frank lets out a long sigh, and slowly nods. Jedediah scratches his head, frowns, and glances at Mop.

"But Frank hardly talks."

"Yeah, well, he only really said 'I'm Jedediah Johnson' a couple times, and that seemed to convince people."

Jedediah looks at Frank.

Frank clears his throat. "I'm Jedediah Johnson," he says in his quiet, gravelly voice, staring straight ahead.

"That *is* pretty convincing," Jedediah says, nodding to himself. He puts his hands on his hips and chews his bottom lip thoughtfully. "Well, if anyone was gonna step up and pretend to be me, I'm glad it was a big, handsome guy like you." He reaches up to clap Frank on the shoulder, and then gasps with sudden excitement. "Oh, I've got it! Tiny! I'll call you Tiny. It's ironic, see? What do you think?"

Frank grunts and shrugs, which Jedediah apparently takes as a sign of agreement, because he gives the man another excited fist-bump, his hand tiny next to the raider's giant fist. Mop, meanwhile, seems progressively more bewildered.

"You're really not mad? 'Cause usually, when you say 'I'm not mad, guys'"—he does a rather poor and high-pitched imitation of Jedediah's voice—"it actually means you're *really* mad..."

"Oh? So you thought I was going to punish Tiny?" Jedediah asks, raising an eyebrow.

"Well," Mop says, trying again in vain to push hair out of his face. "I thought for sure you would punish *somebody*..."

"Quite right," Jedediah says, and shoots Mop in the head.

His body teeters for a moment, topples backward, and lands in the dust with a heavy thud.

The rest of the crew step aside to avoid the fallen body, but otherwise show no reaction—no anger, no horror, not even the barest hint of surprise. Aside from my sharp intake of breath, there's total silence. Jedediah sweeps his eyes over his crew, nods to himself, and resumes twirling his gun.

"Sorry about that," he says, "but, well, you know how it is. Gotta punish somebody, y'know, and it can't be Tiny. He's my biggest and most favorite crew member. Everyone on board with this?" When Jedediah looks around, his crew mumbles quiet assent. Apparently deciding that's not good enough, he whirls abruptly and points his gun at one particular man. "Yes, Eyepatch?"

At the end of his gun is a scrawny man donning—surprise, surprise—an eyepatch over his left eye. The man gulps and stands up straighter, his visible eye bulging.

"Right, boss!" he shouts in Jedediah's face. Jedediah blinks rapidly.

"Woah, 'Patch," he says. "Relax, buddy." He chuckles, and then turns back around. When his back turns, Eyepatch lets his shoulders slump, releasing a gust of breath like a balloon deflating.

"Well, I'm glad we're all on the same page," Jedediah says. "And now…" He splits into a broad grin, putting his gun away and holding his hands up. "Let's celebrate!"

While the raiders celebrate, I sit locked in a basement.

The room is dark and musty, with no windows and a single door, at the top of a set of stairs in the corner. There's no furniture, nothing at all except dust and cobwebs. I already spent a solid thirty minutes shouting and hammering at the door with my fists. Now I sit winded and defeated in the corner, listening to the sounds of revelry above. Despite the bumpy initial reunion, the crew does seem genuinely happy to have their leader back—or else they've grown exceptionally good at faking it for him. And Jed seems happy to be back with them as well. I hear his voice occasionally, cheering and celebrating, cutting through the other noise to reach my ears.

But "Jed" is wrong, I remind myself. It's Jedediah. Jedediah Johnson. The infamous shark, the ruthless dictator. The stranger.

The deception sits heavily in the pit of my stomach. I can't believe I was stupid enough to believe everything he told me, to grow to trust him, maybe even like him. I traveled with him. I put a gun in his hand and expected him to watch my back. I spent a cold night pressed against him. I imagined a future with us together; I let myself believe that he could be the home I was looking for.

The all-encompassing shock has finally left my body, and in its wake, my emotions roil and churn every time I think about it. Anger. Disgust. Disappointment.

Hurt.

It's been a long time since I felt that one. A long time since I let anyone get close enough to hurt me.

I curl my hands into fists and dig my nails into my palms. I force myself to take long, slow breaths, and focus on the rise and fall of my chest until I have myself under control again.

I can't believe I was this fucking stupid. I thought my situation was bad before, stranded out in these hellish western lands, surrounded by raiders. Now I've ended up in an even worse one: held hostage by a crazy dictator who I had almost started to believe was my friend.

I know I should be spending my time productively, trying to think of a plan, a way to escape, but it's too hard. I'm too exhausted, body and mind. It's hard enough to keep my thoughts from spiraling into despair. I don't even raise my head as I hear the door open. Only when footsteps reach the bottom of the stairs do I look up and see Jedediah.

He drops to a crouch a few feet in front of me, and places a folded blanket and a metal canteen on the floor.

"Got you some water," he says, pushing it toward me.

I kick the canteen, sending it skidding back across the floor to hit his foot. He slowly slides it back toward me.

"I know you're upset, but you do need to drink," he says. When I still don't move to touch it, he shrugs. "Well. I'll leave it here. And the blanket, in case it gets cold down here." He scrutinizes me, and when he speaks again, his voice is soft. "I thought about keeping you in a car, but I know places like this make you feel safe."

The memory of that conversation, of the personal things I shared with him, sends a fresh burst of humiliation and hatred through me. I kick the canteen again, this time sending it flying across the room with a clang of metal. Jedediah rocks back on his heels, looking at the fallen canteen for a long few moments before turning back to me.

"I'm sorry," he says. "I really do mean it. Things got out of hand."

"Out of hand," I repeat.

"Well, yeah," he says, gesturing vaguely. "I mean, coming out here was part of the plan, but I didn't expect things with Saint to happen quite like they did, and Tiny pretending to be me required some serious improvising, and...well. You know how these things are. Or maybe you don't. I suppose you'll have to take my word for it."

I stay quiet for a few moments, my anger stewing, until what he said hits me.

"What do you mean, part of the plan?"

"Surely you didn't think I'd end up all the way out here by

accident," he says, half-smiling. "Give me some credit, Clem. Haven't you heard I'm a genius?'"

I say nothing, too busy fighting back an urge to punch him. I may have hit him several times, but that was before; before I was at his mercy, before I saw him murder one of his own men for no good reason. Now I really have no clue who the man is front of me is, or what he's capable of doing. Jedediah glances at my clenched fists, one eyebrow rising as if he's curious to see whether I'll do it. After a few moments pass, he stands up, brushing himself off.

"Well," he says. "We'll have plenty of time to talk about it later. I have to get back to my party." He walks backward toward the stairs, still keeping his eyes on me. "I would invite you, but I'm afraid that might be a little awkward for everyone involved. I'm sure you understand. Don't worry. They'll come around eventually." Before I can even begin to decipher what that means, he waves at me, turns, and climbs the stairs. Without looking back again, he's gone, leaving me even more confused than before.

XXIV
The Grand Plan

I wake to the sound of the door slamming. I scramble up, pressing my back against the wall and facing the stairs. I was on the verge of giving up yesterday, but now, after a night's rest—albeit a shitty one spent on a cold floor—I'm feeling a little differently about the situation. I'm more than ready to launch myself at Jedediah the moment he reaches the bottom of the stairs.

But the man coming toward me isn't Jedediah. It's Frank— or Tiny, or whatever his name is now. He pauses as he reaches the bottom of the stairs, regarding me warily. I stare back at him. After a moment, he swings his gaze to the blanket Jedediah gave me, sitting folded and unused in the middle of the floor. His eyebrows rise slightly, though his face remains otherwise expressionless. He walks over to the canteen, lifts it up, and shakes it to judge the amount of water inside. Finding it full, he shakes his head and mutters under his breath.

He gives me another long, searching look, picks up both the blanket and canteen, and walks over to me. I stay perfectly still as he draws near, my fists clenched. Unlike Jedediah, this man would have no problem beating me down in a fight. But he makes no aggressive moves toward me. Instead, he sets down both blanket and canteen in a slow and almost gentle way, then turns and leaves.

When the door shuts again, I grab the canteen and pull it toward me. I open it, take a good sniff, swirl it around and sniff it again. It smells like water, and a quick taste reveals nothing out of the ordinary. It tastes like nice, clean, bottled water.

As much as I want to reject Jedediah's hospitality, I can't take revenge if I end up dead of dehydration. I swallow my pride along with the water.

As I rest and drink over the day, life gradually returns to my body—and with life, the will to fight.

Later in the day, Jedediah comes for another visit, this time bringing a can of beans. I can smell meat cooking outside, but he didn't bring any. A gesture intended to show that he knows me, I assume, just like the bomb shelter thing. But if he thinks he's going to trick me into trusting him again, he's dead wrong.

I stay in the corner and bristle silently as he sets the opened can in front of me and sits, cross-legged, a few feet away. After a few minutes of silent standoff, the smell of food becomes too tempting. I reach out and grab the can, dragging it over to me. It's warm, and I eat it quickly, while still keeping one eye on Jedediah. He watches me, one hand propping his chin up.

When I'm done eating, I slam the emptied can down on the floor and stare at him. He maintains eye contact, and the corner of his mouth curls up, like he thinks we're playing some sort of game. And maybe we are, from his perspective. Either way, I'm tired of the silence and the waiting.

"You planned all of this?" I ask in disbelief. My voice comes out rusty from disuse, and I clear my throat. "Me taking you, ending up all the way out here." He says nothing, just waits, and I grind my teeth. "How the fuck did you—" I start, and then stop. Everyone has always said that Jedediah Johnson is a genius . . . and there's a question much more important than *how* he did it. "*Why?*"

"Ooh, man, I've been so excited to explain this," he says,

his eyes lighting up. He leans forward, clasping his hands together. "Well, as you know, I had a pretty sweet setup back in Wormwood. Nice mansion, lots of towns to give me whatever I needed, plenty of guards, etcetera, etcetera. But, after a while of that, it actually got rather boring. Who would've thought?"

I study his face, sure that he must be joking, but he looks earnest.

"You got bored," I say flatly. "Bored with...what? Having enough food and water and men to not have to worry about anything? Most people would kill for that."

"Well, yeah," he says, shrugging. "It was nice for a while, but I wanted more."

And there's the truth of it. He can claim boredom all he wants, but in that *more*, and in his eyes, is the real reason: hunger. Hunger on a scale more grand than I could even imagine.

"When I heard what things were like out in the west," he continues, "I thought it sounded perfect. Total lawlessness, and so many little towns in need of my guidance...But my crew disagreed. They liked things the way they were, didn't want to risk it all. So I thought to myself: 'Hmm, how can I get them to follow me across the wastes?'"

"You can't be serious," I say.

"Yes," he says, looking immensely satisfied with himself. "That's where you came into play."

I stare at him. I knew Jedediah Johnson was evil, I knew he was some kind of mad genius, but I never would have expected him to be completely batshit *insane*. And as he spews out this fucking ridiculous plan, he's smiling at me like we're two friends sharing an inside joke. He doesn't say anything else, clearly waiting for my reaction.

"You're out of your fucking mind," I say.

His smile fades, and is replaced with an expression of puzzlement and hurt. His confusion baffles me. Did he really expect me to say something different? Apparently so, judging from the wounded-puppy look he's giving me. I guess he truly, honestly thought I would be . . . what, pleased? Impressed?

"But we talked about this," he says. "When I said the eastern wastes are better than the west, you didn't argue."

"I didn't argue that *maybe* life was better for the townies there," I say, loath even to admit that. "Doesn't mean I think you're anything less than a power-hungry, maniacal piece of shit."

Jedediah sighs and sits back on his heels. He's quiet for a couple minutes.

"You know," he says thoughtfully, "you and I are really quite similar when you think about it."

My eyebrows shoot up despite my determination not to show a reaction.

"In the end, we both want to make the world a better place," he says. He's very serious now, all of the gleeful triumph from before leaving his voice. He speaks more slowly than usual, like he's puzzling the words out as he says them. "And we both know violence is the way to do it."

"You literally burn people inside their homes if they disagree with you," I say, my hands clenching into fists. "We're nothing alike."

"Okay, so, a minor disagreement about methods."

"And you think *tyranny* is the way to make the world a better place."

He frowns at that.

"I just don't get it," he says. "The towns under my care have rules. And protection. And of course I demand a little something in return, but I think that's really quite reasonable."

"Reasonable," I repeat flatly.

"I'm not a cruel man. I just do what I have to do. The same as you, Clementine."

He says it so calmly, so casually, as if it's not even in question. As if the things he's done are truly reasonable—things like burning Old Creek to the ground. Rage rises inside me, and I barely keep myself from wrapping my hands around his throat. The only thing that stops me is the knowledge that he surely has someone outside, waiting to intervene if he's in trouble. When I decide to kill Jedediah, I want to make sure I succeed.

"You're fucking insane," I tell him. "And I'm going to kill you when I get a chance."

Jedediah stares at me for a moment, and then throws back his head and laughs. He keeps laughing as he stands up and moves toward the door. When he's almost there, he finally stops and looks back at me, shaking his head.

"You're not going to kill me," he says, still smiling. He says it with such confidence that I don't know how to react other than with an incredulous stare. "Anyway, I suppose it doesn't really matter if you agree or not. I don't need your help. I've already won."

I stay silent as he walks to the door, steps outside, and locks it.

"We'll see," I whisper to myself in the darkness of my cell.

The next morning, Jedediah's crew stomps around and shouts to one another outside. The words are indecipherable, but they sound busy. I sit and listen carefully, even walk up to the door and press my ear against it in an attempt to hear better, but I gather nothing other than the fact that a lot of movement and noise is happening. After a few minutes, I retreat back to the basement floor to wait. There's nothing else I can do.

Soon the door opens, and Tiny walks down the stairs. A rope hangs from his hands. I stand and back against the wall, my hands curling into fists. I don't give a damn that Tiny is twice my size, and that he'll undoubtedly beat the shit out of me. Whatever he wants to do to me with that rope, there's no way I'm letting it happen without a fight.

The raider descends to the bottom of the stairs, where he

stops, rope dangling from his hands. We stare each other down, and he wraps an end of the rope around one massive hand.

"Wrists," he says, and demonstrates holding them out. I shake my head—that's better than a noose, but not *much* better. He steps forward, and I step to the side. He sighs, and raises his free hand to rub at his forehead.

"I'm guessing you have orders not to hurt me," I say, and spit at his feet. "Good luck with that."

He looks down at his spittle-covered boot impassively, sighs again, and walks back up the stairs without further argument. I stay where I am, bracing myself for whatever comes next.

A few minutes later, Tiny returns with Jedediah behind him. The bastard's usual blasé demeanor is gone for once. He moves quickly down the stairs and stops there, staring at me and tapping one foot against the floor. I set my jaw and glare at him.

"Okay, what's the issue here?" he asks, running a hand through his hair. Tiny stands behind him with the rope in hand, waiting silently. Jedediah looks at him, and at me. When nobody says anything, he throws his hands up with a groan. "Both of you seriously need to work on your verbal communication skills," he mutters, and focuses on me. "Okay, Clem, so here's the deal. I like you, I respect you, and all of that jazz, but I'm afraid I simply must insist on tying you up for the journey."

A journey. So that's what this all the noise is about. I want to ask where we're going, but I won't trust whatever answer he gives anyway.

"Not gonna happen," I say.

"This is really unfair," he says, in a voice like he's scolding me. "You dragged me around in ropes for days, Clementine. *Days*. It's really uncomfortable, you know. And I'm just asking for a few hours in return." I merely glare at him in response. After a moment, he turns and grabs the rope out of Tiny's hands. "Would it make you feel better if I did it myself?" he asks, taking a step toward me. I don't move, which he seems to take as encouragement, moving forward and raising the ropes.

I stay completely still until he's just a step away. As soon as he's close enough, I smash my fist into his jaw. His head jolts to the side, and he swears, stumbling back. I lunge forward again—and a goddamn truck slams into me.

That's what it feels like, at least. I'm smashed facedown on the floor, breath forced out of my chest. I try to struggle, but my arms are pinned down by an ironlike grip. I can barely move, barely breathe with my face pressed against the concrete.

"Careful with her," Jedediah says from somewhere above me. "She barely got me. I'm fine."

Barely got him, my ass. It may not have been my best punch— didn't knock him out this time, after all—but I'm sure he'll have a bruise to show for it. When Tiny loosens his hold on me just a bit, I take full advantage of it by resuming my struggles. He's no longer crushing me against the floor, but he keeps my arms tightly pinned. With all of my struggling, I barely manage to lift my face off the concrete, which just gives me a better view of Jedediah crouched in front of me. He holds one hand against his face, but he doesn't look angry, just vaguely frustrated. The rope dangles loosely from his grip.

"Oh, Clementine," he says, rubbing his jaw. "You really do like to make things difficult, huh?" When I say nothing, he raises his eyes to Tiny and nods. "Okay, hold her."

I struggle the entire time they spend tying me, though it does nothing, especially since I'm starting to lose the feeling in my hands due to Tiny's grip. When he finally releases me, I drop to the floor, breathing hard. I wriggle my hands, testing the binds, and can barely move my fingers.

"Good work," Jedediah says, fist-bumping Tiny. He smiles at me. "Hold tight, I'll be back soon."

They leave me tied on the floor, simmering in my anger,

for five minutes. Finally, Tiny returns to retrieve me. I guess I should consider it a compliment, that Jedediah would dedicate his biggest crew member to personally escort me. Despite my boiling frustration, I know better than to fuck with him, especially after that display of strength before. He's a bit rougher with me after witnessing me punch his boss in the face, dragging me along by one arm with a grip that will leave bruises, but I keep my mouth shut and my face blank.

Outside, I wince at the brightness of the sun. A couple days in a basement was almost enough to make me forget about the intense light and heat, already at a sweltering level at this point of the day. A bead of sweat trickles down my forehead. Never thought I would miss being cooped up in that basement, but this is a reminder that the wastes are just as shitty.

Tiny drags me through the eerily quiet town. The crew has cleaned out the bodies from the last fight, leaving behind nothing but dust and useless junk. While other raiders might leave a mess, Jedediah's crew is thorough and efficient, leaving an empty ghost town in its wake.

The crew waits on the edge of town, lounging around the vehicles. Some are seated on the hoods or leaning against the sides of their cars, others sitting on the ground or standing around in clumps, most of them talking among themselves and roughhousing. There's an atmosphere of thinly veiled energy and excitement—whatever Jedediah has planned, they seem pretty thrilled about it. I listen as we approach, straining for a hint about where we're headed. Are we going "home," to the eastern wastes? Or somewhere else entirely? I hear nothing that helps me guess.

As Jedediah approaches, the crew snaps to attention instantaneously. Their conversations die, their postures straighten, and anyone seated scrambles to their feet. The friendly banter and play fighting dies down, and their eyes all move to watch him.

They stand, and listen, and wait for instruction. The immediate shift is almost absurd, and all at the approach of a single, rather scrawny man who is humming cheerfully to himself as he walks.

I have to marvel at the hold Jedediah has over his crew, the seemingly effortless authority he exudes. These men and women are all hardened raiders. Every one of them is bigger than him, older than him, or at the very least tougher than him. Most look like they could snap their leader in half with one arm tied behind their back. And yet, they all look at him with such deep respect—perhaps even awe. They look at him like he's more than a crew leader. I can see why they call him a king.

"All right, boys and girls, we all good here?" Jedediah asks, looking around. Despite my surprise about his crew's behavior, he acts completely casual. I suppose he's grown to expect it at this point. "All buildings cleared out, all bodies searched, all crew members accounted for?" Several crew members mutter assent, some variations of "yes boss" and "all covered," and Jedediah nods with a satisfied grin. "Great. Let's move out." He swirls a finger in the air, and they move to obey.

I still have no clue where we're going, but apparently everyone else does, because there are no questions asked as everyone piles into the vehicles. One by one, the roars of the engines start up. Tiny, Jedediah, and I are the last to pile in, squished up against one another in the backseat of a car. I'm forced to sit in the middle.

Tiny sits on one side, stoic as usual and keeping his eyes fixed on me like he's expecting me to try something even with my wrists tied. He takes up so much space that he practically fills two seats, forcing me to squish up against Jedediah in the seat and a half left over. I try to wriggle away, but there's nowhere to go. At odds with Tiny's seriousness, Jedediah bounces in his seat, alternating between staring out the window and shooting me grins. He seems to expect me to share in whatever he's pleased about, though I'm far from happy and haven't a fucking clue what's going on.

The ride is completely silent, with the exception of Jedediah occasionally asking a question—usually some variation of "How much longer?" or "Are we almost there?" The two raiders sitting up front repeatedly remind him we'll be there tomorrow. Jedediah keeps looking at me, practically begging me to show some curiosity, but I don't give him the satisfaction. It's not like I can change where we're headed, or that the knowledge will do me any good. No matter where we go, my goal is the same: to kill this madman before his bullshit plan gets any further. Wherever we go, I'll find a way. So, I'm perfectly content to stay silent, especially if there's any chance that it will upset Jedediah.

We travel all day. I steal an occasional glance out the window, careful not to seem *too* interested, but never see anything other than empty wastes. It's impossible for me to tell where we're going, and nobody drops any hints. Even Jedediah quiets down after a while, and then dozes off. Tiny, as usual, remains silent.

When we stop for the night, they move me to the trunk. I fight and kick, scuffling with Tiny as he drags me out of my seat. But in the end, the fight drains out of me, and Tiny carries me and dumps me in the trunk without much effort. Jedediah stands beside him, looking down at me. I glare at him, trying to channel as much hate as I can into my gaze.

"Sorry about this," Jedediah says. His expression makes a good show of genuine regret, though I know better than to believe anything he says or does at this point. "But, well…you know how it is." He blows me a kiss, and Tiny slams the trunk shut.

In the darkness, I will myself not to break down. It's cramped in here, and uncomfortable, and the air tastes stale...but the physical discomfort is nothing in comparison to the overwhelming sense of humiliation. It's been a long time since I've been made to feel like a helpless child, and the feeling claws and chews at my insides. My chest feels tight, and my eyes burn. I shut them, forcing back any hint of tears. Like hell am I going to give Jedediah the satisfaction of knowing he's gotten to me. I just need to be patient. Bide my time. And when the opportunity comes, I'll fucking kill him for doing this to me.

In the morning, I'm more sore than ever, my old lingering injuries added to the fresh bruising from my scuffle with Tiny. I inadvertently wince as the huge man drags me out of the trunk, but cover it with a scowl. I put up a struggle, though it's an admittedly pathetic one. Once I'm planted back in my seat, though, exhaustion takes hold. Despite my intentions of being difficult, I soon doze off.

"We're here!"

Jed's cheerful announcement jolts me awake. I raise my head and look around, trying to gather my wits in preparation for whatever is in store. But nothing could prepare me for what I see when I'm half-dragged out of the vehicle. I stand there, blinking in the sunlight and staring up at what is apparently our destination.

"What the fuck is this?" I ask. The building is a fucking mansion, huge and imposing and absurdly luxurious for the wastes...*especially* the western wastes. I didn't know a place like this could survive in this violent cluster-fuck of a region. I've never seen anything like it before. The only thing that comes close is Jedediah's home in Wormwood, but even that pales in comparison to whatever the hell this place is. At least Jedediah's place is functional, practical, more of a fortress than anything. This place is a goddamn palace. There's nothing functional about it—no fence, no guard towers, no gates. It's like whoever set this place up was so cocky they thought they'd never have to worry about defending it.

"This," Jedediah says, grinning up at the building and radiating pride, "is the former dwelling of the former Queen of the Wastes, or so they say. Supposedly, she was the big boss in the west before Saint came along and shook things up." He looks over his shoulder at me and his crew, who are exiting their vehicles and joining me in staring. They may have known where they were headed, but judging by the looks and whispers, they weren't prepared for this either. Jedediah is nothing but pleased, throwing his arms wide as if to embrace the sprawling palace. "And now, it's mine."

A rather unimpressed silence follows the announcement.

"Never heard of this so-called queen," I say. Jedediah turns to frown at me, and then at his men who seem similarly lost. He lowers his arms and sighs.

"Seriously?" he asks. "The fucking Queen, guys! She was a huge deal! People said all roads lead to her palace, she was stunningly beautiful and widely beloved, etcetera? She disappeared a short while ago and nobody knows why? None of this ringing any bells?"

He looks around at his men, who shrug and shift uncomfortably. Finally, though, Eyepatch brightens up.

"Oh, *oh*, is she the one who bathed in blood to stay beautiful forever?" he asks.

"Y'know, I *have* heard that," Jedediah says, nodding. "And that she had some way of purifying water, but that one's gotta be bullshit. You know how these things get twisted up." He shrugs, and turns back to the huge palace. "Anyway," he says, "the point is, this place is fucking awesome. It's the perfect home for the new ruler of the western wastes."

XXV
The New King

This place may be impressive on the outside, but the inside is like something out of a horrifying fever dream. The Queen's former abode was clearly once luxurious, but apparently the Queen losing her throne was not a peaceful matter. Now the place reeks of death and fear. The front doors are ripped off their hinges. The entrance room is coated in blood, the paintings on the wall splattered with it, the tile's color indistinguishable between the bloodstains and the dust blown through the open doors. A toppled statue rests in the middle of the room, riddled with bullet holes. And of course, there are the bodies, decomposing in the heat. The place reeks of rotting flesh, so thick that I choke on it.

Jedediah's crew is quiet and grim as they enter the building, guns at the ready, expecting trouble. But Jedediah strolls ahead, humming loudly as he walks through the carnage. Tiny drags me along just behind his leader, following as Jedediah walks right over the grisly scene at the entrance and through a set of ripped-apart double doors on the other side.

Through those doors is the throne room. I recognize it only by the huge painting on the wall, depicting a gorgeous woman seated on a dignified chair. The Queen and her throne, I presume. Now, though, the room is less defined by the throne than by the piles of bodies.

Whatever happened in here, it must've been huge and wild and vicious, and of course there was no one left to clean any of it up afterward. There are bodies everywhere, some evidently raiders and others wearing a crown emblem, along with other unidentifiable wastelanders. Jedediah picks his way among the half-decomposed bodies, making his way to the center of the room, where he stops abruptly. He turns in a circle, surveying the room, and stops facing us. He spreads his hands wide once more.

"Ta-da!" he says. "Our new headquarters."

His words echo around the room, emphasizing just how silent and dead this place is. His crew shifts uneasily, much more disturbed by the carnage than their leader is. Jedediah's smile fades, and he lowers his hands.

"Don't you love it?" he asks, puzzled.

"Er, yeah, it's great, boss," Eyepatch says. He clears his throat. "It's just... a bit messy."

"We're going to clean it up, of course. The place stinks," Jedediah says with a roll of his eyes. "Well, rather, you guys are going to clean it up. I have other important things to do. Plan-making for conquering and such." He turns his back to us and finishes his stroll across the room, where he plops down onto a dilapidated wooden chair. After a moment, I realize that must be the throne, though it looks absolutely nothing like the portrait on the wall behind it. It's just a shoddy wooden thing, one leg half-broken so the whole thing slants forward, and clearly has never been as grand as the throne in the picture. Jedediah leans back in the chair, placing his hands on the armrests and crossing his legs at the ankle. He looks very, very pleased with himself. "See? It's perfect."

There, sitting in his "throne," Jedediah Johnson finally looks like the man I always thought he was. I may have been surprised when I first saw him, and surprised by him many times since then, but now it finally fits. A man sitting on a throne in a room full of bodies, and smiling about it. *That's* the real Jedediah Johnson. That's who he is. Not the man the legends say he is, and not the Jed I traveled across the wastes with, but this man.

I stare at him as his crew spreads out, grabbing bodies and wreckage to drag out of the room. They're quiet as they work— not happy about moving into a new place occupied by half-rotted bodies, I guess. Or maybe they're finally realizing that their leader is a complete lunatic who has gotten them in way over their heads. Either way, they still do as he says.

"Maybe I'll drop the name and just start calling myself 'the King,'" Jedediah muses, tapping his fingers on the armrests. He catches me looking, and grins at me across the room. "Westerners are all about their nicknames. What do you think?"

"I think it suits you," I say.

While Jedediah's crew busies themselves cleaning up the carnage, I'm dragged along by Tiny, joining Jedediah on a tour of the place once he's done lounging on his throne. Jedediah insists on checking out each and every room. Most of them are filled with the same gruesome scenes we witnessed in the throne room, but Jedediah grows progressively more excited by each one. In one he finds a small handheld radio, which he insists on carrying with him, clicking it on and off as we walk, though there's nothing but static on any of the stations. Remembering Saint's broadcast, I wonder if the Queen ever listened in when she was still around. I wonder how many people are still out there, with no idea what's happened, waiting to hear his broadcasts again.

Aside from the gore, the place *is* impressive. There are guest rooms with real beds, bathing rooms with huge tubs, a dining hall with actual silverware. The latter seems to have had real plates at some point too, though now the room is covered with shattered ceramic and glass, spoons and forks scattered across the floor.

But all of it pales in comparison to the master bedroom. It must be where the Queen slept, and it's even more luxurious than the room Jedediah left behind in Wormwood. Thankfully there are no bodies in it, though someone has done some impressive finger-painting with blood on the walls, and the pictures have all been torn down and ripped apart. The dresser is tipped over, the floor covered with feathers from some thoroughly murdered pillows, and the mattress on the bed is riddled with stab wounds, but even so, the room is incredible.

Jedediah, oblivious to the mess, stares at the room in awe. He drops the radio he was playing with on top of the fallen dresser, crosses the room, and flops down on the middle of the huge bed.

"Yeah, this will do," he says, half-smiling at the ceiling. After a moment, his head lolls to one side, and he looks over at me and Tiny. "You can go now, Tiny," he says, flapping a hand. The huge man hesitates, looking down at me. After a moment, Jedediah's eyebrows draw together. "I said you can go," he repeats, his voice growing hard. Tiny releases his grip on my shoulder. He sighs once, loudly, before leaving us.

"What do you think?" Jedediah asks once the two of us are left alone, and after I spend several quiet seconds contemplating how hard it would be to kill him with my hands still tied. I raise my eyebrows at the question.

"Does it matter?"

"Of course," he says, as if the question surprises him. He gestures impatiently. "Come, sit."

I stay where I am. He lets his hand drop and sits up, stretching his arms above his head and scrutinizing me.

"Are you still angry?" he asks.

"What?"

"I asked," he says, raising his voice, "are you—"

"Am I 'angry'?" I repeat, cutting him off. "That I fell for your stupid act? That I started to believe you might not be a total monster?" I grind my teeth, humiliation burning deep in the pit of my stomach. "What the fuck do you think?"

"Well, 'monster' is a little strong. Lying and tricks aside, I thought we kind of bonded," he says with a shrug. My blood boils. I take a deep breath, trying to force my temper back before I do something stupid.

"You're the man who burned down my home. Killed my family. Did this to my face," I spit at him. "If I had known that, we would never have 'bonded.'"

"And I'm the man who traveled with you across the wastes," he says. "The man who saved your life, whose life you saved. You asked me about my life and told me—"

"Because you lied," I snap, before he can continue. The reminder of those conversations churns my stomach. "If I had known who you were, those things would never have happened."

Jedediah sighs again, rubbing at his temples as if to ward off a headache.

"Well, you kidnapped me from my home with the intention of exchanging my life for money," he says. "And I forgave you."

"You literally fucking planned that yourself!"

"Well...you got me there," he says. "But still. You didn't know that at the time."

I let out a wordless sound of frustration, unable to put into words how aggravating he is. He looks almost amused.

"I'm still the same person I was, Clem," he says. "You're just mad because you started to like me."

"You are *not* the man I thought I knew," I say.

"How so?"

"I…" I begin, and pause, fumbling for an example. "For starters, the man I knew wouldn't have shot one of his own crewmates for no goddamn reason," I say, thinking of Mop.

"Just because you don't understand doesn't mean there was no reason," he says, and for once he actually sounds annoyed. He sighs and lowers his voice, jabbing a finger at the door. "You don't know what it's like to be in charge of these kinds of people, okay?"

"These kinds of people are *your people.*"

"And sometimes I have to make hard decisions to keep them that way."

"Hard decisions," I repeat. "Like burning down Old Creek. Is that what you're trying to convince me?"

"Clementine—"

"Like locking my family in their home and burning—"

"You killed my father."

That shuts me up. I stare at him, words dying in my throat.

"What?" I ask. He says nothing. "What the fuck are you talking about?"

"That raider you killed," he says softly, once it's clear I'm ready to listen, "in Old Creek. He was my father." I open my mouth, shut it again, and he continues. "And I was upset. I was angry. I had just started taking control of the eastern wastes, and my hold was still fragile, and I was…I was young, you know, and I was scared, and I couldn't…" He pauses. "So I burned Old Creek to the ground." He leans back, resting his hands against the mattress. He half-shrugs, like he's trying to act nonchalant and not quite pulling it off. "I'm not proud of it."

I search for words and can't find them. All I know is that my anger is dying down, suddenly and swiftly, to a small shriveled ball of confusion and shame. I killed his father. I killed his father just like he killed my parents, and he forgave me for it. He could've killed me a hundred times now, a thousand times, and he didn't. Even with that knowledge, he was kind to me. He wanted me to stay with him.

I take a deep breath.

"I didn't know," I say finally, not sure what else to say.

"Well, obviously. I didn't tell you until now."

"Smartass." The comment comes out automatically, as if my brain forgot for a moment that things have changed, that we have all the reasons in the world to hate each other. Jed and I pause for a moment. Very slowly, the corner of his lips curls upward.

He stands up and crosses the room to me. Without hesitation, he takes out a knife and cuts through the ropes binding my wrists. I rub at the chafed skin as blood flows back into my hands.

"Well," he says. "I'm going to go celebrate my conquest of the western wastes." Seeing my questioning look, he shrugs. "So easy I might as well have done it already." He pauses for a moment, looking up at me. I stare down at him. He's probably right; there's no way these western townies or raiders will stand a chance against him. He'll conquer them as certainly as he conquered the east.

I could stop it now, before it happens. I could wrap my hands around his throat and squeeze the life out of him. He'd be dead before Tiny or any of his other goons knew what was happening. For a moment I start to raise my hands, but I force myself to stop. Killing him would mean...what? I once thought it would save the wastes, that people would love me for it, call me a hero. I thought it would lead me to a home. Now, I'm not so sure that's true. Without him, the western wastes will remain in shambles, and perhaps the east will become the same. There will be no home for me there.

Is it possible there could be one for me here, with Jedediah? With *raiders*? Is a home worth betraying my past and everything I thought I knew?

I don't know what's right. Not for me, and certainly not for the wastes. I don't know what the right direction to aim is, not anymore.

"You know, I really did think about leaving this all behind," Jedediah says, pulling me from my thoughts. "When I told you that I wanted to stay with you, that I didn't want to go back, it wasn't a lie. But..." He shrugs. "People need me," he says, his voice very quiet and somber. "Really. Even if they don't know it."

He steps past me without waiting for me to respond.

"You can do whatever you like," he says over his shoulder, and leaves me there.

The Queen's palace is full of shitty whiskey and fistfights. Eastern or western, it seems, all raiders celebrate much the same. Most of the revelry takes place in the throne room, which has been successfully cleansed of bodies and the most obvious of the bloodstains, though the scent of death still lingers. Jedediah left up all of the paintings and sculptures and other decorations depicting the former Queen, in various states of destruction.

I lurk in the back of the room. Jedediah's crew cast me suspicious looks, and suspicious double-takes upon seeing that I'm not restrained, but they leave me alone. Maybe they think I've joined their side, or maybe they think I can't possibly be a threat, or maybe they think nothing and just follow Jedediah's lead.

The raider king watches the party unfold from his throne, body sprawled out across it in a very unkinglike way. Every so often he raises a half-empty bottle of whiskey to his mouth and takes a long swig—or pretends to, rather. I watch carefully, and note that he doesn't actually swallow afterward, just wipes his mouth with the back of his hand. Every so often, he "accidentally" spills some, so the level gradually lowers.

Part of me is tempted to go talk to him...or shout at him, or throttle him, or *something*, but most of me is still too busy processing everything. Our last conversation explained a lot, and also raised so many questions. I've held a grudge against him for what he did to my family for years...and he seemingly forgave me in a matter of days for doing the same to him.

What the hell am I supposed to do with any of this? I don't need this kind of emotional complexity on top of all the shit I'm already dealing with. I don't even know why I'm still here. I should leave this all behind, forget about the infuriating enigma that is Jedediah Johnson. I should go...where? To the eastern wastes? So I can go back to barely surviving off bounties, and always feeling like an outsider?

Maybe I shouldn't leave. Maybe I should stay, and support Jedediah. Maybe he's been right the whole time, that having him in charge is better than lawlessness. Maybe that's what this place needs right now: a ruler with an iron fist, a ruler not afraid to embrace the violence of the wastes.

Maybe I should stay. Maybe I should kill Jedediah in his sleep, just like I killed his father.

When someone taps me on the shoulder, I nearly punch them in the face out of sheer instinct. Thankfully I restrain the impulse, because I have a feeling Tiny would hit back a lot harder. As I stare at him, he wordlessly holds up a pack of cards.

"What?" I say. "Seriously?" He says nothing, just continues holding the cards up. "Did Jedediah send you?" I ask. He shakes his head.

For some reason, I'm inclined to believe the quiet giant, and playing cards with him sounds a lot better than drowning in my thoughts.

Tiny carries a table and two chairs to a corner of the room, and scatters the raiders already hanging out there with a look. Within moments, we have a corner to ourselves. I sit while Tiny deals out cards. No words are exchanged, but I pick up on it quick enough; we're playing War.

It's a mindless, easy game, and I spend most of my time watching Tiny. His huge hands handle the cards with a surprising gentleness—though he's clumsy, frequently dropping cards and struggling to shuffle them. Despite the rough way he handled me as a prisoner, there's no hint of anger or aggression toward me now. I'm still suspicious that he's doing this just to keep an eye on me, but most of the time, he's watching his leader instead.

"So," I say, and Tiny turns to look at me. "How long have you worked for Jedediah?" He shrugs, his eyes going back to the cards. "A long time?" He nods. I pause for a few moments, running my thumb over a card, which has a bloodstain in one corner. "You knew his father," I guess, and after a moment, he nods again. "You worked for his father, and now for him."

"Hmm," Tiny agrees. I eye him, wondering if he knows what Jedediah knows. I could ask him, but instead another question jumps out of my mouth.

"Is it true that Jedediah's father killed his mother?"

Ever since I found out who he really is, that question has been lurking in the back of my mind. How much of what he told me on our journey was true? How much of that persona was really him?

Tiny pauses. His eyes flick behind me, toward where I know Jedediah is sitting. For a moment I think he's going to ignore the question, but just when I'm about to give up and continue playing he gives a small bob of his head.

So it's true, then. I almost wish it weren't. This would be so much easier if Jedediah had lied about everything.

I flip over another card over and collect his when I win.

"Can I ask you something else?" He continues shuffling

his cards without looking at me. "Do you think Jedediah is a good man?"

He pauses, his hand resting on a card. He taps one finger against it, considers for several long seconds.

"Doesn't matter," he says, finally.

"Hmm," I say.

"Hmm," Tiny agrees, and we continue our game.

At the end of the night, I find myself back in Jedediah's room. I expected him to be at his party until dawn, but instead he slips in a few minutes after me, and flops facedown on the bed.

"You're not going to convince me you're drunk," I say. He laughs, the sound muffled by the bedding, and turns his head to face me.

"So, you're still here," he says.

"Yeah."

"For how long?"

I shrug. He rolls over onto his side, propping his chin up with one hand.

"Does this mean you're back on my side?"

"Was I ever on your side?" I ask, raising my eyebrows.

"Sure you were. You saved my life more than a couple of times, I seem to remember."

I want to say *That was different*, but really, is it? If someone walked in right now and came at Jedediah with a knife, I have the feeling I'd still leap to defend him, even if I willed myself not to.

I lean back against the headboard, sighing, well aware that I still haven't answered his question.

"You honestly believe that you're going to make this place better," I say.

"I wouldn't be doing this otherwise."

"And you honestly think you can pull it off."

He shrugs.

"Nobody here can stand up to my crew," he says. "They're the best." As usual, his confidence is at an absolutely ludicrous level. But this time, I believe he may be right. Jedediah has only a few dozen men and women at his disposal, but they're the best of the best. Even if that raider army held together as a unified group—which they didn't, in the end—I don't think even *they* could have fought Jedediah's crew. And who else could possibly stand up to him? "You still think I'm wrong," he says, watching me think.

"No," I say, and am surprised at how confidently my answer comes out. "I think...I think you're right. I think this place needs guidance. I think it needs a ruler."

His eyebrows rise in clear disbelief.

"Well, this is an awfully convenient time for you to change your mind," he says.

"I've been thinking about it a lot," I say. "About how you were with all the townies, and with the raiders, and with me..." I trail off, not sure how to put it into words. "You're the kind of man that people can believe in."

As he searches my face, his eyebrows gradually lower.

"Huh," he says. "You really mean it."

In response, I reach over and squeeze his arm. The touch feels strange, almost taboo, after the events of the last few days, but I let it linger for several seconds before pulling back. Jed smiles at me, and contentedly curls up in bed, making no move to get closer to me.

As he starts to snore, I grab the radio and slip out of the room.

I stop in the hallway with it clutched tightly in my hands, listening for any approaching footsteps, but none come. It's just me, and this radio. An awful lot of people listened to Saint's broadcast not too long ago. I wonder how many wastelanders are still tuning in, waiting for news about him...or someone else like him.

Me, a radio, and a decision I have to make.

Jedediah Johnson is a liar, a shark, a tyrant, and certainly out of his damn mind. Yet still, people love him. Follow him. Trust him. Does he deserve that trust? Does he deserve the loyalty of men like Tiny, or women like me? I think it's time to find out.

I click the radio on and raise it to my mouth.

XXVI
It All Comes Tumbling Down

The morning begins with a bang.

Several bangs, actually, along with a very loud thud. My eyes fly open at the noise, but I remain still, staring at the ceiling. An explosion shakes the building, and some dust and bits of plaster rain down from the ceiling and onto the bed. Beside me, Jedediah finally sits up, clutching the blanket to his chest.

"What?" he asks the air, not awake enough to form a complete sentence. When the air doesn't answer, he scrambles out of bed. Feet still bare, hair sticking up in tufts, he crosses to the door and yanks it open, looking up and down the hallway outside. "Tiny?" he calls out.

I sit up, but stay where I am. A burst of gunfire comes from outside, followed by a yelp from Jedediah, and another burst of gunfire. I scramble to my feet, rushing for the door—but a moment later, Tiny bursts inside and slams it closed behind him. Jedediah is clutched in his arms like a child's toy, looking rattled but unharmed. Tiny sets him down, and he sways on his feet. He gathers himself after a moment, gives Tiny a cursory fist-bump, and turns to me.

"People are here," he says, rubbing at one of his eyes. "Angry people. Lots of angry people. Raiders, and townies, and… fuck. Everyone. All these westerners." He crosses the room to the window, looks outside. When he turns back, his face is very pale and confused. "Why are so many angry people here?"

"Broadcast," Tiny says.

"A broadcast?" Jedediah says, and seems to finally realize. "They heard I'm here, and taking over. They...shit. *Shit*. This isn't how we do things. We're supposed to take it slow. Divide and conquer. How did this happen?"

Tiny says nothing, but his eyes quickly find the radio sitting on the dresser. Jedediah's gaze follows, and pauses there. He opens his mouth, hesitates, and whirls to Tiny again. "Frank," he says, his voice very serious. "Go make sure everyone is together. It's gonna be a fight."

Without a word, Tiny is out the door, slamming it shut behind him and leaving us alone. Jedediah, meanwhile, rushes over to the bed and rummages under it. He grabs a bag I never saw him stash, and his shoes. I turn away from him and walk to the window. I can't see anything from here, but I can hear the noise—a lot of gunshots, and a lot of yelling. I don't need to see it to guess what's happening. That broadcast I sent out last night must have reached a lot of people and pissed them all off, raiders and townies alike.

"You called them here," Jedediah says from behind me. I turn to find him staring at me with naked confusion and hurt on his face. "After everything you said yesterday?" He pauses, searching my face. "I didn't think you were that good of a liar," he says, sounding almost impressed. "Damn."

"It wasn't a lie," I say. I take a deep breath. Words aren't my strong point, but I want to say this right. "I think the wastes need a leader. Whether you're the right man or not, I'm not too sure, and I don't think I'm the right person to choose anyway. So, I'm going to leave it up to you." Jedediah stares at me wordlessly, and I continue after a brief pause. "If you deserve to rule the wastes, then prove it. No crew to do your dirty work, just you and your damn words. Start from scratch and make your way to the top again, if you can."

"How exactly am I supposed to do that with no crew?" he asks, searching my face.

"Do what you've been doing," I say. "Make people love you." I grit my teeth, wrestling with the next words, but they tumble out of my mouth anyway. "You're way too damn good at it. Don't force your way in with a crew. You have to do this on your own. If you let the people choose for themselves, they might just choose you."

He scrutinizes my face. Whatever he finds there makes his expression soften. He opens his mouth, shuts it, opens it again—as if, for once, he's the one struggling to find the right words to express himself. He takes a step toward me.

"Clementine," he says. "You should probably know—"

At that moment, something huge slams into the door—once, and then again. We both turn toward it, and Jed steps in front of me. A moment later, a man bursts through the door, ripping it off its hinges. He's big, dark-skinned, scarred, and . . . familiar. He pauses, looking at us.

"Oh," Tank says. "It's you two."

"Hi there," Jedediah says, sounding as casual as ever, though I can see the tension in his body. I'm tense myself. Nobody was supposed to make it to this room so quickly. Now we're trapped, and I'm unarmed and unprepared.

But here's Tank, and standing in the doorway is Kid and the rest of the crew.

"Well, well," Wolf says behind her, "if it isn't our old friends." He steps into the room, an assault rifle aimed at me—clearly prioritizing me as the threat. "You fucking piece-of-shit liars."

"Seriously? This is the guy?" Kid asks, jerking the barrel of her shotgun in Jed's direction. She eyes him up and down, looking thoroughly unimpressed. "A lot smaller than Saint."

"And *this* scrawny fucker thinks he can come along and attempt the same damn thing right after we kill Saint," Wolf says, shaking his head. "But you know what really pisses me off? This fucker had the gall to talk himself up in the *third person* while he was with us. What kind of crazy asshole—"

"Yeah, he's a crazy bastard," I say, cutting him off. They all look at me, and I take a deep breath. I'd much rather fight my way out of this situation, but right now talking is my only option. "But maybe that's exactly the kind of leader the wastelands need."

Wolf turns to me, surprised.

"Wait," he says. "Aren't you the one who sent out that broadcast in the first place? Bringing everyone here to take this guy down?"

"Yeah...well...it's a complicated situation."

"Listen," Jedediah says, and I relax. He'll take charge now; he'll convince them, like he convinced me. "I'm going to do things differently around here. I'm *not* going to be a second Saint—"

Bang.

I don't even have time to react. My eyes stay on the raiders in the doorway, who mostly look as surprised as I am—aside from Kid, who has stumbled back a few steps from the recoil on her shotgun. Slowly, very slowly, I turn my eyes to Jed.

I missed him stumbling back. I missed him hitting the floor. He's sprawled there now, facedown, surrounded by a metric fuck-ton of blood. It's pooled around him, splattered on the walls, on the bed. On me too, I realize, looking down at myself in stupefaction.

"*Kid,*" Wolf is yelling, though it sounds very distant to my ears, "are you fucking serious? I told you we were gonna do it *right* this time. I had this whole fucking speech planned out—"

I feel numb. Distant, like I'm watching this scene unfold in a dream, like I'm not really here. This can't possibly be happening. This isn't how things were supposed to be. Jed wasn't supposed to die. I wish that I had a gun, that I could mow down each and every one of these raiders. I can vividly imagine it: slicing Tank's throat, planting a bullet in Wolf's forehead, ripping Kid limb from limb. If I only had a weapon—but I don't. I can't. And what would be the point?

I guess I should've expected this. I'm the one who brought them here.

I thought it was the right decision—to give Jed a chance to prove himself. I was so sure he could do it too. I thought I was giving a choice to myself, to him, to the people. Now, that choice has been snuffed out. Was it the right thing to do? Was it best for the wastes, or will people be better off with him in the ground? Jed could've almost certainly led the wastes to a new age...but would it have been an improvement? I'm not sure. We all know he was a good leader, but whether he was a good man, and whether that matters, is something I don't think I'll ever be sure of.

Dolly watches me from across the room as the rest of her crew bickers. I meet her eyes for a moment. I picture myself walking over and knocking her out, taking her gun, killing each and every member of her crew while she watches. I could make her feel the way I feel—like some vital part of her was just ripped out of her and thrown away forever.

I savor the mental image for a moment, and then walk past Dolly and into the hallway outside. Nobody stops me.

XXVII
Afterward

A fight rages in the rest of the Queen's mansion, westerners embroiled in a bloody tussle with Jedediah's men. There are western raiders with their brutal weapons, townies with their makeshift tools, some who are difficult to tell apart but working together—mostly. I see five of them surrounding Eyepatch, who still manages to kill two men before finally going limp.

I walk past the scene in a half daze, ignored by all. My mind keeps flashing back to that gunshot, to the sight of Jed's body surrounded by blood. Somewhere inside of me is a violent rage, and a sickening sadness, but both are smothered by numbness. I walk, barely aware of the danger around me until a knife flies right past my face, hits the wall, and clatters to the floor.

I stop, and my wits finally return, the sound of the fight wiping away my haze. I grab the knife and gut the man nearest me before he knows what hit him. It feels good, doing what I'm best at, and so I keep doing it, hacking and slashing my way through the fight, cutting down townies and western raiders and Jedediah's crew members alike. For a while, it's enough to keep me numb. I embrace the violence, lose myself in it.

No rules, not anymore. They've gotten me nowhere.

But gradually, the rush of it fades away and leaves behind...

nothing. I pause over the body of my latest victim, breathing hard as I watch the life bleed out of the man. He was one of Jedediah's men—I'm sure I'd know his name if I committed enough thought to it, but right now looking at his face just sickens me. I wipe my knife on my pants and step back. So now I do . . . what?

I don't know. I feel like all desire and purpose have drained out of me, so I turn to the next possible thing: logic. I can't stay here. Step one is to get out of this bloodbath. And then . . . And then figure out what's next, I guess.

Of course, there are a few people who try to stop me on my way, mostly western raiders who are eager to fight regardless of the reason why. I take them out easily. Fighting feels mechanical, instinctual, mindless. As my body goes through the motions, my mind is still back in that room, staring at Jed's body facedown on the floor.

More than angry or sad, I am tired, and lost, and afraid to find out what comes next.

It takes a familiar face to jolt me out of my haze again. An unexpected face, waiting around a corner: Cat, the poacher. The bounty hunter freezes, but I waste no time in holding my knife to her throat.

"Wait," she yells, before I can cut her open.

Surprising both of us, I do. I'm not sure what initially gives me pause, but upon getting a better look at her, that pause stretches out further. She's in bad shape—out of breath and covered in blood, and the wound on her leg seems to have reopened. Her face is ashen, and she sways on her feet.

"What the fuck are you doing here?" I ask, still itching to slice her throat, but holding myself back.

"Looking for you," she says. "And Jedediah." I stare at her. "I know you're with him now, and listen, I've seen the goddamn light or whatever too. I'm sick of these crazy-ass western wastes.

I want Jedediah's ass back on that throne, and my ass back in the east. That work for you?"

"Jed is…Jedediah's dead," I say, my voice deadly calm. Letting any hint of emotion out could start a flood of it, and I can't afford that right now.

"Well, shit," Cat says. "Fuck it all then. I just wanna get the fuck out of here."

I lower my knife.

"Yeah," I say. "Me too."

Regardless of everything that's happened between us, I'm not eager to go back to being alone—especially not now, when I'm stranded in the middle of the torn-apart western wastes and surrounded by warring raiders. And as far as allies go, Cat seems like my best bet. At least she's not a raider.

"Thank fucking Jesus," she says.

"The closest exit is—"

"Well, hold up, first we need to find Bird."

Of course, it has to be complicated. I sigh, already regretting my decision to be civil.

"I didn't realize I was signing up for a rescue mission," I say.

"Well, I'm not leaving her behind," Cat snaps. I open my mouth, about to argue, ready to explain to her how impossible it will be for us to get out of here alive without the side mission to rescue her insane companion, but I stop myself. I would have done it for Jed, I realize.

"Fine," I say, mentally cursing at myself even as I agree. "I'll find her. You wait outside."

"It'll be faster if we both look."

"It'll be slower if I have to rescue you too."

I can see that her pride wants her to argue, but she glances down at her injured leg and shuts her mouth. She nods curtly.

"We have a spot where we were supposed to meet," she says. "I'll be waiting there."

I nod at her, and she leaves. More than anything, I want to follow her out, get myself free of this situation. But instead, I plunge back into the fray.

I go to the place where I'd go in Bird's position: the worst of the battle, the spots where the fighting is thickest. Filled with a renewed vigor, I punch and slash and shoot my way through the fight, picking up weapons when I can find them, using my fists when I can't. It would be easy to let myself go here, to give myself over to violence, but purpose keeps me going. It helps me stay aware. Maybe that's what I've been lacking, all this time.

But my purpose proves a lot more difficult than I initially thought it would be. Bird isn't anywhere to be found. I consider the problem in between taking out raiders and townies. Bird is tough, and dedicated to her partner. She would find her way to Cat if she could. And she should be able to. She may not be as good as me, but she's still pretty damn good, and these westerners should be easy enough to take out. So if she can't, that means she's hurt. Or dead.

For now, I have to ignore that second possibility. Instead I focus on the former idea. So maybe she's hurt. If she's hurt… then I'm looking in exactly the wrong kinds of places.

I disentangle myself from the fighting, pausing to kill an idiot townie who decides to pursue me, and instead start to check the places I haven't been looking. The quiet places; abandoned rooms, hallways occupied only by corpses, cramped closets, places where an injured woman with some serious issues might drag herself if she was in trouble.

And finally, in the dining room, I find her.

She's curled up under the table, rocking and shivering, cradling an arm against her chest. Sitting on the floor near her is a bloodied knife. My heart sinks. If she's hurt badly, getting her out of here will be the least of my concerns. There's no way we'll make it across the wastes with both her and Cat useless. But getting a closer look, I realize there's no blood on her, no sign of actual injury.

"Come on, we need to go," I say. She doesn't even look at me. "Cat's waiting." She pauses at that—only to resume rocking, ducking her head lower.

My first instinct is to leave her behind. I'll tell Cat I couldn't find her, or that I found the body. Hell, I should probably kill her myself just to make sure the lie doesn't come back to bite me. I tighten my grip on my knife, but then pause.

I'm not leaving her behind.

"Fuck," I say, shoving the knife into my leg holster. Who knew a journey to the west would turn me into a goddamn bleeding heart?

Sighing at myself, I lower to a crouch beside Bird.

"Let me see it," I say. When she doesn't respond, I grab the arm and yank it toward me—maybe a little more roughly than necessary. She smacks my face with her free hand, making high-pitched sounds of protest. I release her after I see the problem: a rip in her sleeve.

"Ugh," I say. "Can't you subdue the crazy long enough for us to get out of here?" Of course, she doesn't respond to that, just resumes rocking and whimpering to herself. Grumbling, I reach down and rip off a piece of my shirt. I fight with her for the arm again, and wrap the piece of fabric across her revealed skin, circling it twice and then tying it off tightly while she smacks me in the face. Once it's done, I shove her back, struggling with the urge to bash her head in. "See? I'm trying to fucking help," I say, pulling back.

She pauses, looking at the arm and seeming to finally realize what I was doing. She flexes her arm, scrutinizing the knot, and then looking at my dirty, bloodstained shirt.

"Unsanitary," she proclaims quietly.

"Oh come on," I say. "It's good enough for now, right? Considering the imminent danger?"

She grabs the bloodied knife off the floor, scrambles to her feet, and races for the door. Cursing under my breath, I follow.

Bird weaves an unpredictable path through the building with occasional pauses to stab someone. She's so fast that I can do little but struggle to keep up, and take out anyone who gets in my way. I want to ask if she has any idea where she's going, but I can't spare the breath.

Her path seems random, but after several minutes of winding her way through rooms and halls and stabbing her way through raiders, she bursts through a door into open air. I follow her outside and skid to a stop, blinking in the sunlight. I take a moment to catch my breath—and it then hitches as I realize we're not alone. Cat is standing nearby, waiting as she promised, but she's not the only one. Beside her stands Tiny, huge and silent, his eyes locked on me.

"Bird!" Seemingly oblivious to the hulking man standing nearby, Cat grabs her partner by the shoulder, yanks her close, and plants a noisy kiss on her mask. "You asshole!" Bird ducks her head and rubs bashfully at the spot on her mask.

Tiny stares at me over the tops of their heads, waiting for the sickeningly affectionate reunion to finish before he steps forward. I keep an eye on his gun, but he doesn't reach for it.

Instead, he juts out a fist and lets it hang in the air. After a moment, I bump my own knuckles against it, and we both let our hands fall.

"I'm sorry things turned out this way," I say. I'm confused about a lot of things right now, but I do mean that.

"Hmm," he says, and then stares out at the wastelands ahead. He doesn't look as torn up as I'd expect, just vaguely troubled. I wonder if he feels as uncertain as I do about Jedediah's death, and whether it's for the best. There are still a million questions churning through my head, but right now, there's only one that's important.

"So what do we do now?" Cat asks. Silence hangs in the air for a few moments before I realize all three of them are looking at me, waiting for an answer. I blink at them, startled. Gradually, the initial shock fades and a strange calm settles over me. They're looking to me to lead them. This feels . . . right, somehow.

"I think we start in the east," I say.

"Start?" Bird asks.

"The east is gonna be a fucking mess," Cat says, almost simultaneously.

"So we put it back together," I say.

"How are we gonna do that?"

"One piece at a time." I glance around at them. Cat and Bird shrug at each other, and Tiny just watches, silently waiting.

"Gonna be hard," Cat says. "Been a long time since they've been without a leader."

"Oh, they're gonna have one," I say.

Behind us, I distantly hear the fight continuing inside the former Queen's palace; the sound of the raider army and Jedediah's men tearing one another apart. Jedediah's crew will be done for, especially with their leader gone. The raider army will be left limping, and likely dissolve into individual crews again. Everything restored to its natural balance—but in the wastes, balance never lasts for long. It's too ripe with opportunity.

I smile out at the expanse of wastelands in front of me, vast and empty and waiting. So many little towns out there, left alone and uncertain about what comes next. Both the east and the west will be left bleeding from all of this. Someone has to rise to the challenge of handling the aftermath.

People need me. Even if they don't know it.

Like with most things, I think Jed had the right idea about that. Time and time again, I've found myself wrong about people. I overestimate them, and end up disappointed—like the townies we've encountered who fell apart at the first sign of trouble, like those raiders who killed Jed before he had a chance to speak, and like Jed himself in the end. He got greedy, he got cocky, and he paid for it.

I won't make the same mistake.

I've always placed so much value on freedom. But what does that really give people? The right to die free, and little else. Townies know nothing about the world beyond their own walls. How did I ever think they were capable of making their own decisions? All the towns that turned me away when I would've helped them...All the people who saw me as a monster when I was just trying to protect them. Clearly, they have no idea what's good for them. But I do.

So, I think it's time to do what's best for them—even if they hate me for it. I'll save them, even if they don't deserve it. I can't help but care, but I'm tired of chasing love. All I need is a few people to support me...a few whom I'm already starting to gather. The rest will fall in line. They'll respect me, at least, and that will be good enough.

All this time I've spent searching for a new home, without realizing I could *make* one. By force, if I have to.

"The King is dead, long live the Queen?" Cat mutters, looking at Bird. Overhearing it, I grin.

And we set off to make our new world.

Acknowledgments

First of all, thank you to my critique partner Leigh Mar, who was the first person to read the first draft of *Raid*, and who gave invaluable feedback and encouragement that helped shape it into an actual story.

Thank you to my amazing agent, Emmanuelle Morgen, for always believing in my writing and for preventing me from panicking when deadlines loom a little too close for comfort.

Thanks to Lindsey Hall, whose insightful editing made this book bolder and immeasurably better. Thank you to Lisa Marie Pompilio for designing the badass cover, as well as to Ellen Wright, Nazia Khatun, Sarah Guan, Gleni Bartels, and the rest of the team at Orbit, who have been amazing during the publication process for both *Bite* and *Raid*.

As always, thank you to my family for encouraging me to chase my dreams, and for not judging me when those dreams included writing violent books about cannibals. A special thanks to my mom and gramma for all the support, and to my dad, who checked Barnes & Noble every day for a week to see if my book was back in stock yet.

And lastly, thank you to everyone who read and enjoyed *Bite* and/or *Raid*. Hearing from you always makes my day!

extras

orbit

meet the author

K. S. MERBETH is obsessed with SFF, food, video games, and her cat. She resides in Tucson, Arizona. You can finder her on Twitter @ksmerbeth.

interview

When did you first start writing?

Writing has always been my passion, and I've been doing it for as long as I can remember. Ever since I was a kid I've been carrying around notebooks, dreaming up new stories, scribbling ideas in the margins of my notes for class. When I was young I wasn't dedicated enough to sit down and write daily, but I didn't go a single day without thinking about whatever story I was working on. Really, I don't think I've ever had any choice but to write. If I didn't, my head would probably explode from all of the ideas rolling around in there.

Where did the idea for* Bite *come from?

It's a common theme in postapocalyptic stories that when everything goes to shit, people lose their humanity. Many of these worlds are overrun by groups of killers who are so vicious and violent that they might as well be monsters. And yet they're not monsters; they're still human, and therefore should still have backgrounds, feelings, and motivations. I became very interested in writing about these types of characters, finding out more about who they are and how their lives led to this point. So, I came up with the idea of writing a postapocalyptic story with typical "bad guys" as the main characters.

In postapocalyptic worlds, there are often zombies or monsters hungering for human flesh.* Bite *turns that idea on its head.

extras

When did you first know you wanted to write a book featuring cannibals?

After seeing a few films featuring cannibals as villains, I found myself fascinated by the idea. Cannibalism is such a taboo, and people tend to have such an intense disgust and discomfort toward it. I was intrigued by the idea of a world in which people would be forced to commit such an act to survive. Even further, I was interested in the challenge of creating sympathetic characters who also happen to be cannibals. I first explored the idea in a creative writing class in high school, where I wrote a short story called "Love Bites" about two cannibals falling in love in a postapocalyptic world. The idea was so fun to write, and garnered such a strong reaction from my classmates, that I knew I had to explore it further.

Did you have to do any research in preparation for writing Bite?

I'm sure there are a number of weird Google searches in my browser history, like "severing a finger" and "long-term effects of cannibalism" and "what does human flesh taste like." I also looked into guns and ammo, grenades, etc., but most of my research went into finding realistic challenges that Kid and the crew would face while trying to survive in the wastelands. I browsed a lot of survivalist Web sites and looked into things like heat-stroke, dehydration, water purification, and what kinds of canned food would still be edible.

There was a wide-ranging cast in Bite. Who is your favorite character?

I adore the whole cast of *Bite*, and more than any one character in particular, I love the crew's dynamic together. I really love Kid, of course, and I enjoyed writing her journey and her growth. If I have to pick a favorite, though, it's Dolly. I love every aspect of her: her elegant badassery in fight scenes, her total awkwardness in social situations, her wholehearted dedication to Wolf, her maternal protectiveness over Kid. She's a very odd character, and that made her entertaining to write about in every situation.

What is one piece of information that you know about the story or characters that you loved but couldn't fit into the book?
Early in the book, Tank mentions that Dolly once broke Pretty Boy's nose, but nobody ever explains why. The story is, when Pretty Boy initially learned that Dolly was once a prostitute, he attempted to proposition her by offering her a nice gun. She punched him in the face and took the gun. He never tried to make a move on her again.

Lastly, we have to ask: If you could have any superpower, what would it be?
I have to go with telekinesis. It's super cool and I could definitely kick some ass with it. Realistically, though, I'm not really sure whose ass I'd kick...I doubt gaining a superpower would actually give me the motivation to become a superhero or villain. But at least I could use my power for things like getting food out of the fridge without leaving my computer desk.

if you enjoyed
THE WASTELANDERS

look out for

AFTERWAR

by

Lilith Saintcrow

*History is written by the victors; but when you've been
fighting your fellow patriots, your own brothers
and sisters, does anyone really win?*

A harrowing gut punch of a novel, Afterwar *tells
the story of a dark future where America has
been devastated by a second civil war. As the fighting
draws to a close, the camps are liberated, and the
fascist regime crumbles, the work of rebuilding begins.
But can a population who's spent years divided
and hell-bent on victory at any cost ever
be truly reunited?*

Afterwar *is bestselling author Lilith Saintcrow's
answer to the dystopian genre: a timely and all-too-realistic
glimpse of a future that we hope
never comes to pass.*

CHAPTER ONE

Details Later

February 21, '98

The last day in hell ran with cold, stinking rain. A gunmetal-gray sky opened up its sluices, mortars and bigger artillery shook the wooded horizon-hills at 0900, and roll call in the central plaza—down to two thousand scarecrows and change, the dregs of Reklamation Kamp Gloria—took only two and a half hours. Pale smears peered from the red-painted kamp brothel windows, disappearing whenever the Kommandant's oil-slick head and unsettling light blue gaze turned in their direction. Stolid and heavy in his natty black uniform, Kommandant Major General Porter stood on a heavy platform; the raw edges of its boards, once pale and sticky with sap, were now the same shade as the lowering sky. The skeletons in dun, once-orange dungarees stood unsteadily under a triple pounding—first the Kommandant's words crackling over the PA, then the thick curtains of rain, and last the rolling thunder in the hills.

Not just partisans, some whispered, their lips unmoving. Convicts and kampogs learned quickly how to pass along bites of news or speculation, despite the contact regulations—worth a flogging if you were caught talking, a worse flogging if more than two kampogs were "gathering."

Nope, not just partisans. Federals.

Feral rumors, breeding swiftly, ran between the thin-walled Quonsets, bobbing over the reeking, sucking mud like balls of ignes fatui down in the swampy work sites, drifting into the empty stone rectangle of the quarry, flashing like sparks off the sicksticks the uniforms and jar captains carried. Raiders, Federals, knights riding dragons—who cared? Hope wasn't a substitute for a scrap of moldy potato or a filched, crumbling cube of protein paste.

On the second floor of the joyhouse, in a room with dingy pink-ish walls, cheap thin viscose curtains twitched a little, and the narrow bed underneath them shuddered as he finished. The bedspread had been freshly laundered, and the white, sharp smell of harsh soap and dead electrical heat from the industrial dryers filled Lara's empty skull. It was a darkness full of small things—a glimpse of the dusty silk flowers in the tiny vase on the nightstand, a twinge from her discarded body, the burn of slick soylon fabric against her cheek, the indistinct mutter of the PA as Kommandant Porter, the God of Gloria, spoke. Someone would later tell her the Kommandant, his hair swept back and his mirror-shined boots splattered with that thick, gluey mud, had made a speech about how the shivering pogs had paid their debt to society and were to be taken to a Re-Edukation Kamp. Porter audibly hoped they would remember the struggle and sacrifice the uniforms had suffered to remake them—brown immies, any-color degenerates, white politicals since the brown ones were shot, traitors all—into productive members of the Great United States of America First.

It didn't matter. Nothing mattered then but getting through the next sixty seconds. Lara heard all sorts of details later, without meaning to. Right now, though, she lay flattened and breathless under the weight on her back, life and hope and air squeezed out.

"I love you," the Kaptain whispered in her left ear, hot sour breath against her dark hair. It had grown back, first in the sorting shed and now here, though the ends were brittle and fraying. She was lucky to be in the pink room; the plywood stalls down-stairs could see as many as six, seven an hour between first roll call at 0500 to midnight, no breaks, no lunch. Up here in the rooms named for colors, though, there were special clients. A special diet too, more calories than the average kampog, especially a twenty-niner, could dream of. Exemption from even "light" labor in the sorting sheds.

Some of the uniformed guards, or the jar kaptains—the highest class of kampog, because why force a uniform to work in the stinking jar-barracks, where you lay three or four to a shelf-bed—brought "presents." Tiny containers of scent, either liquid or paste, not enough to get drunk on. Lipstick—it was edible, more welcome than the damn cologne. They often brought food, the best present of all. Cigarettes to trade. Some of the girls here drank the colorless, eye-watering liquor the uniforms were rationed, instead of trading it away for more substantial calories.

It let you forget, and that was worth a great deal. A few minutes of release from the tension was so seductive. The poison dulled you, though, and dull didn't last long here. Soaking in bathtub booze was a good way to drown.

"I love you," the Kaptain repeated, the hiss of a zipper closing under his words. The mattress had finished its song of joyless stabbing, and it barely indented under her slight, lonely weight. "I've organized a car, and gas. A good coat. I'll come back and get you." He bent over to arrange her, pushing her shoulder so she had to move, wanting her to look at him.

Rolled over on her back, Lara gazed at the ceiling, the damp trickle between her legs aching only a little. More raw lumber. Paint was a luxury—the red on the brothel's outside was left over from something else. The only other painted building was the Kommandant's House on the outskirts, with its white clapboard walls and picket fence. Lara had even seen the high-haired, floral-dressed wife once or twice, sitting on the porch with a glossy magazine back when the war was going well. Some kampogs used to work in the house or the garden, but that stopped when the siege of Denver was broken. Even the Kommandant's family had to go back to the cities, retreating eastward.

The Kaptain was blond, his bloodshot blue eyes showing his worry over the war. He was her special client, and his status meant she didn't have others. Black wool uniform with the special red piping, the silver Patriot Akademy ring on his left third finger mimicking a wedding band, the back and sides of his head shaved but the top longer. He'd begun growing it out a little while ago.

When the war turned.

He examined her while he buttoned his outer jacket, settling his cuffs, made sure he was zipped up completely. A hurried visit, for him. How many hours had she spent in this room, blessedly alone, and how many with him talking at her, unloading his worries, his thoughts, words dripping over every surface, trying to work their way in? Most of her energy went toward being impervious, locked up inside her skull. Building and maintaining walls for the steel bearings rolling inside her, so their noise could drown out everything else.

"I'll be right back." The Kaptain bent over the bed again, and his lips pressed against her cheek. There was almost no pad of fatty tissue over her teeth—still strong, they hadn't rotted out yet. Childhood fluoride had done her a good turn, and with McCall's crew there had been pine needles. Berries. Ration bars with orange flavor and minerals all in one nasty, grainy mouthful.

She was lucky, really, and how fucked-up was it that she knew? The question was a waste of energy. Here, you couldn't afford to ask. Every effort was channeled into one thing only.

Survival.

"I love you," he whispered yet again. Maybe he needed to convince himself, after all this time. His breath made a scorch circle, a red-hot iron pressed against shrinking flesh. Branded, like the Christian Courts were so fond of decreeing. *B* for "bandit" or *P* for "partisan," or the ever-popular *A* for "scarlet woman," because "adulterer" could possibly be the man, and you couldn't blame *him*.

The Kaptain slammed the door on his way out. Yelled something down the hall—an order, maybe. Quick, hard bootsteps, scurrying back and forth. Looked like he was clearing the top floor. The girls up here might be grateful for the respite, unless they were waiting for a special to bring them something. If they were, they'd assume Lara had pissed the Kaptain off somehow, or something. They didn't quite dare to band together against her—it wasn't worth the risk—but the top-floor joyhouse girls were pariahs even among kampogs, and she was a pariah even among *them.*

Exclusivity, like luck, was suspect.

I'll take care of you, he'd promised. *Wait for me.* Like she had any sort of choice. So Lara just lay there until he went away, his presence leaching slowly out of the small, overdone, dark little room. Nobody wanted bright lights in a joyhouse. A lot of the specials may have even honestly believed the girls in here were glad to see them, glad to be somehow saved.

As if anyone here didn't know it only took one wrong move, one glance, or even nothing at all, and into the killing bottles you went.

It didn't matter. She drifted, letting her ears fill with the high weird cotton-wool sound that meant she was *outside* her skin. Just turned a few inches, so she could look at whatever was happening to her body without feeling.

After some indeterminate period of time—maybe a half hour, maybe more—the throbbing beat of the ancient wheezebox downstairs thumped-ran down to a stop. Without that heartbeat, the expectant hush inside the red-painted building turned painful.

When Lara pushed herself up on her sharp-starved elbows, stealing back into her body bit by bit from the faraway place where not much could hurt her, the first rounds took out two of the watchtowers, splashing concrete, broken glass, slivers of red-hot metal, and rags of guardflesh down into Suicide Alley along the electrified fence.

The Federals—and Swann's Riders—had arrived.

if you enjoyed
THE WASTELANDERS

look out for

EXTINCTION HORIZON
The Extinction Cycle

by

Nicholas Sansbury Smith

USA Today *bestseller Nicholas Sansbury Smith's*
first book in his thrilling post-apocalyptic series
about one man's mission to save the world.

Master Sergeant Reed Beckham has led his Delta
Force team, codenamed Ghost, through every kind of
hell imaginable and never lost a man. When a top secret
Medical Corps research facility goes dark, Team Ghost is
called in to face their deadliest enemy yet—a variant strain of
Ebola that turns men into monsters.

After barely escaping with his life, Beckham returns to
Fort Bragg in the midst of a new type of war.
As cities fall, Team Ghost is ordered to keep CDC

*virologist Dr. Kate Lovato alive long enough to find a cure.
What she uncovers will change everything.*

*Total extinction is just on the horizon, but will the cure
be worse than the virus?*

1

April 18, 2015
DAY 1

The six-man team emerged onto the tarmac at dusk. The shadows they cast moved with calculated precision. They passed under the idle blades of Black Hawk helicopters and crossed between the crates of supplies waiting to be shipped to hot spots around the world.

Any onlooker with even limited military knowledge would know the silhouettes did not belong to the average grunt. Their body armor was thinner and their muscles were sculpted in a way that reflected constant training and exercise. Further scrutiny would reveal that these men carried modified weapons.

But no matter how well trained the eye of an onlooker might have been, none would have known the shadows belonged to the Delta Force operator team code-named Ghost, because technically, they did not exist—technically, they *were* ghosts who were activated only when the most critical situations emerged.

Today was one of those days.

It was April, but Master Sergeant Reed Beckham hardly noticed the budding trees and vibrant colors around him. He was still trying to figure out why Command had canceled leave after a six-month tour of Afghanistan. He was supposed to be at a bar in Key West with his buddies, pounding beers and taking afternoon naps under the brilliant white sun. Instead of boarding a charter flight to the Keys, he found himself following his men into the belly of a V-22 Osprey at Fort Bragg.

When Colonel Clinton had told him the team would receive a full briefing on a flight to Edwards Air Force Base, Beckham hadn't been concerned. That wasn't unusual. On most missions, they were briefed on the fly before dropping into a hot zone. This was a source of great pride amongst his men.

Drop. Take out target. Repeat.

They had the process down, like a well-oiled machine. That machine never broke. The Delta Force operators on Team Ghost were so well trained they could prep for whatever bullshit the world had to throw at them in just minutes.

But that bullshit typically didn't involve what Clinton had said next: Beckham's team was to escort a CDC doctor to Edwards AFB, where they would rendezvous with two officers from the Medical Corps. From there they would receive more orders.

Beckham was team lead for a strike team composed of six men. They weren't in the business of escorting doctors. They weren't babysitters. They were operators who snuck in and out of dangerous places and took care of business the old-fashioned way. He led the type of missions the good old US of A loved to watch on the big screen.

Only Beckham wasn't Chuck Norris, and his men weren't actors. When they were shot, they bled real blood. They didn't get a second chance. He'd promised his team from day one that he would do everything in his power to keep them alive—that he would die before they did. For the average person, it was a promise that couldn't be kept. But for Beckham, it was sacred. It meant everything to him. He wore his promise like a phantom badge into every mission, right above the picture of his mom.

Patting his vest pocket, Beckham stared into the troop hold and watched his men board. Each and every one of them was capable of completing a mission single-handedly, and they were all responsible for making the same life-or-death decisions Beckham did. But he was their leader. He'd never lost a man under his command. Everyone on Team Ghost had come home in one piece. They'd been shot, stabbed, and hit with shrapnel, but they'd always survived. He'd felt every one of their injuries as if they were his own. Their pain was his pain.

The training bible had taught him that his men always came second to the mission, but in Beckham's book, the men surrounding him were just as important. His first squad leader had said, "My mission, my men, myself." Beckham had rearranged the order a bit.

This mission was no different, and the facts surrounding it gave him an uneasy feeling as he grabbed a handhold and climbed into the Osprey.

"Welcome aboard. I'm Chief Wright and this is my pilot, John Bush," said a voice from inside the dimly lit space. Beckham focused on a stocky crew chief standing with his hands on his hips and the slim pilot who stood beside him.

"Holy shit," the chief muttered. He took a moment to give Ghost Alpha and Bravo the reverse–elevator eyes look, starting with their black helmets and then scanning their clear shooting glasses, headsets, tan fatigues, vests stuffed with extra magazines, body armor, and finally, their boots. Then he moved on to their customized weapons, stopping on Beckham's own MP5 submachine gun with an advanced combat optical gunsight mount. The crew chief twisted his mouth to the side. "Damn, you all look like you're about to drop into a war zone."

"We just came from one," Beckham replied. He wasn't exactly in the mood for small talk. He was exhausted and had been looking forward to some R&R. On top of that, he was anxious to get moving. The sooner he knew what was going on, the sooner he could plan for the dangers—and, ultimately, victory.

The chief's features darkened. He narrowed his eyes and in a stern voice said, "We're still waiting for the CDC doctor."

extras

Beckham took a seat across from Sergeant Will Tenor. This was Tenor's first mission at the helm of a strike team. He was a solid leader and quick thinker—the perfect pick to lead Bravo. Beckham scrutinized the man discreetly in the dimly lit section of the Osprey. The younger Delta operator held his helmet in his hand and cleaned the interior with a cloth, a pre-combat ritual. A modified M4 with an ACOG attachment rested next to him.

Tenor didn't give off any impression of being nervous. His stern face was framed by a solid jaw and topped with a strip of hair perfectly groomed into a Mohawk. He flashed Beckham a confident smirk, as if he knew he was being sized up. That was Tenor's way of saying he was ready to go.

The other men wore the same confident looks, but Beckham scanned each one of them to ensure none had shown up with a hangover. He started with Staff Sergeant Carlos "Panda" Spinoza, the team's demolitions expert. The thick man had a booming voice and the whitest teeth Beckham had ever seen. But he rarely smiled or spoke. Battle had hardened him years ago. He gripped an M249 Squad Automatic Weapon (SAW). The weapon had saved Team Ghost a dozen times.

To his right sat Staff Sergeant Parker Horn, also holding a SAW. The star college football player hailed from Texas. He'd earned the nickname Big Horn at Texas Tech, where he'd crushed the school's sack record. He was a staggering six feet two, with a thick skull and wide shoulders. He looked innocent enough at first glance, with his freckled face and strawberry-blond hair, but beneath his fatigues he was a hard man. Delta had made an exception by allowing Horn on the team. With a tumultuous background, history of a broken home, and arms covered in ink, Horn wasn't the model recruit, but Beckham had vetted the man himself. He'd read his file. He knew how Horn worked under pressure, when his life and those of his men were threatened. His valor in the early days of Operation Iraqi Freedom had earned him two Purple Hearts and a Bronze Star. Beckham knew instantly he wanted the man on Team Ghost, and he had never regretted the decision for a minute. Horn was one of the most talented operators he'd ever worked with.

Horn wasn't the only one. All of Beckham's operators were talented. Each of them had scored 95 percent accuracy or better in shooting tests at a thousand yards. They'd all survived the grueling endurance tests that would have left other men dead. They were the best of the best. Beckham's team was America's first line of defense that no one knew existed. Unseen and unheard, they were truly ghosts. He could count on every single one of them when the shit hit the fan.

A flash of movement from the tarmac distracted Beckham before he could examine the youngest members of his team, Staff Sergeant Alex Riley and Sergeant Jim Edwards. Both men carried Benelli M1014 twelve-gauge shotguns as their primary weapons.

Standing, Beckham watched a short man with an enthusiastic stride and slicked-back hair climb inside the compartment with the aid of a stern-looking African American MP. The soldier had the eyes of a hawk. Beckham stifled a snort. He knew the type. They took their jobs very seriously—sometimes too seriously.

Holding out his hand, Beckham said, "Welcome, Doctor..."

"Ellis. Doctor Pat Ellis," the man said, shaking Beckham's hand vigorously and turning to the rest of the team with a smile. "Most people just call me, uh, Ellis."

"Excuse me, sir," the MP said. "We will have time for proper introductions later. We need to get moving immediately." There was urgency in his voice.

"Just waiting on you guys," Beckham replied firmly.

The MP didn't look amused. He took a seat, and Chief Wright hit the button to close the cargo-bay door. The crew chief gave a thumbs-up and pounded the inside wall. "Good to go," he said. Groaning, the metal door crunched shut behind them.

Beckham watched Dr. Ellis like a coach sizing up a recruit. The civilian moved quickly down the troop hold, carrying a leather bag clutched against his chest. He searched the empty seats, stopping next to Horn. The operator ignored him, pulling his skull bandanna up to his nose as if to say, *This seat's taken.*

Ellis hugged the bag closer to his chest and moved toward Tenor. The man dropped his gear bag into the open seat next to him. "Sorry, taken."

Beckham chewed at the inside of his lip. Typically his men were better behaved, but they weren't used to babysitting.

"You can sit here," Beckham offered.

The doctor's face lit up when he saw the open seat, and he rushed over to it, plopping down just as the V-22's engines hummed to life.

"Thanks," Ellis said.

The roar of the aircraft's motors rippled through the walls. Ospreys were known for more than their speed and versatility; they were known for their noise. Beckham had always thought they sounded like a large lawn mower with too many ponies and a dire need for an oil change.

Beckham handed Ellis a pair of earplugs and said, "Better put these on."

"Thanks," Ellis remarked. He grabbed them and held them out in front of his face as if he'd never seen them before, then slowly slipped them into his ears. Then, with the utmost precision, he reached for his harness and buckled in with a click.

The whoosh from the rotors filled the cabin, sending vibrations through the craft. The doctor's eyes widened ever so slightly, but not from fear. He looked excited, like a kid riding on a roller coaster for the first time. The aircraft pulled to the right as the pilots maneuvered it onto the runway. The rumble of the engines intensified. Moments later they were ascending into the sky.

Beckham leaned over to look out his window. Below, the shadow of the aircraft glided across a vast, green field. They were still low enough that he could make out the shapes of several horses running freely through a pasture. The rolling hills and crystal clear creeks snaking through the terrain were serene, but Beckham still felt anxious.

The view quickly vanished, and the horses faded into tiny black dots moving slowly across the distant landscape.

"Which one of you is Master Sergeant Beckham?" asked a voice from the other end of the aircraft.

Beckham raised his knife hand. He craned his neck to see the MP pulling several tablets out of a bag.

"Take one of these, each of you," the man said. He walked down the aisle and handed the devices out in turn. "Once you submit your electronic signature and fingerprint, you will have access to a classified briefing from Colonel Gibson, commanding officer of the United States Army Medical Research Institute of Infectious Diseases. Mission details will be provided at the end of the briefing."

The MP stopped and handed Beckham his tablet.

"What about me?" Dr. Ellis asked, his voice more eager than before.

"I'm sorry, sir, but this briefing is for military personnel only. Master Sergeant Beckham will ensure you have all the information you need to help make this mission a success, but I should remind you that you are here *only* as a consultant." The MP returned to his seat at the other end of the craft and melted into the shadows.

Ellis spoke louder. "How can I consult if I don't know what's going on?"

Beckham glanced over at the doctor and gave him a reassuring nod as if to say, *Don't worry, I'll tell you everything I know.* But that would have been a lie. He didn't like the fact he had to drag a civilian along with them, and neither did his men. Even if Ellis did bring a medical opinion to the mission, civilians typically ended up becoming liabilities and only slowed his team down.

Beckham looked out the window to catch a final glimpse of the sun as it made one last valiant effort before disappearing over the horizon. Darkness filled the aircraft until a bank of lights blinked on above them.

With a quick flick of the touch screen, Beckham activated his tablet. He linked his headset to the device with a small cord, and a message appeared immediately.

586

extras

Beckham looked down the aisle at Horn and Carlos and then across the way at Edwards, Riley, and Tenor. Their faces were all illuminated by the same white glow radiating off their tablets. One by one they removed their gloves and signed the display.

It was odd being warned about the repercussions of sharing any classified information. In fact, it was downright patronizing, especially for a Delta Force operator. Beckham had given his entire life to his country. Chosen Her over a wife and kids and spent time away from the small bit of family he had fighting in faraway lands. But there was something else about the message that went far beyond insult. Its very existence made him uneasy; something didn't feel right about this mission.

Whatever *it* was.

Beckham considered what he already knew. The facts were slowly coming together. Their leave had been canceled only a few days after returning to Fort Bragg from Afghanistan. That told him brass wanted a team that had been in the field recently and was sharp. The lack of a formal briefing from Command told him that someone higher up was in charge. The CIA instantly came to mind, but that didn't explain Ellis and the involvement of the CDC.

Without further hesitation, Beckham signed the display and pressed his index finger over the scanner. He was anxious to know what they were dealing with.

A video image of an older officer popped onto the display. The man was sitting in a large leather chair, his light blue eyes narrowed at the screen. He wiped a single bead of sweat off his forehead.

"As you already know, I'm Colonel Rick Gibson, commanding officer of the United States Army Medical Research Institute of Infectious Diseases. I'll make this briefing as quick as possible. Time is of the essence. At 1000 hours this morning, we lost contact with a top secret facility on San Nicolas Island, off the coast of California. This installation, which is known as Building Eight, is home to some of the most important medical research in the country. The scientists working inside deal with Level Four biohazards, the most severe contagions and chemical toxins known to man. Officially, this facility doesn't exist." He paused, throwing a glance over his shoulder, as if he didn't want anyone to hear him.

Beckham felt his muscles tightening, an involuntary reaction he experienced whenever he felt nervous. He waited for the officer to continue.

Looking back to the camera, Gibson said, "So what does this have to do with your team? Protocol is to activate an emergency operations team, contact CDC, and deploy a response. Along with Doctor Ellis, from CDC, and the assistance of two men from my division, you gentlemen are that response. I'm not taking any chances in this situation, and I'm told you can get the job done."

A lump formed in Beckham's throat. He didn't know what the job was yet, but he had a feeling it would take him inside Building 8. Level 4 contagions were his worst fear as an operator. He'd much rather face a building full of insurgents than walk into a viral hot zone.

"These next videos will give you an idea of what we are dealing with," Gibson continued, his image fading. "This was recorded on the twenty-fourth of March. Location is a WHO field hospital in remote Guinea. The patient tested positive for the Ebola virus."

Beckham tightened his grip on the tablet as the image enlarged. The body of a frail African man lay coiled on a cot. A pair of nurses protected only by masks stood by his side, one of them bending over to wipe a trail of blood leaking from his right eye. The thin blanket draped over the patient's bony body looked like the apron of a butcher, speckled with dark red blood.

Beckham had seen images of patients infected with Ebola before, but not this bad. This man hemorrhaged blood from every orifice. The nurses' attempts to dry his forehead with a red-soaked sponge ended when he lurched forward, black vomit streaming out of his mouth.

Beckham blinked and then focused on the man's ghostly stare. Something about his detached eyes reminded him that the enemy, in this case, wasn't human. It was a microscopic contagion, one that he couldn't simply shoot or blow up. The revelation scared the shit out of him.

"The second video was taken inside the isolation wing of a hospital in Guinea's capital city, Conakry. One hundred and four new cases were confirmed on the twenty-seventh of March. Of those patients, ninety-eight have died since the recording."

Beckham watched men in white bio suits approach a pair of guards holding AK-47s. After checking for clearance, they opened the glass doors. Inside, the videographer panned the camera across the room, revealing dozens of beds, all of which contained the same scene: blood-soaked blankets and patients hemorrhaging out their insides. A doctor waved the camera away, yelling, "Get that thing out of here!"

The video fizzled, and Gibson reappeared on the screen. "I'm sure many of you heard about this outbreak in recent news. The virus is thought be a stronger version of the Zaire strain, the worst type known to man. It has spread to Sierra Leone, Liberia, and Mali. We have confirmed cases in Europe, the Middle East, and Asia. It's just a matter of time before this strain hits US soil."

Beckham's eyes shot up. He scanned the faces of his men. They all wore the same bold look, seemingly undeterred by the images.

Glancing back down at his tablet, Beckham saw Gibson's features had changed. The man checked his wristwatch. Then, with a new sense of urgency painted across his face, Gibson looked up. The creases on his forehead deepened.

"As you can probably guess, the researchers at Building Eight were working on a cure. Doctor Isaac Medford, the team lead, contacted me two days ago to say he had made a breakthrough. He'd extracted chemical samples from a weapon called VX-99. Many of you may have heard rumors of its use in Vietnam. Some of them are probably true. Anyone injected with a single dose is transformed into something that makes the criminally insane look like Girl Scouts. The weapon was designed to make supersoldiers. It was used in 1968 on a platoon of marines; they were to take a small but heavily defended village. Instead, the entire platoon turned on one another and turned the jungle red. They killed in the most barbaric ways. Most of the marines were found without their weapons, having used their bare hands to murder each other and the VC that ambushed them. The chemical was discontinued after its use was found to have irreversible effects, as you are about to see."

Beckham felt several pairs of eyes on him from across the aisle, but he did not look up. He focused on his tablet. The smiling image of a soldier dressed in uniform appeared. Gibson continued his narration. "This is Platoon Commander First Lieutenant Trevor Brett. He was awarded a posthumous Bronze Star for his actions during a classified mission in Vietnam. His family believed he died a hero. His file simply says KIA. But this is far from the truth. Ten years after his last mission, Lieutenant Brett showed up in a rural village outside Son La, over one hundred miles south of where his platoon had dropped in and injected VX-99."

A map appeared, with a red line leading from the upper mountain area to the city of Son La. Beckham recognized the area instantly. He'd spent several weeks of leave there when he first joined the military.

"Remember that red line," Gibson said.

Next, an image of a man in torn clothing emerged. Even though the picture was blurry, Beckham could tell there was no humanity left in him. He'd seen others like him in the slums of Mogadishu, the remote villages of the northern, tribal areas of Afghanistan, and the filthy alleys in Fallujah. War zones tended to produce the look quite often.

"This was a photograph of the lieutenant taken by a British journalist in 1980. Take note of his appearance. His lips, eyes, skin."

Using his fingers, Beckham enlarged the image. Brett had been transformed into a monster, with hair clinging to his head in clumps. His skin was almost translucent; blue veins crisscrossed his exposed flesh. His eyes had developed some sort of second layer or membrane that was reminiscent of a reptilian eye. His irises were yellow, and his pupils had morphed into slits. But the most striking change was the man's lips. They had bulged into a grotesque sucker that reminded Beckham of a leech.

"And his necklace," Gibson continued.

A new image filled the display. Some sort of cord lay across the surface of a metal desk. Beckham thought he saw dried pieces of flesh. But was that possible?

As the image magnified further, his stomach lurched. He'd never seen anything like this. He'd heard of men keeping ears and other trophies, but there were more than just ears on the lieutenant's necklace. There were other things—unspeakable things. Now Beckham knew why Dr. Ellis wasn't allowed to watch the briefing. If anything got out about this chemical weapon, the military would not only be paying out large settlements to families but politicians would be hosting a barbeque on the Hill, grilling anyone connected to VX-99. Gibson would likely be the pig being slow roasted, with an apple in his mouth.

"What you saw are the effects of VX-99. Like I said earlier, the idea behind the serum was to create a supersoldier. What we got was Lieutenant Brett." Gibson paused again and then said, "That red line on the map of Vietnam I told you to remember? That was the path Brett followed for ten years. Murdering and eating anyone he came across. VX-99 didn't simply transform him into a monstrosity; it transformed him into a criminally insane soldier, one that stayed alive all of those years with a single goal: to kill."

Once again Gibson's tired face faded, replaced by a video feed of the ocean. Beckham found himself wondering what Brett's fate had been. There was no way the marine ever saw the light of day again. He'd likely died a long time ago after enduring countless tests by the Medical Corps.

What a fucking way for a soldier to go out, Beckham thought as the camera panned to a beach.

"Your target is a sample of Doctor Medford's research. My men will know exactly what they are looking for." Gibson crinkled his nose. "I know what you're thinking. Why not just bomb the place? We would if we could, believe me, but I need to know what Medford created. It could be invaluable for future Ebola research. I *need* that sample."

Beckham mastered his anger with a deep breath, tuning Gibson out for a moment to think. This mission meant Team Ghost was cannon fodder. That wasn't new or unexpected. He'd signed the papers. He knew from the beginning what he was getting himself into. But this? His team was being sent into a potential hot zone with no real intel besides some shitty briefing about events that had happened nearly fifty years ago.

Ghost had dropped into remote locations with less information than they had now, but those missions had never dealt with Level 4 contagions. This was a different type of enemy.

The tension in the troop hold lingered like a thick fog of humidity. Beckham didn't need to scan his men again to know they all felt it. Never once had he questioned a mission before. Orders were always orders. And no matter how bad things were at Building 8, he still had a duty to his country.

Breathing deeply through his nose, he quelled another surge of anger.

"As I stated before," Gibson continued, "the target is on San Nicolas Island. Everyone working outside Building Eight has been evacuated. When you arrive, the only personnel left within a twenty-mile radius will be the scientists locked beneath the surface."

Beckham studied the screen. Sapphire waves crashed onto the shores of San Nicolas Island under the moonlight. The video, taken by a low-flying chopper, gave a full view of the terrain. Snaking across a background of brown sand was a landing strip with a cluster of buildings nestled around the perimeter.

Gibson continued, his voice growing more anxious. "My men will have a GPS locator with them. They will guide you to Building Eight. It's off the beaten path, away from the rest of the facilities. They have never been there, and neither have I, due to the sensitive nature of the research," he said with a slight pause. "It's one of our smaller labs, with a staff of only fifteen. Navy personnel on the island do not even know Building Eight exists. They've been told they were evacuated due to a toxic spill."

The video transitioned into a building layout. Beckham assumed the blueprints were of Building 8, but it was difficult to tell with the dim lighting in the cargo hold.

Gibson continued to narrate. "My men will give you access to the facility. Your mission is to protect them and retrieve the sample of Medford's work."

Protect his men? Beckham thought. *From what?*

Gibson coughed deeply into his hand and very politely said, "Excuse me. There are three levels in the lab. Your target will be somewhere on the lowest level, where Doctor Medford would have stored the samples. Level One is decontamination. You won't need to worry about activating the chambers because you will be equipped with CBRN suits, but keep in mind that if there is a loose contagion, you are only safe inside your suit. A single tear will compromise you."

Level Two popped onto the screen. "These are the personnel quarters. Navigate your way to the far end, where a final hallway will take you to Level Three. There are four labs on the final level. Each is color-coded and represents a different toxic level. You are looking for the red one. That is where Medford would have been performing his tests."

Gibson's profile reappeared. "Make no mistake, gentlemen—the likelihood of anyone inside being alive is slim to none. You may be walking into a morgue." He paused briefly and then added, "In approximately one hour from this briefing, you will land at Edwards Air Force Base. From there you will rendezvous with two men from our Emergency Operations Center: Major Walt Caster and Major Brian Noble. Major Noble is a virologist and a damn good one. You will then be fitted for your protective suits and further briefed. After securing your equipment, you will proceed to San Nicolas Island by helicopter. By this time tomorrow, I hope to be congratulating you all via conference call after you acquire the sample. Good luck."

The video fizzled out, and Beckham looked up to meet the intense stares of his team. Their eyes pleaded for reassurance, for Beckham to say something inspirational.

He sat there trying to think of something, but his mind raced. Suddenly, a single image froze there: He could see the black, detached eyes of Lieutenant Brett as vividly as if he was staring right at the man. He finally understood why they'd been activated. They were protecting Gibson's men from a possible Brett.

A distant voice snapped Beckham from his thoughts. The youngest and smallest member of Team Ghost, Sergeant Riley, stared at Beckham from across the aisle. An overhead light illuminated his youthful features, reminding Beckham why the man had earned the nickname "the Kid." With light blue eyes and an enthusiastic and contagious laugh, Riley was the team's little brother. He wore a constant cheerful grin.

"Guess we aren't going to the Keys after all?"

"No," Beckham replied grimly.

Riley pulled a bandanna with an illustration of a smiling joker's mouth over his own and let out a deep laugh. "Good. I didn't want to go anyways."

Several of the other men chuckled. Big Horn reached over and smacked the kid's armored knee. "Think of this like a game of football. That's what I do," he said, crossing his arms. "War is easier when you compare it to something you're good at."

Riley fidgeted with the bandanna. The kid was still new and he was probably nervous as all hell.

Beckham didn't blame him. Shit, he was nervous too. He considered telling Riley that everything would be fine, that the mission was just a routine recovery, but that would be a lie. Beckham had never lied to his men and wasn't about to start now.

Stiffening his back, he locked eyes with Tenor, his co-lead. "We're gonna get in, grab the sample, and get out." Turning to Riley, he said, "And *hopefully* we will have some leave left when this is all over."

Riley let out his infamous and reassuring chuckle. It reminded Beckham of the time Riley had climbed onstage at the Bing and danced in his underwear, which had actually been closer to a thong. At least they had the kid to lighten up the mood when it grew dark.

"So do you guys want to tell me what the hell is going on?" Ellis asked. He squirmed under his harness and looked toward Beckham.

The other men grew quiet, and the noise from the V-22's motors reclaimed the troop hold. They would let Beckham respond.

Closing his eyes, he took in a short, silent breath and rested his helmet on the metal wall behind him. *Need-to-know info only*, Beckham thought as he blinked and stared at the bank of LEDs above.

"You're on a reclamation mission, Doctor. Target is a sample of experimental work that the Medical Corps was doing at a secret location."

"What kind of sample?"

"Classified," Beckham replied.

"That's just great," Ellis huffed, settling back into his seat.

Satisfied with his cryptic answer, Beckham closed his eyes again. With any luck he would snag a nap before they landed. And if he was *really* lucky, he wouldn't dream of any hemorrhaging Ebola patients—or worse, of the monster that Lieutenant Brett had transformed into.

orbit

Follow us:

 /orbitbooksUS

 /orbitbooks

 /orbitbooks

Join our mailing list
to receive alerts on our
latest releases and deals.

orbitbooks.net

Enter our monthly
giveaway for the chance
to win some epic prizes.

orbitloot.com